Summer Sure to Die

By the Same Author

Stories

Tales of Arcadia

The Hampshire Romances

Edmund Persuader
Tomazina's Folly

A Novel

The Marriage of Raphael Kerr

A Novella

Elissa Wyatt

Summer Sure to Die

A Tragedy of Rebirth

COMPLETE IN TWO VOLUMES,
OF WHICH THIS IS
VOLUME I

Stuart Shotwell

MERMAID PRESS OF MAINE

This is a work of fiction. Names, characters, places, and incidents either are the froth of the author's imagination or are used fictitiously. Any resemblances to actual persons, living or dead, or to current or recent businesses, events, or locales is entirely coincidental.

The author gratefully acknowledges the many works quoted in this novel, all of which he believes are in the public domain. The sources of most quotations are listed in the acknowledgements at the end of the book, which list is an extension of this copyright page. If proper acknowledgement of any source has been omitted, the author requests that notice thereof be sent to him via Mermaid Press, so that he may make good the omission in future printings.

This is volume 1 of 2.

Publication Data

Shotwell, Stuart (1953–).

Summer Sure to Die/Stuart Shotwell

p. cm.

ISBN 978-0-9841032-5-6 (volume 1 : alk. paper) — ISBN 978-0-9841032-7-0 (volume 2 : alk. paper)

1. United States—20th century—Fiction. I. Shotwell, Stuart (1953–).

II. Title.

Conceived, written, edited, designed, typeset, and produced by Stuart Shotwell.

This book is distributed directly from the publisher at www.stuartshotwell.com. Mermaid Press of Maine regrets that it is not able to acknowledge, consider, or return manuscripts submitted in any form.

For C. J. McC.
and W. K. S.

Nobis placeant ante omnia silvae

Contents

Act 2

VOLUME 2

Act 3

Act 4

Act 5

P*reface*

THE FIRST DRAFT of this book was written in 1981. The second draft was completed in 1996, and the book as such then came into existence in a few exemplars. Fifteen years later it was taken up again and typeset. Then the typeset version lay in a drawer for more than a decade. Given the now ancient provenance of the book, the author considers it an early novel, somewhere between *Opus* 5 and *Opus* 10, if the reader will pardon that presumptuous nomenclature. Its flaws are so deeply woven into its structure that they cannot now be corrected; the writer would have to put time into reverse—unlive his life—go back to those distant eras when he was concerned with the book—and write it again in order to fix what he now clearly sees to be its failings. In doing so, he would only introduce new flaws, of course; for personality is always the greatest limitation of writers, the wall against which they throw themselves, no matter how wise they may become. This is true of any writer, even any artist, any creator. It is true of every human being; but the creative individual in particular is, or should be, constantly throwing himself or herself against the limit that personality imposes. Technique and talent are nearly incidental considerations; one's personality overrides them. And this book is not the field in which that struggle must continue for me.

This rule extends from technical considerations even to the moral quality of one's writing. One cannot write material that is morally better than one is; and one generally writes far worse. Moral depth can be simulated, but a deep reading will always plumb the deception. And more importantly, though readers can in most cases credit a writer with personally possessing at least some of that good of which his or her writing demonstrates an understanding, they can be justified in doubting the possession of any good not so demonstrated. But so few writers are at pains to demonstrate or even simulate morality that the question of detection is really moot. If, as in Copleston's paraphrase, the final cause of becoming is the realization of the Good, then the final cause of writing and of art in general ought also to be the realization of the Good. But, as noted, this is a view with which few writers will be found to agree. The point is that my moral growth since I conceived this novel has been considerable. I believe it to be a deeply moral book—but it makes its moral point only feebly, and its protagonist only dimly glimpses the Good. But so feeble and dim was my art and vision forty years ago.

To turn from a moral to a mechanical point: For the assistance of those readers who have not performed the scholar's shuffle so vilified by Yeats, the back of volume 2 contains a list of passages quoted from other authors and of foreign expressions used.

On the subject of acknowledgments, I take note of the support of those dear to me. My old and ever-honored friend and my brother carry the dedication of this book; I shall say no more of them, but others must be mentioned. In what bottomless well my wife finds her approval of me, I have no idea. My parents, who passed on without ever knowing of this book, were kind to me beyond my deserts; and my other siblings were and still are as well. My daughter has always borne with the foibles and vanities of her father with a patience and kindness beyond her years. My mother-in-law, Eileen, much missed in the world, read and corroborated the passage in which the wedding takes place; and that is indeed the stamp and seal of authentic Irishry. (Of me, she seemed to think that being half Irish and a quarter Catholic was better than being none.) And I would like to mention two other friends and readers, named John and Jon respectively, both philosophers in the most eminent sense of the word, and yet both men of so many parts they cannot be summarized. The time and attention of all these good people is a gift I will never take for granted.

Lastly, I must thank those readers of my other books whom I have found, or who have found me, over the years. They have become a great blessing to me. If this offering, too, can please them, then it will have done more than I could have hoped when I wrote it.

Summer Sure to Die

frigora mitescunt zephyris, ver proterit aestas
interitura, simul
pomifer autumnus fruges effuderit, et mox
bruma recurrit iners.

—Horace

Thaw follows frost; hard on the heel of spring
Treads summer sure to die, for hard on hers
Comes autumn, with his apples scattering;
Then back to wintertide, when nothing stirs.

—Housman

Continuo enim perficiuntur angeli, quod absque perpetuis
statuum mutationibus nullatenus fieri potest; in genere varia-
tiones et mutationes illae se habent sicut vices temporum in
mundo, nempe sicut vices temporum anni, quae sunt ver, aes-
tas, autumnus, hiems, et iterum ver.

The angels are continually being perfected, which cannot possibly occur without unceasing alterations of states. In general these variations and alterations are like the changes of times in the world; namely, the changes of the times of the year; spring, summer, autumn, winter, and again spring.

—Swedenborg

Act I

This Will Be the Summer

Who does not pause and look back in mounting a hill?

—Eliot

Wer hat uns also umgedreht, daß wir,
was wir auch tun, in jener haltung sind
von einem, welcher fortgeht? Wie er auf
dem letzten Hügel, der ihm ganz sein Tal
noch enimal zeigt, sich wendet, anhält, weilt—,
so leben wir und nehmen immer Abschied.

Who has turned us about like this, so that we are—no matter what we do—in the stance of one who goes onward? Like the man who, on the last hill that shows him all his valley one last time, turns, stops, lingers—so we live, ever saying farewell.

—Rilke

Before us lies eternity; our souls
Are love, and a continual farewell.

—Yeats

Wednesday, June 17 / One

Because our land shows this readiness to be changed, all signs
of permanence upon it raise a tender attachment instead of awe:
some of us, at least, love the scanty relics of our forests, and are
thankful if a bush is left of the old hedgerow.

—Eliot

Perhaps, in the vaguest region of his mind, he made a comparison
between the changing horizon and human existence, for everything in this life is continually flying before us. Shadow and light
are blended; after a bedazzlement comes an eclipse; every event is
a turn in the road, and all at once you are old.

—Hugo

The hills are shadows, and they flow
From form to form and nothing stands;
They melt like mist, the solid lands,
Like clouds they shape themselves and go.

—Tennyson

IN THE LATE spring, when the trees had put on their full burden of leaves, but were still of a green pale and unhardened
by the heat of sun, Ryan again stood at the head of the valley.
Twenty years old, he was a wave about to break—poised,
curled, leaping up the shore; and having swept forth out of
a childhood as vast from this vantage as an ocean between conti-
nents, with the urgent wind of success ever at his back, the quick-
sands of adulthood seemed destined to part before him. His life
still hung in a crest; the shore had not yet risen beneath his feet and
cut his footing away; he had not yet stumbled out of his element
and seen all hope, all high intent dissipated; he had not yet looked
back and seen his childhood through the world's eyes—a mere

backwater. Nor seen that on the far side of this isthmus of twenty was another ocean to cross, a bitter one.

Not yet.

Or he was the valley, and the valley was he. Not a valley among alps, only among the mild hills of Massachusetts. Hemmed in by suburbia, a relic of the great estates, the last of its size so close to the metropolis, his symbol: the old besieged by the new. In a few years these acres, over two hundred in all, would take on the value of those about them, would be assessed at a hundred thousand dollars apiece; and the taxes, beyond the capacity of any but a dishonest wealth, would drive the possessor to divide his land and destroy the estate that had belonged to his family for two hundred years. But in 1981 the valuation was still low, set at an obsolete agricultural rate.—The assessors were all old friends of the family.

If the future, in the geography of metaphor, is a mountain—the ascent though purgatory—the steep crooked trail—the abode of those who have seen and know—then the past is a valley. Tip over metaphor's brimming bucket, fresh drawn up from the dark well of literature, before it has been fouled with the poisons of interpreters, and the idea splashes cool and clear over the mind. Let that bucket sit a while in the stare of the critical sun, and all kinds of notions will spawn and breed in it. The hollow, enclosed, protected home, the sheltering walls, the gash, cleft, nurturing furrow in the earth where the seed of generations lies—what you will. To call this particular place a valley would be to overstate. It was rather a glen, or a dale, if those words any longer have meaning in an age when the ubiquitous developer has appropriated them for use as filler on street signs—when every town has its Mount Glendale Ridge Road, its Fair Oaks Drive where a grove of pines once flourished, its Alpen Lane where muskrats grunted in an oily bog. Let Ryan refer to it as The Valley, or, with full consciousness of the archaic and ludicrous flavor of the word, as The Vale. These words were charged with real meaning for him, which, if too heavy a burden for the modesty of the land in question, is at least an improvement over the meaningless jargon of the developer. Someday a broad and sterile street would run through this place, called perhaps Happy Vale Road; in the face of that eventuality, Ryan can be forgiven for his hyperbole. The other residents of the town shared in his exaggeration; for they not only called the place a valley, they termed the house a mansion and its nearby pond a lake.

Within the circle of those hills lay Ryan's childhood. Dangerous for him, because he did not own the land; nor did his family. In a sense, he did not own his childhood. It was in the possession of the Tates. He had life rights—they would never deny him those. But the Tates held title to it.

His pain was to discover that his past was alienable; that the valley was susceptible to change. His pain it was—or his tragedy—or (a less pretentious word, for after all, we each have our sufferings) simply his *role*—this boy called man, this in some ways enviably anachronistic being.

So if he is the valley, who is he? Look around him. On either hand as he pauses are the wings of huge gates, made of iron wrought—one might even say overwrought—in the last century. One rainy summer morning in 1942 they had been left open by a chauffeur irritated because the gatekeeper, called up to train for his later death in the Ardennes, had not been replaced. If that last driver of the Tate family, old Charles, had known that those gates, which had swung on noiseless hinges every day for fifty years, would because of his omission never be shut again—he would have tugged at the brim of his gray cap and grumbled, but he would have shut them.

Now they were partly buried in the accumulation of sand laid down on the busy road nearby for over forty winters. Rust had blistered their black paint as the metal beneath had slowly fixed oxygen and burned. A clumsy high school boy, taking his first turn at the wheel of a snowplow, half-asleep and half-blinded by snow on a January morning, had bent one wing backward; it seemed the tortured limb of a great butterfly or moth, an insect of the sort that carries heroes to the moon in fairy tales.

On either side of the gates the wall began. It closed in the land of the Tates like a dike, running unbroken around the property.

Except for this point where the drive pierced it, and one other spot where it had crumbled at the persuasion of frost and thaw, it stood sound and firm despite its age. It could not have been built in these times—Mr. Tate liked to point that out. It would have cost many millions; even in the last century, using cheap Italian labor, it had taken ten years of intermittent work and constrained the then master of the place to dabble at a job for the first time in his life. Its footing was four feet below the ground, its coping eight feet above; its stone native to the place—the rifled hoards of the settlers who had farmed the land even before the Tates had come, and before that the treasure of a supernumerary glacier, routed up from some far-off bedrock in its passage over the New England hills—green with age and stained and softened by moss in the shadowy stretches under the branches of the hemlocks. Safely nondescript. The Tates' wall had always been there, in the recollection of the old residents of the town—of which, it is true, there were very few, since the place was one of those bedroom communities in a continual state of upheaval, absorbing the transferred nouveau riche and loosing them again to California or to Dallas. But the stones were a fixture, and fixtures are safer because they are less noticed; less noticed, less likely to become a target. That wall was to become the developer's pride someday; brochures for sprawling, flimsy houses—offered at a price that some nations of the world could not have matched with their gross national product in a year—would feature it in color photographs captioned with vague words like "prestige," "elite," and "harmony." For those without a past, the only way to win the association with tradition that they crave lies in perverting tradition completely.

A case in point: Compare that wall to the dreary stake fence that surrounded the old gatehouse now. The gatehouse itself was of brick; it had been a kind of combined carriage house, guard house, and quarters for select servants; from the main house the call had come down almost daily in the old days for a carriage, or an auto; and the horses or later the horseless had been brought out of one of the wide bays—now windowed off and made a studio for a dilettante artist, wife of an investment banker. Mr. Tate had sold the gatehouse in the early fifties, when he came into his own. It had seemed prudent; the place had not been used since the gate-keeper had gone to war; and Lloyd Tate had never regretted letting it go into other hands. Anyway, it was outside the wall. Since it lay quite close to the road, some recent owner had required a fence around what little yard he possessed. Mr. Tate, when asked which occupant of the gatehouse had thrown up that suburban abomination, would officially disremember. New owners were always taking over the gatehouse, remodeling it, and throwing parties at which they showed themselves curiously oblivious to the stolid serviture still professed by the washed, gaunt bricks, strangely unaware that divorce, displacement, or debt would soon drive them out.

But yes, the cedar fence. Cedar stakes weather; they dry out; they ultimately rot, contrary to the claims of those who sell them. Stone protected the valley, and stone did not rot or rust. Stone argued, if it could not purchase, the permanence of the earth. Or at least as much of the earth as it enclosed here; Ryan asked no more.

For several minutes he stood just outside the gates. It would not be too much to compare him to a man pausing before he sets his hand upon his bride on his wedding night. He looks first; for there is so much to see, and he still is under the illusion that it is his.

Even the driveway was of some interest to him. He could see about five hundred feet of it, before it ascended a slight rise, then dipped and turned among the screening trees. It was of an antique type, thick chunks of stone and gravel caught in a smooth flux of gleaming tar; and yet it showed not the slightest sign of wear; or at least, of new wear. Old wear was permissible. Old wear spoke tradition, honored usage, respect; new wear neglect, abuse, indifference. He had not quite memorized the pattern of crazings in the pavement at his feet, but as he surveyed it he was sure that it was not new.

And yet Ryan did not rely for his reassurance only on those objects that defied change with nothing more daring than mere lifelessness. Although he delighted in the stones of the wall and the texture of the asphalt, even in the fractures in those substances, which to him spoke resistance, immalleability, he felt a still sharper pleasure when he lifted his gaze to the trees overhanging the drive.

It drove the water to gather on the rim of his eyes. For look, the trees lived, more surely than rust ever burned, raising their heavy arms to the sun, all crowding their foliage into a collage of green shades, a chaos of growth that distance and the careful eye could with difficulty resolve into individual forms, like topiary figures at first unfamiliar: Norway maples showing their truncated cone, the symmetrical spheres of the sugar, the steeples of pin oak, the astonishing pavilions of the beech, the canopies of white oak borne up on columns four feet thick. The trees lived, thrived, grew stronger every year, drove their roots still deeper into soil and rock with a grip no human, no wind could dislodge. When he looked down the drive, the late afternoon sun rubbed a pale gilding over the green above, and cast in relief the shadows below; everywhere life blossomed, in the flowers of the maple themselves, in the throats of the birds that roved on their business through the branches, in the wings of insects tuning for the summer heat.

His satisfaction spoke.

"Nothing has changed," he said. "Nothing has changed."

Doom is a mere notion, a gothic grotesquerie. Doom is the concept, existing solely in our minds, to which we transfer the blame for the destruction to which we have dedicated ourselves with our own willful blindness.

"Nothing has changed," says Ryan. He is only stating his premise, not his conclusion. If nothing has changed, then nothing ever will—that is his logic. But his logic is faulty; and besides, his premise is false. He is only twenty. He has not yet acquired that penetration of vision that sees, as if in some accelerated superview of existence, how the trees are failing in their battle against age and pollution, their branches dropping from powdery sockets; how the surface of the earth, worn by water and frost, buckles at their roots; how even the cherished stones are withering into dust and sand as we watch. Grip the earth for Ryan, trees; he would like your grip—like to thrust his hand to the wrist in as much soil as you can cleave and cling to. And yet it would do him no more good if he had that ability than it does him now to stand at the head of the valley, rootless—motile and transient in the eye of time as a mere dancing gnat.

Cars flash along the road behind him. In their windows are momentary faces; many who catch sight of him turn their heads to keep him in view as they are carried by him—women who feel they may be safely curious about men only when in motion away; or the young businessmen who may someday own those subdivisions of the Tate grounds, eager to know who stands with so proprietary an attitude between the gates, measuring Ryan up so that they can one day say, "There was a guy who used to hang around here"—pleased that they are in possession and that he is not.

Like the stones, though less successfully, he offers to those onlookers the illusion of solidity. And like the trees, his strength is dynamic: it exists only in motion. Even though he has halted on the very end of the driveway, he seems to be drifting still, coasting forward under the continuing impetus of the motion that brought him there, about to yield to it and go on; and in fact he does begin to move again, and in pilgrim's progress approaches that first, distant turn in the drive. He is nearly six feet tall; at less expansive times he does not move so erectly, but leans his height forward as if shouldering away some difficulty he disdains because it slows others. He is not arrogant, but he can be impatient at times, and to some his impatience seems a kind of arrogance. Now his head is up; his gaze takes in sky and treeline and avenue ahead; he does not push, he glides, with an effortless, ceaseless pace that betrays the power in his leg—too much power, it seems, for the thin cloth over his thighs, where the wales of the corduroy (pale green, but less yellow than the green he admires) have been polished away from within, have moulted under the pressure and energy of long walks in all weathers. A professor of English had once compared his legs to Clintons—the iron bars that link and synchronize the driving wheels of a locomotive. His torso and arms, beneath a jacket that matches his trousers not only in color but in disrepair, are sound, strong, yet without the hypertrophy one might suspect in the legs.

An athlete. Not a breath too much. He could run this driveway and need no more air for the task than he now needs for this
lingering, fond return to his past, his eyes turning again this way
and that as his singleness of purpose finds fulfillment in the sight
of the trees; in the sunlight that spills through and over their shifting, deep screen; in the muted sound of the almost flaccid leaves
rustling in the inquisitive breezes.

His face is not unattractive. It is unexceptional, and yet unex-
ceptionable; a face that love or a desire to love might transfigure
(whether he was lover or beloved) into that of a handsome young
man. One particular feature of it is, if specifiable, indescribable:
something in it—the dark hair above the brow and the broadness
of the brow itself, the hazel eyes, the faint heat in the cheeks, its
square, angled lines—speaks the indomitable Irishry; a something that brings an appropriate smile to the lips of those of his
own extraction, to find in this American man, lately boy, the
character of their countrymen. Ryan Kinsella, Irish both sides,
was in theory not ashamed of his provenance; in principle gloried
in it; was officially delighted with the audacity that had pinned
the rhyme of his mother's maiden name between his other names,
thus: Ryan O'Brien Kinsella. In practice, however, he often found
his Irishness a burden. To have such ancient roots might indeed
have been great comfort to him, in a land where the immigrant
used to view the Americanization of his children as the final proof
of his success in life—where people once boasted of having lost
their parents' culture in the melting pot. But what good are roots
if they are not beneath you? What good are roots if you, the stock,
have been torn and tossed to some different land? They may even
be a new source of pain: for they are yet more proof of change.

All the same, there were times he truly loved the Irish in him.
He detected it, or thought he did, in his ebullient love of spoken
opinion. Not that he was brash, an empty mouth: often he was
compelled to be the watcher, and he had become good at listening.
The world in general had little use for his higher skills, admiring
only those elements of his personality he considered superficial or
accidental. More gleeful palms had struck him on the shoulders

in admiration of his legs than had seized his hand in respect for the work of his brain. Therefore he aspired to live alertly behind a quiet but affable mask, to be the secret who sits in middle and knows, to conceal rather than to reveal his knowledge, for he had found that his superiority often ostracized him, no matter how humbly he disclosed it. But try as he would, the Irish in him would rise like a bubble working in a dough, and he would engage with those about him freely and brilliantly, undoing in a minute or two that comfort with his presence he had cautiously nurtured by means of restraint and courtesy. He would uncover his intellect; he would betray the true condition of his mind—one constantly ranging, and judging, and forming opinions. It is ill enough to be a pariah through some failure of intellect or education; Ryan had often found himself excluded because of his own inextinguishable brightness. And yet this Irish that made him speak was like a relief valve. Without it he would have smothered in the steam generated by the heat of his own ideas.

And here, in the valley, he did not have to conceal anything. He had been a visitor here since before he developed the skills of discretion and concealment, and the Tates knew who he was; or at least they knew him almost as far as he knew himself. They knew he loved his books; and they knew too that he retained the almost animal delight a boy takes in his physical strength, running until he drops, having never dreamed that his will to move the muscles of his limbs could ever outdo and exhaust the beating of the muscle within his ribs. They knew he shone in the innocency of his upbringing and that he hated untruth; and they knew too that in the coils of courtesy he would readily abandon truth to spare another's feelings. He was a lone bird, like nothing so much as Vergil's rascally crow, lonely, stout-shanked, strutting noncha-lantly across the road and ignoring social obligation as it hurtled toward him; and yet like the crow he was also gregarious, feel-ing the regard of his peers like sun between his shoulder blades. He possessed a natural sense of social forms that stood him well, easing the way he meshed with others as oil eases a drive chain running over a sprocket; and making him seem, even to those with whom he shared no common interests, an amiable individual. He was old-fashioned, in fact of a fashion so antique that to most people it could not be identified as a fashion at all—his character seemed an agglomeration of the random extravagances of eccentricity, although it was actually built on a very solid footing of tradition. And yet he adhered to modern mores. Here only did the Tates' knowledge of him diverge from reality; he had done much at college he had not communicated to those at home. Like a hero returning from the war, seeing scenes of carnage replayed in his mind's eye over the images of welcoming mother, fondly silent father, soft sisters untouched, and even over his future wife, hearing the screaming shells even over the siren singing of peace— Ryan felt the tug between what had happened and what the people of his past believed of him, how they conceived of him. He was a rebel against expectation; and yet still he rebelled only within a narrow province.

In a few minutes he had walked the quarter-mile from the gates to a point at which the house was about to become visible. Reversing himself for a moment against the undertow of memory, he slowed, stopped.

The scent of the newly mown grass on either side of the drive stung a smile to life on his mouth: Hal the gardener had been at work that afternoon. Hal was an institution in himself. He had seldom spoken to Ryan in the presence of the Tates, as if refusing to acknowledge him. Long ago that aloofness had hurt Ryan; as he had grown older it had simply puzzled him; and now, in the confidence of his prowess, he found the thought of it amusing. Hal would watch him sidelong as he edged the rhododendron beds or as he rode the red lawn tractor back and forth, week in, week out; as if he feared the boy would break down a bush, or cause unruly tufts of long grass to sprout in his footsteps. If Ryan surprised him alone, face to face, coming around a corner, he would finger the unmown stubble on his chin, nod his head when compelled by a greeting, his eyes wide and bright, and slouch by, leaving a smell of gasoline, of leaf mould, and, perhaps, even of beer. Ryan often wondered if the man was outraged that one of his own class should consort as an equal with his masters—there was that recognition in his glance, as if he had come upon a conspirator he dared not openly acknowledge; and, never taking an opportunity to whisper together with his colleague and allay his suspicions, mistrusted him as one tainted with a shared crime.

But Hal would be gone by now. Hal would be sitting in front of a television somewhere, a beer not far from his hand, and the night, for Hal, would already have begun. Ryan looked at the trees again and forgot him.

From here on, the trees no longer overshadowed the road. Only lone specimens grew along the border of the drive, forming an alley no less striking for being obviously natural in origin. Most were maples, although a few oaks had found their way among the ranks when the surrounding growth had been trimmed aside sometime in the last century and these survivors had been chosen. The final tree in the series was an enormous copper beech, which outdid all the others in height and symmetry; it was this that obscured much of the front of the house from Ryan's present vantage.

To his left the border of grass gradually expanded until it became a lawn of great size. Beyond this lawn, farther still to the left and east, the woods began again, climbing the gentle slope of the valley; on the height of the ridge the soft, blurred green of the deciduous trees merged into another wood formed of the dark spires of aged white pine, seeming both sensuous and tortured. Beneath them were dry, cool corridors among the trunks; beneath them was a pungent carpet of red-gold needles everywhere, springing back beneath the footstep; beneath them were days spent in the wars, intrigues, dangers that spill from a boy's mind like limpid water from a spring that runs always over and is wasted.

The valley was too small, really, to hold so much. So much had happened here; so much, he felt, was still to happen. The key was here—some great skeleton key, cold and real as iron, that he would be able to seize in his fist, found exactly in the spot lit by a spark of recollection. The key would unlock his way into life, undoing the essential mystery of why he was not who he was not. The good of his childhood lay here. And yet he felt like an old dog scenting the myriad paths and forms of the capering rabbits beyond the milky screen of his cataracts, hearing the faint thump of swift small feet, remembering the pleasure of the chase, emitting a faint whine as he realizes once again that the prey is now forever beyond his pursuit. So memory was all about him, detectable but uncatchable. Here was where he had . . . and here was where . . . and the time they had . . . But he could not truly hold it in his mind again. He sniffed the odor of memory and left it to blow by on the wind.

If sheer multitude and magnitude of recollection make a man old, Ryan at twenty stood older than many at forty.

He allowed himself at last to turn his head toward the house and to begin to walk again. He caught his first glimpse of the place again beneath the trees, expanses of ivied stone featureless from this distance among the moist brown of the trunks. He smiled at himself. How long had it been? Only six months since he saw it last, at Christmas; and yet he celebrated this homecoming like Odysseus. Because much was over, and much was beginning; and this summer, this summer ahead was the bourne around which he would turn his course; this summer he would be here. He wondered faintly and briefly if the Tates had ever enjoyed this return as much as he did.

The drive finally flowed into a loop before the house, circling around a grassy omphalos trimmed with Belgian block. When he came out on this open area, he halted once more and looked everything over.

His eye began with the half-dozen chimneys standing too high over the crowded squares of the slate roof; he heard the fires in the hearth in winter, smelled oak taking flame. He swept his gaze over the attic dormers, and his hands once more clenched on the black grime that lay unseen on the high beams beneath the slates, in the playground of rainy afternoons. The soft flesh on the inside of his fingers prickled with splinters of wood; his nostrils burned with the acrid dust and with the reluctant odor of timbers hardened by a century and more of stuffy heat; in his ears was the silence of the vast empty space, overwhelming with its breathless drone even the living pulse of rain above. Like the chimneys, the roof was too high, too heavy, made more massive by its belting of broad gutters in the Yankee style, flashed over with copper sheets, from which leaders green with copper rust descended.

Beneath all this stone and metal the living force of the house looked out at him, in the form of white curtains faintly agitated, from the dozen windows of the second story, the dozen-less-two of the first—each recessed rectangle framed by immaculate black shutters, glazed with six panes over six within muntins so crisply painted they seemed limned by an artist's bold charcoal. In the center of the first story, where the windows were lacking, the great central door of the house stood open, its screen obscuring the shadowy hallway within.

And over all, the ivy, fanning across the façade from four vines as thick as Ryan's thigh, sea-green over the pale gray granite; the ivy's love was like Ryan's love, clinging with infinitely many thread-like fingers at the pointing of the stones, clinging too tightly with its fine, insidious grip, driving fissures invisible but deep into the strength of the beloved house.

But enough of that. No: the rhododendrons in their beds raised fat new buds, promising dense bloom. The dogwood at the east corner of the house shook its pinwheel blossoms in the trembling air. Everywhere was the traffic and commerce of the birds— blackbirds darting from nests in the deep ivy, robins hopping about under the sprawling, flat-topped English yew beneath the library window, sparrows tossed upward by a surge of air as they flitted over the gutters. Song, incessant, the variable melody on the sibilant soft bass of the breeze.

It was not his home, but he was home.

Wednesday, June 17 / Two

Friend of my bosom, thou more than a brother,
Why wert thou not born in my father's dwelling?
So might we talk of the old familiar faces . . .

—Lamb

A S THE HOMECOMER paused, he saw those who belonged; they were sitting on what they referred to—in misleading modesty—as the porch. That such a feature could be called by such a humble name was typical of Tate understatement.

It had been built off the short wing at the left end of the house. This wing enclosed an ample kitchen and several other rooms that a Tate bride had once persuaded her husband-to-be to view as indispensable to his new way of life: a butler's pantry, a storeroom, a deep closet in a chimney corner for hanging smoked meats; and after he had improved upon her improvements by adding an office into the plan, she had insisted that a better dining room was needed. The existing one had looked north; she had wanted more light. Accordingly the architect had to redraw yet again, including a dining room—which became the focus and purpose of the addition. It did indeed face south, displacing all other rooms to the north side; French windows lit it, opening out onto a roofless patio.

It was this patio that gave rise to confusion over nomenclature; for the Tates, and Ryan from time to time, were confounded by guests who referred to it as such instead of as "the porch." There was in fact another patio, called by that name, on the north side of the house, flagstone embedded in a matrix of old, cream-colored grout. But the porch was no mere square of paving stones. It was founded deep as the house, of a similar granite; its paving, of herring-bone brick, was two feet above grade; and round its perimeter was a balustrade of lathed limestone, opening onto four wide-treaded steps that dropped to the edge of the drive.

If that Tate bride had come of age in the seventies or eighties of the twentieth century, she would not have allowed such a porch to be built. Nor would the architect have conceived it. Decks were then the rage: structures as cheap and light as the times, well-fitted to a civilization living in contempt of its own future, unable to understand that the next century would be the inevitable consequence of the current one. True, these decks were made of a wood touted by the lumber companies as better than redwood or cedar—no, as virtually eternal—for it had been injected with a toxin of heavy metal and arsenic to discourage the two greatest powers with which humankind competed, microbes and insects. In the late twentieth century these spindly abominations, these decks, grew up beside every house. They were pleasant places. The leisure hours of life could be spent there, consumed in drinking and eating, in quarreling, or even in watching television. Was the quality of the Tates' life any better for having a monolithic porch instead of a deck? A heresy, perhaps—but the Tates would have said yes.

There they sat even now: Lloyd Tate and his son. When Ryan perceived them, he approached silently around the sweep of the drive and halted before the steps, expecting they would soon notice him; and so stood for a minute, watching them, with a faint smile both affectionate and ironic.

Mr. Tate was surveying the newspaper he held open before him, his graying head turning lightly on his neck, bobbing and dipping as he scanned the bonds and stocks, the mergers and acquisitions with a dubious air. From time to time he uttered some vague sound of recognition or vindication, or loosened his fierce grip on the paper—a compensation for the slight palsy that affected him from time to time—then rattled the sheets for an instant, and turned to the next page. His profile might have stood well on a coin: a fine, aristocratic nose beneath the thick, drawn eyebrows, a cheek without a jowl, and lips so lacking any remarkable feature as to be archetypal, nondescript, generic, merely functional, practical—a mouth useful for pursing suspiciously at newspapers, frowning at witnesses, or smiling in cool irony at lawyers for the plaintiff. The chin was not too angular; if it had been, the face would have been bitter or even savage. The chin, with its slight weakness and gentleness, balanced out the patrician nose, pragmatic mouth, and penetrating eye.

For his eye was keen. Yet that keenness might or might not reveal itself, as the occasion demanded. At this moment he wore his reading glasses, which were rimmed with thick and practical plastic; occasionally he peered at the print over these, not through them, as if continually testing the mere necessity for any optical prescription; and this constant checking of his natural against his assisted facilities gave him the air of a hawk staring out from time to time from behind the mask of a sleepy owl. Witnesses had found this habit unnerving; they felt that when he wore those conspicuous spectacles they were invisible to him; but when he held his notes aside and swivelled his head sharply about in their direction, and his eyes appeared to them over the rim of the reading glasses, naked and piercing as the tips of two blades beneath the arch of cold gray eyebrow—they would fear for a moment that they were transparent, and give one furtive glance toward their counsel. And that one glance was often of damning effect. It told juries and judges too much. It was the reason Lloyd was often able to shift a judge or a jury's opinion as if he were shaking chaff to the side of a box.

Nor was that keenness mere empty truculence. There was brain behind it; in fact, Lloyd could have been described as a man of intellect. Not an *intellectual*—not a man living wholly within the world of ideas, accepting with indignant pride those few crumbs of recognition cast him by the world of deeds. Ryan was in training to be an *intellectual;* Lloyd Tate's son was in training to be an *intellectual;* but Lloyd was a man who employed his intellect in the real world—a world built up, it was true, out of the artificialities and complexities of society and twentieth-century civilization, but no less brutal for all that. If his clients and those who accused his clients wore white collars, there might yet be some widow living in want somewhere because of their light fingers—or because they had caused some bank to teeter, or because they had issued worthless paper, or because their ambition had erected a house of leveraged debt that was destined to collapse into its own crumbling foundations. Among such men Lloyd Tate's intellect was of a unique and effective type. It could see, without disclosing that it saw; it could plan moves within moves, like the mind of a chessmaster looking ahead toward the endgame; it could disarm with trivialities and strike up under the most careful guard with impertinacies; it could soothe the vulnerable or unhinge the hitherto imperturbable by disclosing to them for the first time that their role in life was to be crushed in the mill of law.

He was, furthermore, a man of some culture. He had once impressed a judge with a summation into which numerous scraps from the feast of literature had been mixed to form a gourmet dish of leftovers. Not that he paused to identify and flaunt his allusions, but that the judge felt the effect of them and knew he was being treated to something extraordinary in the way of courtroom rhetoric. And Lloyd's culture was not purely literary. For instance, he held two season tickets to the symphony—the same two seats he had held since he had entered Harvard in 1942. His partners at those concerts had changed constantly over the years: fellow members of the bar, clients, his wife, his son, once or twice Ryan, who had come up on the bus from college on a Friday afternoon, unable to resist Brahms or Beethoven; but Lloyd was a regular, insofar as his court schedule permitted.

Although he could appear formidable in the forum, in private Lloyd Tate was a genuinely gracious man. In ordinary company, with the disguising glasses tucked into his jacket pocket, the keenness of the eyes would be sheathed; and although he would never have been called a mild man, he revealed unexpectedly—and therefore more touchingly—the human weaknesses of love and need for companionship, for a listening ear. Ryan always felt, looking at him, that Lloyd Tate was conscious of having made a great mistake once in his past; which had borne mercy and fellow feeling in him.

Among friends Lloyd occasionally indulged in a peculiar mannerism: he was facetious. This humor was of an insistently familiar, back-slapping kind that reached out and brought into his circle whoever would submit to be so brought. Ryan enjoyed it; by partaking in it he felt included—included where even Lloyd Tate's son was not, by his own choice. Besides, Ryan's wide reading had left him with a head full of phrases that were largely unusable in any but facetious conversation.

This mannerism had not developed with age; it had survived from childhood. Only Lloyd's parents could have recognized it as one with the enthusiasm he had brought home from his first semester at Lawrenceville, after learning and culture had poured into his brain the way water under hydrostatic pressure finds its way inevitably into a hidden cavity in soil. He had developed a love of highflown diction; like Ryan, he had soon learned that it could only be tolerated in company if it was jocularly delivered. The boyhood foible had become an adult idiosyncrasy. His parents were no longer alive to explain and thus excuse this mannerism to his son, who had long since grown thoroughly weary of it as affectation. Lloyd, in these childish moods, might have been said to delight in clichés, the more absurd the better; gaining a jovial pleasure from the irritation it caused the boy, who abhorred all trite language.

Perhaps this mildly perverse delight is only natural in fathers, who, after all, have much to endure before their sons reach twenty, and who find few ways of avenging themselves without causing themselves redoubled trouble. On the whole, Lloyd's relationship with his son was extraordinary. He was always paternal; he never became his son's companion or confidant; nor was he yielding and indulgent. Yet in general he treated his son with an affectionate reserve and respect that had continually built in the boy a confidence that he himself mattered, that his ability to choose his own way in life was unquestioned—that he had, in fact, chosen the right way. And his interests were far different from those of his father. Lloyd would no more think of frowning on his son's intended career than he would frown on the inevitable dawn. Both were beyond his right, as well as his ability, to control; more than that, he would have rejected the power to control either, had it been offered to him, as a form of tampering in something sacred and larger than his own understanding—nature, or the life of another. Although he had his opinion of that career, and his anxieties concerning it, he hid his thoughts and fears successfully, trusting, perhaps, to the Tate wealth—not vast, but quite comfortable if well managed—to prop his son up where livelihood failed.

Even now Collin Tate was practicing that livelihood. He was pressed back in the low-slung Adirondack chair, his spine so straight and his head so high that even from his seat he projected height, pride, purpose. Unlike his father, he was gazing at nothing—looking forward into the air, across the lawn west of the house toward the woods; staring so intently that Ryan, although he had often been deceived in this way before, turned, momentarily curious, to see what held that vision, and saw only the trees, their leaves shifting about and constantly creating and recreating vague shimmering patterns of shadow.

He saw what Collin saw; but in Ryan was a vaguer knowledge of what lay before him. He could have described that play of light—could have pointed it out and communicated his perception brilliantly; but in him it underwent no amalgamation with other thoughts beyond simple memory, nor grew into metaphor; it remained a discrete pleasure, one with the other sights of his *nostos*, his homecoming, but inexpressible as more than that. For Collin that rippling curtain of shadow and light was intrinsically symbolic—of what, depended upon the need of his expression. Later the shifting shadow would become something new and other, a metaphor. He was always catching and cataloging such sights against future use. In fact, as Ryan returned his gaze to him, Collin pulled a small notebook from the pocket of his jacket (no threadbare corduroy, but a fine light tweed, the latest cut) and removed his eyes from his contemplation of the distance long enough to jot down in it, with a silver ballpoint, the image and its potential meaning; wrote it at once, knowing, with the instinct of the writer that never trusts memory, that it would otherwise elude him later. He wrote; he hesitated; he added more; he drew a line, an arrow indicating transposition; carefully recapped the pen; and replaced both pen and notebook in his pocket.

The sunlight glowed on his hair and face. A painter would have been accused of melodrama had he caught the aura formed around the golden hair, the abstracted features; but truth, if stranger than fancy, is also, or can also be, more beautiful. Collin was often seen in such attitudes. Nothing self-conscious compelled him to adopt them, nor was he aware of his appearance at such moments; but often, in a group, if the wind of conversation fell, the next comment made would be addressed to him, or would concern his expression, or the way he sat—"Collin is not with us," "Look at Collin," "A penny for your thoughts, Collin."

For Collin—in his own description—was a poet. And although there was much that argued against him, he was no dilettante. It was true that he had never in his life worked a day for a dollar. He had never been hungry, never the least in want, never gravely ill, nor much alone, nor at all concerned about his future, or dubious about his past—never guilty, never ashamed; had never committed a crime or an immoral act; never, perhaps, been deeply in love. Such things are the poet's credentials in the popular mind. Collin himself had sometimes wondered whether he ought to have some of those experiences, whether he might not write better poetry if he had them. He might well have done so. And yet the world at large has confused the typical lot of its poets with their necessary training. In former times it consigned them to garrets where they were supposed to repine or to sip prussic acid; in the era in which Collin lived, it sent them instead to one dreary academic term after another on jerry-built campuses surrounded by cornfields, as writers-in-residence, sentenced to teaching their love of poetry to others—reduced from worshipers of an ideal to panderers, explaining not attitudes toward beauty but positions of intercourse with it. "If you wish to make me weep, you must first have suffered yourself"—so says the Epicurean hog. But the mind is capable of an intense life even in the mildest of circumstances. In fact, great poetry is written in gardens as often as gutters, on stipends as often as breadcrusts. Collin's expensive jacket and his silver pen were his father's contributions to his craft—superficial, but well-intended, something, Lloyd felt, that people in Collin's line ought to have; thus playing Maecenas to Collin's Maro, though like most Maecenases he found baffling the poetry that his largesse made possible. Collin had little Shakespeare and less Greek. Between his art, and his father and Ryan's understanding of art, there was no common ground.

No, Collin was a poet of the present. He could recite Ashberry and Merwin, Sexton and Rich, men and women of whom his father had never heard. He had no interest in tradition; regarded it with some vague fear and suspicion, because he knew little of it; had never explored it, because it did not speak to him. And he found disquieting the notion that all has been said before. When reading, in a college humanities course, how a fine fire crept under Sappho's flesh, he was disturbed that this ancient had preempted an image he had used in one of his own poems; and that he, though as original as she, was robbed of the reward of his originality simply because others would assume he had been acquainted with her work at the time when he had written his own. He did not, like a newer poet of older times, remake her image in his own experience, as he could remake the shadow of the trees. For him the images that lay in the storehouse of tradition were laurels that had withered; he did not possess the rejuvenating touch that would make them green again. To him old poetry smelled of damp and must.

But if his ignorance of the past arose in part from a certain brashness common to his age, he was not entirely without humility. He was conscious that he had far to go before he achieved his aspirations—which were clear in his mind, and simply stated, if difficultly achieved: to create a perfect body of published work; to win an uncontested rank among the foremost of living poets; and to carry off a great prize. No less than the Nobel would really do.

And while accomplishing this, to live a life in which no biographer could find a flaw. "The poet," he had often told Ryan, staring beside the other and speaking in a tone of almost indignant dignity, "must be pure. The life and the work are one. There must be no flaw in either. The work can be kept, hidden, changed until it is perfect; but the life cannot be rewritten. It must be controlled at all times. The poet must live in constant awareness of what his image will be in the eyes of posterity."

"If you seek a superhuman purity of life, then that itself *is* your flaw," Ryan would observe. "That is your *hamartia,* my friend— in the original sense of the word, that is where you miss out. How can you write for the human condition if you are trying to be better than human? You have to be down in the muck with the rest of us in order to do that. Your basic poet is an outrageous brute, swilling and whoring and making a fool of him—or her—self. In order to be human, you have to be at least part animal. Look at Byron. Man or beast? A little of both. Look at—" And here he would rehearse the sins of poets both ancient and modern, or at least as modern as the nineteenth century.

"No one has done what I mean to do," Collin would respond. And his eyes, usually so clear and luminous, would lour at Ryan's affectionate smile.

Luminous they were now, striking on Ryan as though impelled by a sixth sense to turn. They did not frown, though Ryan wore that same mild smile that would have irritated Collin, had he known the thought behind it.

If earlier Ryan had looked fondly on stone and tree because they had preserved the forms his memory dictated for them, how much greater his gratitude upon seeing these two beloved people in the attitudes their characters had established: the father peering, the son at gaze, half-seeing. To all outward appearances they had not changed. The father's gray hair—death's frost, assumed early in anticipation of the unbroken winter to come, like the coat the hare takes on and sheds each cold season—with this Ryan had been long familiar. And in Collin, how could there be a difference? Now he started, and rose from his seat, his whole being becoming awake and a welcome, turning toward Ryan in friendship—his standing up was an event, for in physique he was the inverse of Ryan, a full two inches taller, heavier in the chest and arms, more spare in the leg—and to Ryan, all seemed the same. The carpenter ant, working in the rank darkness of the oak, does not alter the outward shape of the tree—until the day of the storm, when the trunk topples. The idea tunnelling through the brain behind the luminous, abstracted eye as yet showed Ryan no symptom, no pain, however faint; it was not even hypothesis yet; it was still only a dimly reflected image of a beautiful object, harmless still.

"Ryan!"

The word enveloped itself in silence, of only a few seconds in duration, but full of mutual history. Collin stepped forward, his hand already outstretched; Ryan came to meet him, striding up the steps, so much more quickly and lightly that he was standing on a level with Collin when the two gripped hands. The handshake, an instant longer than mere salutation required, reconnected them, put them back together in space and time, like two atoms that had been destined to decay colliding and combining to form a stable molecule.

In the moments before Collin had seen Ryan, Lloyd had folded his newspaper, and in indecision over the competence of the incumbent attorney general had turned, as he usually did in states of uncertainty—which were rare with him—to his clothing for comfort; which was not indecisive in the least, but immaculate, and well tailored. He always dressed more formally than might be expected of a modern suburbanite at leisure; a trait with which he had influenced his son, and Ryan as well, although the means of the latter could not support much more than a travesty of it. He looked up from watching his hand smoothing the sleeve over one forearm; and as Ryan and Collin greeted one another, he struggled to repress an instantaneous grin.

As Ryan turned to greet him, Lloyd Tate rose from his chair and thrust one hand up and before him dramatically. "Hail!" he said, the smile overwhelming his control utterly now as his will dissolved in pure affability. "Hail to thee, staunch gladiator in the wars of life! How goes the battle?"

"Morituri te salutamus!" answered Ryan, with such a gesture as he thought might have been appropriate for the myrmidon of some unspecified tyrant in the range between Augustus and Hitler. He chose Latin because Lloyd did not share Collin's antipathy to it. Lloyd still possessed a handy mental library of Latin tags and scraps—an index version, as it were, of Ryan's erudition. He could in fact still blunder his way from *Arma virumque* to *caelestibus irae;* and occasionally fetched out these disused relics to vary his banter. Today, however, his absurdity went in another direction. "Remember the Alamo!" he cried.

"Rejoice, we conquer!"

"Don't fire till you see the whites of their eyes!"

"With this or on this!"

"That'll be about enough of that," said Collin. But he silenced them only momentarily, while they were otherwise occupied in grinning at one another and shaking hands heartily.

"These summer evenings, Ryan!" enthused Lloyd. This too, was an old theme.

"Yes, the summer evenings! And tonight is the full moon, the midsummer's moon."

"June seventeenth is still spring," observed Collin. Then he restrained his father by changing the subject: "Dad—Ryan doesn't know yet."

"That's right," realized Lloyd; and his frivolity dissolved, replaced by another kind of pleasure, which yet marred the smoothness of his genial brow with a line of care and caution, of anticipated misgiving.

"Know what?" asked Ryan.

"Constance is here. And my mother."

Long silence; during which Lloyd and Collin reread in Ryan's face the strangeness of the event that even they had not fully assimilated.

"Here?" said Ryan finally.

"At the house. Not this minute, actually. They're out shopping."

"And your mother too?" said Ryan. He could not withhold his eyes; they flickered over Lloyd's face.

"Mother too," said Collin.

"The planets have conjoined," said Lloyd. "The Scorpion is in the house of the legal Lion, along with the lovely Virgo. Which is to say, the Twins are in the ascendant."

"When did they get here?"

"A week ago," said Collin. "I called you to give you the news, but you weren't back. I didn't want to just leave word with your parents. I hope you don't mind; I wanted to tell you myself."

"Of course not," said Ryan. "How long are they staying?"

"Indefinitely. Constance has come back to go to college here."

"Just like that? Out of the blue? What college is she going to?"

"She hasn't even chosen one yet, or been accepted."

"The fact is," said Lloyd, "this plan was all hatched about ten days ago. My spouse called me up from overseas and asked me if I'd be willing to help pay for Constance's education. I said yes, on conditions. A few days later she was here. She made it clear from the start that I could only have Constance in the house if she stayed here too. I think she hasn't a penny to her name, to tell you the truth; I've heard rumors that she made some bad investments over there. If you'd ever told me that I would allow myself to be used in this way, I would have scoffed at you. But the girl is . . ."

His voice trailed into silence.

"The girl is what?" said Ryan, smiling at Lloyd's lapse. Now both father and son smiled too; the elder even triumphantly.

"She's a goddess," said Lloyd.

"What do you say, Collin? Has the hyperbolical fiend got hold of him again?"

"It's not the word I would have chosen," said Collin. "But I think in this case we can let it stand."

"Her appearance, her physical appearance," puffed Lloyd, "defies all previous description."

"The photographs really were inadequate to the task of capturing her real, living presence," agreed Collin.

"They were a joke! Ludicrous! Ryan—the figure!"

"But aside from physical appearance—" said Collin reprovingly, beginning to take over the description.

Lloyd would not relinquish it, however. "Yes," he said, "the charm! The sheer overpowering charm of the girl! Modesty, gentleness—but not without sauce. The Old World education, you know."

"She *is* very old-fashioned," laughed Collin, apparently thinking of some detail. "You'll like that, Ryan. She's like something from another century. She can't even drive yet. She hasn't learned how. She sits about in long skirts and plays Spanish guitar like something out of an old picturebook. She doesn't even own a pair of jeans, if you can believe it. She needs modernizing, but she'll do all right now that she's back here."

"Who cares about jeans?" asked Lloyd. "You couldn't possibly find fault with her clothes.—All dresses and skirts, Ryan. I highly approve. I never liked pants on a woman."

"You're a Neanderthal, Dad. This is the eighties."

"I'm not a Neanderthal. I just have my preferences. Why should that make me a Neanderthal?"

"Why don't we compromise at Cro Magnon?" asked Ryan.

"*Et tu, Brute?*" cried Lloyd. "I tell you, boys, don't modernize that girl. You'll spoil her."

"Modernization is one sin Ryan's never been accused of," observed Collin wryly.

"If you do, she'll just be another one of those girls you see everywhere nowadays, wearing those headphones—what do they call those things?"

"Walkmen," suggested Collin, with the same dry humor.

"Yes. She'll be just another coed wearing a Walkman."

Collin laughed aloud. "Coed!" he repeated. "When was the last time you heard that word, Ryan?"

"Actually, I was reading a manuscript from the fourteenth century just last week—"

Lloyd pretended to wince at the gibe." You'll have to invent a new language to describe her, my boy," he said to Ryan. "That will be your job."

"It's the job of poets to invent languages," said Ryan. "Scholars only report their labors afterwards." He reached out suddenly and gripped Collin's hand again, shaking it impulsively. "I'm very happy for you," he said. "For both of you. I know the situation must be strained in some ways, but I'm very pleased you have this time to spend with her."

"Yes," said Collin, clearly pleased at Ryan's sympathetic understanding. "It's really Dad, you know, who has the hard time of it. He's been very kind to put up with Mother. All the old feelings, the old memories . . ."

"It hasn't been that bad," said Lloyd. "She's been behaving herself. I really think she hasn't any choice. She's never worked a day in her life, and she has been estranged from her parents for twenty years; she can't look to them for support. I'm damned if I don't feel a little sorry for her."

This confession was met with an awkward silence.

"So, Ryan," said Lloyd, to change the subject, "You bear your own good tidings."

"Nothing to compare."

"You're out. That's something."

"I'll never be out. I've got a life sentence in Academia State Penitentiary. Solitary confinement and lousy food, but the library is excellent."

"It must be nice to be done with your first degree, at least," said Collin.

"Only meat is done," said Lloyd. "What you mean is that it must be pleasant to have been graduated from one's course of studies."

"He gets like this every time you come around. Have you noticed?"

"It's an effect I have on some people. Stuffiness oozes from my pores."

"So, when do you leave for merry old England?" asked Lloyd.

"Just before the term starts."

"Surely there's no point in working till then?" asked Lloyd. His tentative phrasing could not conceal the anxiety behind his question. For a moment both father and son averted their eyes. Their tact gave Ryan greater pain than any indifference.

They had had this brief discussion at the beginning of every summer for four years. Each year it was abbreviated more and more, as Lloyd sensed more acutely the financial and moral necessities that compelled Ryan to work at some menial nine-to-five summer job. The first year he had been full, articulate, even lawyerly in his argument. "It distresses me no end to see so fine a mind arrested in its education for even a few months," he had said in summary.

"How so, arrested?" Ryan had responded. "I'll appreciate the cerebral trades all the more for having slung hash for students at the summer program. Learning to value the life of the mind is a necessary part of my education too. I've seen too many who take it for granted."

"But how much can you make, Ryan? Is it really worth it?"

"A pittance, I suppose. *Pauca, sed mea.*" He could not have communicated to Lloyd how perilously his education depended upon his summer earnings. He knew that Lloyd would gladly have given him money, merely to see him at his ease on a summer day in company with Collin; but there existed no mechanism in their relationship that would have permitted such a gift; and Lloyd must have sensed that in raising money matters with Ryan he was treading around the edge of a very deep bog of Irish pride.

(Once Ryan had overheard Lloyd querying Collin as to why the Kinsellas were chronically struggling. "An instructor's pay can't be utterly contemptible for a man and wife and an only child," he had observed. "They live frugally—they have no extravagances. What happens to it all?"

"You don't know the whole network of aunts and uncles and cousins, Dad," Collin had pointed out. "Some relative is always getting sick, pregnant, evicted, or arrested. It's an endless tale of woe. So far as I can tell, Ryan's parents are the only respectable and secure branch on the whole flimsy tree. And they're a soft touch. Just last winter one of Ryan's cousins was mangled in an automobile accident. Of course he was driving an unregistered car and he had no insurance of any kind. Who do you suppose paid the bills?—And you know what it costs to send someone to a school like that. Ryan wasn't recruited on a soccer scholarship.")

Collin, perhaps in unconscious emulation of his friend's principles, had been, at least at the beginning of every summer, similarly determined to make money and "help out," as he put it; but his father's assiduous scorn of his earning power, underscored by steady doses of cash, and the lure of the long days of poetizing in peace, all combined gradually over the first few weeks of the vacation to dispel his frailer ambition. The day Collin ceased bypassing the front section of the paper to examine the classifieds Lloyd allowed himself a sigh of relief. The summer routine, at least as far as his son was concerned, was then secure.

And this time too, Lloyd was making his attempt. "The point in my working is the same as it has always been," said Ryan.

"But what kind of job could you get for three months?"

"It's called a summer job, Mr. Tate."

"'Summer job'? A contradiction in terms!"

"If there's any way, Ryan . . . " said Collin, leaving the sentence unfinished. "Constance will be here—or at least in and out, if they go to stay somewhere else. Think what you'll miss. Of course you'll be welcome to come whenever you can, but it won't be the same as having you here all the time."

To his own surprise, Ryan hesitated. They were equally amazed, but rushed to drive home the wedge. "Those summer evenings, Ryan!" expostulated Lloyd. "The long walks through the hills at even!"

"Think of your parents," urged Collin. "They can't possibly want you to work. You'll be going overseas—you'll be gone for several years, at least."

"They have been wanting me to skip the job this summer, actually," admitted Ryan.

"Of course they have. And you can't claim you need the money anymore. You've got a scholarship. Your father's a professor now; that must mean some extra cash."

"If it were up to me . . ."

"It is up to you. Promise you won't work." Ryan saw that Collin was angling for a promise from him in order to destroy any route of retreat.

Ryan's resolve wavered, for two reasons. The lesser was that for the first time in years his parents' economic difficulties had eased somewhat. Most of his mother's family were healthy and employed; the particularly troublesome cousin was free on probation, and if still an unproductive citizen, at least out of harm's way vegetating on a back stoop in Dorchester. But the second, and ultimately more compelling reason, was that Ryan had remembered summer—summer as it had been before responsibility had fallen upon him.

Summer dawns aching with coolness, which even the middle of night seemed to anticipate with the pale stain that spread with almost visible haste in the east; the sudden influx of heat in the early hours of the morning; the changing, ripening light before noon, and thereafter its full, stark, fertile wealth. The lulling monotony of the cicada; the secrets of shade, of cool stream and pond, of evening lingering longer than one had a right to hope. And fellowship, bounded by an end still distant in thought, still some indeterminate time away; speech, physical company, the presence of youthful companions a drug in itself.

Ryan said nothing. If he had spoken, his words would have formed themselves according to the old pattern of demurral, and he would have been compelled by them to relinquish his vision. Better not to speak at all. Or perhaps he was overcome by possibility and was unable to utter what he felt.

He knew that this summer, this particular summer, was a turning point. In the next few years his profession would close in upon him and constrict him; there would be research, opportunities for study or travel he would pursue out of a sense of obligation to his future and to those who had helped him in the past. He would work through the season in libraries in foreign lands, breathing dead, conditioned air, exiting only at night, tasting summer's heat after the day was spent, in an atmosphere acrid with city smog. Even now he had articles to write, although their urgency was not persuasive. Of course he rejected this knowledge of the future; he sought constantly for ways in which that which had been might always continue. And yet he could not help but feel the lifechange hanging over him like a threat; and rather than face it, he faced backward, toward childhood.

He was not called upon to decide at this moment; it was just as well, for a greater persuasion had yet to arrive. Before that, however, a lesser one appeared at the French windows that opened onto the porch: Mrs. Overton, the housekeeper.

Lesser in compelling force at least; for in actual size, far larger. Ryan saw her first. He thought at once of the great gray goose one of his professors kept on his farm in Little Compton: it liked to peer out of the hatchway of its roost like this before waddling forth, affectionately demanding, both to mother her humans and to seek sustenance from them, even those unknown.

Mrs. Overton, too, was gray. She wore gray frequently as the basic primary layer of what she called her "outfits;" although the gray she wore did not predominate over her appearance, since it was enlivened—perhaps overwhelmed—by any number and variety of scarves, belts, aprons, and items of costume jewelry, which shrieked fluorescently in any but her own sight. Still, her eyes were gray; her hair, which she wore plaited loosely about her head, was graying, like Lloyd's, whose age she shared. Yet it was far grayer than his; in it, as in every part of her, age had made its inroad quickly. It was as if she had yielded to the years at their first encroach upon her fitness. She had gone soft everywhere: hips, belly, bosom, joints, brain, and heart; although it was difficult to imagine, looking at her, that she might ever have been otherwise than large and pillowy. Today she wore an apron of blinding yellow that covered her from chin to shins—a huge and featureless expanse of solid color above which her gray head seemed absurdly small. Her cheeks, whose redness overpowered her sallow face much as the apron outshone the gray she wore almost as a livery, had pressed her eyes into slits—the effect of a broad, open-mouthed smile. "Ryan!" she cried, in an alto sing-song, "Ry-an! Ry-an!"

He rose out of his reverie with a grin, which he tried unsuccessfully to stifle. Collin, too, in facing her, turned the long way about, needing an extra second to try to control his features. From the time they were very young Mrs. Overton had woken this uncontrollable mirth in them. She was intrinsically ludicrous; and although they loved her and were fiercely loyal to her, they could barely contain themselves from laughing in her face. "Mrs. Over-a-ton," they had called her, between themselves; and later, "Mrs. Overdone"; because everything she did was in some way exaggerated or excessive; and because Ryan found the Shakespearian allusion deliciously ludicrous. They had lived in a state of mild terror that she would someday perceive and comprehend the cause of their hilarity; but of this there seemed never to be any danger. She was used to their grinning, their wincing, their shared, humorous, painful glances; she understood only their courtesy, which testified to their affection for her, even if it was strained and—like its object—overdone.

Mrs. Overton offered any observer a ready handle on any of several stereotypes: the weak-minded widow; the silly fairy godmother; the jolly housekeeper, feeding on unquenchable delusions of her importance to her employer; the dispenser of cheap religious clichés, in her case acquired osmotically from a sister who had been for years a devotee of a bland Protestant church; the mother hen, bluff in her affection for her adopted son and his friend; the scatter-brained cook. Ryan's affection for her was built on one such conception: he saw her as pathetic. This she was; and yet the quirks he found pitiable and ludicrous in her were not simple, and not her own; they were shared with the majority of humankind.

Age and death were absorbing mysteries for her, which all the same she could never confront. She took one of the yellowest of the Boston papers; and before all else she read the obituaries. Not just read them—perused them minutely; even though seldom in their columns did she find any name she recognized, since her home had been in California for most of her life. Over details of accomplishment, of failure, of circumstances of decease, over husbands, wives, children, grandchildren left behind she would cluck and murmur, shaking her head, with the same concentration Lloyd Tate devoted to the affairs of the nation and the commonwealth. She was fascinated by human life at its most basic level, as he was at its grander, more self-important plane. To her it seemed that humankind had been placed on earth to make babies and dead bodies; what happened between infancy and the grave bewildered her, but she sought in that intervening term for some clue to the beginning and the end; and she never found it. Perhaps she was looking too hard. Perhaps her interest was answer in itself. Perhaps there was no reason for birth and death beyond the mere fact of their occurrence, no point in life beyond the truism that it does in fact proceed and elapse. Still she would probe; still she would wonder; like some ineffectual tragic chorus, wringing its hands helplessly amid scenes of domestic annihilation, she would whimper inarticulately as she watched the way of the world.

Television soap operas were to her as the old classics in the library were to Lloyd—the confetti with which she charged the cannon of her intellect. In the little office off the kitchen a tube was enthroned upon the stacks of old newspapers or gossip magazines that waited to be browsed through or clipped apart. At certain times of the day she worshipped before its flickering light, wide-eyed, both titillated and horrified. To her it seemed that what she saw was not, could not, be the creation of some squandered talent; it was real. Even the coarse videotape format in which it was recorded argued that. If compelled to do so, she would admit that "it was all made up"; but she could not have lived less in the lives on the screen if the set had been a peephole into true space and time.

If these stories were an addiction for her, they were nearly her only one. The news was almost as interesting, of course; but other programming she condemned as "silliness" and "fluff." Some shows she even found distressing. There had been times, when Collin and Ryan were growing up, that they had been lured by the sight of that blank tube to take over the office and watch the television; for neither in the rest of the house nor in Ryan's home was there any television set. Mrs. Overton would come upon them watching some old film in black and white, and after at first expressing her pleasure to have "company by the TV," retreat in amazement at their choice. " I don't understand how can you watch someone who's dead," she would exclaim. Her phrase became a standing joke to them; the joke mutated into a dozen different forms; became a taunt in their ongoing quarrel about the ancients and the moderns—"How can you read someone who's dead?" (or from Ryan's side, "—someone who isn't dead?") For years they could not comprehend what fear operated in her. The dead remind the living that they shall die, that their present efforts someday shall be retrospect, obituary. Mrs. Overton felt this mutely, unconsciously, as an animal knows to run from fire; but Collin and Ryan, with youth's easy ignorance, kindled the fire higher, laughing at her scruple as bizarre.

Her other vice, beside the soap operas, was a mild nosiness. She felt she knew everyone's life already, of course; but she liked to have confirmation of her knowledge by watching what they did, hearing what they said, and especially "how they met." To witness a greeting was a great entertainment. She had been known to linger in bus stations for the sheer pleasure of forming conjectures on the lives of those who came and went, on the sole basis of the way they said their hellos and goodbyes. Lloyd had caught her loitering on the wrong side of doors on innumerable occasions over the years. He accepted it as a harmless habit, although he took precautions when necessary. His own office, at the far end of the house from the kitchen, was entered through a short hall on one side and through a bathroom on the other, so that either approach could be sealed with two doors. The boys chose an even better expedient to ensure privacy: they scheduled any confidential talks for the peak hours of the soaps, or for nighttime, since Mrs. Overton drooped early.

Beyond her vices lay her virtues. She loved the men of the house; she considered herself hardly less than Lloyd Tate's true mate. Who grew his vegetables? Who shopped for and cooked his food? Who saw to his laundry? Who made sure that the cleaning woman who came once a week kept this enormous house spotless?

Who nagged that slouch Hal Minot when the flower beds needed edging? Not "that awful girl," at least, Lloyd's legal spouse; she had been gone seventeen years, since before Mrs. Overton's arrival. Collin she may well have adored more than any of her own four children, who largely neglected her and despised her, except when they thought her useful as a babysitter or as a source of gifts at weddings and christenings; they were part of the mystery of life that she accepted rather than explored, like her lost husband, who by her own account had not treated her well.

And Ryan, him too she idolized, although she knew virtually nothing accurate about him. Her own imagination was so much more complete than the account he gave of himself to such as her. He was a gentleman; he was ever courteous, soft-spoken, with that Irish laugh that came up through the house wherever you were the way a gleam of light finds its way through the space between clouds, like a solid shaft of sound. And accomplished he was; she was given to know that he had done wonderful things at college. He had a fellowship; he would be a professor someday. In her mind's eye she had him in tweed already, pipe in hand, holding forth as he leaned on the mantel by a crackling fire while fresh-faced students gazed up at him from their places on the floor. She considered him a philosopher—having once heard him explain that he was studying philology, a word which, in the inevitable practice of those of her education and mentality, she corrupted into the nearest familiar term without further inquiry. He would look like the professors on the soap operas, although he would not, of course, chase skirts. She was most comfortable with stereotypes. She readily made Ryan into one; she gave him pause to wonder, as he saw her trying to remake not only him but herself into a cliché, if he was guilty of the same thing.

He met her now for the obligatory hug and kiss. She caught him to her breasts with the unconcern of a woman who has long since ceased to feel any sexuality, or perhaps has never felt it; and Ryan, as a young man who never forgot his own, responded in the way of his kind by imitating rigor mortis and loosing the male equivalent of a nervous giggle—a snicker, half-muffled as he pretended to buss her on the cheek. On hearing this, Collin snickered too; further injuring Ryan's self-restraint, so that as she held him at arm's length for examination and he looked into her shining, soft, almost cow-like eyes, he snickered uncontrollably again.

"Mrs. Overton," he said pointlessly, in a voice muted by his fear that he would betray his hilarity. Collin guffawed.

"It's so nice to have you back!" she said.

"Nice to be back." Conversation with Mrs. Overton had a way of falling into ruts. He made a faint attempt to escape her, but she retained her grip on his shoulders, first tousling his hair, then letting him straighten it, and tousling it again by stroking it against its natural lie.

"We've just been trying to persuade Ryan not to work this summer," said Lloyd.

"Of course he won't work," said Mrs. Overton. "He has worked hard enough. Besides, he has his scholarship and everything. When do you go away to start teaching, Ryan?"

"I won't be teaching for a while yet," said Ryan. He had tried to explain the *cursus honorum* of academic life to her before, without success.

"But you are going away?"

"Yes, ma'am—"

"And when is that?"

"End of the summer. I'm not sure of the date yet."

"Well, that gives you a little time, anyway."

"Yes, it does—"

"Time for cookies, and cake, and homemade ice cream."

Collin snorted. Ryan nodded weakly. "Yes, ma'am," he said, with what solemnity he could.

"And watermelon, and cherries, and peaches—" She stopped suddenly and looked at Lloyd and Collin. "Has he heard our news?" she asked.

"First thing, Mrs. Overton," said Collin.

"Of course," said Lloyd simultaneously.

"Yes, I have," said Ryan. All three of them were trying to forestall an effusion; but it came anyway. Ryan was at least permitted to escape, as Mrs. Overton clasped her hands together in front of the broad, rounded shelf of her chest.

"The most beautiful thing you ever saw! A treasure! So precious! Absolutely a treasure!"

Some sacrifice had to be made to create a diversion. "I hear the missus is back too," interjected Ryan, as if unaware of the effect this would have on her oratory.

She halted in her rapture and her whole being became a sniff of contempt. "Unfortunately," she said. He seized the conversation, hoping to keep it out of her hands.

"We'll have to steal Constance away, won't we, Mrs. Overton?"

"Excellent idea," Lloyd put in, doing his part.

She had to smile; Ryan was grinning at her in his way, with that soft, asking smile that worked so well. "You're right," she said.

"And you will be an essential part of the plan," said Ryan. "We'll meet at midnight to discuss it; you bring the food."

She laughed out loud and gave him a push, which the sheer massiveness of her arm rendered rather less playful than her intention. She was an excellent cook; her self-image had burgeoned on the flattery of the household, just as she herself had grown fat on morsels consumed while cooking. "Speaking of food," she said, "I assume you're staying to dinner."

"I can't."

"Ryan!" protested Collin.

"Honor thy father and mother. I've only been home a few hours. The only way I could slip away was to tell them I needed a little fresh air after the trip up. Of course they knew I was coming here."

"Roast beef," said Mrs. Overton. "New potatoes. Fresh asparagus. Tempt you?"

"Don't tempt him to sin against his parents," said Lloyd.

"I was just teasing him. He knows that—don't you, Ryan? He's not always such a good boy."

"Tomorrow night," said Lloyd. "You'll come; we can at least play second fiddle."

"Thank you. We'll have to see."

The breeze had been lifting the branches of the trees and shaking the soft tassels of the oaks, rustling the great limp leaves; it fell at this instant, and they all heard the whine of the car and the faint growling of its tires on the old asphalt.

Wednesday, June 17/ Three

So like a courtier, contempt nor bitterness
Were in his pride or sharpness; if they were,
His equal had awak'd them.

—All's Well That Ends Well

H ERE THEY ARE," said Collin. Mrs. Overton stepped back, as if contemplating a retreat into the house; but her curiosity impelled her to stay. "You can never tell," she would say often, "what a handshake will bring."

They turned, Ryan more casually than the others, to face toward the sound. In a moment a cream-colored Mercedes appeared around the bend in the drive; it approached with the effortless but uninteresting motion of such luxury cars, the movement of overharnessed power, a kind of controlled glide. The faces of two people were visible behind the lightly tinted glass, turned toward one another in discussion, although that of the driver was directed partly forward. The car slowed and then stopped before the front door; the murmuring engine shut off; and then, after a delay of some seconds, the doors on each side opened, releasing the trailing end of a conversation, the crackling of paper shopping bags, the jingle of keys.

Within his anticipation Ryan felt some deeper perturbation he could not identify, some sense of change, confusion, loss, accession, beginning, doubting hope. A new force had moved into the order of the Tate house; he feared for the stability long established there. As the women began to get out of the car he almost wished to be disappointed in them, and yet at the same time he was disappointed at his own wish.

They had not noticed the group on the porch. As soon as they were out they turned toward the interior of the car and began

43

gathering and extracting the shopping bags. Collin went down the steps to help.

He said something. Ryan did not hear it—some humorous, soft word. The younger woman turned her face to him and lit up with affection—she laughed, spoke some similar banter. Ryan felt distanced, excluded, as if she were still behind the tinted glass.

But this feeling, like that unspecifiable dread of his anticipation, he forgot in looking at her. He had once, in driving along a narrow country road in some town whose very name was unknown to him, momentarily glimpsed the face of a beautiful woman walking in the opposite direction. He had felt as if he had seen a sculpture that had come to life, the soft glow of blood suffusing translucent marble, lips and eyes darkening into vitality, nostrils filling with breath. A face incorruptible, and yet glimpsed only, as the car went by, though its glance was turned toward him as if in recognition or supplication or fear. He had felt he had looked into Helen's face; there had been a tumult in his head, as if nothing mattered, not his destination, not the road over which the car rolled on without his bidding. He would have stopped and gone back, but he knew that even if he had found the woman and spoken with her, the face that he had seen would be gone, would have resolved into some frailer, mortal visage, bearing the mark of time. The memory was preferable, and yet he had kept it, as he kept all his memories, not so much as a touchstone of the present but as earnest for the future.

The face of Constance Tate was like that glimpsed face. And yet it did not flit; it remained real in his sight. She turned away again, bent over to retrieve something, straightened up; and shook, with a slight, unconscious motion, her thick, heavy hair away from her face; and so brilliantly dark it was, in the shadow cast by the house as the sun went westwards, that it could have been some liquid that had blotted his vision at that point on his retina. She placed something on top of the car, and her waist—viewed from the side as she stretched upwards—was so slender he felt almost an awe of it, as he might have in coming upon a flower thought to be extinct.

He could not connect this woman with his former images of her. The photographs had not prepared him for this. They were only snapshots, some yellowing already, all of them dog-eared. Collin, over his father's protests, had declared himself their guardian, and in his care they were often handled, scrutinized, discussed.

First, a little girl of five, in a sailor suit, frightened and wide-eyed, holding fast to a hand that must have been that of her mother (of her mother, only an elegant shoe, a mesh stocking, the hemline of fifteen years ago, a bracelet of pearls, a diamond ring, immaculate nails); in the background, the shoes and flared pantlegs of sailors in some European navy or merchant marine, as if she had been taken to see the ships, her picture snapped, a little sailor girl among the big sailors; dark hair cut in bangs, the uncanny opposite of Collin, who was already apollonine even at that age.

Then a school photo, at eight or nine: a blissful smile amid a crowd of smiles, a smock among school smocks.

A teenager sipping a soft drink, her face half-obscured by the glass, in some outdoor café, a transistor radio on the table, a folded newspaper, her mother's coffee, purse, white gloves, the chair pushed back where Mrs. Tate had risen ("I've got one more picture on the roll, Constance."—"No, Mother!"— "We'll send it to your brother. Come on. Put that glass down!")

And then, from a year ago, another café, with motorscooters and cars flashing by in a blur in the background: this time both of them, Mrs. Tate now a woman over forty who looked thirty-five, slim, dressed with the precision of beauty that knows it is aging. But Constance was an astonishment. She wore a tight black dress that made her waist seem belted into the strait stem of an hourglass as she leaned forward slightly, one elbow casually on the table, a bouquet of flowers in her lap. The neckline of the dress was cut to reveal, as though she had been dressed up by another—by her mother—to show off the body that had bloomed into fullness between the last photograph and this. By contrast her mother looked shrunken. A similar contrast in their hair: Mrs. Tate's drawn back, tight, from her bronzed face, Constance's falling in profusion over her neck, shoulders, arms, as if abandoned in the confidence that it would lie well where it fell. In the daughter's eyes, in that much-studied photograph, Ryan had read trust, trust of both present and future; trust untroubled; the trust of youth; and this he could appreciate. And yet in the eyes of the mother he saw something he understood perhaps still better, the need to hold on to what one had, to what was good.

Collin murmured something more to Constance. Her gaze lifted at once from his face and sought out Ryan where he stood on the porch. She smiled in the delight of recognition, and then looked over the top of the car at her mother. "Mother," she said, "Ryan's here."

He saw that her mother was her usual confidant. And yet Sondra Tate did not share her pleasure at the news. She glanced up, quickly and narrowly, and over the intervening distance her gaze met Ryan's—hers, instantly adversarial, though softened by a certain attraction that seemed to wonder at itself; Ryan's, willing to be generous, but wary. From that very first instant he felt a mutual curiosity and repulsion.

He had long known Sondra Tate's beauty. One day as children, playing in the vast attic of the house, in order to add realism to a game of pirates, he and Collin had smashed the lock on an old trunk—a treasure chest—and found a package of hastily folded newsprint. The paper was dated January, 1964, the time of the separation. In the package were two objects. One was a photograph of the Tates, beyond doubt taken on the day they were married. In June of 1960—in later times Collin and Ryan had computed this fact—Lloyd Tate had been thirty-six and Sondra Burnham had been twenty-two. They had known each other only three weeks. Though they wore little that marked a bridal, she carried a bouquet tightly gripped—which was the second object in the trunk, now withered and scentless. And their visages shone outward, wearing not literal but mental veils, a modesty over their joy. Yet her joy was the stronger than his, because better undergirt with joy's deep foundation, pain. Her parents would have nothing to do with her marriage—nor any longer with her—for not only was Lloyd Tate no Catholic, he was nearly an atheist ("An agnostic," she had explained, but the distinction meant little to them). As for his parents, they were dead. It was a civil ceremony, the expedient of those whose families prove uncivil or who find death has made the family blessing irrelevant. The boys were frightened of the photograph, and yet too fascinated to resist it; perhaps in this they were like Lloyd Tate, who had cast off many of the tokens of his brief life with his spouse, but evidently could not part with these two items, perhaps saved from her own abandoned possessions— hiding them from himself, thrusting them into the disused trunk as if he wished to forget where he had put them. Indeed he was angry years later when he found that Collin had the photograph in his possession, concealed in his closet. Resistless beauty, a fertile matrix of contradiction and confusion—in the photograph a woman, no schoolgirl, looking older than she was, as now she looked younger, winning a little grace from time on both ends of her youth. The boys had often brought it forth to view and discuss. As the years passed, Collin had liked it less and less; and Ryan more and more, seeing in Sondra Tate's face more and more the face of his friend, until the bone structure of that face had grown, changed, set for the last time, and the mother was alone in the past with her own version of beauty, always to Ryan's mind unalterably wondrous.

And now she was back. It seemed she was not to be kept in that trunk of memory, either as image or in the flesh. But now her beauty had become a species of clear, hard good looks. She walked, stood, dressed well; she had it all down by heart, the way a woman of forty-three should carry herself, turn her head, pierce those she saw with a fierce but unrevealing glance. Her beauty seemed to have become a superficies, had come to seem, in fact, skin deep and no more, as if the hollowness within her had expanded and expelled the ability to love, to risk all for love, that had so lit up her face in that photograph. Natural and unconscious action had been carefully schooled out of her bearing. The freshness of the daughter pointed up this lack in the mother all the more sharply. In her response to others Sondra Tate deferred to caution, not the moment's emotion.

Yet she was still not completely lost to herself. This Ryan felt keenly as he studied her face. From instant to instant the vulnerabilities and uncertainties that flickered in her blue eyes and over her countenance revealed her to be human, not self-control incarnate. He had often thought about what she had given up—a husband of intellect and distinction, a connection with an old family, wealth, a beautiful home, the security of life at the nucleus of an apparently normal family. Over the years he had met many women in the town who had sacrificed their inner life entirely for such superficial rewards: women who lived solely for an illusion of affluent complacency in which even they themselves could not believe. Any one of them, offered the option by the Mephistopheles of some suburban tragicomedy, would have traded their dull husbands for Lloyd Tate, with his wit and inbred courtesy, would have readily exchanged their status as the newly rich, as well as the expensive yet featureless houses that went with it, for this place they called a mansion, with its right to pretension; would have given up children who looked even at twenty as bored and restless as their parents at forty-five, for these two offspring, still dreaming and believing in their own futurity.

Sondra Tate had opted out of this. That argued some need in her greater than one for which the superficial could suffice. And of that Ryan approved, even as he, drawn to the Tates, wishing to become one with them himself, scorned her for rejecting her alliance with the family that was to him the center of, the very reason for, memory itself.

He descended the steps of the porch, feeling it would be rude to await their coming. Lloyd followed him, and Mrs. Overton took up a position in the doorway, through which at some point in the subsequent conversation she escaped, unnoticed, having seen what she wanted to see, avoiding further contact with Sondra Tate.

As Ryan approached, the two women put aside their shopping bags; Constance immediately, Sondra with more reluctance, as if still bridling at the protocol required of her by this sojourn in her husband's house. The golden eyes of the daughter were on Ryan's, the face raised to his as she stepped toward him; the blue eyes of the mother were challenging, registering, waiting, occasionally sweeping sideways, refusing any accession to courtesy, feigning interest in anything but him.

Introductions between Constance and Ryan would have been foolish; Collin looked on in silence. Ryan put out his hand, but Constance took his arms lightly in her own hands, holding him at the biceps, and raised herself slightly on her toes to kiss his cheek.

He felt sistered; stupified, he smelt her, both the perfume and the woman beneath it; could not speak, but smiled, a genuine smile, enfeebled by his wonder. Included, adopted, taken in as her honorary brother—an honorary Tate—without question, he could not have approved of her more.

And she, releasing him, looking into his face, must have thought suddenly that he was still a stranger; for her brows took on a twist of shyness, alertness. "You're Ryan," she said, as if both to excuse her forwardness and to reassure herself. "I feel I've known you forever."

"And I know you," he answered, thinking even as he spoke that what he said was a fiction. An intelligence familiar to him from Collin's eyes looked up at him, measuring what he was; and then an affection borrowed from her love for her brother accepted him without further inquisition.

"Mother," said Collin, "this is my old friend, Ryan Kinsella. I've mentioned him in my letters quite a bit over the years. Ryan, my mother."

Constance stepped aside. Ryan advanced to shake Sondra Tate's hand.

"Of course I know Ryan," Sondra said. Her voice was smooth, modulated, even, and yet he sensed that its velvet was that of the cat's paw. Her grip was not utterly limp, but neither was it firm, withholding the acknowledgment of him that circumstances compelled her to utter. "We've heard about your accomplishments," she added. "Rhodes Scholar, varsity man, all that—very impressive. We hadn't heard you were so dangerously handsome."

"I hadn't heard it either."

She seemed surprised at his answer, as if displeased to find his good will would be so difficult to win by cozenage. He gave her nothing; his smile was inscrutable, illegible; and yet it won a faint smile from her, perhaps because she sensed in him an opponent worthy of her skills. That smile, when it came now, at last, was real, though not radiant as her daughter's; and Ryan guessed that this would be the pattern of her character, this alternation between the calculated shock tactics of the hard, artificial self she had erected through the years and the spontaneous effusions of the self still in contact with human pleasures and frailties—love of others, doubt of its course.

"I like you," she said bluntly.

"I admire you," he answered, the upright line of his back flexing almost imperceptibly in what might have been the hint of a bow in another culture, another time.

"There's a great difference between liking and admiring."

"Perhaps we should work to bring them closer together."

She looked at Lloyd, her eyes wry, laughing. "Here's an original," she observed. "Is he always like this?"

"Ryan is nothing if not original," said Lloyd.

"Because I am originally nothing," explained Ryan.

"You can't fool us," said Constance. "We know all about you. Soccer"—she could not restrain a glance at his legs—"and Greek and Latin—and being Irish."

"You've summed up the totality of my being in four words. Can you do the same for yourself?"

"I'd have to think about it. You may have to wait for an answer.—Collin said he hoped you'd be spending some time with us this summer."

"As much as you two will allow me to spend with you."

"So the job is definitely out," said Collin.

Ryan hesitated. "Collin has been presenting some very persuasive reasons why I should forego employment this summer." The faint humor of his tone implied a reference to Constance. Sondra Tate caught it.

"We'll be pleased to get to know you better, Ryan," she said. "But if you're going to be with us, make sure you don't fall in love with my daughter. Men your age often make that mistake."

"Mother!" protested Constance.

It was Ryan's turn to be surprised; but he concealed his discomfort at her brusqueness and returned her salvo. "Only men my age?"

He saw at once that the irony of this remark cut hard: that she smarted under it.

"Men your age in particular."

"And why should the interest be limited in that way?"

"Because the young never love anyone old. They're fascinated with their own youth. They find it easier to believe that life continues after death than that it continues after thirty. People my age are the walking dead as far as you're concerned."

"I assure you, you're wrong, Mrs. Tate; my views with regard to loving across the boundaries of age are extremely advanced, however callow I may be otherwise. As for people 'your age,' no one would believe that *you* are the mother of someone twenty years old."

She watched him narrowly, then softened somewhat. He saw he had made an inroad; but she concealed her approval under another gibe. "And I would find it incredible that *you* are only twenty, considering how articulate you are, except that when I look at you I can see you must be.—But I don't care what you think of me. Don't try to lay down a smoke screen, Mr. Kinsella. Just remember what I said about my daughter."

"It's too late, Mother," said Collin. "You said it yourself. No red-blooded male could help falling in love with her at first sight. Obviously he's desperate about her already; you'll just have to learn to live with it."

Both mother and daughter looked at Ryan uncertainly, as if disconcerted by Collin's jest. He surveyed them both with an absolutely neutral coolness. They were reassured. "I pity him if he is," said Constance. "He'll find me very unworthy."

"You see that my daughter's chief—her only—flaw is a lack of self-esteem," said Lloyd.

"Which you're doing your best to supply, Papa," she said, smiling brightly at him. Her affection brought the conversation smartly about on a new tack. "Did Collin pick you up all right at the station?" she asked.

"He was waiting for me."

"Then I won't worry that we inconvenienced you too much."

"Not at all. Any time you and your mother want to borrow the car, I'm sure we can arrange something."

"Oh, Lloyd, we got you a present," said Sondra, beginning to rummage through the array of shopping bags about her. From one she drew forth a large lampshade. "Here," she said.

"What's that for?" asked Lloyd suspiciously.

"The lamp on the sidetable in the living room."

"What's wrong with the old shade?" muttered Lloyd, Collin, and Ryan in approximate unison. She laughed.

"Well, listen to the three old bachelors! Lloyd, that lampshade is twenty years old. I distinctly remember it."

"Our children are twenty. Should we trade them in, too? My mother bought that lampshade—Lord, it was thirty, forty years ago. It's just as good now as it was then."

"Oh, I agree entirely—just as good. That's why I bought a new one. You need the contemporary look there."

"Age doesn't make fine things bad; it lends them dignity."

"An antique is an antique, dignified or not."

"Antiques have come into fashion since you were last in America, Sondra. Besides, if forty years makes an antique, I'm an antique, and so are you, gallant compliments not withstanding. The fact is, the lamp doesn't need a new shade."

"It's a beginning," said Sondra.

"A beginning of what?" said Ryan gruffly.

She ignored his interjection. "The least you can do is let me try it out," she said to Lloyd. "Come, Constance, help me carry in these bags. These old men have forgotten their manners."

There was a general movement to gather up the bags, during which Sondra went inside, carrying the shade and little else. The screen door slammed behind her. The others paused a moment before they followed, waiting until she was well out of earshot.

"She really is a sweet person," said Constance apologetically. She was apparently used to pleading on behalf of her mother.

"Very sweet," agreed Collin facetiously. "Or at least, sweet people think so."

"It's called projection," said Ryan.

Lloyd added his commentary: "She's sweet, all right. I'll tell you just how sweet: Have you ever bitten into a lemon you thought was an orange? That's how sweet she is."

"But lemon and sugar together make for a good drink, Mr. Tate," said Ryan.

"You mean my daughter's sweetness more than makes up for my wife's acidity, I take it. It's true. And I'll be damned if Sondra doesn't know it."

Ryan felt this was a dangerous topic; Collin and Constance apparently agreed with him. To curtail the discussion, they turned for the front door.

Once more Ryan entered the antechamber of the deep house where memory dwelt. Nothing had changed in this front hall; there was little that could have. It was not large; when the screen door creaked and thumped and clicked fast behind the four of them, they almost filled the whole area. To the right was the door to the library, and next to it the stairway that bent its way upward by several landings—both door and stair of old, varnished oak, stained dark by time but in perfect repair. To the left was a matching door that led to a coat closet and powder room; beside this, running the remainder of the length of the wall, was a table that held only an art nouveau lamp, and now Sondra's purse, an alien object, cast aside as she swept into the house. Ryan noticed it particularly, and was surprised by the vehemence of the displeasure he saw on his face in the mirror over the table.

He looked away, up to the ceiling—at dark beams against cream-colored plaster; he heard, a reassuring cacophony, the clinking of the thick, brown floor tiles as he and his friends walked across them. The grout had crumbled long before Lloyd was born; Ryan had heard him explain once, on being asked why he never had the tiles repaired, that he could remember waking often at night to hear, distantly through the house, his father crossing those tiles to close and bolt the great oak door; that the sound they made had come to have an association with security, routine, tradition, paternal vigilance.

The living room, too, had its tradition. It had been equipped by the same bride who had urged the building of the new wing. Once it had been the dining room; under her direction the heavy curtains that obscured the view on the backyard had been discarded forever, and the polished furnishings she bought for it—the height of fashion in her time—still gleamed with a soft northern light that seemed the lingering glow of the previous century. On those rare occasions when Lloyd invited the partners of the firm and some of the younger attorneys to a dinner, invariably some tactless upstart would ask him if he would be willing to sell some piece from the collection—assuming, perhaps, that Lloyd must be interested in them only as he was, as collectibles, commodities to be traded, articles of investment, for which no profitable offer would be refused. Lloyd would explain that these furnishings had been the Tate possessions since before the century began, an almost inconceivable longevity of ownership in a culture that was continually renewing and remaking itself, continually abandoning what it had just achieved.

The great couch that dominated the room was the only concession to modern times. About five years ago the previous sofa had become disreputably shabby, and Lloyd had discovered that recovering it would cost several times the price of a new piece of furniture. His innate sense of thrift overcame his reverence for the past. Hal Minot took the old couch to the dump, and the new one arrived by delivery truck from one of the swank stores intown, extravagantly comfortable, and boldly if accidentally attractive. After sulking about this loss for some time, even Ryan was compelled to admit that the new couch possessed a certain Tatish style. It was flanked by two other modern appurtenances, the speakers of a stereo system; but since these antedated Ryan's acquaintance with the room, he had never found them offensive.

A little light from the westering sun fell into the large room through the French windows; and on the square of orange it created on the old buff-colored carpet, Sondra had taken her stand, an iconoclast setting her torch to a church. The men put the shopping bags aside like so many bearers dropping delicate scientific equipment whose value they did not appreciate; the new shade sat on its lamp, confronting them.

"Sets the old furniture off, don't you think, Constance?" said Sondra.

"Sets *me* off," said Lloyd. "Honestly, Sondra, what in God's name went through your head?"

"I'm trying to put a little life into this old shack," she answered. "Constance, give me your opinion." She needed her daughter to back her up if she was going to be able to effect such a drastic change with impunity; but Constance, after looking cautiously at the three scowling men, refused her help.

"Actually, Mother, the old one"—she picked it up—"*was* rather pretty."

"What do you mean, 'was'?" said Lloyd. "It still is, and it's going back on the lamp."

"It's broken," she said softly, showing him where the aged silk had split under the pressure of Sondra's fingers.

"Oh, for heaven's sake," he said in disgust.

"You see, you'll have to keep this one," said Sondra.

"Maybe we can find one you like better, Papa," said Constance, looking at her father appeasingly. Evidently the word *Papa* was so new to him that its charm had extraordinary power to dissolve his anger.

"Do that for me, Constance. I'd be grateful. It will be difficult living with *that* thing," he said, gesturing toward the new shade. The ambiguous motion of his hand took in Sondra as well. She darted a glance at him, cold and ugly with remembered quarrels, and a taut silence fell, a continuation of those seventeen years without speech.

"Well," said Ryan, "I guess I should be dutiful and go home."

"Sure we can't talk you into staying to dinner?" asked Lloyd.

"I'm sorry—"

"Not even with the inducement of my daughter's company? Be careful what you say."

"I'm sure Constance would be disappointed in me if I forsook my parents even for her company," said Ryan, neatly avoiding Lloyd's trap. Constance smiled her approval. Further protests were made, but he overcame them, saying his farewells briefly.

"You're coming back tomorrow, of course," said Collin.

"That goes without saying," insisted Lloyd.

"Of course he is," said Constance.

"Eleven o'clock," said Collin. "A picnic by the pond. Bring your bathing suit."

"Summer!" said Lloyd. "All my favorite young people enjoying the summer! Maybe I'll retire and join you."

"Please do," said Constance, touching his arm. He beamed at her, immensely pleased.

"I wish I could," he said. "But there's no rest for the wicked, you know. I labor so that the young and innocent may rest. Besides, what would you do with an old fuddy-duddy like me?"

"Feed you sandwiches and cake," said Constance. He laughed.

Ryan turned to go. "Tomorrow, then," he said.

"So, you *are* coming," insisted Collin. "I thought we could persuade you."

Ryan went back through the hall and out the screen door; Collin followed him. "Remember your promise, now," he told Ryan. "No job this summer."

"I don't recall any such promise."

"Well, you made one. You'll just have to trust me on that point. Look, Constance is here; we've got to keep her entertained. You know what a dreamer I am; she'll get bored of watching me stare off into space. You've got to keep the conversation going when I nod off. What do you say?"

Ryan paused, scuffing the asphalt lightly with the toe of one shoe before he answered; Collin stood on the step, watching his face. "I suppose between you and my parents I'll probably find sufficient excuse to avoid job-hunting, at least for a while," he said finally.

Collin grinned. He joined Ryan on the pavement in order to speak to him confidentially, lowering his voice. "So, what do you think?"

"She's extraordinary, buddy. I'm so glad she's back—glad for you."

"And what about my mother? She can give as good as she gets, don't you think? It looks like you two will have some fun sparring this summer."

"She seems pretty tough," said Ryan.

"Tough isn't the word," said Collin.

"No, it isn't," agreed Ryan. "As a matter of fact, I hate to say it, but there are definite indications your mother has balls."

Collin's guffaw was abrupt and uninhibited; it was matched by similar laughter from the doorway, where Lloyd, following them, had overheard the remark. Grinning, Ryan turned away, waved one final time, and started off down the drive.

❁❁❁

When he had passed out of earshot, Lloyd joined Collin outside. Father and son stood looking after him.

Lloyd chuckled softly. "So," he said, "do you think Constance and your mother are ready for Ryan?"

And then they both laughed together again.

Wednesday, June 17 / Four

Marry, sir, she's the kitchen-wench, and all grease; and I know not
what use to put her to but to make a lamp of her and run from her
by her own light. I warrant her rags and the tallow in them will
burn a Poland winter; if she lives till doomsday, she'll burn a week
longer than the whole world.

—The Comedy of Errors

How now?
Even so quickly may one catch the plague?

—Twelfth-Night

O heaven! were man
But constant, he were perfect: that one error
Fills him with faults; makes him run through all the sins:
Inconstancy falls off ere it begins.

—The Two Gentlemen of Verona

RYAN, HOWEVER, WAS not to escape without assuming the burden that had been gathered for him. Just beyond the loop of the drive a parking area had been cut out of the lawn when the gatehouse had been sold, years ago; Lloyd had intended that it should reduce congestion around the circle, but it was so inconvenient that he himself never used it. He had made it the sole condition of his purchase of a car for Collin that his son should use this neglected parking area; and here stood Collin's car, a small, inexpensive import, beside Mrs. Overton's hulking and nondescript American sedan. And here Ryan came upon Mrs. Overton herself, rummaging through a pile of debris in the back seat of her Pontiac.

At first he saw only her enormous hindquarters as she leaned into her car. He had hopes that he would be able to evade her, and had in fact turned off the drive toward the main lawn when she straightened with a huff of breath and noticed him. At once he knew that he was expected; that she had left her kitchen on autopilot and stolen out to this post in the intention of waylaying him. He might have merely waved hastily and taken to his heels, but his pity won out—he paused, she called, and he approached her, already summoning his resources to effect an early escape. The key to which was controlling the conversation, which in turn required speaking first. "I was just on my way home, Mrs. Overton. My mother is cooking something special, and I took a little longer—"

"I've got your clippings," she said, wagging her finger at him. From the roof of the car she took a large bundle bound with several greasy rubber bands. She held it out to him.

"Oh," was all he could say. He took the packet, and in his momentary state of revulsion, lost his advantage.

"Just some things I thought you might be interested in. There's an article on teaching Chinese I know you'll like."

"I don't know Chinese, Mrs. Overton."

"Well, it's a language. You're so good with languages!"

"Thank you—very much—I'm very touched that you . . . think of me so often." He hefted the bundle as he said this.

"Now, tell me, what did you think of our lamb?"

He felt the old irrepressible mischief rising. "Lamb? I thought you were having roast beef."

"You scamp! You know what I mean."

"Oh, you mean *that* lamb. Well—what can I say?" He chose a word from Mrs. Overton's vocabulary. "She's wonderful. I'm very pleased for Collin, and for Mr. Tate."

"All that education, and all you can say is 'wonderful'?"

"Well, I hardly had a chance to speak to her. But she seems very nice."

Mrs. Overton nodded grimly. "I know what you mean," she said. "*She* took over. That cold, heartless, calculating *thing!* She always does—you'll see, she always does. Always drawing the attention to herself, like a two-year-old. That poor girl hardly gets a word in edgewise.—I tell you, Sondra Tate has only come back for one thing: the money. She's run out. Spent it. Spent it all! Did you know he gave her every cent when she left here? Just to get rid of her. Just to avoid having her around his neck. He hardly had enough to pay me my first week's wages when I came here. And so unnatural! So unnatural of her, to run off to Spain and leave behind such a beautiful, healthy boy. And keeping those poor lambs apart all these years—so unnatural!"

"Well, it's nice that she's finally come back—"

"Nice? Come on, Ryan—we're old friends. Let's not talk nonsense. The woman's a monster. And she won't stop till she gets what she wants. Do you know how little money she has? Only two hundred dollars. In traveler's checks."

Ryan was surprised and displeased: he pictured Mrs. Overton spitefully rooting through Sondra's purse.

"The important thing," he advised her, "is to keep a grip on yourself. She can't rattle you if you don't let her. You've been here a long time—"

"Longer than she ever was! She was just a girl when he married her—not much older than Constance is now. All fire and carrying on—and how long did she last? About four years—not even that. I've been here seventeen years. All she ever wanted was his money, and once she had that, she left."

"I don't know," he said suddenly. "Maybe she wants his money. Maybe she wants something more." They looked each other directly in the eyes.

"Him?" she said, her voice quavering slightly. "You think she wants him? You think she really wants to stay? I can't believe that."

"The important thing is to stay calm. Nothing's happened yet. At least she brought Constance back. That's a good thing, isn't it?"

"She's just using Constance to get what she wants!"

"Maybe so. But none of us are going to be taken in by that. It's just as I said before: the trick now is to keep Constance, and let Mrs. Tate go her own way."

Suddenly Mrs. Overton smiled—laughed, in fact, in her usual high chortle, which always seemed somewhat muffled by the deep fat on her body. She seized him by the earlobe, grinning, and whispered, "That's your job!"

"What do you mean?" he asked, pulling his head to one side to escape her grip.

"I said, that's your job! Go to it, Ryan!"

He was disgusted. "I'm going home," he said severely.

She winked at him. "You'll come back tomorrow!"

"Don't you get any ideas, Mrs. Overton," he said warningly.

"Ideas?" she chortled. "I don't need to get any ideas. Not with you on the job."

He turned abruptly and left.

❁❁❁

Ryan was a walker. He looked upon a good walk as a kind of a mobile solitude for the purpose of reflection; and he knew that the route back to his parents by road would be too brief for his long thoughts. Upon escaping Mrs. Overton he crossed the expanse of the front lawn and made for the hill that formed one wall of the valley on the southern side of the property. As he passed into the fringe of the wood he had to make his way among the trunks of maples and oaks, threading a path through the light-starved saplings that grew in the moist underworld beneath the canopy, seedlings stunted until some giant parent should fall and allow them light. The debris on the floor of the woods rustled and cracked as he went upward; when he came into the higher pine woods, the silence of his tread was a conspicuous change.

Or would have been, if he had noticed it. Nothing here had altered since his last passage through it; he found nothing to jar and arrest him, only soothing sameness. In the pinewood the golden sunlight fell, where it could, in oblique shafts through the green boughs overhead, making illuminated columns out of the drifting pollen.

He had quickly put aside his disgust with Mrs. Overton. Pity had taken its place. He glanced at the packet of clippings in his hand with a faint, painful smile.

She had her plans—but then again, everyone did. As the outsider, he had always been judge and jury, advocate and arbitrator at the Tates'; appealed to by all constantly, he had even from time to time effected a conciliation in a minor feud. It was likely this role would continue with the addition of Constance and Sondra to the scene. Mrs. Overton wanted to use him just as Sondra was using Constance.

And who was this Constance Tate? He felt he had been allowed only a brief look at her, a few words before Sondra took over, striking directly at him, provoking his irony; by sheer force of brash willpower taking his attention from her daughter, who was infinitely more interesting to him. Sondra had been obnoxious— and yet piquing, intriguing; almost making him forget what a threat she was to order, tradition, the way of the past. In fact, at first he found it hard to concentrate on Constance as he walked, so much more insistent was the impression created by Sondra. But then he fell into circular queries concerning the daughter that occupied him for some distance through the wood.

Spain—she had grown up in Spain; and he knew absolutely nothing about the place. As any good classicist in the Anglo-American tradition in his time, Ryan knew German as a matter of course, French as a matter of courtesy, Italian as a point of pride, a smattering of Modern Greek as a part of his credentials; for Spanish alone he reserved his indifference. If the birthplace of Martial, Seneca, Trajan, and Hadrian had a later history, it was unknown to him. He could quote Shakespeare, Goethe, and Dante, but Cervantes was beyond his ken.

Constance had lived in Seville and Madrid, Ryan knew, but those places were little more than names to him, except for what he knew of Seville's Roman years. She had attended an English school in Spain—but what did that mean? Surely she had absorbed a large part of the culture of the land in which she had lived; her Spanish was reported to be impeccable, fluent. In the field of literature, which normally would have been the first he could have explored and shared with any new acquaintance, she must have mastered a curriculum about which he knew absolutely nothing. He knew that she played classical guitar, but not as a passion, according to Collin. From what Collin said of her, she seemed curiously without any strong personal interests.

She shared a common religion with Ryan, at least nominally. But here, he suspected, they were both such indifferent Catholics that the connection would mean little. His Protestant father, as if feeling that the buffets and hurricanos of the spiritual were a threat to intellectual life, had led the family into a haven of secularity. Ryan knew the forms, and respected the feelings, of his ancestors' church; admired its antiquity, venerated its tradition, but was baffled by its articles of faith, and neglected its attendance. Mrs. Tate, he guessed from remarks Collin had made, observed her religion only as a matter of show; and Ryan guessed that the mother had kept the daughter from too much involvement in the Church almost as she would shield her from a dangerously romantic young man.

These subjects were like dams against which the current of his thoughts ran, only to be deflected against another. Since he could create no coherent picture of her, he reverted at last to considering his future opportunities for doing so. He thought of the morrow; questioned whether his only pair of bathing trunks was presentable; wondered whether he had a beach towel that was not utterly bald and ragged; and for a time dealt exclusively with these anxieties, so common to him from years of contact with the Tates.

Then it struck him that Constance, too, would wear a bathing suit. Swimming, Collin had said. The pond would be cold still, but they had never been able to resist it when the warmth of June came on. He thought about her in a bathing suit; and for several minutes saw nothing more before him, in a meditation part cerebral and part physical.

A bluejay jeered above him. With a sense of reluctance he came back to reality. He found that during his minutes of preoccupation he had continued walking; he had left the pines behind and entered the deciduous trees at the southern end of the valley. The growth here was so dense—sassafras, sumac, saplings of pin oak and maple—that he had unconsciously let his feet follow the old path in order that he might remain oblivious to his surroundings as he penetrated the thicket. At the end of this path he now stood, looking out into a clearing—to his fond mind, so liberal with definite articles, *the* clearing—a meadow of hay grasses, now only soft green shoots and the straw of last year's growth. A rough ring of several enormous trees hemmed the place in; one, of particular immensity, he and Collin had styled "The Oak" in times gone by; it was perhaps the largest tree on the property. He wandered into the open and made for its company; the bark, growing over a trunk that had long since buried its heartwood and its knots deep within, was regular, if still corrugated and uncomfortable; it lent him a kind of assurance now as he put his back against it.

He surveyed with some comfort the first daisies, purple clover, paintbrush, and yarrow that tufted the expanse of pale meadow grass; but he frowned at the weed trees that had sprouted in the field in recent years. A little work with a saw or a machete would take care of them; he would do it himself if the Tates would not listen. He had dropped several hints to Mr. Tate in recent seasons, of gradually increasing broadness—that the meadow should be mowed, or it would cease to be a meadow—but Lloyd had not been to this clearing in fifteen years, and for him it was out of mind. The bluejay shifted its perch and scolded him again.

"Bathing suit," said Ryan to the jay. "She'll be wearing a bathing suit. What kind of bathing suit do you think she'll wear?"

The jay jeered at him.

"Bikini," Ryan said. And he understood with that one word the events of the last twenty-four hours.

At this time yesterday he had lain in bed holding a woman in his arms—a woman old enough to be mother to Constance, and who, unlike Sondra Tate, looked her age; whom study and labor, anxiety and loneliness, the burden of seeing beauty and obtaining knowledge without being able to share it, pressed hard upon; so that she clung to him with grieving, painful strength, thrusting her body, from contorted face to flat, barren pelvis, against him as if to force herself into the very physical space he occupied.

This woman he loved; that was why he shuddered in disgust as he thought of Mrs. Overton's fingers on his ear, her wink of would-be conspiracy. Such insinuations were revolting beside the grief and sacrifice of Eve.

Eve Mornay had been one of his professors in his freshman year. She taught art history. He, thinking he had thrown off the morality of his parents, was like an adolescent goat gamboling in the green fields of this great coeducational institution—every woman was beautiful, and no woman was out of his reach; he had taken his seat in the lecture hall at a height slightly above Professor Mornay's eye level, leaning forward over the desktop, fixing his eyes upon her as if he meant to learn the language of art not by listening, but by reading her lips.

He saw that at first she found him disturbing, even rude. He knew he was like a dark blot among the bright, lazy, indifferent faces of the children of affluence, a chimney sweep among the golden girls and boys, his glance reminding her that she, too, would come to dust. She saw, and he saw how she saw, that when he entered and took his seat, looked around at his classmates, he was silent, unsharing, young, proud, aloof. He knew, or imagined, that she held his green corduroy in contempt. He guessed, and rightly, that it irritated her that he took no notes—brought seldom even a pencil, or paper, or a book to her class, unless it was a volume he had needed earlier in some other course. This she had resented—art was no pastime; it was serious; and he could tell that she had vowed he would smart for his presumption at the first exam.

All the same she had to catch herself from lecturing almost to him alone. For he was listening, intently, and he felt that his interest, so much did it exceed that of his classmates, could almost draw her gaze to his. He had a secret. She did not know it until he took the midterm.

He was longer writing than anyone else, although at the time he did not notice. She had to come up among the empty seats of the hall herself to claim his blue book when everyone else had gone. For a moment he did not recognize her; he was still away in his thoughts. He wrote a few more hasty words and surrendered the book to her.

She turned her back as soon as she had it. Perhaps she thought that she had in her hand the means with which she would chastise him, bring him down from this level above her; and yet perhaps too, she had come to dread the necessity of it. When she had gone a few steps he spoke to her.

"Professor Mornay."

Facing him, she looked suddenly weak.

"Could I switch to your section?"

She drew up, considered.

"Why? Isn't it a little late in the semester to be switching sections? Mr. Holmes . . ."

"Mr. Holmes isn't worth listening to."

"The purpose of the sections is to discuss—"

"Mr. Holmes isn't worth discussing anything with."

"But you're there to share ideas—"

"Mr. Holmes doesn't have an idea in his head."

He was so sure of himself, so persistent.

Another pause, longer, and increasingly awkward. She was studying his eyes, as if seeing their color for the first time, memorizing it.

"I'll tell Mr. Holmes I have a scheduling problem," he suggested.

A shorter pause. She was regrouping, gathering her old prejudices about her.

"All right, Mr.—"

"Kinsella. Ryan Kinsella."

"I'll tell you what, Mr. Kinsella—wait until I've corrected your midterm. Then you can see if you really want to be in my section."

"I'll make a deal with you."

"I don't generally make 'deals,' Mr. Kinsella."

"If I get an A on that exam, I switch to your section."

"You're very confident."

"Read it and then judge me."

"Very well. I will." She turned again. Her manner was somewhere between dismissal and retreat.

When she read the exam she found out his secret. His secret was that he was more intelligent, more educated, and more in love with art than any of his classmates.

In the months after that, in her sections and in her lectures, they both sometimes forgot that the other students existed. The others seemed mere auditors, he and she the true students, in the root sense of the word. At times she seemed to catch herself and reproach herself for this obsession with him; at others she did not seem to care whether anyone noticed their mutual fixation, the way their eyes met and remet across the thick warm air of the lecture hall.

When the course was over, they forbore. For three years, until he was a senior. It was a delicious kind of self-denial, bittersweet; she, watching him growing into the community, watching him become recognized not for his highest worth, which she had detected if belatedly at least certainly in his very first year, but for this lesser skill, this magic in his legs; he, seeing how she yearned, in the midst of their long and intense conversations, for another kind of knowledge.

She had told him, when she first discovered he was a soccer player, that she detested sports. And yet for three seasons, in wind, in rain, and even in snow, he could look up at any time, as she had looked up into the upper row of the lecture hall, to see her face shining and distinct in the crowd, exulting when he won, and when he lost, weeping without mercy on herself, as if he had been slain. He told her once she was his good luck—a chance remark, a bantering comment in passing; but she seemed to take it on as a serious responsibility, greeting him uneasily when they next met after a game she had been unable to attend, apologizing for her absence if the score had been good, mute with self-recrimination if the outcome had been bad. In truth he had needed little luck.

After his final season, in the peak of his popularity, he saw that she was unable to discipline herself at all. If she met him on campus in the company of another woman, she instantly began to brood, a selfish indulgence not in her ordinary character. Why should not she, too, walk there, beside him? After all, she knew better what he was.

She lost all will to conceal her wish. It was not enough to meet him by chance in the Blue Room and sit together over coffee. She asked him to walk with her afterward; she put her hand within his biceps and held him to her. She invited him to dinner, downtown at first, and later in her own apartment. The talk often turned to sex, as if the conversation were out of their control. He saw these signs with a disbelief, an awe of the union they foretold. On his side was no foresight, no looking ahead to the end; he was too young for that. What would happen, would happen. And when he had confidence, when confidence came to him in the quiet sadness and elation of his graduation, he took her offering.

They went away to New York together. He gave his parents the flimsiest of excuses about staying with a friend—several times they saw her colleagues or his classmates, once even one of his cousins on the street; and the hotel charges went to four figures before they were through, all of which she had to pay, and willingly paid, too willingly paid. But in New York there were the museums, which were a refreshing salt bread for the mind after the honey of the meeting of their bodies, a leavened loaf they shared as eagerly as the sweetness.

And yet abruptly, in the midst of the feast, she had told him he must go away. Yesterday it was. She could not explain her urgency to him. He had left her this morning, in the Port Authority, and brooded from the instant he could no longer see her face straining after the sight of his, that in spite of her insistence that it was not so, it was his youth that had made her send him from her. Had she found him, in the two weeks that had seemed to him the most serene of his life (the loneliness and sexual hunger sated with a finality that had only yesterday been revealed as illusory)—lacking in some maturity that she needed? He had asked her this, last night; she had bitterly denied it.

"It's not that you're young," she had said; "It's that I'm old."

"It's the same thing," he had answered.

"No, no," she had said, weeping, "Can't you see? It's not. Can't you see I'm being smothered in this—smothered by my own age?"

She had wept in the bus station, too, clinging to him, crying so bitterly, refusing so bitterly his insistence that she change her mind, that he knew she loved him far more than he loved her. He could not love her that much—there was some reason why not, some reason she had sensed; and until this minute in the woods it had been cipher to him.

This then was the reason: that youth cries to youth. That young flesh, the encaged vigor of his twenty years, turned with delight toward the promise of other youngness. Constance had swept Eve out of his mind so abruptly and utterly that he knew, considering his apostasy, that the love he had felt for Eve had lacked an anchor that might be cast down anywhere in the course that lay ahead of him. And Eve herself had felt that too; felt she held a buoyant and drifting spirit, who for all his passion and affection was still blind to his own need, his own purposes.

"Bikini," he murmured to himself; and saw by contrast Eve's body: thin, its flesh neglected. Her soul had fed so exclusively on rich learning that it had brought on a physical famine in the wasting frame. Her mind had been a teacher and companion to his mental age; her body he had amazed and delighted, but in the end his youth had overwhelmed it. When she held him she was not young again, but old, older than she was when alone.

The jay took to wing and joined its peers protesting in the trees around the clearing; a breeze rustled the leaves and lifted and let spring back the uttermost tips of the overspreading limbs of the oak; and finally Ryan came to a resolution.

He would not forget Eve thus in the space of a few hours. He refused to do so. She had told him to, when she had suddenly and convincingly ended what had been well begun these past two weeks in New York. He had no intention of falling in love with his friend's sister—let anyone who wished make such an imputation. It would be selfish of him to infringe in the slightest way on the time brother and sister had together to become acquainted, to become truly brother and sister. Unless, of course, he was invited. If he was invited, he intended to accept the invitation. Let Sondra Tate jibe at him; he could hold his own. And if Constance Tate should appear at the pond tomorrow in the most revealing of swimsuits—he had two eyes in his head, and he would know what to do with them.

And yet in all this he would refuse to listen for even a moment to any whispering of infatuation. And what strengthened his resolve most of all was the thought that if he permitted himself to become captivated by this beautiful young woman, if he undertook some quixotic pursuit of her, and if he failed—then everything would be changed. Things would never be quite the same between the Tates and him again. To gain her would be to gain everything good in life—and he did not think, for even a flickering instant, of any material gain, he thought only of the consolidation and legitimization of his ties to the past he loved—but to lose her after trying would ruin everything.

It was not worth the risk.

He had once, when he was hardly more than a toddler, jumped off the roof of the porch of his parents' house in the confidence that he could, with the wings he had made for himself out of cast-off boards, fly over the highway he was forbidden to cross and visit Collin. He did not remember being hurt; he only remembered his mother's terror. As he leapt from the shingles she caught a glimpse of him through the window whose screen he had dislocated; she raced with a shriek downstairs and out the door; he was lying baffled in a disheveled flowerbed, staring at the colors nodding over his face.

And now he jumped again, trusting to wings as ineffectual, to strength as frail.

"Whatever happens," he said, striding across the clearing, "I will not fall in love with Constance Tate.'"

Wednesday, June 17/Five

If ever household affections and loves are graceful things, they are graceful in the poor.

—Dickens

No consecration of a home is so holy as that of a kindly, self-denying, trustful spirit in him who is the head and life of his house.

—Harriet Martineau

She was always asking him what he was doing, where he was going, with whom he had been; and although there was no reason at all why he should not tell her everything, he inclined to be secret with her because of her curiosity.

—Hugh Walpole

"Why do you softly, richly speak
Rhythm so sweetly scanned?"
Poverty hath the Gaelic and Greek
In my land.

—Rachael Annand Taylor

Better to dine on humble greens served with love than on the best beef served up with hate.

—Proverbs 15:17

IT WAS NOT much farther through the wood before the sound of the traffic began to intrude upon the silence of the valley. With a suddenness that brought a form of disappointment, the stone wall appeared through the undergrowth. Ryan's long acquaintance with the route had led him to a point at which the handholds were well known, and he climbed the barrier without hesitation.

From the top of the wall he could look down a weedy slope to the state road, a two-lane highway over which the rush-hour traffic now surged. The prolonged, modulated, screaming drone of the passenger cars was broken by the roar of a flatbed semi, running in excess of the weight limit, which jolted and clanged by with a hostile shriek of air brakes. From several cars a well-kempt professional countenance peered up at the figure standing nonchalantly atop the Tates' wall. A state police cruiser passed; Ryan watched it narrowly until it was out of sight—the troopers had often stopped and questioned him over the years, seeing him descend at this unlikely spot. The local police, by contrast, knew him and his friendship with the Tates and would at most have waved.

When he was sure of no interference he dropped to the foot of the wall and from there, half-helping and half-resisting gravity, plunged abruptly down the slope on a line tangential to the highway; it led him to a dry culvert, about four feet in height, a safe and convenient passage under the road. He and Collin had used it since boyhood; it had allowed their free passage from one house to the other. He crouched his way through it, ignoring the muffled clangor and rumble of the traffic overhead.

On the other side of the road he doubled back along the highway until he reached a quieter side street; and a short distance down this lane he came to a little house on a quarter-acre lot under dark, overhanging trees.

Here he could not have said, as he paused again, that everything was unchanged. Even in the foreground a dozen details provoked his irritation. The mailbox had been vandalized, bludgeoned wantonly until it was nearly useless, and the post was awry. New potholes had blossomed in the short driveway and the winter's frostheaves still bulged: the patched asphalt reminded him of a runway cratered and buckled by shellfire. The old Valiant parked on this dubious surface still defied the miles and years, true to its name, but its brown paint was pinker and its rust had metastasized farther over the winter; one tire was dangerously bald—the sole whitewall. The little yard on both sides of the driveway and around the house was a maze of weeds uncut for years.

The house itself was a kind of weed—a thing that fulfilled its own purposes, but was out of place in such a garden suburb. Nondescript, a generic brown, in a style it shared with innumerable other lot houses built in the twenties, it clung meekly to its place waiting to be rooted out. Neglect had marked it at all points. A wisteria vine, for instance, once regularly pruned into submission, was now scaling the peeling clapboards—had even pulled one loose—and threatened the electric supply; one feeler had penetrated into the attic by a broken louver and had spread a fan behind the panes of a small window.

The greater part of his irritation at this sight was a disgust with himself. He had long since given up expecting his parents to deal with the continuing crisis in the yard; they lived an inward life, in an interior space cluttered with the debris of their intellectual passions; what passed outside their house was like most of what passed outside their minds, observed with an ingenuous helplessness and then avoided. It was up to him to tame this unruly piece of nature and neglect; but he spent his free time not in performing this duty, but at the Tates'. Whenever he looked on this wreckage he reproached himself with the thought that while he was idling away his hours on Lloyd Tate's well-kept preserve, his parents stayed behind in a squalor borne all too cheerfully.

The Kinsellas had endured professional setbacks that had broken and embittered many a scholar; and yet they considered themselves blessed beyond their greatest hopes. Daniel Kinsella had labored as an instructor for twenty-six years, seeing preferment pass him by at every opportunity until just this past year, when he turned fifty years of age. He had then been made assistant professor. Maureen had also been a teacher, years ago; but she had been driven out of her post when she was pregnant with Ryan. ("Those were less enlightened times," she liked to say, as if to convince herself that since then the world had made up its mind to a more just behavior.) Without Ryan they would certainly have become unhappy; but upon his birth, and increasingly as the years unfolded his powers, their joy and their purpose in life was revealed through him—or so they felt. He was singular; he was brilliant; he was affectionate, dutiful; he was a mystery; he dwelt with them and yet for all their study constantly amazed them, ruling over them through the rapidity and range of his powers of apprehension.

Their sense of blessedness led them into excessive charity. It was a kind of addiction for them to listen to the hard tales of those who had allowed themselves to be embittered; they took a mournful pleasure in murmuring soft soothing sounds that carried the lilt of Boston Irish; in nodding knowingly to one another, sharing a glance with which they secretly pledged to contrive some gift of cash from their own income. It was as if they were aware that their happiness had too narrow a foundation; as if they felt they might purchase protection for that foundation with nothing more than compassion—genuine, it was true, but almost too ready— and with the money that meant nothing to them. It is easy for the blessed to bless; for those who have been hurt, it is hard to undo the fist of the hand. The contrast of their charity to that of Lloyd Tate could be illustrative. There were many years of their married life in which they had given more to charity than he—a shame to him, had he known it; but the reason lay in the sense of injury that he carried in him, which they did not. Although he was blessed with the power of wealth, he could not thread the needle's eye of his own grievances against life and bestow that wealth as readily as could the Kinsellas.

It was these people who had urged their son to forego working this summer. At his graduation two weeks ago they had made their case, painting a picture in shades of gray of the drudgery of his childhood, the loneliness of his early education—they had quite surprised him with the accuracy of their depiction. He had not known till that moment that they were fully aware of what he had given up, working to succeed in their eyes, following their own model of sacrifice. They talked of the scholarship he had won as if it had sealed his lifelong success—pointing out that it would carry him through the next phase of his training, that beyond it he would win grants, teaching assistantships, and ultimately a post— by which they meant, in their eager and self-forgetful naiveté, a real post, not the whipping post his father's job had been. For Ryan, they thought, everything would be better, because—well, because he was Ryan. The world would not treat him as it had treated them.

He had sat listening absolutely stony-faced to this appeal; when they were through he smiled, a hard, almost a cold smile, and shook his head, only slightly, as if to show that their arguments were not even worth a full reply. "It's really for us," said his mother suddenly, realizing the hopelessness of the case, and seeing the necessity for another kind of exhortation that had not previously occurred to them.

"Yes, really, it is," added Daniel, seizing upon her idea at once. "We'd really like to see a little of you before you go away." The selfishness of this motive would have been more persuasive than their previous arguments if it had not been *ipso facto* less credible to him from his knowledge of their characters.

And now, looking at the house where they lived, where they even this minute awaited his return, he felt ashamed that he had been turned from his resolve to work by someone who had no claim over him—by a being to whom as of yet he could hardly assign any character at all. All the same, he did not waver again. In a situation such as this, where one resolution had broken down, he offered compensatory resolutions, on a smaller scale, but numerous, to make up for that which had lapsed. The chief of these new vows was that this summer he would find the time to set his parents' yard to rights. The subsidiary resolutions were vaguer, flitting from his mind almost as quickly as he conjured them up: he would be sure to write every week when he was in England; he would use some of the Greek prize money to buy some new used tires for the Valiant; he would redouble his vigilance over his tongue lest his parents discover the truth about that art history professor who had been so attentive at his graduation; and so forth. It was a catalog of his filial sins; and for a moment, confronted by his parents' helplessness in coping with even the most rudimentary social obligations of suburban life—mowing the lawn and trimming the hedges—he vowed to see all his trespasses made good in the care of their grounds.

When this necessary, if futile, mental exercise had been completed, he approached the door of the house. The steps creaked and sagged under his tread, the screen door—which served more as vain warning than physical barrier to insect intrusion—groaned as he opened it.

He stepped into the kitchen. His mother had heard the familiar complaint of stair and door, and turned from the stove to greet him. Her cheeks, showing the rose of her race, were flushed from the heat of cooking, a little plump, like the rest of her, and above them the hazel shone in her eyes, the hazel that she had given to him.

"Ryan," she said.

"Back," was his laconic answer. A smile escaped him before his chronic reluctance to share his thoughts with her reasserted itself. Her face was always full of question, curiosity, affectionate interest; but the more she asked him about his life, the less she was likely to learn.

She had always been baffling to him. In her youth she had learned Shakespeare and Chaucer by the yard, and her mastery of English literature was stainless, a living thing that regenerated itself in her constant reexploration of the excellencies of the field. While Lloyd Tate gloried in meaningless schoolboy tags trotted out with scant recollection of the context, Maureen overflowed authentic Shakespeare at every waking moment, constantly weaving the Bard's blank verse into life in the little house. Ryan and his father sometimes protested this relentless Elizabetheanizing of their existence, but more often they despaired of resisting it.

Though her own peculiar genius was patent and undeniable, Ryan often thought that her studies had been a kind of dark ale to her brain, so that she knew in every organ, waking or sleeping, the taste, the bitter hops and the sweet dark malt of poetry, but was stupified by it. The cause of his uneasiness was that so often she was unable to retain what he had told her of his life. She constantly confused the simplest events and the most unmistakable personalities, mixing up new compounds in the laboratory of her mind, so that within the period of the same conversation in which he had narrated some happening or told of some acquaintance she would question him or comment on what he had said in terms so disparate from the originals that he could only with difficulty guess to what or to whom she referred. She knew the difference between Gremio and Grumio, between Dromio and Dromio, between Valentine of Verona and Valentine of *Twelfth-Night;* but in her mind his Latinist friend Todd became the Dantean scholar Ted; Ned Strathmore, a fellow soccer player who was wasp from mandible to tarsus, became Nick Stathopoulos, gaining unbeknownst to him a completely new ethnic heritage; and Eve became Elsa or Eva, acquiring in addition to a new name a husband and children (a fictitious family Ryan would find useful to leave unchallenged). As for his professors of the past four years, she could sooner have recited the polysyllables of the chief Mexican volcanoes than remember their names. He felt oftentimes that she could not remember the incidents of his life because she did not care enough about them. Consequently he told her little.

And yet she yearned toward him, hoping he would share his life with her; and for all his frustration, there were times he pitied that longing and spoke almost freely to her. They were lost, gone almost immediately, these insights he gave her—though they might reappear again in mutated form in her conversation at any time to astonish him.

And what son has ever dealt openly with his mother? It is a kind of stubborn pride in a boy not to tell all; and so it was still with Ryan. With his father he chaffered his secrets more readily; not only was his father's mind more retentive, but his fondness for his son was salted with a pinch of gentle humor, which made it more palatable. In his father's presence he would speak on despite his knowledge that his mother's misunderstandings were accumulating as she stood by listening. Maureen Kinsella had learned to "let

Ryan tell his news to his father"; she knew she would hear more that way; and although she had observed her son's reluctance to speak with her, in the goodness and passivity engendered by her excessive intellectuality she never took offense at it.

And she knew more of him than he knew she knew. When he strode now to the kitchen table, seeking to avert his eyes from her by examining the mail that had been set out for him, she saw again the child moving on its sturdy legs; the restlessness of the glance was familiar to her from her years both fighting it and using the hunger of the mind that caused it as she herself taught him to read, write, to weigh what he heard and saw, to quest unceasingly along the endless shelves of the library of human lore; she knew his evasion of her, and yet loved him for his stubbornness, which was her word for his secretiveness. The lives of the Kinsellas, parents and child, were so tightly intertwined that he could hardly breathe without her knowing or guessing the motive. At this moment, for instance, she caught the faint inclination of his head toward the corner of the kitchen by the stove—something no one else, not even her husband, would have perceived, which indeed was suppressed before Ryan himself was aware of it—and she knew the meaning of that unconscious motion. In that corner, as recently as a year ago, a dog had lain that had been Ryan's companion since he was five years old. The old reflex was strong: the boy in him still wondered why Argus had not come to greet him.

It was only the superficial elements of her son's life that Maureen could not retain—the names of the characters that moved into this scene or that of his life in the outer world—tenuous to her because they were Rosencrantz and Gilderstern to his Hamlet. She saw how her failing irritated him; but she felt that his irritation was merely a pair of dark spectacles that hid a look as loving as her own. Perhaps she was right in this; but love beneath irritation is in the end a crippled love for both giver and receiver.

At this moment she saw that he had a secret. She could not have told how it was that she knew; but she turned instinctively and crossed the kitchen to call her husband, in whose presence some clue might out.

The kitchen in the Kinsellas' house was modeled on the same scale as the rest—that is to say, the architect had allotted as little space to it as he could. The floor space was taken up by stove, refrigerator, table, and a few cupboards. In the partition wall was a broom closet, the door to the cellarway, and a doorway to the short hall linking the kitchen to the interior of the house; these filled out the width of the house to the left. Its depth was taken up by a living room, originally a parlor with its own disused door to the outside; and a study beyond that, once the living room. Stairs from the central room ascended to a half story that held two cramped bedrooms and a bath under sloped ceilings.

Such was the extent of the Kinsella residence. Twenty-eight years of marriage had packed it with thousands of books, with dozens of photographs of Ryan, no few of Collin, of relatives and colleagues—filled it with threadbare rugs, treacherous furniture, and dusty knick-knacks, to say nothing of the implements needed for all the chores of life, whether cooking, cleaning, bathing, grooming, or coping with laundry.

So small was the house that Mrs. Kinsella had only to open the door of the kitchen in order to call to her husband; only twelve feet separated the point where she then stood and the entrance to the study.

"Danny," she said softly, "Ryan's back."

Ryan heard the sudden creak of the swivel chair as his father leapt up from it; then the scuffing of an armchair being pushed out of the way as he came through the living room. Maureen moved back into the heart of the kitchen and reached to the sill over the sink to turn down the classical music murmuring on the radio. That simple act gave her away to Ryan—he sensed that she was setting the stage for his talk with his father, that she must have guessed something from his demeanor. He bent all the more over the mail they had saved for him during his absence, browsing through it with a telltale nonchalance.

"Ryan," said his father from the doorway.

"Dad," he responded, looking up casually.

"You'll have to thank your friend Eve for me." Daniel Kinsella hoisted the glass he held in his hand and rolled his eyes behind his frail, wire-rimmed glasses in a show of delight. "This"—he paused over the word—"is the best. Ever."

Ryan had told Eve about his father's infatuation with sherry—how he had denied himself his favorite drink out of a conviction that anything he especially craved was unaffordable, though from time to time he was able to indulge in a glass of the turpentinous liquor served under that name at faculty functions, and allowed himself a rhapsody on it. She had sent a bottle of something good. His mother added some praise of the record Eve had sent to her, a new copy of the Mass in B-Minor to replace the one she had worn out on their phonograph; but Ryan hardly heard her. He was noticing that his father was not really drinking the sherry at all, only wetting his lips with it occasionally, as if it were too rare and valuable to actually consume—as if to let it evaporate on the lips were sufficient. He smiled at his father's foible.

"Glad you're enjoying it, Dad," he said. He started leafing through a journal on the table. "Since when do you get *Classical World*, anyway?"

"Since I made professor," said Daniel. "Sort of a funny story, really." He straightened his round, stooped shoulders, wet his lips with his sherry, cocked back his head on his thin neck, and was forestalled by his wife.

"He's just been to the Tates, Danny; we should ask him about that."

But Ryan had primed himself. "Here's an article by Clarkson, Dad," he said. "'Ontological Certitude and the Gate of Dreams in *Aeneid* Six.'"

His father took the bait with open mouth. "Clarkson!" he cried with disgust. "'Ontological Certitude!' Scatological is what he is, and that *is* a certitude. Wait till my book comes out. Clarkson will go scampering for cover with his certitude between his legs.— What, he's written on the Gate of Dreams? Should be interesting. See if he can make the same mess out of that that he made out of the Palinurus episode. Let me see that, Ryan—I haven't had a chance yet—"

"Sure, Dad," said Ryan, instantly offering it. Only the physical intervention of his mother spoiled his ruse; she turned and intercepted the journal as it was about to change hands. Ryan had anticipated this, and meant to distract her with a question about dinner; but she was as single-minded as he.

"No, Danny," she said, "You'll get carried away. You always do about Clarkson. 'Old Mantuan! Old Mantuan! Who understandeth thee not, loves thee not.' It's just before dinner. And Ryan's home."

"You're right," said Daniel. He raised his glass. "To hell with Clarkson anyway," he grinned, "And good health to your friend Eve.—Would you like some sherry, Ryan?"

"No, thanks," he answered, though he would have enjoyed it. He was aware that whatever he drank would be that much less for his father.

"You're sure? There's plenty of it. Can't talk you into it?"

"No, thanks."

"Just a little?"

"Really, no, thanks."

"Would you like a little juice, Ryan?" asked his mother, going to the refrigerator. "I have a little apple juice."

"No, thanks. I'm really all right." He sat down at the table.

At that instant a cat flung itself at the screen door and hung on the tattered mesh, mewling. "Here's Cassie," said Ryan. He rose to let her in, but his father started past him.

"No, no, you just have a seat, Ryan—I'll get the door. Come on in, Cassandra," he said, opening the door for the cat, an enormously fat orange tiger. It padded past Daniel disdainfully and began to rub against Maureen's shins.

"You just sit down," his mother was saying to Ryan. "You've had a long trip today. You must be tired."

"It's not as if I walked it, Mother," said Ryan. He sat down lightly in the chair, with the air of one ready to dart away at the least excuse.

"Poor Cassie," clucked his mother, "You must be starving." In a minute the smell of catfood had obscured even the odor of the sauce on the stove as the cat choked down her meal. "You sit down, too, dear," Maureen said to her husband.

"But I'll be in your way," he observed, surprised at the invitation. She usually chased him away when she was cooking.

"That's all right," she said. "You and Ryan just sit here and talk." Daniel sat down; Ryan leaned under the table and patted the cat, hoping that his father would start some topic of his own if he kept himself out of sight. Cassandra stopped gulping her meal long enough to hiss at him, which jeopardized his pretense of affection; and his father played into his mother's hands.

"So," he said gamely, as if still reluctant to leave the subject of Clarkson, his *bête noire,* but conscious that he should take an interest in more mundane matters. "How are the Tates?"

"All right," said Ryan. The *bête orange* put its ears back, and Ryan gave up and emerged from beneath the table.

"That's good to hear. What's Collin doing this summer?"

"Same as usual, I guess," said Ryan. "Working on his writing."

"He's very dedicated," said his mother.

"He has to be," said Ryan.

"A lot of boys would say they were going to work on their writing and just never get around to it. But you say he really does."

"That's right."

The topic seemed to be going by safely; but then, in one of those uncanny shots that made him wonder again at the myth of women's intuition, she turned to him and said, "Has he heard from his sister lately? What was her name—Prudence? It's so sad they never had a chance to grow up together."

"Constance."

"That's right. Constance."

Ryan stretched, a little too casually, and plunged in.

"Yeah, she's come home," he said.

They stared at him.

"What?" said his mother.

"Constance. She's come home." Their silence and surprise made further explanation inevitable. "She's going to go to college here. She and her mother have come back to the States. They're staying at the Tates' for a while."

"You're kidding!" exclaimed his father.

"No, I'm not."

"Well—did you see her?"

"Yeah, she was there."

"Well?"

"Well what? She's okay. She's a nice girl. She's Collin's sister, for heaven's sake. What did you expect? Fangs?"

"Isn't that wonderful!" exclaimed Maureen. "How wonderful for Collin!"

"He's pleased," said Ryan, letting irony show in the understatement.

"And they're staying there—at the Tates?" asked his father.

"That's the place."

"Mrs. Tate too? They were divorced, weren't they?"

"Never, actually. It's kind of weird. She seems a little ornery."

"Mrs. Overton used to tell me all about it," said Maureen. "'Such a mad marriage never was before.'"

"Well, what about Constance?" asked Daniel.

"What about her?" countered Ryan.

"Well, I don't know," said Daniel. "Is she good-looking?" His father smiled softly at him; his mother stood holding her breath, spatula in hand. He shrugged.

"All right, I guess."

His mother protested. "All right, you guess! Is that all you can say?"

But Daniel grinned broadly. "That good, eh?" he said.

His humor was infectious; and besides, Ryan saw that he had been caught. He laughed aloud; his father's smile grew still broader, and his mother suddenly understood. "Oh, Ryan," she said, "is she really beautiful? Collin's such a handsome boy—I'll bet Prudence is just beautiful.—Is she? Is she really?"

"Now, Maureen," said his father, "you'll have to get this straight. The girl is Constance. And didn't you hear Ryan? She's all right. The girl's all right."

"What does that mean, 'all right'?" complained Maureen. Father and son said nothing, although they exchanged wry glances. They were on the same side suddenly. "Oh, I wish I could see her," she said, perceiving their conspiracy and despairing of a straight answer.

"You sound as if such an eventuality were totally impossible," said Ryan. "Whereas, in fact, nothing is more likely. You're sure to see her at some point this summer." His own certainty made him wince all the more as he thought of Collin and Constance standing in this cramped kitchen.

"How?" asked his mother. They knew his aversion to bringing his friends home.

"I'm sure Collin will bring her around some time," he said vaguely.

"But the yard is such a mess . . ."

"Do you think that will stop Collin? He doesn't care about the yard. He never has and he never will. And besides, I'm going to straighten it up a little this summer."

They scoffed anxiously. "When will you have time to do that?" asked his father. "You'll probably be working six days a week, like last summer, and we'll never see you."

He hesitated. Neither of them said a word, but they watched him keenly.

"I was thinking," he began. "Maybe if you're really serious about my taking a little time off—"

"We are," urged his father.

"Because—I mean, if you're not, I can always get a job—I can get a job tomorrow, I'm sure—"

"No, no," they said hastily.

"Well, then I would have time. I could fix up the yard, maybe work on the house a little. Do those articles I've been trying to get to. But only if you really think we can afford it—"

"Of course we can—can't we, Mither?—We've got plenty of money. We've got more money than we know what to do with." He raised his glass of sherry demonstratively, as if that proved they lived on the pinnacle of affluence.

Maureen smiled almost deliriously. "That's what we were hoping for," she said. "You deserve a rest. 'No profit grows where no pleasure is ta'en.'"

"But you work on those articles of yours," warned his father. "Those are important. And you don't want to get rusty."

"Rusty!" laughed his mother. "How could a boy ever get rusty with a head stuffed full of Latin and Greek till it's ready to burst! It would be like his forgetting how to breathe if he forgot his Greek."

For a minute no one spoke further on the subject; his parents basked in the mere idea, afraid he would suddenly retract his proposition. Then Maureen thought of something puzzling.

"What made you change your mind?" she asked. "I thought we'd never talk you into it. You even said something about working before you left for the Tates just now."

He shrugged. "I had a chance to think it over."

"You had two weeks to think it over, since graduation. Now all of a sudden—"

"It was the walk," he said. "I always think better when I walk."

"You didn't do any walking when you were staying in New York? I always find myself walking quite a bit when I go there."

"You never relax there, though. You always have to watch where you're going, what you're doing—who's coming towards you, who's behind you, who's walking next to you. You don't have the luxury of thinking. Not if you want to stay alive."

"You didn't have any trouble, did you?" she asked, distracted by this new worry.

"No. Saw a few weirdoes, nothing unusual."

She resumed the previous thread of the conversation with an aptness unusual in her. "I think best when I'm lying in bed at night," she said. "Didn't you think about it then?"

He thought about how he had spent his nights, and the contrast between the reality and her conception was so sharp that it cut him with a kind of humorous pain. "Too noisy," he muttered. "Too noisy to think. Besides, I was too tired."

"Tired from what?"

"Walking around."

"Well," she murmured confusedly, "I wish I knew what it was that changed your mind." She stepped out of the room to the cellarway, which served as a pantry, and rummaged noisily on the shelves over the basement stairs.

He noticed his father watching him with an impish grin.

"That good looking, eh?" said Daniel quietly. The irrepressible smile returned to Ryan's face.

"I made up my mind before I ever set eyes on Constance Tate," he insisted.

"But you'd heard she was back," smiled his father.

"It's possible that I had."

"Well, whatever her hand in the matter—I'll drink to Ms. Tate any time."

Maureen, reentering the kitchen, misunderstood Daniel's remark. "Yes," she said, "it's wonderful that she's home."

Daniel let the previous topic die with her misapprehension. "What colleges does she have in mind?" he asked.

"I don't know. I imagine I'll hear tomorrow. They've invited me over for a picnic."

"You'll hear," said Maureen matter-of-factly, "but you won't tell. But it's nice of them to have you over."

At this point Ryan absently drew the packet of clippings from the pocket of his jacket and set it on the table.

"More from Mrs. Overton's clipping service?" asked his father.

"Yeah."

"There'll be a quiz tomorrow," intoned Daniel in his lecture-hall voice.

"You're right about that," said Ryan. "She'll want to know what I thought of this and that and the next thing." He opened the bundle and looked through the headlines. "'Latin Revival in Full Swing at Local High Schools,'" he read. "I think she's given me that one a hundred times. 'A Friend of Poets: New Biography of Lady Gregory.'"

"She hit the mark with that one," observed his father with surprised approval.

"Sheer accident, Dad. Or maybe it was 'friend of poets' that caught her eye—my role, you know." Daniel saw the likelihood of this conjecture and chuckled. "'Meadow Maintenance: A Quick Guide,'" continued Ryan. She must have heard me grousing about how Mr. Tate should have the clearing mowed. 'Day Tours from London'; 'The Shetlands: Rocky Idyll for the British Isles Traveler'; 'New Violence in Belfast'; 'Tramp Steamers Are the Way to Go.'"

"Tramp steamers!" repeated Maureen, in a sort of sputter. "For tramps, maybe."

"'Choice of Footgear Important in Sports'; 'Olympic Committee Sets New Guidelines'—Does she think I'm trying out for the Olympics?—'Marshall Scholars Announced'—Poor woman is totally confused. 'Italy over Denmark in Soccer'—there's a timely article—'Summer Sale on Bras'—no, wait a minute." He turned the scrap over. "'Racing Results,'" he read. "This one must have gone into the wrong pile. Let's see: 'Ivy Business Schools Tops in Placement'—that does me a lot of good. 'Tips for the Traveler: What to Bring Back and How.' 'Parents Teaching Own Child Arrested'—"

"Oh, I'd like to see that," said Maureen.

"Don't worry, Maureen," said his father. "Statute of limitations is up."

"No, it isn't, Dad. You'd better watch it, or I'll turn you both in."

Daniel chuckled.

"Well, that's just the beginning. They really are overwhelming. I suppose I'll have to devote my summer to digesting this junk."

Daniel clucked in sympathetic disgust. "The wastebasket is right over there," he said, gesturing.

"Do you want the rubber bands, Mother?"

"Oh, yes, I can always use the rubber bands," she answered. He stripped off the bands and handed them to her; then he deposited the clippings in the wastebasket, looking after them sadly.

"She *is* a very nice woman," he said.

"She certainly is," said his father. "Why don't you give her one of your offprints?"

Ryan laughed.

"Oh, Danny, stop it," said Maureen. "She's a good soul. She means well."

"And she's been supplying us with rubber bands for years," added Ryan.

"Dinner's about ready," said Maureen. "Danny, we'll need the chair."

W*ednesday,* J*une 17/* S*ix*

That place that does contain my books, the best companions, is to me a glorious court where hourly I converse with the old sages and philosophers.

—Fletcher and Beaumont

INNER AT THE Kinsellas was held at the little table in the kitchen. A third chair was brought up from the basement, where it was kept during Ryan's absence from the house; it was a third mismatch. Maureen's traditional grace was given, quoting Sir Toby Belch—"Thou art a scholar; let us therefore eat and drink." The cat made amends by sleeping in Ryan's lap through dinner, and provided his parents with an excuse to refuse his help with the dishes. "Don't disturb Cassie—you're both tired—just sit there." He sat still only because in doing so he was indulging them, not himself.

He dreaded a return to the subject of the Tates; so he started another one, as inexhaustible, although sometimes infinitely more unbearable. "So, Mother, how's the clan?" he said.

Maureen sighed. Daniel was silent; one felt he craved a pipe, a prop, at a time like this.

Maureen was the second of seven children. Only one of these seven, Ryan's Uncle Billy, lived still childless, a widower; and he had failed to share in the O'Brien fecundity only because shortly after his marriage his wife had been committed to Metropolitan State Hospital, where she had remained until her death in 1980. "You can't make a family on Sunday visits," Uncle Billy used to say defensively, every time he heard of another O'Brien on the way.

As for the rest, they bred as if they were the sole hope of the race. Maureen's older brother, Frank, had twelve children by his wife, Mary; Millie had five by her husband, Joe; Luce had nine by Ted; Ginny had seven by Bob; and Jack had nine by another Mary. This prolixity gave Ryan forty-two first cousins, ranging in age from thirty to three years of age. Several of these cousins were now creating further branches for the great O'Brien tree, and further confusion for Ryan, who was often compelled at family gatherings to ask of his mother in idle wonderment whether some toddler was a cousin or a cousin's child.

Maureen knew; she knew them all. Sometimes she hesitated; sometimes she paused to reconsider the links between her son and her siblings' offspring; but she never failed of an answer. She would forget the name of Ryan's occasional visitors before their brief stay in the house was over; but her own kin she could remember to the *n*th removal.

"Well," said Maureen. (The word was not an estimate, but a beginning.) "Your uncle's still working up in Chelsea. He burned himself somehow—the torch blew up or something—but he didn't miss more than a day or two. Aunt Mary's still working at the church. She's mostly thinking about Pippin's wedding. Pippin's all in a fluster about it. —Only a month away, you know. The eighteenth of July, Ryan. Hold the date open.—Young Mary had a little girl; she wants to go back to work right away. John, you know, has that little baby—"

"John?"

"He married that high-school girl last fall, remember?"

Ryan signified his recollection with a noise regretting his question.

"Tom's still out on probation, but he can't drive yet. Beatty is still at home with the baby; no husband in sight, poor thing. Danny hardly ever goes to school, I guess."

"I don't blame him," said Ryan.

"Then there's little Corrie, and Ruthie. Good as gold."

"But not as bright," Daniel put in.

"No, not as bright," agreed Maureen. There was no getting around that. "Let's see—did I forget somebody?"

Ryan and his father looked blank.

"Oh, yes, young Frank. He hasn't changed."

"You mean he's still drunk, unemployed, dishonorably discharged, and divorced?" said Ryan. Daniel snorted faintly, repressing laughter.

"I should think you would find a more charitable way to speak of your own cousin, dear."

"Then we'll say he's thrilled about his new treatment program, exploring many exciting new job possibilities, proud of his refusal to serve as one more cog in the great American war machine, and dating some very nice girls."

Daniel's chortle was perfectly audible this time.

"'Beshrew me, the knight's in admirable fooling,'" Maureen said quietly, and went on, unruffled. "Then there's your Aunt Millie—"

"Uncle Joe is still unemployed," assumed Ryan.

"They closed that plant in Natick. What's he supposed to do?"

"Retrain. Rethink. Get moving."

"It's easy for us to say."

"Indeed it is, Mother. I'll say it to his face if you like."

"You wouldn't. You're too nice a boy."

"I could really straighten that crew out, if only I wasn't too nice a boy."

"Who is there, now? Tom, you know—"

"I know," said Ryan quietly, the humor absent from his voice. Tom was dying of lymphatic cancer at the age of twenty-two.

"Why don't you skip to some of the good news, Maureen?" suggested Daniel. "You can't do the whole Catalog of Ships."

"Yes, how about some good news of the great O'Brien clan?"

"Well," said Maureen, thinking. "There's Damie. He's some kind of a chess wizard, it seems."

"Really?" asked Ryan, intrigued. Damien was Aunt Luce and Uncle Ted's boy; he was about five years younger than Ryan, and had always attached himself to his older cousin with a sort of hopeless awe on the occasions when they met.

"And Parnie's built himself some kind of computer. It can add and subtract, it seems."

"How about Bridget, Maureen? Out at UMass? There's good news from her, isn't there?" asked Daniel tentatively. He was afraid his memory would betray him.

"Oh, yes—she's been accepted into a veterinary medicine program."

"And Stevie," said Daniel, "your Uncle Jack's Stevie, Ryan—took Latin this last year."

Maureen laughed mildly. "Mary says he wants to be just like you."

"And how's my sweetheart?"

"Roseleen?" Another smile. "She drew a picture of you. Mary's going to send it, she says. For Uncle Roo. Roo, she calls you."

"I've been thinking, Dad—you remember Sir Thomas More, how he educated his own wife?"

"Jane Colt, yes. Taught her Latin. She was quite young when he married her—called her his *uxorcula*. A good system for obtaining a spouse that suits your interests."

"Hardly a foolproof one, I should think," added Maureen with a sniff, thinking Ryan's facetiousness could use a dash of cold water. He persisted, speaking with a wry smile to his father.

"Don't you think you could take on another pupil?"

"I don't know; she's awfully young."

"She's three already. That's a late start. But you'll have time: the wedding won't be for about eighteen years."

Daniel saw that only a frivolous answer would suit his son's mood. "All right. We'll get her going on Aeschylus next week."

"Start at the top," agreed Ryan.

"I can't believe you didn't meet a girl you liked in four years of college," said Maureen abruptly, as if voicing some long-standing perplexity.

"I did, Mother. That was just the problem. I met too many of them."

Daniel grinned.

"Say, Dad, what was that story about *Classical World?*

"Oh, that," said Daniel, sitting up straighter.

He told it with enthusiasm. It was a funny story, even if its ending was obscured by Maureen's irrelevant comment, as the punch line was being delivered, that they were considering making a donation to Ryan's university. He spent some effort dissuading them from this folly. Before several more minutes had passed he had them promising to use any spare funds towards a new car; but he knew it was only talk. He asked for a clarification of the subscription story; conversation turned to the book Daniel was writing, which entailed much expounding, quoting of Latin, asking of Ryan's advice; and as Ryan became more involved in the matter, Maureen became less interested; she saw she would hear no more of her son except what she did not understand.

She went off to bath and bed; and the men suddenly felt their discomfort in the hard kitchen chairs and moved to the study.

❁ ❁ ❁

This library was one of the smallest rooms in that small house; and yet it was one of the largest rooms on earth for Ryan, for it had the best vantage. From here he had looked out over the whole universe and seen back into time; each of its books, however drab and soiled its binding might be, was a portable window to him, opening on a view of life and thought that had often been brighter than the present that transpired around him.

And there were books enough here for anyone's education—about two thousand of them. Some were packed tightly along the sagging shelves that lined the wall; some bricking up even these shelves, in scholar's bond, or rising in jerry-built towers along the margin of the room, mortared with the creamy yellow of articles photocopied years ago; and others, those most urgently needed in the *ars longa* of scholarship, were stacked on the desktops themselves. Even the small fireplace held torches passed: in a box perched on the grate were Aristotle's *Poetics,* a full edition of Henry, a battered Longinus, and Jebb's life of Bentley.

Only two spots in the room were free of this bibliomanic clutter: in one, on the mantle, was an antiquity—a colorless potsherd stolen from the Acropolis by some glib student, who had high-lighted the faint theta of Themistocles upon it with a pencil. And in a square of shelving newly purged of debris was a contemporanity—a framed diploma, advertising Ryan's claim to the *privilegia et honores et iura et insignia* won for him by the work that had begun within these walls. As he entered the room, Ryan noticed that his father had set this document so that the tutor might admire it, not the pupil.

Their desks had been pushed face to face, on some day Ryan barely remembered, when the wine-colored carpet had still been visible, before the flotsam of papers cast up by study had risen around these two pieces of furniture like seaweed around the hulks of twin rowboats on a beach. Face to face father and son had studied, as if equals from the first. Now Ryan slid into the oaken swivel chair with the grace of familiarity—it was a tight fit between his desk and the bookcase behind him: a groove on one shelf, ground out by the back of his chair, betrayed his bad habit of leaning against the tension of the springs and wedging himself in that narrow space when reading or pausing over his writing. He tugged the chair closer to the desk—its wheels gave a distinctive squeak, and the patina of lemon oil and grime on its arms reminded him how he had used to jerk the chair back and forth and finger the oak when translating aloud for his father.

In fact, it all came back to him strongly—the endlessly familiar lexicons, the ekeing out meaning from alien tongues, the prejudices of English and German scholars; and he thought to himself that he might be judged innocent if, as a boy, he had felt at the Tates' house the way one feels encountering an enclave of one's compatriots in a foreign land—for there they spoke English, and nothing but; they spoke leisure, and play, languages in which children are naturally fluent.

"See your diploma?" asked Daniel, nodding at the shelving over Ryan's head.

"Yes," said Ryan, making not even a feint of turning about politely to look. "Looks like the frame your diploma used to be in."

"It does," agreed Daniel noncommitally. His diploma had been gathering dust upon itself in the tight, hot attic for years. He showed some discomfort under Ryan's even stare. "Show you that piece by Thomlinson?" he suggested.

"Okay."

Daniel began digging eagerly in a pile of offprints. Ryan watched him, suddenly struck by the puzzle of the man, his dogged devotion to his son, his scholarly blindness, his ignorance of his blindness, the mystery of such gentleness in a world of brutal gears and rollers that caught any outstretched hand and drew love to destruction in its mill. Then his father looked up, grinning. "Here it is," he said.

Daniel Kinsella's great life work was nothing more grandiose than a commentary on Vergil. Hundreds had written such commentaries before; hundreds would after him, until even great Vergil went *ad patres*. And yet to Daniel it was a more noble cause in which he wrote—"that someday the student may cry *Tu se' lo mio maestro e 'l mio autore*," as he put it in the first draft of his introduction—than the goals of literary criticism, which he considered sterile and self-serving. The state university where he worked viewed the project as so plebian that it would not allow it as scholarship under the publish-or-perish code, which altereth not. It was in spite of this disdain that Daniel had risen almost inadvertently to his belated professorship.

As a teacher Daniel Kinsella was an animated, humorous, only occasionally querulous wight, who had early in his career come into favor with the athletic types who packed their schedules with introductory courses—he gained a reputation as an entertainer, as a man who never had the heart to flunk—he grew popular. Not that he was a mere sundial students utilized to count their wasted time. He was strict in his insistence upon written exercise, and in a subject as mechanical as Latin at the lowest level, his students quickly saw results—some of them for the first time in their school careers—and admired the man for supplying the discipline they had always lacked. "Kinsella really draws 'em in," his colleagues had to admit, both pleased and contemptuous. And so, as a good "draw" sometimes preserved those who did not publish even from the peril of the tenure joust, he had survived until the faculty could do little more than knight him and certify his nobility. The athletic department, perhaps, had had something to do with his tenure and professorship; but of this he had no inkling; perhaps no one did; perhaps it was a truth too well papered over by the files of the academic bureaucracy to be recovered and known by anyone.

He had few pretensions himself. He insisted on being called Mister Kinsella, not Doctor. On those occasions when it was necessary for him to attend the annual convention, he spent more time asking after his son and his son's professors, or calculating the time for and cost of telephoning his wife, than he did amplifying his own importance in the scholarly world. His greatest defect as a scholar was one that afflicts many: the delusion that Vergil was a possession solely his own. But they say God smiles on these.

Ryan had long since become a better scholar than he was. As the son spoke now to the father he chose his words carefully, disguising his knowledge more than revealing it, for he loved the man too much to let him doubt his own powers even for a moment. He skillfully supplied examples of this or that usage, prodded Daniel's memory with his own feigned forgetfulness, and sometimes showed him a passage in illustration of a minor point that actually held the key to a far more important one—which the senior scholar would at length perceive, and, seizing the text from his son's hands, expostulate on eagerly, while Ryan watched and listened, his face taking on his father's paternal mildness. The discussion would suddenly be cut short—Daniel would seize a pencil and a scrap of paper, or flip through his greasy typescript for the appropriate passage, muttering "Book 6, 307 and 308—inversion of natural order—yes, yes—ties in nicely with Book 2, 531, 538, and 539."

Each enjoyed these little victories in his own way.

By the time the grandmother clock in the living room struck eleven, Daniel had absorbed as much as he could. He, too, went off to bed. In a few minutes more the last sounds ceased upstairs.

Ryan sat in a stupor. As he let the gates of his consciousness swing ajar, the day's events crowded through and filled his thoughts.

The telephone rang. Fortunately it was visible amid the debris; he cast himself on his knees and snatched the receiver up before the second ring, afraid his mother might wake, might come down and intrude. He felt vaguely that he could not bear another such intrusion today. In tugging the cord out from beneath a stack of paper he set off an avalanche more threatening than the ringing, but no one seemed to waken upstairs. He drew the telephone back to his desk and sat down again before he answered.

"Hello," he said. The earpiece gave off a faint hum, as of long distance.

"Hello," said a soft, familiar voice.

The tears sprang to his eyes.

"Eve," he said, "My God, what are you doing?"

She was silent for a moment. He heard her take a deep breath, trying to control herself. "I just called to see if you got home all right."

"Well, it was a rough journey," he said. "The highwaymen pursued us from Stamford to Old Lyme, but we came clean away. Only a few bullet holes."

Then, slowly, she laughed.

"You *are* a dear," she said.

"You've just learned this?"

"I always knew it. But I learn it again every time I talk to you. Thank you, Ryan, for making everything so easy."

"I wish I could say it was a pleasure."

"No, it was not a pleasure," she agreed. "But it was a necessity."

"I don't believe that. You know I don't."

"Sometimes you have to let go to keep what you have, Ryan."

He grew almost angry. "That's the stupidest thing I've ever heard! Has it ever occurred to you that that is a total paradox, a contradiction—a falsehood—a lie? If you don't hold on, if you don't make the effort to keep something—whether it's knowledge or love or life itself—it just goes, it just fades away."

"That's the way life is, Ryan. You have to accept that. Things do pass us by. We pass them by. We have to give them up."

"But what if they're good? Isn't love good? What if we want to hold on to it?"

"You loved me—you loved me a little in New York—"

"I loved you a hell of a lot, Eve! And I bet your backside is still sore."

She laughed faintly but persisted, would not be distracted. "And if I want to be able to go through my life remembering the last two weeks, without ever seeing you tired of me, stealing glances at younger women, then I have to let you go. That's the only way I can have you, if I let you go. Don't you see?"

"Have you ever considered writing lyrics for rock and roll? You've got the idiom down pat."

"I never listen to rock and roll—"

"Well, what you're saying sure isn't the *Ode to Joy*. It's trite and it's dreary—it's one long discord, and it doesn't make any sense. Not to me."

"Don't you realize that millions of other men and women have gone down this same path a million times already? Younger man, older woman. I'm so tired of it."

"What are we, statistics?" he asked. "Have *you* ever gone down this path before?" It was a rhetorical question, but she answered anyway.

"No."

"Well, then," he cried in exasperation, "that's all that counts!"

"But I know what would have happened," she said. "It happens to everyone in this situation. You're young. You're just starting a brilliant career. You need someone your own age. I'd grow old while you were just coming into your prime. You'd be forty, and I'd be—"

"I can count too, God damn it!" he said, in a voice close to a terse shout. "I can add twenty and twenty, and forty and twenty."

"The point is, Ryan," she said, with a crack in her voice, "that life is too short for us. It's too late for us. If I had another twenty years—if—"

"The point is," he interrupted, getting a grip on himself, "that I love you, Eve. I have never met anyone like you." He spelled it out for her. "You—are—unique. I was never happy, never at ease the way I was with you in New York the past two weeks."

"It's just because you were alone before," she said. He gave a short, desperate laugh.

"Was I alone that time you caught me underneath the bleachers?"

"No," she admitted. "But you were lonely."

"That's a good reason for being unhappy, isn't it?" he said. "Being lonely? And for being happy, when you find someone you can talk to, walk with, make love to, really make *love* to?"

"The best reason in the world," she said. "And you will find someone like that. What we had in New York is just a little preview of what you'll find with someone else."

"Eve, I could live the rest of my life looking in vain for someone with your brains. Do you think I'm going to fall for every—" He fell silent, and she was silent, for a long while, perhaps a half a minute, a pause lengthened by the audible hiss of the telephone line.

"I'm just determined," she said, "that you'll be my friend. That you will send me offprints of all your articles, write me about every good and every drab day at Oxford, and someday, send me a wedding invitation. I would like to come to your wedding."

He groaned. There was another silence.

"What's happened?" she said suddenly.

"What?"

"You've changed. Something's different. Something's happened to you."

"Of course something's changed. My girlfriend kicked me out of bed this morning."

"That's not what I mean."

"Sorry, Eve—it's still me, Ryan. I still love you as much as I can in my own immature way—I know it's not enough for you—"

"What did you do today?"

"Well, first of all, I had a traumatic leave-taking with a—"

"After you got home. What did you do? Did you do what you said you were going to do?"

"What was that?"

"Go visit your friend."

"Yes, I did."

"How was it?"

"Fine. It was fine. Everything was fine."

"How was he?"

"Fine. In good spirits. What can I say?"

"What else did you do?"

"Nothing. Came home. Talked to my parents again. Had dinner."

"What's wrong? There's something wrong."

"My God, Eve, what is this?"

"There's something different. I want to know what it is."

"There's nothing different, for God's sake. How can anything be different in twelve, fourteen hours?"

"What did you do after dinner?"

"Talked with my father about his commentary. Right up until a little before you called. Are you satisfied?"

"Did you let your parents talk you into taking the summer off?"

He hesitated. "Yes," he lied, or half-lied. Her voice regained a hint of her old affectionate warmth.

"Oh, I'm glad," she said. "*I* couldn't talk you into it, I know. I'm glad they did."

"Why is everybody trying to push me around?"

"For your own good, dear one."

The distance hummed in their ears, a bitter, insistent, whispered, electronic taunt.

"But that's not it," she said.

"Not what?" he responded, playing dumb.

"What's changed."

"I'm taking the summer off. Isn't that enough of a change?"

"That's not it," she persisted. "There's something in your voice."

"Eve, this conversation is beginning to sound like a seance."

"What happened at your friend's house? Tell me."

"Nothing. I saw him, his father—"

"Is that all? Anyone else?"

"The housekeeper. She gave me some—"

"Anyone else?"

"Eve, I've had enough. Even my mother doesn't do this to me."

"I've done a lot of things to you your mother doesn't do.—I'm asking you one last time, Ryan Kinsella, and you'd better tell me the truth."

He closed his eyes and put one hand on his forehead. He could hardly believe what was taking place. It was like a conspiracy against him. His mother had closed in on it in the same way. He knew exactly what Eve would do with it—what everyone else had done with it.

"Yes," he said, purposelessly attempting one last evasion. "His mother was there."

"His mother? I thought you said his parents were divorced."

"No. Separated. It's no big deal, Eve."

"What about his sister? Doesn't he have a twin sister?" He had talked a good deal about the Tates when they were in New York together. It was a vice of his.

"Yes, he does," he said.

"Well, was she there?"

"Yes, she was there too."

There was a very long silence.

Finally he said, "So what?"

"So, tell me about her."

"What's to tell? She hasn't even started college. She's just my friend's sister."

"But you'd never seen her before, right?"

"That's right. Never."

Another silence.

"Well, what does she look like?"

"Like her brother, a little bit. She's all right. Not bad-looking, I guess."

"She isn't pretty, is she?"

"I guess not, I don't know."

"Not at all pretty. Because she's gorgeous, isn't she?"

"Eve . . ."

"Ryan, I'm happy for you."

"For God's sake, Eve!"

"I couldn't have hoped for anything better. Is she a nice girl?"

"For God's sake . . ."

"Tell me, please, Ryan, it's important to me. I want to know. I want to be able to imagine you with her."

"Eve, I'm going to hang up the phone now."

"No, just a minute, tell me—"

"I'm going to hang up the phone. I'll give you fifteen seconds to say your farewells, but I won't listen to this nonsense. I've heard it from everyone and I've had it."

"Can I call you again?"

"Please do. When you've got this nonsense out of your head."

"Are we going to be friends?"

"We're going to be best friends, forever."

"Remember, if you get married in the first year, they'll take away your scholarship."

"How do you know?"

"I was on the committee once. It's true."

"So who's getting married?" he exploded.

"I love you, Ryan. I'll call tomorrow. Is late all right? What about your parents?"

"My parents think you're just a friend. Married, with children." She gave a little, bitter laugh. "Did you tell them that?"

"I don't have to tell lies to my parents," he said. "They're just like you. They dream it all up. Just give them one little bitty fact, and they fantasize the rest."

"Maybe if you told them more—"

"If they knew that I had had carnal knowledge of a woman—"

"And I wasn't the first."

"I'm serious Eve. I don't know what it would do to them."

"Well, then, look, you call me. Will you? Promise to?"

"No promises," he said. "I can't call down there every night. I can't afford it. I'll write you."

"Reverse the charges," she said.

"You can't afford it."

"I have the money," she said. "I have a job, remember? I admit that I blew my life savings in the past two weeks, but I still have enough money for the phone." Then she added, "Blew my life savings, figuratively and literally."

They were silent.

"Call me, Ryan," she said.

"I will," he said finally.

"And Ryan . . ."

"What?"

"I can't believe . . . how well you're taking this."

"You mean you're astonished that I manifest any maturity at all?"

"I mean anyone else your age would have told me to go to hell when I called."

"Not without some justification. It's your example: I'm rising to the level of your example. I want you to think I'm really more mature than I am." She laughed a little. "Say, Eve," he added, "tell me your opinion. We're going to be just friends, right?"

"Just very good friends."

"Right. What's your opinion of very good friends getting together once in a while and . . ."

"I don't think that would be such a good idea."

"I haven't even said what I'm talking about yet."

"Don't. You'll have to wash out your mouth with soap if you do."

"Look—"

"No. Really, really, Ryan. Sweetheart. No."

"No?"

"No."

"We'll see how you feel about that in a few weeks."

She laughed. "Goodnight, Ryan."

"Goodnight, Eve."

She seemed to pause before she hung up, but she did hang up. He made sure she was gone before he replaced the receiver at his end of the line.

He was very tired. He wanted to sleep. He wanted to lie down and in his dreams walk back through the valley of youth, where there was play and no work, and the promises of love and passion had not become twisted by age, by time, by life. There isn't enough time for us, she had said; and he saw, once again, how impossible it was that the brief life given to him could hold all he wanted of learning and love.

"That's why we have to make use of every minute," he murmured to himself. He looked up at the books on the shelves, old friends, but men and women dead. "That's why we have to live together, in the valley, and not let anything stop us from enjoying life. We have to hold on to it." He thought of her bizarre words again—"If you want to keep what you love, sometimes you have to let it go"—and he scowled in revulsion. Sick words—words of a brain lying to a heart—words of a poor broken mortal who had already given up, given up living at the mere age of forty. What was wrong with her? Why couldn't she grasp life with both hands? Why did she push it away? If she had really loved him, found what she needed in him, if he had been everything she had always wanted, she could not have given him up—her own need, her own passion would have compelled her to cling to him no matter what her mind said to her. Surely there was some lack in him. He must lack something because he was young. But if he had not been young, she would not have loved him; he somehow sensed that. If he had been her age, she would have assumed he was the way she was, adust, over with.

You have to keep looking forward, he thought. *Otherwise you become like her, a defeatist.*

But he himself was the one who looked backwards so much. Was he in some danger of becoming stuck in his past the way she was? His fist pressed, knuckles down, against the desktop. He would make the past new. He would prove this summer that nothing had changed in the valley, the essential things were always there, mutual respect and affection. Let Eve pine for what had never been. In the valley, people knew how to enjoy life.

He rose from his desk and went out into the living room; returned, shut off the light, groped his way into the kitchen, let in the cat, and locked the door. His bed seemed infinitely far away all of a sudden, beyond all the minor chores of preparation for sleep. He stood in the dark kitchen of his home, of his parents' house, thought of the two of them overhead, in their bed asleep, how they would go on before him into death. Was it possible that he would ever look forward to death like that, the way he looked forward to sleep now, as a blissful oblivion after the crosses and hurt of human life? Perhaps everything just went wrong, forever, until you were just sick of it.

He shook his head violently. No. That was Eve-talk. He cast about for some image to dispel that gloomy thought, and he fixed upon Constance, arching her back to put her packages on the roof of the car. And that, more than all the anchors of his frightened life—more than tree and valley—had power to dispel the horror of resignation and defeat. For beauty has power, the more ephemeral, the more speaking.

And as beauty is powerful, so is it dangerous. But he did not consider this, as he stopped for that last moment in the kitchen, wearily leaning against a counter. He looked forward to tomorrow, to seeing Constance, as a means of petrifying the past; he did not think how the forces that transmogrify flesh into stone can also then shatter it.

Wednesday, June 17 / Seven

Die Ehe ist die feinste Kunst auf Erden.

Marriage is the finest art on earth.

—Fock

The tongues of mocking wenches are as keen
As is the razor's edge invisible.
Cutting a smaller hair than may be seen,
Above the sense of sense; so sensible
Seemeth their conference; their conceits have wings
Fleeter than arrows, bullets, wind, thought, swifter things.

—*Love's Labour's Lost*

Thou art a lord and nothing but a lord;
Thou hast a lady far more beautiful
Than any woman in this waning age.

—*The Taming of the Shrew*

BOUT THE TIME Ryan ascended to his narrow bedroom under the eaves, Lloyd Tate also made his way toward the place he slept. But he did not, like the younger man, crawl with almost stupified gratitude between the sheets, to blink once in the splendor of moonlight and become Endymion. A man-boy of twenty will absorb sleep as a pumice drinks oil; a man of fifty-seven does not go so gently out of the day.

He sat in his robe in the armchair after he had washed his face, cleaned his white teeth, brushed his white-peppered hair. His spare reading glasses were at his elbow, along with one of the first of the techno-thrillers that were to be popular in that decade; he did not notice either. Rather he turned out the light and sat in the dark, holding a tumbler of brandy untasted in one hand.

His gaze was naturally drawn towards the window. On this night the moon was full, and its light formed an amazing chaos among the still leaves of the trees. The sight soothed him. He had lived in this house from the time of his birth—he had seen that random shifting of the light intensifying in the growth of the trees over half a century. On other such nights he might have watched it until sleep oppressed him in his chair and he turned toward the bed where his parents had lain before him, and their parents before them.

But tonight his wife was in the house. And she was not in his bed. She had not been in this room since that night in early January—it was 1964—when they had had their last fight, and she had thrown a few clothes in a suitcase while he watched, feeling relieved, jubilant, triumphant, and terrified. She had not been in this room since she had gone away on that day, since he had felt the burden of her presence lift from him, knowing that it was not only burden but blessing, and that although it had bent his back, it had conformed itself to him till it had become almost comfortable, and that its removal was a stimulus to unbearable pain.

He thought about his wife. For Lloyd Tate, lawyer, rationalist, master logician, whose mind was a shears that had slashed through the mobius strip of many a case, so that he could twist and rejoin the ends to his own ends—thinking about his wife was an exercise in avatism. He hardly thought; he felt; he hardly knew what he felt; images came back, tones and words; caresses, the feel of flesh, scent, mingled with a stain of anger, hers and his, his and hers, hurt, and wonder at his own hurt.

He saw her sitting on the edge of the bed in the hotel room on the night they were married, her face turned up to his, intoxicated with delight in him. And then the features merged into the mask he knew best, her eyes narrow with scorn, mocking and bitter; he heard again her voice, which had once been charged with fair wit, a leaping blossom of the mind that gave them both pleasure, but instead had become a weapon that like some cursed sword of story could not be returned to its sheath without first tasting blood—blade and handle identically sharp. And again, turned up, the face, in ecstasy, as she clung to him, opened to him, meeting his motion with hers, and they were both children finding their way through a maze of passion, hoping and dreading to find an exit. Her face at the end of the dining room table—he took such pride in her, in her humor and her brilliance, in her beauty, in the sexuality that wafted from her as a faint convection that made reality waver—turning gradually into the mask, the mask of anger like madness, her inscrutable anger. She was a fruit that had fallen into his hands: it gleamed, it breathed its sweetness; its taste on his tongue was ripe and noble; and yet it choked him, so that he had to cough it out, expel it summarily before it took his life.

Get a grip, old boy, he thought to himself, shaking his head. He lifted the glass to his lips, but did not drink; held it there a moment, and slowly lowered it, looking no longer at the moonlight on the trees, but at the darkened patterns on the surface of the liquid in the tumbler.

The old delusion came strong over him—she, strong and wise and gentle, at his board and in his bed, gracious, giving, his partner against the world. He saw the lie, he knew it for such; and yet his loneliness said Yes, and his age, and his view ahead.

She had never been those things. She had been a hurricane, brooding over his life, drawing in strength as she sapped the pressure of his energies and his skills. He had woken up next to her anger, lain down next to her anger, and found nothing to do about it, no way to alleviate it, neither any way to stay clear of it—for its roots were ancient, in deep contempt, in hard neglect that had nothing to do with his love, that his love could not assuage. Her love for him had been the great puzzle of his life—offered him, then denied; denied when he had everything to offer—the house, the valley, wealth, a place in the social life not only of town and city and state, but of the nation if she wished it—and the two children, whose increasing beauty as the years went by only stung him the more with the longing for what might have, should have been.

The important thing, he thought, *is not the way a woman looks to you, but the way she looks at you. And the trouble with marriages is that people build them backwards. Love at first sight—that means delusion at first sight. You see a woman, you're suddenly convinced she's everything. That she can be strong, kind, gracious, giving; can listen to you, can talk to you. So you marry her; and you find out she's not giving, she's not kind—she's locked up behind an ugly, pathetic hardness you can't get through, no matter how patient you are, how gentle, how persevering, how tolerant. But you go on believing in her, believing in the kind of person you think she should be, could be if she weren't so hurt, so broken by life. You impose your belief, your great need and delusion on her, not letting yourself see who she really is. She can scratch your eyes out, lie to you, break her promises, and you go on forgiving, forgetting, because you're so sure she's really someone else, deep inside.*

Beware of that, he thought. Beware of that "Deep down inside she's—he's—really a very good person." How many times had he heard that from some wife whose husband had shamed her one more time with his drinking or his womanizing? Deep down inside the worst criminal is a good person. The trouble is, that goodness is often so deep and so lost it can never be retrieved. *When it gets that lost, you have to give it up. You have to recognize the limits of your powers of self-delusion; you have to let reality be.*

He could have given up a lot to be with her. When she had first started to feel those vague yearnings to go somewhere else, to be somewhere else, to live some other kind of life, he knew he could have given up a lot—everything—to be with her, if she had been the kind of person he needed, the strong woman, the gently strong woman. But fortunately his delusion had stopped there. He had followed her in her sickness as far as he could. He saw those formless, pointless yearnings after change and travel for what they were—phantoms, restless phantoms of her disease, her unease with herself.

"No," he had said, "if I'm going to be alone, if you're going to cut me off forever with your anger, I want to be alone here, in this house, this place I love. I'm going to stick to the things I know and the work I can do. I won't throw over my friends to follow you and be lonely in some other land. Stay if you like; go if you like. Here I stand." He had stayed at home these seventeen years, weaving and unweaving the warp and woof of loneliness and law; and she had seen the cities of humankind.

And that was one choice he had not regretted. He regretted her; he missed her; he missed his delusions about her, because he was no longer allowed to have them, not after she had gone; but he was glad he had stayed here in the valley.

The boy had been a great solace to him—say more, the boy had been another life to him, a different life, offering a different role for him that took him out of his yearning for the lost role of husband. And how extraordinary that boy had become—a son such as a father could never have dared hope for: handsome, bright, serious, true to his own ideals. He loved to listen to the boy prattle on—at twenty years old, a sophomore in the true sense of the word, in perfect health, with absolute leisure, possessing all the privileges of the rich with none of the obligations—discussing death as soberly as a Church Father. It seemed a reflex of his son's superior character that even the friend of his boyhood had been extraordinary, and was now proving himself so in the eyes of the world.

Lloyd Tate smiled faintly as he thought of the two of them. What was the phrase? *Divus adulescens.* Divine youths, the two of them. Like two gods, a dark and a fair. And young! (He smiled again.) So young! And here was the girl, as godlike as they. What could a parent do but watch, admire, try to conceal his delight in these wonderful beings busy about their youth before his very eyes?

Couldn't Sondra see it too? Wouldn't it melt her, make her perceive what she had given up in leaving here, teach her what mattered in life?

No. That was his delusion speaking again, his hope.

Hope, he thought, imagining himself summing up his case before a breathless jury, *Hope itself can be the most destructive life force of all.* False hope had led him on through all that pain, back then; he would not let it be his master again.

And yet even as he sat there, confirmed in his old resolve, he raised his eyes to the moonlight and felt empty and old. Awful as his marriage with her had been, what had he traded it for? He was aware that his parenthood was in this summer reaching some kind of a watershed. The boy would be a boy no more on the other side of it. And what would the father have then? Whom to console him? A silly housekeeper?

All he would have was his lonely age to live through. Unless he counted on something that was as unreal as the dream of a kind Sondra, a dream of another partner; something that in the seventeen years since she had flung herself out of this bedroom had not come to be.

He thought of her, now, the woman who lay in that bedroom down the hall. She was still, even after her long absence, to his mind the most beautiful woman he had ever seen. Her anger had never marred her beauty, not in his mind. Yes, she was older; but so was he. His tastes, his understanding of beauty had grown more elastic with age. Perhaps if he could lie next to her now, if he set his hand upon her, he would find that her belly was not as firm as the belly on which he had set his hand on that first night twenty-one years ago; but it was the belly that had swollen with their children. Perhaps her breasts, too, had lost their firmness. But they were the breasts that had suckled those two hungry little faces.

He was sure she was still the most beautiful woman on Earth. He never expected to think otherwise. That thought had held him, stopped him, every time he had drawn up the papers for divorce; that had always quenched his anger.

He wanted to go, now, to rise from his chair and steal down the hall—he knew the lock on that door did not work, and besides, she was too proud to use it. A woman like that could defend herself with a laugh. And she would laugh, too, if she woke up and saw him standing there, in the dark, looking at her in the faint light the moon cast through the open window.

But he wanted, very badly, to see her; to see her flesh.

He put his glass down.

He thought, once again, of the way she would look. She had come to the head of the stairs to call Constance shortly before she went to bed; she had been wearing only her nightgown. Her shoulders were bare—square, well-made shoulders, with no flab on them, only a few freckles the Spanish sun had sprinkled on her skin. The fullness of the white silk gathered on her collarbone had hidden the shape of her breasts; but when she was lying down, the silk would lie starkly against the curve of her figure.

He sat for some time, leaning forward in his chair, his elbows on his knees, vaguely irritated by the acrid smell of the brandy in the glass on the table beside him. Finally he rose and went to bed.

But before he did so, he locked himself in his own room.

Thursday, June 18 / One

I know him as myself; for from our infancy
We have convers'd and spent our hours together.

—*The Two Gentlemen of Verona*

RYAN RECEIVED A postcard the next day.

His mother had as usual already read it by the time she brought it back from the mailbox. He knew she had because she looked both guilty and curious as she handed it to him. They had always disagreed about postcards; she felt that anyone who had the chance to read them also had the right—"Otherwise they'd be sealed in an envelope."

"Mail is mail," Ryan would answer. "Sealed or not, mail is mail. If you read my postcards, you've ripped open an envelope of privacy."

As a punishment, he both provoked and avoided satisfying her curiosity as much as was in his power. He grinned as he read the card, but would not give her any satisfaction when she queried him about it.

"Who's it from?" she asked.

"Someone," he muttered, pushing his way out of the kitchen and taking refuge in the study.

It was in Todd's handwriting—a gentlemanly, if spider-like, script.

First assignment. Alcaics.

When high pressure holds off the clouds, and the air
of late spring is brisk with a northern cold still untempered
by the heat of the solstice that is only a few days away, the
heart feeds on phantasms, seeming to itself brass-bound
and invincible.

He showed it to his father. "Todd says every classicist should write impeccable Latin verse," he explained. "He wants me to practice."

Daniel laughed. "A bogus Horatian ode!—What can we do here? *Serenum* would be good for 'high pressure' . . . "

"You work on it, Dad. I'm on my way to Collin's."

He left his father puzzling and reaching for a pencil.

❁❁❁

The blue of the sky that hung over the slated peaks and high chimneys of the Tates' house seemed to hum with the vibration of its own clarity, like a consecrating bell. Deep, vast, clear, and cool, it linked him with immensity, eternity, and so with the delusion, fate.

He was too old a friend to knock; at most he was accustomed to signify his arrival by calling for Collin when he entered. But he thought how Constance and Sondra would not be used to that familiarity, and once over the threshold he hesitated. At that moment muffled footsteps reached him from the living room. Sondra Tate appeared in the doorway, carrying a magazine in one hand, which she tossed casually onto the table in the hall.

"Good morning," Ryan said. Before she could answer, a clock began chiming noon in the depths of the house behind her.

"Good afternoon," she corrected him.

"A good afternoon, and a beautiful one," he said.

"Yes. A little cool."

"But not a cloud in the sky."

"I've been inside all day, actually," she said. "I haven't thought about it. Shall I call Collin for you?"

"Don't trouble yourself. I can find him." He turned toward the stairs, but halted when she spoke again.

"It's odd," she said. "You're less of a stranger here than I am."

He had no desire to begin a protracted conversation with her. He could feel himself being drawn in, and tried to think of something evasive and neutral. "It must be difficult for you, coming back after all these years."

"Yes," she said. "It is, somewhat. But of course it's a very pleasant place."

"Do you plan to stay long?"

"I don't know."

"Well, it's nice that Constance and Collin are having this chance to get to know one another."

"Yes, they do make quite a pair, don't they? Darkness and light."

"Brunette and blond, yes; but in personality I would think Collin is actually the darker one."

"He seems to be. Dreamier, anyway."

She said no more for the moment; after what he took to be a decent interval he was about to say something to conclude the conversation and escape, but she spoke again. "I don't see how you fit in here. If you don't mind my saying so. You seem so different from Collin. It seems an unlikely friendship somehow."

Something bristled deep inside him.

"In what way do you think I'm different?" he asked.

She hesitated.

"Of course you're right," he admitted, before she spoke. "We are very different. But difference doesn't keep people from liking one another."

"You don't think so? I think differences are the most trying part of any relationship."

"I think differences are only a difficulty if you let them be. That difference in age we were talking about yesterday, for instance. If you come to such a relationship with a preconceived idea about the importance of age, you'll make it fail."

"Yes," she agreed. "But it's so much easier if the difference doesn't exist at all. Which is why young men like you chase young women like Constance instead of women my age."

"We're back on our previous theme, I see."

"I'm not saying this strictly to tease you. I have some experience with age difference myself."

"And did it matter to you?"

"Actually, no. It was not the age difference between Lloyd and me that caused problems. Or at least not the most serious problems. There were other differences."

"Of course," said Ryan.

"What do you mean, 'of course'?" she asked, seeming to bristle in her turn. "What differences do you see?"

Ryan was not pleased at the position in which he found himself, but felt compelled to answer. "Well," he said, "take the lampshade, for instance."

"What about the lampshade? Do you mean we have a difference in taste?"

"No, I mean not just that. You seem to have a different way of going about things, that's all."

"You mean I'm direct?"

"Yes—"

"Confrontive? Abrasive?"

"I wouldn't—"

"It's just that I don't believe in sitting by when something is glaringly wrong. I think you should change something if it's wrong."

"But people don't usually go into someone else's house and change the lampshade because they don't like it. They make an allowance for the other's right to his taste, no matter how bad they may think it is."

"I don't," said Sondra.

"But if you don't let someone have the lampshade he wants, then it won't be long before you're trying to change his entire personality."

"If you can't live with him, what option do you have?"

"But don't you think that's wrong?"

"Not at all. You *should* try to change someone if he's not being all he could be."

"But don't you think that's dangerous?"

"In what way?"

"I mean, isn't it a truism that you can't change other people? That they have to change themselves? If you try to change them, you just drive them away. That seems to be the usual pop-psychology cant on the matter, anyway. It seems to me there's some truth in it."

"Sorry, I don't buy it," said Sondra. "If you're going to act responsibly in a relationship with someone else, you have to try to help them reach their full potential."

"As defined by you?"

"Yes—if you have an insight into them that shows you some defect in their personality."

"But that's playing God."

"Somebody has to," she said dryly.

He was very surprised. "Pardon me," he said. "I had thought your views of religion were somewhat less cynical."

"Because I go to church every Sunday? That still leaves room to wonder why God doesn't seem to do anything for us. Besides," she added in the same dry tone, "how is he supposed to help all these poor hapless Protestants, or agnostics like Lloyd and Collin? They don't even pray to him."

"Well," Ryan said, "I guess my view of the matter is more democratic. I think people should be allowed to run around being themselves. And since, as you suggest, even God feels the same way, why shouldn't we follow his example and let people make their own mistakes?"

"Because without direction, they never learn from their mistakes.—Do you believe that people learn by blundering through life? Do you think there's any meaning to the accidents that happen to them?"

"Maybe so. I don't know."

"Well," she said definitively, "I don't. I believe in God. I believe we live after death—maybe. But I don't think that God arranged our lives down here so that they add up to any great tapestry."

At that moment they heard, distantly, Constance's voice in the hall upstairs calling, "Mother!"

Sondra turned toward the stairs and said, "Yes?" Evidently Constance did not hear her, as there was no reply.

"I'll go tell them you're here," Sondra said.

"Don't take the trouble," he began.

"It's no trouble. I know you want to get on with your picnic, and I'm getting ready to go out. We'll have to continue our discussion at some other time." She started up the stairs, but turned to him. "I can see that you and I have several interesting differences ourselves," she added.

"There you go," he countered. "Differences are interesting. Why try to level them all?"

"Maybe the mere act of trying to level them is interesting in itself."

"True, but that's not sufficient justification."

"We disagree," she said, with her cool smile. Then she went up the stairs and left Ryan standing by the door.

Apparently she met Constance in the upper hall almost immediately. He heard her speak. "That friend of Collin's is here," she said.

Ryan heard only a muffled reply.

"Don't go anywhere without telling me," said Sondra.

A question.

"In the hall. And see if you can talk him into buying a new jacket. That thing he's wearing is ratty looking."

He thought Constance said, "Oh, Mother!"

He heard Sondra's footsteps proceeding onward, perhaps to her bedroom. Constance came at once to the stairs and descended them with the light-footed tread of a dancer or a child. When her feet touched the first landing, she stopped for a moment and smiled at him.

"Good morning," she said. A hint of spontaneous, welcoming laughter.

"Good morning," he answered, with similar humor. He made as if to dust off the sleeves of his jacket. The mime, so elaborate and deliberate, told her not only that he had heard her mother's insult, but that he had shrugged it off. Her laughter now was a diminutive cousin of the pealing of the cosmic bell. She descended the rest of the way and came close to him, too close, smiling, perhaps even relieved.

"Don't pay any attention to her," she said. "I like your jacket. It's perfect." She caught at his sleeve and felt the cloth. "Perfect for Cambridge."

"Oxford."

"Oxford! Oxford, I mean!"

"Yes," he said in continuation of her theme, "it has the regulation leather patches on the elbows." He showed her. "Where it wore out, you know, on library desks—chafing against the spines of books as I lounged about the stacks—slashed as I elbowed my way to the top of the class. As Mrs. Overton would say, its warp is woofing. It smells like a German encyclopedia—like tweed—like Professor Herrington's Latakia. It reeks of erudition. I like it, myself." He paused. "Actually, it's the only jacket I have."

She gratified him with a giggle.

"Where's Col?"

"Working on a poem. He'll be down in a while." Her sudden seriousness should have warned him.

"Well, we can't disturb the poet laureate, can we?"

He saw a vexed wrinkle between her brows and realized he had gone too far.

"You'll have to forgive me when I poke a little fun at Collin," he explained. "We kid each other all the time. Sometimes I kid him when he isn't even there. It probably seems like spite to someone who isn't used to it. You can't tell me he's never made fun of me for being a bookworm."

She smiled. That was as far as she would betray her brother. "Shall we wait in the living room?"

He waved her ahead with exaggerated gallantry.

When she had taken a seat on one of the sofas, and he in one of the armchairs, it struck him for the first time in years that the room was enormous. She seemed so slight among the cushions of the couch, so far away across the oriental. The strangeness of this new perception made him wonder if the house was really as much his as he liked to think.

They smiled shyly at one another.

"He's very kind to me," she said, looking down. "He lets me stay in his room when he's writing. I think it's amazing he can stand having someone in the room with him. He says he's never been able to write when anyone else was in the room, but he doesn't mind when I am." She was obviously proud of the distinction.

"I'm impressed," said Ryan. "I can't tell you how many times I've blundered into his room looking for him when he was busy composing the Great American Poem. He always chased me away in disgrace, and I always felt bad about it."

She started to speak, almost eagerly, then hesitated. His expectant look encouraged her.

"Do you know that story about Coleridge writing 'Kubla Khan'?" she asked.

"Exactly what I always think of."

She leaned forward, her eyes bright, sharing the thought. "And that horrid man came in and stopped him after 'And drunk the milk of Paradise.'"

"Yes, yes—how does it go . . . 'Beware! Beware!' . . ."

"'His flashing eyes, his flowing hair—'"

"No, 'Floating—'"

"'His flashing eyes, his floating hair.' Yes."

She was on the edge of the couch, he on the edge of his chair. They each sank back, suddenly shy again, but pleased.

"That's Collin when he's writing," said Ryan. "'Beware his flashing eyes.'"

"From now on I'll be afraid to sit in the room with him," she laughed.

"Well, the key thing is the interval."

"The interval?"

"Yes—if you bother him for five seconds, the inspiration will survive it; for five minutes, you'll kill it dead beyond resurrection."

"I imagine you're right."

"What do you do in his room? Read?"

"Actually I just lie there on the bed. Look out the windows, or watch him—he doesn't notice me. The view is so beautiful up there. It's like being in a tree house, with those heavy trees hanging so close around the windows. He says I inspire him. Just being there, he says. I can't imagine it. But then again I can't imagine inspiration anyway. I've never been inspired in my life. I have absolutely no imagination."

"Who told you that?"

"Everybody says it. My mother, especially. She says I'm the dullest girl that ever lived."

"Does *she* quote Coleridge much?"

She laughed at the idea. "She says that's the kind of thing that makes me dull. She's so sharp herself. She can take any idea and use it as a dagger."

"If you're so dull, how is it that you inspire Collin?"

She smiled. "I'm his muse, I guess." The vexed line appeared between her brows again. "I remember," she said suddenly, "in one of his letters, Collin said something about how you didn't like his poetry."

"Oh, that's just the old battle. I'm very old-fashioned, you know. I like rhyme or blank verse—some kind of structure, preferably metric. He writes very modern stuff. We're always sparring about it. I've been trying to convert him for years, and he thinks I'm totally absurd. It's just a difference in training— outlook—whatever. Form! Form! I tell him. Freedom! Freedom! he chants back at me. I'm sure you'll be drawn into the fray this summer."

"Well, I can appreciate what you're saying, I guess. But I think he writes the most beautiful poetry I've ever read." She had to smile at the wry look on his face. "I guess I'm biased," she added.

"It's possible."

"But you *do* like what he writes, don't you? I mean, aside from your quibble about the form?"

"Yes," he said, surprised as her intent golden eyes drew an admission from him he had never made, even to himself. "I think he has what people like to call 'a unique voice.' I think he'll be recognized. And certainly the themes he writes on mean a lot to me."

She was pleased. They left the subject at that conclusion. After a minute Ryan sought for some way to bring her eyes back to his.

"So . . . How do you feel about your native land?"

"I like it. Everything seems so big here—the cars, the highways"—she laughed—"even the shopping malls."

"Your mother certainly seems to be putting the size of the malls to good use," he said. She smiled softly. He went on: "I have a friend in England who wrote me the same thing about the largeness of things in America. Only the beer bottles are smaller in the States, he said—and just as well, since the beer's so bad."

She turned in her seat toward the French doors. One was open; a breeze drifted in, a chill draft from this northern side of the house. She seemed to be seeking something far away.

"I miss Spain," she said suddenly. "That will always be my home."

He felt a nameless threat.

"I hope the valley feels a little like home to you, too."

"It's a beautiful place."

"I wish you'd grown up here," he said, sitting forward. "I wish you had done everything we used to do." He succeeded in drawing her attention back from the distance.

"What did you use to do, the two of you?"

He made a gesture of futility at the idea of cataloging everything. "We rode our bikes, we swam in the pond, we played in the woods. We talked—we argued for hours on end. We still do it."

"I wish I could have shared those things," she said, matter-of-fact and wistful at the same time.

"You can this summer, anyway. We'll make it all up to you."

"It sounds wonderful."

"But the question is—what are your plans? Are you staying the whole summer?"

She rolled her eyes upward to indicate the source of her uncertainty. "It's still being settled. I think my mother would like to. *I* certainly would like to. It really depends upon whether my father and mother can stand each other."

"Collin tells me you're going to go to college here next fall." She shook her head.

"Not next fall. There's no possibility of that. Maybe second semester. There are so many things to do—tests to take, applications to fill out, fees to pay, people to see—I don't know if even the second semester is realistic. From all the literature I've seen, we've missed every deadline there is. My mother thinks she can bully her way through every obstacle, as usual, but I think she's wrong."

"Well, I'm sure you'll enjoy it once you get there."

"I think I will. I need to catch up to Collin."

"Really? You must have had a pretty good education. Although I suppose I should ask you whether you did, rather than just make that assumption."

"It was reasonably good. But Collin has read so much more than I have."

Ryan was unsure what to do with this statement. "Collin?"

"Yes. He has shelves and shelves of poets in his room I've never even heard of."

"Oh, *that*. If it's any consolation, no one else has heard of them either. I wonder whether Collin has ever heard of Coleridge."

"I'm getting a lot of mileage out of that one quotation," she said with another smile.

"Seriously, you can't feel inferior to Collin because of his obsession with modern poetry. It's his specialty. You have your specialty, too."

"No, I don't. I have no specialty. I have no—no passion like Collin's poetry. Like your Greek and Latin. It's one of the things that makes me dull. The only thing that ever has ever come close to a passion for me is Collin's poetry. That's why I want to learn as much as I can about the poets he likes. It's the only way I'll ever get closer to his poetry."

"Wait a minute—what about your guitar? You play guitar, right? That's a specialty."

She made a motion of dismissal. "I love it," she admitted, "But I'll never be any good at it."

"Well, if it's not guitar, it's something else. Everyone has a specialty. Maybe it's not something they produce—a book, a symphony, a piece of woodworking. But there is something unique about everyone that can be their passion, if they only recognize it. Maybe for you it's—it's Spain. Maybe it really is the guitar, if you dismiss the idea that you have to measure up to some impossible standard you set for yourself. Maybe it's lying in the sun daydreaming."

"That hardly compares with writing great poetry."

"Who says it doesn't?"

"You're stretching for a point. You know you're being absurd," she said gently.

"Not at all. I believe what I'm saying. Let me ask you, what do you think my passion is, my specialty?"

"Classics."

"You might think so. It is, in a way. But sometimes I think classics is just a vocation—just a job. It's something I do, it's not something I am."

"You said yesterday I'd summed up your whole being by saying classics and soccer and being Irish."

"And I was joking."

"What is your passion, then?"

He sat back in the armchair and paused a moment.

"My passion—is this place. The valley. If I could be here, in the kind of life and fellowship Collin and I had together when we were young, I would be happy."

"But how can that . . . that impossible fantasy compare to something so . . . noble as writing poetry?"

"Because you measure the intensity of the passion itself, not the product."

"Now you're beginning to sound like Collin."

"I am a lot like Collin. We're flip sides of the same coin. We both believe that you find happiness by recognizing what it is that you most like to do and pursuing that single-mindedly. It's a certain purity of vision."

"If I could do anything," she said slowly, looking out the windows again, "I'd stay with Collin. I'd read all his poetry. I'd go with him to all his readings. I'd work to support him. I'd type his manuscripts. That's how much I believe in him."

"That's wonderful, but you may have some competition some day," he said. She winced visibly. He continued. "Maybe you should focus on something that *you* do, rather than pin your happiness on something someone else does. Then your happiness is in your control. That's where it should be."

"What about your fantasy? How can you—be here always? That's pretty impractical. It's not even remotely in your control, either."

He smiled. "I know," he said. "That's why I study Greek. I'm going to need the consolation of philosophy. The secret to happiness doesn't lie in getting what you want—it consists in not having any wants at all. Or at least in being content with the things you do have. Unfortunately, I haven't progressed as far as that stage yet. Maybe I just haven't been forced to."

They heard footsteps on the stairs; the tiles rattled, and then Collin stood at the entrance of the living room. "It's a little too cold to swim, isn't it?" he said.

"Not at all," said Ryan. "You've been moping around in this dark house too much. It's warm out there in the sun."

"Bring your suit?"

Ryan tugged a crumpled swimsuit from the pocket of his jacket. Constance laughed at the sight of it.

"I've got mine on underneath," she said.

"Constance is quite the water rat," observed Collin.

"Is that so?" asked Ryan, pleased. "Are you a good swimmer?"

"Not really. But I love the water. Fresh water especially."

"I'd better bring my suit too," said Collin. "You two see what Mrs. Overton has put together for lunch; I'll meet you out front."

Thursday, June 18/Two

I have been half in love with easeful death.

—Keats

Hey nonny no!
Men are fools that wish to die!
Is't not fine to dance and sing
When the bells of death do ring?
Is't not fine to swim in wine
And turn upon the toe
And sing heynonny no,
When the winds blow and the seas flow?
Hey nonny no!

—Traditional

Were it not madness to deny
To live, because we're sure to die?

—Etherege

THEY HAD TO commandeer Hal Minot's wheelbarrow to carry the picnic basket, which weighed a good eighty pounds. Collin packed the towels and blankets around the bulging wicker and trundled it off, singing snatches of rock and roll, as Constance and Ryan followed.

The path to the pond began not far from the stone porch. Not a path, but a passage; not a trail, but a tunnel under boughs. At one time a carriage road had been cut through the wood to the pond so that Collin's great-grandparents could welcome their friends to parties by the water. The broad slab of granite where company had boarded the carriage was still there beside the drive. But the woods had inched the margins of the road inwards; now three could not walk abreast down the way. No light shone through the trees here; the hemlocks and maples closed tightly overhead, the innermost ceiling a rough lattice of branches starved of sun, as if the underside of the canopy had been withered by the passage of some unhappy spirit. Usually the path was eerily quiet, the abrasion of air on the leaves above being muted. But now it echoed with Collin's ebullient and yet abstracted song, and returned startled sussurations at the clattering and clinking of the shifting china, remurmured surprisedly with a woman's soft laughter.

At midpoint the passage bent; and this, together with the initial plunge and final upsweep of the tunnel, prevented a view from one end to the other. Only when they passed that curve could the opening into light ahead be seen, dazzling, for the noon sun fell on the water beyond and cast its rays partly into the shadowed mouth of the path.

"Isn't this beautiful? Isn't this just so beautiful?" asked Constance as they stepped out of darkness.

"It is," said Ryan.

For he saw that the woods still crowded the margin of the pond; the sun still glistered in the textures brushed up by the breeze on the surface; the ripples still ran against the beach of imported sand; the cyclopean stones still lined the margin; the willow, a hundred yards away at the far end, still wept into its own black shadow; and in the center of the pond the rock, glacial memento or ledge that had defied excavation, still raised its tempting bourne.

A mere cup of water beside Earth's great reservoirs; but deep, black; black and deep; like a footprint left by hasty night as it vacated the land. But unlike airy night, unbreathable.

"You should see this place in the fall," said Collin, giving up his song. "All reds, yellows, oranges, golds—reflected in the water—beautiful."

"You should write about it," said Constance.

"I should. Actually, I have; but I should again."

"The saddest sight you'll ever see," said Ryan.

She turned to him. He was standing slightly apart. "What did you say?" she asked.

"I said, the saddest sight you'll ever see. The pond, in autumn."

"Why sad?"

He looked at her curiously, a mirror for her incomprehension. "Because autumn is sad."

"How so? I've always loved autumn."

"So do I. But it's sad all the same. Death—change—the final beauty before winter—isn't that sad?"

"But I think of cool fresh air, clean rain—back to school, a new beginning. I don't think about death when I think about fall."

"You don't think about how short life is, how the things you know and love are all passing away?"

"Not at all."

"I envy you. At least I think I do."

"You forget, Ryan," said Collin, "that Constance has never seen a New England autumn."

"Is autumn so different here?" she wondered.

Collin paused a moment, and the other two felt they were waiting for something.

"Yes," he said. "The past crowds in on you. You can't avoid it."

"But is that sad? You have such beautiful memories. Aren't they pleasant to think of?"

"'Tears, idle tears,'" quoted Ryan, "'I know not what they mean, tears from the depth of some divine despair rise in the heart, and . . .'" He groped for the line. "What do they do? Gather—'gather to the eyes . . . in looking on the happy Autumn-fields, and thinking of the days that are no more.'"

"Yes," said Constance immediately, "but even Tennyson says the autumn itself is happy."

"But they recall 'the days that are no more.'"

She turned and addressed her appeal suddenly to Collin, as if he were the referee of her own opinions. "But you have the future. You have your poetry—all the things you'll accomplish."

"I understand your point," said Collin. "As a matter of fact, I do think of the future, a lot of the future. I think you'll find that's one of the great differences between Ryan and me. I'm an American—I look forward, towards the West, toward the Frontier, which is still there in spirit, at least. Ryan looks back to Europe, toward the past." He paused, and then added, in a tone Ryan called his "quoting voice," a few words that were apparently from one of his own poems: "'He thinks the past cannot be surpassed.'"

"It's true I look back to Europe, but so do you," Ryan responded readily. "At least I know I'm doing it. You can talk about Whitman and Chicago and sprawling America, but you live in this little slice of the Old World. Face it, Collin: We're both New Englanders, and New England is still part of the Old World."

Collin smiled faintly, a soft, indulgent grin. His silence, too, was damning, as he gave up the discussion and lifted the basket out of the wheelbarrow. Without warning a rivet pulled through the soft wood of a handle, and the hamper tilted dramatically as he set it hastily on the sand; a clatter, as of shattering plates, brought a change of subject.

"We'd better check to see nothing has broken," said Constance.

"Spread out a blanket," said Collin, easing open the lid.

They knelt around the basket. As they unpacked it they found that nothing had suffered damage. In a few minutes they had the contents spread across the blanket: two bottles of suntan lotion, six plates, seven bowls, five glasses, and a complete silver setting for four; roast beef sandwiches, hard boiled eggs, chicken, cold asparagus; an assortment of homemade breads and biscuits, with several sticks of butter; an enormous earthenware bowl of strawberries, a half-dozen apples; bottles of mineral water and juices, cans of soda; insulated containers of vichyssoise, coffee, and tea; a small plastic tub of salad made of fresh peas and lettuce from Mrs. Overton's garden; a tin of cookies, still radiating heat from the oven; and a few black slabs of a chocolate cherry cake.

"Good old Mrs. Overdone," said Collin fondly.

Constance whispered amazedly in Spanish, then added: "How does she expect us to eat all this?"

"You'll be surprised. These Irishmen can really pack it away."

"She's a dear, sweet, blessed soul," intoned Ryan. "And sure she'd be goin' to heaven, if only she'd put a few bottles of good stout in here." He and Collin both favored a particular brand of stout as a general-purpose beverage.

"Forget it," said Collin. "She'll still be trying to feed us soft drinks when we're tottering at the brink of the grave."

"Do you object to alcohol?" Ryan asked Constance, as the thought suddenly occurred to him.

"Not at all." Her reassurance seemed too eager.

"Tell him," said Collin.

Her glance flickered away for a moment. "It's just that—" she began.

"It's just that Mother drinks too much, is what she's trying to say."

"Not exactly *too much*, but more than I wish she did. But she's not an alcoholic or anything."

"Too much is too much," said Ryan. "What's your definition of an alcoholic? Someone who drinks too much, right? You don't have to apologize. You should meet some of my relatives. My cousin Frank. My cousin Joey. I have a cousin Mary who's fourteen—they just caught her snorting cocaine in the girl's room."

"Ryan has eight zillion cousins," explained Collin, beginning to organize the food and protect if from the sun, which had grown almost hot. "Tell Constance about your cousins, Ryan."

"Got a few weeks?"

"Give me a quick overview," she said. She seemed grateful to him for turning the conversation.

"I can't even *remember* all my cousins."

"I don't believe it."

"It's true," affirmed Collin. "No one could remember all his cousins.—Does your mother remember all your cousins, Ryan?"

"I think so. But who would ever know it if she forgot one or two?" While he continued to speak he watched regretfully as they busied themselves making the food inaccessible; they apparently had no intention of eating as yet. "There are my uncle Frank and aunt Mary's kids. He's a welder in a shipyard up in Chelsea. She does the housewife thing. They've got Reena; young Frank—he's the drunk; Pippin—she's getting married this summer; let's see—Mary, my cousin; John—he married a sixteen-year-old girl last year and they have a son—"

Constance's eyes widened; she stopped clattering the plates and listened.

"Then there's Tom; he's been in jail four times for car theft. And Annie. She has a two-year-old, but she isn't married yet. No, wait, that's Beatty—Beatrice, you know. And Pippin—oh, I already said Pippin. I can't remember what Pippin does."

"And they're all your aunt and uncle's kids? It must be a big family."

"There are more, too. Corrie and Ruthie. They're twins. Goody-two-shoes. Sort of dull. Teenagers."

"You certainly do have a lot of cousins! I'm impressed."

Collin laughed merrily, and Ryan snorted.

"Those are just the children of my uncle Frank and aunt Mary. My mother had four sisters and two brothers. Uncle Frank and Aunt Mary have twelve kids, I think. My Aunt Millie has at least five. Aunt Luce has about nine. Aunt Ginny and Uncle Bob—there's a terrible marriage!—they have seven kids. Uncle Jack and his wife have nine. Uncle Billy got married to a woman who wound up in Met State—"

"A mental hospital," explained Collin.

"—She died just last year. They didn't have any kids.—And then lots of my cousins have kids. Sometimes it seems like they have millions of kids."

Collin laughed again. "All with Celtic names. Tell her some of the names, Ryan."

"I don't know how Celtic they are, really. Lots of saints mixed in there. Elaine, Caitlin, Sean, Andy—let's see—a few Mary's, a Meggin, a Pat, a Donovan; Stephen—"

"Have you met all these cousins?" Constance asked Collin.

"God, no. A few."

"A few of the more presentable ones," said Ryan.

"Yeah. Bridget, for instance. I saw her around Amherst once or twice last year. She said she was studying veterinary science.—Right?"

"Sounds good," said Ryan, unable to confirm this fact, though his mother had mentioned it the day before.

"She's actually sort of attractive. So was Cissy. I met her a few years ago."

"Before she ran away, you mean.—Her twin brother Randy was paralyzed in a car accident," Ryan explained to Constance. "It really changed her. She left home not long after the accident, and she hasn't been seen or heard from for three years."

"She had a tough time," said Collin.

"They all did. My Uncle Ted had to have his leg amputated—he was hit by a forklift at the place he worked. Pinned against a loading dock—they didn't have to do much cutting to get the leg off, I guess. Their oldest son, Matthew, became a priest. He was the pride of their lives. Then he fell in love with a streetwalker and left the church so he could marry her. Now he sells insurance."

"You're not serious! Not a real—"

"A real bona fide prostitute. She's not one anymore, of course. She's really nice, actually. She's a lot nicer than some of my cousins who look down their noses at her. Her name is Candy."

"I can't believe all this," said Constance.

"It's true," said Collin. "It's as good as a soap opera."

Ryan scratched his head lightly. "It's better than a soap opera, if you like that kind of thing. I can't handle it, myself. They overwhelm me. When I'm with them, they make me feel like one more attraction in the O'Brien freak show."

"But you're . . . " Constance began, then faltered.

"Different? Not really. Well, I guess I am a little different. I'll have to hand it to my mother. She really raised herself up out of that family. Out of all the drinking and the crazy stuff. Although it had a lot to do with her marrying my father. Somewhere not far back our branch of the Kinsellas became Protestant. Don't ask me how. But my father has never been a very religious man. I think that loosened some of the ties my mother had with the O'Briens. They sort of pity her for marrying out of the Church."

"Then your parents are like ours," said Constance.

"In that respect, anyway. That's about where the resemblance ends."

"Ryan's mother knows Shakespeare by heart," commented Collin.

"Really?" Constance asked eagerly. "I love Shakespeare."

"You should go over there and chat with her sometime," observed Collin, with a sarcasm that made Constance look at him wonderingly. "You'll be ready to believe the Bard has been reincarnated in female form. You won't catch *her* watching the soap opera."

"That you won't," agreed Ryan.

"I can't imagine what that must be like," said Constance.

"Having a mother who is not anti-intellectual, you mean?" muttered Collin. She winced, but let the remark pass, turning toward Ryan.

"Do you talk with her much about Shakespeare? I mean, can you share it with her?"

"She shares it with you—it's sort of a one-sided thing. She'll put down a frying pan and say, 'What if he really means us to think she's still alive when Lear says "The feather stirs; she lives!"' You know by the use of the pronoun without antecedent that she's talking about *him*, Shakespeare. She's always said that the fascination of Shakespeare is that he's in love with ideas. She's still in love with ideas, too—at a remove, anyway. As long as they're his ideas."

"Speaking of soap operas, what were you and Mrs. Overton watching yesterday?" Collin asked Constance.

"I didn't want to watch it, really. She wanted me to."

"Wait," said Ryan. "You weren't—watching *television?*"

"Yes," she admitted. He hid his face in mock horror.

"You just lost ten points, Con," said Collin.

"I really didn't want to at first," she pleaded. "I was reading a magazine from one of her piles and she turned on the set and begged me to keep her company."

Collin chortled. "You should have seen these two. As cozy as you please in the office there, sipping tea in the glow of the tube."

"That was before the movie came on. Then she got very upset all of a sudden. I couldn't understand why."

Ryan nodded. "And she said, 'I don't know how you can watch people who are dead,' right?"

"Exactly! And she went running out of the room. Just because some movie star was dead. Isn't that the strangest thing?"

"Totally bizarre," agreed Collin curtly.

"Well," mused Ryan.

"Well, what? Admit it, it's bizarre. She does strange things sometimes."

"I'm not too sure I haven't felt something similar. Certainly not in regard to movie stars—I don't give a damn about movie stars, if you'll pardon my language."

"It's all right," said Collin. "Constance has heard the word 'damn' before somewhere, I'm sure. It was probably the first word she heard from Mother's lips. And we know you're totally free of the taint of popular culture. We'll never accuse you of liking movie stars. In fact, I'm amazed you even know what they are."

"Oh, I do know a little of the wider world," said Ryan, playing along with the satire, which was not without some truth. "Even my ivory tower has a window."

"Facing east, away from Hollywood.—So what's your interpretation of this peculiar remark of Mrs. Overton's?"

"Well," he said again. "Put it into another context. Take a contemporary poet instead. Housman, for instance."

"Contemporary poet!" scoffed Collin. "When did he die, anyway?"

"Oh, I don't know. Before the war."

"What war? The Vietnam War? The Korean War? Or the Trojan War?"

"The Second World War, you ignoramus," said Ryan mildly.

Collin raised his eyebrows and looked significantly at Constance. "The man's been dead for over forty years, and Ryan calls him contemporary!"

Ryan laughed. "Call him whatever you like."

"Antique," suggested Collin, not without something like a sneer.

"All right, antique. Like the lampshade—or like your mother, as your father pointed out yesterday. The point is that he's dead; and every time I read his poetry—bitterly sad stuff—I think about the fact that he's dead. How can you help it? All he ever thought about when he wrote it was that he was going to die, and he made sure you remember that when you read him. What was it?

> This is for all ill-treated fellows
> Unborn and unbegot
> For them to read when they're in trouble
> And I am not.

"'Am not' in trouble, and 'am not' in existence, implying that to exist is to be in trouble."

"Thank you, Mr. Critic," said Collin.

"So you *do* think about death when you read him," continued Ryan, "because he's so obsessed with it. But even if he weren't, even if his range of themes was a little wider, let's say, like Yeats— even when I read Yeats, I feel that way."

"What way?"

"Well, I think about all that he did, all that he lived through, thought, wrote about, all the beauty he produced and got down on the page—and he died in spite of all that, of course; and there's just something terribly sad about it. When I read him I think to myself, live as long as I can, I'll never produce anything this beautiful; and death took even him, the way it will take me. When I read him, even if it's a poem about love, or passion, or happiness of some sort, I think about the fact that I'm going to die."

"That's awful!" said Constance. She looked to Collin for support, but he was now suddenly silent.

"I think that Mrs. Overton feels the same way about her movie stars," continued Ryan, oblivious to Constance's distress. "When she sees one she knows is dead, she forcefully recalls her own mortality. She's frightened. She runs out of the room. I myself don't feel frightened, in my version of the phenomenon. I just feel sad. Sad that we enjoy life, and then it's gone."

"But why dwell on it?" protested Constance. "I mean, we all die—so what? What can we do about it? We can't change it any more than we can change"—she opened the palm of her hand and looked at it as she spoke—"the color of sunlight. As a fact, it just doesn't interest me. It's pointless to think about it."

Ryan raised his eyes to hers in a glance so penetrating and inscrutable that she turned to Collin again, beseechingly. She found on his face an expression identical to that on Ryan's. It was as if she sat between her brother and a mirror; the fearless between the frightened.

"But look," she cried feebly, raising both hands now and gesturing around them at sky, water, earth. "How can you think of death on such a beautiful day?"

They looked. At sky, at shivering water, the gently swaying limbs of the trees.

"How can you *not* think of it?" asked Ryan in a soft voice.

"Exactly," said Collin.

She folded her hands in her lap and was speechless.

"I think you're right," Collin continued in a minute, referring back to Mrs. Overton. "That *is* the explanation for her behavior. The context was so mundane that I completely overlooked the universality of the reaction."

"What puzzles me," said Ryan, "is why I feel that way only when I consider someone who really accomplished something— someone who could justifiably write *vixi*, 'I have lived,' across his tombstone. Why not when I think of the unknowns, the millions who lived and died and left no mark? Isn't that loss even more frightening and sad? How can my reaction be so undemocratic?"

"Maybe it isn't. Look at Mrs. Overton. She has her fascination with the obituaries. That's very democratic."

"But *I* don't. And I wouldn't be caught dead reading them." He smiled at his own joke.

"Because you'd be ashamed to take such an interest in the minutiae of death," suggested Collin. "So for you it takes another form. Have you ever seen a photograph of those graveyards in France that stretch on for acres and acres?"

"The crosses 'row on row'?"

"Isn't that unbearable too, the same way Housman's death is? Or the photographs of the death camps?"

"Yes," agreed Ryan.

"In a way, I find the death of the unknowns even more frightening."

"Because you don't want to die as an unknown."

"Exactly."

Collin again paused a moment. "And I won't either," he asserted softly.

"No," said Constance suddenly, "you won't. Great poetry survives death. And that's why I don't feel sadness for the poets when I read it."

"You think fame is a consolation for death, then?" asked Ryan.

"'The future for the dying past,'" said Collin in his quoting voice.

"The future is dead too, old man. The future will die one way or another, and human fame will be washed under."

"By what? A nuclear holocaust? Sometimes I think the bomb was invented for pessimists like you. Or the environment? Toxic waste?"

"It doesn't matter by what—it doesn't matter if the great catastrophe happens or not. The greatest catastrophe for you would be if nothing happened—if the human race went on multiplying infinitely, and populated the entire universe. When a billion billion poets have been published, who will have time for your work? Who will have time for our Shakespeare when a hundred thousand Shakespeares have lived and died? You mock me for reading poets in a dead language. It will be people like me who will read you when English is dead. And that won't take long to happen. Who reads Chaucer now?—A handful of scholars, lecturing to a few thousand college students cribbing their way through a few excerpts in an anthology."

He had Collin's range now, and the big guns were pounding.

"You want to live forever," he went on. "What's forever? Three hundred years? Six hundred years? Chaucer was walking the earth six hundred years ago, living and breathing and arguing with his friends the way you and I are arguing now."

"And he's still being read," said Constance.

"Not by today's new poets," said Ryan. "They don't have time for him. They think he's old-fashioned. He has nothing to teach them. It doesn't occur to them that six hundred years from now a fresh crop of arrogant young poets will declare *them* old-fashioned."

Collin was almost scowling.

"You don't believe that anything human lasts, then?" asked Constance. "Don't you think that's immoral? I mean something human has to continue. Didn't Collin tell me you were a Catholic?"

"No, I'm not," said Ryan. "I'm a 'pagan, suckled in a creed outworn.'"

"Well, I'm a Catholic," said Constance quietly. "Maybe not a good one, but still a Catholic."

"So, what does that have to do with the topic at hand?" asked Ryan.

"If you're Catholic, you have to believe that there *are* human things that last. Human love lasts, for example."

"Only insofar as it partakes of divine love," added Ryan. "Or at least that's what the theologians say." Constance looked at him, seeming unsure whether he was quoting again, or mocking her, or putting words into her mouth. She continued anyway.

"And the beauty that humans create lasts too. In poetry, in art, in music—it lives forever. And those who create it are blessed. I believe it."

Collin smiled softly, returned to good spirits at the sight of Ryan's discomfiture.

"Is that an argument?" asked Ryan.

"No. It's a statement of faith."

"Then I can't argue with it. Not even the Devil can do that. But your faith won't get your brother off the hook."

"Why not? He has faith too."

She looked keenly into Ryan's eyes now, her own golden gaze armed with certainty. He felt such satisfaction in what he considered the splendid innocence and ingenuousness of her viewpoint, that he abandoned the argument entirely. In fact, as he looked away, feeling a vague, hungry, burning sensation, he almost forgot what he had been arguing about. But as he retreated he fired one last round.

"If he isn't writing poetry for the *moment*—for the joy it gives him *now,* as he does it—then he's deluded," he said.

"Well, of course, that *is* the greater part of it," said Collin. "The act of creating."

"I'm glad we can all agree that what happens *now* is very important," said Constance. She was scolding them.

"Poor Constance," said Collin. "She isn't used to hearing death discussed with such detachment."

"Is it detachment?" asked Ryan. "At any rate, we're boring you. We'll have to be better company."

"Yes, please," she said. "Talk about fun. Talk about life. It's actually getting warm out here. I might even go for a swim, or at least get some sun."

"I'll talk about fun," said Collin. His change of tone announced something important. "How's this for fun? You remember that poetry workshop I wrote you about? The one at Nahamus?"

"You decided not to go?" wondered Constance hopefully.

"No, I decided I would."

"Then that's no fun. At least, not for me and Ryan. Why do you call that fun? Not that I would stop you from going. I just wish I could go too."

"That's the whole point. Listen. It starts on the twenty-fifth of July, and runs a week. I've talked Dad into not renting the cottage for that week. The main house will be rented, but not the cottage on the cliff."

Constance sat up, her face radiant with pleasure. "Oh, Collin!" she cried.

"And what I would like to know, is: How would you two like to spend that week at the beach? I'd be gone during the day, but you could do all those beachy things—get sunburned, read junk fiction, get salt in your hair and sand in your clothes, sweat one minute and freeze the next—in other words, make yourself as miserable and uncomfortable as possible. Would that be fun, or what? Ryan can keep you entertained and translate the native dialects during the day. At night I'll be back, and we can cook clams and lobsters and drink good beer and fall asleep in front of the fire."

She leapt to her feet and did a rapturous dance, shaking her shining hair about her shoulders. "Could we? Could we?"

"You seem to have a volunteer," noted Ryan.

"What about you?" asked Collin.

Ryan stared at Constance, who had stopped dancing and was frozen, breathless, waiting for his answer. "Are you kidding?" he asked.

"Does that mean yes?" asked Constance.

"How could I say no?"

"You couldn't," she said.

"Obviously he couldn't," said Collin. Ryan detected humor in the comment.

"Then I'll say yes."

"It's settled," said Collin. But Constance hurled herself back onto the blanket and caught Collin's sleeve.

"What about Mother?"

He gestured unconcernedly. "We'll tie her up and leave her in a closet somewhere."

"Seriously—"

"Why should she object?"

She cast a furtive glance at Ryan.

"You don't know her," she said. "She can't live a week without me. She'll probably tag along." She added a groan at the mere thought.

"I'll get Dad to work on her if necessary."

"Would you? He might be able to do something."

"Don't worry about it. We'll take care of her one way or another." As she sat back on her heels, reassured, he added: "Now, is that talking about fun, or what?"

"But you two have to promise me—no more talking about death. Who's going to die? We'll all live forever, all three of us."

"Let's not go overboard," said Collin.

"Well, we won't know we're going to die until it happens, right?" she teased him.

"Good point," he agreed facetiously. "Try that out on Peter Pan over there."

"No," she said. "No more death."

Ryan laughed. "It's going to get mighty dull around here. What are we going to do if we can't confront the great issues of existence?"

"You let me take care of that," she retorted.

"All right, you be the cruise director. What's first? Shuffleboard?"

"No," she said. "A swim."

"It *is* awfully hot," Ryan admitted.

"Put your suits on," she said. "Last one in is a rotten egg."

Without any further comment or warning she stood up and drew her dress off over her head in one sudden motion.

"Jesus Christ!" exclaimed Ryan.

Which was more dazzling, her tanned skin, or the blinding whiteness of the bikini—a minimum of cloth stretched taut over taut flesh? She laughed, her eyes sparkling with humor.

"Excuse my language," he said. "I've never seen a naked woman before. Or should I say, a naked Catholic?"

"It's not that bad," she protested laughingly. She knew how she looked; and yet she was not showing off. She moved naturally, unself-consciously.

"Bad?" said Ryan. "Did I say it was bad?—I do trust you have a license to wear that thing. There must be some law against carrying ill-concealed weapons."

Collin threw back his head and laughed.

"Mother was right," said Constance. "You Americans are prudes." She knelt in front of Ryan on the blanket, and her beauty, her sexuality, her perfume, filled his sight and his senses. She smiled into his face, too close. "What was that you were saying about death?" she asked.

"I forget."

"Good. Are we going to live forever, or not?"

"Better than that," said Collin. "We're going to live right now."

"Personally, I think I've already died and gone to heaven," said Ryan. "If I really believed the angels dressed like that, I might decide that heaven was worth a Mass." She laughed again and stepped back from the blanket.

Ryan had long since shed his jacket, but now he drew off his shirt as though suddenly overcome by the heat.

"You have a tan already," said Constance in surprise.

"Played a few pickup games this spring, mostly without a shirt. What did you think—I'd be all white, wasted away by my studies?"

"Collin's pretty white," she said. "He needs a tan."

"He's been slaving in his garret. People think *I'm* a drudge— I'm a dilettante compared to him."

"You put on some lotion," she said to Collin, who was also shucking his shirt.

"Yes, Mommy," he answered. He went into the woods to change.

Ryan pulled his suit out of the pocket of his jacket and stood up. Constance laughed suddenly. "'Yes, Mommy,'" she repeated.

"The boy's mixed up," observed Ryan.

"He's the nicest person I've ever met," she said. "Don't you think he is?"

"I don't know all the people you've met. But I guess I'd probably agree with you."

"And he really is handsome. I'll bet all the girls at school go after him."

"I imagine."

"He says he doesn't have a girlfriend."

"Wasn't there someone—Cindi, or Coco, or something?"

She was silent, and he could see her swallow hard. "He didn't say anything about anyone. But there's a whole bunch of poems he hasn't shown me."

"Why do you ask? Are you jealous?"

She blushed. "No," she said. "I just wanted to tease him about it if there was somebody."

"That's the best way to find out. Tease him for not having a girlfriend. I guarantee you'll see those poems within twenty-four hours."

She looked at him wonderingly. "It's scary how well you know him," she said. He grinned a close, secret grin. The expression was a specialty of his; it made people wonder how much more he knew that he was not telling.

He went into the woods to change.

On his way back, he paused and peered through some bushes on the edge of the beach. The bushes were in bloom; their scent hung about him in a cloying cloud as he watched Constance dabbling one foot in the water.

"'Tell, if thou canst,' he murmured to himself, "'whence doth come This Camphire, Storax, Spiknard, Galbanum. . . . I'll tell thee: while my Julia did unlace her silken bodies, but a breathing space . . .'" She had a beauty that stung him now like the final line of a fine poem—the salt stood on the rim of his eye, and he thought not of life at all, but of how this magnificence of flesh would pass, would become like Eve's body someday. All the tawny skin firm over the fine proportions, the rippling muscle and the round breasts, the heavy mass of hair; and all this and the mind within that lit it, gentle, but not retiring; forward, humorous, affectionate.

Just then Collin came out of the woods across the way and stopped, watching her too. The intensity of his interest disturbed Ryan. He stepped forth out of the undergrowth and Collin looked toward the sky.

"Last one in has to push the wheelbarrow back," said Ryan.

"The water's cold," said Constance doubtingly.

"You'll never get in if you hesitate," said Ryan, dropping the bundle of his clothes on the sand.

"Look out, Con, this guy's a nut."

It was Ryan's practice to plunge in as quickly as possible. He now ran full tilt at the water, past Constance, who cried out as he splashed through the shallows beyond her. Then in a low dive he bored the surface and went under.

The cold was like a barrier. He swam obstinately downward and outward, propelling himself some thirty feet before he emerged for a breath. Then he turned at once for the shore.

"How can you do that?" she asked as he staggered back through the shallows.

"Take the plunge," he said. "It's the only way."

"He's right," agreed Collin. "Just run right at it and get it over with."

"I don't see you following his example."

"Hey, I thought you were the great proponent of living for the moment," said Ryan. "Go for it. Go all the way. That's the way to live life, right?"

"I like to go slowly."

"Aw, come on," said Ryan. "I know what that means. That means we have to coax and plead with you for half an hour, and then you chicken out."

"I'm not going in like that, all of a sudden. It's bad for you. It's too much of a shock to your system. You have to try it a little at a time and see if you can stand it."

"Take the plunge," urged Ryan again. "Live life to the full! My God, I'm more of a practitioner of your philosophy than you are."

"I'll come in," said Constance. "Just give me time."

"What are we going to do about her, Collin?"

"Throw her in," said Collin.

"You wouldn't dare!" she cried.

Collin approached her, feigning menace. Ryan and Constance both laughed, certain he would not actually throw her in; but he suddenly caught her and took her up in his arms. She shrieked and struggled, but clung to him at the same time; and then he ran headlong into the pond, and threw himself, and her as well, into the water. She emitted one last shriek of dismay as they went under with an explosive splash.

"Oh, you!" she gasped when they arose from the water, sputtering and choking with cold. "I'll kill you!"

She flung herself at him, seized him, and dragged him under again. He was laughing as the water closed over him, and he stood up again to throw her under in revenge.

She had had enough—she was too cold, he was too strong—and she tried to escape. He caught her by one ankle and upended her as she struggled up the shallows. She could only laugh, turn on him, and blind him with a flurry of splashes. He wrestled her down again; they rolled about in knee-deep water, each emitting cries of mock hostility—until she suddenly paused to clutch the top of her bathing suit, which was about to slip from its place. Collin forbore, and she scrambled out onto the beach.

They stood staring at each other, breathing hard. Constance readjusted her suit and seemed almost to blush in spite of the chill. But Ryan saw that both she and Collin were smiling, faintly smiling.

"I'll get you for that," she said.

"'Talk about fun. Talk about life,'" responded Collin.

"Is that what you call fun?" she said, although the tone of her reproach signaled its humor. "Is that what you call life? Drowning me? Beating me up?"

"You're still breathing, you hellcat."

She looked at Ryan as if she had suddenly remembered he was there. "Would you have done this?" she asked, slicking back her hair. He held up his hand woodenly in a feeble imitation of the Boy Scout salute.

"Me, ma'am?" he said. "Never."

"He just didn't think of it first, that's all," said Collin. "Come on, Ryan. I'll race you to the rock."

"Maybe you'd better catch your breath," said Ryan.

"No, I'm ready," said Collin. "Come on, don't wimp out on me. I'm starting—catch me if you can." And with this he dove into the water and began pulling for the rock. Ryan followed somewhat reluctantly.

He caught up almost immediately—the momentum of a good dive won him that. In recent years he had never lost a race against Collin, being in better training year round; but now he was surprised at his friend's speed and power. All his own strength could barely keep him abreast. And yet he felt he was competing not against vigor, but against frenzy.

What's wrong with you, Collin? he wondered suddenly.

They were nearing the rock when Collin pulled ahead. Ryan could not catch him. When he glided the last few feet, Collin was clinging to the granite, gasping, too exhausted for the moment to pull himself out of the water.

Ryan found the familiar toeholds in the rock and climbed out. "Come on," he said, offering his hand to Collin. With that assistance Collin clambered out and sprawled panting in the sun.

"Are you all right?" Constance called from the shore.

"Of course," answered Ryan.

"Who won?"

"I did," said Collin, propping himself on one elbow.

"I'm coming out," she said.

"It's a long way," said Ryan. "If you wait a minute, we'll come back."

But she waded in, holding her hands just above the surface of the water. When she came to the edge of the shallows, she committed herself and began a slow, graceful crawl toward them.

They watched her closely. Her strokes were light, but her form was good; she had evidently been coached at one time.

"She says she can't swim," said Collin ironically.

"Right. She looks really good."

About halfway she stopped to pull up a strap, giggling at the necessity. When she reached them they showed her where the holds were and helped her up.

The rock became very small. She sat down between them.

In a minute Collin lay back in the sun. Ryan found Constance's presence beside him almost too intense, and he lay back also; but then she did likewise, even though the rock afforded so little space that she was in contact with both Ryan and Collin along nearly her full length. So far from being ill at ease was she that she even took each by the hand as she lay there.

"Isn't this wonderful?" she said, with an almost wistful pleasure.

It is wonderful, thought Ryan in surprise. *This moment, this* now.

"Just the three of us, friends," she added.

"It's like when we were kids," said Collin. "Isn't it, Ryan? Magic like that. Remember those hot summer days, swimming here, diving from the rock—the time we made that raft, remember? It was all like this, magic."

"You're right," said Ryan. He felt a bliss stealing over him.

"This is going to be a beautiful summer," said Constance.

"Like those summers again, but with you here this time," said Collin. "The way it should have been."

"Let's promise to do everything together," said Constance. "All the things you used to do. And no fair leaving me out just because I'm a girl. Promise."

"I promise," said Collin.

"I promise with pleasure," said Ryan.

"And I promise." She gave each of their hands an extra squeeze and held them tight. The sun streamed over them, the water lapped quietly at the edges of the rock; her perfume, still faintly detectable, tingled faintly in the air. If Ryan opened his eyes to look up at the cloudless blue sky, he saw at their periphery the outline of her face, her throat, her breasts rising and falling beneath the white cloth.

Summer! he thought. *A whole summer!*

❁ ❁ ❁

They lay so still on the warm rock that Constance fell asleep. Her grip softened. She moaned ever so slightly, and her head turned to rest against Collin's shoulder. He sat up. She awoke, smiled, withdrew her hands, and rubbed her eyes, stretching on the rock.

Ryan propped himself on one elbow; he had a pain in his back where a lump of granite had dug into him. In this position his gaze rested naturally on Constance's lower torso. The bikini there was drawn so tightly over her hips and her belly was so lean that as she stretched a gap appeared between the cloth and her abdomen, into which he could see without any hindrance. He shifted so hastily that he nearly fell off the rock.

"Take it easy," said Collin. Constance sat up.

"There isn't much room here," she said, as if agreeing to someone's complaint.

"How about a few dives and then we swim back?" suggested Collin.

"I'm not much of a diver," she demurred. "You go ahead, though."

Ryan and Collin made several dives, both showing off. They teased Constance by scattering water over her each time they climbed out. Finally Collin stayed in after a dive, holding on to the edge of the rock with one hand. "What do you say about some lunch?"

"I thought you'd never ask," said Ryan.

"But no racing back," said Constance.

"No," agreed Collin. "We'll take it easy."

Ryan used the side stroke, Constance the breast stroke with her head above the surface, and Collin the backstroke; they stayed together the whole way. Ryan saw that even as they swam the happy smile never left her face.

Thursday, June 18/Three

Awake forever in a sweet unrest.

—Keats

FTER THE FEAST they fell asleep in the sun. Ryan awoke in a short while, disoriented. Constance was applying suntan lotion to Collin's back; she smiled sleepily at the look on Ryan's face.

"I don't know why I'm so tired," he said. He had never been idle long enough to realize that exhaustion is the natural consequence of having nothing to do.

"I know what you mean," she said, massaging the oil into Collin's shoulders. "I think I've still got jet lag. Collin and I were up pretty late last night. He was reading me Ferlinghetti. Have you ever read him?"

"I've never even heard of him."

"I've been talking about him for years, you nitwit," interjected Collin.

"How about Kunitz?" Constance asked Ryan.

"I make it a point never to read anything in paperback."

"Are you serious?"

"They didn't have paperbacks before about 1940," explained Collin.

"Oh, I get it." She sat back on her heels and pushed the hair away from her face with the backs of her hands. "If I asked you to, would you listen to Collin read Ferlinghetti? Just once?"

"Sure."

Collin laughed faintly, cynically. "I admire your powers of persuasion, Constance. I've been trying to get him to listen to Ferlinghetti for six years. It only took you about six seconds to talk him into it."

"You have to smile when you ask, that's all," she said.

"Yeah, Collin. Why didn't you ever smile when you asked?"

"Hah! You'd better watch it. I have an ally now."

"We should have brought the Ferlinghetti with us," said Constance. She began smearing lotion on the back of Collin's legs, which were beginning to look dangerously pink.

"Next time we will. You can charm him and I'll pour good poetry into his ears."

"And I'll bring a copy of Sappho or Catullus," added Ryan.

"Stuffy, boring old nonsense!" scoffed Collin. "Thee and thou, lovey dove."

Constance laughed. "Don't start up again, you two."

"On second thought, Catullus would scorch your ears, Constance," said Ryan. "I wouldn't dare corrupt you."

"What do you mean?"

"He's pretty risqué."

"Really? How so?"

"Say some dirty words for Ryan," suggested Collin, "so he knows you're not innocent."

She rattled off a string of Spanish words that Ryan had never heard before. Collin laughed.

"He doesn't understand a word you're saying."

"Don't you know Spanish, Ryan?"

"*Si, señorita.*"

"That's the sum total of what he knows. You've just heard it all."

"*Olé,*" added Ryan after a moment. "*Mañana. Tacos. Tortillas. El Toro. El Greco. Toda la vida es sueno.*"

Collin snorted, and Constance laughed out loud.

"Are you finished?" Collin asked her a minute later.

"All done," she said, adding a final dab to his ankles.

"Good. I think I'll turn over."

She made as if to throw the bottle at him in outrage. "You're the worst," she exclaimed, sprawling on the blanket once more.

"You're right about that," agreed Ryan. "You stay away from him, Constance."

"You're just as bad. Always kidding!"

"You love it," said Collin, beginning to spread lotion on his arms.

"It's true," she said. "I've never had any male friends who liked to kid around. All they wanted to do was grab me."

"Really?" said Ryan. "Why?"

She elbowed him, giggling. "Cut it out."

"Any guy ever grabs you, I'll annihilate him," said Collin.

"You'll have to get to him before I do," said Ryan.

"I've got first dibs. I'm her brother."

"All right. But if he's still breathing after you annihilate him, I'll finish him off."

"Thanks, macho dudes, but I can take care of myself."

"I'll bet you can," said Ryan.

"It runs on the distaff side," said Collin.

Drowsy silence met this remark. "I also fall asleep really fast," said Constance after a minute.

❀❀❀

Somewhere between waking and sleeping, Ryan lay on the blanket beside her, watching the fringe of green treetops on the rim of the sky beneath his heavy lids.

If he concentrated, he could conjure her image up in his mind and make her walk beside him. He saw her again in white, or descending the stairs, sitting on the sofa, stripping off her dress, sunning on the rock. But if he lost control of his thoughts, she might appear anywhere, alone or with Collin or her mother, she might even merge with Collin in a fraternal amalgam, then become discrete again.

If the brushes of fantasy and memory are vivid and colorful, they are yet broad. In these waking dreams, her features were a blur, her beauty inchoate, an aura rather than a limned design. And although her sexuality was not absent, it was subdued. These were like the dreams of boyhood, of a love that knew nothing of the abrasion of flesh on flesh. If she had been here ten years ago, on the shore of this dark water of memory, he could not have dreamed more chastely of her than he did now, when he had under his belt a quadrennium of discoveries in the *philosophia amatoria*. As the afternoon slipped, slipped toward evening, the others sometimes woke, ate, or drank, changed position, exchanged a few words of small talk with him or each other in murmurs, or lay in silence without seeking sleep. But Ryan clung successfully despite these interruptions to the dream state he had attained. Once he rose and plunged into the pond; but when he had lain down again, when the sun had soaked into his limbs and trunk and head again, the dreams returned.

The shadow of the trees at length stole over the three by the pond; they sat up one by one.

"What time is it?" asked Ryan, groping for his watch.

"After five," said Collin, consulting his.

"I suppose I should go home."

"Can't you stay for dinner?" asked Collin.

"Of course he's staying for dinner," said Constance.

"I wish I could. My parents are too good to me, though."

"Well, they *are* going to spare you one of these nights, aren't they?" asked Constance.

"If I arrange it well in advance, I think they'll be able to bear it, yes," he said. But neither took the hint and specified a day.

They gathered their belongings and heaped them in the wheelbarrow, moving slowly and reluctantly, each as if only in imitation of the others. As Collin stowed the picnic basket, he gave Ryan a sign behind Constance's back. Immediately they began walking for the pathway, leaving the wheelbarrow and Constance behind.

"Hey—guys," she called. They turned.

"What?" asked Collin.

"The wheelbarrow, remember?" She knew they were teasing her.

"We made a solemn promise to let you share in everything," said Ryan. "Do you want us to break it already?"

"No," she said. She tossed her towel on top of the pile and picked up the handles.

"Oh ho," exclaimed Collin.

She propelled the barrow over the sand and started up the path without difficulty. Ryan and Collin made elaborate faces of surprise at each other after she had passed, pursing their lips and raising their eyebrows. She was stronger than they had thought.

By the time they reached the top of the path, however, the arrangement had been altered. Ryan was pushing the wheelbarrow and Constance was riding in it, perched on the front lip, shrieking every now and then when he threatened to overturn her. Collin strode beside them, occasionally feigning an intention to upset the wheelbarrow, passenger and all. They had no sooner crossed the grass to the steps by the porch when an upstairs window shot open in its casing and a voice called out.

"Constance, what are you doing? Do you want to get yourself killed?" They could see Sondra's face behind the screen.

"It's all right, Mother," said Constance.

"It's not all right. You get out of that thing. I can't believe you two young men would do something so dangerous. Constance, come up here and get ready for dinner. Your hair is a mess. I don't want your father to see you that way."

Constance clambered out of the wheelbarrow, and after the three young people had rolled their eyes and smirked enough to salve their self-respect, she ran away inside. Collin and Ryan returned the picnic basket and went up the back stairs through the cool, dark house to Collin's room.

At the end of the upper hall—or of the main upper hall, at least, since the second floor was even within its restricted plan labyrinthine—was a small bedroom that looked over the western side of the valley. Once it had been a maid's room, near the kitchen stairs and adjoining a small, spartan bathroom; and yet, like much of the house, it was wainscotted in oak. Into this isolated room Collin had moved his things about the time he started college. The view was the finest of any room in the house, especially when, as now, the sun sank lingeringly toward the west and washed the tops of the trees in the land below with a yellow light, giving a felted texture to the mass of moving leaves. This was what Collin contemplated from the desk by the window when he worked at his writing.

The desk itself was narrow. Most of the top was taken up by an electronic typewriter of the best make, the ultimate writer's tool in the days before the personal computer. Beneath the other windows were bookshelves, some of unfinished pine rather roughly patched together by Hal Minot, inhabited almost exclusively by American poets and novelists in paperback editions. One corner was owned by an old wooden icebox that Collin used as a dresser. An antique double bed took up most of the remainder of the room; its disproportionate size compelled visitors to use it as a kind of couch, since there were no other places in the room to sit except for Collin's desk chair.

They changed back into their clothes. When Ryan was dressed he looked at the photographs tucked into the frame of the mirror over the dresser. "You need new pictures of her now," he said.

"Yeah," said Collin, rattling the hangers in the closet as he searched for the right shirt. "We'll take some film to Maine, for sure."

"What's the story on her staying here, anyway? For the whole summer, I mean? She said this morning that it depends on how well your parents get along."

"She'll stay. I don't care what my parents do. I'll see to it she stays." This was uttered with a determination that bordered on the savage. Ryan was surprised once again at the intensity of Collin's emotion.

"Well, what's your mother's plan?" he asked.

Collin grinned softly, his vehemence dissolving. "You won't believe it, but I think she wants to play the wife again."

"Actually, I do believe it. I suspected as much immediately. Mrs. Overton seems to be terrified of the possibility."

"Does she? Poor old thing. There isn't room for both of them here, that's for sure." He was silent. Finally Ryan prompted him.

"Well, what are you going to do about it?"

"Do about it? What should I do about it? What business is it of mine, really? She is sort of a bitch—if you can pardon a son calling his own mother that. She can definitely make life hard at times. But let's face it. I won't be around the house forever. If that's what Dad wants to do, let him. He's lonely. As long as Constance is here when I come home, at Christmas, holidays, in the summer, I don't care if my mother is too."

They both thought about this change in their lives.

"God!" exclaimed Ryan suddenly. "Remember those weird ladies your father used to date when we were kids?"

"Ugh!" said Collin.

"Where did he ever find them, anyway?"

"Class reunions and stuff. They were the losers nobody wanted."

"Your father definitely deserves better."

"You've got to admit, my mother's in great shape. She only pales in comparison to Constance. And he must still love her somehow. He's never divorced her. Although that could be because he thought she would claim alimony or try to get the house away from him or something. You know him. He's pretty Scotch."

"If only she were a little less—bitchy, to quote her son."

"That's her problem all right. It's as if she can't control herself. She wants to cozy up to my father, but all that nastiness keeps coming out. Like that bit about the lampshade. I really do think she was trying to be nice, at least when she first got it for him. But then she winds up cutting him down for still having the old one. Being obnoxious is a compulsion with her. That's why Constance likes you and me so much. We only tease her half the time. Her mother's on her back day and night."

"Well, she's certainly using Constance to get to your father. Did you catch that stuff about not wanting your father to see her with her hair messed up?"

"Yeah."

"So you're really not going to do anything about it?"

"What would you suggest? It would be like trying to stop the sap from rising. If you were a fifty-seven-year-old bachelor and some good-looking forty-odd-year-old woman were after your tail, wouldn't you just go with the flow?"

"Well, if you put it in exclusively sexual terms—"

"That's not all there is to it. My mother's a very intelligent woman. Well educated. Bryn Mawr. All that."

"She's sharp all right. Sharp as a knife in the back."

Collin scoffed. "Don't worry. It's the lampshade that's got you upset, that's all." He sat on the edge of the chair to tie his shoes. "You should like this, Ryan. It's our big chance to rewrite the past. It's the only one we'll ever get."

"I know. We're already doing it. It's strange, though. We both grew up as only children, and all of a sudden you're not an only child any more. I envy you in a way. For having a sister. Especially a sister like Constance."

"Do you?" asked Collin in a strange tone of voice.

"Yes," said Ryan, a little surprised.

"That's funny," said Collin, advancing toward the door. "I envy you—because Constance *isn't* your sister."

And before Ryan could even grasp his point, Collin had gone out, leaving him to follow.

They went down the front stairs. The Mercedes was just driving up as they came out the front door into the late afternoon air. Ryan was trying to think of something to say to put Collin back in humor; and he was worried at finding himself on the point of leaving without an invitation to return.

But Collin's spirits rebounded without Ryan's assistance. "Remember," he said, "You promised to sit still for Ferlinghetti." This sudden reversion to the topic of poetry was not a nonsequitur in Collin's world.

"That's true," admitted Ryan.

Lloyd greeted them with a hearty "Good evening!" He looked at Collin in surprise. "My boy—you're burned. How was your picnic?"

"Excellent, Dad. Mrs. Overton tried to kill us with food, but we held our own."

"And Constance? Did she enjoy it?"

They heard a light rattling of the floor tiles in the hallway, and Constance ran out of the house, without stockings or shoes.

"Ryan," she began, "I wanted to say goodbye.—Oh, hello, Papa!" She embraced him and kissed him warmly. "How was your day? And don't tell me it was no fun."

"We're not allowed to talk about things that aren't fun," said Ryan. "Like death and jobs."

"It's going to be a quiet summer for you two, then," said Lloyd. "But we can talk about your picnic," he said to Constance.

"It was the most beautiful day of my life," she exclaimed. She turned to Collin and Ryan. "Don't you think so? Wasn't it for you?"

"It was right up there in the top ten," said Ryan, realizing as he said it that it was the truth.

"Right up there," echoed Collin.

"Well, come inside and tell me about it while I pour myself a scotch," Lloyd said to Constance. As they moved toward the door Ryan backed out of the way, putting up one hand in a kind of salute.

"*Au revoir*—Mr. Tate—Constance—Collin—splendid day," he said.

"Why don't you stay for supper?" asked Lloyd.

"Usual reason. My mother doesn't recognize me—you know how it is."

"Papa, can't we just rent Ryan for the summer?" asked Constance.

"I'd love to, sweetheart. I once offered to purchase him out-right, but his mother quoted Shakespeare to me and I couldn't come back with anything good. That was the end of it."

"Say, Ryan," said Collin suddenly, "poker game tomorrow night. You coming?"

"If I'm invited."

"Of course. It's just Chuckie and Ringer and Steve—you know Ringer, don't you? You met him at Christmas."

"Yeah, I remember. Short stories?"

"The very man."

"And me, too," said Constance, tugging at Collin's sleeve.

"What?"

"I'm playing too. I'll be there too."

"You will? Do you play poker?"

"You're teaching me tomorrow morning."

"I don't know, Constance. I don't know if you really want to."

"Remember what you promised. Look, I was willing to push that wheelbarrow back from the pond."

"I'm just afraid it will end the same way, with us pushing you."

"Collin!"

He suddenly twisted his arm behind him as if she had forced it there. "Brutal coercion!" he said. "All right, you can come."

"Ryan, did you ever foresee the day that a woman would have all three of us wrapped around her finger?" asked Lloyd.

"It must be these summer evenings," said Ryan.

"Oh, no!" groaned Collin.

"These summer evenings! Oh, these summer evenings!" cried Lloyd, grinning and throwing out his arms melodramatically.

"Will you guys cut it out?" said Collin.

"But it is beautiful, isn't it? The summer?" Constance said, appealing to him as the *arbiter elegantiae*.

"Yes," he agreed, "the summer is beautiful."

"We got him to admit it!" exulted Ryan.

"Constance got him to admit it," Lloyd corrected him.

"Get out of here, Ryan," said Collin. "Save yourself. She's turning us all into mush."

"Yes, I must escape," agreed Ryan. He turned away, and then thought of something else. "What is it, penny-ante?"

"Nickel. We've got chips, so don't worry about getting change."

The change was not Ryan's worry, but he was determined not to let his friends guess how dangerous this kind of casual game could be to his finances. "Goodbye," he called one last time. "See you tomorrow."

"Goodbye," said Constance. "Pick some night to have dinner with us."

Ryan paused.

"Some summer evening!" added Lloyd.

"It's not even summer yet," protested Collin.

"When's the solstice?" wondered Lloyd. "Sunday, isn't it? We'll have to wait until then. Come to dinner Sunday, Ryan. We'll have a celebration. A Midsummer-Night's dream."

"How can it be Midsummer Night if it's the first night of summer?" asked Collin.

"Don't ask me. It just is. It always is."

"Actually, I think Midsummer Night is the twenty-fourth in England," said Ryan. "But I should think the solstice would do."

"That's a wonderful idea!" said Constance. "I was in a production of *Midsummer-Night's Dream* in school. We could all memorize something from it and give a recitation."

"Sunday is Father's Day," remembered Collin. "Will that cause a problem, Ryan?"

"My father detests Father's Day. It's one of the few days he would be pleased to have me out of the house, so he can glory in its nonobservance."

"Then it's settled," said Constance. "Tell your parents you're coming."

He waved as nonchalantly as possible and turned away to hide his pleasure.

Friday, June 19/One

Every braggart shall be found an ass.

> *—All's Well That Ends Well*

Mad brewage set to work
Their brains, no doubt.

> —Browning

Nothing is capable of being well set to music that is not nonsense.

> —Addison

IN THE FOLLOWING morning it seemed to Ryan that the day would not begin until evening twilight. Before he even rose from bed he tried to truncate the interval with extra sleep, but found he had outgrown the ability he had possessed as an adolescent to hide from life for ten hours at a stretch. He was prowling about the house by 6:30.

He made a point of being congenial to his parents, since he felt keenly how little his thoughts were with them. They glowed in his attention as if they were his children and not he theirs. They pestered him to relax, aborting his half-hearted efforts to proceed with study, snuffing every train that might have provided a fuse for his customary energy—in short, stripping him of every faculty he had to enjoy his hours at home.

Hung on the wall of the Kinsella living room was an obscure lithograph of an improbable whaling expedition. It had been in the house when Daniel and Maureen had closed on the place years before, and had remained continuously in the same spot until it had made its presence indispensable by forming a permanent shadow on the wallpaper. In it was depicted a clipper ship among floes of ice; on one iceberg a leviathan, having run inexplicably aground, lay under the attack of tiny men in whale boats. Overhead, flying penguins circled like vultures. The scene caught Ryan's eye on this day, and he sympathized with the whale. He felt as stranded, as helpless, as idle; his parents the Lilliputian tormentors launching their harpoons beneath his blank, staring eye. He had never experienced this strange disability, idleness. His sense of self was so dependent on work or intense play, on activity of some sort, that he felt vaguely threatened, as if the real Ryan were melting and fading away in the stuffy hollows of his parents' house.

What business he had during the day consisted of three items. The first was to call Eve. He had not weaned himself from the sad huskiness, the intelligence and affection of her voice; and yet last night he had not been able to call her. Yesterday had been too enjoyable, too young; at the thought of calling her then, he felt a dread of her defeatism; he was repulsed at the thought of another long, weary, late-night call, of their disembodied voices mingling in some void between them.

But now he resolved to make the call. He sat down at the telephone in the study after shooing his parents into the kitchen and closing both doors behind him. He stared at the books on the wall; he thought about this and that; half an hour passed. He heard stealthy footsteps in the living room and threw open the study door indignantly.

"I just wanted my concordance," said his mother guiltily. She stole past him into the office and picked up a large green volume with a broken spine. His father stood at the kitchen door, fretful with curiosity.

"Did you make your phone call?" he asked.

"I'm going into town," said Ryan. "You want anything?"

His second task for the day was to deposit the check from his Greek prize examination, holding back enough to finance his potential losings at the poker game. But the teller at his bank refused to let him make only a partial deposit. He did not have enough funds in his account to cover the difference; she rebuffed him with an incantation about regulations, ten business days, the check clearing. He asked to talk to the manager. Unfortunately for his bank account, the manager was a female hardly older than he was; she was swayed by his charm, his courtesy, his vigorous indifference to her increasingly feeble repetitions of bank policy, and especially by his open face. The tellers in the little branch office watched the drama playing out in the wings with raised eyebrows. Finally Ryan walked away with a fraction of his prize money in his pocket. The Irishman had persevered.

Returning, he confronted the telephone again. He breathed deeply and dialed. The receiver buzzed rhythmically, once, twice, three times, four times. The instant the fifth ring ceased he hung up quickly and exhaled. "I meant to call you Thursday," he said, practicing. "I called Friday, but you weren't home. I didn't get back until too late on Friday night." Then he wondered why he felt so guilty.

His final order of business was to call Collin and ask him what time the game was to start. He hoped his friend would simply order him over at once, but luck was not with him. Mrs. Overton answered. "Oh, he's gone out, Ryan, to buy some soda for the party tonight."

Ryan chafed his brow with the palm of his hand to help him suppress a chortle. "He did?" he commented finally. "Well, when do you expect him back?"

"I don't know. He just left a little while ago."

"Did Constance go too?"

"Oh no—she's here. Do you want to talk to her?"

He was tempted, but he thought it would be gauche to trouble Constance to come to the phone to give him information he could obtain from Mrs. Overton. "No, that's all right," he said. "I just wanted to find out when the game was starting tonight."

"Eight o'clock. I asked Collin on purpose to find out when the cookies had to be ready.—What? Did you say something, dear?"

"No—just clearing my throat."

"Do you have a cold? I'm sure Collin will get some ginger ale. That will make your throat feel better."

"He's getting ale, but I'm sure there's no ginger in it. I'm fine, Mrs. Overton. I'll be there at eight o'clock tonight."

"Maybe you shouldn't stay up late if you have a cold."

"Tell Collin I'll be over at eight."

"You take care of yourself!"

"Goodbye, Mrs. Overton."

"Goodbye, dear."

He hung up. Now he had nothing left to do but think.

❀❀❀

After dinner he struck up a conversation with his father, then struggled to keep up his end of it. When it finally failed, he wandered out into the yard, thrusting at the weeds with his foot and idly imagining his assault upon them. The evening grew chill quickly. He went back in to put on his jacket. "Are you leaving already?" his mother asked him. And suddenly he was. He would while away his time in the woods.

When he dropped over the wall into the valley he left the aimlessness of his anticipation behind. His mood changed; he felt that controlled excitement he knew from title games, even from prolonged sexual activity, when the heartbeat reached an early peak and then slowed, like an engine turning over at a fast idle, ready to throttle up at an instant's notice. He was ready. His mind opened, receptive to the challenge of ideas; his senses seemed keener, larger. In the valley there was no wasted time even in delay.

He climbed up through the woods to the clearing. Some instinct cautioned him, and he stepped silently through the last thickets. Looking about in the twilight, he was at first almost frightened, then doubted his vision, then grinned delight.

A doe was browsing beneath the great oak. He had not seen a deer in these woods since he was four or five. It was an omen—that is to say, it fit his mood. He felt a breeze rise at his back and carry warning of his presence to her. Her long neck swung up; she stared at him, fascinated, with round black eyes; she gave a harsh warning noise like an asthmatic cough; and then she was a bobbing white tail disappearing in the shadows of the undergrowth, a receding, hasty stamping and crackling of brush and leaves.

The pine grove was still, a cathedral deserted after vespers. While he was crossing it he checked his watch. Ten minutes still required annihilating. He found a pine he knew: it grew on the crest of the ridge, higher than any others. He scaled it, heedless of the pitch that stained his hands and shoes, and cleared the canopy.

From his perch he could see over the crests of the pines and then over the deciduous trees on the slope beneath him, away to the center of the valley, where stood the house, lights within it lit already in preparation for the party, its exterior bronzed by the refulgence of sunset. Old, passive and impassive, immovable, unshaken by the breeze that swayed the pine to which he clung, it cooled now with another nightfall. To the southwest he could just catch a glimpse of the sheen of the pond, already mirroring the approaching dark.

His watch marked off the minutes of his delay slowly. Just as he decided that his courtesy was overscrupulous, he saw a car drive up to the circle before the house and stop. He descended the tree with jealous haste.

❁❁❁

Whereas Ryan had had few other acquaintances besides Collin before he went to college, Collin had met many people his age in school and out. Ryan still felt a residual resentment of others who intruded on the valley; but he grew ashamed of his envy when he arrived at the house. In the entrance hall Collin broke off a discussion with his friend Ringer to throw open the screen door and welcome Ryan in. His other friends were of second rank; they came and went, into favor and out, mere accidents of acquaintance, transients of affection.

"Where were you today?" asked Collin. His question, however welcome, was only rhetorical; Ryan knew better than to answer it.

"Hello, Ringer," said Ryan. "Ryan Kinsella."

"Right, right," said Ringer, peering closely at him. They shook hands stiffly.

"You've met before," said Collin. "Last Christmas. When my father had the open house."

"Oh, right," said Ringer, brightening somewhat. He evidently remembered the party, at least. He himself had a face thoroughly forgettable, because so like other collegiate faces. His hair was clean cut but his cheeks unshaven; his clothes were expensive but worn in slovenly disarray; his manner was polite, and yet in its careless affectation of courtesy insufferably rude.

But he was a writer. His adviser knew someone at the *New Yorker;* it was rumored that the editors were only waiting for Ringer's final revision of one of his stories before setting him on a pedestal in the gallery of the published. Collin retailed this gossip with grave approval from semester to semester, but somehow the revision had not taken place, or perhaps the contact was mythical. At any rate, Ringer was still unpublished, although the tawny redolence of the literary cub still clung to his reputation.

"So, where were you today?" asked Collin again. "It was a bore without you."

"What did you two do?"

"Nothing. Stupid little chores. My mother dragged Constance off shopping again.—She got a new dress for tonight. She wouldn't show it to me."

"Where is she?" asked Ryan, noticing as he spoke that another car was pulling up outside.

"Putting it on. She'll probably be a while. Are you coming for dinner Sunday night?"

"If you're sure—"

"Don't give me that. Remember the promise. That's all Constance has been saying all day. 'Where's Ryan? Doesn't he remember the promise?'—Hello, Steve!"

Steve wandered up to the screen door, blinking in the light spilling out of the hall. His eyes were very poor; he seemed to have to explore his way through even familiar surroundings. Collin had described his driving as frightening even by daylight.

The password, repeated all around, was "How y'doing?" Collin and Steve shook hands; then Steve lurched forward, peeping at Ryan from behind startlingly thick glasses. "My God," he said, "The *Rhodes Scholar.* How y'doing? Congratulations, man. I couldn't believe it when I heard. What a stroke of luck!"

For Steve, luck could explain away every human excellence. He was a year older than Collin, the editor of the literary magazine, grooming Collin to replace him after the next year's issue. He ground out a passable piece for the magazine every year, viewed with indulgence because he was "a great editor"; but aside from that he did little but organize other people's work. Everyone else's success seemed pure luck to him—so and so had published in the *Coke Mountain Review* —amazing good fortune!—Collin had a half-dozen poems to submit to the magazine—lucky he could find all that time!—so-and-so had won a Marshall—some people had amazing good fortune! In another twenty or thirty years Steve would digress during conversations with clients planning college funds for their children to say that he had majored in creative writing when in school, but had had no luck with editors—had no contacts—never got a break. His hearers would note his faint envy of men and women who were in all likelihood less content than he was and wonder briefly whether it was real or assumed.

"How y'doing, Ringer," he continued, true to form. He had been among the first to develop Ringer's mythos. "How goes the rewrite?"

"Coming along," said Ringer inscrutably.

"Great! I'll never get over it. . . . Where's your father, Col?"

"Out. He took my mother to a dinner party." Collin looked significantly at Ryan as he said this.

"Your mother?" puzzled Steve.

"Back from Spain. My sister's here, too. You'll meet her in a few minutes. She's playing cards with us."

"Poker? The lady plays poker?" Another curiosity of Steve's personality was a tendency to sexism. He was almost conscious that it would not do; he often made faint and failing efforts to conceal it when in the company of females. "Since when do women play poker?"

"This one has been playing since this morning."

"I don't know about this," said Steve.

"Don't be a jerk," said Collin flatly. "Come on, let's go upstairs. Chuckie can find us when he comes."

"Well, I hope you got my beer," grumbled Steve.

"Of course I did," said Collin as they started up the stairs. Ryan was detained by Ringer.

"Wait, you got a Rhodes?" asked this supercilious literary jock. He must have heard the story at Christmas, but now made a point of showing he had forgotten it.

"Yes."

"Not bad! Not bad at all!"

And having subordinated Ryan's honors to his own by expressing his approval, he suffered him to lead the way upstairs.

Ryan turned into the first room off the hallway. It had been their playroom once. The toy boxes and playthings were gone; it now held little more than several chairs and a great round wooden table. As part of his ritual of return he went first to the window and looked down on the drive and the grassy circle directly below. Then he sat in one of the chairs at the table and felt the thick patina on the golden brown oak with the flat of his hand.

Around him the others were joking and laughing, but for a few minutes he did not hear them. He was remembering what the table meant. The top was made of jointed boards two inches thick, still showing every dent and bruise of their battles and councils—it had been Arthur's Round Table, the broad back of the eagle Landroval, and the deck of the Argo and of the ship of Odysseus. It had held the splendor of their armory, wooden swords and shields, daggers of glittering foil, and helmets fashioned of heirloom silver bowls; on this surface they had laid out maps of Middle Earth and drawn up schemes for the recapture of Toad Hall. Once the poker chips stacked ready here today had been a dragon's tricolored wealth, spilled out of an embroidered pillow case across the oak; he could still see it in the sunshine of his memory.

"I hope you're not planning to stick to Mrs. Overton's menu," said Collin, intruding on his reverie. He gestured toward the array of soft drinks Mrs. Overton had set out on the table along with the vast platters of cookies.

"There was a time that was all we wanted, Collin," said Ryan. "Remember that time you came back after two weeks away at Nansett and told me to meet you at the clearing?"

"And I had a soda for each of us. Two root beers, I think it was. We sat there under the oak and toasted our reunion."

"I wouldn't trade even the best Irish stout for a taste of the root beer we drank then."

"I know what you mean," said Collin. He dug into the enormous tub of ice in the corner, fished out a bottle of expensive imported stout, stripped off the top, and took a deep swig. "But one of these days even you will have to admit," he added cheerfully, "that change isn't all bad. There are some pleasures that improve as one reaches legal majority. Beverages, for one."

"Females, for another," said Steve, with a lewd wink at Ryan.

Collin was in a generous mood and refused once again to be drawn out. "Yes, females, for another. I definitely appreciate women more than I did when I was growing up as the only son in a bachelor's house."

"Write me a poem about it," said Steve.

"I will. I definitely will.—So what will it be, Ryan? Mrs. Overton and root beer, or Constance and stout?" He offered Ryan a frosted, dripping bottle, and after a moment's hesitation, Ryan took it with his characteristic smile.

"An incontrovertible argument," he said.

"Exactly," said Collin. "I don't blame old Mrs. O for wanting to keep us little boys forever, but that doesn't mean we have to go along with it."

Ryan was not entirely sure. "It takes a lot more than a bottle of beer to make a man stop being a boy," he observed. "In fact, it usually has the opposite effect." But he took a first pull on the bottle with great pleasure.

Another car pulled up outside. Collin leaned out the window and called, "Hey, Chuckie! Come upstairs!"

It seemed Chuckie Worth appeared almost instantly; only the dull scuffle of his feet as he took the stairs three at a time preceded him. He was just back from a Junior Year in France, sporting all the souvenirs. Some were visible—a mustache, a black beret, a thick *cahier* of poems stained with coffee, a satchel of cassettes representative of the latest French hits, a leather jacket that reeked of *Gaulois* cigarettes—and some were attitudinal or behavioral: a contempt for the looks of American women, a tendency to declare in mid-sentence that English was stupid and inexpressive, and a habit of using verbs as reflexive that had never known a self before. Collin took the notebook eagerly and enthused; Steve produced a beer; and Ringer began disputing Chuckie's contention that the French tapes should be given priority. Ryan saluted Chuckie with his bottle and Chuckie nodded back cautiously; like all Collin's friends, he found the cawing of this classical crow a little daunting.

It was Steve, the organizer, who compelled them to sit around the table; although thereafter they did not immediately begin play, but variously talked about writing, shuffled the cards, bought poker chips, drank beer, cracked jokes, and ate Mrs. Overton's cookies. Ryan was in no hurry to begin losing money; for the moment he was content to listen to the shop-talk of the others and wonder at what a strange disease writing was, how it pierced its way gradually to the vitals like the quill of a porcupine, poisoning even the humblest human with self-centeredness. He was glad to be proof to it; his knowledge of tradition held him pinned fast under its tremendous weight; he was sure he could not have wriggled a pinion free even to flap it brokenly in faint imitation of the ancient great ones.

The dispute over music reemerged. Ringer wanted jazz, though none was available; Chuckie shook out his satchel on the table; Steve and Collin chose rock and roll. Ryan knew better than to cast his vote. The tapes were sorted, stacked, the first inserted, and Collin's finger was poised over the play button; and then there was a sudden silence as Ryan stood up.

He had taken a seat facing the door in anticipation of this moment; and yet when Constance appeared he felt almost confused, as if he truly were again a boy of eight—but a boy before whom the High Queen of the Fairy had appeared and made him fey of her beauty; as if Helen had looked down from the walls into his camp; or Hero cried out to him as he rose dripping from the straits. If he had seen such a woman as such a boy, if such a magic had fallen on his brain, he would have stored the vision away in his heart as the inhabitant of a treeless country saves a particularly large and fine piece of firewood—burning it only occasionally for warmth, or to cook up the fantasies on which he fed, husbanding its latent energy, smothering it when he was fortified against chill and hunger, lest it be wasted and consumed. But seeing her now, he could not damp the burning; for now he had some knowledge.

Knowledge has a bad reputation as a robber and despoiler of the mystery of beautiful things. If science describes the stars as spheres of plasma in fusion reaction, the night sky is no longer the same; and yet other mysteries remain to infuse the night with the aweful—the mysteries of enormous distance, vast time, the hiddenness of godhead. To a boy all the attributes of feminine beauty in a handsome woman are sources of ignorant awe—breasts, waist, the apple roundness her buttocks become as she leans over, or the conventions of hair and dress. But even when those mysteries are known, they remain wonders to quicken the pulse; and they give rise to other mysteries not unrelated to the bafflements of the night sky: the search for oneness, the struggle against mortality, the craving for the ideal.

The others stood up; with the exception of Collin, more out of astonishment than courtesy. They all had sisters; but this was a most unsisterly apparition.

"Am I too formal?" she asked shyly. She wore a blouse of black gauze over a low-cut black dress.

"Not at all. We like feeling shabby," said Ryan. She laughed, grateful for his humor.

"Constance," said Collin, "this is Chuckie Worth, Ringer Cornfield, Steve Woodruff. Gentlemen, my sister, Constance Tate."

"Very pleased to meet you," she said graciously, extending her hand to Ringer, who stood nearest her. He stared at her in brute stupefaction.

"Shake hands, you dope," said Collin.

Ringer managed to raise a limp hand to her firm handshake. He said nothing; neither did the other two guests. She withdrew her hand almost instantly, sensing his lack of response, and realizing that for some reason the common courtesies of meeting had been aborted. To cover her embarrassment, she went instead to Ryan and laid one hand on the crook of his arm.

"Where were you today, you naughty person?"

"Not doing anything I wouldn't have gladly given up to be with you two."

"I know what you mean. My mother took me shopping. It was a bore—but I got this. Do you like it?" She stood back, brightening as she showed her dress to him.

"You're beautiful," he said.

There was an appreciative mumble from the other guests.

"I'd much rather have been sunbathing. Did you see Collin's burn?"

They all looked at Collin.

"Well, you can't see it now," she explained. "It's all over him.—How does it feel?"

"I'm surviving," said Collin.

"Have you started yet?"

"Only the drinking. You sit over here next to me." He had kept a seat for her beside him; she went around the table and sat there, opposite Ryan, at whom she smiled with pleasure. Collin's three friends sat down in heavy confusion.

"I've bought you some chips," said Collin, pushing them toward her. She pulled a slip of paper out of the ruffled sleeve of her blouse.

"Is that where you keep your aces?" asked Ryan. She laughed.

"It's my list of hands. I haven't learned the order yet."

Steve overcame his confusion enough to roll his eyes in an attempt at sexist disgust, but no one paid any attention.

"You can always come to me if you have questions," said Ryan. "If you think you have a good hand, just show it to me, and I'll give you the nod."

"And fold your own," observed Collin. "That's why I put her next to me. All right, boys . . . I mean . . . ante up." He turned on the stereo and in a moment a guitar began to climb stridently through a pentatonic scale.

He dealt and they began to play. For the first hand, the betting was surprisingly heavy. Even Ryan was drawn into it, astonished to find himself with two jacks and two queens; but Constance beat him with three tens. When she showed her hand the other players murmured their incredulity.

"You made almost a buck off these suckers," exclaimed Collin. "I told you it was easy."

"You've got a great face for poker," said Ryan. "That's what they call an angel face. 'Who? Me have three of a kind?'"

"I didn't think three of a kind was much of anything," she responded ingenuously.

❁❁❁

As the night went on Constance played avidly, concentrating more than the young men; she was quick to fold when her hand was worthless, cautious when her hand seemed promising, and keenly opportunistic when she knew the cards were right. She kept track of the game eagerly, reminding each dealer of his turn—a duty that became more important as those who were drinking began to show confusion over the formalities, talking loudly and playing poorly. Furthermore, Ryan observed, she used every psychological device to encourage the betting when her hand was good. More than once he folded a pair, realizing that she had drawn something strong, and sat the hand out while she fleeced the others mercilessly. Collin, too, read the clues easily, but often insisted on pursuing bad luck. And yet her interest was not mercenary: she had no sense that she was playing for money. The chips were mere plastic to her. She was only having fun at something new and doing it well.

Ryan had thought in the first moment of general confusion upon Constance's arrival that this was going to be a very different poker party. Steve, who had unwrapped an enormous Jamaican cigar before she appeared, had surreptiously replaced it in his pocket. Ringer had actually sat up straight, turned down the flap of his collar that had been twisted upwards, and combed his fingers through his hair. Chuckie had taken off his beret and crumpled it, as if feeling for the first time that perhaps he was laying it on a bit thick. But it did not take long for these three to regain their customary insouciance; and Ryan soon saw the signs. Steve produced his cigar once more, fidgeted with it, and laid it on the table like a threat. Chuckie began swearing copiously in French. Ringer drew a platter close and ate his way through a heap of chocolate chip cookies, scattering crumbs down his front; he repeatedly interrupted the game to turn up the volume for his favorite songs, and then neglected to turn it down.

Such thoughtlessness was the chief reason Ryan disliked most of Collin's friends. He could have forgiven them, for Collin's sake, their diametrical differences from his own views on literature; but that refusal to consider anyone's feelings but their own, which seemed to be infixed permanently in their personalities, he found deeply repellent. It was not just that they were always leery of his aggressive intellect, interpreting his jealousy as hauteur. He sensed vaguely that their disdain for him was in part a reflex of their feeling of inferiority, and he almost reveled in it. No; beneath this understandable and superficial friction he felt the chafe of a more basic rudeness in them. He had once brought up the issue with Collin, insisting these new friends of his were not gentlemen in the best sense of the word; yet Collin had only laughed off his objections, admitting their occasional tactlessness, but insisting they were good people at heart. Ryan could only wonder at Collin's blindness and let the matter go.

He was not surprised, now, to see these three outsiders, as he thought of them, behaving badly. They seldom spoke to Constance, or even made more than a mumbled reply when she addressed them. The conversation they conducted at high volume over the blaring stereo was addressed to Collin and to one another; they spoke of school and acquaintances without making any attempt to include Constance in the discussion. She was a good-looking woman, and as such they inspected her from time to time; but that was all they could see in her. Whatever notice they did take of her was offensive in itself: Steve stopped once in the act of dealing and polished his glasses to ogle her better, and Chuckie's swearing seemed a blatant attempt to impress. At one point Ringer explained some minor point of poker etiquette in a repulsively superior fashion.

Alcohol did not reduce their egotism. They drank heavily, dipping into the icy water in the tub and repeatedly drawing forth cans and bottles of the weak American brew they liked. Every time one of them stood to fetch another he brought back beer for all three, until the game itself was impeded by empties and by cans still unopened. By turns they lurched ostentatiously to the bathroom, cracking incoherent jokes about piss and bladders. The other three, by staying sober, noticed their drunkenness all the more. Ryan drank only two bottles of stout all evening, and Collin not much more; Constance sipped about once an hour from a glass her brother had poured for her.

On this night Ryan found some satisfaction in observing that the behavior of Collin's friends was annoying even Collin. Clearly he felt his sister was snubbed. He put off his habitual dreaminess to laugh with Constance, to tease her and chat with her, as if trying to make up for the slight his friends were inflicting on her. He stared down Steve's goggled glances. He noticed her discomfort and the tinge of color in her cheeks when Chuckie swore, and read the icy distaste in Ryan's eyes; that was all the translation of the French he needed. And he openly rebuked Ringer for spraying cookies and beer over the cards when he spoke.

I told you so, thought Ryan more than once.

Ryan had noticed two invariable rules of such gatherings. The first was that midnight followed immediately on nine o'clock, especially for those who are drinking, who suddenly realize that they have become inarticulate and belligerent. The second is that if even one writer is present, the talk will always turn to writing. Here there were four. The subject had gone in and out of the conversation all night like a shuttle in a tangled weaving, and finally become inextricably stuck on the matter of poetry. Ryan could have sat in silence through any discussion of that issue out of fear of offending Collin; but he was so disgusted with the three outsiders that he finally joined the topic.

Chuckie provoked the outburst. He had just played one of his favorite English rock songs for the third time, standing by his chair, bottle in hand, singing along with the lyrics in a flat, hoarse voice. "*Merde!*" he said, as the rendition ended, "That's one hell of a good song, *n'est-ce pas?* The lyrics are so—*incroyable!*"

"On the contrary," said Ryan. The tape had ended, and his quiet voice filled the sudden aural void. "They're particularly devoid of meaning."

They all looked up, astonished that he had entered a conversation he had seemed to disdain by his previous silence. He spoke, too, as if he knew what he was talking about; and this authentic expertise cowed Chuckie at first.

"What do you mean, 'particularly?'" asked Ringer. He had control of the cards, and had been shuffling them aimlessly for several minutes, despite a gentle reminder from Constance that he should deal them. "That's a very provocative word, that 'particularly'."

"I mean even worse than run-of-the-mill rock lyrics, which are jejune at best."

"Now, wait a minute," said Steve. "Some of that stuff is damned fine poetry."

"Here he goes," said Collin of Ryan. He took a drink of stout and assumed his Ryan-toleration attitude by raising one eyebrow ironically.

"It's your deal, I think, Ringer," said Constance sweetly. Ringer put the deck down and forgot it; he smelled a good fight.

"This very song is damned fine poetry," said Chuckie now, confident of his reserves. "I'd like to see you write better."

"I write better every time I make up a shopping list. Don't be ridiculous."

"What the hell is wrong with it, I'd like to know?" demanded Chuckie. He lurched closer to Ryan, who did not bother to look at him.

"To start with, it's meaningless."

"What's going on?" Constance whispered to Collin, sensing some change in the atmosphere.

"You'll see," he said. "We can't stop it now. We might as well just watch."

"But what about the game?"

He smiled at her innocence. "Haven't you noticed that the game is just an excuse to blab?"

She looked at her pile of chips in perplexity.

Meanwhile Chuckie and Ryan had continued the skirmish. "How can you say it's meaningless? To anyone with *sensitivity*, it has great meaning."

"Recite the lyrics for me," said Ryan. Chuckie seemed to find that his mind was empty of all but an alcoholic hiss.

"We'll play them again," he said.

"That's right," said Ringer, with the attitude of a man going to the ultimate font of truth, "Put the song on again. It's a great song! Go ahead, Chuckie, find it again." Chuckie made his way to the tape player and began rewinding the cassette. Ryan rose from his chair and went to the closet. Steve watched him, as if calculating his chances in an argument against an opponent who could walk and talk as if sober. It probably did not occur to him that Ryan actually was sober.

"God! I don't believe this!" said Collin, as he realized what Ryan was doing.

From the closet Ryan had produced a small chalkboard, a relic of their childhood. By searching in the cracks on the floor of the closet he even found a neglected piece of dirty chalk. He propped the chalkboard on the top of a bookcase and stood ready.

"Anyone want another beer?" asked Steve.

"Quiet, you guys," said Chuckie. "Here it is."

The song played again and they sat and listened to it. Ryan dashed the words across the chalkboard with a kind of cynical precision that was not lost on his audience. When the song ended again, Chuckie shut off the machine. The silence, after four hours of talk and music, lent a seriousness to the proceedings, and Ryan's grave and yet sarcastic expression, as he turned to face Chuckie, was likely to make those who had spoken in favor of the song cast about for a rationalization.

"It really isn't very good," said Constance, almost to herself.

"This is not your best exemplar of rock lyrics," said Collin. He was reserving some turf from which to make a future defense if necessary.

"On the contrary," said Ryan. "It's absolutely typical." He read the song ruthlessly from the chalkboard.

> When I see your face
> I can't replace.
> The way I feel,
> is it really real?
>
> When I see your face
> I can't replace.
> Like an eagle flies
> high in the skies.
>
> When I see your face
> I can't replace.
> Is it really love
> I'm thinkin' of?

"Perhaps, Mr. Worth," he said, "you would be so kind as to explain to us why the verb 'replace' seems to be used intransitively here? Just for starters."

"What?" said Chuckie. Ryan looked at him coldly.

"What is the object of 'replace'?"

"You mean, what's it about?"

"I mean, 'I can't replace *what?*' What can't this poor person replace?"

"I don't know," said Chuckie, bewildered at such a literal demand. "Replace, replace—you know . . . he just can't replace."

"Her face," said Steve definitively.

"Yeah," said Chuckie and Ringer. "Her face, it's her face."

"Why doesn't he say so then? Why does he just say 'replace'?"

"Because it doesn't fit the music, obviously," said Steve.

"Obviously," said Ryan, in contempt of such an excuse. "We can see a similar criterion operating in the next two lines. 'The way I feel, is it really real?' One is tempted to respond, 'If you don't know, how should I?' Just exactly what is it that he feels? He's rather vague. He sees a face, he can't replace something, and he feels some way that may or may not be 'real.'" Ryan looked around at his three bleary opponents. "Can you shed any light on this?" They were silent. "Once you strip it of its music, it looks— how shall I say it? Particularly empty. The music always glosses over the deficiencies in the lyrics. That's why I don't particularly like rock and roll. Take away the music, and the lyrics are almost invariably inane, at best slovenly and confused." No one could offer an objection as yet. He continued.

"Now, take the next stanza. The same pointless and incomplete couplet, followed by a totally irrelevant simile, introduced improperly by 'like,' not 'as'."

"There's nothing wrong with that," protested Ringer. Ryan did not deign to reply.

"What is it about a flying eagle that bears a remote resemblance to the inability of this individual to 'replace' whatever it is he can't replace? Do we think of eagles ordinarily replacing things? Or is there supposed to be a vague connection between the sight of this someone and the delight felt by the soaring eagle?"

"Yeah," said Steve.

"Of course," said Ringer.

"'This really is hardly worth discussing,' observed Collin.

"Next a repetition of the couplet. Unfortunately, once was already more than enough. Now the grand finale: 'Is it really love I'm thinkin' of?'" Constance found Ryan's affectation of seriousness so droll that she could not help giggling. When he heard her, a smile tugged at the corners of his mouth momentarily, but he did not yield to it. His opponents, meanwhile, sat in suspicious unease. "This question," he continued, "is obviously part of the ancient hackneyed tradition of rock and roll lyrics—a formula that has lost all meaning and is now inserted at will as a filler." He mimicked the whining tones of the singer: "I don't know—is it love? Is it really love I'm thinkin' of?'"

Constance laughed outright, high and sweet.

Ryan continued. "You're right, Collin, this thing really is too jejune to provide material for discussion. As I said before, a particularly empty song."

"Some of the lyrics in opera are lousy, too," said Steve suavely.

"True," said Ryan. "Very bad." He paused and surveyed the words on the chalkboard. "But not this bad," he said. "Never this bad. The only way in which someone could be satisfied with something as pathetic as this, is if he had no knowledge of anything that had been written in the past. Your average writer of rock and roll lyrics is practically illiterate. Does it surprise you that he can't express himself with concision? That would be bad enough, if that were all; but in this case, it's clear that he has nothing to say. He has never experienced enough in life to have something to share with us. We are more intelligent, more articulate, better educated, more experienced—and more sensitive" (with a look at Chuckie) "than this poor fool. I have no objection to stupid, silly, illiterate, boring, insensitive, and possibly drug-damaged slobs expressing themselves—but do we have to listen? That's the question: Do we have to bother listening?"

"Some rock and roll songs really are good," said Ringer stubbornly, evidently abandoning the case in point.

"But you yourself have pointed out the flaw in your analysis," said Collin suddenly. "You can't divorce the lyrics from the music.

The lyrics do gain enormously from their musical setting. When the words 'When I see your face' are sung in this particular song, the music is very evocative. You feel certain at once that he's talking about the face of someone he loves. I don't pretend to defend the whole thing; but it's not total garbage, in its musical context."

"The words are an extension of the music, then?" asked Ryan. "No more, no less articulate than the musical phrases—vague, evocative, discrete bits of meaning thrown out like the sound of the instruments?"

"I suppose you could say that. The song as a whole achieves more than the words or the music considered separately."

"And does it really say something worth listening to?"

"Of course it does. Everything human is worth listening to."

"That I dispute. Theoretically, maybe. Every human being is as good as another, in some abstract sense. But every human being can't write poetry. I know what I'm talking about, because I'm among those who can't. But I can read poetry, and I know the difference between poetry that speaks, poetry that has something to say, and junk like this." He tapped the blackboard as he spoke. "Equal rights under the law is one thing. But in poetry it only gives license to those who mouth confused and stale versions of what we've all heard many times before. If the sum total of this artistic effort is 'Is it love I'm thinkin' of,' I'll stick to Sappho, thank you."

"And you'd deny the man on the street a voice," Steve rejoined bitterly.

"Not at all."

"Everyone is capable of poetry. Every utterance of humanity is poetry."

"The man on the street can utter whatever he wants. I don't have to listen to it. And I define poetry as something intrinsically worth listening to."

"I'd rather listen to the man on the street than that fuddy-duddy old stuff you're stuck on. Talk about stale! Do you claim the ancients never wrote bad poetry?"

"Of course they did. The point is that it's gone. It didn't survive. The problem with modern poetry is that it hasn't undergone that natural selection process. It's unwinnowed. We just can't take the time to listen to it all."

"Well, who can take the time to listen to something written two thousand years ago?"

"If you did you'd write much better poetry yourself. Your skills, your perception, your taste, would all be honed. This kind of thing"—Ryan indicated the chalkboard again—"would lose all attractiveness for you. You'd avoid vague thoughts and words—you'd write only when you had something to say—and you'd say it well."

"It isn't necessary to read the old poetry to write good poetry today," said Collin.

"It's absolutely, critically necessary," said Ryan. This flat statement was met with jeers.

"You're better off forgetting all that stuff," said Ringer, his speech slurred. "It just gets into your head, it just fills up your head with old fuddy-duddy stuff. 'Love' and 'dove' and crap like that."

"So you can fill your head up instead with something truly striking, like 'Is it love I'm thinkin' of,'" suggested Ryan.

"It ruins your inspiration, reading that stuff. I used to read Rimbaud, but after a while it just started to depress me. You can't worry about competing with everyone who went before you."

"You're not competing. You're building on what they did. You're plundering the monuments of their greatness for the stones to build your own."

"Well, look at Rimbaud. He never read that old crap."

"Rimbaud," said Ryan with a touch of indignation, "could write perfect Latin hexameters off the top of his head when he was fifteen years old. That was the kind of training he had. All you modern would-be Rimbauds forget that."

"I have nothing against reading Whitman," said Steve. "Whitman is—Whitman is the ultimate source. For all American poets." His fellow writers solemnly agreed to this.

"The ultimate source," said Ryan, "aside from the Greek and Latin, is English poetry. American poetry is to English poetry as Latin poetry was to Greek poetry—always working in the shadow of a greater brilliance." There was loud, outraged protest at this. Collin's voice rose above it.

"This is too much, even for you, Ryan. The brilliance of modern poetry is in throwing off tradition, in finding a new, simple way to speak the truth about human experience."

"Poetry *is* tradition," said Ryan passionately. "Poetry cannot exist without tradition." They hooted at him, eager to be united against his eloquence.

"Poetry," said Collin in a commanding voice, "is speech that invokes a universal. It has nothing to do with tradition."

"Your definition is too simplistic," retorted Ryan. "It includes even this kind of nonsense we're talking about."

"Exactly."

"But this lyric is too particular to be universal. It's one person's empty attempt to fill a musical phrase so that he can assemble a song and an album, and make a living. What's universal about that?"

"What's wrong with the particular?" asked Chuckie. The heavy lids over his red eyes were drooping by now. "This moment is particular, and it's a damned fine moment."

"Shut up, Chuckie," said Collin, sensing, perhaps, an incipient disaster.

"Why don't we compose a poem right now, about this particular moment? A joint impromptu? Show this *Rhodes scholar* what we think of his poetic theories?"

"Don't try it," said Collin curtly. "You'll just make an ass out of yourself."

Chuckie stood up and swayed over the table.

"So help me God," said Collin, "I'll never speak to you again, Chuckie. Don't embarrass me in front of my sister."

"'The round table,'" said Chuckie, quoting his muse, "'cannot unite us. We cannot—'"

"'Give up our traditions,'" suggested Ryan wryly.

"'—Give up our quarreling. Our words fly about in the air above us like wingèd eagles—'"

"Is there any other kind?" asked Ryan, looking quizzically at Constance, whose eyes sparkled back at him over the hand with which she was hiding her smile.

"'—And do battle in the air above our heads. '"

No one ever knew if Chuckie was finished with his composition. At this point the beer and brown sugar proved to much for Ringer, who hung his head over the table and vomited profusely.

The others immediately leaped to their feet. Collin cried out in disgust, Constance in compassion, Steve and Chuckie perhaps in some anxiety for the sympathy of their own queasy stomachs. When his convulsions ceased, Ringer sat staring, in a drunken stupor, at the mess he had made.

"The critic has spoken," said Ryan.

"For God's sake, Ryan," said Collin, "take Constance out of here, will you?"

"Let me help clean up," said Constance.

"No!" said Collin absolutely. "My sister will never stoop to clean up the vomit of a dog like that."

"Especially not in that dress," Ryan pointed out.

He moved very quickly. In a few moments he was ushering Constance, still protesting, toward the stairs.

"I hope you're ashamed of yourself," said Collin to Chuckie.

"Me? What do I have to do with it?"

"Your poem was an even worse form of vomit than his!"

"What are you so pissed-off about?"

"I ask a few friends over to meet my sister and you behave like a bunch of idiots, that's what I'm so pissed-off about!"

"You don't think he'll start a fight, do you?" Constance asked Ryan, pausing on the stairs.

"No. He'll just give them the dressing-down they deserve."

"What about poor Ringer?"

"He'll survive. I imagine he's survived this kind of thing before."

"Don't you think we really should help?"

"Let's just stay out of the way."

The sound of angry voices followed them down the stairs. The word "poetry" was being flung about like a weapon.

"Why is he so upset?" she asked.

"Don't you know? He wants you to think well of him. He thinks his friends reflect badly on him."

She suffered herself to be escorted to the living room, where she sat on the edge of the sofa, listening to the voices upstairs with knit brows. Ryan took a seat where he could both see the lower hallway and intercept her if she tried to return to help Collin.

Friday, June 19 / Two

It is not poetry, but prose run mad.

—Pope

FTER A FEW moments they heard heavy, drunken steps. Chuckie came lurching down the stairs, notebook in one hand, clattered across the tiles, and slammed the screen door behind him. It seemed he could not even have had time to climb into his car before it started and whined away angrily around the circle, tires scuffling on the pavement.

"He shouldn't be driving," said Constance worriedly.

"You're right," agreed Ryan. "None of them should be driving. Especially Ringer." They looked at one another, imagining horrible possibilities.

Steve's tones rose in volume now, defiant, almost pompous, and Collin's matched his, incisive, articulate, impassioned. A final outburst from Collin, and then Steve's rolling, hasty footsteps—in the upper hall, and then descending the stairs, although with a more dignified rhythm than Chuckie. At the foot of the stairs Steve came to a halt, looking around him, as if so humiliated and enraged that he had lost his bearings. Upon seeing Ryan through the entrance to the living room, however, he seemed to recall himself, and stalked off to his car. In another few moments, he too was gone.

"What a bizarre night," said Ryan.

"I *really* don't think these people should be driving. Don't let Ringer get into his car, Ryan. There's a spare room for him."

"Don't worry," said Ryan. "We'll catch him if we have to."

They listened again. They could hear Collin walking back and forth upstairs; water running distantly; Ringer speaking in a muffled voice.

"Maybe I should get some towels or something," she said.

"You'll only embarrass Collin all the more if you help."

They sat in silence for a minute.

"I hope those boys get home all right," she said. Then, almost to herself, she added, "I hate it when people drink."

"You mean, too much?"

"I mean, at all. Anything is too much."

He refrained from commenting that she had previously expressed herself somewhat differently on the subject.

"It is strange, isn't it?" he said vaguely. "I could never understand it."

"Mama gets really mean when she drinks. She used to start in the early afternoon. When I got home from school she'd be really nasty. It would go on like that until bedtime. Then, after I'd fallen asleep, she'd come into my room and wake me up and apologize. She'd hold me and talk baby-talk to me. Lots of times she'd fall asleep in my bed, and I'd have to undress her and tuck her in and go sleep in her bed. And sometimes she'd do and say really strange things to people, just because she was drunk, and I'd have to try to cover up for her. Once she insulted one of our dear friends, this really nice man who had really helped us a lot. I had to tell him she'd had a bad reaction to some medicine two different doctors had given her. I don't think he believed me. He stopped coming around so much."

She paused, hanging her head, staring intensely at the floor, but seeing something else. Then she lifted her eyes to his anxiously. "I shouldn't be telling you this."

"It's all right. You should tell somebody."

"It's just because she's lonely."

"I'm sure it is."

"Everyone's lonely," said Constance.

"I know," he answered, feeling at a loss for anything sufficiently profound.

"Do you? Do you know?" she asked, almost plaintively. "Whenever I got angry with her, I would say that to myself: 'It's just because she's lonely.' That helped. I was really lonely too, so it was easy to sympathize with her. It helped me forgive her for what she did."

"You were that lonely?"

"The last few years I have been. Mother and I were sort of trapped in our life together. I used to think about Collin so much."

"You had no friends?"

"Oh, sure. I knew girls in school. No one I was really close with, though. And the guys I knew were just a bunch of creeps who were after me all the time."

He took a deep breath, looking at her. His neck felt hot, and he vaguely sensed the pain in his palms where the nails of his clenched fingers were cutting into his skin.

"Creeps?"

"You know. Creeps."

He was unable to say anything. She took his silence for confusion and reluctantly explained.

"The worst was when I went out on a date with this guy who was the son of some general. He was supposed to be a perfect gentleman. We went to a disco and had a really great time. Then on the way home he stopped the car and tried to rape me."

For a minute they were both silent.

"How did you stop him?" he asked, with difficulty.

"Well, I almost didn't. But I was hitting him without really causing him any pain and by accident my thumb went into his eye. I mean, right into his eye. Really hard." She rubbed her thumb against her forefinger involuntarily, as if she could still feel the eyeball under it. "I practically put it out. He stopped right away. He was in agony. But he sort of snapped out of his crazy thing. He even drove me home, holding his hand over one eye."

The story had taken on its own momentum. She went on: "I just jumped out of the car and ran in. I was crying. And by that time Mother was in her crying stage too. She was good and drunk. We just held onto each other and cried. Then she realized that something must have gone wrong. So I told her about it."

She drew her hair back from her face severely with both hands, still staring into the distance. "She went berserk. I mean, I've seen her crazy before, but never like that. I thought she was going to kill someone. She wanted to call the police, the army, the American embassy, even Papa. Everybody in the world. I had to pull the phone plug out of the jack."

The last thing she needs, he thought to himself, *is another person out of control.* He forced himself to sit still. Gradually he raised his hands and, with conscious effort, unbent his fingers. He studied the marks left by his nails.

"How did you get her calmed down?" he asked.

"I gave her another drink. Isn't that horrible? It was the only thing I could think of to do. And it worked, too."

"And the . . . creep?"

"I don't know. I never saw him again. I hope his eye was all right."

Ryan hoped the opposite, and worse; but said nothing.

"The general cut us after that," she added. "I think he found out what had happened. I think he was too embarrassed to face my mother."

She smiled weakly. "Happy times in the Tate family," she said. "At least, distaff side. I don't suppose things like that happen around here much."

"No," he said. "The worst we get is a some drunken, sophomoric poetizing. Pretty dull stuff."

"I like things dull," she said. "They're safe when they're dull. You don't have to worry all the time that something's going to blow up."

For several minutes Ryan sat calmly in his chair, devising hideous mutilations of the sons of Spanish generals. Constance, likewise tranquil to all appearances, seemed to be still thinking on the same topic. "Don't ever tell Collin," she pleaded now. "You know, about what I just told you. About that horrible date. He'd be furious."

"Don't worry, I won't," said Ryan. "Although he's not always an angry sort of person, you know. He only gets upset when something jangles against his idealism. Don't get the wrong impression from the way he acted tonight. He was really provoked; those clowns were really rude to you, I thought."

"I didn't really notice it," she said. "I was having a lot of fun."

"Good. I'm glad to hear it."

At this point Collin and Ringer began descending the stairs. Ryan motioned Constance to stay where she was and went out into the hall. Collin was supporting the drunkard as he felt his way down, clutching the banister dizzily. On the tiles Collin turned him loose, and he staggered toward the front door.

"I'm taking him home," Collin said to Ryan, nearly in a whisper. "Would you mind staying with her? It's not far. I'll be gone about a half hour at the most. Would you mind? I'd just feel badly if she went to bed before I have a chance to apologize."

"Don't worry," said Ryan, keeping his voice down also. "She doesn't think a bit the less of you. I'll be glad to stay with her. Or better still, why don't you stay here, and I'll drive him home?"

"No, I feel responsible," said Collin. "You know what I mean."

"But what about his car? Do you want me to take it and follow you?"

"He can pick it up tomorrow. I'm not worried about that."

"Is there anything we can do? Did you get everything cleaned up?"

Collin frowned in disgust. "Yeah," he said. "I got it all. What a mess!—Just keep her entertained until I come back. Do you mind? I know it's late. I'll only be a half hour. Tell jokes, dance, dribble a soccer ball, do anything. Just keep her awake long enough for me to apologize in form."

"It's never occurred to her that you have anything to apologize for."

Collin moved abruptly away as Ringer opened the screen door. Ryan went back and sat down opposite Constance.

"What's happening?" she asked.

"He's driving Ringer home."

"Oh, thank God! I would have been terrified about him."

"He wants me to keep you awake until he can make his apologies."

She looked puzzled. "For what?"

"For the way his friends behaved."

"That's ridiculous!"

"That's what I told him. But you'll have to reassure him yourself."

"Do you think the others got home all right?"

"They say God looks after fools and drunks. So don't worry about them." His assurance was so final that she relaxed.

"Well, I guess I'm hostess now. Can I offer you something more?"

His smile declined the offer. She laughed suddenly.

"It's all your fault, you know," she said.

"*My* fault? How so?"

"You were the one who started the whole thing about that silly song."

Ryan laughed, but only a little.

"I couldn't believe it when you pulled out that blackboard. It was like being in class or something."

"Something had to be done. That guy was getting away with high treason against Queen Poetry."

"You really don't like rock music?"

He shifted about uncomfortably. "Well, I'm not totally cold to it."

"I love it, myself. Have you ever been to a disco?"

Ryan had never participated in this mania of his times. He was not sure if he felt insulted to be asked, or ashamed of himself for admitting his inexperience. "No," he said shortly.

"Not that I consider myself a disco-brain. I've only been a couple of times. It was fun. I love dancing." She smiled, remembering, and Ryan felt both jealous and gauche. "Not that disco is the same as rock and roll," she added.

"Of course not," he said. He had no idea what he was talking about.

"And you really don't like modern poetry?"

Now he relaxed. "A comparison," he began.

"Yes?"

"You had some of the stout Collin and I were drinking, didn't you?"

"Yes—"

"What did you think of it?"

"It was good. A little rich for my taste, but good."

"That, to me, is what traditional poetry is like. A good, solid, English or Irish brew—rich, sweet, with a tang of hops and a good head, enough of an intoxicant to make you imbibe it with respect. Modern poetry is like American beer—tasteless, hastily brewed, mass-produced, made everywhere with virtually the same ingredients; easily consumed, but all the more insidiously sickening. I'll tell you a fact: if I drink good stout all night, my stomach never complains; but four or five cans of that American drivel, and I'm almost in the same case as your 'poor Ringer.' The same thing is true of American poetry."

"But does everything have to rhyme?"

"Rhyme? Of course not."

"But isn't that one of the hallmarks of traditional poetry? Collin hates rhyme."

"Rhyme is just one means of establishing form. Meter is more important. 'Apt numbers,' as Milton said, emphasis on the 'apt.' He didn't mean doggerel. 'Fit quantity of syllables, and the sense variously drawn out from one verse into another, not the jingling sounds of like endings.'"

"Are you quoting him?"

"Well, yes."

"Off the top of your head like that?"

He grinned suddenly, his disarming Ryan-Irish grin. "I've had this discussion before," he confessed.

"With Collin?"

"Many times with Collin. And with his friends."

"So you think modern verse is just . . . prose?"

"Well, it's peculiar, really. Modern prose is all style and no content; modern poetry seems to be all content and no style. Both are still in a kind of prolonged, mindless reaction to the past. No one really knows anymore how they got to be in such a state. Their formlessness has become self-perpetuating."

"But form . . . I mean, what is it? I don't really understand why it's so important."

"It's everything. It's what makes poetry different from conversation. It makes a painting different from a scribble."

"But other things make that difference, too. Inspiration, the power of creation. Genius, like Collin has. Clarity of vision. Saying something so that we see it in a new way. What Collin said—'Poetry is speech that invokes a universal.'"

"Yes, these things matter too. But without form, both outer and inner form, poetry cannot exist."

"You don't think that what Collin writes is poetry, then?"

He grew cautious. "I think Collin's best poetry exhibits an inner form." He paused, struggling with his honesty, and then added: "But strictly speaking, his writing does not fall under my definition of poetry."

"You'll never persuade me, then."

"God forbid that any of my intellectualizing should rob you of even a moment of pride and pleasure in his verse. He's settled this issue in his own mind a long time ago. He knows what he believes. I flatter myself, though, that I keep him thinking about his poetic principles. He's such a far cut above his friends! And he doesn't even perceive it. Not that he doesn't get irritated with them. You saw how he got angry at Chuckie when he started that frivolous impromptu. But he can sit and listen to the very same people talk about 'craftsmanship,' even though they don't know a transitive from an intransitive verb. It's as if a carpenter didn't know the difference between a piece of plywood and a two-by-four. What kind of house would you expect him to build?"

He broke off suddenly. "I'm ranting," he apologized.

"Maybe," she said. "But at least I'm learning something."

They heard a car engine in the distance. "Is that him already?" asked Constance.

"No, that's the Mercedes."

Car doors opened and closed, the screen door thumped to and fro, tiles rattled. They shared a look that said: This should be interesting. Ryan rose to his feet as Lloyd and Sondra entered the room.

"Still up? said Sondra. Her tone of voice caused a confused alarm in Ryan: it had lost much of its coldness.

In her evening gown she made even a person of Ryan's age reconsider his prejudice against her years. Lloyd seemed almost proud of her; he seemed to be bound to her by some subatomic force, as if caught and in orbit around her, aware of her constantly and making little effort to conceal his preoccupation. They were both elated, oddly elated, happy in some shy way, not believing in the potential of their pleasure with one another; Ryan found them attractive and amusing and yet vaguely repulsive: two adults acting like teenagers back from the prom.

"Hello there," said Lloyd. "Where's Collin? Whose car is that in the drive?"

"It's Ringer's," said Ryan. "He was too—" he hesitated over the word, and finally let it pass, though it seemed harsh: "—too drunk to drive home. Collin took him."

"That bad?" said Lloyd.

"How did that ever come about?" asked Sondra.

"Beer," said Ryan. She laughed.

As if drawn by Constance's greater influence, Lloyd broke away from his wife's side and sagged onto the couch next to his daughter. "What are you doing up so late?" he asked. "Did you have a good time?"

"Oh, yes. It was a lot of fun."

"Win much?"

Ryan snorted.

"I think I was doing pretty well," she admitted.

"She broke the bank," said Ryan. "Ringer and Chuckie were in debt to Collin, Steve was just breaking even, and I was down to three chips."

"Is that why you started that fight?" she teased him.

"I had to do something."

"What fight was this?" asked Sondra. She had gone automatically to the bar and poured two brandies.

"Well," Ryan began. Sondra cut him off.

"I'm asking Constance, if you please. I know I'll never get the real story out of you." Bringing the drinks, she came to the sofa and sat down between Lloyd and Constance. She handed one to her husband, who seemed surprised that she had thought of him.

"Thank you, dear," he murmured.

Constance glanced at Ryan, sharing her astonishment at the endearment; then she realized that her parents were waiting for her answer.

"Nothing," she said, in confusion. "It was about poetry."

"Nothing, and about poetry?" said Lloyd humorously. "Around here, that's what we eat, drink, talk, and breathe morning, noon, and night, Constance. You can't say an argument about poetry is an argument about nothing. Your brother and Ryan have been known to exist for six days on nothing but breakfast, brunch, lunch, and supper of poetry—or argument about it, at least."

"What is there to argue about?" asked Sondra. "You either read it or you don't."

"Wise words," said Ryan. "It's too bad we didn't have you with us earlier. Of course, we could have argued about exactly what you meant for quite some time." He looked uneasily at Lloyd and Sondra as they sat side by side on the sofa. They seemed distant from the present, their bantering answers a cover for some more urgent preoccupation they were concealing even from one another.

"Did *you* have a good time?" he asked abruptly.

They glanced shyly at one another and then looked at their drinks. Lloyd cleared his throat. "A better time than I can remember having had for years," he said.

"No kidding," said Ryan in a flat tone.

"No, no kidding. And what did we do? Just talked. Spent the evening with some very lovely people. Didn't we?"

"It was wonderful," agreed Sondra.

Ryan and Constance stared at each other. There was a lengthy silence, which neither of the older people seemed to notice. Ryan took a deep breath and exhaled it. Lloyd admired the color of his brandy, sniffed its bouquet, sipped it, and relished it.

"Well, I'm glad you had such a good time," said Constance weakly. "Really. It sounds like fun." She warmed to the idea as the surprise wore off. "You should go out more often."

"Thank you, dear," said Lloyd.

"What time is it?" asked Sondra absently, as if she had no intention of ever going to bed.

Ryan dredged his watch out of his pocket and consulted it. "One oh five," he said.

"What kind of a watch is that?" asked Sondra curiously. He showed it to her from where he sat. It was a wristwatch without straps; the crystal was badly cracked.

"My cousin gave it to me," he said. "He found it when he was sweeping out the store where he works."

"How pathetic! You should get yourself a decent watch."

"It only loses two minutes a year."

"I don't believe it," she said. "Lloyd, what time is it?"

Lloyd pulled a watch from an inner pocket of his tuxedo and consulted it.

"That old thing!" she said with a start.

"Someone very dear gave this to me," he said.

"You should get a new one."

"A new one wouldn't do."

She turned her eyes away. *Is she blushing?* Ryan wondered. He decided she wasn't, but she was in any case pleased and a bit flustered.

"It *is* after one," Lloyd affirmed. He swished the brandy around in his glass and then swallowed it impulsively.

"You're not doing any work tomorrow, are you?" asked Sondra.

"Collin and I have a long-standing engagement for dinner with McCrew.—I guess you never met him. He's the trustee for that money my uncle left Collin. He invites us over to his place once a year or so."

"What money?"

"I'm sure I wrote you about that."

"Why didn't your uncle leave anything for poor Constance?"

"He never knew her. He was a horrible misogynist, anyway.— And what are you two doing tomorrow?"

"Just some shopping."

Constance groaned. "Mother! Give me a break! If we shop all day and Collin is gone when we get back, how will I have any fun?"

"If we don't go shopping, how will *I* have any fun?"

Lloyd laughed. Constance groaned again. "Don't be such a pain!" she said.

"It'll just be for a little while. We'll just dash into the mall and dash out."

"I know you and your 'dash in and dash out.' That means try on every dress in the place. Haven't we been to every store in a fifty-mile radius?"

"There's a mall at Chestnut Hill we haven't been to."

Constance rolled her eyes.

"Come on." It was Sondra's turn to plead. "We'll get you a dress for the party on Sunday." She smiled at Ryan. "I hear we're having a Midsummer-Night's celebration." But he refused to be brought into her attempt to mollify Constance, who sulked, but made no further protest.

"Well," said Lloyd. "I should go to bed." He stood, and his wife shifted forward to the edge of the sofa as though she were going to rise too, as if it were a matter of course that they should go up to bed together. "Going up?" he asked her.

"I think I should," she said. "Unlike some of us"—she looked pointedly at Constance—"I need my beauty sleep."

But she did not stand up immediately, and after a moment's hesitation he made his way to the front stairs, leaving his glass on the sideboard as he went.

A general exchange of goodnights. When he was well up the stairs Sondra turned to Constance, leaning over her, and threw her arms tightly around her neck.

"Goodnight, honey," she murmured. "Good night, little sugar-girl, sweet little honey-girl." Ryan noticed that her voice was trembling as if with a suppressed emotion.

"Mother!" said Constance in annoyance. Sondra began kissing her temple and her hair rapturously.

"I know you're mad at me because we're going shopping," Sondra said. "Don't be mad at me. I love you." Still Constance resisted.

"Cut it out!" she said warningly. Sondra ran her hands through her daughter's hair, luxuriating in its softness. "Mother," protested

Constance, "for heaven's sake, I'm going to look like a witch!" But Sondra only caught her close again, leaning awkwardly toward her.

"Can't you give me a kiss?" she whispered softly. "Your mama's happy tonight, baby. Can't you give your mama a kiss?"

This appeal proved to much for Constance. She threw her arms around her mother's neck and hugged her tightly, and then kissed her. Ryan, who was scrutinizing the pattern of the carpet, thought he heard a muffled sob. Sondra straightened up, patted Constance's head a few more times, and then rose from the sofa, keeping her face averted from Ryan.

"Goodnight, Mama," said Constance softly. Her mother paused at the door.

"Goodnight, honey," she whispered. She didn't trust herself to turn around. In a somewhat louder voice: "Goodnight, Ryan."

"Goodnight, Mrs. Tate," he said. His male voice sounded gruff and harsh in his ears after their milder tones.

In a minute her tread had died away in the upper recesses of the house. Constance went to a sidetable and found a brush in a purse there; she restored her hair to its previous discipline in front of a gilded mirror. When all was in order again, she turned to Ryan.

He raised one eyebrow.

"Wait till Collin hears about this," she said.

"He won't believe it. If I hadn't seen it, I wouldn't believe it myself."

They remained in silence, meditating mutually on the possibilities.

Collin found them thus when he returned not long later. He sank into the sofa where his father had been sitting and exhaled a long breath of weariness and disgust. In another moment he noticed their reflectiveness.

"You don't seem too talkative," he said.

Ryan mumbled something incoherent.

"I'm sorry," said Collin impulsively, turning to Constance. He seemed to be presuming that their mood was a consequence of the party. "I really am. They really are a bunch of jerks."

She smiled. "Don't worry about them. I had a good time. I was sorry it ended that way, but it doesn't matter."

"But they were so rude to you!"

"How could they have been rude to me? They hardly said a word to me all night except 'I'll see you and raise you three.'"

"That's what I mean."

"Oh, Collin, don't give it another thought."

"Yeah," said Ryan. "Something much more interesting is going on."

Collin frowned at him. "What?" he asked.

"It was the most incredible thing," Constance began, sitting forward in her chair. "Mama and Papa came back while you were gone. They were so . . . "

While she groped for a word Collin stared at her, mystified.

"So lovey-dovey," she said finally.

"What?" he said again, incredulous.

"Papa called mama 'dear.' And that watch—his good watch—where did he get that?"

"She gave it to him when they were married. Why?"

"He told her someone very dear had given it to him. I think she actually blushed. "

"You're kidding!" said Collin in a whisper.

"Was she really blushing?" said Ryan. "I thought she might be, but then I thought she wasn't."

"Yes," Constance affirmed solemnly. "And I've never, ever seen her blush before. I didn't even know she *could* blush. Then she told me she was happy. She really meant it, too. She was so happy, she was *crying*."

"Crying?" said Collin. "*Crying?* What could have happened? I thought they were just going out to a dinner party."

"I'll tell you what happened," said Ryan. He lowered his voice as he continued: "Your mother got control of herself for a while, and your father was so relieved to find her good-tempered that he got mellow. When he got mellow, it took the pressure off her. So they had a good time for once."

"You mean she finally sheathed her claws?" said Collin. "It took her long enough."

"Yeah," said Constance. "About twenty years."

"You mean forty."

"Why did they ever break up, anyway?" asked Ryan. For the first time he was beginning to sense the positive possibilities in a renewed relationship between Mr. and Mrs. Tate.

Collin shrugged a little dazedly. "I don't know. He once said she was really hard to live with. And another time, I remember, he said she was basically a nasty person."

"He said that about Mama?"

"Well, she is a little savage at times, you have to admit."

"Maybe. But basically nasty, never."

"Well, that was what he said. Obviously he must have believed it, or they wouldn't have broken up."

"But the way he was acting tonight—I don't think he ever stopped loving her."

"Face it," said Ryan. "If she would only make it possible for him, he has a lot to gain. I mean, she's still his wife, for Pete's sake. To him, she's still young. And she's very good looking. If I were him, I would definitely go for it. Or at least give it a try."

"Do you think it would ever work?" Constance asked Collin with some excitement.

"I don't know. What do you think? You know her better."

Her face fell as she reflected. "I don't know. It's hard for her to keep her spirits up. Sooner or later she turns on everyone."

"It seems that way."

"But what if she changes?" wondered Constance. "I've always hoped someday she would. What if she gets a grip on herself and stops . . . being nasty?"

"What a summer it would be!" said Collin. "Can you imagine—Dad and Mother back together, the three of us having a great time—"

"We've got to encourage this in some way. We've got to do something romantic," said Constance.

"It's almost Midsummer Night," said Ryan, caught up by her eagerness. What could be more romantic than that?"

"Yes!" she exclaimed. "When all the lovers are magically reunited."

"We could all take a part. They could be Titania and Oberon."

"Yes!" she cried again, clapping her hands. "That would be perfect! Remember, we said we would all memorize something."

"Who are Titania and Oberon?" asked Collin.

"They're the king and queen of the fairies. At the beginning of the play they're estranged, but by the end . . . And the best part is, I know my part already. We did a performance of *Midsummer-Night's Dream* in school."

"What part did you have?" asked Ryan curiously.

"I was Bottom."

Ryan guffawed at the incongruity.

"Bottom?" Collin muttered quizzically. "That doesn't sound like much of a part."

"It was a great part, actually. The most fun of any."

"But how did *you* ever get it?" asked Ryan. "What about Hermia? What about Titania herself?"

"Oh, we drew lots. There were only girls in the class, you know. Someone had to do it."

"Is that how you got to like Shakespeare?" asked Ryan. "I remember you said something yesterday about liking him."

"Oh, no, we read a lot of his stuff. I had a teacher who must have been a lot like your mother. Fixated!"

"What a waste," said Collin.

"Not at all, Collin, dear," she said. "On this point I'll have to agree with Ryan. Shakespeare is truly great."

"Correction: *was* great. He is now obsolete."

"True greatness is never obsolete," said Ryan. "There's too little of it for that. I've been telling you for years, Collin: you'd sympathize with his world view. That's what makes him great— the scope of his vision, his perception of mortality, to say nothing of his mastery of the language."

"Have you read much of him?" Constance asked Ryan.

"Everything. Over and over. Since I was a wee lad."

"We used to have contests in school. The teacher would give us a line, and if someone in the class could identify the play it came from, the class would score a point. If no one could, the teacher would score a point. Then we would try to stump her. She was good, though. We always lost."

Ryan smiled his idiosyncratic grin and quoted: "'Come kiss me, sweet-and-twenty, youth's a stuff will not endure.'"

"*Twelfth Night,*" she said. "That's easy." As an afterthought she blew him a kiss, and he laughed delightedly.

"Well, we'll see if Shakespeare can inspire two not-so-sweet and not-so-youthful types to get back together," said Collin.

"Shall we do it then?"

"Well, maybe not read the whole play. But if you want to read parts, I guess that would be all right. You can count me out, though. I'll provide a modern counteractive."

"We'd better practice a little," suggested Ryan.

"Yes," agreed Constance. "Sunday is so close. And tomorrow I'll be gone shopping most of the day."

"Shopping? Again?" said Collin. "Don't tell me the whole summer's going to be frittered away in shopping trips."

"I can't help it. I'm Mama's excuse for going."

"And I'm going out to dinner tomorrow night with Dad and that lawyer."

"How about the morning?" asked Ryan.

"Saturday morning," said Collin, and that was sufficient answer. On Saturday mornings Lloyd had always insisted on a great breakfast feast, the stated purpose of which was to allow him to reacquaint himself with his son after the work week. As a child Ryan had often been present at these breakfasts. He had gorged himself on a selection of Mrs. Overton's vast offering, which might include ham and eggs, bacon, sausages, homefries, waffles, pancakes, homemade croissants, donuts, danish, muffins, french toast and cinnamon toast, milk, orange juice; every kind of condiment, jam, jelly, and syrup; and fruits of the season, from grapefruit to strawberries to pears. His part had been simple, amounting to no more than helping himself to another buttered raisin scone and shooting sympathetic looks at Collin as his friend bore up under a tedious barrage of questions about schoolwork and teachers and playmates; an inquisition which, so far as he could see, served no other purpose than to impede the satisfaction of a growing boy's appetite. However, as he had grown older not even the temptation of superabundant food could persuade him to endure the boredom of the weekly report of son to father, and he had learned to avoid Saturday mornings at the Tates. Certainly there would be no time tomorrow morning for anything but the ceremony of the prolonged meal.

"Why don't you two do something tomorrow night?" asked Collin after a moment's thought. "If you can entertain yourselves until I get home, we might be able to manage an hour together."

"We would certainly have enough time to practice our parts," said Ryan.

"More than enough, I should think," said Collin.

"If we get tired of that, Ryan can tell me about his adventures as a big man on campus."

"And you, 'with greedy ear,' could 'devour up my discourse,'" suggested Ryan.

"*Othello*," she said.

"I can see you'll do just fine," said Collin. "And look, Ryan, no fair brainwashing my sister with your propaganda. No 'Introduction to Paradise Lost'."

"You're too late, old buddy."

"Are you serious?" exclaimed Collin.

"Yup. Already hit her with that. While you were driving Ringer home."

Collin shook his head. "You watch out for this guy, Constance. He's fast. Intellectually speaking, that is. He'll ask your mind to go to bed with his on the first date."

"I hate to break the news," said Constance, "but I'm not a virgin. Intellectually speaking, that is."

"I'm glad you added that," said Ryan.

"But I don't sleep around, either," she informed him.

"Intellectually speaking, you mean."

"I mean in any sense. I stick to my principles."

"Well, for my part, I don't seduce women."

"Intellectually speaking, you mean."

"I mean in any sense. Truth is like love. It speaks for itself. There's no point in trying to force it."

She was blushing faintly. "I'm losing track of the metaphor," she said.

"That means it's time to go to bed," said Collin.

"Are you speaking metaphorically?" asked Ryan.

"No, you pedant. I'm wiped out."

"Just when the conversation was getting interesting!"

"It's easy for you. You can sleep late if you want. I have to get up tomorrow and eat half of Mrs. Overton's pantry."

"Aren't you going to offer Ryan a ride home?" asked Constance.

"I would, but he wouldn't accept. The man's a walking machine. Just set him upright on the soles of his feet and he moves like an automaton. I know him too well to bother offering him anything. If he wants to take the car, all he has to do is ask for the keys."

"Are you such a walker, Ryan?"

"I am," he confessed. "And a walk will be good for me. It will clear my head after this wild night of drinking, gambling, and wenching."

"I love to walk. I haven't been getting enough exercise since I've been here."

"The woods—we've got to walk in the woods."

"We will," said Collin.

During this latter exchange they had all risen and begun moving toward the door.

"Well, good night," said Ryan. "I really enjoyed it."

"Especially when Ringer got sick, I suppose," said Collin.

"It was the high point of the evening."

"Let's not talk about it. Ever again."

"It's a done deal, buddy."

Collin stopped by the stairs, but Constance followed Ryan to the door.

"Till tomorrow," Ryan said.

"I feel as if there's something else I want to tell you," Constance said.

"What would that be?"

"I don't know."

"If you figure it out, call me up. Anytime."

"I wish you lived up in the spare bedroom. I don't like the idea of your leaving. If you lived here, then we wouldn't have to coax you to come back."

"I'm coaxed. I'm persuaded. Just let me know when my presence is required."

"I'll call you after dinner," she said.

"Excellent.—Good night."

"Goodnight, Ryan," said Collin. One more glance at the two of them, to hold them in his mind, and Ryan went out, plunging into the dark.

Saturday, June 20/One

Summer is i-comen in,
Ludhe sing cuccu.

—Traditional, c. 1250

Summer surprised us.

—T. S. Eliot

THERE IS A moment when spring ends and summer begins; a day, a dawn, when spring, loitering, lagging, suddenly has taken its cool mornings and fled, and the heat of summer has come. The calendar may say spring is over; but not until that thick heat moves in, until the skin prickles with the first real sweat of the season, has summer truly arrived.

Such was the morning after the unfortunate poker party, when Ryan slept late and awoke in a sweat with the ten o'clock sun full on his bed. Summer's heat filled up his little bedroom like a stench. In Ryan's metaphor, it was like that change when a child playing in the street first called him "Mister." Though he had felt certain of his maturity, a guileless stranger had confirmed it; and his was the choice, to enjoy the alteration of season or regret it.

He would have regretted this particular moment less had he not slept too long (even metaphorically) and woken feeling sick and stupid. He staggered to a cool shower, which refreshed him, however excruciating; and stepped with more vigor, more control of himself, down the stairs to breakfast.

"Summer's here," said his mother.

"It's finally come," agreed his father.

"A great summer," said Ryan. "I'm ready for it."

So he felt, at least for the first hour or so. His life seemed to have expanded somehow. He went and stood in the yard after breakfast, and did not see the weeds, the ragged shrubbery, the decrepit house, or the few misshapen trees that stood isolated and awkward, like ugly prudes caught naked, trying to conceal forms in which no one took interest. His mother and father peered at him by turns through the screen door and saw him looking north. It did not occur to any of them—not even to Ryan—that he was looking towards the Mecca of his life. They thought that he merely went out to absorb the heat that had begun to lift invisibly the dense dew left by the last night of spring; they did not realize that, like an Arab to the call of the muezzin, he had crept forth to worship.

Then he went inside again, through the kitchen to the cooler study. Still under the impetus of his invigoration, he drew out notes, culled books from the shelves, and sat down at his desk.

His work was cut to pattern; he had only to stitch it together. At the convention in December he had talked with an editor who had suggested a topic for an article; and this idea had stuck in his hand, for he seen it at once as a lever and fulcrum to topple one of the self-apotheosized idols of modern philology. He intended to send his article to the unsuspecting gentleman who had urged the idea on him, even though he was confident that it would be rejected in horror. Another journal, smaller and more radical, would accept it eagerly; like Ryan, its editor had not yet outgrown that adolescent state in which independent thought is confused with ruthless iconoclasm. To kill the Buddha you meet on the road is one thing; to track that Buddha down specifically to kill him is something else. The hunting metaphor was appropriate: the wind was up, Ryan had caught scent and snapped his leash; the quarry was even in sight, he had only to close and spring for the hamstring, and a Regis Professor would lie thrashing exquisitely for a brief while until a later paper could dispatch him. It was all there—multiple self-contradictions, consistent misreading of the Greek, research farmed out carelessly to graduate students, an ignominious neglect of Wilamowitz.

But as he laid his hand to this happy chore, the door opened. It was his mother; she brought a letter from Todd; and he could not resist it.

It was a long letter, written very recently; in it Todd related droll academic adventures and demonstrated, in a note added apparently after the letter had been completed, that he must have learned something of Ryan's brief affair with Eve, probably in a telephone conversation with her on the very day it had ended. Like all Todd's letters it had no date, greeting, or signature, beginning and ending with Sibylline abruptness; and like them all it dug out and husked the buried kernel of Ryan's last:

> You upbraid me for using a metaphor that you claim is "hackneyed" and "stale." I find this amusing for two reasons: first, because the metaphor I used, which depends upon a comparison between the span of human civilization and the span of a single life, is a perfectly salable literary ware; and because if either of us were guilty of this sin, it would more likely be you than me.
>
> On the first point, you will agree that in the great marketplace of words, there are some goods that can be offered for sale again and again and bring a profit year after year. Amid all the chaffering chapmen, the hustling hucksters, the bargaining buyers, wedged in among the gaudy booths full of toys that will not last out the day, is always one where the merchandise is traditional, the stock unvaried, where you may purchase a metaphor that stirred sorrow in your grandfather, and his grandfather, and his before his, back before there was a way to capture the shadow of the word in writing. Of course, there are some men and women who have waged war their whole lives against such metaphors: that Humankind is like a human, the ages of humanity being mirrored by the individual's progress from infancy through prime to senility; or that the life of a human is like the day, dawning, tending toward noon, declining into twilight, or like the seasons of the year, from blind, rushing spring to slow-footed Autumn. If we pause before

these wares, fingering them, thinking our mental furniture incomplete without at least one antique to show off the splendor of our newer acquisitions, some tradesman at a neighboring booth, jealous for our attention, will cry them down as hackneyed and outworn. But he has confused merchandise that has grown venerable and noble with that which will become worthless with the passing of time, like his own cheap wares (which, after all, are all he understands). Do not listen to this cheap critic. These metaphors prove fertile because they hold truth, or perhaps because they combine two features of life that are always ready to the mind, just as a brawling man and wife keep begetting children: because at night each is ready to hand. After all, the combination of two inalterables is an inalterable; and more recondite metaphors are less prolific. "As the generations of leaves," says Glaucus, son of Hippolochus, "so the generations of men."

No wonder, then (to move on to my second point) that you linger on at that booth in the fair, that you buy by the armful (for even the most antique words are inexpensive), that you do not look at the stones and trees without thinking of a half-dozen contradictory metaphors. The leaves may come and go, you think, but root and branch remain.

Upon reading this letter, Ryan took the piece of paper on which he had meant to begin the outline of his article and wrote the following:

Todd—
Old man—Sorry no write, but busy. Agree with you about time-honored metaphors. But you never explain why you think I'm more guilty of their use than you.
Yes, Eve and I finally got together—and she has already broken off with me—a sad business. I'll tell you about it over an ale next fall.
But I look up. Collin's twin sister has appeared on the scene quite unexpectedly—is beautiful, bright, sweet. I think this

will be the summer that it all happens. I'll write more when I can.

  —Your colleague, Ryan

P.S. I put my Dad to work on your assignment. Unfortunately, his caesuras are hopeless!

He busily addressed an envelope and sealed the letter in it. And suddenly he found that in the process of writing this massive response the thrill of the chase had died away within him. Summer crowded into the study, and bright life, real life, made things philological and metaphorical look like mere petty paper pursuits. He yawned; his gaze rose from the envelope, from the webs of Todd's handwriting, from the inchoate gatherings of his research; he sat back; he put his hands behind his head, leaned against the bookshelves, and rocked precariously on the two rear legs of the chair. In a moment he was daydreaming.

This was how summer came in for Ryan Kinsella.

Saturday, June 20/Two

For she is chang'd, as she had never been.

—The Taming of the Shrew

ONDRA TATE ALSO slept too long.

Her room was on the north side of the stone house; it stayed cool until just before she awoke. She opened her eyes, struggled up onto one elbow, and looked around herself with the air of a woman who has been long sick and has awakened with an indistinct understanding of her whereabouts.

She saw about her the bedroom in Lloyd's house: the dressing table with all her powders, perfumes, eyecolors, and lipsticks; her shoes, like Cinderella's crystal slipper, still tumbled on the floor where she had kicked them off; and in the closet, showing through the still-open door, the dress she had worn last night, dangling awry on its hanger, reminding her how she had stuffed it in there, dazedly, in a glow of pleasure, confusion, longing that now came back to her even before she remembered the cause: a palpable feeling of security.

She was afraid the feeling would escape her. If she rose she might shed it when she slipped off her nightdress; it might wash from her flesh like faery dust when she showered; it might be smothered when she put on her old habits. She lay back on the pillows and kept still, holding onto it as one gropes vaguely after a pleasant dream. The pattern of the antique paper on the wall, whose infinitely crisscrossing roses she had always detested, now seemed pleasant, as a taste finally acquired overwhelms the palate with its determined persuasion. It was old; it had not changed; it had the Tate solidity behind it.

And the Tate solidity had the power to ease the fear that had tormented her increasingly in the last few months: fear of simple destitution. She would not think of it now, or she would feel it twisting in her again, like a kind of nausea. Yoked with that sickening fear was another emotion, shame; shame that she had come to this, that she had no recourse; that she had been conned, cheated, made a fool of, shown up as a fool, and worse, as a foolish woman.

Not a penny, she thought. Here I lie, without a penny. And for the first time in months, the phrase that had stung her like a taunt had little effect: Not a penny.

Since the time she left Lloyd she had had enough to live on. Even after the considerable sum he had given her had trickled away, she had remained in possession of some soundly invested money, left to her by her aunt, which yielded just enough so that she could pretend, in the society of Seville and even later in Madrid, to more wealth than she had. Julio had put an end to that. He had promised her better earnings, enough to see Constance through an American university and leave Sondra her old competence; he had promised other things, too, and they, too, were gone with him.

She had never known how terrifying poverty was. In a world in which everything is valued in dollars, to be poor is to have no part; in a sense, to be poor is to cease being human. The fear alone had almost broken her. She might have turned to the bottle, and who knows what might have become of her; but she felt such violent shame when she imagined her child dragged into degradation because of her stupidity, that she was impelled to act.

When she finally knew the money was gone, she had cast about for any recourse. The first that occurred to her was Lloyd. Legally, she was still married. Perhaps he could find a way to prove that that no longer mattered; but surely she had some rights she could enforce upon him—she could win some kind of settlement.

Or perhaps not. He was a lawyer. To take him on in the arena of the courts would be preeminently foolhardy. She knew perfectly well that justice went to the strong, and in Boston, he had power that she could not begin to match among the circle of men that ran the law. She knew, all the same, that he was frightened of her, because he was afraid that a settlement might affect the house and land, or his ability to keep them and pass them on to Collin.

But Constance was some kind of bargaining chip. She had always known that he would instantly cherish his daughter, and Sondra had at least some kind of moral hold over the girl. She could come between the two of them; she could manipulate the love that arose between them to secure her own position.

Even if she remained estranged from him, she had reasoned, she might on that grounds make peace with her parents. They were nearly seventy; she had been practicing her religion *pro forma* in Spain; these things might count for something.

So she had packed up very suddenly one day, as she saw the time looming when even bluffing the purchase of tickets would become an impossibility. The uprooting had been violent, after seventeen years; and yet the roots of her friendships in Spain were rotten, for they had been formed of money, and the money was gone. At the very worst, she had brought Constance back to a place where the girl would be safe; and though her daughter had detected some trouble, the full extent of the disaster was unknown to her.

But here in the room with the yellowed roses, Sondra herself felt safe. Not just from the fear of poverty: she could feel another fear easing in her, the one that had made her a prey to Julio. She wanted the roses in her life, even if only to change them, eventually, to sweep them out, to make the interior of this house bright, airy, modern, fashionable; to make this place hers, to find roots that would hold her upright for the rest of her life.

The revelation of last night was that she had seen how she could make herself part of the Tate solidity. Not that Lloyd's attraction to her was any surprise; rather that she had seen a way that she could endure life in this house, a way to readjust her perspective.

It had not happened when they were alone together, over some dinner plumped with calculated romance, or in some moment of weakness—as she had half-imagined it might—when she made herself available and he needed her too much to refuse. Indeed, that had not happened; or at least not yet. They had been in company—he had brought her along out of some reluctant sense of duty to her as a houseguest, perhaps; or perhaps because he wanted to. They had driven out to another town in silence broken only by scant, faintly irritated conversation on the character of this or that old acquaintance they would be seeing: he offering information, she making clear her indifference.

But over dinner, sitting nearly opposite him at the table, she had found herself laughing, first at the humor of others, and then at his wit, which twenty years had sharpened until it almost frightened her. Her laughter seemed to fire him; he kept them all entertained; was unquenchable; told stories of sin and skullduggery in his profession that horrified them even while they laughed. Then, as if his point had been made, he yielded to others.

Afterward, she sat beside him on a sofa. At first they said little to one another or anyone. But she felt an ease with him. She first noticed it when in the course of the evening, several people who had not been acquainted with them made comments that showed a natural assumption that the Tates were in some sense a normal couple. Sondra was surprised to discover that this error pleased her. She had been on the outside so long, a foreigner, an undivorced single woman, a freak; in this social context, all she had had to do was to keep silent, and she was accepted. Lloyd had invited her—that countenanced her with those who knew of their strange situation; and though they were curious, though they might find the oddness of the circumstances repulsive, when they looked at her, they obviously thought their friend Lloyd could do worse.

Little by little, as the evening wore on, she had warmed to the role. She had spoken to Lloyd; she had smiled at him. He had reacted with a trace of suspicion at first; but he was willing to allow for a change in her, if she would make one. It was not hard to pretend that she wanted this role, a life with him.

She had often thought that pretense was the key to life. Everyone was essentially faking an ease in their roles that they could never feel. She remembered a psychiatrist who had told her repeatedly that reality was only a game we play to cope with our lives, that the insane are simply those who won't play or can't. Maybe this thing—love, marriage, companionship with another—was just a game; maybe she could play it, after all. And last night she had tried pretending, first to others, then to Lloyd, and finally to herself, that this role was comfortable. She found herself enjoying the acting—perhaps because she had realized that Lloyd was surprised and pleased; that Lloyd's friends, once they grew used to her, were pleased at the possibilities; that when they came home Constance was deeply moved and excited at this glimpse of possible normalcy.

That feeling of possibility had been heady for her—the possibility not only of giving up her anxiety about money and her loneliness, but pretending her way out of the endless, searing bitterness that had poisoned her life.

Last night at the party she had watched Lloyd, wondering why she had rejected him—his face so proud, keen with intelligence, yet made affable by the softening questions and uncertainties of the heart. He was the handsomest man at the dinner. If she had been able to live with him through the intervening years, even now she would still be proud of such a companion. He had been hers, her possession solely, indisputably, twenty years before. Why had she been so angry at him—then and always?

It was no disappointment in him that had caused her long-ago rage. The reason was inside her, in the bitterness that came she knew not whence and made her drive all love from her path. It controlled her; it made her angry. She looked back, back into her childhood, and it was always there. It had made her break her ties with everyone, one by one—everyone but Constance. It was an obstacle in her inward life she had never known how to rise above. But if she could simply step around it, in pretense—that would be better than enduring its endless perplexity.

Now, sitting propped on her pillows, in Lloyd's house, she felt again the same intense, sweet liberation from the tyranny of her own irascibility. She had to find a means to hold on to this feeling, this fragile knowledge that freed her from her past and from the future she dreaded, of dying by degrees in the acid of her own anger.

She rose from bed and went over to the window. Throwing the sash as high as it would go, she knelt on the floor, leaning her breasts against the sill and pressing her cheek against the screen. She could feel the heat of the day beginning to suck at the coolness within the house. "Summer," she murmured, as if recognizing someone she had not seen for years.

She felt a sudden, sexual quiver.

Last night, sitting beside Lloyd at the party, she had put her hand on his. He had turned his gaze to hers, incredulous. She felt a faint pang of compassion for him, and her eyes softened with tears no art could have put there. His hand lay stiff and unresponsive, though he continued to look at her, astonished. She had looked away, caressed his hand once in a hopeless, apologetic way, and let go of it.

Yet something had happened in that moment. It was ineffable, indefinable. And they both knew it. It was clear in the unison with which they had acted during the remainder of the party, the way they had stayed together, though still speaking little; the way they rose to go together, said their thanks and farewell to host and hostess so curiously like a couple that someone had said, within her hearing, that you would never guess that Lloyd Tate's wife had taken a seventeen-year sabbatical. And when they had begun to drive, suddenly they began to speak—at first about the party, commenting on the quips, the foibles of the guests, the changes in those whom they had known together; and then, finding suddenly an inexhaustible and comfortable topic, the children. As they were entering the drive at home, Lloyd had commented finally: "I've never said this to you, Sondra, because I've never known Constance well enough until now to make this judgment. You've done a wonderful job raising her. She's a sweet young woman; I couldn't ask for anything more in a daughter. And I know it wasn't easy doing that alone. It wasn't easy for me, either, raising Collin by myself. We've done things the hard way, you and I. But at least we don't have any cause to regret the results as far as our children are concerned."

With those words it was almost as if they had put their estrange-ment behind them; as if they had acknowledged it, and now could start over. She wondered now, by the window, if she could almost love him again, as she had loved him when she married him, but without the anger: if she could pretend the anger away, deny that it even existed.

Below her, outside in the back of the house, a door thumped open. Mrs. Overton appeared on the lawn and made her way to the garden plot, which lay almost out of sight beyond the huge rhodo-dendra at the edge of the grass. For several minutes she stooped over her peas and lettuce, puffing and groaning with such gusto that her noise was audible even at this distance over the cacophony of the birds that flew about in the trees. As she turned to leave again, she paused at the garden gate and looked up, directly toward Sondra's window.

You're worried, aren't you? Sondra thought. *Well, you have every reason to be. If I get Lloyd back—if I decide to stay here—you won't last long.*

She stood up. Mrs. Overton seemed to see the movement behind the screen; she ducked her head and hurried on, passing out of sight behind the kitchen wing as she approached the house.

❁❁❁

When Sondra stepped out of her room a little later, she felt a twinge of fear. What if she immediately lost her grip on this feel-ing she hardly understood? What if Lloyd rebuffed her, irritated her, thinking better of his weakness last night? She saw no one in the hall, no one as she descended the stairs. She walked through to the dining room and found the breakfast table laid for the Saturday morning feast, but no sign of anyone.

She twisted the rings on her fingers nervously and wandered back out into the living room, over the grinding tiles, and then, absently and curiously (unable to stand still or remain inside the house alone) she walked outside.

The heat of the sun smote her, the screen door thudded shut behind her—twin blows, one to sense and one to sound. She stopped, threw her head back, closed her eyes, and smelt the heat; it brought the odor of woodland and drying grass, sticky rhododendron sap, the old, black asphalt beneath her neat white shoes; and there was in it, too some yeasty, fleshy smell she could not quite isolate, that made her think, however incongruously, of field hockey practice at college. She kept walking, opening her eyes wide as they adjusted to the light. A robin strutted before her like a little herald of her coming, throwing out its fat breast and chirruping; when she came to the edge of the front lawn it took to wing and flitted busily away along the trunks of the bordering trees. The lawn, under the watchful hills, was dotted with birds hunting and running about; a trusting rabbit grazed at one side, unconcerned by her presence.

Suddenly a memory fluttered in her, white, shy, glimmering as it too took wing.

She put her hands to her belly; and it was flat, tight beneath the white raw silk of her dress. She had been wearing a white dress that day too. She had walked out of the house in this way on a day like this, into the heat of a summer morning, her belly big with the twins. Her heaviness; the weight of her stride; the sense of carrying life, other life, life not hers, not Lloyd's, life belonging not even yet to her children, but to God.

How Lloyd had loved her—always had loved her, but especially when she was full of her children. People said that women had a glow in their faces when they were pregnant; but what about the shining gaze of a man beholding the woman he loves carrying new life? His adoration had been too much for her at times. She had come outside to escape it; and found instead the adoration of all nature, watching her, rejoicing in her, until she yielded to the joy herself.

"My God," she said in a whisper, not realizing she spoke aloud.

She was struck suddenly by the magnitude of all she had given up in fleeing her marriage: such mornings as this, in a home that could have been hers. She put her hands to her eyes, shuddered, regained control of herself. She had missed—an entire twenty years, it seemed. She turned away from the loss and her admission of it with a desperate will to forget, to make good the lack.

Yet in turning she saw Collin on the stone porch, watching her. He had his little notebook open on his knee and a pencil in his hand. He must have seen her talking to herself. She felt embarrassed and surprised at the same time; he was perhaps the only man on earth who could make her feel that way. She walked toward him, thinking she should explain her agitation somehow; he continued to examine her as she came with a look she mistook for clinical, but which was in fact a function of his abstraction—if he was thinking about her at all, it was to regret that she seemed intent on disturbing him.

She ascended the stairs to the top step and there stopped. He continued to regard her mildly. The morning sun made a sort of halo in the sheen of his golden hair; his face seemed studiously neutral, but without a single bad grace or trace of ill temper.

At least my son was spared the infection of my discontent, she thought gratefully.

"Collin," she said suddenly. He waited expectantly. She searched for words. Finally she blurted: "You're so beautiful!"

He raised one eyebrow. "Well," he said. "Good morning to you, too."

"Didn't your father teach you how to take a compliment?" she asked.

"My father warned me to beware of them."

"And your mother wasn't around to teach you how to smile and say 'Thank you?'"

"No," he said quietly. "My mother wasn't around."

She went to him quickly, fighting back tears, of grief in her loss, of joy in her possession. She could not refrain: she caught his head in her hands, stroked his hair—then drew him from his chair, embraced him, kissed his cheeks almost desperately; and burst into tears after all.

He was by this point incapable of speaking.

"Your mother has come back," she said. "I'm sorry—I'm sorry, Collin. I know you detest me for what I did—I don't blame you. But I've come back, and I love you. You're my son. You're Constance's brother. Do you think I'm a stone, that I feel nothing? A bitch? A shrew? I don't blame you." She removed her hands from him with difficulty, drying her eyes with her fingers. In stunned silence, mechanically, he offered her one of the handkerchiefs with which Mrs. Overton always supplied him, ironed and folded. She laughed shyly and gratefully as she took it. "You *are* well bred," she affirmed. "He did a much better job with you than I could have." She managed to bring herself back under control. "May I take this?" she asked, indicating the handkerchief. He nodded mutely. She felt the need to say something more. "It's hard, I know," she said vaguely. He still could not speak; and as he stood there astonished and concerned, twenty and handsome and full of dreams and ideas that seemed like the whispers of gods to him, he was so beautiful that she had to turn away and go into the house.

She compelled herself to sit down at the dining room table. Lloyd would be coming in soon; she didn't want to seem like some bawling ninny. But she did not have time to compose herself before Collin came in behind her and took a seat, looking at her with continued concern and incomprehension. "Are you all right?" he asked.

"Yes," she said, smiling. "I'm very all right."

"You seem keyed up."

"Well, you can understand . . . coming back here after all these years. Finding that the little baby boy I . . . I abandoned . . . is a grown young man. I missed so much. And I can never get it back. And finding a husband who is really kinder to me than I deserve . . ."

"He's a very generous man," observed her son somewhat coldly.

"Collin," she said impulsively, "I was so young—I didn't know what I wanted. I didn't know what was good."

"It seemed to me when you showed up here about ten days ago that you didn't know what you wanted."

"Maybe I knew but I didn't believe it could happen. Maybe I'm beginning to believe it now."

He sat for a long time, perhaps five minutes, and said nothing. If she had been more familiar with him she would have known that his thoughts could have been anywhere; but it seemed that he was scrutinizing her, testing her. She could not bring herself to look him in the eye. She felt a tremendous strength flowing from him, or rather from her love for him; she hoped that it would keep her on the track, it would keep her converted.

"Well," he said finally, " I think we really would like it if you stayed with us. But don't make life hard for us. Exercising a sharp wit is like satisfying a craving; it's hard to get it under control once you start indulging it. Dad likes repartee; but when it's a little too pointed, it only makes him bitter. And I don't like to see him like that."

She nodded contritely.

"Your feelings are changing, aren't they?" he said. "It seems like they've changed even since yesterday."

She nodded again; a little sob escaped her that sounded like a groan.

"What made them change?" he asked plainly.

She raised her eyes to his, then looked confusedly across the table.

"I don't know," she said. "I was with your father last night at that dinner—and suddenly it seemed I had found a way out—a way out of myself. It was as if I had found a way to change a pattern I had hardly even dreamed of escaping from." She looked back at him, embarrassed. "You must think I'm crazy."

"No," he said. "I don't know what to think. I guess I just don't know you well enough."

"You will," she promised. "If we stay . . . we'll do things together, all of us. You'll get to know me better. You'll see I'm not so terrible."

"Yes," he said uncertainly.

She realized she had outrun all the science of his twenty years. He did not know what to make of her. He sat for a minute or two and then rose suddenly, as if wishing to escape from her and think over what she had said.

"Breakfast is at ten today," he said, consulting his watch. "Just a few more minutes. I'll go see what Constance is up to."

"Collin, I—"

"Don't worry," he said.

"Don't worry?"

"I mean . . . about what I think. I'll just judge you by the way you treat Dad. That's all that matters to me." Then he added, somewhat more darkly, "And by the way you treat Constance."

He began to walk out of the room.

"Collin," she pleaded again. He paused.

"Yes?"

"Just call me 'Mother' once."

He regarded her with a gaze that was part kindness and part irony. "All right," he said. "I'll see you in a few minutes— Mother." Then he left her in sole possession.

She tried to compose herself better. Her heart leapt as the swinging door to the kitchen gave its characteristic alert, a peculiar muffled suction; but only Mrs. Overton appeared. She paused as she saw Sondra, frowning almost pompously; then, as if gritting her teeth and girding her great waist for combat, she stalked around the table toward her.

Sondra had taken her own accustomed place at the side of the table. Mrs. Overton had always sat at the foot, presiding over the serving of the meals, except on Saturday mornings, where tradition excluded her. She would have been unwelcome at this *Tate au Tate* between father and son, distracting the two of them and complicating Lloyd's attempts to extract meaningful information from the boy; on the previous Saturday, Sondra had noticed, her place at the foot of the table had stood empty. Now, however, she swept up the setting from before Sondra—plate, silver, napkin, cup, saucer, tumbler, and mat—and transferred them with exaggerated ill grace to the place at the foot. Without a word she huffed away, and the door swung shut behind her.

Clearly she had received orders. Lloyd must have told her that Sondra should have the place at the foot of the table, and he must have ignored the wounded looks and the warning headshakes.

Mrs. Overton could not shirk in this regard; he would be sure to reproach her if he saw she had failed.

Sondra was amazed, overcome. She remained where she was, looking at the foot of the table, savoring this testimony of Lloyd's care, this gesture that proffered a welcome back into the family.

In a moment Constance entered, smiling with some happy, secret knowledge. Sondra held out her hand, beckoning to her. Constance came to her side, drew a chair close, and beamed at her with her old unshakable kindness.

"Good morning, my beauty," said Sondra softly.

"You heartbreaker," teased Constance.

"What do you mean, 'heartbreaker'? You're my heartbreaker."

"You've dazzled Collin somehow."

"What do you mean?"

"He said something very nice about you just now."

"What was it?"

"I can't tell you. You'll just have to take my word for it."

"You mean he said that underneath my nasty exterior I might actually have a heart after all?"

Sondra could tell from the surprised look on Constance's face that she had very nearly guessed his very words.

"Oh, hush, Mama.—What did you say to him, anyway?"

"I'm just feeling a little emotional this morning. I was overcome when I saw him. He's such a beautiful boy . . . and I was sorry I hadn't been here to see him grow up." She almost began crying again; Constance put her hand on her shoulder.

"They're coming," said Sondra, hearing a noise in the other room. "I don't want to let them catch me sniveling." She pulled herself together again and wiped her eyes.

Lloyd and Collin entered from the living room. "Take your places, ladies," said Lloyd. Constance rose at once and went around the table, where Collin held her chair for her. But Sondra sat where she was, fearful of presuming. "Please," said Lloyd, motioning toward the foot of the table. Collin drew out the chair for her, too, and she rose and took the place she had not held for seventeen years.

Lloyd allowed himself one brief, curious inspection of her face. She sank down a little in her chair, at first feeling a dread that her great new knowledge would desert her; but it did not fade; it was strong. She raised her face to Lloyd and smiled at him.

He had to look away. He was immensely pleased. Something *had* happened last night; he had taken this risk, extended himself in the gesture of the table place, and she had shown that so far his trust was not mistaken.

Mrs. Overton served the food in its usual obscene abundance: scrambled eggs, bacon, sausage, a quiche, scones, muffins, turnovers of rhubarb and strawberry picked that morning in the garden, crumbcake, honied rolls, homemade bagels, french toast and pancakes layered in a huge tureen heated in the oven, maple syrup, jams and jellies, fresh-squeezed orange juice, dark breakfast tea and pungent java. Sondra noticed little of it, and little of the malignant looks with which it was served up to her. Her attention was on her family; for the first time in all her stay, she was able to imagine it unbroken.

Collin and Constance told the story of the poker game—he, very drolly, and she, with that unconscious love of fun that was even more winning; he, wincing occasionally and venting his disgust at the uncouthness of his friends, poking good-naturedly at Ryan's foibles; she, compassionating Ringer and attempting a defense of the scholar. Then Collin interrogated his father on the dinner party. He received little more than smiles, nods, muted expressions of satisfaction from both ends of the table. If baffling, this was at least novel and entertaining; Collin smiled wryly at both parents, exchanged glances with Constance, and turned the topic to tomorrow night. He would see to it that Ryan was present; Lloyd had ordered leg of lamb, Ryan's favorite; Constance was to pick up her new dress today. The banter was affable in all directions, for Sondra said nothing, or next to nothing. She laughed from time to time, but her customary acid had sucrified.

She saw clearly now that she was the destructive member of the family. They could be happy, she thought, if she did not spoil it.

The relief of the others was obvious: the meal lasted in high spirits nearly until noon, Constance and Collin laughing and talking, and Lloyd doting on them, occasionally darting a glance at Sondra, as if to confirm his joy with her.

At length they all grew too sated with food even to admire it, to pick at it, or to be tempted to another cup of coffee; they grew too pleased with their own company even to float another topic of conversation. "Well," said Lloyd finally, "I believe you want to take the car." It was his usual signal—the keys were about to be handed over. He also had a certain credit card that she was able to use; on previous occasions, Sondra had badgered him for this, shamelessly exploiting his weakness for Constance. This time she stood back diffidently. He fetched forth the keys from his pocket, and then his wallet, and produced the credit card. "Don't be shy," he said, seeing her hesitation. She came forward, and he handed them over. "Buy something for yourself, too," he suggested.

"I couldn't," she said; though in fact she had bought herself many things already, as they all well knew.

"A present from me," he said, "for tomorrow night. For old time's sake. For Midsummer-Night. For my Titania."

She found herself unable to speak.

"Do you remember how their part opens?" he continued, since she was silent. "I looked it over again last night. Oberon and Titania are feuding over a child she's raised. Let's just say this little present is a peace-offering. We won't feud the way they did. You buy yourself something special to wear, and we'll all celebrate, tomorrow night. What do you say?"

She did not trust herself to voice even one word.

"Well, go on, then," he said, waving her away. "Have a good time, you two. We'll see you later."

"Give your father a kiss, Constance," said Sondra. Constance came to her father and kissed him on the cheek; but he never took his eyes off his wife.

"Go on," he said. "We'll see you later."

Saturday, June 20 / Three

HOLOFERNES. Sir Nathaniel, will you hear an extemporal epitaph
on the death of the deer?

—Love's Labour's Lost

AT ABOUT ONE o'clock that afternoon Ryan had what seemed a brilliant idea. Unfortunately, nothing came of it; but his elation until it proved fruitless buoyed him for five minutes of a hot, dreary day. He had forgotten, last night, to tell Collin of the deer; and he thought that under the pretext of passing on this news, he might make himself available for an earlier invitation to the valley. He called at once.

He woke an unusually depressed Mrs. Overton from a snooze on a soapless afternoon. After a long delay, which could not be entirely a result of her notorious reluctance to climb stairs, he had Collin on the phone.

"I hope you weren't busy," said Ryan.

"Writing," said Collin, with resignation.

"Sorry, old man. It's just that I remembered something I forgot to tell you last night."

"What's that?"

"I saw a deer under the oak in the clearing."

"No!" cried Collin. "A deer in the clearing?"

"A doe—good looking, from what I could tell, no mange or injuries. Took off when she saw me, of course, but some girls do."

"Excellent! A deer in the valley! When was the last time we saw one?"

"I don't know. Eight, nine?"

"At least. At least when we were eight. Wait till I tell Dad!"

"The population must be up again."

"Must be. Maybe we can hunt for it with Constance some time."

"Excellent idea. This afternoon, maybe?"

"As a matter of fact," said Collin distantly. "Look, Ryan, I've got to get back to the typewriter. I'll see you tomorrow if you're not still around tonight when I get home. You *are* coming over, aren't you?"

"If the lady calls," said Ryan.

"She will. Well, I'll see you.

"Okay. Tomorrow if not before."

"And Ryan—thanks for calling."

"Thought you ought to know, buddy."

They hung up. Ryan knew exactly what had happened. The muse had whispered to Collin. Even now he would be hurrying from the phone in the upstairs hall to his room to write about the deer. Ryan looked at the materials he had set out for his article— the texts, the photocopied secondary sources he would cite, a reproduction of a thirteenth-century manuscript, some sheets of cheap lined notepaper—and for the first time in his life he envied Collin the pursuit of that more evanescent creature, Poesie.

❁❁❁

It was nearly six hours later when the phone rang again on Ryan's desk. He had been bracing himself a long time to resist the summons of the first ring. His mother hurtled in from the living room and had almost snatched up the receiver before his hand went down across it with the forbidding rigidity of the gate at a railroad crossing.

"I've got it, Mother," he said flatly.

"It might be your uncle calling. We're going up there for Fourth of July, you know." It rang once more; he picked it up.

"Hello," he said.

"Hello, Ryan?" said Constance Tate's soft voice. He pointed peremptorily at the door and his mother slunk toward it.

"Hi," he said. "Could you wait just a minute?"

"Sure."

Maureen had paused at the threshold and half-turned to gather more information. He motioned to her to close the door.

"Is it Edie?" she asked. He scowled with piratical ferocity. "Well, if it is, thank her for my record." Then she shut the door. He waited until her footsteps testified to her retreat to the kitchen.

"Hello again," he said, instantly affable, transformed from buccaneer to young buck. "How goes it?"

"I was wondering if you still want to come over."

"Does the sea still rush to meet the shore? Does the caged lark still yearn to mount singing into the sky? Does the lover still long for the dim sleepy ground where his love lies buried? Does Ryan Kinsella still want to visit his old friends in the valley?"

She laughed. "And Collin always said you weren't a poet," she said.

"Just imagine if I were a poet, how much better a poet I would be than anyone in all the preceding centuries."

"As great as the sun to the twinkling stars," she suggested.

"As the Leviathan to the minnows," he proposed.

"As the lion to the hyenas."

"As the hound to his fleas."

"Hey, we make a good team," she laughed.

"We can form an advisory board to Collin. Kinsella-Tate poetry consulting services."

"Except we're minnows to him, Ryan."

"You're right. Mortals to his divinity."

"It's true! Are you making fun again?"

"Me? Making fun?"

"My brother was right about you."

"In what regard?"

"He said you never give a straight answer to anything. Are you coming over or not?"

"Any incentives?"

"You mean my company isn't enough?—As a matter of fact, I do have a surprise for you when you come."

"Let me guess. We're going to spend the evening cutting coupons with Mrs. Overton."

"No! This is a real, serious surprise."

"Oh, really? Any hints?"

"It has something to do with a certain great poet of our acquaintance."

"Who would that be?—Oh, no, wait, I think I know who you mean. But isn't Tennyson dead? And does he really count as an acquaintance?"

"You're being sacrilegious again, Mr. Kinsella. I won't allow it. If you're going to be that way, I won't share my surprise with you."

He instantly became serious. "I apologize. I'll be over in fifteen minutes. And I promise I'll be as grave as a churchyard."

"That's better. I'll look for you."

❈❈❈

He was quicker than his word, but she was as good as hers, and was standing behind the screen door as he approached the house.

"Good evening," he said. She opened the door, her smile more than sufficient for greeting. He stepped in, and for a moment she made no motion toward the interior of the house, remaining quite close to him, smiling up into his face. Then she turned away and moved with a lingering, leisurely step toward the living room, a stride that invited him to walk beside her. He noticed the way she moved with some curiosity; it was so different from the purposeful, direct motion she used when her mother or Collin were nearby.

"My mother's gone out shopping," she said. "For shoes."

"On Saturday night? Are there stores open? I confess I'm naive on this subject."

"Oh, the malls are always open. She wanted me to go, but I refused. I told her you were coming over to tell me about your shipwrecks and hair's-breadth escapes."

"I'd like to hear some of yours."

"There isn't anything to tell. I really think that without Collin, I'd just be some dumb brunette going topless at St. Tropez when her mother wasn't looking." This image was so startling that Ryan needed a moment to frame an answer.

"I doubt that. You have your brains independently of him; he didn't give them to you."

"But the inspiration to attempt to use them would probably be lacking without him. You may think I'm giving him too much credit for saving me from leading an utterly boring life, and ultimately being an utterly boring person, but that's exactly what he's done. He knows so much more than I do, and he has such . . . I don't even know how to say it . . ."

"Intellectual integrity?" suggested Ryan, who was never at a loss for a way to end other peoples' sentences. She had flung herself casually on the couch; he settled into a chair opposite her.

"Yes. That's it exactly. His integrity is a challenge to me. I'll never catch up to him, but it's my duty to try."

"Sorry," he said. "I just don't see you as an air-brain."

He was about to begin preaching to her, but she abruptly changed topics and began telling him about her parents. She described Sondra's subdued, affectionate manner this morning, and her sudden tears; the breakfast; the place setting; the gift of the dress—"For tomorrow night," she added in parenthesis. "You *are* coming, aren't you?—Oh no, Collin says that the way to deal with you is just to feign complete confidence that you will be present when required.—About six would be good.—Anyway, we found just the dress she wanted. You won't believe it when you see it."

"I probably won't. I don't believe any of this. It sounds a lot like they might fall in love again."

"Do you really think so?"

At this point they were interrupted by Mrs. Overton, who opened the door from dining room and peered into the shadows at them.

"Oh, you're here," she said.

"Good evening, Mrs. Overton," said Ryan.

"Is it just you two together?"

"Yes, just us. Sitting here talking."

"But it's getting dark. Wouldn't you like me to turn on a light?"

They looked at each other.

"It's not really dark, it's dusk. Besides, I like the dark," said Constance.

"The twilight is nice, Mrs. Overton," said Ryan. "We'll leave the lights off."

"All right," she said in a significant tone. "I'll leave you two alone in the dark, if you want." And she went back into the kitchen somewhat more cheerfully.

"Just don't expect a baby in nine months," Ryan said when she was out of hearing. Constance laughed merrily. "She's terrified, you know," Ryan added.

"Of what? Out-of-wedlock babies?"

"No. She's afraid of a shakeup if your mother and father get back together. She thinks your mother might give her the boot."

"Tell her not to worry. My mother hates to cook."

"It's not just that. I've always had a hunch she had matrimonial plans for your father."

"Mrs. Overton?" Constance looked both amused and horrified.

"Mrs. O. The very same."

"You mean she's *jealous* of my mother?"

"Bizarre though it may seem, I think that's in there somewhere, all mixed in with the soap operas and the cookie recipes."

"What does that have to do with a baby in nine months?"

"Her plan is for—well, never mind. I'd feel like a fool talking about it."

"Oh. I think I can sort of guess what it might be."

They looked at each other awkwardly; then they laughed and were at ease again.

"What about that surprise you mentioned?" he asked, to turn the subject.

She rose and approached a side table. There she picked up a folder that had obviously been carefully laid out for this moment. Her manner reminded him of a votary approaching an altar to take up a sacred relic. "Collin told me to show this to you," she said. "He said he was sorry for bolting away from the phone so quickly today when you called to tell him about the deer. He said this would explain. He said he took some poetic license in saying he saw the deer himself, but that you would understand." She came to his side and offered him a piece of paper, which was apparently the entire contents of the folder.

"My God," he said as he took it. "He hasn't shared one of his poems with me for years." She stole away, as though not to disturb him as he read, and sank into the cushions of the couch again.

On Seeing a Deer in the Woods after Sixteen Years

I have seen the deer.
Not the one that stared
eyesbrown, velvetshadowdappled, hungry
at the staring boy I was once. But
of that deer some part, deerness flowing and shared from
memory to now
unknown to me while I grew, in the wild (a nursery and a
school,
beyond my ken, beneath our human notice)
like the wildness moving in me, beyond and beneath.
(Think of) the generations I was before I was,
to be born here (why here? why now?)
doe with your roundsoft eyes, liquid eyes, golden eyes
I was born to see you return.

I have seen the deer.
On that day did the boy's eyes slay you, deer?
That you went away, that you hid
in the thick thicket beyond the highways, mountains, oceans,
moons
spinning and glowing, grinning and growing over my lack of
you?
(The moons mounting, the years mounting.)
Did I remember you? I thought so.
But not I think till I saw you

gracile in the clearing of our father's wood.
When my eyes met your eyes again
you came to life once more.

I have seen the deer.
What wildness woke! Passion to passion,
fear to fear, we gazed in past and present tangled
as in the net of hunter Time, looking
on and on in each other like a man seeing
in an infinity of reflecting mirrors
not himself confronted but a woman he does not know.
She lifts a slim foot to dash away, to dash the glass,
to tear the web that binds them to each other and the world;
he would cry out, but the deer, the truly deer,
have no names.

I have seen the deer.
Vanished. All my power
unable to recall more than words—
and what are words? The dapple of the shifting shadow
on your goldenness, the hard sharp breath you gave
in flight. The want begins once more, the want for you
that will not end. Humankind has driven
the animal from itself, the animal that would have let me
join you.
I was born to call you without hope.

Ryan read the poem once and then again, and then a third
time in increasing astonishment. At length, unable to conceal his
confusion, he put it on the table in front of him, where it seemed
to catch fire in the westering sun that stole in fragments into the
room.

"Well?" she asked. "Don't you think it's beautiful?"

He looked up into her expectant face and realized that she had
no idea what the poem meant.

"Well?" she repeated. "Don't you?"

"It certainly is extraordinary. I would have called it disturbing before I called it beautiful."

"It *is* very powerful," she agreed.

"Especially . . . because it's about you."

He could see she was surprised. She hesitated; and then asked: "What do you mean?"

He picked up the poem and peered at it again in the fading light. "'Doe with your roundsoft eyes, liquid eyes, golden eyes,'" he read, "'I was born to see you return.'"

"He means the doe in the woods!"

"I don't deny he's playing on the comparison. There are some parts that belong to the deer, and some parts that belong only to you. This line about 'the hard sharp breath' given in flight—it's the sound deer make when they're alarmed and start to run; it sounds almost like a sneeze. But what about this part: 'We gazed in past and present tangled/as in the net of hunter Time, looking/on and on in each other like a man seeing/in an infinity of reflecting mirrors/not himself confronted but a woman he does not know.' You and the deer become a metaphor for one another. And the undeniable tip-off is where he says 'our father's wood'. Who else could he mean but the two of you?"

She was confused and uncertain. "But what's all that about passion?" she asked.

"Yes," he admitted. "What is all that about passion? It seems out of place in any case, whether he's talking about the deer or you. But poets tend to lean on that word *passion* a little too much; maybe it doesn't mean anything specific. 'Passion to passion, fear to fear.' What's the fear? I can't quite figure it out. But it's very moving here at the end where he imagines you leaving again. 'The want for you begins once more, the want for you that will not end.' 'I was born to call you without hope.' It's very sad."

She came from her seat and knelt beside him, reaching for the poem. "May I see it again?" she asked.

He held it out to her; she took it. She was so close to him now that he was aware of her perfume.

After rereading the poem for several minutes she spoke. "What's this at the end, then? 'The animal that would have let me join you'? How does that figure in your interpretation?"

"I don't know. I can't figure that part out either."

"But you still think it's about me?"

"I'm sure it is. Why don't you ask Collin?"

"I'd feel like such fool. If it's really about me and I didn't even see it . . ."

"Well, maybe I'm wrong. Poems are slippery things."

"Yes."

She rose and went back to the sofa, carrying the poem in her hand. "Yes," she repeated. "They are, aren't they?" She seemed to find that thought reassuring. Her smile flashed over her features again. "And you know what Pooh says about them."

"Pooh? No, I don't remember."

She laughed, a little embarrassed. "There, you see," she said, "you and Collin sit around and quote great poets and all I have in my head is Pooh. Actually, I did some baby-sitting last summer for a little English girl who wanted me to read her Pooh. I think Pooh is really for adults; I wound up laughing a lot more than she did. Anyway, there's a part where Pooh has read one of his poems to Piglet and asks him how he likes it. And Piglet says he likes it except for the shillings; he doesn't know what they're doing in the poem. And Pooh says, 'They wanted to come in after the pounds'—he'd mentioned pounds—and he says that's the best way to write poetry, letting things come into the poem when they want to. Maybe that's how the passion got in there, and the thing about the animal. It just wanted to be there."

"Sometimes the metaphor has its own logic, and it overpowers the logic of the poem.—To put what Pooh says more academically."

"Exactly.—You really are good at this, aren't you?"

"Well, I don't know. Our friend seems to have me baffled in a couple of places."

"But I never would have dreamed he was talking about me. Comparing me to the deer. Never, if I had looked at this poem for a million years."

She put it back in the folder and replaced it on the side table. It seemed to Ryan that her air of reverence was gone; she seemed to be trying to put it out of her mind. She sat down again and looked at him shyly. "I'd like to be able to read poetry as well as you can," she said.

"Criticism is just a game. Anyone can learn to play it."

"Do you think I could? When I go to college?"

"If you want. But it's better just to learn to enjoy poetry than to be a critic. There's a big difference."

"Well, reading poetry intelligently is what I'm after. I'd like to be able to know what Collin is really saying."

"Only the poet knows that. There'll still be secrets in his poems that you'll never pierce."

"I'm sure there will," she agreed.

She slipped into a reverie. He watched her furtively, though he could see little of her expression as she sat silhouetted by the last rays of the sun.

"You were going to tell me about your childhood," she said, after a long silence. "I was going to be your Desdemona. Remember?

"Yes—I do. Do you really want to hear my whole tale of woe from the beginning?"

"From when you were born to when you went to college. Collin said you were captain of the soccer team. You can start with that."

"That's starting at the end, though."

"Well, start at the end, then."

"It isn't as glamorous as it sounds. When I went to college, I was only sixteen. I'd always been alone, because I never went to school. My parents taught me at home; you know about that. At college I was a complete outsider. It didn't help that I was so much younger than everyone else. The difference between sixteen and eighteen is enormous. I was a freak, a monstrosity. But I had no intention of living in the woodwork for four years. I was ready to join in and start living life by then. I needed some activity where people would be forced to put up with me whether they wanted to or not.

"Collin used to organize pickup soccer games when he was in prep school, and he'd invite me along; we'd play soccer for three hours at a time. Before I started to play in college I thought I was pretty good, but that first year on the team was hell. I was absolutely at the bottom of the ranks. Most of the other guys had been private school hotshots; they'd played for four years. The coaches barely tolerated me.

"But I put in extra practice after hours, weekends, vacations— even after the season was over. Just basic ball-handling stuff; dribbling, knocking the ball against a wall, trapping it, penalty shots, over and over and over. When spring soccer started the coaches suddenly noticed me. When the fall season got going in my sophomore year, I was starting right wing on junior varsity.

"But I wasn't satisfied with that. I kept practicing. I used to drag one of my buddies from the classics department out on the field to play goalie for me. Todd Schmidt. After I got to know him, it turned out that he was the nephew of one of your father's old law school cronies. Todd was my best friend at school the first three years, before he went to Cambridge. He's a great Latinist, but not much of a goalie. If he ever stopped a shot, it was with his face. I used to beat him to a pulp out there on the field. But he never quit.

"Anyway, my sophomore year I was top scorer on the JV. At the beginning of my junior year there was a soft spot at varsity right wing, and the coach started me there the first game to see what I could do. I was top scorer from day one. That pretty much did it. A few last second penalty shots and everyone on the team thinks you're all right, no matter where you came from or how young you are."

She shifted so that she was prone on the sofa, putting her head on her arms and turning her face toward him. "I bet you could tell a lot of exciting stories about some of those last-second shots," she said.

He evaded the hint. "Actually," he said, "the best last-second goal I ever saw was by a halfback, a guy named Croxy. This guy had arms like an ape. He got a throw-in with one second to go and just pitched it right into the goal to break a tie. You should have seen the look on that goalie's face. You should have seen the look on *Croxy's* face. We all laughed till we cried. What a feeling that is! Winning at the last second by a bizarre stroke of luck. It warps your thinking; you think God is personally intervening to help you. You can't figure why it doesn't work every time; why there are still games you lose.

"That's the great thing about sports. They aren't real life. Everybody gets up again after they fall down. You can lose and life goes on. What's bad is that those bizarre accidents happen in real life, too. And they aren't always in your favor. The bullet that would have missed if it had been an inch to the right. The accident that wouldn't have crippled if someone had fallen a little to the left. The half-second of forgetfulness that puts a car into a tree. It's weird, winning is. You always want it to mean something, to make it prove that life makes sense. But even when we won and won and won and nothing could stop us, I always had the feeling that the winning was just an illusion. The guys that went away beaten— we could have been them. Maybe next time we would be. And it made you wonder, will my life be like that? Will I play as hard as I can and still lose, because of some bizarre thing I have no control over? How can I make sure that my life doesn't depend on some accident like that—that I have something real that matters and no stroke of luck can take away? And even more difficult—how can I live so that someone *else* doesn't have to lose so I can win?"

He was silent for several minutes. Finally she raised her head. "Tell me about everything, from the beginning. From when you first met Collin."

"I'd bore you to death."

"No, you won't. I like listening to you." She seemed almost to snuggle into the sofa, like a child preparing for a story hour. Perhaps it was that unconscious wriggle that overcame his last resistance.

"All right," he said.

He looked around the living room. It struck him how comfortable he felt here; how much more comfortable than in his parents' house. When he began to speak, all that had been openly jocular in his tone fell away instantly. He thought even as he began how it was like that moment when lovemaking becomes serious. He spoke slowly, taking his time; and his voice fell over her softly, in plain statement of fact that was humble in spite of the successes he had to tell, his quiet tone always at odds with self-praise.

Saturday, June 20/Four

There are two tellings to every tale.

—Irish proverb

Should I examine you in the dead languages, would not your living accents charm from me all power of reproof?

—Fanny Burney

When [his son] began to come to years of discretion, Cato himself would teach him to read. . . . He himself . . . taught him his grammar, law, and his gymnastic exercises. He says, likewise, that he wrote histories, in large characters, with his own hand, that so his son, without stirring out of the house, might learn to know about his countrymen and forefathers; nor did he less abstain from speaking anything obscene before his son, than if it had been in the presence of the sacred virgins, called vestals. . . . Thus, like an excellent work, Cato formed and fashioned his son to virtue; nor had he any occasion to find fault with his readiness and docility.

—Plutarch

Tristam, said he, shall be made to conjugate every word in the dictionary, backwards and forwards the same way;—every word, Yorick, by this means, you see, is converted into a thesis or an hypothesis;—every thesis and hypothesis have an offspring of propositions;—and each proposition has its own consequences and conclusions; every one of which leads the mind on again, into fresh tracks of enquiries and doubtings.—The force of this engine, added my father, is incredible in opening a child's head.— 'Tis enough, brother Shandy, cried my uncle Toby, to burst it into a thousand splinters.

—Sterne

Ryan told his story, but there was much he could not tell from within himself, because of mere ignorance or modesty. The true tale was a larger one than he knew.

The first time he and Collin met they were three years old. Mrs. Overton and his mother had struck up a conversation in a market. Ryan remembered that Mrs. Overton said something about a *bad girl* who had hurt Mr. Tate, and he had pictured Collin's mother as a little girl wearing a pinafore and a naughty frown. And that day was the first time he ever heard the word *divorce*, though in the event no divorce had come of the separation. At first the boys sat in the seats of the shopping carts, eyeing one another innocently enough; but when the adults became absorbed in their gossip, the mischief began. Collin chewed his way into a package of cold cuts, generously offering tidbits to Ryan as he tore them out of the cellophane wrapper; and Ryan, never to be outdone in liberality, shredded a package of bread and wrung the contents into lumps to proffer it to his co-conspirator. Soon Collin crawled from his seat to demonstrate how bananas could be effectively pulped by stomping them through the mesh of the cart, and Ryan discovered that tomatoes could be similarly processed.

When the damage was discovered and the appropriate scoldings had been meted out, it was not a far leap to the conclusion that the boys would make compatible playmates. One day not long later Maureen drove the brand-new Valiant up the sweeping driveway to the Tate's house, chatted a few minutes with the housekeeper, soothed Ryan's anxiety at being left, and then went off to a faculty tea.

At first the house terrified Ryan. The living room alone was larger than the entire first floor of his parent's house; and the old beauty of the furnishings made a dim impression even on his toddler's mind, for it stood in stark contrast to the collection of ramshackle chairs and tables at home. But Collin soon taught him by example that the carpeted halls were endlessly fun for running and shrieking, especially when Mrs. Overton pursued them, puffing and remonstrating ineffectually until she could corner them and shame them into behaving. Each room in the labyrinth had wonders to explore—sofas that became trampolines or ocean-going ships, armchairs like the thrones of kings, great caverns under wide four-poster beds, and high closets where a dozen little boys could have hidden together. He soon learned his way about and grew confident he would never be lost in the house; although in later years he often wondered to himself whether he had not lost himself there forever, by finding a self who lived happily only within those walls.

Perhaps Mrs. Overton might have discouraged another visit. The boys were wild together. But by the time Ryan's mother returned, the portly housekeeper had long since yielded responsibility to Lloyd and sagged exhausted into a chair. He met Maureen at the door with Ryan perched on his arm like a happy monkey ready to shake a cup full of pennies. She made her first and best impression then, with the new car, her one good dress, and her round, pleasant, Irish face, and the pride, relief, and happiness with which she reclaimed her tike.

She felt shy of this Brahmin lawyer. He had a stern, harried look that told of his pain for his lost wife and daughter, of his anxiety for his motherless son; but he had been delighted to find Collin romping gleefully with this stout-legged little boy, and set her at ease. "They play so well together," he said.

"Perhaps Collin should visit us sometime," she responded. "We're just a few minutes down the road. I'm sure Mrs. Overton could use a day off."

"I'm sure she'd be pleased to arrange that," said Lloyd.

He paused uncertainly. Maureen looked appropriately encouraging and inquisitive.

"Let me ask you something," he said. "An odd thing happened. Ryan seemed interested in the coat of arms I have framed in the hall here. I thought maybe the griffin and the falcon might have caught his eye, so I held him up for a better look. But it was the letters he was interested in. He read the name 'Tate' to me. I didn't believe it at first, but he spelled it out. Am I mistaken, or can he read?"

"He reads a little," admitted Maureen. She and Daniel had already decided on their plan of educating Ryan at home; at first sight this nonsensical attorney looked just the type to upset it. But he smiled now, barely, a taut, admiring grimace, and ruffled the dark locks of that literary head; and she guessed and guessed correctly that when the Kinsellas' secret became known to him he would keep it.

Mrs. Overton was instructed to inspect the Kinsella's house. She reported that it was small and beginning to decay on the outside, but otherwise wholesome. The Kinsellas were a little odd—they owned no television—but affable; and though they were poor at tending the plants in their yard, they were responsible tenders of their son. With this, Lloyd ordered her to encourage the connection in every way. The Kinsella boy had promise.

The Kinsellas, for their part, scrutinized Collin just as carefully. They found that if the static charge of wild spirits generated by two little boys at play could be grounded and dispersed for a minute, Collin showed himself scrupulously polite, full of a natural modesty and respect of his elders that was a constant surprise in the only son of a wealthy man, a boy who was being raised by a somewhat dizzy and indulgent housekeeper. And as he grew and developed a moral sense, he showed himself fiercely honest— more honest even than Ryan, who became politic at an early age. Collin seemed to view life more simply. An act was right or it was wrong. He could not tolerate anything morally ambiguous. But the boys shared one trait: once they had been pinned to a promise, though Ryan might have resorted to every twist of childish sophistry and pettifogging to avoid the initial commitment, they would keep their word no matter what it cost them. And this was a remarkable characteristic.

At first the boys were transported from house to house infrequently, by Valiant or Mercedes. But one Saturday morning when Ryan was seven years old, Collin appeared in the Kinsellas' dooryard alone, carrying a wooden spear and dressed in a little vest of fleece that made him seem a diminutive hunter-herdsman from a remote place and age. He staunchly refused to come into the house. He had set out from home to find his friend, and with some pride in his accomplishment demanded Ryan join him for the trek home. A call was made; Mrs. Overton was in a panic, Lloyd in high dudgeon with her for letting the boy escape the breakfast ritual; but it was a feat of skill and daring not to be slighted. Daniel went with them as far as the culvert; extracted a solemn vow from them that they would never cross the highway above; and saw them emerge on the far side, ascend the hill, scale the wall, and wave before disappearing into the Tate dominions.

From this time their friendship grew solid. Friday night they spent together at one house, and all day Saturday at the other. From the beginning Ryan preferred the comfort and size of the Tates' home, where cookies and ice cream were in supply to meet even a boy's demand; where they might climb to the attic and make all the noise they wished and yet go unheard and unreprimanded by those below; where they could view the forbidden inanity of the television in Mrs. Overton's office and sate themselves with mocking and scorning the contemptible antics of the grownups who flitted across its blurry screen. To Collin, Ryan's house seemed magically cozy. It was small, but it possessed that finest of comforts, a real mother. He did, however, think curious and awkward the notion in the air there that boys did not need more than two cookies after dinner; and it was often inconvenient that no way could be found to remain undetected in one's wakefulness after ten o'clock at night. But each boy essentially gained a second home and alternate parents. Lloyd and the Kinsellas often spoke of an "other son," and Mrs. Overton counted Ryan as another foster child. Little distinction in treatment was made for either boy in either household. Had Ryan needed scolding, Lloyd would have fulfilled this duty as readily as the Kinsellas would have reproved Collin; yet except for the customary sins of late-to-dinner and late-to-bed, neither side had many failings to correct.

From time to time in the early years the parents of both houses would conspire and concur that enough visiting had taken place for one weekend. They would then be met with such an explosion of indignation, such a wearisome assault of nagging, begging, and finally hopeless and forlorn sulking, that it was hardly worth trying to claim some time alone with their children. When separated in this way, the boys would resort to the telephone, and could be heard ranting in anguish over the inhumanity and injustice of parental collusion. In the end both the Kinsellas and Lloyd Tate would feel that perhaps they had indeed been a little cruel and selfish. They found it was easier to avoid the accusations of tyranny than to endure them to no purpose; and with this kind of assiduous training, the parents at length became sufficiently tractable that the boys lost not an available minute of the weekends.

Though Ryan had no other friends, Collin had several. Every once in a while he would invite one over to share in their play. Inevitably, however, these third parties would disgrace themselves somehow or other—by preferring Spies when the obvious choice was Trojan War, or by raucous and embarrassing behavior at the table, or by a mysterious and pitiable terror of the snapping turtles in the pond. Ryan found these schoolfellows of Collin's to be the most dull and tedious creatures he had ever met. For one thing, they knew nothing of Odysseus; and then when the task at hand was crafting Roman broadswords from old boards found in the attic, they went utterly blank; and if their knuckles were banged when they had been entrusted with the shield of Achilles (an old trash can lid gauded up with poster paint) they cried or grew angry; and worst of all—poor ignorant things—they bored both Collin and Ryan by endlessly retelling empty jokes they had heard while worshipping television. They never lasted long. They had little imagination, less character, and no education.

All these attributes the boys had in abundance, though Ryan always outlearned Collin. Even at five or six, he was sprinkling his jokes with Latin and Greek. At the time when Collin went off to kindergarten, to bang blocks together and cut construction paper into circles and squares, Ryan had been put to the wheel in his father's study. By then he had long since learned the Roman and Greek alphabets and could sound out words rapidly in both. Now he began learning the structure of the languages. Xenophon was his mentor in Greek that first year, and Nepos in Latin, his father teaching him mornings until he had to dash off to his classes at the university. And there was many a time as Daniel labored against the palpable apathy of enormous lecture halls that he missed the keen eyes that saw and the sharp ears that listened, the uncannily quick apprehension that caught every word from his lips.

When Daniel was gone Maureen would sit with the boy. She taught Ryan to write in a clear, neat, and somewhat ornate script; drilled him in the number facts; presented him with geography and history; and cleaned up his orthography from time to time. Later she studied at the university extension and scrambled to stay a lesson ahead of him as she tutored him in the rudiments of algebra and trigonometry. For geometry he read Euclid; nothing more seemed necessary; and its Greek was so simple that he mastered the subject at a very early age, and always retained a fondness for it. Chemistry, biology, physics, and astronomy would wait until he reached college—neither Daniel nor Maureen dared attempt them. To spark his interest in English, he was given Robin Hood, *Treasure Island*, *Prester John*, King Arthur, Andrew Lang's fairy tales, *The Hobbit* and *The Lord of the Rings*, *The Secret Garden*, *Wind in the Willows*, *Lorna Doone*, William Morris and H. Rider Haggard, books that he studied as any wizened scholar his chosen classic. And Maureen read Shakespeare with him not once, but repeatedly, and drew him out on forays from Palgrave's *Golden Treasury* into English poetry from Chaucer to Eliot.

But when he came to Collin's house on Friday afternoon, Ryan brought not his scholarship but a head full of adventure stories. He would sketch out the plot of his current reading, and they would act out the tale, alter it or embellish as they willed, becoming Allan Quatermain or John Ridd, Strider or Lancelot, each as he chose. But it was not until Daniel let Ryan loose on Homer and Vergil, at about age eight, that the boys' world became rigidly fantastic. The first weekend after he had started the *Iliad* Ryan raced over to the Tates' and expounded as much as he knew. He became Agamemnon, and Collin Achilles. They feigned a magnificent quarrel over Briseïs on the sand by the pond, came to mock blows, made peace, shook hands, and went off to sack Troy— launching their invasion at the Scaean Gates, otherwise known as the stone porch. A rotten rose trellis served as a scaling ladder; and victory was postponed another ten years when Achilles cut his heel on a rusty nail in the fragments of the trellis and had to be taken for a tetanus shot. He faced this proceeding with a truly astonishing stoicism, once Agamemnon had explained that he was receiving a transfusion of the ichor of the gods (or the water of the Styx), which would make him invulnerable. A few weeks later, when Ryan was studying the *Doloneia,* Lloyd awoke at midnight to hear the rumble of the wheelbarrow on the lawn. Looking out his window, he found a young Diomedes and Odysseus, complete with bow and arrow, spear and sword, cloaks and bizarre head- gear, trundling off the chariot of King Rhesos. He was grateful when the game playing moved on to the *Odyssey;* what more time-honored occupation for boys than to build a raft and drift about between Scylla (the rock) and Charybdis (the large willow overhanging the pond), where they had tied a rope to a branch and could cling to it as Odysseus clung to the fig tree. His relief was short-lived, however, as Mrs. Overton almost fell victim to live archery in the living room when Ryan was studying the slay- ing of the suitors. During every week of Ryan's progress through these epics, Collin's conversation with his father was full of specu- lation on what his friend would report on the next visit; and after receiving his update, over Saturday breakfast he would complain bitterly that while he was being forced to read *The Goody Family Goes to Town,* Ryan was reading "real stuff" in which spears sank into frothing wounds and gods and goddesses copulated on mountain tops.

The great flaw in the Kinsella's plan was that home became school. Home was where the lexica grew dirty and ragged beneath a little thumb, where reading lessons and reading for pleasure became confused together; where the Teubners and the Oxford Classical Texts waited in the shelves, promising more years of work than his young life could comprehend; where he fell asleep by night with Greek, Latin, English, and later German, French, and Italian, boiling in his brain until he hardly remembered which was his own mother tongue. Yet the boy could not read enough to satisfy his hunger. His father sometimes had literally to wrench the text out of his hands when the day was done. His parents nagged him to turn on extra lights when he read, took him to have his eyes checked three times in one year, and lived so much in terror of his reading at night under the covers that they warned a puzzled Lloyd Tate never to let a flashlight fall into their son's hands.

And this course of study made him a freak. Sent outdoors on weekday afternoons to play in the yard, he would watch the bright school bus stop at the end of the street (he had never ridden on one) and stare enviously at the children running home to what seemed to him to be blissfully uncomplicated lives. On one such occasion when he was ten a grown neighbor went by and heard him chanting—

> O Myriads of immortal Spirits, O Powers
> Matchless, but with th'Almighty, and that strife
> Was not inglorious—

and worrying, asked Maureen if the boy was ill. No wonder the children nearby thought him a misfit, perhaps retarded, and spread the rumor that the Kinsella boy did not go to school because he was crazy.

In their suburb, one of the small old villages outside Boston, not only was the town administration quite small, but failure to attend school was almost unheard of; the local sergeant of police doubled as truant officer. When word eventually reached him that the Kinsella boy did not seem to be in attendance, he paid a surprise visit. Maureen opened the door in answer to his knock. As he stood there on the step explaining his purpose, the sound of the boy and his father reached him; they were discussing something in loud tones in the study. Daniel and Maureen had long dreaded this moment, spun a thousand plans for it, and never concluded what they should say or do. Now that it had finally come, Maureen was speechless.

Then she saw by his name tag that the officer was an O'Brien. Within thirty seconds they had established that he was a grandson of the great uncle after whom her brother Frank was named. She took him right into the study where Daniel and Ryan were, introduced him, sat him down in front of the fire, poured him some hot chocolate, resumed her knitting, and said nothing more. Ryan asked him his opinion of the role of the will in *Oedipus Rex*. Sergeant O'Brien was not sure what his opinion was. Ryan, then nine years old, discussed the critical passage at length, reading it aloud in Greek and tossing off a translation in support of his point. The sergeant took the proffered text and sat over it bug-eyed for several minutes while the debate went on over his head. Ryan strongly suggested he have some of the scones Mrs. Overton had sent home with him on Sunday; and Sergeant O'Brien found he did have an opinion on these, and it was quite favorable. Having won his good will, Ryan badgered him further about Sophocles, but Sergeant O'Brien carefully demurred. "Greek is all right," he said finally. "But what's really important, now, Mrs. Kinsella, is if he's getting Latin. He'll need that, now, won't he?" For such a boy, surely, was bound to be a Jesuit.

"That he will, Sergeant O'Brien," said Maureen. "And I can assure you, his Latin is very good."

"Ryan, recite the man some of that from St. Ambrose," suggested Daniel.

"You mean the hymn for Christmas?"

"That's it."

Ryan rattled off a few lines from memory:

> *Intende, qui regis Israel,*
> *super Cherubim qui sedes,*
> *appare Ephrem coram, excita*
> *potentiam tuam et veni.*
> *Veni, redemptor gentium,*
> *ostende partum virginis . . .*

"Ah, that's beautiful, now," said Sergeant O'Brien. He took another scone. He was feeling beneficent; and besides, the Latin put his duty all in a new light. "You know, now, why I've come," he said to Daniel. Suddenly Daniel blanched and swallowed hard. "Well, don't worry yourself. I'm thinking the boy is a prodigal. A genius. He probably could be in a good Catholic school; but I can see that you're doing the right thing by him, raising him up secret from the world, like; devoting him to the Church." He chewed the scone meditatively. "And if no one bothers *me* about him," he went on, "I guess I'll find a way not to bother *you*."

"That's very kind of you," said Daniel. He felt no need to correct the sergeant's misapprehension about Ryan's intended career.

Yet the officer was right in this: Ryan would have been an excellent casuist. On more than one occasion, Lloyd told him he would make a good lawyer—though Ryan did not quite grasp the irony implicit in the compliment. After he had received the first troublesome inquiries about which school he attended, Daniel and Maureen told him to answer by saying he went to private school. They then tried to justify the telling of this white lie for a quarter of an hour, sinking slowly deeper and deeper into their own conscious guilt; until Ryan finally put an end to their self-torment by coolly observing that his home was a school of sorts, since he learned things there; and it could not possibly be more private. It would not be the last time the boy helped them out of a moral dilemma.

He gradually learned that he was different. Instinct soon told him to suppress his knowledge outside his own home or that of the Tates'. The tension between him and his best friend because of this difference grew greater with the passing years. Ryan had prose and poetic composition in English, Greek, and Latin, and later in German and French. As models he read Addison, Spencer, and others who had something to say and said it well; in Greek there was inimitable Plato; in Latin, Tully. Small wonder that he had no patience with people who could not parse their own language or scan a sonnet. It was he who saved Collin's poems from becoming beads of dangling participles strung loosely on a vague theme, by ranting the term "finite verb" so often that Collin finally cornered one of his teachers and asked what it meant. But if he gave Collin fantasy and verbal integrity, Collin had much to give in return—not only the whole valley and its experience, but stories to tell of school, of other children, of cheating and swearing and who had kissed whom. He seconded Ryan in the only fight he ever had, with one of the tough caddy boys from a neighboring golf course who trespassed on the Tates' land to swim at the pond. He smuggled up to the attic a girlie magazine he had found on the side of the road, and explained to Ryan the details that even unblenching Homer had left out. In short, he brought some of the real world to Ryan, and made him an apprentice of its lore, as Ryan had made him a pupil of the unreal.

Yet Collin's influence did not win out over their fantasy world until the end of their thirteenth year. By then they had to work harder to convince themselves of their make-believe. They needed real props. They had discarded their wooden swords for a cavalry saber of steel Ryan had bought at a junk shop and a blade of tourist Toledo that Sondra had sent over from Spain at Collin's urgent request. Their parents were beginning to feel some alarm that this play had persisted so long into their adolescence, but on those occasions when they met and mentioned it, either Daniel or Lloyd was sure to conclude the discussion by saying, "Wait till they discover girls."

When the change came, however, the motivation was more literary than sexual. About this time Ryan obtained a copy of Yeats' collected poetry. He had read several of these poems before, but the whole volume, which is not a slim one, absolutely overwhelmed him. Much as he loved Homer, much as he respected the despair and moral horror of Vergil, Yeats outstripped either of these in his affection. He read Yeats until he knew a hundred poems by heart entire, and a little at least of every other in the volume. It was as if his life had found its ultimate mentor and spokesman, its guide to lead him on the way down and fetch him up again. His life was lit by the twilight of the Celtic Dawn; he dreamed of a glimmering girl with apple blossom in her hair, of cloud-pale eyelids, dream-dimmed eyes, and when he walked the hills over the valley, thought he paced up Knocknarea. He beat Yeats into Collin's ears at such great length that his friend read and even studied the poems, although he ultimately found them "too old-fashioned" for his taste.

It was odd, but in many ways typical of the life of a child prodigy, that Ryan's early maturity in childhood should become a lingering immaturity in adolescence. He had in fact been holding his friend back. But then Collin found his own literary mentor in Walt Whitman. In that vast, textured, real depiction of American life, he found the richness of vision that up to that point only fantasy had supplied. He could give up fantasy, for he had discovered that life itself—the modern life of everyday—was far more "fantastic," that is, more huge, strange, varied, exciting, and adventurous, than anything he had heard about from Ryan.

His values underwent a revolution. He could not explain what was happening to him; he could hardly understand it himself. Instead he gave Ryan a copy of Whitman's collected poetry and prose, and Ryan dutifully read it from cover to cover. When he had completed his assignment, he reported back to Collin.

"Do you understand now?" asked Collin.

"Understand what?" asked Ryan.

"Why I can't believe in fantasy anymore; why I can't run around the woods with swords anymore; why I can't pretend anymore."

Ryan did not. He withdrew, stunned and betrayed. For two months he spent the weekends in his own room, reciting Yeats between rereadings of Austen. For seven years he and Collin had been inseparable; now he and his companion seemed irreconcilable.

Their friendship might have foundered at that point. It was Collin's turn to take the lead, and he rose to the responsibility. One day he appeared at the door of the Kinsellas' house and declared that he would drag Ryan into the twentieth century "kicking and screaming if necessary." Later he would say, "I never got him quite all the way in, but I did get one foot over the threshold and nail it down."

When Collin took Ryan back to his house that day, everything had changed. Collin talked of things—new, strange things that stirred Ryan's blood as his own recounting of ancient tales had once stirred Collin's. He told of articles he was reading in magazines he now subscribed to—the *New Yorker, Esquire,* and *Atlantic Monthly.* He mentioned popular singers and music, and showed Ryan his new stereo, his records and cassettes. He and Ryan had their first beer together, a brand Collin had somehow procured from Colorado. He was wearing new clothes; he had stocked his shelves with American literature, and found poets in the bookstores of Harvard Square that Ryan had never heard of. His sword he had put in a closet and his copy of Lattimore's Homer was gathering dust.

Collin was now the tutor, and Ryan became both a student and a spectator of his friend's new lifestyle. Collin's other friendships multiplied rapidly. He started throwing poker parties to which he invited people he and Ryan would have scorned in earlier years, older schoolmates who had licenses, cars, motorcycles, even girlfriends—boys and girls who could barely utter four continuous words in their own language but could smoke and drink and dance and drive. When Collin grew bored of the fast crowd, he brought in people with intellectual pretensions of every kind. As Ryan watched and listened to this motley swarm of loungers and hangers-on who were attracted to the great house, he learned what it was that Collin had discovered about life, that it had color and adventure and excitement hidden even within the mundane. He did not forsake his Yeats, but he yielded readily to this new fascination with reality, especially when he encountered it in the form of the opposite sex.

He himself was quite hopeless with women in those days. When he had made his way over to Collin's on a Friday evening, he would chose the most interesting or the prettiest girl in the room and admire her surreptitiously during his visit without attempting to speak a word to her. Then on his walk home (for the sleep-overs had ended with boyhood, and both friends preferred their privacy) he would reconstruct her fine points and flaws in his mind, trying to decide if she might be *the one.* Somehow she never seemed to be. Fed as he was by ideal images, he was surprised to find real human beings built more of failings than of virtues.

From time to time he intruded himself boldly into the conversations in Collin's living room. His knowledge and his opinions were continually shocking to Collin's friends; at times he enjoyed this phenomenon, and at times it caused him pain.

Collin often expostulated with him to stop acting the pedant. "I wouldn't have to be the pedant if they were halfway educated," groused Ryan.

"At least *pretend* not to be a pedant, then," said Collin.

"I will—when they pretend not to be foolish," Ryan retorted.

No matter how alien and unintelligible he might be, Collin's crowd accepted him. They could see the strength of the bond that existed between their host and this strange, laconic figure who came and went at will in the Tate household. And the Tates, of course, were rich; and Ryan lived within their aura. He did learn, however, that it was he who was the misfit, not Collin's friends. And he learned to tolerate them, even sometimes to like them as people, even as he loved Collin. Furthermore, in the year or two after Collin ushered him into his new life, he learned to hold his liquor, to swear authentically, to talk at times like a punch-drunk boxer, and to conceal his intelligence when he wished to do so— all key social skills that he put to use later. Without Collin's tutelage, he would never have succeeded as he had in college.

❁ ❁ ❁

By the time Ryan was fifteen his father had nothing left to teach him. Daniel found that all he could add to Ryan's recitations were stale explanations of the Greek particles, which Ryan graciously endured, though he itched to disprove them out of Dennison. One night he overheard his parents talking in the kitchen. Said Daniel: "He's got that look in his eye, Maureen; the look a man has when he's been drawing very fondly at a bottle, and it's almost empty. He takes one last fond look, and one last fond drink, and then he throws the bottle aside and thinks of it no more."

"Yes," she answered. "I dare say he still respects us. We'd better stop teaching him now, before we earn his contempt."

So one rainy day in early fall Ryan and his father climbed into the Valiant, which was not so new anymore, and drove off to the university where Daniel had been schooled. Professor Ermin was expecting them; Professor Ermin of the old guard, the rear guard that takes the beating in the ongoing campaign for survival that classical philology has become. The earnest young scholars in the vanguard hardly know what sort of philistines and curs are snapping at their heels, what insolent deans and administrators are talking about "phasing out the department"; they have leisure for their arcane studies because the Professor Ermins of the world draw students by the hundred into the great circus of their lectures. Perhaps it is true that these Ermins teach off the notes they took in college; perhaps it is true that scholarship suffers in their hands; but they know Greek and they know Latin, and they keep the department alive. "I keep the lamp burning," Professor Ermin used to boast.

To Ryan when he drove up College Hill it seemed he was ascending Olympus. The men and women were gods and goddesses in yellow slickers; the ivy that rippled like the surface of the Tate's pond in gusts of wind was the amaranth or acanthus, the brick and limestone was ivory in his mind. He was ready to sell his soul if need be to walk on those paths, to pass through those archways, to sit in real classes and know for the first time (and his idealism was to receive a bitter disappointment here) the converse of peers as excited about knowledge as he was.

When they had parked on the narrow street in front of the classics department, he stepped out into a rain-filled gutter. A bell was ringing, classes were changing. A young woman in a hot-pink slicker hurtled into him and rushed away without apologizing, perhaps without noticing this boy of fifteen; but he saw her, smelled her blond hair, felt her chest brush against him as she flung herself on her way, bound somewhere and late. He thought of Dante's first meeting with Beatrice; this was his *Incipit vita nova.*

Daniel had practically to drag him toward the classics building and up the dark stairs of the entrance. He was in a daze; for a moment Daniel was afraid he would be overawed by the setting and make fools of them both. Within the building the gray day was made cheerful by warm light everywhere; a torrent of students descended from upper rooms, their quick footsteps sounding on the narrow, winding stairs; friendly voices carried from the library; in a pigeonhole of an office a stammering freshman could be heard torturing Horace as a graduate student goaded her on. Daniel gripped Ryan by the arm, and the two stood looking about them, one with nostalgic joy and the other with wonder.

When the stairs were clear they went up to Ermin's office. He sat at his desk, looking down his nose at a sheaf of student papers. Ill-health had shrunken his stout flesh, but his spirit was as feisty and full as ever. Introductions, reminiscences, invitations to be seated, closing of the door, clearing of the throat. Then the old professor cocked himself back in his chair as if ready to spring and spoke to the point. "So, young man," he said, "I hear you're thinking of applying here."

"Yes, sir."

"Your father tells me you're a powerful hand at Greek. Is that so?"

Ryan thought of the gods and goddesses in the classes even now beginning around them. He thought of the beauty dashing into a lecture hall somewhere, juggling her books in one arm as she stripped off the pink raincoat, looking for a seat; of a soft sweater over a soft form.

If he meant to win a place here, he had to rise now to the trial. The mist seemed to pass from before his eyes, and he grinned the Kinsella grin. "Try me," he said.

Professor Ermin pulled a copy of the *Agamemnon* off the shelf, opened it to the first choral ode, and handed it to him. "Read in meter and translate," he said. Ryan glanced at the page, snapped the book shut, and recited the ode in flawless rhythm from memory. Then he translated, instantaneously, from the Greek etched in his mind.

"I see you know your Aeschylus," said Ermin noncommittally. He chose an obscure passage in one of the later books of Livy; and though the boy did not have this by heart, he translated it in a bold, amplifying style that raised several interesting points of interpretation. Ermin went back to Greek, choosing the *Oration on the Crown*. Ryan reduced the syntax to sound English sense without faltering. A random page of the *Annales* followed; then more poetry. Perhaps the rusticisms of Theocritus could throw him—no. Perhaps he would stumble on the plateau of Plato, or in the argot of Aristophanes. No. More dramatists. The thickets of Thucydides? A little late Greek? Fragments from Ennius? The *Hymn of the Arval Brotherhood?* Ryan spat idioms right and left. His father sat by, his jubilation tempered by amazement as he considered what his son had become.

A long quiz began on literary history. For this Ryan had been well primed in Lesky and Schanz-Hosius. There was nothing left to do but begin an examination in the secondary literature; but at the first question, Daniel spoke up as on cue, for father and son had rehearsed this between them. "I just had him read the texts, Professor," he said. "I remember you always used to say, 'The texts, the texts are the most important thing. Don't read Wilamowitz until you've read all the Teubners.' It's up to you to initiate him into scholarship." Ryan sat silent, virtuous not only in his knowledge but now as well in his pedagogical virginity.

But Ermin was silent too. Silent for a long time, looking Ryan full in the face; nor did Ryan ever flinch or rest his eyes away. At last the old man's hand went to the phone on the desk. He called the admissions department and asked for the director by name; he made an appointment for a private conference with him; and he hung up the receiver.

"Danny," he said, "I can't do much around here anymore. I'm old, and things have changed. There was a day I could have snapped my fingers and your boy would be in; but now, you know, they don't listen to us much. But I'll tell you something—" and his face went into spasms that foreboded the apoplexy he died of three years later—"if I don't get your son into this university, so help me God, heads will roll! Heads will *roll!* If those—" and he used a noun that was most unclassically Anglo-Saxon—"up there at Harvard get their clutches on this boy, it will be a sad loss for our alma mater, Danny." He took a grip on his temper, eyeing Ryan again. "You have a good chance to make a name for yourself in classical philology," he told him bluntly, "and I want our brand on you. Tell me something, son. If they came to you from Harvard today and said, 'We've got a place for you'—what would you do?"

"I'd tell them to go to hell, sir," said Ryan loyally.

Ermin grinned. Then he caught himself and frowned. "Well," he said, "that would be a mistake." And then, his duty done, he laughed broadly.

He sent them off to see the campus. Ryan peered under the hood of every pink raincoat they passed, and heard not a word his father said. But Daniel was raving anyway, drunken with the success of his parental labors, and feeling already the sting of grief at losing this son and pupil to the care of others. He found a phone booth to call the news home to Maureen; and a fifteen-year-old boy, in somewhat worn best clothes, under a ragged umbrella, swiveled around like a weathervane on the gusty street, furtively watching women too sophisticated even to notice his attention.

Saturday, June 20/Five

It is hardly too much to say that we all of us occasionally speak of our dearest friends in a manner in which our dearest friends would very little like to hear themselves mentioned; and that we nevertheless expect that our dearest friends shall invariably speak of us as though they were blind to all our faults, but keenly alive to every shade of our virtues.

—Trollope

But how is it
That this lives in thy mind? What seest thou else
In the dark backward and abysm of time?

—*The Tempest*

WHEN HE CEASED speaking, Constance still lay motionless on the sofa for a few minutes, face down in the waves of her dark hair. Then she sat up and looked toward him. Night had come on; she was a shadow.

"You have a beautiful voice," she said.

He did not respond. He thought suddenly of Eve. She had listened to him like this too, as if drugged, straining to catch every word, coaxing him to speak and not to stop. And he realized for the first time that his voice could weave a net around a heart.

"I was afraid you'd fallen asleep," he said.

"No, I heard every word."

They sat without speaking for several minutes.

"Well," he said, "you should tell me about *your* past. Since we seem to be in a confessional mood here."

"There really isn't much to tell."

"I don't for a minute believe that. Everyone has a story."

"Maybe so," she admitted. "But I can't tell mine. It's locked up inside me; I can't get at it myself. I know it's there, I can feel it; but I can't get it out. I've tried before. When Collin first started writing to me he asked me to tell my story; but I couldn't seem to gather it all up at once and get it on paper."

"So you intend to tell me nothing?"

She was troubled by this reproach.

"I know what I can do," she said after a moment's thought.

"What's that?"

"Come with me," she said, standing. Then she added archly: "Unless you think it's improper to go to a lady's bedroom."

"Of course it is," he said, rising from the armchair. "But that won't stop me. Anyway, Mrs. Overton will be delighted."

She giggled and led the way. A light had already been switched on in the upper hall; by its light they made their way upstairs to her room. When he had entered she closed the door behind him.

"This *is* a secret conference," he said. "I feel honored."

"You should. I've never shown anyone else the things I'm going to show you now. They're sacred to me. But I know you'll respect them."

She went to her dresser and took a little key from a jewelry box there. As she was turning away she noticed herself in the mirror. "Slight delay," she said, flashing him an apologetic smile. She took up a hairbrush and applied herself vigorously to correcting some imaginary dislocation of her tresses. Ryan watched in fascination. She caught sight of him in the mirror and blushed. He turned away.

It was strange to be here in this room now that she had taken possession. It had been intended for her years ago, but she had never lived in it. Not an item in it was anything but pink—the floral pattern of the paper, the dust ruffles on the furniture, the curtains, even the carpet had predominately rose-colored strands worked into it. Although it had been long disused, it had always been a reminder of the mysterious girl who was absent in a foreign land. A girl become a woman, who stood brushing her hair in front of the mirror that until a short time ago had never reflected her face.

"It's a little too pink, don't you think?" she said, observing him looking about the room.

"Yes. Your parents overdid it."

"You mean my parents decorated it? I thought it went much further back than that."

"The story I heard was that when they knew they were having a child they decorated one room pink and one room blue just to be ready for either eventuality. Then they wound up using the blue room for both of you—I guess that was easier."

"The blue room? You mean Collin's old room?"

"Yes."

"It's not so relentlessly blue as this place is pink."

"There's one thing that isn't pink," he said, nodding at the bed. A lacy, skimpy, and incongruously black brassiere lay on the bedspread.

She laughed and hid it away in her dresser with another arch smile.

"That's what I get for inviting you in here!" she said. "Now," she went on, "it's time for you to be serious. Go on, sit down."

"Where?" he asked, looking around.

"On the bed, silly."

He took a seat there somewhat diffidently, but made no comment.

"You will be serious, won't you?" she asked.

"Yes," he said quietly.

Satisfied, she went to one side of the room. He had noticed that Collin's yearbook picture hung here in a carved wooden frame; now he realized that it bore a connection to the mahogany box that stood on a table beneath it, and to the two candles on the table, which had been mounted in holders he recognized as Tate family heirlooms. The image of the altar occurred to him again.

"Light those candles much?" he asked.

"Once I did," she answered, as she unlocked the box and began to look through it. "Collin had just given me some poems to read. I thought the candles might help set the mood—help me understand what he had been writing about."

She hesitated in making her selection from the contents of the box; but as she chose what she wished and gathered it in one hand, he realized that the box was full of the letters and poems Collin had sent her over the years. Next she stooped and looked through some cardboard letter files underneath the table; Ryan knew that these were her letters to Collin, in his filing system. She must have begged them from him temporarily. Ryan had known they wrote regularly, but still found the volume of their correspondence surprising.

"You two wrote one another quite a bit, didn't you?"

"Once a week for the past three years," she said. "And sometimes two or three times a week, when we were inspired. You can see how much thicker Collin's letters were." She held up one envelope to demonstrate; it was far thicker than the others. "I numbered his, from the first one. There are two hundred and six." He whistled under his breath appreciatively, and she was pleased. "The letters that I wrote are really more *me* than anything I could tell you about myself."

After more hesitation, she culled some photographs from the wooden box. Then she brought them over, perching beside him on the bed.

First she showed him the photographs, laughing softly. There were three, and Ryan was in every one. He laughed aloud. "You see, I really have known you for years and years," she said. "Here you are with your war gear." She indicated a picture from about ten years ago: he and Collin leaning easily on their spears, Collin already a little taller, broader in the shoulder, but Ryan thicker through the legs. "There we are," agreed Ryan, shaking his head. "It's a wonder we weren't locked up. Look at those spears! We made them out of ash and hardened them in a fire. We did everything right. We were perfectionists even in fantasy."

He looked at another photograph. It was earlier—one of Collin's birthday parties, perhaps his fifth. Various rude little boys and a forgotten girl sat around the oaken table; Ryan had a place of honor near the birthday boy. "I wonder what you were doing on that day," he said to Constance.

"I was with a crowd of adults, my mother's friends. That's the way all my birthdays were. They were parties for her, really."

"That must have been pretty boring for you."

"Dreary! *Really* dreary."

The third photograph dated from about five years ago. It showed the boys sitting in a convertible sportscar that belonged to one of Collin's older friends. They were wearing borrowed sunglasses and trying to look suave.

"My God," exclaimed Ryan, "I'd forgotten about that one. That's when I was practicing my act for college, I guess." He turned it over; Lloyd Tate had scrawled, "Coll hamming it up with Ryan." He handed them back to her with an unhappy glance. "It's sad to think that all you had to go on was photos like these," he said.

"Yes, that was all I had," she said. "At least until Collin really started writing me in earnest." She looked the photographs over fondly one more time. "All right," she said softly. She took up the first letter in the stack. It was preserved in its original envelope, in the corner of which she had written "No. 1." She drew forth several sheets of expensive writing paper covered with Collin's script, and glanced over them, as if hesitating to entrust them to anyone else. "Here," she said finally, with a shy smile at him. "It's his first." She thrust the pages into his hands and then fell back on the bed as if to give him privacy. He read:

June 3, 1978

Dear Constance,

  We have written before—I have each of your birthday greetings, Christmas cards, the letter you sent when I broke my leg—so I cannot claim this is the first letter between us. But for all we have said of importance it might as well be. Let this be the first letter, the inaugural letter of our friendship— because I do intend to be friends with you, if you want to be.

  After all, you are my sister. What other woman could be my friend first, before you? Do you ever think how strange it is

that you and I should have been conceived in and lived, pressed
against each other, for nine months in the same womb, been
born between the same legs, and now be utter strangers to each
other, so very estranged that I am sure we would not know one
another if we were to meet face to face without introduction?
Doesn't it seem to you that we were meant to be—"friends"
does not seem a strong enough word. Many share a womb; but
to share a womb *at the same time,* to share every varying ebb
and flow in the tides of the womb for nine months, and then to
be completely severed even from sight of each other, forever—
to how many does this happen? And that you are a woman, and
I a man—doesn't that argue for our being two halves of one
greater unity?

Perhaps you think I am crazy, speaking like this. I don't
even know you well enough to guess how you will respond
to my thoughts. Behind the pleasantries we have exchanged,
we could be any kind of people. That's why I would like to do
away with the pleasantries once and for all, and say, here I am,
your brother. Give me a name yourself if you like. Your mother
gave me Collin, my father gave you Constance. We ourselves
have to give each other names—names in the heart, not names
on the tongue.

I suppose that from the very first I endowed your
name with great meaning. Think—as you must have, often
enough—how the word Constance has come to be given as a
name: by men and women who thought to bestow the attribute
along with it, because they had cause in their own lives to hunger after that which is, more than all else, beyond attainment in
human affairs: the unchangeable, the constant, the permanent.
For me over the years your name has come to stand for the
steady promise of my unknown sister—my constant invisible
companion—always there, waiting to be known and truly
loved, ready to be the confidant of all my hopes. And yet, even
though I know in my heart that this is true, my mind is suspicious of the unknown, and is not above torturing me with the

occasional doubt—can I picture you laughing at this letter, or baffled by it? No—no, Constance, I cannot.

I will tell you, then, the most important things about me. I could tell you what you know or have surmised about me, the particulars that have a place in any effort we make to become acquainted; but I would rather that their place be later. Strange it may seem, but I can put almost everything I want to say in one word: *poet*. I am a poet. But then I have to explain what that means.

It means an eye held open, no matter what the brightness of the vision, or its soul-besieging darkness, to a middle place beyond the real and just this side of the ideal, a zone where objects, events, and emotions partake of both the actual and the theoretical, where they are partly external and partly in the mind; where they are recognizable as that which is familiar, but are cloaked in metaphor that gives them greater meaning, that binds them into the web of life, showing their relationship with every other thing. The eye of the poet must look beyond and within everything without fear and without regret at losing the comforting familiarity of the common vision.

But that is only the first part of the meaning of the word poet. There is the next part, after the eye has pierced to the point of truth and stolen that image away into the mind. The mind must then translate the vision into another medium, which will allow the eye of the uninitiated to see as the poet has seen. The poem is a negative image, in a sense, a die that stamps its reverse into the reader's mind; or better, say it is a transparency that allows the new light of the poet's understanding to shine into that unquiet place.

You think I am an arrogant person, to talk this way. Not arrogant, but impassioned—willing to believe in the profession I have chosen (it would do more justice to my feelings to say that it chose me) no matter how absurd I may seem. You may say, what is this vision? Is it not much like blindness, that cannot see the shapes of things immediately before the eye? I hope to show you, as time goes by, that it is not arrogance, nor blindness. It is a belief in the great sadness that is the beauty of death; in the great joy that is ugliness of life.

But what credentials, you ask, can a young man of seventeen bring to this endeavor? Scant ones, I admit. I have no pretensions of superior virtue: I am just as mired in the demands of the flesh and of petty personal politics as everyone else. Nor do I affect superiority through whatever intelligence I may possess, for I do not believe that an individual's ability to articulate this vision of the middle distance makes him or her a better person "in the eyes of God" (that is, in some absolute sense) than the mute or the unprivileged. My sole credential is my will to speak, my desire to find whatever is best in me, and to put it on the page. And if you find truth written with sincerity and understanding on the page, you may be sure that it exists somewhere, however hidden or halting, inside the writer. People could be found who would gladly point out the faults in my personal life; but no such attack can detract from the value I demonstrate on the page as a human being. And there is no long-woven cloth of words that does not have its glib detractor. I only hope to offer the best in me, such as it is, to the view of those who wish to see it; and I understand how few these are.

I hope that you are one of them. Your answer will tell me at once; and if you choose not to answer, that, too, will tell me. I feel that I have risked much here; but perhaps not: those who have no power to understand our dreams have no power to hurt them. But I know, I feel somehow, that you will understand.

Dear, unknown sister, all my love.

Collin

After this a folded typescript page had been included. As Ryan came across it he realized that it was one of Collin's poems. "Should I read this, too?" he asked quietly. She knew what he meant without looking, and she touched his arm in a way that told him he should. He opened it and found this:

Inaugural Prayer

A tear of rain driven down the glass
divides
into two wandering drops

I would draw a track to unite them
but I stand inside the window
and cannot touch them
can only watch
as each part severed
goes on to trace its path alone
until descent inevitably ends
and other rain, other sun
washes and dries away those courses forever.

Sister, sister
you who were driven from my life
put your finger forth on your side of the glass
and mark a path for us to meet.

To Ryan this poem seemed surprisingly juvenile, although he found the sentiment touching, considering its personal context. But of this reaction he said nothing. In fact, he was afraid of offering any comment at all, lest he disappoint Constance's expectations. He waited to see if she would speak first.

She took his silence as the hesitation of one who has been deeply moved. She sat up and put her hand lightly on his arm. "Isn't it beautiful?" she asked.

"You must have been very pleased and surprised to receive this letter out of the blue," said Ryan. In corroboration she handed him the next letter, her own reply to Collin. It was not numbered, and the envelope had apparently been discarded; it bore a date around a week subsequent to her brother's. Here for the first time Ryan had a full sample of Constance's handwriting. It was better than Collin's, insofar as it was clearer, more uniform, and obviously better schooled.

"I was only seventeen when I wrote it, remember," she said. As before, she lay back on the bed to make her presence less of a hindrance to him. In fact her reclining posture had the opposite effect, but he focused on the letter and read:

Dear Collin,

Your letter makes me very afraid. But not afraid *of* you, or of knowing you. It's just that I am not what you are, a poet. I don't know how to begin to answer you, and you must have mercy on my inability to write the way you do, and remember always that I love you, even though I hardly know you. Don't give up on me because I write poorly. I read very well, and anything you wish to write to me will be read a hundred times and treasured forever.

It is strange that you should write me, because often lately my thoughts have been full of you. My thoughts are all questions. I hope you will forgive me if many of them were petty, personal things. The last picture I have of you is from two years ago, and I would very much like to be able to imagine you as you are now, sitting in the house in the valley as you write. But I could never send you a picture of myself, because there are no good ones. That horrible one that mother sent—I could cry when I think about your having it.

There, you see, I have gone ahead and done what I never wished to do, and written about "the shapes of things immediately before the eye," as you put it. But your poor sister can hardly do anything else. I do not have the vision you do. Please don't think I am just a silly schoolgirl. I love poetry, I always have. I think I must have been made that way to be, as you said, the other half of you, to read what you write. I cannot tell you what your poem meant to me. I cry every time I read it, and I read it several times a day. I have memorized it, I have read it so often. I keep it with your letter in my jewelry box, but if you send me more, I shall buy a box especially for your letters.

I am glad that you like my name. Until your letter I always wondered about it, why anyone would want to name his daughter that. I always thought that our father chose it because he knew Mother was going to leave him, and it was sort of a reproach to her. But what you have said makes me sure that I was called Constance to be constant to my twin brother. I will always be the friend you are seeking. I will have no secret from you. You are right. We were made together, and grew together from the first. We are really one person.

Your name I have always loved. It always seemed magical and musical to me, like the ringing of the bell in the little church near the house where we lived when I was growing up. I can't tell you the number of times I lay in my bed in that house while the bell tolled, thinking that it was saying "Col-lin, Col-lin" over and over. You will think I am being silly, I know. Mother told me that she chose the name because it sounded uppercrust. That was what she said. I prefer to think of it my way. Isn't it strange how she chose your name, and Father chose mine, and when they were divorced I went with her and you with him? But I don't understand all of that anyway. I have enjoyed growing up in Spain, but I have had many American friends, and from the way they talk, it sounds like America would be much more fun for me. And Mother always says the valley is such a beautiful place.

In answer to all you have written about your being a poet, all I can say is that I know you are certainly a poet after reading the poem you sent. I believe in you completely. I could never think that you were "absurd" or "arrogant," as you seem to think. I could only think so if I were absurd and arrogant myself. One of my teachers quoted someone once who said that contempt is voiced most loudly by the contemptible. I know I will never be so contemptible as not to love everything you do and every word you write.

What else can I tell you about myself? There is hardly anything. I am going to the English School here because

Mama says it is better than the other schools. But the classes are longer here and the work is very hard. I have two years to go, because I had to lose a year when I came here—that's how much harder it is. Mother says you will be finished your senior year at high school by June of next year. I wish I could be through then, too. I don't know if I will survive Chemistry. I bet you are good at it, because I bet you are good at everything you put your mind to. What college will you be going to, or is it too early to ask? I had better stop all this drivel, or you will be fed up and never write.

Please, please, dear Collin, write me again. I send you all my love.

Love,
Constance

Ryan's first thought was how addictive such insistent praise and humility would be for anyone, but particularly for someone like Collin, who felt his ego was at risk in every poem. He would know that any poetry he sent Constance would be read repeatedly; that she would weep over it.

Next it struck him how determinedly they addressed one another with endearments. They had clearly meant from the start to find companionship in one another. "Dear unknown sister," wrote Collin. "Please, please, dear Collin," she implored him, and sent him all her love. It was too much; it had the ring of desperation.

And finally, he found curious the strained quality of her prose. Each sentence had been written deliberately, and the patience with extended ideas that Collin demonstrated in hypotaxis she seemed never to have acquired. She herself even observed that she was too easily distracted. Yet he found the style of her letter much fresher that Collin's verbosity, which (he was vaguely aware) was not unlike his own.

She sat up beside him.

"I won't show you Collin's second letter," she said. "Not that there's any reason I shouldn't, but I can't show them all. But I will

show you this. This was the poem he sent with his second letter." She drew a sheet of typing paper from the envelope marked
"No. 2."

"Does he always send a poem when he writes?" he asked.

"Always," she said. "Except once he didn't. That was horrible. At first I thought something had gone really wrong. But
he was just awfully busy with exams and just wanted to get a
note off quickly. It isn't always a new poem that he sends me.
He says it makes him nervous to send me poems he's just written. He might want to change them the minute the mailbox
closes. He quoted me something from Thomas Wolfe once—
you know him? He's one of Collin's favorite writers—about
someone writing a letter to a woman he wanted to see again,
and it got to be about ten pages long; and the minute he put
it in the mailbox, he felt it was the stupidest thing he'd ever
written in his life."

"And she called the guy up the next morning when she got it,"
said Ryan. "He was still in bed, as I recall. So he shouldn't have
worried. And neither should Collin."

"He didn't tell me that part," she said, smiling.

He turned his eyes to the poem.

On Receiving Word

Day broke along
long hills
Birds shook feathered limbs
on the leafy limbs of trees
Stalk and bud of rose
rose bursting in bloom
when I heard constant
Constance was my sister again.

"Isn't it beautiful?" she asked again. He thought a smile might
be sufficient response. Fortunately she did not wait for an answer;
she fed him the next letter, one of her own.

Dear Collin,

When your letter came I was so glad I could barely wait until I had escaped from Mother and could get away to my own room and read it. She always wants to grill me about my day, and there is never much to say, and I always have so much schoolwork to do. She wanted to know why we are writing all of a sudden. I must lock your letters away or she will come into my room when I am at school and read them, and I would hate that.

After I read it I just lay on my bed. I felt as if I couldn't move, not one muscle. I cried just thinking about all the things I had missed. Your childhood sounds so beautiful. Mine was not like that. I can't tell you. I wish I could write the way you do. But even if I could, what would there be to tell? About parties I was taken to, where I was fussed over and sent around from grown-up to grown-up, or left to play with horrible children who made fun of my accent or my English if I forgot. Mama was always trying out new men. I don't mean that the way it sounds, but she always had someone who liked her and thought that because she was American and of independent means that he could get whatever he wanted from her. But I don't think Mama ever really wanted anything from these men but company. She wanted to be able to boss them around and feel like she controlled them, but she didn't want any kind of real, serious relationship, because then they might be able to control her. Or at least that's the way I see it.

Maybe I have made her sound like a bad person. She's not, not at all. She has a temper, and the sharpest tongue I ever heard, but underneath it all she's just a little girl. The older I get the more I see it. We went through a bad phase a while ago, but we're over that now. That's normal, isn't it? She loves me more than anything on earth. If anything ever happened to me she would kill herself. And I know she misses you. She has your picture on her dressing table. She tells me that you look like me, which is of course absolutely absurd.

I keep trying and trying to tell you the important things, but I keep wandering away from what I really want to say. I think of starting over, but I know I would never be able to write anything better.

You ask me about my childhood. I wrote you about the house near the church. That was in Seville. We lived there till I was fourteen. The street was very quiet. There was a little balcony in mother's room that looked over the garden behind us. It wasn't ours, but the old man who owned it let me play there. He really was very sweet. He had no children of his own, and he used to pretend he was my grandfather. Did you ever meet our real grandparents? (I mean Mother's parents.) That is, that you can remember? I was sorry to learn from your letter about Aunt Evelyn. I told mother about it (it was the only thing from your letters I have told her) and she said she was a very nice woman—very intelligent, she said. But she also said that she and Aunt Evelyn never got along.

I'm wandering again. How do you concentrate so well? I envy you that. I'm sure that if I read your letters long enough, I will write better myself.

You mentioned your best friend, Ryan. It must be wonderful to have a friend like that. The oldest friend I have here is an American girl, Joanna Littleford. She's eighteen. She's going back to the States at the end of this year. Her father's some kind of a military person. I've known her for all of two years. Compare that to all the time you've known your friend. But somehow it seems to me that the valley—at least, this is the way I imagine it—is a kind of place where friendships last forever. Will I ever see it? Or will I be so old and gray that it will be too late for me to have friends there, to be friends with you there?

You see what a mess I have made out of your "commission" that I write you about my past. I suppose I am so busy with my present that the past doesn't matter to me. As for the future, my greatest hope is to meet you someday and walk through the valley with you.

Dear Collin, if you think of it, and if you are forgiving enough of the poor return I made you, will you write me a little about Father? And I know it is despicable of me, but if you would send me your photograph? You have no idea how much it would mean to me. I would make a shrine for it. You laugh at me. Laugh all you like—I only wish I could hear your laughter. I would make you laugh if we were together. I know it, and you would think me far more intelligent and far more sophisticated than I really am. Mother tells me I'm ugly sometimes, and other times she tells me I'm the most beautiful thing that ever lived, but mothers always say that kind of thing. Still, I think you wouldn't be ashamed of me. It's only on paper that I make such a pathetic fool of myself.

I have saved to the very end saying anything about the poem you sent. You tell me that it is not enough to say that I cried over it, and that you want an "in-depth critique." I practically cry again in a different way when I read that phrase. Dear Collin, I just don't know what to say. The two poems you have sent me mean more to me than anything in the world. Even if you are fed up with me because I am no poet, and never send me another poem, I will still treasure them all the rest of my life. If you were here and could see my tears you would think that was enough of a response to them, I know you would. You are the voice, and I am the ear. It's the way you said in your first letter, we are two halves. Please, please don't stop writing. I beg you to write me again.

Constantly yours,
Your Constance

Ryan could sympathize with Collin in this respect, that it must have been frustrating to eke out any organized picture of his sister's life from this meandering catalog of thoughts, whims, and feelings. But he envied Collin these letters, the boxes full of them.

"You and Collin have written so much," he commented.

"Collin more than me."

"But look at these boxes! How can you say you're not a writer?"

"Letters hardly count."

"You must write other things too."

"I have a journal. Collin encouraged me to start one. So far I think I've managed to keep my mother from seeing it."

"There—a journal. They say that's the start of a career." His tone changed suddenly. "Will you write me when I'm in England?" he asked.

"Of course I will," she said. "But don't talk about that. It's no fair talking about that—that's after the summer's over."

"I wish this summer would never end," he said, as if to himself.

"Why? Don't you want to go to Cambridge?"

"Oxford," he corrected her.

"Oh, that's right. It's your friend who's at Cambridge. But don't you want to go there?"

"Do you want to go off to school?" he countered. "And leave Collin?"

"No," she said, seeing what he meant." I wish we could all three of us just stay here."

"We'll have to open a university," he said. "I could offer courses in Greek and poetic dissection. You could teach Spanish and guitar."

"And Collin could be poet in residence," she said. "And what about Papa?"

"He'd be in charge of writing grants and funding in general."

"And Mama?"

He was stumped.

"Don't worry," she said. "We'll find a job for her. Purchasing agent or something.—I suppose Mrs. Overton would supply the refectory?"

"Exactly."

It was a happy fantasy, but faded away as rapidly as it had come. She produced the last letter; but apparently she did not mean to show him this in its entirety. Instead she glanced over it and selected one sheet from about a half dozen. He saw it was numbered in the late hundred-sixties, and that Collin had abandoned handwriting with the acquisition of his electronic typewriter. By way of introduction Constance said: "Something you said in your 'lecture' last night made me think of this. I found it again this morning." The sheet she had handed to him began and ended in mid-sentence:

what he knows. The man was absolutely a philistine. Steve and I opened our guns on him and reduced him to a pile of rubble pretty quick. To hell with their damn funding! We were *not* about to listen to that from anybody. What the whole episode really reminded me of was a passage in a letter I had just received from Ryan. The subject is (obviously) not exactly the same, but it's related. Here it is:

We know well that the greater part of humanity passes up proffered knowledge and the profound pleasure of thought—and of reverie—for the hasty satisfactions of mass-produced entertainment. There is no way to reach such people, for their span of attention is not long enough to grasp and retain the various elements of an intricate message. Once such people flocked to the circuses of Rome; now they gawk at electronic violence. But our forebears have so packed our libraries—those tabernacles of knowledge—with wisdom and with delight for the imagination, that time spent before so niggardly an altar as television is almost criminally squandered. Life is too short for television. The doors of the tabernacle are open; you may plunder it of knowledge ascetic or sensual, as your will or your whim or your wants lead you, and never sate yourself. The books, the art, and the music of the past are all the mind needs to thrive and to create anew. And the creative act of the mind (or the re-creative, to put it more accurately) is no less ecstatic than the creative act of the body.

Now, is this or is this not nobly put? A little on the defensive side, but if you study the classics, you get that way, I suppose. I liked the final sentence so well that I wrote a poem using the idea. I would send it to you, but if Mother ever raids your letter box again, she'd probably flip reading it.

Anyway—back to the subject. After we told Bernstein off, we had nowhere to go for money.

This was all that he was allowed to see. He read it several times, intently, and still felt no readiness to give it up. He found himself a little hurt by the comment about classicists. He also was chagrined that he was quoted to Constance out of context. He remembered the letter distinctly; it had not been an attack on the philistines so much as a dismissal of them, made in passing as he encouraged Collin to read more in the older authors.

While he was mulling over the letter, she went to the mahogany box and found another. She gently tugged the one he was holding from his fingers and then offered him another single page, which bore the number 186. "I just thought of this," she said. "It's another one where he quotes you." He took it without a word, wondering as he did so if he would find it painful.

Mr. Dilton wants me to try my hand at short stories. He says I have the knack for the little twist of resolution, and I of course am very flattered and hem and haw and think about it. He wants some entries for a contest someone he knows is running, and he thinks it would be good for the program here if they could rack up some prizes. But fiction revolts me. It just isn't *truth*. I know Wolfe is always going on about getting at the truth in fiction, and God knows he knew what he was talking about; but just look at what a poet he was himself, at least at heart.

So in this quandary, this state of temptation, so to speak, I wrote to Ryan—I suppose because I knew exactly what he would say. He is so predictably sententious about all things modern. I mean, I respect his point of view; but he is so rigid, so stuck in the past. Look at what he had to say. Really, he is a great friend, and I have great affection for him—I know you two will hit it off when you finally get yourself over here—but

I really have to laugh when I reread this. He's so paranoid about new things; I suppose contact with me has made him so. Here he is on his soap box:

> Call me a snob if you will, but I believe that short stories as a general rule are written by people with short attention spans for people with short attention spans. The fascination of the present age with short stories is like the fascination of the Alexandrians with the epyllion, the little epic, as opposed to the great epic. Like the Alexandrians, the writers of today lack the courage, the vision, the patience that sticking to a vast artistic enterprise requires. Had Homer lived in an age so artistically pusillanimous, Achilles would have sulked forever, and Odysseus would have lived agelessly with Kalypso. Had Michelangelo possessed so little persistence, all but a corner of the Sistine Chapel would be bare. Had Melville flagged as his task expanded, Moby Dick would never have been sighted.
>
> Of course, I do not forget the multitude of great writers who tried their hand at the 'eidolon,' the 'little picture' instead of the big one—whether Tolstoy or Faulkner or whoever. They proved elsewhere that they could handle the great work of a novel. But these writers who spring out of nowhere nowadays, with nothing but short stories to offer, no intention of writing anything but short stories—all I want to say to them is, 'Give me the development of a novel, give me character, give me motivation, give me sustained plotting. Your short stories are a flash in the pan—feeble fireworks where I want creative sunlight, a sisterly kiss to the passions of sexual love, a promise that breaks itself in the act of utterance.'

His overreaction is absurd, but he states his case so clearly it's enough to make one forever give up the idea of writing short stories. I wonder what he would write another friend about *my* poetry. He's too kind to do anything in my presence other than mutter a few hints that I should try to write in meter.

To Ryan, to be accused of paranoia seemed a brutal judgment. Clearly Constance did not remember the tone of the letter, or she would never have given it to him; or she was so blinded by her adoration of her brother that she did not think how his candid statements might hurt. Not that Ryan had not heard the same sentiments from Collin himself; but somehow, to see them in cold carbon ribbon, in a letter to Constance, was difficult for him to accept.

For a minute he struggled with his feelings; but then he rose to the occasion and forgave his friend. There certainly was some truth in what he said; the bizarre education his parents had given him had led him to demand more from the world at large than it was capable of giving.

He handed the letter back to her with genuine humility and said, "I'm glad he takes my advice with a generous dose of salt." She did not quite comprehend what he meant, but he thought that just as well. To distract her from glancing over it again, he said, "You'd better put those back in the box before something happens to them." She seemed pleased at the thoughtfulness of his suggestion, and refiled the letters at once. Then she came and sat by him again, but turned slightly this time so that she could see him.

"It was kind of you to share those with me," he said.

"I can't think of anyone else that would understand them better than you."

"I can't either," he said, with more meaning than she appreciated.

"I suppose we should go back downstairs before my mother comes home and finds us in my bedroom together."

"If she's upset, just tell her we'll name the baby after her."

"Ryan!" she giggled. "You shouldn't say things like that!"

"Why not?"

"Because they're outrageous, and you know it. Our relationship is completely Platonic."

"So far," he admitted, with his trademark smile.

She laughed aloud and pushed his arm playfully. He had a momentary impulse to seize her, as Collin had at the pond, and tickle or tease or wrestle with her, but he sensed that she would be frightened if he did.

"No, you're right," he said now in mock alarm. "We'd better go downstairs right away. And whatever you do, don't tell my mother I was in your bedroom." She laughed again, tugged him to his feet, and together they went into the hall. At that moment they heard the Mercedes in the drive; in astonishingly rapid succession the engine was switched off, the car doors opened and closed, and the screen door creaked wide.

"Oh, God," she whispered. "We can't just appear from upstairs together. She'll give me all kinds of grief."

"Are you serious?"

"Yes. I know it sounds weird, but it's true."

"Just tell her Mrs. Overton said it was okay."

"Sshh! What are we going to do?"

Steps could be heard on the tiles; it seemed that someone would soon confront them.

"The back stairs," he said.

"Now you've got me sneaking around," she joked, turning in that direction.

"Don't worry," said Ryan. "Even if we do get caught, they always believe the first lie."

"How would you know about that?"

"I've done this kind of thing a lot."

"Oh, right, Señor Don Juan!"

They crept down the back stairs. They could tell now that Sondra was ascending the front; they came out in the kitchen and tiptoed by the open door of Mrs. Overton's office, where the housekeeper was snoozing in front of the muted television.

"Where should we go?"

"Out on the lawn."

They continued through the kitchen and went out the back door. On the stoop she caught his arm and whispered in his ear. "This is dumb. Mother's window looks over the back."

At that moment the lights went on in Sondra's room and cast a patch of radiance on the center of the lawn.

"Follow me," he said. He led the way along a path between the foundation and the rhododendron by the stoop and brought her undetected to the end of the house. They then went around the porch to the driveway.

"Whew," she said. "That was the silliest nonadventure I ever had."

"Good practice, though," he pointed out. She laughed once more.

"I swear, Ryan Kinsella, you are the most—"

"Incorrigible," he suggested.

"Incorrigible, yes, the most incorrigible and outrageous person I've ever met. Do you ever stop kidding around?"

"You mean you don't think I'm a dull, paranoid old pedant?"

She demonstrated her opinion of this absurdity with another laugh. They strolled on toward the warm darkness of the front lawn.

"You mean you really don't think so?" he persisted. "You don't think I'm a bore?"

"I wish you'd come over and bore me every night like this," she said wistfully.

"Call me up," he said bluntly. "Do you think there's anything I'd rather do?"

"You *are* coming tomorrow? For dinner?"

"If I'm invited, I come. It's that simple."

"Of course you're invited. How many times do we have to tell you? At six tomorrow."

This seemed like the end of the evening. She stopped; he stepped ahead and turned. Was she reluctant to say goodnight? He could not tell.

"I love listening to you," she said. "I wish I had more to give in return."

"You give me all I could ask. Whatever you say, or do, or tell, is more than enough repayment."

"You're so sweet, Ryan."

"The feeling is mutual."

She laughed. "You never let anyone have the last compliment, do you?"

"Not if I can help it."

"I suppose you must be ready to go home?"

"If I have to."

"Honestly, it's impossible to tell what you're really thinking, you're so relentlessly gallant."

"The perplexity is mutual."

"Well, I suppose we'd better call it a night, then?"

"I suppose."

They were silent a moment, close to one another in the darkness, hardly more than shadows.

"Here is this feeling again," she said. "What is it? I have just one thing more to say to you, but I can't figure out what it is."

"I'll wait," he said calmly.

"Oh, no, you want to go, I know. I feel so silly. I'll decide what I'm thinking of someday. It's just this vague feeling, I can't explain it."

"Boredom?" he wondered.

"Oh, shush!"

"Well, I'm afraid I've overstayed my welcome. Let me walk you back to the house."

"Don't be silly," she said. The house was hardly a hundred feet away. "I'd offer to drive you home," she said.

"Except you don't have a license and you know I like to walk anyway."

"Exactly."

"Well, all right," he said. "Goodnight, I guess."

"Yes, goodnight. And thank you, Ryan."

"The pleasure was mine." He turned away.

"Will you go by the road, or through the woods?" she asked.

"I don't know. Does it matter?"

"Go by the woods. The road is too dangerous at night."

"You watch that big pine up there," he said, pointing to the lookout pine silhouetted against the night sky on the ridge. "If you see one lantern in it, I've gone by road; two, and I've gone by woods."

She laughed delightedly at this bit of foolishness.

"One if by road, two if by woods," he repeated. "Not one if by woods, or two if by road; not two if by road, or one if by wood, but one if by road, and two if by wood. Have you got that?"

She laughed again—bright, bright laughter in the dark night. "What nonsense!" she cried.

He began to move away, pausing every few yards to look back and say, "One if by road, and two if by wood."

When he was almost out of earshot he thought he heard her speak. He paused and called back, "Did you say something?"

"No," she said; he could tell she was fibbing. He was almost sure he had heard her say, "Come back; come back and speak more nonsense to me." But now she had turned and disappeared in the direction of the house.

He went on across the lawn and into the woods toward home.

Sunday, June 21/One

I cannot say 'tis pity
She lacks instructions, for she seems a mistress
To most that teach.

—*The Winter's Tale*

OF ALL THE ways of killing time, the cruelest is to torment it to death with boredom and idleness. Yet with only these shifts Ryan endured the day before the party. He had had so little experience with ennui that he little knew how painful it was; in the entirety of his life he had experienced it only during exam weeks. He did not know that by putting the limbs of Chronos on the rack, he only stretched that god to new lengths, and made him all the more superior an opponent to his own patience.

He was dressed in his best clothes—that is to say, the same clothes he had worn for years day in and day out, but washed as of this morning, a process that had skimmed yet more of the wale off his corduroy, and frayed the cuff of his sleeve dangerously close to utter disintegration—and his jacket lay across his desk, at the ready, although the day was far too hot to allow any reasonable person to put such an unseasonable covering on his back—when the telephone rang at quarter past five in the afternoon. Actually, the time was twelve minutes past the hour—he marked it to the minute, because he was looking at his watch, which lay on the pages of the Shakespeare he had been studying in a desultory fashion.

The bell was like a starting gun. His mother started, his father started, the cat started; only Ryan sat still, like some humorless commissar in the belly of a great bureaucracy brooding over the telephone that gives him his power.

"It's Ramscoe," said his father. "It's for me."

"Ryan, I think that's your uncle," said his mother, crossing the living room behind her husband. "I'll get it." Ryan saw at once what their game was. They wanted knowledge, control, the right to meddle. He was not about to let them have any of these.

He waited, letting the phone ring again without anxiety. As far as he was concerned, there were only two possibilities. It was Eve; or it was one of the Tates, wondering where he was. He could not risk missing their call out of his wish to avoid Eve's.

Both Daniel and Maureen were reaching for the telephone when he cast out one hand and gripped the receiver, holding them at bay with a calm, cold gaze. They halted and waited almost submissively. On the fifth ring he picked it up and in a dry, business-like voice said: "Hello."

"Hello?" said Constance's soft voice. "Is Ryan there?" She did not recognize him in his commissar mode.

"Speaking," he said, shooting a glance of command at his parents. They backed out as if he had cracked a whip in their faces, and Daniel shut the door behind them.

"Oh, hello!" she laughed, relieved. "I didn't recognize you."

"It's my secret voice," he said. "I keep it in a drawer in my desk."

"I think it's so formal when people say 'speaking.' Don't you?"

"I suppose. But I had a professor named 'Speeking,' with two *e*'s. He used to answer the phone by saying 'Speeking speaking,' and I can assure you it was quite comical."

She laughed as she imagined it, and perhaps because she did not know whether to believe him, and then went on: "How are you today? Are you ready for a Midsummer-Night's dream?"

"I certainly am. I had one last night, too; so I'm well prepared."

"A dream, you mean? What was it?"

"I mean our talk last night."

"Yes, wasn't that just the nicest time?—But, Ryan," she said, suddenly forlorn, "is there any chance I could meet you somewhere on your way over here? I want to ask you something."

"Name the place. The clearing? Is that too far?"

"I haven't been there yet. I don't know the way."

"You haven't been there yet! Hasn't Collin shown you the whole valley yet?"

"We haven't gotten around to it, really."

"Well, how about the pond?"

"That would be perfect. Is it any trouble for you to come through the woods?"

"You watch for the lanterns. Remember—"

"No!" she laughed, "Don't start that again, please!"

"All right. How does fifteen minutes, at the pond, sound to you?"

"I'll be waiting."

"I'll see you then."

When he had put down the receiver he might have been disposed to sit there a moment and relish the conversation; but a suspicion intruded upon his pleasure. He rose silently, pocketed his watch, took up his jacket, and stole to the door. He threw it open. Maureen was industriously straightening the covers on a worn armchair, and Daniel, much against all habit, was doing the same. They looked up guiltily.

Their duplicity was so obvious, and his mood so quickened and happy, that he burst out laughing at the sight of them. At this they looked even more contrite.

❁❁❁

He was accustomed to think of the valley as a place where many of the great rights and necessities of human life—company, air, light, sky, ample space to live and walk—were allowed to him, though to others of his class they were often circumscribed as luxuries. But he was not yet used to the thought that Constance was now part of these *aedis liberae*. And she changed all. The places sanctified by the past were alive again; her presence unwove memory and worked it anew over a fresh weft.

When he wound down through the woods toward the pond he heard a guitar. He did not recognize the piece; it was classical, rendered in a light, airy style that faltered only occasionally. He slipped out onto the beach slightly behind her, unnoticed, and kept still, watching her.

Apparently she was determined upon simplicity tonight, perhaps to avoid upstaging her mother; she wore a dress in a country style, simple enough but for belled pleats around the hem, which were then in fashion. She had kicked off her sandals and half hidden her feet by thrusting them into the sand. Her head was bent over the guitar, which she held almost as if embracing a living creature that languished in her arms. Her fingers pressed and plucked at the strings, forming delicate arches at the frets, coaxing and caressing where the wires crossed the humming mouth of the instrument.

He thought of all the things he had been trained to think of—of shepherdesses and sylphs, of dark Lorna in Doone Valley, of pale women in Yeats, even of Wolfe's "Dark Helen in my heart forever burning."

She sensed his presence and abruptly ceased playing, turning to him with a startled "Oh!"

"Hello," he said.

"I didn't hear you coming."

"Your playing is very good," he said.

"Not very; but you're kind to say it."

He sat down at a little distance from her.

"How old were you when you started taking lessons?"

"About eight."

"Really? That's impressive." He was about to say, "You shouldn't let all that talent go to waste"; but he hesitated for a moment, and she spoke first.

"Just don't tell me 'You should do something with your talent.' Everyone says that to me."

"Yuck," he said. "How could anyone say such a tactless thing?"

"I always tell them I *am* doing something with my playing— I'm enjoying it. Isn't that enough?"

"It is indeed. You have a sensible attitude."

She looked out over the pond. "It's a beautiful evening," she said.

"Yes, it is."

"Ryan," she said suddenly, "I have to talk to you about something."

"I'm here to listen."

"You have to promise me you'll be serious," she said. "Like last night."

"I promise."

She paused, still leaning over her guitar, and glanced nervously at him.

"It's just this," she said. "I . . . Ryan, do you think I'm stupid?"

He raised his eyebrows in surprise.

"No," he said, shaking his head. "No, I do *not* think you're stupid. In fact, I'm so far from thinking you're stupid that I feel inclined to scold you for even asking such a question."

"There," she said. "It's a stupid question."

"That's not what I mean. I mean that you should recognize and be grateful for your intelligence."

"Oh, I know," she said morosely. "I'm certainly grateful that I wasn't born unfortunate—you know: retarded or handicapped somehow. It's just that I keep comparing myself to you and Collin, and next to you two I'm a zero. Collin's a poet, and you're—you're a genius. There's no other way to put it. And I feel like Bottom, with an ass's head and nothing in it but straw."

"I'm not a genius," he said flatly. "Let's clear that up before we go any further. I like to think I'm a scholar. I try not to be a pedant. But I don't feel in danger of being a genius. Scholars tend to plod along. Some plod faster than others, but as a rule they don't fly. Geniuses fly. And as for Collin—well, yes, he's a poet, or at least—yes, all right, he's a poet. But these are only professions. Why should *you* feel your intelligence any less because *we* have professions?"

"That's just it! You both know what you're doing with your lives. Look at me—I'm twenty, and I still don't know."

"Do you think that's at all unusual? Not knowing what you want to do with the rest of your life at age twenty? Most people feel that way. You'll see that the minute you get to college. That's one of the things college is for. You can explore your inclinations."

"I don't have any inclinations, though."

"Nonsense. Everyone has inclinations."

"Not me," she said stubbornly.

"There are things you like, aren't there?"

"Liking things and being inclined to do something particular with your life are two completely different things."

"Tell me what you like."

"I can't."

"Come on, now."

"I'm serious. I don't have any great passions."

"Everyone does. You can't possibly not have passions."

"Like what? Give me some examples. What are your passions, aside from Greek and Latin? I don't have anything comparable to them."

"I don't just mean professional passions. You have to look at all the things you like and make something to do that includes as many of them as possible."

"So, what are the things you like?"

"Well, I like this valley and everything in it. Collin. Your father. Silly Mrs. Overton. Evenings like this. This pond. The look of ripples on the water. The sound of rain in the night. The wind in the trees. The smell of wool. I like the way a dog smells after it's been snoozing. I like hot tea; a fire; friends; a conversation you hear in the distance that you're about to join. I like books—great poetry. The vista of the past. Homer, Dante, Shakespeare, Yeats, the Bible. Livy and Catullus. Plato, and Cicero's philosophy. I like music. I like the way a soccer ball feels when you boot it and you know it's going to beat the goalie to that left corner and sink into the net. I like the way little kids look up at you, with big eyes. I like a woman's body. I like reading aloud. I like great art—old art. I like bronzes. I like the inscrutable smiles of the *kouroi*. I love trees, stones, walls, roads. I like pavement under your feet as you run. I like things that last. I like flowers, fruits—things that are beautiful for a day."

He paused here, suddenly fearing that his eager response would only dampen her spirits further. "Now, what about you?" he asked.

She thought for a moment, her face troubled.

"I like Spain," she said. "I could almost cry when I think about how much I miss Spain. But then I think about Collin and Papa and being here for the first time—my home, for the first time. I like . . . the valley. I like playing guitar when there's no one around to say I'm playing well or playing badly. I like sitting in cafés in the sun with a coffee, watching the people walk by. I like Shakespeare too. I like Collin's poetry. I like lying on his bed while he works and imagining what's going on in his mind. I love that big house, and all the creaky doors and the tiles that rattle in the front hall, and eating long meals around that big table.—But so what, Ryan? What good will all that do me?"

"It proves that you're drawn to certain things, the same way everyone else is. Those likes and dislikes add up—add up into inclinations—and you'll follow your inclinations into something that has meaning for you."

"I'd like to help people," she said. "I know that. I'd like to leave the world better than I found it. At least in some small way."

"There you are, then. An inclination—an ambition—and far nobler than mine. How will all my scholarship decrease the suffering in the world by one bit? There is something to be said for handing on the torch of knowledge, it's true; but those torches won't feed the hungry or heal the sick. The same goes for Collin's poetry. But you—you could be anything you want. You're not locked into a calling yet, the way we are. You could be a doctor, a lawyer helping the poor—there's nothing stopping you."

"Nothing except my own stupidity. I could never be a doctor. Think of all the things they have to know! And I was so bad at chemistry."

"I don't buy that," he said. "You could certainly do it if you wanted to. It's amazing what people do when they rise to the challenge of acquiring all the facts they need to go out and help people, when that's what they want to do. It's a great inspiration. When you really want something, you'll get it."

"But I don't know where I'm going or what I'm doing."

"You're going to school. That's all you have to know for now. You'll do your best, try out a few fields. You'll find something. And finding out what you don't want to do is worth a lot, too. If you really want to be a doctor, and you can't stand pre-med—"

She cut him off with an exasperated laugh. "Look," she said forcefully, "let's just get one thing straight: I'm not going to be a doctor. I could never be a doctor."

"All right—it was just an example. I was just saying you'll find out what you want to do and what you don't want to do."

"But you're missing the point."

"Well, okay, what *is* the point?"

"Well, for instance—why is it that I can't talk about my past the way you and Collin can? He's always asking me to, and you were asking me to last night. It's as if I have no past. It's as if I look back and except for a few isolated events, there's nothing. There's no magic there, the way there is when you talk, and when Collin writes."

"Maybe it's a consequence of living in the present. Maybe your memories just haven't been sparked. They're certainly in there. You can't help having memories. It has nothing to do with your intelligence."

"But Ryan, it's as if I have some secret locked inside of me that I can't speak. I don't even know what it is myself. I don't mean some dark, terrible secret—I mean just me, who I am. I keep wanting to call out to you and Collin to help me say it, unlock it."

"Well, maybe we will, if we can. But I think the key is in your hand. You can use that key any time you want."

"Do you think it would help if I took a course in autobiographical writing? Collin does. He said that should be my first choice of courses at college."

"My friend," said Ryan with some emotion, "I really don't view this as quite so much of a crisis as you do. If you want to take a course like that, it certainly won't do you any harm. But if you just took a little time to write about your past right now—if you sat down tomorrow, or the next day and organized your thoughts— I'm sure you'd see right away that what Collin does in his poetry is really just a matter of focusing clearly on a particular moment or event and—"

"But I'm not going anywhere," she said almost desperately. "I've come from nowhere and I'm going nowhere. I can write all I like, but there's nothing to tell. You have your Greek, and Collin has his poetry. I have nothing."

"Yes, I have my Greek," he said, finally becoming piqued, though his emotion made him speak only more gently to her, if intensely. "And do you know why I have my Greek? I'll tell you: Because it was shoved down my throat from the time I was three. You set yourself up against Collin and me because we've 'found' our calling, as you put it. I think of you as not opposed to us, but somewhere between us. I didn't find my calling, it found me. Collin, he's almost always wanted to write: I'll agree that he found what he wanted. But you're in between us, as of now. You haven't fallen victim to the necessity of continuing to do the only thing you can do well, and you haven't found the passion that will make you a slave to the opinions of others, the way Collin has. You still have time, to pick some better work between our extremes: something that you can master, not something that will master you. Something you're content with, or can abandon without regret if something happier comes along. No one could possibly get Collin or me to change our ways. Our lives are fixed, determined, cast in concrete, poet and pedagogue. We have no choice. At age twenty our entire lifetime is committed already. Take away his poetry and my texts and we'd languish and die. At age twenty! You've fallen in with some very strange characters, Constance. Don't change your standards to fit ours. Ours are perverted. Yours are healthy."

She sat in silence after this outburst; but he could see she was not comforted by his point of view.

"But I've read so little," she said after a while.

"The education you've already had is superior to the education most people in this country have when they get out of college," he declared. When she made an indication of disbelief, he added: "I'm not exaggerating, Constance. You can't conceive what a pathetic bucket of slop passes for education in this country. What books did you read in your senior year, your last year of school?"

"What, in English class?"

"In English, yes."

"Well, there was *Mill on the Floss*." Her face grew bright remembering. "She was like me," she added.

"And what else?"

"Let's see . . . *Mansfield Park; The Antiquary; Tess; Pickwick Papers*—that's not the right order. For poetry we read Chaucer, Shakespeare, *Paradise Lost,* just about all of Donne, some Blake, Wordsworth—"

"For God's sake," he said, "Go ask your brother if he's ever read even one of those books! I doubt he's even heard of them. And he had a 'good' private school education."

"But he's read all kinds of American things."

"Not in school. He didn't read them in school. You think they give high school students *The Body Electric?* They feed them pap, even in prep school. God forbid they should get near the bursting teat of truth and poetry."

She dug at the sand with her toes.

"I'll tell you what you've done," he said. "You've confused ability to learn with actual acquired knowledge. So you haven't read Whitman. The point is that when you do, you'll have more than enough brains to comprehend him. True intelligence consists in the *ability* to learn, not in the amount you actually have packed away in your head. For all you know, your intelligence far surpasses Collin's or mine— you just don't sling the literary claptrap around the way we do. Everybody confuses those two things. I'll tell you the truth. You may think I'm a snob about people's intelligence—that I make fun of people who are less endowed mentally than I am. And I admit, my education has made such a rare bird of me that it's hard for me to deal with people who've never read anything more complicated than *Reader's Digest,* or *TV Guide,* or the Yellow Pages. But deep down inside me, I'm a leveler: I really do believe that every human being possesses just about the same intelligence. There are exceptions, of course. But basically we're all given the same brain. We all have about the same potential. The only difference lies in our inclination. One person thrives on mathematics; another becomes a sculptor. Is one more or less intelligent than the other? I don't think so. Or say that you find some man who's a wizard at physics, plays the cello like an angel, speaks fifteen languages, is a holy terror on the chessboard. So what? Look at his social life—he has no friends, no family, or he was studying somewhere in a dark carrel while you and I were filling our senses with the outdoors, while Collin was writing, trying to perfect a single line—whatever. Inclination leads him to apply his ability to learn in a given field, and he acquires knowledge in that field, but his acquired knowledge is no indicator of his intelligence—only his education and his inclination. Speaking for myself, I've never met the person I felt to be innately more *intelligent* than I was—though some were better educated. I never read a scholarly study that I felt I could not have written, given time and inclination. I've seen people just as intelligent as I am, if not more so, who were in awe of me because I knew Greek; but they had no inclination to learn it. They were in awe of my *inclination*, that's what it boils down to. And that's silly. The question I'm asking is, do you feel inferior to Collin and to me because you were never *inclined* to write poetry or read Greek? Look, I've never been inclined to write poetry, and Collin couldn't stomach Greek for more than two weeks, so you're no dumber with respect to him than I am, and no dumber with respect to me than he is. Even if your inclinations don't lead you to do anything more with your life than read, and think, and observe, and serve others, you'll always be just as intelligent as we are."

She seemed somewhat mollified, whether by his logic or by the flood of his speech, he could not tell. "As a matter of fact," he went on, "the only foolish thing I ever heard you say was when you questioned your own intelligence. And that was clearly due to overexposure to the foolishness of your current companions."

She laughed. "You *are* quite a pair. But I love you both."

"Well, of course—how could you help it?"

She laughed again.

"And we love you," he continued. "And we respect your intelligence, Constance. Why do you think Collin shows you his poems?"

"But he's always mad at me because I have nothing to say."

"I'll tell you the truth. The day you come out with a good, logical, critical analysis of one of his poems, he'll never show you another. He writes for your tears. Those are all the praise a poet could ever want. Besides—I told you: the jargon these poets trade off when they read one another's works is just a knack. Stick around the people Collin travels with long enough and you'll learn it."

"I wish that were true! I'm so intimidated at the idea of meeting more of his friends. Things didn't go so well when Chuckie and Ringer and Steve were here."

"That was no reflection on you, for heaven's sake. That was their fault. Take Steve—I remember one time he read a sonnet Collin had written as an assignment in school. It was a real, bona fide rhyming sonnet with fourteen lines, though the rhythm was a bit . . . creative, shall we say. Well, Collin shows it to Steve. Steve reads it; gives him the complete critique—rather harsh, as I recall; sits back, puffs on his stogie, and says, 'Say, Col, ever write a poem that rhymes?'"

"No!"

"Yes. He totally missed the rhyme. Missed the attempt at form completely." He grinned at her, and she giggled. "So don't worry. We're all human. And if to err is human, Collin's writer friends are even more human than we are."

They sat in silence for a minute, looking at one another. She seemed reassured at last.

Suddenly he stood up. "Come here," he said. She rose, putting her guitar aside, and came to him obediently, still smiling, somewhat shyly. He went to the water's edge, where a rock jutted out slightly into the water, just big enough for two to stand; he called her there beside him.

"What?" she asked with a smile as she stepped out next to him.

"Look," he said. He pointed at the water. She looked down at the reflection of her face and form against the dark blue sky in the dark, windless mirror of the pond. "What do you see?" he asked.

"I see myself," she said tentatively. She looked at him, smiling and curious.

"I'll tell you what you see, Constance Tate," he said. "You see a very beautiful woman." She looked pleased and embarrassed, but said nothing. "You remember that line in *Midsummer-Night* where Titania has fallen in love with Bottom even though he's wearing the head of an ass? She's completely deluded and enamored. She says to him 'Thou art as wise as thou art beautiful.' Which is of course ironic and humorous because it's true—he's ugly and foolish, and so just as wise as beautiful. But when I look at you, I can say the same thing without irony. Thou art as wise as thou art beautiful. You can't see your intelligence, looking in this pond; but I can see it in your eyes and hear it in the words you speak, as surely as I can see your beauty when I stand face to face with you. So enough nonsense! If you ever wonder, if you ever worry, if it seems you can't keep up, just go look in your mirror and remember those words: 'Thou art as wise as thou art beautiful.'"

She stood with lowered eyes and a hint of red blood in her cheek; for a minute they were silent, motionless. Then she caught his hand without looking at him and squeezed it vigorously. He squeezed back; and he felt an inexplicable, delicious, melting softness inside himself.

Then she looked up with a grin and said: "'Not so neither, but if I had wit enough to get out of this wood, I have enough to serve my own turn!'"

He took up her challenge. "'Out of this valley do not desire to go,'" he said.

> Thou shalt remain here, whe'r thou wilt or no.
> I am a spirit of no common rate;
> The summer still doth tend upon my state;
> And I do love thee: therefore, go with me.

He stepped off the rock, tugging her along with him; their hands were linked a few moments more; and then she went to put on her sandals and take up her guitar.

They walked in comfortable silence through the long tunnel of green boughs toward the house.

Sunday, June 21 / Two

LLOYD TATE, DAPPER in a bowtie and cream-colored linen suit, was the first to greet them. "Hail! Hail!" he cried from the stone porch as they came into view. "Greetings, O Ryan the Rhodesian! Hail, conquering hero! The feast awaits thy coming, and the banqueters are chafing at the bit and biting at the chafing dishes.—But what do my eyes behold? I see thou art accompanied in thy course hither by a fair nymph of the country. Naiad or dryad? Ah, I see she is a devotee of Musica, for she carries an instrument with which to refresh and delight poor heartstricken mortals. Fair nymph, you are most welcome to our revels." This absurd speech was accompanied by various thespian and forensic poses, all ludicrous.

"Oh, here you are," said Collin dryly, appearing through the French doors behind his father. "We thought you'd gotten lost in woods." He too wore a white suit, but outdid his father by sporting a pair of gleaming white bucks, a shoe that had just come briefly back into fashion.

"And what better night to get lost in the woods of Athens than Midsummer-Night?" asked Lloyd. "Where have you been, my children? Plunged in a magic spell? Transformed into wandering players? Dreaming of high pursuits?"

"Dreaming of leg of lamb," said Ryan.

"And strawberry shortcake," added Constance.

"Ascend, then! Ascend to the banquet halls of the fairy king! Oberon bids you welcome!"

"Calm down, Dad," said Collin. He gave Constance and Ryan a wry glance and drew a circle in the air beside his head to indicate Lloyd's insanity.

"Sooner calm the raging seas, the tempest howling in the firmament, than calm my poetic frenzy!" scoffed Lloyd.

"No more Shakespeare for you," said Collin bluntly. "Doctor's orders.—Ryan, why did you bring that silly jacket? It's far too hot for that."

"What do you mean, why did I bring it? Even with it, I'll feel underdressed," responded Ryan, as he walked up the steps with Constance, his jacket slung over his shoulder. "Look at you two. You're the height of *la mode*."

"Nonsense," said Collin. "The guest of honor is never underdressed. You make us look like fools. I was too hot in this thing anyway." He took off his jacket, evincing both relief to be rid of it and reluctance to give up a key component of his stylishness. "Shirtsleeves it is. Come on, Dad."

"Yes, a sensible notion. But I'll desist until fair Titania appears.—You've heard about Titania and her dress?"

"I have indeed," said Ryan.

"We're awaiting her appearance with bated breath. Constance, my dear, don't you think it might be necessary for you to go help the fairy queen don her gossamer wings?"

"She wouldn't let me."

"Well . . . maybe you should just check?"

"No, Papa. She said if she was late we should all just have a cocktail and be patient."

"All right—well, cocktails isn't a bad idea. Come inside, my fellow revelers. Pick your poison." He went inside, leading the way.

"He's gone over the edge," observed Ryan.

"What else is new?" said Collin.

They followed Lloyd inside, through the dining room and into the living room. There the Yankee gentleman of the bar became a gentleman of the old South—presiding at a different kind of bar. He bowed and beckoned, waved the young people close before him, leaned forward conspiratorially, and in a pregnant drawl asked: "What will the Li'l Co'nel have? Mint Julep?"

Constance giggled. "Seltzer with a twist, Papa."

His preparation of this choice was elaborate; she giggled again watching him at work, and exchanged a glance with Collin and Ryan. He handed the concoction to her with a flourish, then peered from under his white eyebrows at Collin and Ryan.

"And ye, my lads?" he asked, already forgetting his southern act and affecting a Scottish burr. "What'll ye be havin'?"

"Stout, Dad. Same as always."

"Stout! Stout again!—Not that stout isn't a fine drink. But when there's scotch to be had, how can a man drink anything less?"

"Stout isn't anything *less,* Mr. Tate," said Ryan. "It's the highest achievement of human artifice."

"Lord, what fools these mortals be!" said Lloyd, fetching forth two bottles from the cooler in the bar.

"I guess it was inevitable that we hear that line at some point this evening," said Ryan. "Better sooner than later. Get it over with, I say."

After Lloyd had served up the stout, he chose a tumbler from the bar, topping it off with single malt and adding but a few ice cubes to temper it, apparently only doing even that much damage to it in order that he might have something to rattle while making the toast he intended. The young people again exchanged horrified glances, but were called to attention by the rattle.

"I propose a toast—which you can't drink to, since it's unlucky to drink to yourselves. I propose a toast to the three dearest, loyallest, handsomest, brightest children a man ever had. To Constance" —with a bow—"and Collin—and Ryan."

"And I'll drink to the best father I ever had," said Collin.

"Happy Father's Day," said Constance, seconding her brother.

"Well, I can't drink to you in the same terms as Collin," said Ryan, "but you certainly are the best—what shall I call you, Mr. Tate?"

"Father-in-law," suggested Lloyd precipitously.

"Wait a minute," said Collin.

"Well, I'm a father of sorts to my son's friend, and I'm certainly in law. So, I'm a father in law. Without the hyphens."

"But the term has other implications, Dad."

"I'll drink to a father out of law, then," said Ryan hurriedly. "A father neither of the blood nor the law—an out-law nonfather. It's an honor to be considered your honorary son, Mr. Tate."

They all drank their respective toasts.

They were each assessing what they held in hand when a sound on the stairs saved them from that awkward silence that sets in after an exchange of effusive compliments. Titania Tate was approaching. Lloyd put his drink down on the bar carefully, and the others followed his example, turning expectantly toward the door.

Sondra was giggling—nervously, but not without some pleasure; evidently she anticipated producing an effect. In this she was justified. When she entered the living room, the only sound was a drawn-out "Whoa!" from Ryan. She paused, looking everywhere but at Lloyd.

She did seem Titania. The dress, slit barely enough to allow her to walk, was a sheath of heavy, gauzy cloth that undulated in shimmering layers when she moved, with a ruffle of gauze at the hem that suggested an elfin train of gossamer, and more gauze at the shoulders that mimicked busy fairy wings. The neck was scooped low to dazzle the eyes of foolish mortals, and the tailored waist left them nowhere to look for refuge. Her hair was held in place by a tiara whose diamonds argued their authenticity persuasively in the sparkling points of rainbow light they showered forth from moment to moment. But as astonishing as her dress might be, what her admirers dwelt on most after they had taken stock of her form was her face—radiant, pleased, softened with the magic of the occasion.

Constance, who had the advantage of having seen the dress before, if not the entire outfit from gleaming slippers to sparkling headpiece, was the first to recover. She clapped her hands and laughed, "Mama! Oh, Mama!" Sondra beamed at her.

Collin struggled to speak. "God! Mother—" was all he could say. Lloyd cut him off by stepping forward with a look on his face such as he might have had if had actually finished those eight ounces of Glenfiddich. But he had rehearsed this moment, and although of all of them he was the most affected, he was the best prepared. He had spent a good hour totaled from odd intervals in the course of the day learning his speech. He went to Sondra, and with a humorous bow took her hand and said:

> Be thou as thou wast wont to be:
> See as thou wast wont to see:
> Dian's bud o'er Cupid's flower
> Hath such force and blessed power.
> Now, my Titania: wake you, my sweet queen.
> Sound, music! Come, take hands with me,
> And rock the ground whereon these sleepers be.
> Now thou and I are new in amity,
> We will tonight at midnight solemnly
> Dance in Duke Theseus' house triumphantly,
> And bless it to all fair prosperity.

The young people applauded with enthusiasm. "Way to go, Dad," said Collin.

"You've outdone yourself, Mama," said Constance. "It's even better than your dress last Christmas."

"As Ryan would say, you look *ravishing*," said Collin.

"Ravishing *is* the word," said Lloyd.

"I feel faint with all this flattery," she said. "Lloyd, would you get me a drink, please?"

Lloyd went at once to the bar to fetch a bourbon. Constance approached Sondra and tugged at key points of her dress, making a few minor adjustments. "It looks gorgeous, Mother," she said. "This gauzy stuff looks fine—I told you it would—it doesn't look rumpled at all."

"I had a nasty time with the zipper," said Sondra. "I should have had you stay."

"Listen to this girl talk," said Lloyd. "Collin, I want you to listen to this. This is the way women talk when they've been living together for twenty years—or twenty minutes, for that matter.

This is what you and I have been missing all these years. This kind of endless, soothing, background chatter about gauzy stuff and zippers."

"Sounds like gibberish to me," said Collin.

"I love it," said Ryan.

"We haven't heard your opinion of the dress, Ryan," said Lloyd.

"Yeah, Ryan," said Collin. "Cat's got your tongue for once."

"Yes, I'm quite crushed at your neglect," said Sondra, looking up from Constance's little ministrations.

"The cat does indeed have my tongue," said Ryan. "A fairy queen, come to life! When you walked into the room, I thought *La Belle Dame Sans Merci* was calling to me to cast my heart away, or Vivien was dancing round me with her fatal book of charms."

"Sounds like gibberish to me!" said Sondra. "Male gibberish."

"But charming gibberish," said Constance.

"Yes," said Sondra, giving her a sharp look. "Ever so charming! But nonsense all the same."

"Well," said Ryan, "poetical nonsense is generally more pleasing than humdrum truth, however pleasantly delivered."

"Then humbug is pleasanter than humdrum?" said Sondra.

"Humble humbug is, as opposed to posturing humbug."

"Then you approve of posturing imposture?"

Ryan drew his wits together. "As a humble humanist, I adopt whatever pose or posture imposes at least a posy of poesy on humdrum existence; if that be humbug, expose it or excuse it."

Lloyd laughed delightedly. "Well done, Ryan! The soul of the Bard is abroad tonight!"

"A humdinger of a humorist!" said Sondra. "The very air is humid with humming when you speak."

"And yet my humility is humongous."

"I still hear a humming.—Can we implore you to leave aside your kazoo for the duration of the evening?"

"Not unless you twist my humerus until my back heaves into a hump—but that would be inhumane."

"Then your hum will never be dumb?"

"When I am numb—or when I become—hummous."

"You must—mean 'humus'."

"But 'humus' has no hum."

"And therefore no pun," cried Lloyd, ecstatic.

"God, that's enough!" groaned Collin. "There's nothing more unbearable than a bad pun."

"*Au contraire,*" said Ryan. "There's nothing more punnable than a bad bear. You see, humming bees and honeybees find bears unbearable, but there are no honey trees in punning bees, and so there bears are unterrible."

"We'll never stop him now," said Collin. "He's gone—he's off—stuff his mouth with something."

At this moment Mrs. Overton appeared at the door and announced, "Dinner is served."

"Dinner will do nicely," said Ryan. "Are you serving *hum*ble pie?"

❁❁❁

They sat around the table in the dining room, cooled by a breeze from the French doors, and Mrs. Overton bore in the feast a dish at a time. Sondra kept up a novel attitude, pleased and pleasant and curiously demure. Constance seemed giddy with pleasure; beside her, Collin was pleased enough to be affable to his mother. Lloyd, in relentless high spirits, joked with Ryan, and Ryan sparred in a jocular way with Sondra, becoming a go-between where no one else could pass.

But Ryan, despite the role he played, felt himself very much the outsider in this family that might actually be beginning to work. Perhaps it had nothing to do with the Tates and their problems. Perhaps it was only his problem. When the son of an immigrant, with his head full of grand ideas about democracy and equality, goes back to the old country and sits at the landlord's table, he still feels like a peasant. Ryan thought with a pang from time to time of his parents—his father at home without him on Father's Day, stubbornly pretending he had no desire to celebrate the occasion;

his mother putting her same dull offering of food on the table, bland stuff seasoned more by the poetry she chanted over it inadvertently than by the ancient and stale herbs she drew out of the spice cupboard. In his imagination his parents seemed suddenly pathetic, vulnerable, inevitably to be overwhelmed and borne down without his help.

Maureen would have been at home in the conversation here, however. If the conversation had a single theme, it was Shakespeare. The half-baked plan to read parts from *Midsummer-Night* was indefinitely postponed, but Sondra recited "All the world's a stage," and "Out, out, brief candle" from her boarding-school days. Ryan quoted so often, and spoke in Bardese with such fluency, that the others were kept continually guessing where the poet had left off and his imitator had picked up. Lloyd remembered a sonnet or two, but not complete; he and Ryan struggled to patch up his omissions. Constance found her lines coming back to her, and contributed the vagaries of Bottom to the conversation, fragment by fragment. At length, however, in a moment when dessert was in the offing, and they sat idle with nothing but their wine before them, Constance delivered her longest and most spirited recitation. Lloyd and Ryan applauded, but Collin sat by in a cool silence. Noticing this, Constance looked stricken.

"Do you really not like Shakespeare?" she asked her brother.

"Not like Shakespeare!" scoffed Lloyd. "Of course he likes Shakespeare. He's a poet!" The battle lines between the ancients and the moderns (as Collin defined them) were not as clear to Lloyd as they were to his son.

"When it comes to Shakespeare, I always think of what Whitman said about him," said Collin.

"And what was that?" asked Lloyd.

"He said something about how his plays were only for the entertainment of the elite, and were unacceptable for America and democracy."

Lloyd looked baffled, and Ryan emitted what might have been a growl.

"But didn't Whitman like *anything* about Shakespeare?" asked Constance, dismayed.

"Oh, he liked some things about him," said Collin.

"Some things?" said Lloyd.

"And so do *you* like some things?" asked Constance.

"Well—I like *MacBeth* and *Romeo and Juliet.*"

"But that's only a fraction of what he wrote," said Lloyd. "How can you like only a fraction of Shakespeare?"

"That's liking only the Ninth of Beethoven," said Ryan.

"Or only a fifth of Scotch!" exclaimed Lloyd.

"Or only the fourth day out of July," rejoined Ryan.

"Or only . . . third base!"

"Or only your own half of a kiss," concluded Ryan.

"In short, Collin my boy," said Lloyd, "it's impossible to love only *some* of Shakespeare! If you love Shakespeare, you love him all."

"Well, I haven't read him all," said Collin bluntly.

"Have you read *Midsummer-Night's Dream?*" asked Sondra.

"No," he said.

"Well, that could explain why you're looking at us as if we've all gone mad. That's what you're supposed to do on Midsummer-Night—go mad."

"Perhaps a plot summary would help," said Collin, making sure to show that he was just barely interested.

"It's about a fairy king and queen," began Lloyd.

"Don't forget Theseus," added Ryan, "and Hippolyta the Amazon."

"And it has two sets of lovers," said Sondra.

"Lysander and Hermia, and Demetrius and Helena," said Constance. "And it has all the actors, like Bottom and Quince and Snout."

"It takes place in Athens," said Lloyd.

"In the forest," said Ryan.

"And Puck, don't forget Puck," said Sondra.

"Robin Goodfellow," said Ryan, in explanation.

"And Peaseblossom and Cobweb—my best friend played Cobweb," said Constance.

"Good God," said Collin dryly, making no attempt to digest this incoherent account. "Just tell me what happens in it."

"It's about love," said Sondra.

"'Ay me! for aught that ever I could read,'" said Lloyd, "'could ever hear by tale or history, the course of true love never did run smooth.'"

"Imagine you had a magical herb," said Ryan to Collin, "which you use to make people fall in love—even people with no inclination to fall in love—"

"You could make Titania love an ass," said Lloyd.

"And you have another drug you use to make them fall out of love, which would be necessary of course, considering all the damage you'd probably do with the first one."

"Just think of all the money you could make if you really had a potion like that," said Sondra.

"Yes," said Ryan, "And you could probably sell the falling-out-of-love drug for far more than the other."

"But what a horrible idea," said Constance. "I mean, it's one thing in Shakespeare; but making people fall in love against their will would be awful. It's a paradox, really."

"I agree," said Lloyd. "Love is the highest expression of the will—the highest gift we can give one another."

"I don't know," said Sondra coolly. "People often deliberately set out to make others fall in love with them. Is that wrong?"

"*I* think so," said Lloyd. "The willful nature of the act implies deceit. It's one thing to let another person know who you are and hope; it's another to scheme to catch him."

"Let the lover beware," said Sondra.

"This is like that conversation we had the other day," Ryan said to her. "About changing people."

"How is that?" she asked. "I don't see the connection."

"If you deliberately set out to make another love you, when you're not in love yourself, you're showing the same willingness to intervene in other people's lives. The same willingness to operate as an active agent in someone else's existence."

"People do that all the time. Haven't you noticed?"

"Yes, people do it, but they shouldn't do it. 'Live and let live,' that's one of life's great rules."

"Are you telling me that you've never consciously attempted to make a woman like you? You've never flirted? Bragged? Dressed up in your best for someone?"

"That's not the same," protested Ryan.

"Yes, it is. You're acting as an agent of change in someone else's life. It's just as if you had a drug you were sprinkling in her eyes."

"It's different. If you put on your best clothes to impress others, you're still allowing them the operation of their will. If you drug them, you're not."

"I don't know, Ryan," said Lloyd humorously. "I've seen some dresses that pretty effectively removed all question of willpower from the picture."

"Oh, Papa!" scolded Constance, smiling.

"You see?" said Sondra to Ryan. "Sexual attraction is a drug. We sprinkle it in one another's eyes every chance we get."

"Do *you* do that?" asked Ryan.

Sondra paused, smiling slightly. "Of course I do," she said.

Lloyd guffawed. "Watch out, mortals!" he said.

Watch out, Oberon, thought Ryan.

"Well," said Collin, "the whole play sounds like chaos to me. I can't make head or tail of anything you people are babbling about."

"That's the whole point," said Ryan. "That's what the play's about—confusion. The confusion about what you want. It's about thinking you want something and going after it, and finding out it's not really what you want after all, and finding something better."

"Well, I don't need to read it, then. I'm not confused about what I want."

"You won't have to read it," said Ryan. "We'll act it out for you, right here before your very eyes. We'll give you a part in it."

"Thanks anyway," said Collin.

At this point Mrs. Overton barged into the room, puffing noisily, and began clattering dishware on the table. She seemed irritated. Ryan and Collin exchanged a knowing look. She gathered up most of the dirty dinner dishes and went back into the kitchen through the swinging door.

When she was gone Lloyd cleared his throat nervously.

"Well," he said, "On this beautiful summer evening—Midsummer's evening—I'd just like to register my appreciation for the presence of the distaff side."

"Hear, hear," said Ryan.

"It really is very pleasant for us three old bachelors to have you ladies with us," added Lloyd.

"It certainly is," said Collin.

"How sweet of you, Papa," said Constance.

"Yes, Lloyd," said Sondra. "It's very kind of you to welcome us as you have."

"Well," said Lloyd, "I hope we'll have your company through the summer."

The silence was abrupt. Constance looked at Collin; he looked at his father in amazement.

"That's very, very kind of you," Sondra said.

"Stay until Collin goes off to school," said Lloyd. "That should give you a chance to find your feet."

"It would be very convenient," said Sondra.

"Convenient?" said Constance. "How can you say that, Mama? It would be wonderful! Wonderful!"

She jumped from her chair to give her father a kiss. He laughed and pretended to duck out of her way, but she caught him and kissed him on the cheek.

"Now we can really *plan* things," she said, looking significantly at Collin. Ryan knew she meant the trip to Maine.

"This would certainly be an ideal base for exploring colleges," said Sondra. "We haven't even begun to do that."

"It would be an ideal base for having fun, too," said Constance. "An ideal base for me to reform these two morbid mortals, Lysander and Demetrius, and teach them what life is really all about."

"You won't have much luck with that," said Lloyd.

Mrs. Overton barged back into the room again. Constance went up to her and seized her hands. "We're staying!" she said. "We're staying all summer! Isn't that wonderful!"

"Oh!" said Mrs. Overton, in a tone she might have used if she had seen something in the road that had been run over.

"Stop rhapsodizing and sit down, Constance," said Sondra. "Let the help do their work."

Constance let go of Mrs. Overton and went back to her seat; as she passed Ryan she beamed at him.

Mrs. Overton, however, went directly back to the kitchen, without retrieving any more dishes. Only Ryan noticed her confusion. He rose from his place and followed her out of the room; the others went on talking about the summer and barely noticed him leave.

He found the housekeeper standing in the middle of the kitchen, pink with rage.

Oh, Jesus, he thought. *We're in for it now.*

He looked around desperately and saw the dessert plates set out—yellow cake made from her special recipe, covered with mounds of bright strawberries. "Well, Mrs. Overton," he said in a sprightly tone, "I thought you might need some help carrying the shortcake out."

"Seventeen years!" she said, "Seventeen years!"

He saw that he was too late to distract her.

"Did you hear that? Did you *hear* that, Ryan? 'Let the help do their work!' Did you *hear* that?"

"Yeah," he admitted. "Pretty tactless."

"Tactless! Tactless! Is that all you can say?"

He looked at her grimly. He suddenly sympathized with her pain too acutely to offer palliatives.

"Look at her!" said Mrs. Overton. "The hussy! The chippy! That's what we used to call women like that! Looks are all she has! And what are looks worth? When *I* was growing up, they used to teach us that there was a big difference between being and seeming. She may *seem* beautiful, but *inside* she's ugly!"

He felt compelled to say something to circumvent her continuing rage. "Judge not, that ye be not judged, Mrs. Overton," he said. "How can we know what's inside her?"

"By her actions, that's how. Her actions! What did *she* do to make this dinner a success? Did *she* go way out there to Fitchburg and watch Cusack dig those spring potatoes from the ground himself?"

"No, but she—"

"Did *she* drive thirty miles up the North Shore to Mitchell's butcher shop, because she knew Mr. Mitchell and Mr. Mitchell alone has the very best lamb in the state?

"No, but—"

"Was that lamb fresh, Ryan? Was it tender?"

He sighed. "Ma'am, you know it was."

"Did *she* go to the only place in Middlesex County where she could pick wild strawberries herself? Did *she* make that mint jelly from my grandmother's recipe?—I remember the time I caught you and Collin with spoons in hand, finishing off a pint jar each of my grandmother's mint jelly. You know you love it!"

"I freely confess."

"And those butter rolls! Did you ever taste the like? Can *she* do that?"

"You make the best butter rolls on the planet, Mrs. Overton."

"And can *she* cook asparagus spears the way I can? Coddle them in olive oil and just the right herbs—oregano, a little thyme from my own garden, the tiniest touch of dill?"

"The dill, yes—"

"'Let the help do their work! Let the help do their work!' I'll tell you what would have happened if *she* had put the dill on that asparagus: you all would have choked on it, that's what would have happened! To say nothing of the fact that I drove all the way into the market in Boston for that asparagus. This time of the season it's usually all tough and woody—but I picked it all over and found the tenderest and tastiest spears in the whole market. Didn't I? Didn't I, Ryan?"

"You did exactly that."

"Ryan, I've done exactly that not only on this night, but on every day I've been in this house—for seventeen years!"

He was a little puzzled. "Found the best asparagus, ma'am?"

"No! Found and cooked the best of everything! For seventeen years! While *she* was off trolloping around Europe! And so she comes back—and he takes her in again—and I cook one of the finest dinners I ever put on that table—and what good does it do me? He gets so full of wine and song that he invites her to stay the rest of the summer! It would have been better if I'd burned every dish. Then he would have been distracted; then the night would have been a disaster. But I made everything perfectly—the way I always do—and I played right into her hands—the way you do and Collin does and dear little Constance!"

He looked nervously at the door. "Mrs. Overton . . . you've got to calm down."

"Why? Why should I calm down? That hussy is out there making goo-goo eyes at the finest man you or I or any of us ever knew—decked out in a dress that cost more than I make in wages in a month—cut down to here and her bosom popping out in your face—playing on his weaknesses—because he does have weaknesses, Lord forgive him, just like the rest of us—and one of his weaknesses is that he's lonely, and he's getting older—and he sees her mincing around—Ryan, can't you see? She's after his money again. She took it all once, she's going to take it again. And no one seems to care but me! No one seems to understand what's happening but me! If you're so smart, why don't you figure out some way to stop her?"

She gave him a moment to think; and what he thought was that she had gone too far. "Because!" he snapped. "Because it's none of my business! And it's none of your business, either. If Mr. Tate wants to fall in love with his wife again, it's his own business, and no one else's."

She glared at him unhappily.

"And I'll tell you something else," he added. "I'm actually beginning to pity her. I'm actually beginning to like her a little bit. I'm beginning to see what it is in her that he sees. Down under all that spleen is something passionate and brilliant and aching for peace."

"Passionate! Aching for peace! She's just a—I couldn't even say what she is. A chippy, is what she is. That's what we used to call women like that. It's not a nice word, but it's the truth!"

"For God's sake, will you keep your voice down?" he whispered.

She leaned on the counter and wiped her eyes with her apron, groaning softly. "Why did everything have to change?" she complained. "We were all doing so well without her!"

For a moment he hoped that her virulence had subsided into despair; he eyed the door, meditating his escape. But now she turned to him with new urgency. "What about Constance? How are things going between you two?"

He turned back to her, indignant. "Forget Constance!" he hissed. "That's your idea—your plan! I won't have anything to do with it!"

"What about last night? I can't believe you've . . . that you've been idle."

"Mrs. Overton—give it up! If Mr. Tate wants Collin's mother to stay here, she'll stay here. And if you have any loyalty as a friend to the Tates, you'll respect that—you'll do your best to help them find their way through whatever it is they have to go through, bad or good. Just cut it out with these cheap machinations. They won't work—and they're beneath your dignity!"

"I can outlast her," she said bitterly, as if retorting to a reproach. "I'll be here when she's long gone, you'll see."

He took a deep breath and succeeded in regaining control of his temper. He gestured to the counter.

"Shortcake," he said. "Let's get the shortcake out there. The cream is melting."

"I'd like to throw one of them right in her face!" said Mrs. Overton. "That would fix her!"

"It would fix you, too," said Ryan.

"Don't you threaten me, Ryan Kinsella! When it comes down to it, you and I are in the same boat. We're not the rich ones, you know!"

"No," he said. "We're not."

He was so angry that he did not trust himself to stay and help her. He turned and went back out through the door into the dining room.

❀❀❀

Mrs. Overton managed to clear the table and serve the dessert with a tolerable pretense of civility. The rest of the evening went off without any further comment from her. After dinner she consoled herself by rattling the pans as loudly as she could, but the sound barely carried to the dining room over the classical music playing on the stereo.

Lloyd broke out the champagne. As Constance drank, she became very silly; her mother scolded her from time to time. But her silliness was very charming, and they were all happy to watch it play out.

Ryan had only had wine of this quality once before, when he had told the Tates of his scholarship last December. The champagne at the marriage of his cousin—where he quaffed sticky, stale California out of a fountain in the courtyard of the gaudy Chateau Villa de Ville, a fountain so dirty he would have forbidden his dog to drink water from it—that champagne was not of the same genus as this magical liquid that shot tiny pearls of gas up the long crystal glass at his nose when he drank. As his head began to whirl, he reflected that he was being ruined for the company of ordinary mortals—learning to despise all those things he could afford, and to appreciate too well those he could not. It was a dangerous way to increase one's knowledge of the world.

And as he watched Constance, he thought, from time to time, how increasing his knowledge of her, too, might prove dangerous.

Monday, June 22,
through
Thursday, June 25

O Colin, Colin! the shepheards joye,
How I admire ech turning of thy verse!

—Spenser

I loafe and invite my soul,
I lean and loafe at my ease observing a spear of summer grass.

—Whitman

AT TEN-THIRTY THE next morning Ryan's mother stole into the study with a letter for him. He was sitting at his desk, his gaze on the faded green cover of *Kristin Lavransdatter.* The book had lain before him for nearly an hour and a half and he had not yet opened it. He had originally picked *Die Sonette an Orpheus,* but on consideration decided that that title might be perceived as obscure and difficult.

He was to bring a book to the pond as part of the deal Constance had negotiated with Collin last night. "How am I supposed to get my poems into shape for the workshop if I spend my days lounging around at the pond with you and Ryan?" he had complained. She promised him he would have early morning, late afternoon, and late evening to work without interruption if he would only spare her a few hours at midday. Still he grumbled.

"Bring those books you've been wanting to read," she said.

"What books?"

"The book by Tull, for one," she reminded him.

"Right," he said, remembering.

"Who's Tull?" asked Ryan.

"One of the leaders at the workshop," said Collin. "I want to bone up on the stuff they've all done before I go."

"Well, bring your books to the pond," said Ryan.

"You two will have to read, too," said Collin.

"Sure," said Ryan.

"I'll read whatever you're not busy with," said Constance.

Now Maureen put the letter on the copy of *Kristin,* directly in his field of vision. "For you, Ryan," she said.

"Uh huh," he muttered, irritated by her officiousness.

The address was in Eve's hand. The return said only "Mornay," which he knew his mother would not recognize or remember. She bustled about for a minute, rubbing dust off books and knick-knacks with her fingers and gathering up the wastebaskets; then she went out. When she returned a minute later, Ryan was still gazing abstractedly at the letter.

"Well," she said, "aren't you going to open it?"

"Why should I?" he asked stubbornly.

As usual, she answered him with a quotation. "'When the oracle, thus by Apollo's great divine seal'd up, shall the contents discover, something rare even then will rush to knowledge.'"

"The oracle can wait," he said.

"But don't you want to know whom it's from?"

"I know whom it's from."

"Who is it, then?"

He tapped the return address. "Mornay," he said.

"Who's he?"

"She, Mother. Eve Mornay."

"Oh, *Eva!* I guess I never knew her last name."

"I specifically remember introducing her as Eve Mornay when you met her at graduation."

"Well, I'll have to try harder to remember."

"A good plan, Mother."

"Just like the day of the week. That shouldn't be hard."

He hid his eyes behind the palm of one hand, wincing.

Maureen turned to the open door of the living room, where his father was reading the paper. "Danny! Ryan just got a letter from Eva."

"Eve, you mean, dear," said his father mercifully, who had of course heard every word. "That's very nice. What does it say?"

"I don't know," said Maureen. "He hasn't opened it yet.—Why don't you open it, Ryan, and see what it says?"

"Because I'm waiting for you to leave and shut the door behind you."

"Oh," she said. She reluctantly took the hint.

Was there ever anything more stubborn and obtuse than a mother? he thought.

After she had closed the door he heard her say, "I swear, Danny, there was never anything so stubborn as that boy. He's a tyrant!"

"Shh, Mither," warned Daniel.

Maureen lowered her voice, but Ryan caught snatches of a one of her favorite quotations: "'I would there were no age between sixteen and three-and-twenty,'" she said, "'or that youth would sleep out the rest, for there is nothing in the between but getting wenches with child, wronging the ancientry, stealing, and fighting.'"

He took up the letter. For a long while he weighed it in his hand and in his mind. He could not decide whether to open it now or to wait. A revolution had taken place in his feelings: last Monday he had woken up in bed beside Eve; this Monday he felt a powerful aversion even to opening her letter. Was she right about him and his love for her? Yet it was not her physical age that had made his feelings change; it was her attitude, that hopelessness that said all was over for her.

No—he found this conclusion revolting. Of course he loved her—he remembered her eager, wistful face turned towards his; the great bounty of her learning, shared without conceit or stinginess; and the sad wildness of her lovemaking, as if she was clutching at her last chance to know passion.

Full of these thoughts, he began to break the seal; but even before he could expose the entire edge of the letter he hesitated and checked his watch. He was reassured to see that he had nearly a half hour. With a mixture of reluctance and shame at that reluctance, he finally pulled out the letter and read it.

June 19–20

Dearest Ryan

You didn't call me as you said you would. At first I was very surprised and bitter because I know you always keep your promises. Remember that time you stood in the rain waiting for me when that meeting went on and on? But then I thought back on what you said and remembered that you said, "No promises." At that point I realized you had been very clever: when you said you would call you meant *someday*. I have been out a few times; perhaps you called then and decided your attempt was sufficient. But I'm not angry. Never in my life could I truly be angry with you. I am only angry with myself for even thinking I had any claim to a man half my age.

But I do wish you would call me. I know you think this is my proper punishment and in a sense you're right. Why should you trouble yourself any more with an old hag of a professor—no, you're right, that's laying it on a bit thick. You were certainly right about one thing. Do you remember when you said that in a few weeks my body would miss you? I have been looking at the legs of every man I see and they are *disgusting*. Now I think about things we did—I can't believe them. Isn't it that way for you? When I think about what almost happened in the subway I practically have a heart attack. What if we'd been caught? I'm sure the driver knew. I can't believe you even tried that. It was degrading and filthy—and now I almost wish I hadn't stopped you.

Ryan, as trite as this sounds, I want to be your friend. I suddenly feel very weak, very vulnerable. After two weeks with you I was stronger than I've ever been. Those two weeks, two weeks. Now they are gone, forever and ever except in my heart, where I'll treasure them and remember them always.

Ryan, sweet Ryan, young Ryan. I feel my life is over in some strange way; but at least there was you, for a while. Now all I have is loneliness, getting up, going to the library, working and teaching and coming home to cello concertos and coffee, coffee, coffee, too much coffee. And you will be in England—where you belong, dear man, not in some dreary American high rise university with a bad library—and going on adventures with Todd—how I envy him your company. If only I could be there, dressed in his skin, watching you and loving you. I'll bet you would say all kinds of things about Eve Mornay and I would scold you for betraying her instead of just saying "Whew! Eve Mornay did that?" the way I'm sure he will.

Two weeks and you turned me into a sex maniac. Chaste as a nun until then—well, it will fade. All things fade away. Soon all the sap will dry up in me again, and I will return to being what I always was—the mousy little female professor with that hard, bitter, acid look women get when they have to fight men for every rung on the ladder. "Oh, do try not to feel too sorry for yourself," you say; "after all, you drove me away, so it's all your fault." Mea culpa, mea culpa—but call me, dear one, call me.

"Stop blathering," you say, "and give me the news if you have any." Here are a few crumbs of gossip: Amwell says they want my book, but they have been bitching about the plates. "Doctor Mornay, do you have any idea how much sixty color plates will cost?"—"This is an art book, remember? If it doesn't have pictures, how can it teach anyone about art? You don't seriously think anyone is going to read the *text*, do you?"—"Well, maybe we could do something in black and white. By the way, about the cover . . . We were thinking an odalisque might be kind of . . . eye-catching, you know."—"It certainly would. Especially on a book about Puritan portraiture."

Also—I have a letter from Todd. He's in Chicago, or will be in July and August. Why don't you get in touch with him?

He's at his uncle's house. I don't know what he's doing—he was very vague; teaching a course, or some manuscript, or something you philologists do and we mere scholars couldn't possibly comprehend. He's such an unusual young man. I didn't like him at first, but gradually I came to feel a kind of fascination for him. I can understand how that girl must have felt. I heard the whole story from Curtin. He said Todd didn't even know her name. Why didn't you tell me about it? Were you protecting your friend's reputation? You see you've started us being friends, and now he'll tell me all the gossip and secrets about you; so you might as well tell me about him. He's already told me something you never mentioned. I won't say anything, just one word: Anna.

I'm degenerating into the frivolous here. I suppose I should tell you what's really on my mind: your new love interest. After I spoke to you on Wednesday night I kicked myself for not asking you what her name is, but I was sure you'd told me once, and I knew I could remember if I tried. I knew it was like her brother's. I kept saying to myself Collin Collin Collin, Col, Col, Col, lin, lin, lin—Collette, Corretta, Lynn? Lindsey, Columel? But I knew I didn't have it. So I went into the bookstore and found one of those Name Your Baby books—I didn't buy it, I just read it there. (Ashley came by and saw what I was doing and just rolled her eyes—Professor Mornay, an unwed mother at age forty-very-odd.) Carol, Carolina, Carrie, Catherine, Cecilia, Charlotte, Chelsea, Christina, Cissie, Clara, Cleo, Concordia (that one almost had me tricked for a minute) but then of course CONSTANCE. No wonder you fell in love with her the minute you saw her.

Please tell me about her. It would be good for you to have someone to confide in, and good for me to think of you with someone else. You might think I was jealous, that I really loathed her and was faking this interest. But it's the cure for what ails me at the moment. What am I good for, if not to see my dear friend Ryan happy at last? Can she deserve you? Can she learn to be good enough for you? How good is her Greek?

Is it as good as mine? I'll bet it is. How about her French? How do they do it in Spain? You think I'm being nasty—call me up, I'll convince you I'm not.

The whole point of this letter is this: I know I deserve to be punished with your silence, but don't do it to me. I ask you earnestly, if you have ever loved or ever respected me, write me, call me. This is a critical period for my future sanity.

Love,
Eve

P.S. It struck me as I was writing this that "Constance Tate" is practically a homophone for "constant state."

Ryan could not read this letter without feeling angry, even as the tears stood in his eyes. What right had she to give up on life? Here was so much pleasure, so much enjoyment in the things of the mind and spirit and flesh; and she chose to sit hunched in a shawl at home, reading the squabbles of scholars, while her bones slowly grew soft in her thin hips.

He rubbed the water away from his eyes with one quick motion, banished it. There were other things in the letter that made him angry too. What was Todd doing writing Eve about Anna? The man knew absolutely nothing about her. He had probably heard some vague rumor and made up the rest, the way everyone seemed to be doing.

And then there was this rot about Constance—"I do *not* love Constance Tate," he muttered fiercely to himself; "I don't now, and I never will." They had a Platonic friendship, she herself had said; and although as a scholar he felt some doubts about the casual use of that word, he knew perfectly well what she meant—he agreed and approved and he wanted nothing more. As for this filth about her, he shuddered as he brooded over it. He had absolutely no sexual feelings whatsoever toward her, he was sure. He paused a moment as if searching his brain and body to detect such feelings. Yes, he was quite sure of that. His affection for her was as pure as Collin's, as pure as a brother's.

That idea struck him now, and he liked it. Collin was with her daily and felt no sexual impulse toward her—why should he, Ryan, be any different? He was a brother to her, just as Collin was. To hell with Eve Mornay and her all-knowing reduction of human affairs to the same stupid pattern of sexual attraction. If he ever made any advances toward Constance, he would destroy the entire summer. How could Eve understand that? He had something to build here this summer that would mean more than any brief sexual satisfaction—he had to show Constance and Collin that all three of them belonged together, that the world could be excluded, and they could live with one another on their own terms. No matter where they went—Ryan to Oxford, Collin to finish his schooling, and Constance to start hers—they had to wind up back in the valley together. That was the only way they could be happy. What was the alternative? To be scattered and overwhelmed by the world, parted by strangers who did not matter, who did not understand—strangers like Eve.

He rose to go, but then stopped as he realized that he had to hide the letter. The only parent-proof container he had was a footlocker in which he concealed his correspondence with Todd and certain women he had known. It was under his bed upstairs, and opening it was an elaborate process requiring two keys locked in other boxes that were in turn locked in a bureau drawer. He could take the letter with him to the Tates', but the thought of it falling into their hands by accident (and such accidents did happen) was horrifying.

He determined to burn it. He cleared the box of books out of the fireplace; from his desk he scrounged up some matches that he had once used to light sealing wax. The flue creaked as he opened it, and a draught of surprisingly cool air flowed down out of the chimney. Striking a match, he kindled the paper. In less than a minute the letter was gone.

When the last ash dropped on the hearth, he regretted what he had done. He thought of Eve's sad face again, of the affection and strange passion with which she had written; but the great black flakes on the cold bricks were irrecoverable. Perhaps he would call her after all, he thought, or maybe write her instead. He would decide when he returned.

With a sort of panic he checked his watch. He still had time, he would not be late—but Constance might be early. She might be watching at the screen door, or pacing under the shade of the trees by the lawn—and wasn't every moment of time with her, of the summer, of life itself, of critical importance? He grabbed his book; took up the ragged bath towel and swimming trunks he had brought down earlier; and exploded out of the office into the living room.

"Going," he said to his father.

"Is something burning?" asked Daniel.

"Yes.—No! Was burning. It's all right." He went through the kitchen.

"Goodbye, Ryan," said his mother. "Have a good time."

He paused at the door, relenting a little.

"You too, Mom," he said. And with this generous salutation he was gone.

❁ ❁ ❁

They lay the rest of the day on the sand by the pond. Collin opened one of his books, but no more than opened it; Ryan cast Kristin's woes aside on the sand as if heedlessness might save him from the same; and Constance—she had not brought a book at all. Indolence was their watchword, and they did not change it, allowing nothing to intrude upon them that did not know that shibboleth; challenging all practicality and usefulness that came within range of their sleepy minds. The day was perfect both as present and as past, because they wanted nothing more from it than to lie on that blanket under the eye of the sun, together, young, without care. It was the very sameness of one minute to the next, of one hour to the next, that pleased them so; it was as if they were bound away to fight a war at the end of the summer, and meant to soak up as much undiluted *existence* as they could in the rays of the sun. They were aware of the minute variations in that sameness in the same way that the shipwrecked drifting on a raft are conscious of a breath of wind riffling the surface of the doldrums about them—occasions when one of them would rise and dive into the pond, or Constance would coat Collin's back with oil—and all felt a faint unease until they were all together again on that patch of blue cloth.

Moments of more audible sociality did occur. Lunch, for instance, when they sat sharing lamb sandwiches and all the other things Mrs. Overton had stuffed into the picnic basket. Or the stone-skipping contest, which Collin won with eight skips; or when Constance and Collin joined in completing the sand castle that Ryan had started at the water's edge. But after these respites from rest, they plunged onto the blanket again, back or belly down, as if drawn there by a greater attraction than gravity. On the blanket their limbs seemed saturated with a delicious heaviness that could never cloy, and their minds floated to and fro, from sleep and back again, in an endless hypnogogic state.

As for Constance, there she was. Ryan did not have to quarrel with his consciousness over his feelings about her. She lay between him and her brother, her bronzed skin slick and smooth with oil, wet with minute beads of clear sweat; smelled perfumed and sweet at first, and as the day wore on, smelled sunned and warm and sleepy; twisted her fugitive locks into a thick braid and pinned them up; tugged, in her half-slumber, at the edges of her bikini, as if afraid it was shrinking over her flesh. Ryan felt as if he inhaled a narcotic smoke in her presence; felt unhealth and dis-ease overwhelming him, but could not tear himself from the pleasant reveries her nearness blew into shape in his brain like rising smoke rings that rolled inwards upon themselves and then dissolved.

And this day was a great success for all of them; for it became, with the previous day spent at the pond, and with those subsequent to it, the epitome of the perfect summer, the image evoked by the word. The sameness for which they strove, which they perfectly achieved, now built out of the chemicals of recollection a hundred, a thousand discrete but identical memories in as many different regions of the brain, linked to as many multiple cues; and as long as Ryan lived (which is not to say much of memory's longevity) the hours of hot, idle summer recurred to him at the pricking of uncountable stimuli—whether of smells: coconut oil; dry sand; the clean, blank odor of fresh water; the crisp, dry blanket into which he pressed his face side by side with his friends—or of sights: the brilliance of sunlight that robbed the world of its color when he opened his leaden eyes to it again; the tops of the high trees around the pond shifting in a kind of endlessly changing green chiaroscuro; the image of a young woman in a bikini, her dark hair tied up off her slender, damp neck—or of sounds: the faint ripple of water, the clucking and chirping song of birds, the occasional *thung* of a frog, the sibilance of breezes and of their own dim breathing—or of feeling: the feeling of flesh, warm and too warm; cold plunges into elemental water; or the other sensations that they all felt but denied (for that time) with success.

The next day found them there again. Which was the day they had built the sand castle? By nightfall they could not remember, and they argued about the question on some provocation, greatly amused at their achievement in attaining the perfect similitude of one day to the next.

They had at first feared for the day. It dawned overcast; but Ryan made sure he appeared at the time Constance had set when they had parted—he would not call first and risk a change of plans. They decided to walk, and went on the paths north of the house, following the stream that fed the pond until, at the far extremity of the property, they arrived at its headwaters in a small marsh. This became one of the individual memories of the summer, stitched through Ryan's larger memory with a binding thread: Constance, cool in a white dress, following Collin's broad back, his golden head turning this way and that as he pointed out the past—the ancient upturned oak, raising an enormous fan of rotted roots where, in a dozen dens and tunnels pierced under the soft mossy loam where it had once stood, were the homes of a variety of animals great and small (in times gone by, of the fox, which they had flushed out on a day ten years ago)—the bridge of boards labeled with their initials in dwarvish runes that led over the stream to the west—the pit of a minor granite quarry, not worked for over a hundred and fifty years, from which stone for the house might well have been taken—the high nests of squirrels, crows, ravens, and owls, the perch of the redtail—the low drumlin they had once thought an aboriginal barrow, imagining a race of hardy autochthons who had passed their spiritual legacy on to the Tates.

But even as they walked, the sun broke through the brooding sky and shot its rays through the canopy of the broad trees; and the light fell, in a thousand shimmering discs (where the leaves made a camera obscura for each piercing ray) over white dress, over dark and golden head. Then they hoped, and talked of the sky, craning to see it, as the clouds were reft away and calm blue remained; and within a half hour they were lying once more on the blanket, and life was once more the same sameness.

❁❁❁

Ryan did make one decision that day, before he succumbed to the seductive indolence of the valley. He perceived that he needed some way to while into oblivion the superfluous hours of the summer. His article he abandoned. It could no longer interest him; he cast about for a substitute.

He decided he would teach himself Spanish. Constance would not know of his project; he would keep his study a secret until he had mastered the language. He walked into town and found in a used bookstore a volume that he thought just the thing, though the copyright was 1930. When he reappeared in the kitchen with this rusted volume under his arm, Daniel was curious.

"Something new?"

"Spanish, Dad."

"Spanish? Why would you ever want to study Spanish, Ryan?"

"It's happening."

"What?"

"Spanish. It's happening."

"Nothing's happened in Spain since the civil war, Ryan! You know that as well as I do."

"And you can read all about that in Hemingway," said Maureen.

"Dad's not talking about *that* civil war, Mother. He means the Roman civil war."

"And you can read about that in Caesar," said Daniel. "Which, by the way, you read years ago. I'm serious. Why waste your time on Spanish? What was ever done in Spanish? What scholar ever worked in Spanish? The only thing I ever heard of that was written in Spanish was a book on the Greek verb. I read it in graduate school. If you're a Latinist, you just need a little imagination, a little elasticity of conception, and the centuries melt away, and instead of Spanish you're reading the Latin of Caesar's foot soldiers."

"Well, of course, Carol's from Spain," said Maureen.

"Who's Carol?" asked Ryan, wary of his mother's nonsequiturs.

"Collin's brother. Sister, I mean."

"Constance?" asked Daniel.

"Oh, that's right. Constance. She's from Spain."

Daniel looked at Ryan with dawning comprehension; and then persisted. "But surely she couldn't expect a serious scholar to do so frivolous a thing as to spend his time learning a—well, it's practically a dead language. No scholarship ever gets written in it. You can't name me a book written in Spanish that any classicist has to know."

"Danny, what's the fuss? Ryan eats languages for breakfast. Everyone needs to do something totally unproductive sometimes. It's a good way to relax. Some people read detective novels. Ryan learns useless languages."

"Mither!" said Daniel, becoming genuinely annoyed.

"Dad," said Ryan sternly, "You're not my tutor anymore. I'll set my own course of studies."

"Well, of course you will, son. I'm not interfering. I just thought—"

"It's none of your business, Dad."

"Of course not. But surely Constance is not the type—"

"This is my idea. It has nothing to do with her."

"You mean she knows nothing about it?"

"It's a good Catholic country," interjected Maureen.

"Nothing. And don't tell her, either, if she should ever show up here. I want to surprise her."

Daniel shrugged.

Ryan made no further attempt to refute his father's narrow arguments. The refutation was in a pair of dark eyes; he could not adduce them.

As he turned to studying the book, he was not without some of his father's arrogance. The language seemed laughably simple; it did not seem capable of the beauties Constance claimed for it. But as the summer went on, Spanish began to weave its spell, as any language will in a truly open mind, in a mind nourished by the belief that all things human are worthy of interest and attention. And Ryan, for all his youthful prejudices, was nourished by such a belief; though he had not yet perceived that what makes humanity worthy is what it shares with the divine.

❁ ❁ ❁

The end of Tuesday afternoon found them saying their goodbyes on the drive before the house. Collin seemed to be in his dream state, and went immediately away either to make notes for a poem or to change for dinner; but Constance lingered at the door.

"Did you hear a car?" she asked.

"No," said Ryan.

She peered along the driveway towards the point where it wound out of sight. Ryan stole a glance at her. She was still in her bathing suit, her towel draped over her neck in a coil, her wet hair falling over it.

"I thought I heard Papa's car."

The Mercedes did not appear. She looked at him and smiled, shrugged. He edged away unwillingly, feeling compelled to depart.

"I have that feeling again," she said.

"You want me to move into the spare bedroom," he suggested.

"I wish you would. I guess what I really want to do is to invite you back tomorrow."

"Do you see me stopping you?"

"Will you come?"

"Name the time."

"The usual. Or better make it after lunch—Mrs. Overton is going up to Maine tomorrow to open the house up for the tenants." This was a duty that had belonged to the housekeeper for years. She felt some proprietorship of the task; Lloyd paid a good part of her wages out of the summer's rental on the cliff cottage. She did not seem to mind that her salary never went up, though the rent rose every year.

"What, then? About one?"

"That sounds good. You aren't busy?"

"As busy as a drone. I'll see you then." He felt he could not linger anymore, so he began to walk away. After a few yards he looked back. She was still standing by the door, watching him, her mouth open as if to call to him. She looked embarrassed, smiled, laughed at her own foolishness, and shook her head. Opening the screen door, with the air of one forcing herself, she waved one final time and went in. He continued on his way; but when he had moved somewhat under the cover of the trees bordering the lawn he dropped poor *Kristin* as if by accident, and in picking up the book managed to glance at the front of the house.

She was at the window of the old playroom, watching him.

❀❀❀

On Wednesday afternoon Ryan's hand gripped the screen door knob at twenty-three seconds past the hour of one. He was proud of his restraint in not arriving early.

No one was in the hall or the living room; from the point at which he stopped by the couch, he could see the dining room was empty; and then, hearing laughter, he looked straight ahead, through the screen door that led off the north side of the living room onto the rear lawn. Some wrought-iron chairs were grouped there under the overhanging boughs of an ash tree; here Constance and Collin were now sitting.

When the rear door clicked shut again behind him they looked up.

"Ryan!" Constance exclaimed happily.

"Just in time," said Collin, standing up and waving him forward.

They were both very well dressed—Collin in an Oxford shirt and new khakis, Constance in something that managed to be both understated and sophisticated. Something about their manner as well suggested the conviviality of a celebration.

"Come have some before they're all gone," said Constance. She indicated the marble-topped table before them, on which stood an enormous, speckled, stoneware bread bowl filled almost to the brim with magnificent cherries.

He took a seat and looked in amazement at the bowl. The cherries seemed to have been individually selected: each was firm and dark red, not the lighter shade that betrays the not-quite-ripe. They had been washed and even now glistened, chill with sweat in the hot noontime, redolent and inviting.

"Isn't this decadent?" asked Constance. "We're going to see if the three of us can finish this whole bowl."

"You two seem in high spirits today," observed Ryan.

"We're celebrating," said Collin.

"Celebrating what?"

"This morning I wrote a damned fine poem. Isn't that worth celebrating?"

"It justifies your entire existence," agreed Ryan somewhat dryly.

"Aren't you the cool one!" said Constance with a smile. "Ryan—even you, with your silly prejudices, would like this poem."

"My silly prejudices? I take it you're referring to my carefully considered critical position in regard to the failures and excesses of modern poetry."

She laughed aloud. "Read it to him, Collin."

"Shall I?" he said, as if considering something foolhardy.

"Why not? How can he enjoy the cherries if he doesn't hear the poem?"

"How can he enjoy life if he doesn't hear the poem?"

"That too," said Constance. "Read it, dear."

Collin took up a notebook that lay beside the bowl of cherries and opened it to the last page. He read; he read well. It had been several years since he had trusted Ryan in this way, and Ryan listened with more of an open mind than in past.

That is summer, the taste of the cherry
the sweetness, tartness etched on the tongue
the round, fugitive fruit
    trapped between the teeth
    and bitten to the stone within
the stain of red as if from a stanchless wound
the unthinking hunger for another
    before the first is fairly finished

The cherry has flesh
So that when the wild birds pluck the fruit
and carry the stone away
    when the chipmunk with its cheeks
    stuffed full of the nuts of the pine
    pauses
    to cram the windfall
    into it jaws
    and abscond
both bird and beast may think themselves acting
    in their own need
    and not in that of nature and the tree

We, too, pluck fruit
    as if the seed were trash
    and the flesh were all

What is summer's stone?
What germ of future fruit
    do we take on unknowing

> as we consume summer's flesh?
> Do we, too, labor in the service
> of a power we do not perceive
> like the seed-dispersing bird?

Ryan was surprised. "Not bad," he said.

Constance clapped her hands. "I told you, Collin! Even Ryan likes it."

Collin beamed despite himself. "It needs work, of course. But for a first draft, it's really not bad."

"Yes—the patheticism may not do in the middle part. About the birds and the squirrel thinking themselves acting in their own need. Your reader will probably argue that they aren't so conscious of their actions. Maybe delete 'think themselves' and just read 'act on their own need, instead of on that of nature and the tree.'"

"I see your point. I'll have to think about that."

"And 'trash' is a little risky. But I like it. Sort of Shakespearean, really. 'Who steals my purse steals trash.' That kind of thing. But the last part—'What is summer's stone?'—I like it, Collin. It's nice work."

"What did you do, instantly memorize it while Collin was reading it?" asked Constance.

"He's Mr. Memory," explained Collin. "It's all those years of memorizing Greek and Latin. One run by him and it's been photographed. I bet he could recite the whole poem if you put him up to it."

"Is that true? Could you, Ryan?"

Ryan hesitated.

"Go ahead, man. See what you can do," said Collin.

Ryan then recited the poem in full, with a few minor changes of wording. Constance and Collin checked his consistency against the typed page.

"See," said Collin when Ryan was finished. "What did I tell you?"

"Incredible!" said Constance. "You *are* a genius."

"Why?" Ryan said. "Because I can remember what a poet has written? Memory's just a trick, a habit. Idiots can do it; actually, they can do it better than geniuses. I could never write something like that, but I can repeat it once I hear it.——Come on, now; let's see what we can do about this bowl of cherries."

"Let me pick some really good ones for you," said Constance. "I know which are the best."

"Constance chose each one of these individually," explained Collin. "She insisted on it when we went down to the store."

She selected a handful and held them out to Ryan. Then she sat back on her chair, carelessly bit a cherry open, pried out the stone and discarded it, and finished the fruit. This process had already stained her lips and fingertips red. Ryan followed suit.

"Ah," he said after tasting the first one. "That *is* summer."

"Where did these cherries come from, anyway?" asked Constance. "None of the fruit seems to be ripe around here yet."

"The West Coast, probably," said Collin.

"Really? The fruit ripens earlier there?"

"The roses bloom at Christmas in some places out there," said Ryan.

"Isn't this despicable? I know nothing about my own country."

"Wait till the native corn comes in," said Ryan.

"Or the Macintosh apples," added Collin. "Out in Amherst there's a farm stand where they have the best apples you ever ate. There's nothing better than a New England apple."

"That's what everyone everywhere says, I'm sure," said Constance. "In Spain we had apples from all over the world. Even from Chile, during the winter. Of course, it's summer there then."

"And it's winter there now," observed Ryan.

"Then let's celebrate the fact that it's not winter here with a little sunbathing. Are you up for that? As soon as we finish these cherries."

"I brought my bathing suit."

"Good.——Collin?"

"Sounds good to me."

They ate in silence for a few minutes, and the level of cherries in the bowl diminished visibly.

"They say this is what life is not," said Collin, indicating the bowl. "But you'd never know it the way we've been enjoying it this past week."

"Yes," agreed Constance. "And don't you admit that it's better to enjoy life this way than to sit around moaning and groaning about death? It's been almost a week since you two got going on that."

Collin and Ryan immediately began moaning and groaning. She giggled and pushed Collin on the arm.

"Thanks for reminding us," said Collin.

"That's half the fun of living, thinking about death," said Ryan. "You know the Tate family motto."

"What's that?" asked Constance.

"Actually, it was grandfather's personal motto," explained Collin. "The real Tate motto is something else."

"You mean on that coat of arms thing in the hall?"

"That's the one," said Ryan. "It's a variation on something from Persius, the Roman satirist. *Vive memor Lethes.* 'Live heedful of Lethe.' Lethe was the river in Hades where you washed away your sins and forgot everything in your past life."

"So what does it mean, exactly? 'Live in the knowledge that your sins will be forgiven'?"

"No. Lethe is a metonomy for death. 'Live remembering oblivion' might be the closest translation. 'Live remembering that you're going to forget everything.' Live thinking on death, looking toward the end."

She shook her head in disgust. "You two are too much! What an utterly absurd philosophy."

"Not at all," said Ryan.

"Look, you silly thing," she said, digging her hand into the cherries and showing him a fistful, "When you eat these, do you think about death?"

"Certainly," said Collin. "Have you ever heard that Zen story about the man who was pursued by tigers?"

"No," said Constance. "Zen was not a big part of my upbringing. How does it go?"

"Well, this guy was being chased by tigers. He jumped off a cliff to escape them, and caught hold of a vine to save himself. While he was hanging there in space, he looked down and saw lions beneath him, roaring and waiting to eat him. The lions were below and the tigers were above; and just then a mouse crawled out on the vine and started to chew it through. And the man looked around and saw a ripe cherry hanging just within reach. So he plucked it, and ate it; and it was the finest cherry he ever ate in his life."

"Meaning?"

"Meaning that I taste death in every one of these cherries," said Collin, taking one that had escaped between her fingers. "Life is in the sweetness, and death is in the tartness. They're there side by side on your tongue. You couldn't enjoy the sweetness without the tartness, could you? How could you enjoy life if you were going to live forever?"

"Exactly," agreed Ryan, prying one of her fingers loose and stealing one of the fruits from her hand. "Live remembering that all your memories will turn to nothing. That's the cold hard pit in the fruit of life. You could write another damn fine poem on that, old man."

"We're cruisin', buddy," said Collin. "We've got her on the run. Keep it up."

"You two are utterly impossible! Incorrigible!" She threw the cherries back into the bowl. One glanced off the rim and hit Collin in the leg, leaving a minute purple stain.

"Look what you did to my pants!" said Collin, affecting outrage. "I could kill you for that!"

She instantly picked up another cherry and pelted him with it.

"You—little!—" he laughed, leaping up. She sprang to her feet, seized a handful of cherries, and darted away, turning from a safe distance to sling fruit in his direction. "I'll get you for that!" he roared, in the same mock angry tone, and set off after her. She shrieked and dashed away, flinging cherries at him wildly as he chased her around the chairs, along the edges of the lawn, and through the trunks of the trees.

In a few moments he had caught her; she laughed and shrieked, crying, "No! No! Don't!" He had no mercy on her; he began tickling her at once. She doubled over, fell to the ground, writhed to escape him; but he held her fast by one arm, digging ruthlessly at her ribs with his free hand. She rolled about and caught at his hands and screamed with laughter, her dark hair tossing on the green grass.

Suddenly Ryan could not bear to watch anymore. He averted his eyes, but the shrieks went on.

The cherries were before him, and he began to eat them with all the nonchalance he could summon.

"That should do it," he said calmly, when Constance was gasping for breath. "She won't dare to malign the Great Leveler again."

Collin relented and stood up. He tucked in his shirt, examined with rue the grass stains he had added to the stains of the cherries, and walked about the lawn restlessly.

Out of the corner of his eye, Ryan watched Constance recover. She lay with her knees drawn to one side, gasping, her hair tangled over her face, over her shoulders, over her heaving breasts, and over the lawn beneath her head, smiling in spite of herself and groaning when she had breath for it.

A memory rose up from the back of his mind, and he looked away and tried to force his thoughts in some other track; but the memory would come, he could not stop it.

The girl—what was her name?—lying on the sparse grass beneath the bleachers by the soccer field, with her back to them, her knees drawn up, breathless.

He shut his eyes tightly, but he could still hear her panting.

Gradually, as Constance recovered, he forced the memory from his mind. By the time she had sat up, he had seized on Persius and was reciting the motto over and over again in his head.

"Come on," said Collin suddenly. "Let's go look at the garden."

"Look what you've done to me," she said as she rose, combing her hair back with her fingers. Her white dress was smeared with stains from the grass and the earth.

Ryan, too, rose hastily now, and turned toward the garden as if for some kind of refuge.

❁ ❁ ❁

Mrs. Overton's plot of vegetables lay to the northwest of the back lawn, sufficiently clear of the trees and shrubs to have the benefit of sun from about ten o'clock till sunset. She griped about the lost hours of morning light, but spread cow manure and compost so assiduously that she made up for the shadows of the maples. When Ryan and Collin were little boys, they had watched in very vocal disgust as she went about this chore. She would don oversize rubber boots—her "dung boots"—and wade directly into steaming manure dumped by the truckload on her garden, grappling it into buckets with her bare hands and scattering it with earnest enthusiasm. Seventeen seasons of her work had built the soil into a kind of black potting medium saturated with nutrients.

They entered this precinct of Priapus through a gap in the rhododendrons where a path had been beaten in the bare dirt by Mrs. Overton's heavy tread. Even before they had passed through the rusty gate in the sagging fence, the stench of baked dung and breathing soil and leafage had permeated their sinuses and lungs. Ryan and Collin went first down the narrow, weedless rows, pointing out the individual crops to Constance. Here were the peas she had already learned to steal from the basket in the kitchen before dinner, splitting the crisp pods for the sugary seeds within; here were beans ready to be broken from the vine and eaten; here was the soft green plumage of the sweet carrots, the massed buds of the broad broccoli plants, the balled cabbages, the rose-blossom growth of young lettuce.

Though Mrs. Overton was well ahead in most of her planting, in this New England climate the squash had not long been planted, acorn and butternut and the expansionist summer squashes and zucchini. She kept a single mound of pumpkins, for the sole purpose of providing a Big Max for the front door at Halloween; it was often more than a hundred pounds, and had to be rolled the long route to its destined place by Hal Minot. These cucurbits had just begun to explode into growth with the recent heat, and had hung a wide awning of leaf over their black hillock. The eggplants had started well, although some insect was making lacework of their olive and purple leaves; the leeks, which Mrs. Overton grew with great success by the score for her winter soups, were already covered over and blanching to a forced whiteness in their trenches; and the pepper seedlings, fearless of the cutworm in their protective collars, raised their pompoms of gleaming leaves.

Beyond the vegetable garden were the herbs. Ryan urged Constance to break a shoot off each variety and test it. She leaned over the bed, sniffing and exclaiming over basil, oregano, rosemary, dill, and parsley, and the others that they could not identify for her. But best of all was the thyme, studded not only with its own tiny blossoms, but with the humming, quivering, hovering honeybees as well—golden, motile flowers, seeming drunk on the fragrance and the nectar.

On the north edge of the garden, just outside the wire fence, Mrs. Overton had assembled a chorus of perennials. These were her own; Minot was forbidden to touch them. Both she and Minot grew prize-winning hollyhocks, and each put down the other by offering gratuitous advice on their nurture; it was a serious feud that occasionally required Lloyd Tate's intervention. Among the flowers that the warm front had coaxed into blossom were floribunda roses and daylilies, edelweis and phlox, some of the irises, a great patch of baby's breath, a few delphiniums, and bee-balm. These made splashes of color against the jealously encroaching wood—reds, whites, scarlet, yellows and oranges, and brooding purples. Among the cultivated plants were wildflowers Mrs. Overton had added to the show in her zeal to outstrip Minot; now blooming were white false indigo, lilac bergamot, sundrops, honeysuckle, pink Barbara's buttons, shinleaf, creambush, hardy geranium, sunny tickseed, and dewdrop; delicate fameflower, vivid fire pink, houseleek, and yellow-trumpet. There were many in the bed Constance had never seen before. Ryan's favorite was the enormous clump of Shasta daisies, not yet ready to bloom.

They stood for several minutes looking about them, saying nothing. To Ryan, Collin seemed restless still; Constance, though a bit disheveled, ineffably content.

"Let's go to the pond," suggested Ryan.

Nirvana beckoned; they began to drift back through the garden toward the gate.

✿✿✿

In its oblivion and muted euphoria, this day merged with those that had gone before and with the one that followed. Nothing changed, except that they each read a little. Constance bowed her head over Whitman with drooping lids; Collin hmmed and chuckled and frowned his way through the opus of "the greatest living American poet"—and then fell into a dream; while Ryan went up the mountain to the haunts of the eldritch woman with Kristin, pausing to watch the dragonflies skimming over the water on their tandem wings.

Outside the limits of the blanket on the sand, the world offered its irritations as before. When Ryan returned home on Thursday, Maureen told him that someone named Mrs. E. Morgan had called. She had somehow gathered that the call was from school; in offering gratuitous conjectures on who this Mrs. Morgan might be, she wondered if perhaps Ryan had not forgotten to return a library book? And so for a while a fictitious Mrs. Morgan, college librarian, took on a thriving life in Maureen's mind. Ryan knew his mother's quirks; he had no doubt the call was from Eve.

He found himself still angry with Eve, he hardly knew why. He would not call. She had sent him away—why should she be allowed to console herself with his conversation, when she had refused his presence? Or so he told himself. Sooner or later she would catch him at home. He would talk to her then.

Friday, June 26

"Alas! your Majesty," answered the prince, "it is not love or marriage that makes me so gloomy; but the thought, which haunts me day and night, that all men, even kings, must die. Never shall I be happy again till I have found a kingdom where death is unknown. And I have determined to give myself no rest till I have discovered the Land of Immortality."

—Andrew Lang

Was death invented that there might be poetry? If so, it is, after all, not so senseless an arrangement.

—William Cory

ON FRIDAY MORNING Ryan received a reply to the note he had sent to Todd. It began with a quotation from his own letter:

"This will be the summer that it all happens," you
say. Have you taken into account the operation of
that fatal confusion of desire that plagues everything human?
Your next assignment, in Lucretian hexameters:

Strange that summer is forced to carry this burden
of dreams, especially these heaviest of human dreams,
love and leisure. 'This will be the summer'—a promise
bound to die, strangled by the very ignorance of desire
that brings it into being. If we knew, clearly, what we
wanted, and could keep it before us constantly, and if we
knew that no true happiness can depend upon any other
being, we would not need the illusions of summer to

> persuade us that in this season happiness is possible. We
> could thrive in autumn's ebb or winter's dearth. But our
> sure knowledge of what we need is obscured by insistent,
> daily irrelevancies. At the end of the vacation the drudge
> stops and says, 'This is what I want—this is what life
> is about, this rest, pleasure, contentment'—and then
> returns to the job that exhausts, irritates, and defeats him.

After reading this through, Ryan scrounged a sheet of paper out of the drawers of his desk and dashed off a reply:

> Must you crack open your craw and caw like a baleful bird
> over my summer? Must you croak like a craven raven, O sable
> maven, over my haven? You prove your lineage from the twa
> corbies as you look down on me in my mortal splendor and
> shriek like a raucous black forager after carrion. I will not
> study your austere philosophy. Avoid thee, Satan! I will not
> succumb.

He signed this, stuffed it into a used envelope, readdressed and sealed the cover, and tossed it into the basket where the family placed outgoing mail. The act gave him some relief from his perturbation, but he sat for several minutes, thinking over Todd's message and muttering irritably. "Fatal confusion of desire! What the *hell* is the old curmudgeon cawing about this time? Do I or do I not know exactly what I want, and exactly what I'm doing? Lighten up a little, Schmidt! You damned Latinists are so *tight!*"

At length he focused on having already secured an invitation to the Tates' for that morning. This was a soothing thought. Constance seemed to have settled on the practice of arranging for Ryan's next visit each day before he went home—a great relief to his pride. Irish pride, perhaps; or perhaps simply the pride of the poor. The Tates had to show they valued him; he could not endure being taken for granted. With Constance's arrival, he felt the need to be esteemed by them more than ever.

When he arrived at the Tates' at eleven, he found his friends sitting with Sondra on the porch around a circular table shaded by a large umbrella—one of her innovations. Collin was bent over the notebook on his lap, jotting something, and paying no attention to the conversation of the two women; which was, from what Ryan caught as he approached, about a friend in Spain.

His entry on the scene changed the atmosphere entirely, in the most gratifying way. Collin sat up and put his notes aside; Constance jumped up to welcome him, tugging a chair into place at the table; and Sondra, inscrutable behind dark glasses, allowed him a cool smile.

He had not seen Sondra since Sunday evening. He had heard she had gone into the city one morning to have lunch with Lloyd, but beyond that he knew nothing of her doings.

"How have you been, Mrs. Tate?" he asked. "I haven't seen you all week."

"I have been well, thank you. And yourself? I see you have a little more sun in your face."

"Mama and I were talking about colleges, Ryan," said Constance.

"We weren't at all," retorted her mother. "We were talking about Señora Landau."

"I mean, before that."

"And which college are you going to favor with your presence?" asked Ryan.

"You're the academic," said Sondra. "Which would you recommend?"

"Any of the better ones."

"By which you mean?"

"There are dozens of good schools in this country."

"You don't limit your definition of good to the Ivy League, then?"

"Not at all. The Ivies are just a group of schools that play football together, and not very good football, for that matter. As schools, a few of them are excellent; some are adequate; and one or two are dubious."

"But what kind of school could I get into?" asked Constance.

"Any school in the nation," declared Ryan emphatically. "Any school would be lucky to get you."

"Your loyalty is appreciated, Ryan," said Sondra, "but it's hardly realistic. And realism is what we need right now."

"I *am* being realistic. Constance could get into any school in the country. I'm sure of it."

"What about Collin's school?" asked Constance diffidently.

Ryan was about to make a blunt reply but caught himself. "Why don't you ask Collin?" he suggested. She turned to her brother.

"I think you might be able to get in," said Collin, with a note of equivocation that surprised Ryan.

"You *think* she *might* be able to get in? You're crazy, my friend. She'd be a shoo-in."

"Would you mind if I went to school with you?" Constance asked Collin.

"Not at all. Don't be silly."

"But what about these test scores?" asked Sondra. "We don't have them yet, and they seem so critical here. Nobody can tell us anything without the scores."

"Well, I can," said Ryan. "She'll score well. There's no question of that. And her background is so exotic everyone will be interested in her. An American woman educated—well-educated—in Spain will intrigue any admissions officer. These people pride themselves on assembling a diverse student body. The trick is to do it without sacrificing academic standards, and that's no problem in her case."

"My grades aren't bad," Constance pointed out hopefully.

"Your grades are excellent, my dear," said Sondra. "Even a fond parent can judge objectively when it comes to numbers. I just think that if you had studied a little less, you'd be a more interesting person. Ryan is too generous on that point. That's what I'm most worried about, after these scores, which are an unknown factor."

"Are you saying you don't think Constance is an interesting person?" asked Ryan.

"Interesting to you, perhaps, along with several million other young men; but that's not what counts when it comes to getting into college."

"You badly underestimate your own daughter, Mrs. Tate. Anyone who quotes Shakespeare off the top of her head has a lot going for her. As I recall, you quoted some yourself just a few days ago."

"Quoting Shakespeare hardly makes me an intellectual. Even if it did, are intellectuals interesting people?"

"By God, I hope so! By definition they are. They trade in ideas, and ideas are the very food of human interest. The person who is not interested in ideas is not an interesting person. We all agreed on Sunday night that Shakespeare is interesting—and the thing that makes him interesting is that his works are absolutely seething with ideas."

"Spoken like a true intellectual, Mr. Kinsella.—But I wouldn't want you to inflate my daughter's estimate of her intelligence, and her college hopes, to unrealistic levels."

"I'm afraid he *has* been doing exactly that," said Constance.

"I hope you haven't done any damage," Sondra said to Ryan.

"There are some parents," said Ryan, "who believe their children are capable of everything, and there are some who believe their children are capable of nothing. To which class do you belong?"

"Neither. I'm somewhere in the middle. I believe my daughter is capable not of *everything,* not of *nothing,* but of *anything.*"

"I don't admit of an intermediate class. You either believe in your children completely, or not at all."

"I agree," said Collin. "It's all or nothing."

"Wait till you're a parent. There is indeed a middle ground. It's called the realistic view. I hope Constance has the skills to be happy in life, though how she could, I don't really know, since they aren't skills that I myself ever had to give to her. I have reasonable expectations that she won't die in the gutter, but I don't expect her to be a tremendous success, either."

"But you think she'll be happy. What greater success is there than achieving happiness?" asked Ryan.

"You're confusing the issue. Success and happiness are incompatible."

"Not at all. Look at Collin. If he becomes a successful poet in the world's terms, as I believe he will, he stands a fair chance of being happy, because that's the way he has defined his happiness."

"Collin's different," said Sondra. "He can do anything he sets out to do."

"Then why give any less credit to Constance?"

"Constance," said Sondra, surveying her daughter as she spoke, "has no ambitions. And one needs ambitions to accomplish anything noteworthy in life."

"I would say that an ambition to be happy, even in a humble way, is an ambition as great as any," said Ryan. "Maybe even greater than others. But why not ask Constance what her ambitions are?"

They looked to her, waiting. She stared down at the table, embarrassed, and cast about for an answer. "Oh, Ryan," she said, "Why are you putting me on the spot? All I can say are the same things I said last Sunday. I'd like to be happy. I'd like to help other people. I don't know. I'd like to go to college; I'd like to spend time with Collin, and Mother and Papa; and get married, some-day." She looked at Ryan now with a smile almost defiant. "Have children," she added. "Do you think that's a despicable ambition? Will you hate me if I never learn Greek?"

"I could never hate you no matter what you did or didn't do. If you murdered someone I wouldn't hate you.—Though if you turned politician, I might have a problem with that.—The point is not what you do, it's how you do it. It's keeping your mind alive, living, learning, growing, all through your life. You can do that in any occupation, though it's easier in some than others. That's the finest ambition of all, because it lights up and gives life to any-thing you do. Go to college, get married, have children, but do it in a way that nourishes your mind and soul, not constricts and suffocates them."

"You seem to know all about marriage," said Sondra in her best ironic tone.

"I know only what I see," said Ryan, "and only what I dream for myself. I want to be married too. I can't imagine going through life without a partner. I haven't thought too much about children, but I imagine that follows easily enough."

Sondra snorted in wry amusement.

"Don't you think that's a sufficient ambition?" he asked her. "I have my other ambitions, too, but this one is central to my life, and it would be central no matter what else I did."

"Yes, but without those other ambitions, your marriage would soon go stale. I know your type."

"You're wrong. I'd be perfectly happy being married to the right person and living in the right place, because by definition that marriage would be a marriage in which learning and growing was central."

"What about your scholarship?" she asked slyly.

"Do you mean the Rhodes or scholarship in general?"

"Well, both."

"I would abandon either if it meant I would never be lonely again—if I could have the kind of companionship I've dreamed of."

"This is an entirely new side of Ryan Kinsella," said Sondra. "Willing to sacrifice his books for a bride? It's hard to believe."

"You were talking about my scholarship, Mrs. Tate, and scholarship is different from the love of books. Scholarship is even different from the love of ideas. I love scholarship, as much as anyone can, but I know I need people more. I learned that from books themselves, from Collin, from school, from my own loneliness. Maybe Collin could maintain his ambition in the face of loneliness, but I couldn't."

"I certainly could," said Collin. "I can't imagine ever being married."

"Collin!" exclaimed Constance in amazed reproach.

"You don't believe me? It's true. I'd be more than happy to have my sister's company, and nothing else."

"That's really very loyal and touching, I'm sure," said Sondra, "but it sounds like a young man to me. I like Ryan's ambition better. I'm sure you'll be married by the time you're twenty-five."

"No," said Collin. "Never."

"I'm afraid you'll have no choice in the matter," she said. "You're too good looking. Some woman will want you, and that will be the end of it. You'll find some way to justify it in your own mind—she'll be your soul-mate or something."

"I've found my soul-mate," said Collin, smiling at Constance, who beamed back at him.

"Well, you may find a woman who can do something for you that your sister can't," Sondra said wryly. He frowned and said nothing; she turned back to Ryan. "But I can hardly believe you would be happy at some occupation where you didn't need to use your mind," she said to him.

"It would certainly be a wise thing to continue to employ it. I think I would go crazy if I didn't; but scholarship itself I could give up."

"But your mind would rust," she said. "And that would be a shame. Look at me: I was at the top of my class—I could have been anything; now I'm on the brink of being absolutely nothing. Look at Constance. I worry that she won't do as well on these tests she has to take as she would have if she had taken them when she was still in school."

"A little refreshing will be all that's needed," he said. "It's incredible how retentive the mind is. What it takes in is buried there, somewhere—you never lose it. You just have to find it under all the useless things. And idleness does tend to sift the useful material to the bottom. 'The mind that lies fallow but a single day sprouts up in follies that are only to be killed by a constant and assiduous culture.'"

They could tell from his tone that he was quoting. "Who said that?" asked Constance.

"I can't remember! Addison or Steele, I suppose. The mind does tend to harden unless you keep putting things—things of value—into it, the same way your arteries harden without exercise and proper nutrition. It's true that most people's minds seem to calcify when they get out of college. But it doesn't have to happen. And it's a process that can be reversed at any time. I'm not really afraid I'll ever let it happen to me."

"And how would you suggest I reverse that process?" asked Sondra.

"Learn something. Read something challenging."

"You won't let me work on reestablishing my happiness first?"

"I'll give you to the end of the summer for that," he said. "Then it's back to the books."

"How are you ever going to find someone you want to marry, Ryan?" asked Constance suddenly. "She'd have to be brilliant."

"You're right," he said. "She'd have to be at least as intelligent as you are."

"I don't know Greek," she said.

"We went through this last Sunday, Constance. Since when is acquired knowledge a proper measure of intelligence? Do you think I have a shopping list of things this future wife should know? What I want is a mind that will engage mine. I don't care if she *knows* nothing, as long as her intellect is alive and alert, and she keeps it that way—not for my sake, but for her own. She will of course learn in the process of keeping it alive, but that's not the same as expecting her to come completely programmed with everything that has been pounded into my head."

"For a young man of twenty you certainly seem to have given a great deal of thought to your future wife," observed Sondra.

"I've had the spiritual leisure for consideration. Twenty years is a long time to be alone without a spouse, if you really want one, and I've wanted one ever since I can remember. It may sound strange—it may *be* strange—but then again, I suppose I *am* strange."

"You're not strange at all," protested Constance.

"He's just feeling sorry for himself," said Collin. "Don't worry—he does this all the time."

"I'm a little surprised that your outlook is so romantic," said Sondra. "I mean, I knew it was, but it goes even further than I expected. It's hard to imagine you pining for a wife at age five."

"But I did," Ryan insisted. "What can I say? I'm the marrying kind. I'm a believer. I'm a romantic."

"You and Constance should get along splendidly, then," said Sondra, turning her sunglasses on her daughter.

"Mother," warned Constance.

"I should hope we get along splendidly already," interposed Ryan, sensing that Sondra was about to make some embarrassing revelation.

"How old were you the first time you got married?" Sondra asked her.

"Mother!"

"I think it was five, wasn't it?—To her teddy bear," she explained to Ryan. "She's an incurable romantic. In spite of—or maybe because of—having me for a mother."

Constance almost writhed.

"Your teddy bear?" asked Collin, grinning.

"I'm sure he made a better husband than you ever will," said Ryan.

Collin laughed. "I'm sure you're right about that. Any woman who wants to marry me will have to bring along her teddy bear to hug while I'm at my desk, writing."

"You'd really give up a woman's affection to write?" asked Ryan.

"I certainly would."

"You're crazy!"

"Not at all. Love is ephemeral—art is eternal."

"You've got that on ass-backwards," said Ryan hotly, forgetting his language. "Love is eternal, and art is ephemeral."

Collin grinned at him in a very knowing and very annoying way. "Which would you take if you had the choice?" he asked. "Making love or making a poem?"

"This conversation is getting too hot for me," said Sondra to Constance.

"You're insane even to ask that question," said Ryan.

"The sexual act, then, I presume?"

"Absolutely. I'd destroy every poem I ever wrote for that act."

"Not much of a sacrifice in your case—but we're speaking hypothetically. A poem can only be written once—the inspiration may escape—but making love can be postponed without prejudice."

"But each individual act of love is unique," said Ryan, "irretrievable, and as much a product of inspiration as any piece of poetry."

Here they both caught themselves; the one because his ignorance of sexual matters would soon become apparent, the other, because his knowledge was becoming all too obvious.

"But love is more important than anything," said Constance quietly to Collin. "Don't you think?" Her sincerity put him on the defensive, and perhaps, his affection for her.

"I don't deny that love is the most important thing in life—I mean, all kinds of love, family, marital, sexual, whatever. But an artist has to put himself above love. He has to view it with detachment."

"Cut this artist-with-a-capital-'A' stuff," said Ryan.

"Why?"

"It's bogus! As if a person were better than human just because he writes poems or paints pictures."

"He *is* better than the average run-of-the-mill human, in a way," said Collin.

"In what way?"

"In his ability to keep a distance from life even as he experiences it."

Ryan scoffed. "He's not experiencing it, then."

"The artist loves the same way everyone else loves, doesn't he?" asked Constance.

"No," said Collin. "He's always at a remove from himself."

"In other words, he's taking notes on a table by the bed," said Ryan cynically. Sondra found the image amusing.

"But what if you had a choice, just as Ryan said," suggested Constance, "Between loving a woman—a woman who loved you—and writing? Ryan said he would give up what he does. Would you?"

"Ryan is not an artist," said Collin, "and has no pretensions to be one."

"But he loves his Greek and Latin," she insisted. "Would you give up the art you love for a woman?"

"But my art is not just sitting somewhere writing poems—it's the entire way I live. My art and my life are one and the same."

"You're dodging the question," observed Ryan.

"Would you?" repeated Constance. "Would you give up your art for the woman you loved?"

"Would I give up my life for a woman? Never in a million years," said Collin with a smile—a somewhat patronizing smile, Ryan thought.

Constance seemed to wince. "I'd give up *my* life for someone I loved," she said.

"That's a bad philosophy to have, my dear," said Sondra.

"I'm serious. I would—if I really loved someone."

"I'm all too aware that you're perfectly capable of doing such a foolish thing. I hope that as you grow up a little more—see more of the world, and of men in particular—you'll realize that you shouldn't stake so much on anyone else."

"I have to agree," said Collin. "While the sentiment is attractive, the consequences of such an outlook would be disastrous."

"I think the consequences of your outlook could be negative, too," said Constance.

"Disastrous, even," said Ryan.

"Do *you* think I'm foolish to be willing to give up everything for love, Ryan?" asked Constance.

"Well—not foolish. But I think that you shouldn't give up your self for someone else. I just don't think it would work. You'd have nothing to offer the person you loved if you'd given that up. That's pretty basic."

"But how can you argue with love?"

"How can you love without a self?"

"Maybe I have no self. Maybe that's my problem. But I certainly love others."

"If you love, you must have a self. Even if it's hidden in there under all the giving to others. You just have to find it and listen to it. As for Collin, don't pay any attention to him. He's an artist, an artist with a capital *A*, and considers himself superhuman; and therefore he's a monster."

"Not a monster at all, you troublemaker," said Collin. "I've explained this to you a million times, and you still don't get it. An artist's life has to be one seamless whole—everything's a part of it. I have no intention of getting involved in squalid affairs—brawling, whoring, being a bankrupt or a beggar—the way some poets have. When people read a biography of my life, they're going to see that I lived with an intensity and dignity that never faltered. And that in itself will be perhaps my finest work of art, my finest poetry."

"Watch him now, he'll be quoting Milton," Ryan said, as if in aside to Constance.

"I will quote Milton, damn it. You were the one who first told me that quote, and it's a fine one."

"I had no idea when I told it to you that you would use it as a weapon against yourself."

"What is it?" asked Constance.

"It runs like this: 'He who would not be frustrate of his hope to write well hereafter in laudable things ought himself to be a true poem.'"

"I don't get it," she said.

The pedant jumped in. "It reflects the deep morality of Milton—his belief that the poet is the *vates sacer*, the sacred seer; that he must be pure in order to write morally pure verse."

"I'm still not sure I get it."

"It means your brother is essentially a Puritan. Didn't the Tates come over on the *Arabella?*"

"But we're all human," said Sondra to her son. "We all make mistakes. What are you going to do when you make a moral mistake? Believe me, it will happen sooner or later. It happens to you the same way an accident happens—no one wants it, but it comes anyway, the way a car jumping a curb mows down a family of four."

"It won't happen to me," said Collin.

"But if it does—*when* it does—you'll have to be able to forgive yourself."

"I won't let it happen. It's that simple."

"Collin, my dear young man, that's simply unrealistic. Being involved with other people is just too complicated and confusing—it happens all too fast—you can't control it. You're bound to make mistakes of some kind or another—you're bound to hurt somebody, if not yourself."

"Mixing Puritanism and poetry makes for a dangerous cocktail," said Ryan. "There's a line my mother likes to quote a lot. 'The web of our life is of a mingled yarn, good and ill together: our virtues would be proud if our faults whipped them not; and our crimes would despair if they were not cherished by our virtues.' Tear out your faults, Collin, and you tear out half the substance of your life."

"Wrong quotation, old man. Remember the title of Goethe's autobiography? You told me about it once."

"What is it?" asked Constance.

"Dichtung und Wahrheit," said Ryan. "Poetry and Truth."

"That is what a poet's life must be," said Collin. "Poetry and truth."

"And did I tell you what the critic said of that book?"

"You know my complete contempt for critics of any kind."

"I do indeed; don't forget, you're talking to one.—He said, *'Mehr Dichtung als Wahrheit';* 'More poetry than truth."

"And what's wrong with my wanting to write a life work that has a moral spine to it?"

"Nothing," said Ryan. "It's your pitiless obsession with the perfection of your own life that's the problem."

"And *I* say," interjected Sondra, "that you're all being silly children. No one is going to give up loving and getting married for writing poems. This is all totally hypothetical nonsense."

"The important thing is what Collin's choice in the hypothetical situation reveals about him," said Ryan. "And about his understanding of love."

"So you're the expert in love, now, are you?" said Collin.

"I'm expert enough to know it's the most powerful force on earth, bar none, for good or ill. I respect it. It's bigger than I am."

"That's because you don't have the proper detachment from it," retorted Collin.

"Neither do you. No one does. No one can. That'd be like standing on the beach and imagining that you were observing the tidal wave with detachment."

"No, it's like standing on the mountaintop and watching the wave sweep over everyone else."

"A very Lucretian image! They say he went mad and died after drinking a love potion. The tidal wave has a way of reaching even to the mountaintop."

"I can control my emotions," said Collin. "I don't claim that I don't sometimes have to struggle. But my will always wins."

"Live a little longer," suggested Ryan.

"You can't conceive of moral control because you—" But Collin caught himself before he finished the sentence.

"And when your 'moral control' deserts you," Ryan retorted fiercely, "it will be the worse disaster, because you'll have no idea what to do with your emotions. You'll be totally at their mercy. You'll be on strange new ground where there are no signposts—"

"Really," interrupted Sondra. "I think you two are getting a little hot under the collar over this."

"This is just the way they are, Mama," said Constance. "Don't worry about it."

"Love isn't a disaster, or at least it doesn't have to be," Sondra said. "For goodness sake, why don't you talk about the things people your age usually talk about?"

"Twenty is a very sophomoric age, Mrs. Tate," said Ryan.

"Usually they talk about death," Constance told her mother.

"'That's what we have been talking about, in a way," said Ryan. "'Love is strong as death, and passion cruel as the grave.'"

"Death!" said Sondra. "What do you people know about death? What does any of us know about that yet? Nothing, thank God! Why don't you talk about rock stars or something? Something *normal?*"

"There's nothing particularly normal about us, I'm afraid," said Collin.

"I can't believe that. You seem to like to lie in the sun at the beach. That seems a perfectly normal thing for a young person to do."

The Mercedes now appeared around the bend in the drive, moving with an unusual haste.

"Papa's home!" said Constance happily.

"My God," exclaimed Collin. "Dad never comes home early. Something must be wrong."

"Maybe he likes the company here," suggested Ryan.

When Lloyd emerged from the car and greeted them, Constance jumped up to hug and kiss him and Ryan rose from his seat for a moment. Lloyd offered the usual extravagant salutations.

"To what do we owe the pleasure of seeing you home early, Dad?" asked Collin as his father ascended the steps.

"Sheer disgust with the city on this Friday—this beautiful summer day."

"Which will eventually become a beautiful summer evening," said Ryan.

"And those summer evenings!" said Lloyd.

"Ryan, will you *please* not start him going," said Collin.

"Sit down, Papa," said Constance. "Let me take your briefcase and get you a cool something to drink."

"You dear girl!" rhapsodized Lloyd, surrendering his briefcase to her.

"Anything in particular?" she asked.

"Mrs. Overton must have some lemonade in there. She always has a full supply in the summer."

"Bring some for us all, dear," said Sondra. "And you, sir, take off that jacket and loosen that tie before you stifle."

"Thank you," he said. "I will." But though he took off his jacket, his personal dress code would not allow him to actually slacken his tie.

"Well, what have you people been doing?" he asked as he sat down.

"Discussing the great, weighty topics of existence," said Sondra.

"I can imagine," he said, with mock solemnity. The sparkle in Lloyd's eye as he shared this joke with his wife was tantamount to a wink.

"Aren't you looking forward to growing old and dull, Ryan?" asked Collin dryly.

"You mean getting to be really ancient, like forty or something, and having no interest in the great weighty topics of life?"

"Exactly. It must be sort of like a having a lobotomy."

Lloyd laughed. "Ah, Youth!" he said. "Wait till you learn, my boy, that living and dying, one or the other, is irrelevant; hopes and dreams, ambitions, desires, are meaningless; human life can be summed up in one word: responsibility."

Though he couched his complaint in his customary facetious hyperbole, he spoke with a wistful fervor that impelled even the two young men to sit silent with some respect.

"That reminds me of something that's always puzzled me," said Ryan after a time.

"And what's that?" asked Lloyd. "I can't imagine what would puzzle you for long."

"It's the epigraph to a book of poems by Yeats. 'In dreams begins responsibility.' It makes absolutely no sense to me. My responsibilities have nothing to do with what my brain does at night. I could see it if you turned the idea around and said, 'Dreams begin in responsibilities,' because you do dream about your responsibilities. But they hardly begin there."

"Ryan, my boy, I'm amazed at you," said Lloyd. "He's not talking about dreams you dream at night. He means your yearnings. The things you dream about having. They bring responsibilities down on your head like plagues. You yearn for company on the road of life—for a roof over your head—for a career— you get them and you find yourself bound up in responsibilities tighter than that poor fellow in your Greek myth chained on the rock. And the eagle is tearing at your liver—the eagle that says, 'Where is your freedom now? What you yearned for were responsibilities, not freedoms. For responsibilities you sold your freedom.'"

Young man and old stared without comprehension at one another.

With striking immediacy, Constance now reappeared with a tray, beaming happily.

"Here comes one of your responsibilities now," said Ryan.

"Yes," said Lloyd. "And that's the rub. You love your responsibilities.—Maybe you do understand a little of the problem after all."

"Dear Mrs. Overton anticipates our every want," said Constance. "She had the tray set out and the pitcher of lemonade in the refrigerator." She set the tray down and began serving out the drinks.

"I have an idea," she said then. "Let's be like Peter Pan and stay young forever."

"An excellent idea!" said Ryan.

"We went through this the other day," Collin reminded them.

"There *is* one great advantage to growing old," said Lloyd.

"What is that?"

"You find that there are increasing number of beautiful women in the world."

"And how does that come about, Dad?"

"Because as you grow older, your definition of beauty is constantly expanding to include women of your own age. Your notion of age is static when you're young. Old is old to you, and young is young. But as you age, your concept of age becomes dynamic—it changes to adapt to your own self-image. Confess it—when you're twenty, you think any woman over about thirty is too old to be good-looking. But when you get to be thirty, you'll find that you're willing to look at all the women up to about forty. Then when you hit forty, you find that women up to about fifty can be very attractive. And so on. The effect is that as you age, you find the pool of attractive women grows in size continually."

"I look forward to finding that pool and diving into it some-day," said Ryan. As the others laughed, Ryan looked across the table at Sondra; and for a moment he thought he could see the laughing death's head beneath flesh, bone under taut skin, the darkness of the sunglasses suggesting vacant sockets. He looked away, repulsed and disturbed.

"Speaking of diving into something," he said, "what about the pond? It's an excellent time for a swim."

"You're right," said Collin, and began drinking off his lemonade rapidly.

"Papa?" said Constance. "Will you join us?"

"Not me. Or at least, not now. Maybe later. It feels good just to sit in the fresh air, even if it is a little warm."

"That air conditioning is terrible," agreed Sondra. "Bad for your lungs, bad for your skin, bad for your head. Though it is a necessary evil at times."

"You should listen to us," said Constance to her father, "and stay home all the time. Or at least come home early more often."

"You're right, I should listen to you, dear. But it's so very hard for men to listen to women."

"And why is that?"

"Because we've been trained from an early age not to hear them. To discount every word they utter. I've been noticing this phenomenon a lot in court lately."

"But how can you just not hear us?"

"Well, as a matter of fact, I was thinking of a book that Collin and I read together when he was little. There was a character in it who was—I suppose you might say he was considered the village idiot. No one could understand a word he said. He was perfectly harmless, but unintelligible. The main character in the book somehow fell in with this strange person and wound up spending a lot of time with him. Then one day when he wasn't listening closely—when he had his thoughts on something else—and this outcast was speaking to him, he realized that he could understand every word the fellow said. And what he heard was highly intelligent.—Do you remember this, Collin?"

"Vaguely. I can't remember the name of the book, though."

"But the point really is that when men focus their attention on what women say, they see it only through a thick filter of prejudices and alien values. For instance, men talk a lot about being rational and being logical; but often that turns out to be some kind of bludgeon they use to shut women up with. If what they're hearing doesn't fit through the logic-filter, they don't hear it. If you tell me to come home early, I immediately think of responsibilities that make that impossible. I think to myself, that just doesn't make sense. But in fact it makes perfect sense, if I stop to think of how I need refreshment from work—if I think how much I enjoy the company of my family."

"So what can I do to make you hear me, Papa?"

"I don't know. Nothing, I think. I just have to learn to listen to your wisdom around the edges of all my filters."

"Well, I think you should go swimming. If not now, a little later."

Lloyd smiled fondly at her. "I'll take it under consideration," he said. "In the meantime, you young people should go on down to the pond and enjoy yourselves."

"We'll expect you," she said. She rose to go change into her swimsuit; Ryan and Collin rose too; and in a few minutes the three of them were on their way to the pond.

❁❁❁

Lloyd and Sondra remained behind on the porch, watching them out of sight. Then she took her dark glasses off and looked at Lloyd.

"Quite a threesome, aren't they?" said Lloyd.

"You can say that again. The things they find to talk about! We started off discussing colleges, which you would think would be just about the hottest topic you could find for this age group. But we moved on to the nature of intelligence, marriage, sex, and life versus art. All the things they know nothing about."

"I can just imagine. The conversation never flags with Ryan around, I can tell you. Always a fresh point of view, and willing to express it. He's—well, I wouldn't say glib—but he has a sort of a mixture of eloquence and loquacity. Sort of a rapid, prosy way of talking—very erudite, very expressive."

"He'd make a good lawyer," suggested Sondra.

"I used to think so, but eventually I concluded that he'd make a terrible lawyer. The jury could never follow him, and he could never talk down to it. I know plenty of *judges* who couldn't keep up with him. Let him be a teacher. It'll be sink or swim in his classes. But that's really the most exciting kind of teacher to have." He paused and looked at the sky, as if assessing the position of the sun. The sweat had broken out on his brow. "It used to be that Collin couldn't keep up with him. Ryan could talk circles round him. It was very interesting to watch. His favorite tactic was *reductio ad absurdum:* he'd keep chipping away at Collin's argument with little sophistries and false assumptions until poor Collin found himself asserting something he didn't believe. The Socratic method, as it was practiced by Socrates. But for the past few years Collin's been able to hold his own pretty well. He knows what he believes better than he did, and he's more wary of sophistry."

"I didn't realize that Ryan was quite the romantic he is. I suppose it stands to reason, considering what he studies."

"Oh, he'll do all right," said Lloyd. The pragmatist in him was not worried about Ryan.

"But he seems so serious about marriage. At his age, too!"

"It couldn't have been too serious a discussion," Lloyd observed dryly. "They didn't mention death."

"Oh, yes they did, toward the end. Don't you think that's a very strange topic for people their age? If Constance started talking about dying in that way, I'd take her to a shrink."

"Well, as Ryan would be the first to admit, it's purely sophomoric. They'll get over it in a year or two.—But you see why Collin and I enjoy having Ryan around. The conversation never seems to lag. He always has an opinion. A true Irishman, I guess. He's been good for Collin, and Collin's been good for him."

He wiped his brow with his handkerchief. "What do you say?" he added. "Maybe we should have a swim."

"We could just sit in the shade on the back lawn and have some lunch," she said. "With a pitcher of something really cold. I make a devil of a martini."

"That sounds a little less strenuous," he said in agreement. They rose together and went inside.

Saturday, June 27,
through
Sunday, June 28

*Virginibus Tyriis mos est gestare pharetram
purpureoque alte suras vincire coturno.*

It is the custom of Tyrian maidens to carry a quiver
and to bind the purple buskin high on their calves.

—Vergil

RYAN BREAKFASTED AT the Tates' Saturday morning, but left at noon. The family was going to Ipswich to visit a cousin of Lloyd's who wanted to meet Constance. Ryan lingered until they were actually getting into the car; then he went up into the woods.

He was in no hurry to return to his prison. The clearing was a golden-green splendor; the oak waited, as it had always waited, and for the moment Ryan too was in the mood to wait.

At the south side of the meadow was a little hillside, from which projected a ledge covered with wild grasses and moss. He sat here and watched the wood around him, becoming gradually aware of the quiet life swarming everywhere in it.

So, he thought of a sudden. *What about all of this?*

He held a defensive conversation with an imaginary interlocutor.

—*All of what?* he thought.

—*All this with the Tates,* came the answer. *With Constance.*

—*What about it? There's nothing unusual about it. We're just friends. That's all.*

—You don't have any unusually strong feeling for a certain gorgeous babe with dark eyes?

—We're friends! I'm just another brother to her. Besides, she has shown no sign of . . . sexual desire. I can be pure, too. I can live at that level. No problem. And if I put the move on her, it would just embarrass everyone anyway. It would screw up the whole summer. And I'm going away in a couple of months. So there's no future in it. Even if we did hit it off, we'd have to exclude Collin, and that would be weird.

The skeptical voice was silent.

It's possible to just be friends, he thought. *That's all I intend to do.*

After a few more minutes he rose somewhat hastily and went home.

❁❁❁

The heat that had been occasionally oppressive over the previous week was tempered that night by a heavy rain. When Ryan went out to retrieve the Sunday paper, he noticed—or at least imagined—with some disgust that the weeds in the yard had already responded to the drenching and teemed thicker and higher than ever. Though the temperature had fallen below eighty degrees, the humidity had increased; a mist crept from the earth, as though from the mouth of Aornus; a haze lingered overhead, and above it sat a lid of motionless and unbroken clouds.

Ryan's mood was as comfortless as the weather. The local paper his parents took was so poorly written, so frivolous and thin a pastiche of narrow views and uncritical thinking, as to leave him depressed when he had read it, whether the news itself happened to be good or bad on any given day. The function of the Sunday edition, in particular, seemed to be to encourage the reader to squander any time that would otherwise have been available for constructive reflection; it was replete with pointless features, magazine sections choked with trivia, news stories of the past week digested and regurgitated, and comic strips so inane as to confound the reader before they amused. The clouds brooded; Ryan picked his way restlessly through the paper; had no appetite; and at length wound up stretched out on his old rack in the study.

But his ennui terminated abruptly a little after one o'clock. Collin called. "Come on, old man," he said. "We're going to go deer stalking. Put something on that may as well get wet; the woods will still be soaking. It's too dreary a day to hang around the house, but it'll be perfect for finding that deer." Ryan did not even feign to need persuading.

He did not change—his old clothes could hardly be ruined; though he did go along the roads to the Tates in order to arrive in dry condition. In the living room the lights were blazing to dispel the gloom. Lloyd and Sondra, settled into opposite ends of a sofa with separate copies of the *Times* crossword, were engaged in a pleasant rivalry to see who could finish the puzzle first; as nearly as Ryan could judge, they were an even match. Though they invited him to sit down, he and Collin drifted into the hall to wait for Constance, who was changing out of the clothes she had worn to Mass.

While Ryan and Collin were still discussing the overcast sky with the indignation of young sunworshippers, Constance came down the stairs. She had chosen a dress to suit her part in the hunt: of green cotton cloth, with skirts to the knee and a bodice over a white blouse with puffed sleeves. But the decisive touch was her footwear: she wore boots of suede that covered her calves, bound crisscross at the shins with leather laces.

"Fantastic!" gushed Ryan when he saw her. "You look like the picture of Venus in her hunting outfit in my father's old copy of Greenough's Vergil.—Where did you *ever* get the boots and the dress?"

This was not a serious request for information so much as an exclamation; but Constance began a detailed explanation, glowing with pleasure. Collin soon interrupted her.

"I think you've overdone it," he said flatly. "You look like something off the cover of one of those drugstore romances."

"Exactly!" crowed Ryan enthusiastically. "It's romance, Collin! It's adventure! Fantasy, fancy, imagination! Where's your sense of fun, you dreary old goat?"

"I just think you're going a little too far, that's all," Collin told her.

"What are you, an old fogey at age twenty?" scoffed Ryan. "What better outfit for the maiden who's going to lure the deer out of the wood with her roundsoft eyes?"

"Don't quote my own poetry back at me. You know I hate that," said Collin.

"My apologies.—Look, just tell me, is this lady beautiful or what?"

Collin looked at Constance with a strange, hurt expression. "Come on," he said abruptly. "Let's go."

But Lloyd called from the living room; he wanted to see what Constance was wearing. He enthused in his florid way for several minutes before they could escape.

When they set off toward the woods, Collin led the way. He seemed impatient; but to Ryan's surprise Collin's mood seemed to have no effect on Constance. She capered along next to them, and at every evidence of his irritation, she smiled knowingly at Ryan.

As they entered the woods she stopped. "Wait a minute," she said. "We need spears. We can't go hunting without spears."

"You're absolutely right!" cried Ryan, in a near frenzy of approval. He immediately began searching about through the clumps of young trees and brush on the edge of the wood for suitable stock.

"Give me a break!" said Collin. "What is this, a complete reversion to childhood? Can't we just go on a walk to observe nature like mature adults?"

"The ability to act immature upon select occasions is the true proof of maturity," opined Ryan.

"I am *not* going to go through the woods carrying a stick in my hands like a ten-year-old."

"It's just a game," said Constance coaxingly.

"It's a game I gave up years ago. I have no interest in playing it now."

"Well, Constance missed her chance," said Ryan, tearing a somewhat rotten sapling out of the ground and breaking it to length over his knee.

"I don't believe this," moaned Collin.

"It's just for fun," said Constance.

"Here," said Ryan, handing her the rude spear he had made for her, and taking up a weapon of his own, a kind of shillelagh formed of a yardlong shaft surmounted by a clump of knotted roots. "Yours is for stabbing trees and stuff. Mine is more for mashing enemies."

"It's perfect," she said, hefting her weapon. "Collin, are you sure you don't need one?"

Collin subdued them somewhat with a cold stare. "Stabbing trees and mashing things. Are you *ever* going to grow up, Kinsella?"

"I hope not.—Say, pardon me if this doesn't fit into your plan for the perfect poetic life. Reality has a way of being messy. Friendships, love affairs—the grist of poetry—none of it runs as smoothly as you like."

"Don't lecture me, Mr. Critic," said Collin. He sighed resignedly and led them onward through the rain-soaked woods.

"He'll rue his pride when the Orcs attack us," said Ryan confidently to Constance as they went. "It'll be up to us to defend him then."

"I'll give my life for him if necessary," said Constance.

"True-hearted maid!" exclaimed Ryan.

Even Collin had to laugh, if painfully, at this extravagance.

Up through the woods they walked. The rain had brought out a dozen different kinds of mushrooms through the mould, from delicate Indian Pipes to wide Fairy Rings. Their way wound through the pillared halls of the pines, where Ryan and Constance dashed about among the trunks, hiding from time to time to spring out at Collin, or defending him against imaginary foes. In these mock skirmishes, Constance cast her spear against the trees as Ryan and Collin had done as boys.

"Did you see that?" marveled Ryan after one such throw. "This lady's a natural, Collin. Too bad she wasn't around before you got old and staid. We could have had a lot of fun."

"If you two don't stop making such a racket, we'll never find that deer," said Collin. "She's probably miles away by now."

"Good point," Ryan admitted. He and Constance fell quietly in behind Collin, and the troop proceeded into the southern part of the valley with more caution.

Whether because of their earlier commotion or because the deer was ranging, their hunt had no success. Ryan discovered a matted spot in the long grass in a thicket of wild olive where the doe must have spent the rainy night, and they found droppings here and there, but they neither heard nor saw her.

"Well," said Ryan, when it became clear the doe was elsewhere, "at least you've had a chance to see the clearing, Constance."

They were at that moment standing in the place, looking about themselves. "And I can see why it's a magic spot," she said.

"The saplings have got to be cleared out. Those over there. You used to have much more of a sense of space and sky; the margins are beginning to close in. It used to feel more like a meadow or even a field; now it's kind of like a hole in the woods."

"But it's still wonderful. Why don't we have our picnic here tomorrow? The weather's supposed to be good."

"A perfect idea."

"Collin? What do you say?"

"I've really got to get some work done," he said grimly. "I can't spend the whole summer in picnics and fantasies."

"Well, sure," said Constance in a mortified tone.

"Didn't Mother say something about going somewhere with you tomorrow?"

"Oh . . . yes. Shopping. Where else?"

"Again?" said Ryan.

"She wants me to get a wardrobe together for college visiting. You know, those dreary wrap-around skirts and preppy-looking shoes."

"So a picnic is out of the question anyway," said Collin. He waved away a blackfly that was harassing him. "Besides," he added, "it's awfully buggy here at this time of year."

"Well, how about Tuesday? I'll bet the bugs won't be so bad if the weather is dry.—Come on, Ryan, help me persuade him."

"You have to eat, don't you?" said Ryan. "A picnic won't take all that much longer than stopping for a sandwich."

"We'll probably wind up down by the pond again, and I'll waste the whole afternoon."

"There won't be that temptation if we have lunch here. Constance and I will be responsible for bringing the basket up here, setting up, and taking everything away again. You just show up here at twelve noon Tuesday, have your lunch, give us the pleasure of your company, and leave whenever you like."

"It'll be a good break for you," said Constance. "It'll refresh you. You'll work better in the afternoon."

He considered with evident reluctance.

"All right," he said. "If you take care of everything, I'll show up at noon."

"Excellent!" exclaimed Constance. She and Ryan pumped hands triumphantly.

Collin turned for the house, and Ryan and Constance followed. A light shower now began, and as they made their way through the pine woods, they could hear the rain singing in a hushed voice among the bobbing tassels of the evergreens overhead, and occasionally penetrating with a staccato patter onto the humus of needles below.

Monday, June 29, through Tuesday, June 30

The shadie Pine in the Sun's heat
Was their coole and known Retreat;
For then 'twas not cut down, but stood
The youth and glory of the wood.

> —Vaughn, after Boethius

A wind sways the pines,
And below
Not a breath of wild air;
Still as the mosses that glow
On the flooring and over the lines
Of the roots here and there.
The pine-tree drops its dead;
They are quiet, as under the sea.
Overhead, overhead
Rushes life in a race,
As the clouds the clouds chase;
 And we go,
And we drop like the fruits of the tree,
  Even we,
  Even so.

> —Meredith

RYAN HAD ONLY his image of Constance running about the woods to carry him through a Monday without his friends; but to his surprise, this proved almost enough. He ransacked the shelves for the copy of Greenough's Vergil and found the picture of Venus in her hunting boots—a very comical drawing it seemed to him now: the artist had entangled the hem of the goddess's hunting dress in a thorn bush, as though to supply a reason that she should accost her son, and Aeneas himself and the faithful Achates—fitted out most unclassically with wild, bushy beards—goggled at her like happily retarded mountain men. Though Ryan found he had outgrown the picture, he left the book open on his desk; it reminded him of Constance, light-footed in the pinewood, calling to him.

He had another distraction late Monday morning. About the time the first ray of light cut through the overcast, Maureen brought him a second letter from Eve. After he had expended some effort in driving his mother away, he sat by himself in the study, contemplating the envelope for nearly five minutes. Then he tore it open abruptly.

Fri 26

Dear Ryan,

As I have heard nothing and you have not replied to my letter or phone call, I know you are punishing me. I am very sorry for everything that happened, everything I did. You know me—you know I am not one to do such a thing lightly or cruelly. You know how much I love you and need you: I would never have told you to say good-bye to me as a lover forever if I did not love you. But just because I love you does not mean I am ignorant of the fact that my love can never be fulfilled. All I am trying to do is to remain friends with you. I know this is very trite and stupid ("We can still be friends, can't we?") but I mean it. I mean it because I love you as much as ever. That will never change.

I know I do not write with passion. My words seem so stilted and flat to me. I write like the staid old humanist you first met in Art Appreciation when you were only sixteen. Did I ever tell you what it was like reading your first exam? It was like discovering that a god in human guise had come and taken a seat in the third row. After that, I felt I was delivering every lecture to you, for your approval. And after every class you simply walked out the door—you never joined the stampede to the front to ask questions and argue about grades and make appointments—and even while I stood there, fielding questions and acting so professional and professorial, my consciousness was full of the knowledge that you were leaving, that I would not see you again until the next lecture, and my heart would be sinking inside me. One time in the section you did have a question to ask. Do you remember? Even then you hung back, casual and aloof; I hoped I could get rid of the others and have you all to myself, but I could see you looking at the clock, edging toward the door; and I turned to you, interrupted myself, and said, "I'll just be a minute more." Everyone was so surprised—especially you—I felt it. But maybe you weren't surprised. Maybe you knew you deserved the attention.

If I had known then that I would someday be in your arms—that you would someday make love to me—what would I have done? Denied it completely. Have you ever noticed that the more strenuously you deny to yourself that you could ever love a particular person, the more likely it becomes that you will? The men I have known that I identified as possibilities always remained just that, on the verge of being interesting. But you, a boy whom I could not possibly love— and even when I loved you, whom I had no intention of ever sleeping with—you became the one who made all the others fade away into a dreary, dispassionate sameness. When did I really love you? I don't know. When you won the championship, I think. Yes, I was part of the same silly idolatry as those two girls. But unlike them, I worshiped you from afar. I had no expectation that I could be your lover. Tell me the truth, Ryan—have you ever shared your thoughts with anyone the way you shared them with me? I don't think so. I know that, before I met you, it was not only that I had no one to talk to, it was as if I did not even have a language with which to speak all my thoughts and feelings.

I confess I am a little jealous of Constance. But it is only my flesh that is jealous. My flesh envies her your embrace. Has she felt it yet?

I have been distracted by memories and jealousies here; I am really only writing to ask you again to call me. Call me some evening and let's talk the way we used to. Why can't we do that? You know I can afford it if you reverse the charges. Please call me. I have Todd's address and some news about him that will interest you. If for no other reason, call for that.

Yours,
Eve

This letter was calculated to appeal to his affections, and almost succeeded. He remembered her from that course: standing with hunched shoulders all alone on the stage, repeatedly thrusting her bangle bracelets back up over her thin forearms, delivering her lecture clearly and brilliantly from a page or two of notes—all mind, she had seemed, an intensely cogitating cerebrum housed in a nervous, tightly strung frame. She was the first truly brilliant woman he had ever met outside his own home; he could hardly help being fascinated, even infatuated, at the time.

He set the letter down and drew paper and pen from his desk. But before he could frame his thoughts for a reply, irritation overcame his affection and pity once again. If only she would stop these stupid innuendoes about Constance! Her obsession on this point reminded him of the kind of muddled ideas his mother and Mrs. Overton fixed upon. She was only trying to soothe her own conscience by pretending that she had given him up to another, more appropriate partner. Her flesh was jealous, she said; and yet he was determined that his friendship with Constance would not be one of the flesh. She tried to tease his interest with the news of Todd's article, which he had already heard from Professor Philpin, and a gift of Todd's address, which he already had; he found it insulting that she should offer such rewards to him at all. And what was the point of calling her, if all she wanted to do was to wallow in misery over the phone? He detested any such purpose.

Yet even more irritating than these sins was the one sentence that was perhaps the most ingenuous in her disingenuous essay: "Have you ever noticed," she asked, "that the more strenuously you deny to yourself that you could ever love a particular person, the more likely it becomes that you will?"

He brooded over this sentence for some time, though it caused him annoyance of claustrophobic proportions.

"No," he finally muttered aloud to himself, "I haven't ever noticed any such thing."

He surprised himself by inadvertently snapping in two the pen he held in his hands. He threw it in the wastebasket, and the crumpled sheet of writing paper soon followed.

❁❁❁

Constance called at nine Tuesday morning. When she told him how much they had to do before the picnic, he suggested that he come over at once. "You'd better," she agreed. "Mrs. Overton's already working on filling the picnic basket. If we don't take it away from her soon, we'll never be able to carry it."

At this point Ryan's telephone slipped from a pile of papers on which it had been teetering and fell to the floor with a crash and a clang.

"What was that?" asked Constance.

"That was the phone," said Ryan, still holding on the receiver. "I was already on my way to see you, and I pulled the phone off the desk." She laughed aloud.

He left the house in such a hurry he forgot the rhubarb meringue pie his mother had baked for the occasion; she had to call him back. Carrying this, he had to go by road; but he put the detour to good use, as the daylilies were just now beginning to bloom, and even though it went against his conscience to pick wildflowers he plucked several for Constance.

When he turned the bend in the drive, he saw her sitting on the front steps, her chin in her hand and her elbow on her thigh, waiting for him. She saw him at once and stood, with a half-suppressed waving motion of her hand, and came to meet him.

"Good morning," he said. He held out the lilies.

"For me?" she said happily. She gathered the flowers into her hands and held them against her face, searching for their fragrance. Where they lay along her throat and cheeks they lit her skin with an orange radiance. "That's so sweet of you, Ryan. No one has ever given me flowers before.—And what's in the box?"

"A pie. Just what we need, right? More food. My mother insisted on making it. It's one of the few things she really makes well. Mrs. Overton is always jealous—she doesn't have the recipe. But she loves the pie."

"Then we'll give her a big piece. That will distract her while we drag the picnic basket out of the house."

This scheme was effective. Mrs. Overton put up only faint resistance to Ryan's suggestion that they cut her a piece of the pie at once. Then she had to sit down with a cup of coffee and test it; and while she was busy cooing and chewing, Ryan and Constance made off with the basket and set out for the woods.

It was a summer morning; it was a morning when all was warm and busy, all nature thriving and bustling, bird and insect and even leaf—even the lawns seemed to be almost crackling with growth, the individual blades of grass yearning toward the sun with an audible song. Hal Minot was puttering about in his dour fashion, and after suffering a greeting from Ryan, stared at the young people in mingled disgust and envy. "Spoiled, do-nothin' kids," he muttered.

"You're getting grumpy in your old age, Hal," said Ryan.

"You will too, cub," growled Minot.

"But that's a day or two away," retorted Ryan. "For now I'll be happy." Beside him Constance laughed, smiling so radiantly at Minot that for a moment the old curmudgeon seemed confused.

"I think that's the longest conversation I've ever had with him," said Ryan as they crossed the lawn.

"He's still watching us," reported Constance. "What do you think he's thinking?"

"He's remembering when he was young," said Ryan. "And believe me, he doesn't do that often.—What a day! What a day! I feel the way I used to when we'd won a game. It was as if we'd just won everything in life that really mattered."

"Maybe you had," she said. "Maybe we both have, in this moment."

He looked at her suddenly, but she was gazing elsewhere, at the blue of sky and the green of trees.

When they reached the clearing, they spent some time tramping about through the grass looking for the ideal spot. Each time they found one, the grass looked thicker or softer somewhere else. The best place was a circular patch of moss and tufted grass, but it was spoiled by a weed tree that had shot up directly in the center. Ryan offered to return to the house to fetch a pruning saw from Minot, and after reviewing all the alternatives, Constance agreed this was the best plan. Not too much later the soft sassafras was crumbling under the teeth of the saw; then Ryan dragged the tree out of sight while Constance spread the blanket.

Together they unpacked what they could of the basket. "There's no point in uncovering anything," Ryan observed. "The ants will arrive in a second if we do." So in the end they sat on the blanket in a comfortable silence, watching the light change in the wood as the sun climbed higher.

Occasionally their eyes met, and they smiled at nothing in particular. "I hope you don't mind that I'm not feeling too talkative," she said at one point.

"Not at all," he said. And they smiled at one another again.

"I feel like I'm waiting for something," she said. "But not really waiting at all. Like something is already here and it's happened and I'm totally comfortable with it; only I don't know quite what it is."

"I know what you mean," he said, with an agreeable, puzzled smile.

"I don't think it's that we're waiting for Collin. Do you?"

"No. Not at all. I feel full of something—contentment, happiness, joy, something—that hasn't quite burst free."

"Exactly."

They gave up guessing at it; and summer sang on.

Some time later Ryan, who was sitting slightly in front of Constance on the blanket, touched her on the ankle. She looked around in surprise, and saw him staring across the clearing at the shadowed margin of the wood.

The deer had come into the meadow without noticing them. She was browsing, in the nervous and insatiable manner of her kind, at leaf above and grass beneath, the whole world her manger if she could only trust to solitude long enough to eat the fodder before her nose. She strode along the edge of the meadow, tearing as if for final succor at a sprawling vine, and then halted at a straggling bush of wild rose, which she stripped and ate, thorns and all. The two humans watched for several minutes, admiring the narrow breast, the long, swiveling ears, the legs that seemed too spindly to move with such strange grace, and the luxurious, plumelike tail.

Suddenly she became aware of their presence. She threw her head up, trained anxious brown eyes and downy ears on them, and remained frozen, watching them watch her. Then their scent reached her; her nose twitched; she stamped one hard little hoof and gave a snort of warning and indignation; and then she was off, bouncing her white tail and hindquarters high in the air with the contemptuous gesture with which her race had taunted many a hunter.

Constance leaned forward and seized Ryan's hand in both of hers as he turned to her. She smiled as one who has seen a wonder, a unicorn. For a long moment they looked at one another, and then she loosed her grip and sat back again.

"Do you think it might come back again when Collin's here?" she asked.

"I don't think so. She won't come back here again today, I should think. She'll be sleeping around mid-day, anyway."

"Wasn't she beautiful?" she marveled. He grinned his Irish grin, making her laugh aloud. "Now I've seen her too," she said.

"I'm glad about that. Now Collin can say we're both crazy."

They sat quietly once more, listening to the woods. In the murmuring silence of the summer morning, time crept on unnoticed; until Constance checked her watch.

"Eleven-thirty," she said. "I wish there was some way to spy on the house from here and see if Collin's coming."

"We can climb the big pine," suggested Ryan. "You can see the house from the top. We used to do that all the time when we were kids."

"Where is it?"

"Back up on the hill, in the pine woods."

"Let's do it," she said impulsively.

"You're bound to get pitch on your dress," said Ryan. She looked down at her dress, which was in a modified peasant style, with frills along the hem that mimicked a petticoat.

"Oh, who cares?" she said recklessly. "What are dresses for, if not to get dirty? Even if Mother kills me, it'll be worth it."

They went up into the other wood, and in a few minutes stood under the giant pine. "Wow," she said. "This is some tree."

"Yes," he said. "There are only two problems with it. As you can see, the branches don't start at ground level; and there are parts of the climb where the limbs are so close together you have to squeeze your way past them."

She peered up into that shady spiral staircase with awe. "I don't know," she said. "Maybe I'll only go part way up, and let you go the rest of the way and see what you can see."

"Whatever you feel comfortable with. If you don't want to go at all, that's all right, too. We can always walk down to the house and barge in on the scamp."

"No, I'd like to give it a try. It's just that once I went to the top of the cathedral at Cologne with my friend Joanna—it was terrifying! All those winding stairs! But we made it to the top. And once we were there, it was wonderful. You could look out on the whole city and see little boats going by on the river. We stayed there a whole hour just to be away from Mother. She was furious when we got back down."

"Well, this is probably a little like that. It's not a hard climb. You just have to be careful."

She swallowed hard, but her eyes shone with excitement. "Okay," she said. "Let's do it." She scrutinized the lowest branches, which were about eight feet off the ground. "How do I get started?"

"I'll give you a boost. Can you do a chin-up?"

"I can do eight," she said. "I was class champion."

"You're all set, then." He motioned her under the lowest branch.

"So how do we do this?" she asked again, still unsure.

"Like this," he said; and without further ceremony he bent over, seized her around the knees, and straightened again, raising her instantly into the air. She gave a startled gasp and clutched at the bough. "Nothing to it," he observed.

"Say, Ryan," she said as he held her off the ground, "do you know the mark of a true gentleman?"

"What's that?"

"He doesn't look up a lady's dress when she's climbing a tree."

He laughed. "Ladies don't climb trees."

"What are you suggesting?"

"I'm suggesting it's high time you got a good grip on that branch and hoisted yourself onto it. Besides, what would I see that I haven't already seen much better when you were wearing that bathing suit?"

"Good point. And who wants to be a lady, anyway?"

"And who ever said I was a gentleman?"

Her giggle was cut short as she applied herself. The weight eased from his arms and shoulders as she pulled herself into the tree with a flash of white frills.

She scrambled to the next massive limb and clung to it. "Mother *would* kill me," she exclaimed. "And so would Collin, if he was acting the way he did Sunday."

"Then stay in the tree if they show up," said Ryan. He sprang up, seized the branch, and lifted himself up beside her.

"I've got to get rid of these clogs," she said.

"Good move."

She carefully kicked her shoes off onto the ground and then clambered upward, laughing nervously under her breath. "This reminds me of when Tigger climbed the tree," she said. "Do you remember that?"

"I'm afraid I don't."

"There's some line like: 'For the first ten feet he said happily to himself, 'Up we go!'"

And so up they did go, up a tangled gray staircase into the sky. The view of the ground beneath was soon blocked by the heavy sockets of the tree limbs; they talked only of this grip and that dead limb to be avoided; she laughed at the pine pitch on her hands and thrilled at the jays that shrieked at them from a dozen feet away; and they were alone together in an ever-more-dizzying green world, fleeing higher and higher.

After some time she stopped. "The trunk's getting very thin," she said. "It shakes when I move."

"Oh, not *very* thin. If you like, I can get by you and see how much farther we have to go before you can see the house."

"Would you? Can you do that safely?"

He climbed past her and went another twelve or fifteen feet higher. "You can see fine from here," he said. When he received no answer, he climbed back to where she was.

They clung to opposite sides of the tree, looking into one another's eyes. A warm breeze broke through the evergreen canopy, and the world swayed around them; her face paled with a terror she seemed yet to find delicious even as she groaned and shifted her grip on the pine with a shudder.

"You okay?" asked Ryan.

She laughed gamely. "My mouth is so dry," she said hoarsely.

"Oh, that's only terror. It's just a little farther."

"Dear Ryan," she said, "you wouldn't lie to me, would you? Is it really just a little farther? Is it really safe?"

"Another dozen feet. I swear it."

"I'd hate to come all this way and miss seeing the whole valley. The tree won't break, will it?"

"Don't worry. Wood is pound for pound stronger than steel."

"Oh.—What does that mean, pound for pound?"

"That means that this trunk is at least as strong as coat-hanger wire."

She laughed a little deliriously. "All right," she said, "In that case, I'll do it."

She forced herself upwards. He pointed out that she was clearing the crowns of the neighboring trees; and at last she took a good post and stopped. She did not dare look away from the trunk, which she now had in a fast embrace, utterly careless of the pine pitch. Ryan knew she had reached her limit, whether she could see the house from where she was or not. He had stayed a little below her, to reduce the weight on the crown of the tree, which swayed dizzily with every puff of air and every little shift of their positions. Now she turned her face resolutely in the direction of the house.

"Oh my God!" she cried faintly. "There it is! It looks like a doll house! Oh, Ryan, Ryan, hold me, hold onto me! Oh my God, I'm terrified!"

He swiftly climbed higher and wrapped his arms around the trunk and her upper thighs, locking her tightly to the tree with his embrace.

"Can you see?" she asked.

"I can see fine. Pretty incredible, isn't it?"

"Ryan, I'm so terrified!"

"You couldn't be too terrified if you keep telling me you are. As long as you can still talk, you don't have to worry."

"I suppose," she agreed. Then: "Isn't it beautiful?"

"It is indeed."

And they looked around at the panorama of shimmering canopy, distant hills, and the stone house, sitting snug in its roost of lawns, imposing even in miniature. "You can see Boston in that direction," Ryan pointed out. Several skyscrapers were visible in the summer haze on the eastern horizon.

"Oh, I'm so glad I did this," she said. Her voice sounded steadier. "Are you all right? Are you comfortable where you are?"

"I'm fine. How are you doing?"

"Fine—a little nervous. Thanks for just holding onto me."

"The pleasure's mine, madam."

She giggled. "Is this where you hang your signal lanterns?"

"This is the place."

"And you used to climb up here when you were kids?"

"Yup."

"Oh, doesn't the sun feel wonderful! And the breeze . . . when it doesn't bob you around like that and make you sick. Are you sure we're all right?"

"I wouldn't want to be here in a hurricane, but this is a good healthy tree. It's strong as a whip."

"And about as thick.—Look, there's Collin!"

She had caught a glimpse of him through the border trees; Ryan could see that he was striding rapidly toward the spot where his car was parked.

"Where's he going?" asked Ryan.

"I don't know. That's very strange." Though they lost sight of him, in a moment they could see his car backing out of the parking space and speeding off down the driveway.

"He must have some errand to do before he comes for lunch," said Ryan.

"Maybe he has to mail something." She hesitated. "If I tell you something, will you keep it a secret?"

"Of course."

"I saw an envelope on his desk addressed to some poetry editor. I think he's trying to get some of his poems published."

"He's been sending them out for years," said Ryan. "Didn't you know that?"

"No! Are you serious? He never told me that!"

"Yeah. He must have about fifty pink slips by now."

"Pink slips? What are they?"

"That's what he calls his rejection letters."

"So why hasn't he ever told me about this?"

"I don't know, but I think we could find a better place to discuss it."

"I suppose we *should* climb down," she said reluctantly.

"Maybe so. He'll probably be back pretty soon."

"Well, you'll have to let go of me." She laughed again. "You probably think I'm a bore talking about my mother all the time, but I can't help thinking of what her face would look like if she could see me now, in the top of this tree, with your arms around my legs."

"She probably could see you, if she looked out the front window, though she probably wouldn't believe it if she did."

"Hi, Mama," said Constance, waving daringly and giggling.

"I *have* noticed that she seems to intrude on your thoughts whenever you start having fun."

"I wonder why that is.——By the way, are you going to let go of me or not?"

"I haven't decided."

She laughed and moved about in his grip. His insides seemed to churn suddenly.

"What's the matter?" he asked. "Isn't this chaste enough for you, with this tree between us?"

"I'm sure it's all that's protecting me from being ravished right here in the treetops," she answered. He had to laugh.

"I think you're safe here," he responded. "From that, at least. All right, I'm going to let go now. Are you ready?"

"Go ahead."

He loosed his grip on her and began his descent; she followed at once, keeping a distance of several limbs between her bare feet and his last handhold.

"'The journey downward is easy,'" he muttered at one point.

She apparently missed the allusion. "It really is," she agreed. In a few minutes they reached the lowest limb—he jumped down and then turned to help her.

When he set her down she assessed the damage. Her hair, in which several long needles had fastened like pins, was in tangles; her dress was torn where she had been pinked by jagged pine twigs; and she had a long smear of pine sap on the fabric over one thigh, where Ryan had crushed it to the oozing trunk. She laughed. "From now on, this is my tree-climbing dress," she said.

"Collin is going to wonder what we've been doing. I wish I'd brought a comb."

"If I had a knife I'd whittle you one out of the jawbone of a wild boar. But I don't. You'll just have to be beautiful in disarray."

She managed to restore her hair to some order with a few deft strokes of her hands. As they made their way back to the clearing she said, "Now *that* was an adventure. Thank you for being so patient with me."

"It was my pleasure. Besides, we owed that to you. You didn't have a chance to climb that tree when you were ten."

When they reached the picnic place she drank a glass of iced tea thirstily. Not much later they heard a whistling in the wood: Collin was approaching.

"In a good mood today," noted Ryan as his friend came into view.

"The very best of moods," Collin responded, showing them a bottle of cold champagne and three crystal glasses.

"To what do we owe this unwonted sanguinity?" asked Ryan.

"Yes, Collin—what is it?" added Constance, jumping up to take the glasses.

"Nothing but a good morning's work—enough to free me for the afternoon, I think." Constance cheered this news. "My God," he said, looking closely at her, "what have you been doing?"

"Oh, we, uh—we climbed a tree. To see if you were coming."

"What, the lookout tree?" He looked at Ryan with some horror.

"Climbed it like a monkey," said Ryan.

"You're kidding!"

"Right to the top."

He surveyed her in astonishment. "You're kind of a mess, honey," he said. She blushed and looked unhappy.

"I know. I should go home and change."

"Don't be ridiculous," said Ryan.

"Under the circumstances, it's not worth it," said Collin. "Let's eat, drink, and be merry."

"For tomorrow we must die," finished Ryan.

"If you guys start that again, I *am* going back to the house," said Constance.

❀ ❀ ❀

When Ryan strode back into his parents' that evening, sunburned and relaxed, not even his mother's news could change his mood. "Eva called," she said. "She wants you to call her collect."

"Hello, Mother," said Ryan pointedly. "The pie was delicious. Mrs. Overton raved about it. You should have seen her—torn between ecstasy and jealousy."

"Did you hear your mother, Ryan?" asked his father uncertainly. "Your friend Eve called."

"Right.—What's for dinner?" He rattled around among the blackened pots steaming on the stove.

"After one of Mrs. Overton's great picnic feasts, you're asking about dinner?" said his mother.

"He's a growing boy, Maureen.—What did you have, Ryan?"

"A lot of some things and a little of everything. Chicken and potato salad and sandwiches and cookies and pie and strawberries and champagne."

"Champagne!"

"Great feed, Dad. Wish you'd been there."

"Invite me sometime," said his father, chuckling at the idea.

"You're to call collect," said Maureen. "Don't you think that's thoughtful? It must be important."

"Oh, very important."

"Then what did you do?" asked his father.

"Lounged around in the grass, talked about things."

"I can imagine," chortled Daniel.

"Constance drifted off at one point."

"Must have been the scintillating conversation you two young scholars were having."

"It was the champagne, I think.—Then we got too hot and had to go swimming. After that, we hung around the pond."

"It sounds like a wonderful day, dear," said Maureen. "I'm so glad you're having a real summer for once."

"So am I."

"'Sweet recreation barr'd, what doth ensue but moody moping, and dull melancholy, kinsman to grim and comfortless despair, and at her heels a huge infectious troop of pale distemperatures and foes to life.'"

"Exactly the way I would have put it, Mother."

"Well, that's because you're a genius, just as he was."

"Genius *schmenius;* I'm hungry, is what I am. Don't forget to call me for dinner."

"I think we can bear it in mind," said Daniel fondly.

"Going to make that phone call?" asked Maureen.

Ryan mumbled incoherently and went on into the study. He closed the door and settled into his chair happily.

"Right, I'm going to make that call," he said with a laugh.

Instead he spent the time before dinner letting the memories of the day glide through his mind like the notes of a soothing song.

Wednesday, July 1, through Friday, July 3

O larger is remembrance than desire!
O deeper than all longing is regret!

—Michael Field

WEDNESDAY EVENING. THOUGH twenty-four hours had passed, Ryan was in much the same mood—again savoring the past day's sun, the swimming, his friends' company. He sat in the study; the house was quiet but for the sounds of distant traffic on the highway and the occasional insect rasping outside the screens. His parents had gone to bed, and he was alone.

His thoughts avoided that great secret within him as though it were a precipice; he let them instead expand in every other direction. When the telephone rang, he was willing to talk even to Eve. He picked up the receiver.

"Hello, Eve," he said in a mild tone.

"Ryan?" Her voice sounded slightly frightened. "How did you know it was me?"

"How are you?"

"Thank God I've got you at last."

"You had me before this," he said.

"Oh, I know—I know. You're punishing me, aren't you? For sending you away."

He took a deep breath before he answered. "No, Eve," he said, "I'm not punishing you for that. I'm punishing you because you're a quitter—a coward."

"I know, I know," she said, with a faint sob. It was clear she would assent to anything to keep him on the phone.

"Do you agree with me?" he asked.

"Yes—" she said at first; but she was too smart to be caught in the first meshes of his subtlety—"No, no, I don't. What I did was brave, Ryan. If you only knew . . ."

"If you had any courage, you would have loved me."

"I *do* love you, Ryan."

He sighed again. "I know you do," he said after a moment, reluctant to spar with her. "And I love you, too."

"Well then, can't we just be friends?"

"We are friends."

"Why don't you return my calls, then?"

"Because I'm mad at you."

"Why are you mad at me?"

"Because you're a coward." She had no answer; she began to cry. He felt terribly ashamed of himself.

"Eve, Evie—for God's sake, don't cry—please."

"All right," she said hoarsely. "I'm sorry. It's hard for me." There was a long silence while she recovered herself. "You're the only person I ever loved," she said. "I mean, let me put it like this: you're the only man I ever loved, loved in every sense."

"And you threw me away. That should make you feel good just about now."

"I had to do it. I know you'll understand—someday, when you're happy."

"That would make it easier, I suppose. But what if I'm never happy? What if I live out my life alone, and think to myself, I could have been with Eve, if she hadn't sacrificed herself so that I could find someone better who doesn't exist?"

"No!" she cried with a surprising fervor, a surprising horror in her voice. "That won't happen!" He realized that she had never considered this possibility, and he seized upon it.

"That will be wonderful, won't it? Two lives wasted, all because of your delusions of—of omniscience. You can't control my life by altering yours. You think you're saving me, Eve, but you're really dragging me down with you."

"That won't happen! You'll find someone else. I know you will."

"Why should I? Did you? You just told me you never did."

"But you're different—"

"How different? I'm just like you—a freak. My brains, my education, my whole view of life make me a freak. Let's face it, no one will have you, and no one will have me."

"Oh God, Ryan, stop it! Stop it right now! You're just torturing me!"

"Now you see why I'm angry with you. That's the way I look at it."

"But you're wrong. You're only twenty. You have years and years to find someone you love."

"That's what you said to yourself when you were twenty, isn't it? Do you remember how you told me, last time you called, that life was too short for you? That you needed another twenty years? Well, I've got a secret for you—life is too short for everybody, and that includes me. People like you and me don't have a big choice of whom we love and live with. In another twenty years I'll be just as wretched as you are now."

She sobbed bitterly. He felt ashamed once more, for he knew that he really was only tormenting her. He was telling her honestly how he had felt two weeks ago—but did he feel that way now? If she were to be overcome suddenly by his argument and beg him to come back to her, would he go?

Now she stopped weeping abruptly, as if she had thought of something.

"What about Constance?" she asked.

"Is that why you're so interested in Constance?" he asked. "Is Constance the salve for your conscience? Do you say to yourself, it's all right to abandon Ryan, because someone else will snap him up? Well, I've got news for you: I don't love Constance Tate. I never have, and I never will."

But now she laughed softly as she cried again.

"Dear one," she said, "if you could only hear yourself.—Say that again."

"What?"

"Say, 'I don't love Constance Tate.'"

"I don't love Constance Tate, and I never will." She gave a strange, burbling, delighted laugh, and ceased crying altogether, sniffing and almost chuckling.

"If you could only hear yourself," she said. "Ryan, I don't know whether you know it, but you love Constance Tate more than you ever loved me." She chuckled outright.

He felt almost as if he had received a physical blow. He could not utter a word for a full sixty seconds, while she laughed and sniffed and continued gradually regaining control of herself. "Thank God," she said at one point. "You had me so scared there for a minute! You're *so* clever. You knew exactly what would scare me most—if I thought you would ever have to suffer what I did. That would kill me. I couldn't bear to think of you being that alone. But when you say that—'I don't love Constance Tate'— just like that, I know nature has gone its own way. You've found someone your own age." He wondered suddenly if she had gone mad, or if he had. Was there not a negative in that sentence? Did the words not mean what he knew them to mean?

"I said I *don't* love Constance Tate—*do not* love her. Do you hear me? Do you understand?"

She laughed softly. "Yes," she said, "I do understand." A final sniff and laugh. "Now tell me, are we going to be friends or what?"

"We are friends—we've always been friends—we always will be friends, if you don't go totally out of your mind."

"I may," she admitted. "But I haven't yet."

"So what more do you want? You've relieved yourself of the necessity of coping with me as a lover, and we're still friends. What are you worried about? What am I supposed to do for you?"

"Talk to me, Ryan. Just talk to me, the way you used to."

"So now you're the one who wants to recapture the past."

"I guess so. I'll admit it. Why shouldn't we?"

He thought of talking with her like this, by the hour, late at night over the telephone, and he felt a powerful revulsion; but he said nothing of it. "So, all right, talk. What do you want to talk about?

"I don't know."

He refused to speak, leaving the burden on her.

"Do you want to hear my news about Todd?"

"What? His article in the *Hermes-heft?*"

"Oh, you know about that." She was disappointed. "Did you get a letter from him?"

"No. Not about that, anyway. I've known about that for ages."

"Well . . . his address. Do you have his address in Chicago? Do you have a pencil handy?"

"I've got his address already."

"You do? Really?

"Yes. From last summer."

"Oh. Well."

They were silent.

"You haven't forgiven me, have you?" she asked sadly.

"I'm trying," he said, more in ruth than truth.

"Ryan, for heaven's sake, tell me about Constance. We'll never be at ease with each other again, until you do. Can't you talk about her yet?"

"What's to say? She's my best friend's sister. She's good-looking, has an affable personality—"

"Bright? Is she bright, Ryan? She doesn't have to be as well-educated as you are, but if she's quick, if she likes to learn, that's more than enough."

"She's bright, yes. I wouldn't choose that word—it's a little condescending—but if you like it, all right."

"I'm very glad, Ryan."

"I'll tell her you said so. I'll say, 'My slightly screwloose friend *Professor Doctor* Eve Mornay is glad to hear that you're a "bright" individual.' I'm sure she'll be very glad that you're glad."

"I'm glad for you, Ryan."

"What does her brightness have to do with me?"

She positively giggled this time, as if he were playing a pleasant game with her.

"Is she blond or brunette?"

"Brunette."

"And what about her eyes? What color are they?"

"I don't know. Brunette eyes. I don't know. Dark. What did you expect, red?"

"Dark eyes, dark hair. What does she look like? What about her figure?"

He began to be irritated. "I'll send you her measurements. And her IQ, too, if she knows it. Would you like her SAT scores? She'll be taking the tests soon, I understand."

"I'm sorry, Ryan. Have pity on me. Two weeks ago you were mine, and now you're hers. You've got to expect a little lag in my feelings of possession. Have you made love to her, Ryan? Is she good?"

In the darkness of the little room he saw red. Rage welled up in him; he gripped the receiver tightly, struggling against the feeling as well as he could, trying to remember all the sweet, sad things about Eve that might help him control his anger; but the fury overcame him, and half-enraged and half-frightened that he might say something truly hurtful, he slammed down the phone.

He felt dizzy. His heart was pounding as no windsprint had ever made it pound, a crazy, bounding pulse. He slipped to his knees and crawled across the floor, following the phone cord to the jack on the wall; one ring sounded before he wrenched the cord from its socket. Then he sat back, leaning against the wall, trying to calm himself.

He wondered at the power of his anger. All he could think of was Constance, clinging to the crown of the high pine, and he beside her, holding her gently yet with all his might, so that so precious a being should not come to any harm . . . and he despised Eve and her simplistic views. Eve had had her chance, and she had given it up. He would not talk to her, or write her, until she had learned to respect at least that one subject.

He had been invited back to the Tates' tomorrow, to spend another day at the pond. He trained his mind to think on that and to forget the words that Eve had spoken in her curiosity and her twisted affection and jealousy. Tomorrow would be oblivion. He must store it up; on Friday Mrs. Tate was to take Constance visiting colleges, and Collin would certainly write all day. Then there was the Fourth of July, and his parents wanted him to go to his aunt and uncle's.

As he sat in the dark study he wondered at the strange, new feeling of misery inside him. It seemed so like Eve's misery. Where had it come from? He could not tell; he felt only the nearness of something large looming in his future, some pain or joy as yet without a name.

❃ ❃ ❃

On Friday he received a letter from Eve.

July 1

Dear Ryan,

I'm sorry. I'm sorry, but I know you love her. I've been very rude, I've been crass. I promise not to do that again. Don't you remember, once you used to joke like that? But only about people that didn't matter, I guess. Now you can't joke about her. That only persuades me all the more that you love her.

When you need to talk, I will be here. I will be very humble, and never say rude things.

Forgive me for not understanding. I have never seen you love somebody so much—how could I know how I was hurting your feelings?

Love,
Eve

He told himself that this was an improvement. And in his mood on Friday morning, he could forgive her the error on that topic anyway. On Thursday the Tates had invited him to celebrate the Fourth with them—not just Constance and Collin, but Mr. Tate as well had insisted on it yesterday, and Mrs. Tate had been almost petulant in seconding the invitation.

Daniel and Maureen had tried to dissuade him, suggesting a claim on him on the grounds that he would be leaving for England soon. He countered with tradition: he had not missed an Independence Day at the Tates for a dozen years in a row. His father would not stoop to playing further on Ryan's conscience and sense of duty to his parents; and although his mother started to do so, her reasoning quickly became tangled in counterproductive appeals to his love for his relatives. "Uncle Frank and Aunt Mary have been asking after you, Ryan," she said. "They'd really like to see you before you go away. I know there's the wedding, but the whole clan will go to that, and there won't be much chance for us all to sit and talk. They'll have the barbecue and light some roman candles, the way they always do. Your cousin Mary has a new baby girl—Kathy, her name is—and her husband Tom will be there; he's back home for a stint. And Reena's coming, too, and Pippin—you know she's always been sweet on you; and young Frank they say is on the wagon; and John and that poor little girl he married last year, they have a little baby boy; and Annie's Meggin and Caitlin; and thank God Tommy will be somewhere else, I hear; and of course Beatty and Allie and Danny; and Corrie and Ruthie, you know they think you're wonderful."

"Everyone will be there?" said Ryan.

"Everyone. Except for Tom."

"I really think I have to go to the Tates. It's kind of a big deal. Constance has never celebrated with us. We have to keep up the tradition, you know, and I'm part of it. Anyway, you two always go to Uncle Frank's by yourselves."

"Oh, Ryan," moaned his mother, seeing that she was losing the struggle, "just promise me you won't try to get out of going to the wedding."

"Okay, Mother."

"Do you promise? Promise you'll come to the wedding with us?"

"All right, I promise."

And Maureen had to content herself with that.

Saturday, July 4

I have played croquet until I am tired of it, and have come to think it is only fit for boys and girls. The great thing is to give them opportunities for flirting, and it does that.

—Trollope

THIS YEAR THE holiday dawned true to form: hot and overcast. By noon the temperature had peaked at ninety-four degrees, despite seamless clouds that showed no sign of either dissipating or dispensing rain. Both the heat and the overcast were a tradition, and never altered anyone's intention to enjoy the day; in fact, Collin's first words to Ryan when they met by the front lawn at about two o'clock were a cheerful "Cloudy, as usual."

"As it's supposed to be," Ryan affirmed happily. "Need any help?"

Collin was laying out the croquet court on the front lawn with the aid of a tape measure and a crumpled slip of paper on which his father had jotted the regulation measurements a decade ago.

"I've about got it," said Collin, forcing a wicket into the thick turf. "You might go see if my father needs any help with the barbecue."

"Help blowing himself up, you mean? I'll see what I can do."

Ryan went through the house to the back lawn. He did not see Constance, either inside or out; but he quickly spotted Lloyd, who stood before the stone barbecue on the eastern edge of the lawn like some pyromaniacal priest before the altar of his chosen god, or like Hephaistos himself, readying the forges for his Cyclopes.

The resemblance to the cultist was perhaps more apt. For Lloyd, the Fourth of July was an orgy of sentiment. Despite his pragmatism, he found pomp and melodrama reassuring. His life had veered at times into excesses of emotion and loneliness; rituals guided, sanctioned, set limits; they created the illusion of a family where there was only a broken home. The tradition of the holiday as observed in the Tate household had evolved out of activities once chosen on a whimsical basis and then repeated religiously and augmented over the years; and Lloyd and Collin and Ryan were as fanatically devoted and superstitious about the continuance of the various rites of the day as the devotees of the ancient mysteries.

Per tradition Lloyd was dressed in seersucker trousers and an Oxford shirt with garters on the sleeves. When he saw Ryan approaching, he doffed an ancient Panama and bowed ceremoniously, peering over his half-glasses the while. "Greetings, Rhodesian," he said. "I prepare for the ritual roasting of the hecatomb of hamburgs and hot dogs."

"So I see," said Ryan nervously, as Lloyd turned and drenched the blazing charcoal in the barbecue with another heavy dose of lighter fluid from the can in his hand. "You know," Ryan said, "you really shouldn't spray that stuff into the flames like that. The fire can travel right back up into the can and blow it up."

"My boy, you tell me that every year, and every year I agree, and forget all about it. I haven't succeeded in immolating myself yet, at any rate." He gave the charcoal another burst from the can. Ryan resisted the urge to shy away, and stood fast beside him; but when Lloyd had set down the starter fluid, Ryan surreptitiously removed it from his reach. The flames were now snapping lustily, threatening to singe Lloyd's bushy eyebrows as he heaped more briquettes on the pyre.

"Is there something for me to do?" asked Ryan.

"Yes—I think you could put the beer and soft drinks on ice," said Lloyd, indicating a stack of beverage cases, several huge bags of ice, and the oversized galvanized tub that did service as a cooler. Ryan went about his task in the usual fashion—that is, by first dumping in the ice, then recalling that the bottles and cans should have had priority; by next trying ineffectually to bury the containers in the ice; and by finally removing the ice and starting over. Even this exercise in frustration had the feeling of a ritual.

During this process Mrs. Overton began lugging out trays and baskets of various supplies—paper plates and woven plate holders; the Tate silver; bottle openers and can openers; toasting forks, spatulas, and tongs; the barbecue grill, which had been polished with a wire brush until it shone; crystal beer mugs; bowls for the potato chips and homemade rolls; dishes for the ice cream; and various implements of no reasonable affiliation with the menu, such as nutcrackers, corkscrews, lobster picks, pie servers, a cake tin, and a small piece of chain that had once served to keep toddlers out of her garden. It was a strange mixture of the practical and the pointless, the plebian and the luxurious. Ryan helped her by fetching down the ice cream freezer from its high shelf in the dark pantry. He was pleased to see that she bustled about with more of her old happiness than she had exhibited since Sondra's arrival.

The housekeeper had gone busily away into the kitchen for the rock salt; Lloyd was prodding the charcoal diabolically; and Ryan, standing by a picnic table, was inspecting the mechanism of the freezer for rust and grease. He was not facing the door of the living room, nor did he hear it open; but suddenly his attention was drawn there like the needle of a compass freed to find the septentrion.

She wore dark blue, with a playful plastic bangle on each wrist, one of red and one of white. She was watching him with a smile that did not fade, but softened and brightened from moment to moment as she paused, as she left the step, as she swished the skirts of her dress toward him with a self-consciously happy, feline tread; as she came close, too close, and beamed up into his face and seized his arm. "You're here," she said, "you're really here. I was afraid you'd get dragged way by your parents."

"Not a chance," he said. "Tradition is tradition." She let go of him shyly, and said nothing, still gazing up into his eyes, so close to him that he could not even make a pretense of fiddling with the ice cream freezer. "Climb any trees lately?" he asked. She laughed softly and paced away, circling halfway around him before she turned back. Her intense excitement was infectious, like that of a child on Christmas morning.

"I've been looking for a sequoia to try next," she said. "Those are the big ones, aren't they?"

"Anything less would be anticlimactic," he agreed.

"But they don't grow around here, do they?"

"Oh, I think we have a few down at the end of the valley. But they're only about three hundred feet tall. Little sprouts."

"Ryan, when I think of what we did, I practically faint! I went out on the front lawn this morning and just looked at that tree. I can't believe I was up in the very top of it. I swear, the trunk up there is only *this big!*"

He laughed at the circle she made with her index finger.

"You were wicked to take me up there," she teased.

"Stick with me and you'll do lots of wickedly fun things like that," he said.

"I intend to.—Did you see my bracelets?" She showed them off. "Have you ever seen anything so hideous? Twenty-five cents, in a big bin. There were thousands of them.—Have you seen Collin? Oh, Ryan, he wrote the most beautiful poem last night. I cried my eyes out—he was disgusted with me."

"I bet," said Ryan.

"No, he really was. Or at least he said he was. But then I did my best and told him what I thought—and he changed a line."

"Uh oh. He'll never show you another."

"Oh, stop it. I was very proud of myself. There was just one line you couldn't really understand—it had a squinting participle. And I could tell it wasn't supposed to be ambiguous."

"I hope you didn't use that term, 'squinting'."

"No—no, I didn't. He seems to get irritated when I start talking about grammar."

"Overexposure to pedantry, I suppose."

"What is that thing?" she asked suddenly, looking at the ice cream freezer.

"This? You make ice cream with it."

"Oh, come on, Ryan, what is it?"

"I'm serious. It's an ice cream freezer. Every Fourth we make ice cream the old-fashioned way. It's a tradition. See, you put the cream and eggs and all that stuff in this can—put these paddles in, see, they scrape the inside of the can and churn up the mixture; you put the whole thing in this bucket, add ice and a little rock salt, and crank the thing around and around with this handle."

"And it makes ice cream?"

"Well, it don't make scrambled eggs."

"Why don't you just put the batter in the freezer?"

"It has to be quiescently frozen."

"What does that mean?"

"I don't know, really. Frozen by degrees, if you'll pardon the pun." She laughed and came dangerously close to him again; so close that they both forgot the freezer.

"Do you like my ribbon?" she asked, showing him the thin blue strip hidden in the wealth of her hair.

"I like your everything. Even your perfume."

"Constance, my dear!" cried Lloyd, catching sight of her. "Ready for the festivities? You look ravishing!"

She curtsied to him; he saluted with a spatula, and then turned back to the barbecue again to cope with an eruption of flame in the charcoal.

"What are those things on his arms?" Constance asked Ryan in a puzzled whisper.

"Those are sleeve garters. Pretty strange, huh? Kind of a weird Fourth of July tradition he has." She pressed her hands to her mouth—her shoulders shook—and she looked at Ryan with marveling, laughing eyes over her fingertips. He suddenly choked on a wild laughter of his own, and they avoided one another's eyes, trying to recover without drawing Lloyd's attention, nearly leaning against one another in their sudden debility.

"God!" she exclaimed after a minute. "I can' t believe it. Sleeve garters! What an amazing man he is!"

"Constance, what kind of trouble are you causing out here?" called Sondra. The screen door slammed behind her. Ryan and Constance at once stepped apart. As her mother approached, Constance ran to her and whispered in her ear. Sondra looked at Lloyd and her eyebrows rose.

"Lloyd," she said, "why in heaven's name are you wearing those things on your sleeves?"

"What?—Oh, these things, you mean? Tradition, Sondra. My father and my grandfather wore sleeve garters on the Fourth of July."

"But you look like . . . a gambler or something. All you need is a green eyeshade and a croupier."

"Sondra, you simply must acclimate yourself to conditions around here. The boys would be horrified if any aspect of our yearly rites were altered. It's like a superstition."

She let the topic drop; Lloyd turned back to the barbecue, which was beginning to give promise that it might eventually sink into a heap of seething embers. "How are you today, Ryan?" Sondra asked.

"Very well, thank you. And you?"

"Hot. Insufferably hot."

"Better than being hot and insufferable."

"Or rude and insufferable. I may just melt like the Wicked Witch of the West."

"It was water that made her melt, not heat. Perhaps we should all go swimming?"

At this ambiguous remark, she said to Constance, "Stick your tongue out at him or something."

"Well, now," said Lloyd as he joined them, "Where's Collin?"

"Setting up the croquet court, I think," said Ryan.

"No, he finished that," said Constance.

"I saw him with all kinds of strange things," said Sondra: "The wheelbarrow, burlap bags, rope, pieces of cloth."

"Those are for the races," said Lloyd happily.

"The races? You mean we have to get even hotter than we are?"

"There's no enjoying the Fourth of July without a little perspiration," said Lloyd. "Fortunately, we form an even number.—Here comes Mrs. Overton. Now all we need is my wandering boy."

"Even number?" asked Sondra, exchanging a mystified glance with Constance. Lloyd smiled and gave Ryan a conspiratorial wink.

"Did you bring the book?" he asked Mrs. Overton, although he could see it in her hand.

"Yes, sir," she said. The presence of Sondra had not dampened her spirits yet; she actually smiled at them all and paused to admire Constance. "Oh, what a pretty dress! And I love those bracelets. What are they, Italian? I bet they were very expensive."

"They weren't too bad," said Constance, embarrassed for Mrs. Overton, and aware that Ryan was grinning beside her.

"Here comes Collin," said Lloyd. "Where have you been?"

"Doing all the work, as usual," said Collin. "Did you get any stout, Dad?"

"It's on ice. Ryan took care of it."

"Good. I'm dying of thirst."

"Not until we read the Declaration. The party can't start until we read the Declaration," said Lloyd.

"All right," said Collin, acceding to tradition.

"Everybody take seats," said Lloyd. "I'll just check the barbecue one last time." He hurried off.

Sondra and Mrs. Overton sat down, leaving the young people in a little knot together. Constance caught Collin's arm and whispered to him.

"Ryan says he always wear those things on his sleeve," she said, as if she could not believe it without further corroboration. Collin smiled a little painfully.

"Yes, I'm afraid so. Isn't it incredible? So horribly gauche!— But you look gorgeous, Constance. Are you sure you want to wear that dress?"

"Why? What's happening that I shouldn't?"

"Hasn't anyone told them yet?" Collin asked Ryan.

"If you haven't, I haven't."

"Then we'll leave them in the dark," said Collin.

"Collin!" she protested. "Tell me!"

"Time to sit down," said Collin.

They found Sondra and Mrs. Overton were actually speaking to one another. "It's always this hot on the Fourth," Mrs. Overton was saying.

"Just the sort of weather to sit still and say cool, don't you think?"

"Oh, it would be nice, if we could do it; but not on the Fourth; not with *him* giving the orders."

"Why, what is it that we have to do?" asked Sondra.

"Well, first——" Mrs. Overton began.

"You just wait and see," said Collin. "It's not bad, Mother; don't worry. You'll have fun."

"We call it the Fourth of July Triathlon," said Ryan.

"Is that anything like a marathon?"

"Oh, marathons are for wimps," said Ryan. "Compared to this, anyway."

"We've fallen in with a gang of jocks," said Sondra to Constance.

Lloyd returned and the talk ceased. He took up the book Mrs. Overton had brought, opened it to a well-worn page, and looked the text over, humming faintly. Ryan knew Lloyd was in a serious mood for the moment, because he hummed in a minor key. "Have to change this," he said, nodding generally at Collin, Ryan, and Mrs. Overton. Tradition was about to receive modification. He produced a pencil from his pocket and used it to mark several passages. "All right," he said. "I'll start off. I'll take the first two paragraphs, and the last one, as usual. Counsel's prerogative. Constance, you take from 'He has refused' to 'formidable to Tyrants only.'——It's marked here, don't worry. Sondra, you take from 'He has called' to 'Convulsions within.' Collin, 'He has endeavored' to 'Civil Power.' Ryan, 'He has combined,' to 'all Cases whatsoever.' Mrs. Overton will take the rest, up to the last paragraph. It could be more evenly divided, but it's better to stick to the divisions of sense as well as we can."

"Oh, we're reading the Declaration of Independence," said Sondra, catching on.

"Of course; we always do. We read the account of the first Thanksgiving at Thanksgiving, and the Gospel at Christmas, so it seems only appropriate. After all, if it hadn't been for the intelligence and courage of these our Founding Fathers, we would still be living in thrall to the British king."

"There's a queen, now, sir," said Mrs. Overton.

"Same principle."

"But I like her," said Mrs. Overton.

"She is a very nice person," admitted Lloyd generously, "but a cruel Tyrant nonetheless.—Enough." He cleared his throat, struck his best attitude, and began to read "When in the Course of human Events"; and it really was a pleasure to hear him in his courtroom voice, calling upon the jury of world opinion to vindicate his fellow countrymen. He spoke slowly, with precise enunciation; each sentence became another blow struck in the name of the oppressed, crying out in a voice of reason against the tyrant who had repeatedly demonstrated his insanity. Not a jury in the world but would have acquitted.

Constance received the book in her turn, and read nervously but fluently. Sondra read in a neutral tone that betrayed no emotion, but solid education; and Collin very slowly, as if afraid he would stumble among the obsolete phrases. Ryan was a Patrick Henry before he had finished his part, and would willingly have read the rest of the text without stopping. His oratory was utterly negated, however, by Mrs. Overton's halting and curious performance—it was obvious she did not understand what she was reading until a few seconds after the words had passed her lips, a delay which fed a continual struggle between her intonation and the late echo of sense: she frequently returned to correct errors in emphasis in a manner that proved utterly confusing. Though her delivery was provoking, Lloyd showed no impatience with her. Several years ago, when Collin had complained about her reading, Lloyd had rebuked him by saying that the document was the possession of every American, plain or fancy; and that Mrs. Overton's voice sounded as pleasant in his ears as the voice of the most polished orator—or at least, it did when she was reading that particular piece of prose. In any case, the impression left by her halting phrases was erased by his final flourishes—he especially enjoyed "our Lives, our Fortunes, and our sacred Honor"—and he closed the book reverently, and remained standing for a moment in silence. "Now," he said finally, with a smile, "on to the games!"

They adjourned to the front lawn. As they went, the men teased Constance and Sondra with hints or with a smug and portentous silence. "The first event," said Lloyd when they had reassembled, "is the three-legged race."

"No, Dad, the sack race is first," said Collin.

"No, son, it's the three-legged race."

"It *is* the three-legged race," said Mrs. Overton.

"Ryan," said Collin, "am I right, or what?"

"You're right, The sack race is always first."

"I am the *Magister Ludorum*," said Lloyd. "I say it's the three-legged race. The teams are: Collin and his mother, Constance and her father, and Mrs. Overton and Ryan."

"How do we do this? What is this?" asked Constance worriedly.

"You poor blighted child," said her mother. "You've never learned what a three-legged race was?"

"Are we going to time the individual teams, or can we all run together?" asked Ryan.

"I think this year we can all run together, " said Lloyd.

"But who will tie up the last team?"

"I think Constance and I can manage that."

Preparations began. Collin had already set out the course, and each of the teams had only to sit on the chairs provided in order to have their ankles wrapped with strips of cloth and bound with rope. As Lloyd lashed Ryan's right leg to Mrs. Overton's, she winked at him. "Shall we win again, Ryan, or shall we give them a sporting chance?"

"Let's hold back just a bit to see how well they do," he said.

"Listen to this guff," said Collin.

"Remember when you and I used to race together, Collin?" asked Ryan.

"And we always won, too."

"No, you didn't!" exclaimed Mrs. Overton. "Your father and I always won."

Ryan recalled those years: Mrs. Overton had enjoyed being linked with Lloyd a little too much and a little too openly, been too broadly humorous, and embarrassed everyone else. So one holiday Lloyd had made her Ryan's partner in the race. Thereafter it was the Tates against the non-Tates, with victory varying as luck would have it.

Constance and his father were bound together next. In the meantime Ryan and Mrs. Overton practiced under the trees. When they had reached the far side of the lawn, Mrs. Overton gripped his arm suddenly and whispered fiercely to him. "We've got to win, Ryan—we've got to show her up."

"We're in it for fun, Mrs. Overton," he said, "not to show any-one up. But I'm all for winning. If you really want to win, you'll have to do exactly as I say."

"I'll do it. You tell me how to go about it. You're the athlete."

They drilled. He taught her that the most important object was not to fall down, to remain standing even at the risk of being slow; and next to time their strides perfectly and ignore the progress of the others. He even had her practice recovering from a fall with him. She could not possibly have appeared more undignified than she did flopping about on the ground trying to coordinate her movements with those of Ryan; but apparently she did not care if she lost face now, so long as she gained it when the race was run.

"Hey! You're practicing!" said Constance as they made their way back to the starting line.

"How else do you expect us to get to Carnegie Hall?" asked Ryan.

"Is that cheating?" Constance asked Lloyd, who was still try-ing to tie Collin and his mother's ankles together.

"Oh, who needs to practice?" he said. "We'll be naturals at this, you'll see."

"My stocking has a run in it already," said Sondra to Constance. "How about yours?"

"But Papa, it's not fair for them to practice, if we don't get a chance, too."

"That's the way the world is," he answered.

"I'm glad you're a lawyer and not a judge," she said.

"I would have been a judge a long time ago, if it hadn't meant a cut in pay."

"Oh, yes, my stocking has a run in it too," said Constance. "Darn, how did that happen so fast?"

"Forget about the run in your stocking and try to get a run in the race," said Ryan.

"Don't worry about the silly run. It's a good omen," said Lloyd. "And I'll buy the winner a free pair of pantyhose."

"Is that supposed to inspire me?" asked Ryan.

"They don't make pantyhose for legs as enormous as yours," said Constance.

"I quit then. What's the point of running?"

She giggled and swiped at him playfully, almost losing her balance.

"Everybody ready?" asked Lloyd. "Now, on the starting line."

Keeping as aloof from the others as they could, the teams maneuvered to the rope that Collin had stretched through the grass. Ryan steered Mrs. Overton to an outside lane, where they would have more room.

"I think my foot is turning blue," said Constance.

"I wish I'd thought to bring the beer," panted Collin.

"After the race we'll get it," agreed his father.

"Look at them," said Constance, laughing at Ryan and Mrs. Overton. Ryan was conscious that he and the housekeeper made an absurd sight, he with his powerful legs, poised as if to proceed without consideration of their hindrance, and she on her fat, wobbly hams; he six feet tall, she as squat as a barrel. Lloyd restrained himself as he saw this, but the others did not. At their laughter, Mrs. Overton glared pop-eyed down the course, and Ryan shook his fist in mock defiance.

"You just wait," he said. "We're going to whup you good, Constance Tate."

"I wish I were tied to *you*," she said, shaking her delicate fist at him. "Then I could knock you down and wrestle you."

"On your mark," said Lloyd.

"Now remember," said Ryan to Mrs. Overton in a whisper, "stay cool and go on my count."

"Get set!"

"On my count, remember," he whispered.

"On your count," said Mrs. Overton, as grim as if her life depended on it. Ryan almost burst into hysterics.

"Go!" cried Lloyd.

Collin and his mother immediately fell down, laughing; Constance and her father bolted off, staggering, he shouting and she shrieking; and Ryan, counting "One, two—one, two—one, two," strode up the lawn with Mrs. Overton with relatively little effort. Though they were aided by the looseness of the bond, which had slipped as they had practiced, their success was more a result of their humorless coordination. When they had crossed the finish line, Ryan untied their legs and sprinted over to tease Constance, who was still lurching about with her father, hanging on his shoulder and laughing helplessly. Collin seemed to be trying to drag Sondra down the field by her ankle; she was laughing so hard she could not regain her feet. At the finish Constance and Lloyd fell to their knees, completely winded. "All that work for second place!" he gasped. "Constance, we did a terrible job."

"That'll teach you to mock an Irishman and his yokefellow, Ms. Tate," said Ryan.

"Have mercy!" she laughed breathlessly. "Get this rope off my leg!" She and Lloyd rolled about, trying to get their legs forward so that they could reach the bond.

"Do we have to continue this travesty?" asked Collin. He and Sondra had advanced no more than a dozen feet along the course. "We concede defeat. Can we take the rope off?"

"Go ahead," said Lloyd.

"At least we placed," said Sondra, sitting up. "I hope the next event isn't as horrible as this."

"Ryan, will you be so kind as to fetch the beer?" asked Lloyd. "I'd send Collin, but we may die of thirst before he gets that knot untied."

"Of course," said Ryan.

"I'll help you," said Constance. She tugged the wrapping off her leg, rubbed her ankle, and caught up to him. Her brow was damp with droplets of sweat, and a few hairs had stuck to the skin at her temples. She was limping slightly.

"Are you all right?" he asked.

"Oh, I'm fine," she said, smiling.

"We'll use this," he said, seizing the wheelbarrow where it stood on the edge of the lawn.

"Give me a ride again," she said, casting a glance over her shoulder. "As soon as Mother can't see."

When they had passed out of sight around the house, he paused; she climbed in and crouched down, facing him. He raced away with her—she laughed and clung to the sides, and they careened around the house, intoxicated with the heat of the day and their own vigor. When they reached the tub of ice, he lurched to a halt and let her crawl out.

"It must be wonderful to be in such good shape," she said, as he hefted the cooler into the wheelbarrow.

"Yeah, but I'm nothing compared to Mrs. Overton. She's in such ripped condition she terrifies me."

Constance burst into a peal of merriment, and finally the laughter Ryan had repressed bubbled out of him. "Did you ever see anything so absurd?" asked Constance. "She was so intent. But she's such a sweet person. I feel so terrible laughing at her."

"Now you know how Collin and I feel. She's a very dear old soul—" and he lowered his voice, looking around—"but she's the silliest thing that ever was." He picked up the handles of the wheelbarrow and trundled it away; she brought the tray with the glasses.

Everyone called for refreshment. Collin and Ryan downed their stout, Constance and Mrs. Overton soft drinks, and Lloyd and Sondra some vapid American brew. Constance entertained them all—a sketch she was, nearly skipping with excitement, teasing Ryan and Collin and making fun of her own failure in the first event.

"All right," said Lloyd, where he sat under a tree with Sondra, "time for the sack race."

"I can't believe you're really going to do this to us," said Sondra.

"What is a sack race, anyway?" asked Constance.

"You have to climb into one of these sacks," said Collin, showing her one of the ancient grain bags he had brought out earlier. "Then you have to run the course while you're wearing it."

"This is absurd! Ryan's going to beat us easily!"

"He *is* rather good at it," admitted Collin.

"I insist he be handicapped," said Sondra.

"What do you say, sport?" asked Lloyd. "Will you yield to popular demand?"

Ryan lifted his mug, which he had just refilled. "I'll race with my stout in hand," he said. "If I spill a drop, I'm disqualified."

His proposal was agreed to. "For this race we're going to time each individual," said Lloyd, bringing out an antique stopwatch. "Everyone tries harder that way. There's no temptation to give up when you see someone else has gone ahead of you." The start and finish lines were the same as before; he took his position at the latter.

"I'll go first," said Mrs. Overton. She seemed eager to rack up a lead immediately. She brought a burlap sack to the starting line and put her plump legs into it, hoisted it up over her rump, and poised herself for the signal. Ryan and Collin were seized by paroxysms at the sight: the one sat shaking with stifled laughter; the other rolled over on his side in the grass and lay paralyzed, unable to watch. Constance, sitting between them, emitted a strangled, sputtering gasp, and hid her eyes.

"Go," cried Lloyd. The valiant housekeeper, somehow sure she was racing for honor and glory, began hopping and puffing toward the end of the course. Even as he struggled with his laughter, Ryan wondered which she would reach first, the finish line or her cardiac limits. She finished the race as red in the face as her own rare roast beef, dropping the sack and stepping out of it with a glare of triumph.

"One minute, forty-two point five seconds," announced Lloyd. "Sondra, you're next."

In an effort to distract herself from her mirth, Constance sprang up and went to help her mother. "Let this business be a lesson to you, my dear," moralized Sondra as she climbed into the sack. "The real winner is not the one who crosses the finish line first. It's the one who is able to appear ridiculous with the best grace. That's what we're really testing here. In some ways that's what society itself is all about."

Mrs. Overton returned and threw herself heavily to the turf beside Ryan and Collin. They still had not recovered. Collin forced himself to sit upright, and Ryan sagged back against a tree trunk; their faces were contorted, and their cheeks marked by tears. Ignoring one another, they tried to concentrate on Sondra.

When Sondra had prepared herself, Lloyd gave the word. She jumped forward, fell immediately, and began laughing uncontrollably. Constance, too, gave a sprightly laugh; and Collin and Ryan, each seizing the excuse, succumbed to gales of amusement out of all proportion to the apparent cause. Mrs. Overton puffed and grinned triumphantly.

Sondra regained control of herself with an effort and demanded a restart. This was granted her, and now she leapt nimbly across the course. What she lacked in speed, she made up for in grace; what she lacked in seriousness, she made up for in the clever satire of her own efforts. "Well done! " exclaimed Lloyd when she crossed the finish line. "One minute forty-five seconds!"

"Well done!" grumbled Mrs. Overton under her breath to Ryan and Collin. "How can it be well done if it's worse than my time by two seconds? He didn't tell me well done! The man's bewitched!"

"Ryan next," called Lloyd.

Ryan wiped his eyes, rose, and strode to the starting line, glass in hand. He pulled one of the old grain sacks up over his legs, took another swig of his stout, and declared himself ready.

"Wait!" cried Constance. "That mug is only half full."

"You must be an optimist," said Ryan. "It looks half empty to me."

"A beer glass always looks empty to an Irishman," said Collin.

"We can't let you race like that," said Constance. "It would be too easy for you." She ran to the cooler and seized another bottle of stout.

"Wait a minute," protested Ryan. She wrenched the cap off the bottle with an opener and darted forward to pour the stout a little too enthusiastically into the mug. Foam and brown stout poured down the outside of the glass. "Wait a bloody minute!" exclaimed Ryan.

"We've got to make this fair," she said.

"Fair? You call this fair?" He held up the dripping mug, now filled to the brim.

"You can't spill a drop," she warned him. "And no fair waiting till the foam subsides. Or drinking any of it on the way, in case you were contemplating that."

"I'll get you good for this, Constance Tate."

"You'll never make it," said Collin. "She's got you, Ryan."

"We've all got him this time," said Sondra.

"It's not fair," said Mrs. Overton loyally. "No one could do that."

"Enough horsing around on the course," said Lloyd. "Are you ready or not, Ryan?"

"You just wait," said Ryan to Constance.

She mimicked a saccharine simper. "Oh, and by the way, Mr. Kinsella," she said—"Best of luck."

He snapped his teeth at her in mock menace, and she ran away giggling.

Lloyd called him to his mark and gave the signal to start. Off went Ryan, almost effortlessly, holding the glass in one hand and the top of the sack in the other, at a rapid pace. He traveled by enormous leaps, landing silently on his toes, absorbing the shock so well with his calves, and adjusting the mug in his hand so carefully throughout that he spilled not a drop of the drink.

"Oh, no!" cried Constance. "He's going to do it! He's going to win!" She ran after him down the course, calling out mock insults and trying to distract him.

He was nearing the finish line when the sack tripped him. He pitched headlong across the grass, dashing stout in every direction. A shout went up from the onlookers.

"Disqualified!" crowed Constance. She hopped about him in a victory dance, hooting and taunting him with ludicrous insults.

He endured this for a few moments and then abruptly scrambled free of the sack and dashed after her; away she sped, as light and swift as the deer—flew to her brother for protection, and crouched behind him.

"Save me!" she begged him.

"I hardly see how I can do that," he said matter-of-factly. "It's my turn to run next."

"I'll get you another stout," said Constance to Ryan, her tone suddenly propitiating. She jumped up, dodged him, and ran to the cooler.

"It won't win you a pardon," said Ryan.

She hurriedly poured him another drink, the very image of sweetness and submission; and then contrived to spill some on his knee as she was handing it to him. He set down the glass and lunged at her—she shrieked and jumped away—she was all invitation, with her laughing dark eyes, the wild flush of heat and exertion—he seized her by the arms; and she laughed, and yielded, and made no attempt to struggle. If she had playfully resisted, he would have wrestled her down and, for lack of any other way to consummate the game, would have ended up tickling her; but she made no motion at all, and he released her.

"Many a man there is, who is six feet under," he declared, "for far, far less than you have dared."

"Quiet over there," Lloyd said. "We're trying to run a race."

"You two stop flirting and be serious," said Sondra.

"This *is* serious, Mama," said Constance. "Serious flirting.— I'm sorry, Mr. Kinsella," she said, in a tone that made her apology only an escalation of the skirmish. She picked up his glass and offered it to him demurely once again—and once again tried to splash it on him.

"I'll get you for this," was all he could think to say.

"How? By beating me at croquet?"

"I'll knock you through the wickets," he threatened, leaning close to her. She brought her face inches from his.

"I'll conk you with the mallet," she rejoined.

"I'll drive you into the ground and use you for a stake!"

"I'll kick you in the shins!"

"Go, go, Collin!" shrieked Mrs. Overton suddenly. Constance turned away to watch, instantly refocused; Ryan, too, turned away, but saw little of the race.

His brain seemed to be in a roar. The heat, the exertion, the alcohol had scant effect compared to the shock and intoxication caused by the person standing beside him.

What's the matter with me? he wondered dimly, even as he cheered Collin, echoing her cheering. *I really like this woman,* he thought; *That's what it is; I really like this woman. And she likes me; she likes me a lot.*

Collin fell at about the same spot Ryan had, but more disastrously, rolling and twisting himself into the sack so tightly that it cost him ten seconds to rise and hop across the finish line. He barely bested his mother and Mrs. Overton.

"Constance, you're next," said Lloyd.

"No, Papa," she said, running over to him. "You go next and I'll time you. I'm going to go last and beat everyone."

"You?" said Collin. "You don't really think you can beat me, do you?"

"Not only will I beat you, I'll beat you by fifteen seconds."

"Listen to this, will you? Fifteen seconds?"

"Come on, Papa, let me go last," she pleaded. Lloyd could not resist her entreaty. He gave up the stopwatch and took up the sack. But his performance was notable more for its dignity than its speed. He came in last.

"All right, let's see what you can do," said Collin to Constance. She thrust the stopwatch back into her father's hands and dashed back to the starting line. Both Collin and Ryan razzed her mercilessly, but she only grinned at their insults. She kicked off her shoes, donned the sack, and crouched at the starting line.

"Go!" cried Lloyd.

She hopped nimbly along the course and crossed the finish without missing a step.

"One minute twenty-four point two seconds!" announced Lloyd.

Constance stepped out of the sack, threw two fists above her head, and cavorted, taunting her brother and Ryan.

"Crow all you like," said Collin to his sister. "Croquet's next, and it just so happens that no one can beat me in croquet."

"We'll see about *that*, won't we, now?" she retorted. "Just like no one could beat you in the sack race."

After replenishing their various drinks, they moved on to the croquet court. Collin seized the mallet that he knew would give him first turn; Constance took second, Mrs. Overton third, Lloyd fourth; and Sondra and Ryan wound up at the bottom of the order. Collin's first shot took him handily through the wickets, and he proceeded halfway around the court before he had to yield the turn.

"He is sort of good at this, isn't he?" Constance said to Ryan suddenly.

"He wins every year," said Ryan.

"Really? Why didn't you tell me that before I started bragging?"

She made respectable progress in her turn, though she did not catch up with her brother. The others played about as well—all but Ryan, who was so distracted by some banter of Constance's that his first shot went completely wide. "Why bother with the mallet?" said Collin. "Why not just kick it through?"

"I'd have better luck if I did," was Ryan's rejoinder.

"How did you ever win all those soccer games, Ryan?" asked Constance. "I thought you were some kind of jock. It sure doesn't look like it, the way you blew the sack race and the way you hit that ball."

"In serious sports, we don't allow beautiful, obnoxious women on the playing field," said Ryan. "If we did, neither side would ever score."

"Well, you won't score with me, either, if you keep talking like that."

"Whoa!" exclaimed Collin, raising his eyebrows and looking at Constance.

By now it was Sondra's turn again, and she found her ball in proximity to Ryan's. "I forget," she said. "What do I get if I hit him?"

"You get a free shot from a mallet's length away, or you can send him."

"Oh, yes—what's sending him again?"

"You put your foot on your own ball and hit it so that it knocks his away from the court," explained Collin.

"Yes, I remember now." She putted her ball solidly against Ryan's and set it up to send him.

"Mama!" exclaimed Constance. "You aren't really going to do that!"

"Certain people *do* reveal their true personality in this game, don't they?" said Ryan.

"This is my only chance to ever get vengeance on you," Sondra told him.

"What did I ever do to you that you should need to take vengeance on me?" asked Ryan.

"Nothing yet. But I have a hunch that sooner or later this summer you're going to do something positively dreadful. Then I'll be glad I made a pre-emptive strike."

"I think this is what they call a self-fulfilling prophecy," he said. "Besides, vengeance has a way of backfiring. You'd better watch out." She paid no attention.

She had once been a good golfer—now she swung as if she were teeing off on a three-hundred-yard fairway. Just after she struck, however, her foot slipped off her own ball, which spurted after Ryan's. Both balls had sufficient momentum to roll off the lawn into a gutter at the side of the driveway; and following the slope to the nearest drain, they traveled another thirty feet from the court. All but Sondra laughed surprisedly at this result.

"Serves you right, Mama," said Constance.

"Need I say I told you so?" said Ryan.

"How did that ever happen? I thought my ball was supposed to stay still!"

"By all the laws of physics, it should have," said Ryan. "But somehow you contrived to circumvent them. It's just an indication that vindication never pays."

"Well, stop vindicating yourself, then," said Sondra.

She and Ryan went over to examine the situation.

"You two don't mind if we just continue playing, do you?" asked Collin. "I think you're both out of this game."

"It ain't over till it's over," said Ryan. "You watch, I'll make my comeback yet." He took a careful fillip at his ball, which had become wedged in the grate covering the drain; it popped free, bounded up the gutter, slowed, stopped,, and rolled back to where it had started, an inch or two from Sondra's ball. Collin and Constance and Lloyd found this hugely funny.

"I think we'll just go on and play," said Lloyd. "Do let us know when you plan to rejoin us on the court."

"I think I can make sure that never happens," said Sondra. Without even making a pretense of striking her ball against Ryan's, she swung her mallet directly against his ball and shot it out of the gutter, across the driveway, and onto the lawn at the side of the house.

"Oh, how nasty, Mama!" said Constance.

"Nasty is too kind a word for that," said Ryan. "Dastardly, perhaps. Heinous. Evil. And only one punishment will suit—the one decreed by the *lex talionis* and the *circus vitiosus*. An eye for an eye, a tooth for a tooth, and a cheat for a cheat." He drew back his mallet to shoulder height and sent her ball smartly after his own.

"You guys are hopeless," observed Collin.

"Go on without us," said Ryan. "I, at least, will be back. Just as soon as I dispatch this troublemaker."

He and Sondra went briskly across the driveway—she gave a sudden, girlish laugh, dashed ahead, and knocked his ball farther along the side of the house.

"All right," he said. "This time you're going to get a lesson you'll never forget."

"Who's going to give it to me?"

"I am."

"You and whose army?"

"You remind me of your daughter all of a sudden, Mrs. Tate.— The army of my righteousness, that's whose army."

He gave a tremendous blow to her ball that sent it out of sight of the croquet court altogether.

"This," she said, "is war."

She hurried after the balls and arrived enough ahead of him to give his playing piece a swipe that sent it into the same hinterland as her own. She smiled triumphantly. "Did you ever hear someone say, Ryan, that vengeance doesn't pay?"

"Did you ever hear anyone explain that the soft answer turneth away wrath? That if your enemy smites you, you should turn the other cheek?" So saying, he ran after her ball and slashed at it again, dropping it directly in the middle of the back lawn. She retaliated by hitting his in the same direction.

They were now completely out of sight and hearing of the other players. The two balls lay within a few feet of one another; they each dashed up to the other's ball again, poised a mallet over it, and looked at one another.

He was struck suddenly, as he paused, by how attractive she was. Her face was glowing, her eyes were lit with that deviltry he had seen often in her daughter's; and the very motion of her body, of limbs and curves and even the tossing of her well-kempt hair, struck him suddenly as youthful and sensual.

She smiled, forgetting the game for a moment. They both straightened up and leaned on their mallets.

"Well," she said, "I guess we've made royal fools of ourselves."

"I guess so. And worse than that, we've lost our chance to beat Collin. Which would have been good for him."

"The question is, are you having fun?"

He laughed. "Actually, I am. And you?"

"I'm enjoying this much more than being beaten."

"You mean you just decided to play your own little game on the side, since you were likely to lose again playing against everyone else?"

"Something like that. I didn't really plan it, but now that you mention it, I suppose you're right. I always did dislike games where I was doomed to lose."

"A very natural reaction."

"Is this the last event before the barbecue?"

"Yes. From here on out you can relax."

They surveyed each other in silence for a few moments before she spoke again.

"Say, Ryan, there's something I've been meaning to say to you."

"Yes?"

"Do you remember the warning I gave you the first day we met? About not falling in love with Constance?"

The smile faded from his face. "I do," he said.

"You're not forgetting it, are you?"

"I'm not likely to."

"Because it's one of those things . . . like croquet is for me. It's no fun if you're doomed to lose."

He regarded her with a humorless stare. "'The dooms of men are in God's hidden place,' as the poet says."

"Don't be offended by my reminding you."

"Let me put it this way, Mrs. Tate. I'm no more at risk of falling in love with Constance than I am of falling in love with a woman your age."

She managed to laugh off this sting. "Don't be silly. And speaking of that, do call me Sondra, will you? When you call me Mrs. Tate, I get the feeling you think of me as an aged hag."

"I've formed the habit already," he said ambiguously. "It'll be a difficult one to break."

"Try. For my sake."

At this moment a ball came flying around the side of the house. It was soon followed by Collin, with Constance, Lloyd, and Mrs. Overton behind him.

"What are you doing here?" asked Sondra.

"I'm poison," Collin boasted.

"What's that?" she asked.

"That means that instead of winning outright I've decided to hunt down my opponents. If I touch you, you're out."

"And here are the rest of us, tagging along behind," said Lloyd, "no better than slaves tied to the triumphal chariot of the proud victor."

"By God," said Ryan, "there's still a chance to win. If we get around the house, back on the court, and through the wickets, we can beat this bully."

"Dream on, Kinsella," said Collin.

"Whose turn is it?" asked Sondra.

"Mine, I think," said Ryan.

He stepped up to his ball, rapped it smartly against Sondra's, and prepared to send her.

"Treachery!" she cried. "You can't do that to me!"

"When the ship starts to sink, it's always the women and children who are thrown overboard first, to lighten the load," he said. "A sacrifice is necessary, or the sharks will take everyone. Besides, you were the one that got us into this mess." He swung his mallet; the two balls collided with a crack under his foot, and her ball rolled toward Collin's.

"Serves you right, Mama," said Constance.

"How can you say that?"

"I believe I was next in our original order," said Collin.

"Go for it," said Ryan.

Collin clacked his ball against his mother's with one stroke of the mallet. "You're out," he told her. "Prepare to die, Ryan."

"You'll never catch me, old man," said Ryan. "Not if I have to drive this ball on before me from here to Timbouctou." And with this he poised himself for an attempt to take himself out of Collin's range. Standing over the ball and hoisting the mallet high, he put all his strength into the swing, actually lofting the ball four or five feet off the ground. But in the effort, the handle of his mallet shattered just below the head—his aim went awry, and the ball struck the house just beneath a kitchen window, rebounded, and was lost in the shrubs.

The whole picture was so comical that everyone burst into laughter.

"Well," said Collin finally. "What do you say? Do you concede? Or do we have to pursue this farce to the bitter end?"

Ryan examined his broken mallet and looked around at the spectators. It was clearly time for new entertainment. "It goes against the grain," he said, "but at least I bend the knee to a noble foe." Constance and Lloyd applauded; Collin lifted his mallet high in celebration of his victory, and Constance ran to him and kissed him on the cheek.

"I told you I'd beat you," he said.

"You were right. I hereby proclaim you champion of the croquet court. We're even, anyway. You won one, I won one, and Ryan one won. With a little help from Mrs. Overton, of course."

"I understand this is the last of the games," said Sondra.

"Yes, the games are finished, but something infinitely more strenuous than games remains," said Lloyd. "That is, making ice cream. But fortunately you and I and Mrs. Overton don't have to do anything but watch. Collin and Ryan will do the work, and Constance will help hold the freezer down.

"I'll get the booze," said Ryan. "We'll need plenty of that."

"I'll help," said Constance.

They dispersed to various chores. Ryan and Constance gathered the croquet pieces and went off around the house together; Mrs. Overton fetched the ice cream batter, and with Collin loaded and packed the ice cream freezer; and Lloyd and Sondra arranged the lawn chairs more congenially.

As Ryan walked beside Constance he felt intense euphoria. She smiled blissfully at him.

"I never would have thought that Collin would be so very much better than all of us at croquet," she said.

"He always has been. He has some hand and eye coordination I lack, that's for sure. Who came in second?"

"I would have, if he hadn't poisoned me. I was right behind him."

"And your father?"

"He was next. Mrs. Overton was last, poor thing, though she didn't seem to mind. The minute mother went around the house, she became quite jolly again. I think you must be right about her being jealous.—Oh, Ryan," she added, touching his arm, "I'm so glad you get along with my mother. It's wonderful to see you two kidding each other. I know she really likes you a lot."

"She has an odd way of showing it," he said.

"Oh, that's just the way she is.—You know, I've never seen her happier than she has been these past two weeks."

"And what about you? How have you felt?"

"I never dreamed I could ever be as happy as I am now."

They were silent until they had retrieved the beverages and the glasses; then, before starting back around the house, they paused together as if on cue, and looked at one another.

"And you?" she asked. "Are you happy, too?"

He felt a deep perturbation as he looked into her smiling face, the same premonition of unrest he had had several times over the preceding days.

"I've never been so happy either," he said.

❁ ❁ ❁

Collin was the first to turn the crank of the ice cream freezer. He continued until his sweat was adding drips of brine to the slush in the tub. Ryan then took over. When he was tiring, Constance insisted on taking a turn. She cranked until her face was bright pink and the back and sides of her dress were drenched.

"Oh, Constance," said her mother, "You're completely soaked. That dress is ruined."

"Two dresses in one week," she said in a low voice to Ryan.

"Change into another, and we'll ruin that, too," he responded.

"What are you two whispering about over there?" asked Sondra.

"What's wrong with a little sweat?" asked Ryan.

"What's wrong with it?" exclaimed Sondra. "I was taught that even saying the word was vulgar. Men perspire, women glow— only horses sweat."

"This is the eighties, Mrs. Tate. Sweat is sexy."

"Ugh!"

When the turning grew difficult—they traditionally beat the ice cream much too long—Constance stood straddling the edges of the bucket, one hand on Ryan's shoulder for balance, while

Collin wound the crank as though to shear it. At last they gave up, packed the can in clean ice, and left the ice cream to set.

"Well, what now?" Sondra asked the young people.

"Swimming," said Lloyd.

"Swimming! This day is one surprise after another."

"Mama never goes swimming," said Constance.

"It's true. I don't think I've been swimming in decades."

"It's a tradition," said Lloyd. "We all go swimming on the Fourth of July. "

"Except me," said Mrs. Overton. "I just won't endure getting my hair wet." She pushed her somewhat dirty bouffant about warily, as if afraid to dislodge it from her head completely. "Besides," she added, "I don't even own a suit."

"Well, then, we certainly don't want you to go swimming," said Sondra. "As for me, I think it's high time I gave it a try."

"Really, Mama?" asked Constance. "You're really going to come swimming with us?"

"Why not?"

Constance pirouetted with glee like an eight-year-old. "Amazing!" she exclaimed. "The whole family, actually doing something together!"

❁❁❁

The pond was cool and gray beneath the luminous overcast. Lloyd and Sondra merely waded in and dog-paddled about, chatting in low tones together; the young people swam out to the rock, and Ryan and Collin dove from it several times. Mrs. Overton sat on a log on the beach. She was now in a full sulk.

"Mother looks good in a bathing suit, don't you think?" asked Constance in a whisper. From his perch on the rock beside her, Ryan surreptitiously surveyed Sondra in her suit, a one-piece with a low-cut back.

"She doesn't exactly make the eyes scream with pain," he admitted. "Your father doesn't seem to mind the way she looks, either."

When they swam to the beach, Mrs. Overton came forward. "I think we ought to get the barbecue going," she said urgently. Her concern was greeted with puzzled indifference.

"There's no rush," said Lloyd.

"Well," she said impatiently, "I'll go back and start getting everything ready."

When she had left, Constance muttered, "Poor thing," in an aside to Ryan.

"She'd better get used to the situation," said Ryan. "She can't last forever if she fights it. She's got to adapt."

"Change, you mean? I thought you were the one who didn't want anything to change. Now you're expecting her to?"

"If she adapts, she won't rock the boat."

"I see what you mean," she said.

After lingering for some time by the pond, they all returned to the house. Collin lent Ryan a clean shirt; on which Ryan was complimented as he had never been for clothing of his own. Constance reappeared after a long interval with dry hair and another blue dress, of a different style and shade.

By then the first hamburgers were on the grill, sizzling over a bed of coals that would have daunted a fakir. Lloyd presided, cheerfully burning everything into unrecognizable lumps of carbon. No matter; Ryan and Collin ate with their usual wolfish gusto, impervious to Constance's teasing. For a young man, food is an especially serious business. They ate potato salad, tossed salad, tomato salad, and macaroni salad; wheat rolls, corn bread, and brown bread; baked beans; carrot sticks and celery sticks, both dipped in a mixture of sour cream and powdered soup; all of which was washed down with black stout.

"You boys eat like the red-blooded Americans you are," said Lloyd, "except for that mucky stout. The stout is totally unpatriotic."

"Good taste is never unpatriotic," rejoined Ryan, "just as true patriotism is never in bad taste."

"Ryan, you're speaking gibberish."

To which Ryan responded by saluting Lloyd with a fresh bottle.

"You two are drinking a lot," worried Mrs. Overton.

"On such a hot day alcohol has no effect," said Ryan. "We could drink cases of the stuff and be as clearheaded as you, Mrs. O."

She sniffed uncertainly.

Despite their appetites, even Collin and Ryan felt the need to pause before turning to the ice cream. By now the evening was approaching. When the smoke from the barbecue died away, mosquitoes and gnats swarmed over the lawn from the woods, driving the party indoors. For several hours they played parlor games, talked, lost track of time; and the darkness came on.

Lloyd had a illegal source of fireworks—a newsstand in South Boston where imports from the South were sold under the counter. He and Collin now dashed about on the lawn, firing off Roman candles, blowing tin cans into the trees with enormous firecrackers and cherry bombs, and igniting some odd and unsatisfactory flares. The others watched from the driveway. "Why aren't you out there, running around like a little boy trying to get his fingers blown off?" Sondra asked Ryan.

"It's just not part of the tradition. Mr. Tate had to solemnly promise my mother that I wouldn't have anything to do with firecrackers if I was allowed to spend July Fourth here. That was when I was eight, and he still feels the prohibition."

"It's a good thing," said Constance. "You'd probably be missing a nose and an eye by now. Although it does look a little like fun"—her sentence was here emphasized by an enormous bang from the lawn—"in a terrifying sort of way."

"Would you like to try some sparklers?" asked Ryan. "Those are safe enough."

He lit them for her. She danced around the driveway, with a clutch of sparklers in each hand, drawing glowing circles in the air.

When the last incendiary had burned itself out, they retreated from the mosquitoes and the reek of sulfur and returned to the living room. Mrs. Overton continued into the kitchen, exhausted, and they saw her no more that evening. After a few minutes, Ryan thought he detected a consensus among the Tates to end the party. He rose and said he would be leaving.

"Don't go yet!" pleaded Constance. "Just because these old fogeys are fading is no reason we have to." But her pleas were not seconded by anyone, not even Collin. Ryan persisted, and she gave in. "Come on, Collin," she said finally, "let's walk him to the end of the driveway, or across the lawn, whichever way he's going."

"All right," said Collin.

Ryan said his goodbyes to Lloyd and Sondra and in a minute more was walking up the driveway in the warm night with his friends.

He almost invariably took the route through the woods, by night or day, because it was shorter. But he knew that if he went by road now, Constance and Collin would accompany him farther.

"Now *that*," said Collin, "was a Fourth of July."

"The first of fifty or sixty we'll all have together," said Constance, catching both Collin and Ryan by the arms as she walked between them.

"Doesn't it seem pathetic when you look back, Ryan," said Collin, "and think about all those years without Constance and my mother joining in?"

"It does," he agreed. "It seems quite sad."

"You poor miserable bachelors," Constance said. "But that's right, Collin, you're going to be a bachelor forever. I'll just have to devote myself to you to make sure you're not poor and miserable anymore."

"That sounds like a good arrangement."

They walked on in a silence broken from time to time by the reports of fireworks drifting to their ears from distant fields. The darkness was lit by the lurid glow that far-off street lamps cast upon the clouds, which were thus dimly visible overhead, seeming to lour still closer to the earth. Ryan and Collin knew the turning of the way by instinct and guided Constance between them. Her hand held Ryan's arm above the elbow with a gentle but unhesitating pressure. "You're walking too fast," she said.

"You're right," he said. "And at a time like this, I couldn't possibly walk too slowly."

"Yes," she answered. "Don't you wish this driveway never ended, and we could just walk like this together forever and never stop?"

"The same way I wish childhood would never end—or friendship, love, the summer, life, the whole human race."

"Well, at least we won't live to see the end of the human race," said Collin.

"At least not in all probability," said Ryan. "Someone else will have to suffer through that. Can you imagine looking back on all of human history and culture, the last person left to mourn it all? We're lucky in that respect to die younger than the rest of our species."

"Those who die young are lucky in general," said Collin. "They die still perfect, uncorrupted. They're mourned as perfect and yet as incomplete, because they never had the opportunity to demonstrate that they, too, would be failures, like everyone else."

"Guys," said Constance in a rising, warning tone. "It's bad enough we're going to reach the end of the driveway; let's not turn it into a metaphor for death. You two turn everything into a metaphor for death."

"Every parting *is* a little death," said Ryan.

Now, quite suddenly, the gates loomed out of the darkness. Constance let go; for a moment the three friends stood apart, peering at one another's silhouettes; and then Constance came close to Ryan again.

"Thank you," she said.

"For what?"

"For coming. For being who you are."

"In the first case, the pleasure was all mine; in the second, I take more pleasure in my friends than they can ever take in me."

"Oh, quit all that nineteenth-century mumbo-jumbo," said Collin.

Constance still stood close to him, hesitating.

"Yes?" asked Ryan.

"Oh, you know, it's the same old feeling," she said.

"That troublesome something that eludes recall?"

"Yes."

"Don't be silly," said Collin. "Just say goodnight."

"Well, goodnight, I suppose," said Constance.

"Goodnight," said Ryan. Then he added the phrase that had on several other occasions reminded her that she had not set a date for his returning on the morrow: "I'll see you," he said.

This time, however, she missed the hint. Collin had turned to go and had even taken several steps along the drive toward the house. "What are you waiting for?" he asked Constance. "Do you want to tease Ryan again?"

"Don't climb any trees," she told Ryan. He laughed and turned away.

"Goodbye, old man," he said to Collin.

He went through the gates; they went toward the house. He turned; in the gloom he could just see her turn, too, to take one last look at him.

❁ ❁ ❁

After Lloyd and Sondra had been left in the living room, neither made any motion to end the evening. They sat in silence for several minutes, side by side on the couch, sipping their drinks. The dull, oppressive heat still clung to the interior spaces of the house; at the screens great insects thumped and buzzed and fluttered, caught in the disarming and distracting radiance of the lamps within. To Sondra it seemed the woods behind the house had become a temperate jungle teeming with rasping, vocal life. She began to say something about it; but as she looked at Lloyd, she saw he was about to speak.

He hesitated. "You were about to say something?" he asked.

What she had intended to say seemed too trivial. She said something else instead. "I was just going to say how much I enjoyed myself today."

"Yes," he said vaguely.

Several minutes passed. She knew he had something to say, and waited to hear it, though she was increasingly feeling her weariness.

"Tell me," he said, "what do you think of the children's plan to go to Maine alone?"

She sat up abruptly, stiffened, fidgeted. The subject made her feel threatened somehow. It was that Ryan; Constance seemed to like him immensely. Sondra had never seen her so at ease with a male acquaintance.

"Collin will be gone most of the days," said Lloyd, as if guessing her thoughts. "That will leave Constance and Ryan alone. Not that the boy's not a perfect gentleman. You couldn't ask for a more considerate companion. I have no problems with it myself, but I was wondering how you felt."

She had never liked the idea. She had half-formed plans to thwart it with college visits. Her impulse now was to insist that the scheme be abandoned; but she looked at Lloyd and held her peace a moment longer.

Why was he so keenly interested in this question? She could see that he was, though he looked away into the middle distance, or into his glass, swishing the liquid about.

"There's this to be said for it," he added in an indifferent tone. "Mrs. Overton always takes the last week in July to visit her sister-in-law; she has a little place on the shore in Rhode Island. If the children were gone, I wouldn't have to worry about how to feed them without her around."

She saw at once what was going through his mind. If Mrs. Overton and the children were gone, they would have the house to themselves. Her heart skipped a beat; she sat in silence still, and did not know how to answer.

"Are you really worried about Ryan and Constance?" asked Lloyd.

"Yes," she said.

"Why? You couldn't ask for a nicer boy."

"He's so serious! I wouldn't mind if it was just a little crush on both sides—a little summer romance, a few kisses and holding hands—maybe I'm being naive to even ask for such a thing. Nowadays the sex just seems to go along with it all. I wouldn't even *really* mind that, as long as they were sensible about it. But you should hear him talk about marriage. This is one very serious and very odd young man. Constance would get completely tangled up with him. She worships serious people. Look how she behaves about Collin and his writing. I just want her to have some kind of a normal college experience—not go off to school all emotionally tied up with someone who would never work out for her."

"Ryan would never work out for her? What do you mean?"

She looked her surprise at the mere question. "What do *you* mean?" she asked. "He's as poor as a churchmouse. You've seen that jacket he wears."

"Jacket? Who cares about his jacket? He's going to be a well-respected scholar. I guarantee it. At a prestigious university, too. Mark my words. That may not add up to wealth beyond the dreams of avarice, but it's respectable enough. He'll keep his wife and family alive."

"I'd like to see Constance do something better than just stay alive. I'd like to see her really independent financially."

"Look," he added, changing tack, "he's going away at the end of the summer. Even if they do fall in love, it's not likely to last. He'll be in England, she'll be involved in college—all those new faces and new friends. Let things take their own course."

She weighed the risks. She knew that Lloyd wanted that week alone with her. Maybe if they had that time together, something would happen, something that would change everything.

"You think it will be all right?" she asked.

"Don't worry about it. My God, Sondra, they're so young. People that young just don't form serious attachments."

"I was twenty-two when I met you," she said.

"There's a big difference between twenty and twenty-two.— Let them get it out of their system now, if you're worried about it. Then they can be comfortable friends later in life."

She thought for another minute or two, but felt only more tired and confused. "All right," she said finally.

"You won't object to their going to Maine, then?"

"No."

"Good. I'll tell Collin in the morning. He'll be very pleased. They all will."

He rose and stretched. "Going up?"

"I guess it would be a good idea," she said.

They put their glasses on the bar and turned out the living room lights. She preceded him up the stairs; when she stopped at her door, he had to step past her.

She turned to face him, and her motion brought them very close together.

"It will be nice to have some time together," she said.

"Yes," he agreed. His voice was faint, faltering.

She kissed him on the cheek. His face was rough with the day's growth of beard.

"Thank you," she said. "For today."

"Well, as our young friend says, the pleasure was mine."

He hesitated an instant longer. She thought just for that moment that he might put his arms around her; but he turned away.

"Goodnight," she said.

"Goodnight," he answered, without looking at her.

She had the fleeting feeling that he was pulling himself away from her with an effort. As he went down the hall toward his room, he seemed suddenly old and tired. He looked like someone who carried something even more burdensome than present confusion and future uncertainty—he looked like someone who carried that heaviest of all impediments, the things that might have been but are not.

Act 2
The
Sophomores

Alles was durch meine Kinderjahre
namenlos noch und wie Wasser glänzt,
will ich nach dir nennen am Altare,
der entzündet ist von deinem Haare
und mit deinen Brüsten leicht bekränzt.

Everything that throughout my childhood
remained nameless, gleaming like water
I will name after you at the altar,
the altar kindled by your hair
and lightly crowned with your breasts.

—Rilke

Sunday, July 5

ROSALINE. Is the fool sick?
BEROWNE. Sick at heart.

—Love's Labour's Lost

TO THE UNENLIGHTENED observer, the young man in love is one of the most puzzling spectacles on earth.

When Ryan awoke and rose the next morning, he did not eat breakfast. He thought he did. He went into the kitchen and sat at the table while his parents pored over the Sunday paper; when Maureen asked him what he wanted, he told her, and she cooked it, and put it in front of him; and he took up his fork, and pushed the eggs this way and that—he took up his knife, broke his toast, and covered the pieces with jam; he poured himself juice and let the glass sit untasted; he performed the stunted modern ritual with the tea mug and tea bag, added a little honey, and then set the whole business in the sink. Some part of his consciousness congratulated itself for thus carrying on as if there were nothing wrong—for forestalling his parents' concern for him.

But they were concerned anyway. When he went out of the kitchen into the study, their eyes followed him as far as the door; then met over the Living section and the Focus pages; then fell simultaneously to the ruins of his breakfast plate, which left no doubt, despite its disorder, that nothing there had been consumed; then met again in consternation.

Daniel Kinsella stood up. Maureen would have risen too, and followed him, but he made a sign, and she stayed where she was. Daniel would have more luck in the lion's den than she would. Besides, she could hear everything from where she sat.

Ryan had tilted the chair back on two legs and put his shoulders up against Grote and Mommsen and Gibbon. It seemed to Daniel as if the boy had been thrown there by a Sumo wrestler. He was whistling some broken, bizarre . . . well, it could hardly be called a tune; certainly his father had never heard anything quite like it before.

"Ryan," said Daniel.

Ryan stopped whistling and looked up. His eyes were glazed, slightly unfocused, as if he had a fever. One possible explanation occurred to Daniel.

"Have a lot to drink last night?" he asked.

"No," said Ryan. The surprise was convincing.

"Is something wrong? Do you feel all right?" asked Daniel.

"Sure. I feel fine," said Ryan; and he looked away into some unseeable perspective and with apparently unselfconscious rudeness resumed whistling the same broken tune.

As Daniel Kinsella stood there, looking at his son and listening to that peculiar melody, he felt a terrible foreboding. This wasn't just some ailment or quirk; it seemed to him that something was very wrong with his son.

"Ryan," he said, "you've never given us any trouble, in all these years. You've been our pride and joy."

"You have a generous memory, Dad. I can think of a few occasions when I caused you some worry."

"They were trivial, whatever they were. But don't give me any grief now; tell me what's bothering you."

"Nothing, Dad," said Ryan. "Nothing at all."

"But you didn't eat your breakfast," said his mother from the kitchen.

"Yes I did," said Ryan emphatically. He now fully believed he had.

"Ryan, if you don't tell us," said his father, "We'll feel we're to blame."

"You're only to blame for being silly, Dad. There's nothing wrong."

Ryan looked off into the distance and whistled that broken song. His father saw that they would have no answer from him, not now, not for many a day, and he turned to leave. Then he paused.

"What . . . tune is that, anyway?" he asked.

Ryan looked at him, all incomprehension.

"The tune you've been whistling," said Daniel.

"I haven't been whistling," Ryan said. "Oh," he added, as if suddenly realizing that he had been. "*That,* you mean. I don't know." He shrugged. "Close the door when you go, will you, Dad?"

Daniel closed the door behind him and went back into the kitchen. He looked at Maureen and shook his head. A crinkle of worry had appeared on her brow. They sat at the table for quite some time, but they did not read the paper.

❁❁❁

After his father had left, Ryan gave no further thought to his parents' concern. He had not really thought any coherent thing since he had left the Tates' last night. His mind had been filled with a miscellany—bits and pieces of friendship, scholarship, soccership that burst and vanished in his mind like Fourth of July fireworks—flaring colors that drew his attention away from the ground of his emotion.

But now he turned his attention to the notes he had been whistling—insidious sounds, insidious because they had broken free from his subconscious. He thought connectedly for perhaps half a minute before he realized what they were. On the night of the poker party, Collin's friend had played that dreary, raucous rock song:

> Can this be love
> I'm thinkin' of?

That's all it is, he thought. Some stupid little jingle that's stuck in my mind.

And then it seemed there was no sound anywhere around him in the world. He was alone somewhere . . . he was beneath the lookout pine. Here was Constance, coming through the great shadowed columns of the wood in a white dress; her eyes sparkling, bright with tears and laughter. She stood before him now, and to him she seemed a priestess, a devotee of Athena Parthenos, in the pillared grove of some pillared temple; and he reached out one hand, his right, and touched the side of her head, and stroked her soft hair downwards, just once.

That was the Gesture that was to haunt him, this its origin, its first dreaming. He did not dream of holding her light, slender body within his arms; he did not dream of kissing her; he did not dream of making love with her; he dreamed only of the chaste *gesture* of reaching out to her as she stood before him, her face affectionate with a soft smile; he dreamed only of touching her head with his hand.

Then the fantasy was gone. He was in the study again. While he had been daydreaming, he had rocked forward so that all four legs of the chair were again on the floor; he found himself sitting with his mouth slightly open, slightly dry, and his head bowed. And he realized at last, as he looked about him, confused by the sudden and vivid power of his reverie, that he was in love with Constance Tate.

He put his face down on the desk in a daze, and the tears crept from his eyes silently. He felt that he loved her so much that if he could not make her love him, he could not bear to live; or if he did bear it, it would only be a shadow life, a role conducted for the benefit of others.

And the reason for this, as he saw clearly now, for a moment, was that she was the incarnation of all he had ever craved in his life. She was the valley, she was the softness and richness of life there, its pleasures of conversation and companionship; she was bright hot sun and cold clear water, the deep-driven root and the high-thrown bough, she was fantasy, reality, the merging of child and present, the eternally present child in him—the way she had run about in her high-laced boots, laughing, playing, delighted, never jaded or wearied or pompous with her own attempts to have significance among the slew of ciphers that was humankind—the way she had climbed the tree sanctified by childhood—the way she pressed close to him, raising her face to his affection, catching at his arm . . . Imagine, he thought, if she loved him, if she sought out his company, wanted to be with him before all others, if they lived together in that brief time before all was over forever. And more than that, imagine if he had the right to love her, to express his affection; to work and care for her and make her happy with his mind and his voice and his flesh. She was all that he needed to love, hungered to love; and if he had her love, he could go anywhere on earth and live in the valley until he died; she was its earth and its people, she was the stone of the house, and she was her brother. She was the stock whereby he, the wild scion, might be engrafted and bear fruit on an old and dear tree.

He was stunned by his discovery. He could not conceive now how he had always imagined that he would want someone like Eve. Someone who shared the pedantic clutter of his knowledge, who could say, "It's an *i*-stem" and "the Homeric mythos," who could add to that hoard of erudition in his mind the coins and jewels of her own privateering across the seven seas of scholarship. And for what? His whole being turned away from the thought of such a life partner; and in so doing, took the first step in a slow but decisive revolt. Eve had been a companion to him, but their talk had been barren, their love had been sterile, by contrast to the fertile conversation and loamy affections of the valley. They had talked and talked, and where had it led them? To bed; and where had that led, ultimately? To parting, confusion, anger, because essentially they did not share the same spirit. He felt that with Constance he shared his whole self, his past, his memories, and all he loved; and he shared his potential with her, because he believed that their minds could grow together continuously within the unbounded reaches of their affection. What was it she had said? "It was as if she had some secret locked inside of her that she could not speak; the secret of who she was." Her secret, her being, was what he loved, and what he would cherish in her, though she never gained the tongue to speak it. Her image played through his mind again, and he groaned.

He knew boldly and at once that he must marry her. It was the perfect and the only right consummation of his childhood, and he was not the only one who had sensed that from the beginning. And now that he thought of it, he told himself that they could all still live together in the valley, literally, and never leave. He would have his job teaching—though it was not easy to get a job in his field, he knew his resume would coruscate with awards and published articles by the time he received his doctorate. There were colleges all over the area—it did not matter to him in which he taught, so long as he came home every night to the valley. If somehow he could buy the gatehouse back, and he and Constance could live there . . . and Collin would continue living and working in the main house, and publish, make a name for himself . . . and Mr. and Mrs. Tate (in the omnipotence of his fantasy he decreed it) would be reconciled.

Constance should go to college, of course. But it was important, it was crucial, that he marry Constance before they went on to those next years of learning and growing, so that she would not by some terrible turning of life—so treacherous, so unpredictable life was—would not learn to love some other way of living, some other place, or worst of all, some other man. Of himself he felt no doubt, or of her if once she loved him and vowed to love him; but without those vows, what would they be to one another in the difficult times ahead—a lover present only in a long-distance phone call or a letter?

And what of his plans for the summer? He had been wrong about how it had to be done. He saw now how he had been lying to himself. He had said he would be a brother to her, as Collin was. He had sat in this chair not more than a few days ago and denied that he loved Constance Tate, denied it to Eve and to himself time and again; and Eve had told him bluntly that he was wrong, that he did love Constance, more than he had ever been able to love Eve Mornay. No wonder he had been so angry with her—she had casually confronted him with the truth he had been denying to himself. How had she been able to tell? Was it just a lucky guess, a jealous suspicion? Perhaps it was. He would never really know.

But however it was, she had hit upon the truth. Not that he had any intention of writing to her or calling her to share his feelings with her; he knew he could not bear to talk about this with anyone, not with Eve any more than with his mother.

As he thought of his parents, he realized he had given the state of his emotions away. In the future he would have to conceal his feelings more carefully. He imagined he could probably cover over his lapse by simply eating a hearty lunch; though he was surprised to find that the thought revolted him.

Now suddenly his thoughts turned to the great game that those in love play in their heads, the great game of Whether or Not, the game they can never win by themselves. The point of this game for Ryan was to determine whether or not Constance loved him as he loved her. The playing pieces were looks, words, touches, situations, hopes, promises kept and broken; the tactics were confusion, misplaced rationality, desperation, and hurt; and the only rule was that certainty was impossible: a positive indictor would always be canceled by a negative indicator. The mere attempt to isolate a datum by observing the beloved closely would change the entire system and make that datum suspect.

She enjoys my company, he thought. *I'm sure she does. She invites me over all the time. And the way she looked at me yesterday, especially . . . and the difficulty she always has saying good-bye—that's a good sign.*

But then the answering voice came: *She feels pretty much the same way about her own brother.* (Suddenly Ryan felt disgusted and exasperated at the mere thought of being classed with a brother in her affections.) *And she didn't come up with an invitation last night, remember?* said the voice. *That probably means she's getting bored with you. Maybe she just had her fill of you yesterday. Maybe you mean that little to her.* (In the game of Whether or Not, last night always counts for more than the three previous weeks.)

But she respects my advice, he thought. *She sought it out specifically, that evening at the pond.*

Respect of that sort might not be any good, the voice pointed out. *You don't want to be seen as some aloof figure whose good opinion she doesn't need to cultivate. And what if you bored her or frightened her off with your pedantic response? You talked quite a bit at the time. It's very possible you said something totally idiotic.*

He protested: *But sometimes people in love test the ones they love by telling them their worst fears about themselves. She might have been doing that. That would be a good sign. And what about the way she's always touching me? Always taking my hand or my arm, or coming so close to me that I feel dizzy? Smiling at me, waiting for me, being thoughtful of me?*

She does all that for Collin, doesn't she? asked the voice.

But what if she's only particularly kind to Collin so she can disguise how she feels for me?

A mental scoff met this too-ingenious ploy. *Then why is she so much more reserved with you than she is with Collin?* the voice pointed out. *What about those tickle-fights she has with him? She just gave up when you and she were on the verge of something like that just yesterday.*

Maybe it was significant that her resistance collapsed. Even if it was *reserve, wasn't that reserve perhaps a good sign? Maybe she felt she might lose control emotionally if she yielded to that kind of physical play with me.*

Uh huh, said the voice.

And what about that time I caught her looking after me out of the upstairs window? he thought.

Maybe she was laughing at you. You can never be sure.

But what about last night? Last night even her mother accused her of flirting. And Constance said, "This is serious flirting." That's a good sign. That's certainly a good sign. You can't deny that.

Unless she meant something else you don't understand. Which is always a possibility.

He gave up his dialectic in frustration. This round of the game seemed to have ended in the paradoxical score of love, but love on his side only. In this game, one never knew the other player's score.

After all was calculated, she was only twenty, and he was only twenty. How many people married at twenty anymore? People seemed to wait, as if their lives would go on for ever. He guessed that if she really loved, she might not want to wait any more than he did. But she had always been so crushed and contained by her mother—she might want a time to feel free, to feel that she had an independent self.

And did she have even now a self independent enough to defy the disapproval of others—her mother, for one? He knew her mother would fight like a wildcat against a marriage. Of Lloyd, he could not say. He thought Lloyd's only objection would be that it would be far healthier for Constance in the long run to have time to grow independently of anyone. How could Ryan counter that argument?

And how would Collin feel? Would he be pleased, angry, bemused, jealous? Ryan knew his friend well enough to know he might be all of these things together. And one word, one frown, one skeptical glance from him, and Constance would be hurt and doubtful of her course. Somehow he had to convince them all that they must live out this summer for the rest of their lives.

In this first hour of the morning, as he sat alone in the study, he laid the mental tracks on which his mind was to run for the foreseeable future. It was a circular railway; it ran nowhere but back into itself, through terrain sometimes pleasant and some-times frightening, in a climate that might be clear or might be so sopped in swirling, treacherous fog that any kind of painful thing might lie athwart the tracks ahead and Ryan would not be able to see it until he smashed into it headlong. Between journeys on this cerebral railway he had long pauses in the station—which he spent idling in fantasy, dreaming of walking with her, sitting with her, in the house, in the woods, by the pond, talking with her—long, long conversations he had with her, in his head or under his breath.

His acknowledgment of his affection transformed him. Now he lived in a state of suspense and pain. He was convinced that this love was greater than any other focus of emotion he would ever know as long as he lived. It was as if he had been carelessly play-ing some game of chance and suddenly realized that everything he loved and owned, all his years of study, his life itself, was riding on the wheel that now, as he watched it, spun slower and slower. Who

could blame him if he held his breath and hoped that the wheel
would never stop spinning? So long as he was ignorant of her true
feelings, he had not lost everything. He truly believed that if the
wheel stopped and he found he had lost, the summer would die out
of his life forever.

His pain was thus a suppressed panic that he would lose all.
He was very close, very close to having everything he had ever
wanted: he thought of her upturned face and knew he was very
close. He had been so careless! So very careless. How many glib
and teasing things had he said that she might have misinterpreted?
But how awful it would be to lose all spontaneity now, now that
he knew how critical his behavior had become. He was desperate
to control the situation, and yet he knew instinctively that it was
beyond his control, and that he would have to let her form her
judgments and act on her feelings as she was internally led. And
yet not to act would be unbearable.

He rocked back in his chair and stared out the far window of the
study. It was slightly dirty, and the paint around the mullions was
peeled and cracked and mildewed. A honeysuckle vine had taken
over that side of the house, and threatened to close in the window
altogether; but he could see an indistinct pattern of leaves farther
away from the house, and it soothed him somehow and released
his mind into fantasy for a brief time.

He saw her waiting for him by the gates of the valley (in his
daydream those gates had been rehung, repainted, and repaired);
she was holding a nosegay and stepping nervously back and forth
from one wing of the gates to the other, anxious because he was
not with her; and then she turned, saw him—her face lit, she
drew herself up, stood more erect—her deep breath slightly lifted
her breasts beneath the white cloth of her dress—she awaited his
approach with a eagerness nearly unrestrainable; and when he
came to her, he touched her head with the gesture, and she looked
into his eyes and nowhere else. Then they turned and went back
into the valley together. She pressed close to him, holding his arm
tightly, as though afraid he would vanish.

Then he saw himself walking along the gravel shore of a
mountain lake. The water was as blue as the cloudless sky, but
even colder, so clear he could see steely fish swimming, like shadows behind dim glass, deep in the motionless masses of the tarn.
Across the lake a mountain of gray basalt, glittering with old
snow, rose from the water's edge; but on his side of the lake ancient
firs rose on the rim of the beach—beneath them a wild upholstery
of moss and ferns, a screen of shrubs hiding the deep couches of
the deer. He caught sight of her ahead of him on the shore, leaning
disconsolate against the hollow trunk of a fallen tree; she heard his
steps, she raised her face, incredulous—leapt up and ran, calling
his name, down the crumbling shingle; but when she neared him,
she stopped and waited for his calmer, more sure approach; waited
for him to stop before her and touch her with the gesture.

And fantasy followed fantasy. The germ of each was the gesture, in a different setting, a different moment where she came to
him or he to her or both arrived together; sometimes the fantasy
included a direction in which they turned as one afterward; but all
his love, all his hope was focused on that one brief motion of his
arm and his hand and the beatitude of the love in her face. It was
not a possessive or condescending motion; it was only the quiet
extension and expression of his love, offered to her without any
condition but that of her mutual desire.

In these broken, fantasized minutes of chaste passion he began
to sense something strange, something larger in himself than
he had ever known before. He thought of the errors the world
had committed against him, and they seemed unimportant. His
parents, so loving and yet so flawed; his teachers at school, who
acted the part of the wise, and yet seemed to be driven by the hor-
mones of a teenager, like actors mouthing words they could not
comprehend; his peers in college, so unimaginative, so unable to
seize their opportunities, so unaware of the violence and wanton-
ness that ran through all creation like a hidden crack in a black
obsidian; his friends, his acquaintances—even Sondra Tate, so
resistive, so restless, so determined to seize control and make

everyone's life her own; and it was as if he were beginning to gather all these into his embracing compassion.

This was a stirring he could not identify. It was grim and yet it was forgiving. He called it, when he knew it well enough to give it a name, *the reaper's joy*. It was the labor and reward of the Harvester, striding up the field, gathering human life into the sweep of his scythe; fruitage and loss at once; triumph despite the illusion of futility.

This first morning it moved him finally to such an ache and irritation that he suddenly bolted from his desk.

He was dizzy, but he had to go out. As he walked unsteadily through the kitchen, he looked at his parents, with a cool and aloof compassion; and they looked back at him with dread in their eyes—not dread of him, but that same dread a parent feels who has learned his child possesses some defect that will bring suffering with it. He went out without speaking.

❀❀❀

When next he noticed where he was, he was ascending the hill through the woods. The massive, regular trunks of the pines seemed to him now like the columns holding high the arched roof of a cathedral. Light fell through the canopy in long shafts that met the humus in pools of blurred and dappled gold.

This really is a sacred place, he thought. *Sacred as the grove of Athena.*

"Sacred," he said aloud. The word was muffled and alone in the summer wood.

What are you saying, Ryan Kinsella? he thought. He remembered the passage from Plato where Socrates confronts his accuser at the trial. "Was there ever a person, Meletus, who believed in the existence of human affairs, but not in human beings? . . . Did anyone ever believe in horsemanship, but not in horses? Or in flute-playing, but not in flute-players? No, my good sir, . . . there never was such a person. So now please answer this question: Was there ever a person who believed in things that are divine, but not in divine powers themselves?"

If this place is sacred, he thought, *then sacred to whom? To what? If I feel something sacred about this place, then must there not be something divine in the universe?*

And it's not just this place, he thought. *It's my life—suddenly—now—because she's in it. There's something sacred about my life.*

But what god is it then? Aphrodite? Pan? The jealous god of Israel? The gentle god of Christ? The god of my mother's people? The god of my father's people?

The myths were empty; the names, the concepts, all seemed empty and inadequate compared to what he felt.

He thought of where Constance probably was at this moment: at Mass in the stone church not far from the village green. Worshipping a god he could not believe in.

He looked about him and listened.

I believe in here, he thought. *I believe in now. I believe in the love I feel.*

"If you exist," he whispered, "tell me—is this right, that I love her?"

He listened; listened, perhaps for the first time in his life, inwardly.

"Should I love her?" he asked again. "I want to know because . . . the way I feel is so . . . I feel I could die of this." *Or live of it,* he thought, *be wrenched into life as I never have been.*

He listened.

And in the silence, inside his listening, he heard love.

That was all he heard. No words, no interpretations, no judgments—only love.

So is that an answer? he wondered. And he wondered still more: *Is that a god?*

He sat down, feeling dazed. He sat like a drunk, with his great legs bent and to one side, as if they had suddenly ceased to be of use.

What is this? he thought. *Am I praying? Am I being answered?*

He knew suddenly that this was it. There was no theodicy, no theology; there was no less pain, no less mystery; there was no reason revealed, no dogma, no creed that could make him hate or kill; there was only this love.

It felt like that reaper's joy. It was the slowest and the quickest, the saddest and the most heartening of emotions; it was delight mingled with pain, the pulse of song mingled with the ache of silence. What he felt was the human resonance of that thing larger than the human, to which all must vibrate, whether they know it or not.

Monday, July 6

Come over the hills and far with me,
and be my love in the rain.

—Frost

I need not tell a New England boy what a museum of curiosities is the garret of a well-regulated New England house of fifty or sixty years' standing. Here meet together, as if by some preconcerted arrangement, all the broken-down chairs of the household, all the spavined tables, all the seedy hats, all the intoxicated-looking boots, all the split walking-sticks that have retired from business, "weary with the march of life." The pots, the pans, the trunks, the bottles—who may hope to make an inventory of the numberless odds and ends collected in this bewildering lumber-room? But what a place it is to sit of an afternoon with the rain pattering on the roof! what a place in which to read *Gulliver's Travels,* or the famous adventures of Rinaldo Rinaldini!

—Thomas Bailey Aldrich

RYAN HEARD NOTHING from the Tates for another twenty-four hours. Which time he spent, after returning from the woods, in the stuffy study, with the door closed, the desk bare before him, watching nothing, though his eyes and his lips sometimes moved. He came forth to eat, or to climb to his narrow bed and lie awake still longer hours, caught in the cycle of agitated thought and soothing dream.

Occasionally he experienced entire minutes of acute panic, as he considered the possibility that the Tates might never call him again. But Constance did call, on the morning of the sixth at about eleven. He heard her voice for the first time fully cognizant of its meaning for him; it seemed to him a music through whose

445

overtones he could walk, within whose echoes he could dwell. As he listened, playing the game Whether or Not, every word, every breath, was a potential source of reassurance or discouragement. Somehow he found himself exchanging much the same silly talk with her as before, though now it seemed freighted with meaning, seemed bold flirtation. He was conscious of his restraint—he wanted to tell her what he had discovered about his feelings—and yet he was sure that doing so would be the destruction of his hopes.

She, too, seemed subdued when they met. He noticed it in her gait when he first observed her from across the lawn. He was approaching the house; she had been sitting on the steps of the stone porch with an unopened book on her lap; but she left her seat at once and walked along the drive to meet him. Though she had obviously seen him, her gaze was averted; his greeting, when he approached her, was answered only with a preoccupied and somewhat painful smile.

"Are you all right?" he asked impulsively.

"Oh, yes," she said. "I'm fine. Is there some reason I shouldn't be?"

"Well," he said, attempting humor, "I see you're wearing your tree-climbing dress. It's the first time in our acquaintance I ever saw you wear a dress twice. Something must be terribly wrong."

She tried to smile again. "Actually, you've hit part of it," she confessed. "Mother found it this morning and had a fit. I didn't tell her how it happened, but she called me a tomboy and a couple of other things—pretty bad things. She hasn't been that mad at me for a long time. So I washed it and sewed up the holes—see?— and now it's going to be my rough-house dress."

He laughed softly. "All my clothes are rough-house clothes," he said. She brightened with his smile, and suddenly changed the subject.

"I hope you weren't in the middle of something when I called," she said.

He checked the effusive denial that rose to his lips. "Oh, I wasn't really busy at all," he said.

"Because I know you have other things to do. I asked Collin yesterday if he thought it would be all right to call you up, and he said you always liked a little time alone." She stole a quick glance up at the window of Collin's room. Ryan realized that she had walked down the drive away from the house, even moving slightly perpendicular to his own path, in order to reach a point out of earshot of that window.

"Constance," he said, "you should know by now that I enjoy your company. I don't come over here out of charity. I come for purely selfish reasons—because I like coming here. So don't ever hesitate to give me a call because you imagine I'm bored with the valley or too busy to come."

She was visibly relieved. "I'm the selfish one," she said. "Collin has his work, and you have yours; but I don't have anything to do but play." She paused painfully a moment before continuing. "He got mad at me this morning because I fell asleep on his bed while he was writing. It's the first time he's ever thrown me out of his room."

"So there really was something wrong, then."

She only nodded, as if she did not trust herself to speak.

"Two things," he said. "First of all, it's summertime. I'm with you. I don't have anything to do but play either—Collin was the one who talked me into that. I haven't forgotten that promise we made, and I intend to keep it, as I'm sure Collin does; he's just worrying about getting his portfolio together for that workshop. That's all right. You and I can go for a walk, or just sit somewhere and talk together, while Collin does what he has to do. Secondly, he won't be mad at you for long. You know he won't. And even if he does lose his temper from time to time, I never will. Not as long as we both shall live."

She looked up and smiled radiantly. For a minute they simply stood, looking at one another; he with his hands by his sides, she holding one hand in the other before her narrow waist. For Ryan, it was a dizzying moment. *Should I say something more?* he wondered. *No, no,* he told himself.

From far off in the south came the growl of thunder.

"A thunderstorm!" she exclaimed. "I haven't seen one since I came here."

"Are you afraid of thunder?" he asked.

"Who, me? The girl who climbs trees and sweats like a horse? I love thunderstorms."

"Great! Let's go climb the look-out tree before the storm gets here."

She laughed and rolled her eyes in horror at the thought. "It's a good thing I can tell when you're joking," she said. "Or at least, I can usually tell. Otherwise I'd think you were crazy."

"What we could do, actually, is go up in the attic and watch the storm through that big dormer. Collin and I used to do that when we were kids."

"Really? Is it safe up there?"

"See those lightning rods?" he asked, pointing up to the roof.

"Is that what those are?"

Another roll of thunder turned them toward the house. He tried to steal a glance at her unobserved as they went, but met her eyes. They both laughed shyly. "I'm so glad you came," she said impulsively. "Even if it rains all day, we'll have fun. But I'd better warn you: my affliction is worse than ever. Now I feel I have something to say to you all the time, but I still don't know what it is."

"Maybe that means you're closer to discovering it."

"I hope so. It's beginning to drive me crazy."

They went inside. Lloyd and Sondra were in the living room, he marking up a crossword puzzle in the paper and she languidly reading a fashion magazine. A few college guides lay on the coffee table; she seemed to be avoiding them. Her greeting seemed somewhat acid—Ryan thought that perhaps he was implicated in the destruction of the dress; but Lloyd's welcome was as hale as ever.

Constance had never seen the attic. The entrance, hidden at the back of a closet, opened on a steep and unlit staircase that led up, straight and strait, for some fifteen feet. The treads were only six inches wide, and the risers nearly a foot in height; to ascend was more akin to climbing a ladder than walking up steps. "We might as well be climbing a tree!" exclaimed Constance as she groped her way upward in the dark.

The attic, by contrast with the stairwell, was enormous. Beneath the steep peak of the roof was a single space the size of a Viking hall, intersected by the timbers of the internal frame. The rafters were oak, dirty brown with age, fitted at the angle of the roof with tongue and fork joints trunnelled together; perpendicular to them ran the purlins, crowded close together to bear the weight of the slate roofing, and beneath them the collar ties, held up by knee-braced queen posts. The floor was chestnut, now a rarity, but once a common wood—dried and hard, with a layer of acrid dust everywhere upon it, except where the footprints of years gone by were preserved. Here and there were openings where one might gain access to the subfloor, and traverse another interior structure through a space almost large enough for a man to walk upright.

"I had no idea there was so much space up here," she marveled.

"It's not too hot for you, is it?" he asked. The temperature was daunting, the air stuffy and heavy with the odor of wood and dust.

"The heat is sort of nice, actually. For a while, anyway. What's all this junk?"

"Exactly that—junk."

They looked over a sea of broken furniture, discarded steamer chests, lamps, baby cribs and toys, games in battered boxes, clothing eaten by moths and squirrels, obscure prints and paintings in crumbling plaster frames, and swelling waves of Harper's Monthlies and National Geographics. On one beam the best-selling novels of the last century were ranged in powdery oblivion, from *Ben Hur* to *St. Elmo*.

"This is your ancestry, Constance," he told her. "This is your family history. A century's worth of castoffs."

"Amazing! My mother would have fun throwing this all away—if it wasn't too dirty to touch. Look at that thing! What is it?"

"It's the head of a wild goat," he explained. He dragged the mounted trophy out of a dusty pile and showed it to her.

"Is that a——?"

"A cigar in its mouth, yes. Ancient by now, but it still stinks. We put it there."

"You did? You and Collin?"

"Oh, there's quite a story behind this one."

"Will you tell me it?"

"Sure."

Another roll of thunder called them.

"Let's watch the storm for now," he said. "I'll tell you later."

He showed her to the big dormer and they found a high perch on a horizontal beam. From here they could look through the multiple lights of the window toward the wooded hills over which the storm was approaching.

The black belly of the thunderhead overrode the lingering bland gray of the overcast that had lain upon the land all morning. Even as it brought darkness, it brought too the eerie illumination of its lightning. The thunder began to follow each distant and general flash in almost continuous peals, echoing off the earth and rumbling over hills and lawns and through the house. As the light of day sank rapidly into pseudo-night, the first clearly defined bolt fell, an ornate and jagged blast, with side forks and bizarre upturnings, as if the unleashed electricity sought out the energy of the clouds as well as following the unseen discharge of the earth. The clap of thunder seared their ears. Constance seized his arm involuntarily, but then let go with a laugh.

"Room for one more?" asked a voice behind them. They turned to see Collin by the stairway.

"Plenty of room," said Ryan, guiltily conscious, for the first time in his life, of a disappointment in seeing his friend.

"Oh, Collin, you're just in time," said Constance. She patted the place on the beam beside her.

"How can you sit on that filthy thing?" he said as he approached.

"I'm wearing my play dress."

"So I see."

He found a piece of cardboard to protect his clothes from the dust, laid it on the beam, and scrambled up beside them.

"We just saw a huge bolt fall," said Constance.

"Right over that far hill," added Ryan.

As they watched they saw the tops of the farthest trees shocked by an invisible wave of wind. In a few seconds a furious gust struck the trees that bordered the lawn, tearing loose dozens of broad leaves and setting them swirling toward and over the house. The windows strained and rattled in their casings, and the wooden frame of the roof, massive and solid though it was, creaked in this place or that due to the unequal pressure exerted upon it.

After the dry wind, instantly the rain. The panes shuddered, smeared by driven water, and the slates roared. The gutters filled instantaneously with leaping streams beaten into froth by occasional stones of hail. The lightning fell very close now, per- haps somewhere in the valley itself; the brightness of the bolt flared over the flooded window, and the thunder shot its fusillade through the watchers. At once another bolt stabbed the earth, much closer, probably on the far edge of the lawn, with a fire that lived in ragged afterimage on their retinas even after the tre- mendous crack had turned to a dwindling echo rolling over the hills to the north. Constance had gripped both Ryan's hand and Collin's, and Collin was just beginning to chide her fear when the storm's discharge flung another writhing fork to earth just beyond the trees that edged the lawn—perhaps even striking one—and threw a wild horizontal lash over the rest of the windbreak. They recoiled as a simultaneous crack of thunder rent the air.

It seemed the next bolt should strike the house, but the light- ning came no nearer. More fell, before them, among the hills; but soon the rolls of thunder sounded behind them, the wind abated, and the rain slowed from a tempest to a mild downpour.

"That's about as close as it gets," said Ryan. His words sounded distant and muffled to him; he was too conscious of the hand that held his.

"Gotta go," said Collin suddenly. As he disengaged his hand from Constance's, she released Ryan's also.

"Aren't you going to have lunch?" asked Constance.

"You two go ahead," said Collin. "I'll be down in a while."

"The inspiration has struck with the lightning," said Ryan to Constance as Collin went away downstairs. She turned to him with a smile.

"I think I've been forgiven," she said.

"Of course. You're his muse. And after the cursing and whining and carrying on, a writer always forgives his muse for nodding off. He has to. It's an ongoing relationship. He can't quit."

"Ryan," she said, "I'm so grateful to you. You have a way of lifting up my spirits no matter how low I am. You just keep tickling away at me until I have to laugh."

"I guess that makes me *your* muse, then. Or your *amuse*."

"We'll make it your official position. You're hired."

When he thought about that moment later, he was frightened to realize how close he had come to reaching for her as she dazzled him with that affectionate smile. But she had jumped down from her seat on the beam before he could make that mistake, if it indeed would have been a mistake.

"Let's get some lunch," she said.

❁❁❁

Collin joined them in the dining room. They talked over the dishes until late afternoon; then Constance served them high tea in the grand style, complete with tarts and cake baked by Mrs. Overton. After that Collin invited Ryan to dinner; but Ryan did not stay.

He was caught in his own casuistry: Whether or Not forced him to go. He thought, suddenly, that he might be overstaying his welcome. Better to leave Constance craving his return, never to let her decide he could be tedious.

It was gratifying to have her follow him to the door, wishing he could stay; he hoped she would press him a little more, so that his scruples might be satisfied. But they passed Sondra in the living room, and she darted him a chilly glance; and that glance hardened his resolution.

"Well, if I can't talk you into staying," said Constance at the door, "can I make you promise to come back tomorrow?"

"Sure," said Ryan.

"Don't make any plans," called Sondra from the living room.

"Why not?" said Constance over her shoulder.

"Because we're going to take the day and look around a little."

"Where?"

"I haven't decided yet."

"Bogus!" exclaimed Constance under her breath.

"Did you say something, dear?"

"Nothing I wanted you to hear, Mother."

"Don't get snippy, Miss Tate," said the acid voice in the living room. "It's unbecoming."

Constance made a face.

"How about Wednesday?" she asked Ryan.

"Sounds great."

"We'll do something special. Have a picnic again or something."

He smiled and went out; but when he had stepped into the driveway he paused and turned back.

She was leaning against the post of the doorway, smiling mysteriously at him, veiled by the screen.

"Did anybody ever tell you," he said in a low voice, "that you look beautiful when you're snippy?"

She laughed, and he turned away and left, carrying that bright sound with him.

❁❁❁

As he walked home along the steaming roadways, he wondered why he had refused the Tates' invitation. He puzzled over the quibbles of Whether or Not; and he thought again of that look Sondra had given him. *Why did I react the way I did?* he asked himself. *That was exactly what she wanted me to do. Why should I care what Sondra Tate thinks? I don't want to marry her. I want to marry her daughter.*

It's the old whip, he thought: *the Irish pride.* "The immigrant's curse," his father always called it; the feeling that one is just not good enough. And a true Irishman reacts by damning all and sundry to hell, and stalking off full of loathing for the high and mighty, and for himself—and for God, for that matter, who made the world the way it is, or at least stood by and let humans make it that way.

To hell with Sondra Tate, thought Ryan, kicking a stone in the road with a savagery that surprised him. *She thinks I want to climb the ladder. Well, to heck with her. This is America, and I don't have to climb the ladder. I'm every bit as good as she is—no, by God, I'm better. I've worked for what I've got. My parents have worked for what they've got, little as it is. My whole clan . . .*

He thought about his clan. It was not a pleasant business, thinking about the O'Briens. It was not an easy business. They knew about his friendship with the Tates. ("How are those rich friends of yours, Ryan? With the big fancy house?"—"Shut up, Tommy.") Some of them, his Aunt Ginny and his Aunt Luce especially, told him to take what he could get. ("But don't lose yourself, Ryan, don't lose your pride. Remember, you're an O'Brien.")

Remember I'm an O'Brien, he thought sullenly as he approached his parents' rundown house and heard the classical music from Maureen's radio drifting faintly on the damp evening air. *Remember I'm an O'Brien.*

He paused before the stoop and listened to the music; it was Bruch's *Scottish Fantasy.*

I'll remember, he thought. *I couldn't forget if I tried. Blood, fiber, and bone I remember.*

He ascended the steps and opened the screen door.

"Oh, here you are," said his mother. "Have a good time?"

"Do you ever forget you're an O'Brien, Mother?" he asked her.

She had trouble apprehending his strange question. "What?" she said.

"That you're an O'Brien. Do you ever forget it?"

She looked at him now as if she knew exactly what thoughts were going through his mind; as if she had had the very thoughts he was having many times in her life.

"No," she said.

He went past her. Neither of them attempted—or needed—to say anything further.

Tuesday, July 7

Unhappy is he who in love-longing
must always live.

—Anonymous

RYAN WAS STUDYING Spanish the next morning at about ten when Constance called.

"You haven't left?" he said hopefully.

"We're about to. My mother wants us to look at some college in Worchester. Then we're going out to Amherst."

"The whirlwind tour, huh?"

"I don't think we'll come back till late. But I had two things to ask you. First, can you come for a picnic tomorrow? Collin says that since you and I did the last one, it's his turn to throw a picnic for us. He's already got Mrs. Overton slaving away."

"Sure. What time?"

"We're supposed to meet him at the pond at noon. Maybe you can come a little before?"

"Quarter of?"

"Sounds good. He's says it's supposed to be formal."

"Formal?"

"Dress-up. You know."

"My tux is at the cleaners."

She laughed.

"Find something else. It doesn't matter too much."

"It matters to Collin. How formal does he want us to get at noon on a July day? We'll vaporize. Well, I suppose I'll find something."

"And the other thing—you were going to tell me the story about that old goat's head."

"Oh, that's right—we forgot all about that."

A pause.

"So? Go ahead."

"Right now? Do you have the time?"

"I don't know. Mother could come downstairs any time. But at least you could start."

"Well, it's not that big a deal, really. We must have been about eight or ten. There was a big mansion on the other side of the golf course—you know where the golf course is?"

"It's down at the end of the valley, right?"

"That's right. Way up on a hill on the other side of it was the Pike estate. Acres and acres of land; exotic trees from all over the world. Terraced gardens going down the hillside. The house was huge—turrets and arches and porches and windows with curved glass. Tunnels that went down from the drive under the house into the gardens."

"Wow. It sounds like quite a place."

"It really was one of the most beautiful houses in the state."

"How did these people get so rich?"

"I don't know. The usual way, I imagine. Took it from someone else. Anyway, it all came down to a little old lady, and she died; and the heirs didn't want the house. They wanted to subdivide the land and sell it off to build other houses—cheap to make, but expensive to buy. So they tore down the mansion."

"You're kidding!"

"No. Just brought in the wrecking crane and went to it. Half the county heard about it and went to watch. Collin called me up and we ran over there—cut right through someone's golf game, I remember.

"It turned out the heirs hadn't even bothered taking the stuff out of the house. I guess they must have taken some things; but if they didn't think they could sell what they found, they left it for the wreckers. You wouldn't believe what started showing up when the wrecking ball hit. Sofas, chairs, bookcases full of books, paintings. God, the woodwork in that place! I could cry thinking about it. Mahogany banisters, oak paneling. It was like a museum.

"When the wreckers had knocked down the house, the crowd just swarmed over the wreckage, grabbing anything it could. It was a weird scene. We spotted that goat's head and toted it off as fast as we could go. When you're ten years old or whatever, something like that is a big prize.

"So we put it up in our clubhouse. That's the whole story. I'll just never forget it, somehow. The waste of it all. All that work and wealth being destroyed so someone else could do less work and make more money."

"It sounds horrible."

"It was. But then again, it was kind of a lark for us, getting that goat head out of it."

"What about the cigar?"

"The cigar—well, that—"

He heard Sondra calling her.

"Oh—my mother's ready."

"Say, have a good time."

"Right! If you had any idea—Coming, Mother!—Look, Ryan, I'll see you tomorrow."

"Fine. Quarter to noon."

"Ryan?"

"Yes?"

"You don't think anything like that would ever happen to this place, do you?"

"They'll have to drive the wrecking crane over a few warm bodies first."

"Just a minute, Mother!—It just all seems so fragile sometimes.—Coming!—Look, I've got to go."

"See you."

"Bye bye."

He hung up and stared at the phone. *It is fragile, baby,* he thought. *That's the first step, figuring that out. Now let's do something about it.*

As if on cue, as if she had been waiting until he finished speaking, his mother knocked on the door of the study.

"Yes?"

She entered, holding out a letter. "For you," she said.

"Thanks," he said. "You don't have to bring it in, you know. You can just leave it with the rest of the mail and I'll check for it when I get around to it."

She looked at him open-mouthed, as if she could not conceive of such a lack of curiosity; but after she had seen the letter safely into his grasp, she left without any further argument.

It was from Eve.

July 3

Dearest Ryan,

I send you my greetings and all my love and to Constance, too. I hope you are happy, but if you are not yet, I will give you advice—I will betray my own sex and help you enslave Constance. My advice is simply this, Ryan: talk to her. Find some place and some time when she has to listen to you without the interruption of others, and speak to her, as you spoke to me once, of the words and dreams you love; tell her those wonderful stories about your childhood, and of how you hope to live. Talk of love, but not of your love for her; there's no need for that. And don't worry if she seems to drink in your sweet voice greedily, as if it were the nectar of some goblin fruit, or if she seems to offer nothing in return, if she seems not to think of loving you.

Because when your voice is silent, when she is apart from you, she will begin to miss it. She will begin to hunger for your voice and your presence—oh, Ryan, when you are serious! How sweet, sweet your voice is when you are serious! She will begin to seek you out more and more, thinking that she's fully in control of herself, that she goes to you only to selfishly indulge her addiction; but the day won't be far off that she will listen to you late, late into the night, and give herself utterly to you, and wake beside you a slave of your voice and your body.

And when you see in her eyes that she loves you more than she loves herself, her life, her own future, when she would give all those things to make you happy—be kind to her, Ryan. Don't despise her sacrifice, when she makes it. Because it is only her love for you that drives her to it, the love that you created in her with your own sorcery.

Your
Eve

"What kind of bullshit is this?" he said under his breath when he had read the letter. "Christ, Eve, have you started reading romance novels in your old age?"

But he read the letter again; he read it again several times.

Wednesday, July 8

Simmer's a pleasant time,
Flow'rs of ev'ry colour;
The water rins o'er the heugh,
And I long for my true lover.

—Burns

O N WEDNESDAY COLLIN called Ryan to make the invitation official. "A formal picnic at noon," he said. "Afterwards we change in the woods for sunning and swimming. I understand Constance broached the idea already."

"She did. Let's do it."

"All you have to do is meet Constance and escort her to the pond."

"No problem. Say, glad your writing is going well."

"How can you tell?"

"I can always tell. You're affable. Human. Awake, alive, and somewhat present."

"You've never suffered from writer's block, or you'd have more mercy."

"You know I don't believe in the disease. You either have something to say or you don't. If you do, say it; if you don't, shut up. That's the way I look at it."

"You don't know what you're talking about, as usual. If you collected all the blocks currently stalling writers in this country, you could build a monument to rival the Great Pyramid."

"Cute conceit, buddy. Just don't get inspired by it and run off and write another poem."

"That would be a new trick—to be inspired by writer's block."

"Are you kidding? Sometimes I think all these modern writers write about is how they can't write. Which all comes of having nothing to say."

"Well, that's never been a problem for you," said Collin, laughing indulgently. "Noon, at the pond."

"See you then."

The formality of the picnic posed a problem. Ryan went through every closet in the house and found a shirt that had been given to his father ten years ago as a castoff; it had been too big for Daniel Kinsella, but it now fit Ryan perfectly. With a tie, it would pass.

In the event, the splendor of the Tate siblings proved such as to make Ryan feel his own fashion irrelevant. Collin wore a pressed white linen suit and hat, and Constance wore a white dress that, but for its set of whimsical pockets at the hips, would have served a bride of simple tastes. When she and Ryan arrived at the pond, Collin stared in amazement at her.

"It goes without saying that you'll die a horrible death if Mother catches you wearing that here," said Collin.

"I know. This dress is my death warrant," said Constance.

"What your mother doesn't know won't hurt her," said Ryan.

"Well," said Collin, "welcome. It may be a short life, but we'll make it a merry one."

He had set up a card table in the shade and spread over it a checkered cloth; three folding chairs were grouped around it, and three places were set with silver. A bottle of wine from the Tate cellar breathed already in a silver bucket; the luncheon was still packed in baskets, wrapped in more checkers.

"The genteel country picnic," said Ryan. "You've outdone even Mrs. Overdo." Collin smiled with satisfaction and motioned them forward.

"Ryan, if you'll serve the wine . . . Constance, be so kind as to set out the chicken and potato salad; I've take care of this basket here." In a few minutes the table was crowded with food, and they raised their glasses and began the feast.

Collin was in his best form—present and engaged. Constance seemed to respond to his mood with deep happiness, even exaltation. Ryan ate but hardly tasted, listened but hardly heard, spoke but hardly knew what he said; he was most conscious that Constance was beside him, within reach of the gesture, if he had dared, if he had had the right, to make it. He felt that if he only had had that right, he would have been utterly content in this moment. Collin talked on—of their plans for the trip to Maine, of the coming workshop, of his poems; Constance told her misadventures on the previous day; but Ryan for once was scattered and distracted. It was as if he and Collin had changed roles.

But by the time they made their way through lunch and arrived at dessert—sherbet, served out of a frosted thermos—they had reverted to their usual parts in the play. Collin had relapsed into silence, and Ryan had begun to feel more collected and focused. They all sat for some time without speaking, relaxed and watching the sun creep nearer to their shaded spot, feeling the beach begin to beckon, and along with it the oblivion of that worship. It struck Ryan now, in this moment, how beautiful this brother and sister were. Collin gazed over the pond, up at the gleaming sky; she, in a similar abstraction, bent her head over the ruins of the picnic, with a little smile playing about her face. His golden head and her dark one, sharing in their different ways a stark beauty of feature, the intense, candid eyes and smile.

"Don't you wish," said Constance suddenly, "that you had lived in the olden days, when life was really like this—the way it is at this exact moment?"

"You mean life isn't the way life is?" asked Ryan.

"You know what I mean. When life really was like this—people were genteel and polite to one another, they had manners—they sat here just the way we're sitting here, on a summer's day, at peace with themselves and each other."

"The rich people maybe," said Ryan. "They could afford picnics and good manners—though whether they were really at peace is another question. Anyway, most of the world was on its knees scrubbing floors or breaking stone somewhere. The poor couldn't afford courtesy and gentility."

"But even the poor had a higher standard of behavior then, don't you think?"

"What do you mean by behavior?"

"Well, morality is what I mean, I guess."

"You mean the poor had higher morals than they do now?"

"I think everyone did."

"I don't think so. Some people were moral and some were immoral. Things haven't changed. People don't change much, overall."

"Ryan," she said, laughing, "I can't believe you're telling me that the good old days really weren't better."

"I'm not saying that. I do believe that if we could be transported back about two hundred years, and if the technological expectations that fill us with such discontent were erased from our minds, we'd be a lot happier. But the relative morality would not really be any different."

"But don't you really think that people on the whole were more moral two hundred years ago?"

"People are people. How do you quantify something like morality? You could look at crime rates, but that's about it. Everything else is all pretty soft evidence."

"But don't you think the definition of what was immoral was different?"

"Sure. But were standards then more moral or less? Maybe there's more crime and violence now, but in those days they used to treat unwed mothers as if they were subhuman. Was that right? The English took the food out of Ireland and left the poor to starve. Children worked in factories. Animals were abused on the streets and on the farms. Was all that right? Nowadays utterly unthinking people on Wall Street grow rich off the labor of women and children in sweat shops in Asia. Certainly that isn't right. When you try to gauge relative morality over the centuries, it's all pretty much of a wash, it seems to me."

"But Ryan, Ryan," she said, laughing in surprise, "how can you say that? I thought you were as romantic as I am."

"I'm a hundred times more romantic than you. But venerating certain values of the past is not the same as believing all the values of the past were good or that everyone subscribed to those values. It seems to me that the one thing history teaches over and over is that people are pretty much the same in all times and all places. And the lowest common denominator is pretty low. I've seen scholars claim that we can't possibly understand Roman culture because we could never comprehend the mindset that would allow slavery in a society. But we had slavery in this country a hundred and twenty years ago. It seems to me we have slavery today. We just call it by another name. The names change, but people are the same. 'The past is a foreign country,' someone once said, 'and they do things differently there.' I think it's not so much that they did things differently as that the whole complex of standards they lived by is different—not better or worse, just different. That makes it impossible to decide whether they themselves were better or worse than we are, and leads to the working hypothesis that they were neither."

"But don't you believe in the old ways?"

"Do you mean the real ways or the fictional ones? Do you mean the same old petty values we have today, or do you mean chivalry, and heroism, and rescuing fair damsels from the tops of trees?"

"I mean chivalry, of course."

"Well, of course I believe in *that* stuff."

"Thank goodness! You were beginning to worry me."

"Are you kidding? If I had my way, I'd be John Ridd in *Lorna Doone*, and put all these cheap modern romances to shame. "

"Then let's pretend we *are* living a hundred and fifty years ago," she said. She was showing every sign of beginning to rhapsodize when Collin interrupted her.

"You'll have to count me out," he said. "The good old days weren't for me."

"Oh, Collin, why not? I think you'd fit right in."

"Then you don't know me. We're different in that respect. You've got your head as full of nonsense as Ryan. I have no desire to live in the past."

She was disappointed; but persevered with a smile, albeit a softer one. "Why not?" she asked. "What's better about the present?"

"The poetry, for one thing. If I lived two hundred years ago, I'd be chained to writing in rhyme and meter. I couldn't express myself."

"You could express yourself better," insisted Ryan. "'Splendid the songbird's measured cadence rings: Not *chains*, she singing says, they've shed their *wings*.' It might take more work, but you'd create a finer music."

"And what about sex?" asked Collin, going on the offensive and turning to Ryan. "Would you like to live in a time when people were frigid prudes in ignorance of their own sexuality?"

"There never was such a time," said Ryan.

"You can't deny that prudishness and hypocrisy were greater in the past. Think how premarital sex was frowned upon—and not long ago, either. Who thinks twice about it now?"

"There's a case to be made for keeping sex within the bounds of marriage," Ryan found himself saying, somewhat to his own surprise.

"My God, Ryan," cried Collin, "you never cease to amaze me! If you can make a case for that, I'd certainly like to hear it."

"I'm not claiming I subscribe to that point of view, but I do respect it. Just think what life is like in the typical college dorm. People all around you getting caught in bad relationships, and sex only making the relationships more complicated and difficult to escape from. You see people so psychically bruised by the time they find a good relationship that they can barely bring themselves to act on what they've found."

"On the contrary, they would never find those good relationships without the bad ones. The bad relationships are learning experiences."

"It seems to me the bad relationships are just patterns people get stuck in and repeat over and over. It's as if they learn how not to love, and keep repeating their mistakes *ad infinitum*."

"But how does postponing sex until marriage stop that?"

"It doesn't, necessarily. I'm only saying I sympathize with the morality that tries to prevent that damage."

"It's not damage. It's experience. It's knowledge."

"Sticking your hand in the fire is experience too, but you don't have to do it to know that fire is destructive."

"So you think sex before marriage is like sticking your hand in the fire?"

"I'm saying it *can* be. I'm just saying I sympathize with the moral position that tries to avoid sex before marriage, that's all."

"But you wouldn't insist on marrying a virgin, would you?" asked Collin.

"Of course not. But if the woman I loved *were* a virgin, I wouldn't scorn her for it. I think you would."

"I certainly would," huffed Collin.

At this point the irony of the discussion proved too intense for Ryan. He had spent the last four years of his life pursuing every sexual relationship he could; and Collin, he was fairly certain, was still wholly inexperienced.

"Look," Ryan said, "all I'm trying to say is that if this were a perfect world—"

"Which it isn't, and never was," said Collin.

"And never will be," stressed Ryan. "But if this were a perfect world, premarital sex would be unnecessary. Because premarital sex is only touted now as a means of preparing oneself for marriage, of learning about sex and love before one is locked into a relationship, a marriage."

"Maybe for you," said Collin. "But those of us who don't view marriage as the ultimate purpose of life will have to disagree. There is no such thing as 'premarital' sex for us; there is only sex, pure and simple."

"Sex pure and simple?" repeated Ryan, puzzled at the juxtaposition. "Look," he went on, trying again, "I don't mean to be Panglossian, but let me do a little thought experiment just for the sake of making the point. If this were a perfect world, at age sixteen, or twenty-one, or whatever, you could marry the person perfectly suited to you, and learn about love and sex together, and no past affections for other people would ever come between you. And that would be the perfect union between two people."

"So what relevance does your experiment have to the real world? Since, as you admit, the world isn't perfect."

"But don't you think it was closer to perfect once?" pleaded Constance with a shy smile. Her interruption threw the discussion off course.

"I'm sorry, I just can't bring myself to believe in the perfect world of the past," said Ryan "As I said, I'd rather have lived two hundred years ago; but that's because I would rather live without television and without nuclear weapons, not because I believe people were more nearly perfect then."

"One disadvantage of living in ancient times," said Collin in an ironic tone, "would be that you wouldn't be able to have the illusion that any previous times had been better than your own."

"On the contrary," said Ryan. "The Greeks and Romans were always looking back fondly to a prehistoric Golden Age."

"Really?" said Constance.

"Oh, yes. They figured everything had been perfect once and had just gone bad. There's a passage in Catullus that sounds a lot like the kind of ranting you hear from religious leaders now about how society is going downhill."

"So?" she said. "Recite it for us."

"In Latin or English?"

"English, please."

He thought for a moment, and then with occasional hesitation said: "'After the earth had been stained with crime so hideous it would be a sin even to tell of it, and greed had driven Justice from the heart of every man and woman, brothers plunged their hands deep in the blood of their siblings, children ceased to grieve for their parents when they died—in fact, the father himself longed for the death of his firstborn in order to make the boy's bride-to-be a new stepmother for the dead; the mother lay in love with her heedless son, impiously fearless of polluting the gods of her household; all things, good and bad, were confounded in a hideous madness, and turned the just mind of the gods away from us. And this is the reason they no longer deign to meet us, or permit the bright light of day to touch them.'"

"That's pretty intense," said Constance.

"So what's your point?" asked Collin.

"My point is that every culture has its delusions about what went before."

"I don't," said Collin.

"Well, I don't feel I do either," said Ryan, almost impatiently.

"But all those things *are* sinful, that you mentioned," said Constance. "Brothers killing siblings, and incest."

"Yes, but the point is that there was no period in time when those things didn't happen. People have a way of thinking that once upon a time humans didn't do those things."

"But there are many things that are accepted now that were once considered evil," said Collin.

Ryan was close to abandoning any attempt to follow a topic. The conversation seemed to be running according to some agenda he could not identify. "So?" he said.

"So in that respect, there are fewer evils today than in previous times."

Ryan laughed. "You mean we make the world better by declaring that evil things are no longer evil?"

"I mean we abolish taboos and free our minds from ignorance and prudery."

"But the reason that those taboos existed still remains. For instance, in the case of premarital sex, the taboo existed in order to protect people—especially women—from the misery of having children when they didn't want them or couldn't provide for them. It's fine to declare that premarital sex is no longer taboo, but just because we have contraceptives now doesn't mean there aren't thousands upon thousands of wretched girls on the streets carrying babies they don't want and would be better off without. Or take incest. The taboo against it has not existed in all cultures. The Egyptian royalty married in their own families. But the genetic reasons for the taboo seem to be pretty valid. You can declare that the taboo has no function anymore, now that technology has provided us with contraceptives—but babies are still going to be born retarded and disabled because they were conceived in an incestuous relationship."

"The genetic reasons are not the only ones," said Constance.

"No, of course not," agreed Ryan.

"What other reasons are there?" asked Collin. Constance looked to Ryan to explain her thoughts.

"Well, all right," said Ryan. "It's true that it's possible to imagine a situation—this is purely theoretical, of course—where incest would not be harmful. As a matter of fact, maybe it's not purely theoretical. There was a case recently where a man and a woman met, fell in love, and decided to marry. When they told their families, they discovered that they were in fact full-blooded brother and sister."

"Are you serious?" asked Constance.

"Yes, this is a true story. I don't remember how the situation had come about, but it did occur."

"What happened to them?" Collin asked.

"Well, they couldn't get married. There's a law against it. But there's no law against a brother and sister taking up residence in the same house, which they proceeded to do; and I trust people left them alone. Now, in a case like that, they have my complete sympathy. They would be wise to adopt children, rather than have their own, if they can adopt without being married. There incest is as beneficial and constructive as any expression of affection. But in actual fact, in a million cases out of a million and one, incest is a situation where one person exploits the other. That's what makes it so ugly. That's a better reason for the taboo than the genetic one, you're right. It's almost always damaging to the family and the individuals; or it's a part of a family situation that's unhealthy to begin with."

Collin had no rejoinder. He sat staring out across the pond, brooding.

"I'd still rather have lived in days gone by," said Constance, when she saw her brother had abandoned the discussion.

"Well, we can't, I guess," said Ryan. "Unless we imagine— unless we make them happen. As we have done today, at this picnic Collin staged for us." They turned to him, but he was not listening. "Look at him," said Ryan. "Dreaming again."

Constance laughed, went around the table, and kissed Collin on the cheek.

"Thank you for the picnic, sweet dreamer," she said. He looked irritated and held her away.

"He's mad at us because we're romantics, Constance," said Ryan.

"I'm afraid you're right," she said. "But he loves us anyway."

"I'm so sick of you two babbling all the time," said Collin coldly. The others laughed affectionately at him.

"Time for some sun, I think," said Constance, beginning to undo her dress.

"For God's sake, Constance," said Collin, "go do that in the woods."

"Why? I've got my bathing suit on underneath."

"It isn't decent, that's all. Don't do it."

"So much for abolishing taboos," said Ryan.

Thursday, July 9

His whole converse is with the celebrated poets—with Horace and Persius, Juvenal and Tibullus, but as for modern rhymers, he has but an indifferent opinion of them.

—Cervantes

IT WAS NOT until the very end of Wednesday that Ryan received his invitation to return; Constance reminded him of his promise to listen to a reading of poetry. She proposed the morning; Collin countered with the evening. She did not look happy at this, Ryan noticed. For a moment her eyes met his, and he thought she might say, "Well, come over early anyway"; but Collin was vaguely lecturing the air to the effect that some people had work to do, and she looked away guiltily and said no more. Ryan thought further that he might simply say to her, "I'm not busy tomorrow. Why don't we . . ." But somehow he found himself saying good-bye instead.

The course of Thursday, then, was a purgatory. His sole entertainment was his Spanish lesson and another assignment from Todd—a puzzling one that made him think his friend and Eve were in communication. It ran:

Choose your meter:

> Romanticism is a characteristic that can coexist with
> many disparate qualities in a personality. Yet in itself
> it attracts other romantics, who flutter to its darkness
> heedless what strange attributes accompany it in the soul.
> Thus it is a poor—it is the worst—basis for partnership.
> She loves him because he sighs; but he is a fascist and she
> a Quaker. Will she notice before it is too late?

"What's the word for a lady Quaker in Latin, Dad?" he asked when he had shown the assignment to his father.

"Well, Quakers are Friends. So I guess it would be *Amica.*"

"Could be kind of ambiguous, don't you think?"

"How about just saying she was a member of the *Societas Amicorum?*"

"Gets a little cumbersome."

That was as far as he took the discussion; he put the card aside and promptly forgot it.

As he walked over to the Tates after dinner he saw a score of monarch butterflies taking advantage of the late warmth and the last rays of the sun to feed on the blossoms of the roadside milkweed. By the time he reached the gate and started up the drive, the roadway was in rich summer twilight; an occasional mosquito pestered him, and at one point a bat swept overhead like a bird with its wings on backwards, or a sculler facing the wrong way but toiling to win his race all the same.

No one responded to his light knock at the screen. He let himself in and took the stairs three at a time. The light shone from Collin's room at the end of the long hallway; he could see the upper portion of the bedstead, the carved black walnut headboard and the posts that rose nearly to the ceiling; and Constance lounging on it, leaning on an elbow. She had a happy, postparandial glow on her face, augmented by the literal glow of the falling sun, which lit the room. He came all the way to the door before she saw him. When she did she smiled instantly and warmly, and held out her hand to him as if inviting him to take it.

"Welcome," she said. She sat up, found a new position leaning against the headboard, and motioned him to find a place at the foot.

"Shut the door, will you, Ryan?" asked Collin by way of greeting. Ryan saw at once he was determined to be casual. He was reading some brochures—evidently something that had to do with the workshop—and did not put them aside until Ryan had closed the door and perched on the edge of the bed.

"Well, what shall we read first?" Collin asked. He went to the bookcases and began scanning them over. "Any favorites, Constance?"

"I liked Ferlinghetti," she said diffidently. "And Cohen."

Collin pulled several slim volumes one by one from the shelves as he worked his way along the wall.

"You know what you really ought to do?" said Constance.

"What's that?"

"Read one of your own first."

He looked at her. "Why?"

"Because if you start reading other people's poems, you'll read them all night without turning back to your own."

"That's probably true. All right."

He put the books on his desk for the moment and opened a deep drawer. Ryan had a glimpse of several notebooks, each thick with crisp, white, typed sheets. These notebooks seemed to be a of special issue affected by poets: a clever concealed spring clamped the backing on the loose sheets inside, forming a mimic of a bound book, but differing in this: that by carefully prying apart the covers, the writer could free the pages for reshuffling or replacement.

"Is that the one with the quotation?" asked Constance.

"Yes," said Collin.

"Show him the cover."

Collin held out the cover of the notebook, and Ryan took it with curiosity. On the black liner inside had been glued a square of white paper with a neatly typed epigraph. It took him a moment to realize that he was reading not Collin's writing, but his own words, retyped from some old letter whose subject he could not now remember. After the extract from his writing, which was in quotation marks, was an added comment by Collin. The whole read as follows:

> "That wisdom I knew and disobeyed has been expressed
> by none so well—though many have understood and uttered
> it—as by Steele: 'It is an endless and frivolous Pursuit to act

by any other Rule than the Care of satisfying our own Minds in what we do.' This, before repressed and silenced, is to be now my motto. Because in seeking to satisfy his own highest standards a person may, by labor and by the odd felicities of inspiration, achieve some part of his or her dream."

And the dream that is mine is to tell the sadness in everything that is indistinguishable from joy.

"Should I be flattered?" asked Ryan. "Did one paragraph in the mountain of verbiage I've poured over your head in the past few years actually receive approval?"

"You should indeed be flattered," said Constance.

"I don't know," Ryan told her. "These writers are notorious packrats. They'll take quotations even from people whose views they despise."

"It's a good quote, even if I do despise your views," said Collin. "Do you remember it?"

"Just dimly. I don't recall the specific letter."

"Maybe Constance can find it for us. She's been pestering me to let her read your correspondence," said Collin dryly, glancing at Constance. She seemed pained by his revelation.

"You must be very bored, then," Ryan said to her. "Or at least I know you *will* be bored, if you do wade through those letters." To Collin he said: "I trust you have no intention of inflicting them on her?"

"None whatsoever," he said. "They're too full of your propaganda. I wasn't influenced by it, but she might be."

"You should trust my judgment," she said. "I *do* have a mind of my own."

"I'm sure Collin has no doubt of that," said Ryan. "He's just trying to spare you my ranting."

"Speaking of which," said Collin, "do try to restrain yourself when you hear this poem."

"Poor Collin," said Constance. "He's stuck between a sister who can't articulate and a . . ."

"A friend who can't shut up," said Ryan, finishing the thought.

"I wasn't going to say that," she said with a reproving smile.
"No, you're too polite."
She prodded him playfully with her foot.
"Stop it," she said.
"When you two are ready . . ." said Collin.
They faced him and listened.
"This one is called 'Autumn: Memory and Moral,'" he said. With that prefatory he began to read, in a strong, clear voice that even Mrs. Overton might have distantly heard, if she had not been drowsing in front of the television. He did not act, or affect, or sneer, or cast hostile, defiant looks at his audience, or commit any other of the many errors poets both good and bad commit in reading their works; his voice was only an instrument through which the words spoke to the listener.

> We ran up the hill
> away from the house toward the sky
> two boys with spears
> of ash hardened in the fires
> of burning leaves
>
> We ran breathless
> under trees of burning leaves
> seeking the clearing of renown under the sky
> where autumn spun the long grass
> gold
>
> The cold stung our ears
> and chilled the breath in our throats
> as we loosed our shouts
> among the oaks
> and woke the trunks
> to echo
>
> *If we knew*
> as we played

as children
in the bright death world of autumn
that all things die
and we did not care

why should that make us pause
now?
Let us
play, play on defiantly
though the day is short, too short
and already we hear
a voice the wind makes unfamiliar

calling us
to return

He had chosen appropriately: Ryan could remember well the days of which he spoke.

Ryan slipped off the edge of the bed and extended a hand. "May I read it?" he asked.

"The critic has to have the text in his paws," Collin noted sardonically; but he gave Ryan the poem.

Ryan sat on the bed again. Constance moved closer, perhaps a little anxiously, though she did not look over Ryan's shoulder.

"Basically, I like it," said Ryan after a few minutes. He had qualifications for his liking that he kept to himself; but he did have a criticism he could share. "But one thing that troubles me," he went on, "is that the readers will want to see this 'If we knew' as contrary-to-fact, even though it's not. That is, they'll read it as if it said, 'If we had known as we played . . . that all things die and that we did not care," and wind up confused about what you're doing. They'd be less likely to make that mistake if you reworded slightly. Maybe something like this:

We knew
as we played

as children
in the bright death-world of autumn
that all things die—
and still we did not care

*So why should that make us pause
now?*

"Let me see," said Collin, holding out his hand for the poem. Ryan gave it back.

Collin reread it carefully.

"Well," he said, "I see what you're talking about, Mr. Critic. But I don't see it as a major problem, or even really a problem at all. As you say, the passage *isn't* contrary to fact. A poet has to be able to rely on his readers to understand English; he can't head off every possible misunderstanding."

"But he should where he can. His poetry will be more forceful and effective if he does."

"Maybe it would be more forced and mechanical."

"I think the poem is splendid just the way it is," said Constance

"There, you see?" said Collin. "The ingenuous listener is always of more value than the critic who claims hypothetical misreadings."

"I'm afraid we're both biased," said Ryan, smiling at Constance as he spoke. "Having been one of the little boys with a spear in his hand, I can't comment objectively. I do like the poem. I think that bit about the 'clearing of renown,' and 'spinning the grass into gold' is rather nice. And the symbol of home works rather well."

"He's just bursting with compliments tonight," Collin said to Constance. "How about you, Constance? Any further thoughts?"

"Nothing I could really put into words," she said. "Aside from the fact that I liked it. I hope you won't be mad at me if I can't really say anything about it."

"I won't be mad at you. But I do think that if you try harder, you'll find you do have something to say. Everyone has something to say, even about poems they like." He gestured toward the books piled on his desk." There isn't a poem in these books I wouldn't change if it were my own, even though I like the poems themselves very much." He rose and put the poem in her hands. "Go ahead," he said. "Try it."

She looked nervously at the page. "Well," she said, "I like the way the boys run up the hill toward the sky. You can sort of feel that elation they feel, the idea that they're just going to run right into the sky. Their spirits are soaring."

Collin listened and said nothing. She plunged on. "And the way the cold stings their ears. And the way they shout in the cold; and the sound of their voices among the trees. And 'the bright death-world of autumn' is good."

"And how do you feel about the meditation on death?" asked Ryan, teasing her.

"Well, I'm very much in agreement with it. Let's play, play on. This was my point all along, if you'll remember. But I think Collin has captured just what he said he wanted to capture, the 'sadness indistinguishable from joy.' Life is short, and that's sad; but life is also very beautiful, the more beautiful because it is so short; and because it's beautiful, it's joyful."

"Our propaganda is getting to her, Ryan. She's beginning to see that life is short."

"I've just been thinking about going to school," she said. "I'll be twenty-one before I even start. I'll be three years behind you, and five years behind Ryan."

"It's not a race," said Ryan.

"But it is, in a way. I want to be with you two, not dawdling along behind.

"We'll wait for you," said Ryan.

"Yes, Ryan will make time stand still for all of us," said Collin. There was a silence.

"Through?" asked Collin.

Constance nodded apologetically.

Collin now took up one of the volumes he had selected; and since no further discussion seemed to be forthcoming, he began to read.

If Ryan seemed to listen now with good grace, it was because he was really not hearing anything. As Collin read on, one poem seemed to become another; extravagant poems about love, full of images of moonlight and breasts and talk of self-denigration or anger, flowed into dreary poems threatening madness and suicide, and these into poems boasting and punning endlessly about the writing of poetry, all mixed together with the trivial and the inscrutably and irrelevantly private references of writers utterly unknown to Ryan; he heard ranting feminist poems, ranting male chauvinist poems; politically activist poetry, politically apathetic poetry; poems lamenting the death of the earth, and poems celebrating the birth of the new age—one after another helter-skelter, as Collin chose his favorites at random in the books he had before him. From time to time an image or even an entire poem might burst out of the sameness of verbiage like a flare blossoming above a tangled morass, but such moments were few.

The poem to which Ryan was truly listening lay beside him on the bed. He sat at the foot, and she leaned on the pillows. He daydreamed, as the words of the poets rose and fell and passed unheard through the evening air, of another time, a future time: how he would approach as he had this night, seeing her lit by the sun through the doorway of Collin's room; how she would turn, and reach out and touch his arm lightly as he caressed her head with the gesture; how she would smile a greeting.

After some time had passed, he realized that she had fallen asleep beside him. Collin was in the middle of a long, cheerless, and incomprehensible poem, and had not yet noticed. Ryan nudged her leg. Her eyes sprang open and her body stiffened; she listened to Collin intently until she was sure she had escaped his notice; and then, as she reconstructed what had happened, she shot Ryan a grateful glance.

"You two are awfully quiet," said Collin when he had finished.

"Read another of your own," begged Constance.

"I think Ryan would probably prefer to hear real poetry," said Collin.

"Leaving aside the question of what is real poetry and what isn't, I prefer to hear yours."

"Please, Collin," added Constance.

"All right. But you'll have to take what you get, Ryan."

"Do your worst, buddy."

Collin went through his sheaf of poems until he found the one he wanted.

"This one is called 'For Walt Whitman.'"

For you
who showed me that the mazes of faery
lead only back upon themselves
and taught me
that I would find love and danger alike
treading the labyrinth of the human mind

For you
who bid me combat for the sake of truth
the dragon seed of a thousand lies
that sprang from the furrows of my mind
lent life and arms by the fantasy I loved

For you
who (when the faery staff broke
and the faery voice deceived)
led me on the search for my own heart
on the streets of the earth

For you I write
(difficult old man
with the bitterness in your cup)
and thanks to you
instead of the impossible
I dream the truth

"There's the old battle cry," said Ryan. "I won't take you on. Not now, anyway."

"Wise man," said Collin, in humorous and condescending approval.

The two friends eyed each other, smiling faintly, two fighters scarred from years of equal combat, half-reluctant and half-eager to start up the war again. Constance seemed to feel a distraction was in order.

"Well, if you're not going to discuss that one," she said, "why don't we call it an evening and raid the kitchen?"

Friday, July 10

But see, while idly I stood looking on,
I found the effect of love in idleness.

—The Taming of the Shrew

Yet mark'd I where the bolt of Cupid fell:
It fell upon a little western flower,
Before milk-white, now purple with love's wound,
And maidens call it, Love-in-idleness.
Fetch me that flower; the herb I show'd thee once:
The juice of it on sleeping eyelids laid
Will make or man or woman madly dote
Upon the next live creature that it sees.

—A Midsummer-Night's Dream

Idleness overthrows all, in the empty heart love reigns, love tyrannizeth in an idle person.

—Robert Burton

In all these torments, and for a long time, he had discontinued his work, and nothing is more dangerous than discontinued work, for it is a habit which a man loses—a habit easy to give up, but difficult to reacquire.

—Hugo

O Mortal man, who livest here by toil,
Do not complain of this thy hard estate;
That like an emmet thou must ever moil,
Is a sad sentence of an ancient date;
And, certes, there is for it reason great;
For, though sometimes it makes thee weep and wail,
And curse thy star, and early drudge and late;

Withouten that would come an heavier bale,
Loose life, unruly passions, and diseases pale.

—Thomson

All our miseries derive from not being able to sit quiet in a room
alone.

—Pascal

Idleness teacheth much evil.

—Ecclesiasticus 33:27

Idleness is the devil's pillow.

—Proverb

Absence of occupation is not rest,
A mind quite vacant is a mind distress'd.

—Cowper

CONSTANCE HAD INVITED Ryan back for breakfast on
Saturday. All day Friday he sat in the study as if it
were a prison cell. His parents tried to coax him out
on various errands, but he just stared them down with
a weariness and ennui they found uncharacteristic
and therefore deeply disturbing. In the latter part of the morning
his mother brought him a letter from Eve; he opened it over the
Spanish textbook.

July 8

Dear Ryan,

Dear one, if you only knew how difficult life is for me,
you would write, at least one word. I will not bore you with a
long letter. I only ask you to send one word to me—I enclose

a postcard, and you can check the Yes box or the No box: Tell
me, is she yours yet? It would mean so much to me if I knew.

Amwell is being much more reasonable.

I have talked to Todd a few times.

Oh, Ryan, Ryan

Your Eve

A postcard was indeed enclosed, addressed and stamped. It was
a photograph of *King and Queen,* a sculpture by Henry Moore.
Ryan had long ago conceived one of his unshakable prejudices
against Moore, and Eve knew of this aversion; one of the sculptor's
pieces stood on the campus, and they had often sparred about it
when they passed through the college green. Now she was teasing
him, but he had no patience for it.

He turned the card over and looked at the two check boxes on
the back in a stupor. After a minute he realized he had taken up a
pen and was marking a heavy *X* in the No box. He was grinding
the ballpoint into the fibers of the card so deeply that he had almost
cut through it.

He tore the card in half. An hour later, when his parents had
gone out, he burned the card and the letter in the fireplace.

Saturday, July 11

Verum ergo illud est, quod a Tarentino Archyta, ut opinor, dici solutum nostros senes commemorare audivi ab aliis senibus auditum: si quis in caelum ascendisset naturamque mundi et pulchritudinem siderum perspexisset, insuavem illam admirationem ei fore, quae iucundissa fuisset, si aliquem cui narret habuisset.

True it is, then—the observation that I heard from our elders, who had it from their elders, who said it was a common saying of (as I recall) Archytas of Tarentum: If someone had ascended to heaven and had seen in deepest detail the very workings of the universe and the beauty of the stars, these wonders would bring him no pleasure; whereas seeing them would have been the most joyous of all experiences, if only he had had someone to whom he could speak of them.

—Cicero

I T WAS THE long-standing custom of Lloyd Tate and Mrs. Overton to go over the household accounts before the great breakfast on Saturday morning. Their conference was held in his den—a place that deserved the name, for it was a kind of lair for him, and Mrs. Overton somehow found him less accessible, more redoubtable, when she appeared before him there. The room, which was entered through a door in the eastern wall of the living room, was large, like all the other rooms in the great house, but so gloomy and heavy with ancient drapery and dark paneling—looking out, as it did, only on the north—that it seemed close and small. Much of this space was dominated by a massive antique desk—Lloyd called it his "acre of mahogany"— which squatted facing the door near the center of the dark maroon carpet. Ryan used to say that it had been carved out of an enormous stump rooted to the spot and the house then built around it, like the bed of Odysseus. The old carpet on which it crouched had borne the years well; where the rug had worn out, small orientals had been laid over it, and it seemed it would survive forever, gradually absorbing the new layers thrown down upon it, overpowering even the dyes of recent accretions, as the deep hue of the berries beneath soak upward through the layers of a thick pie crust. The bookshelves behind the desk were loaded with the law, an armory as deadly as that of a man-o'-war, each volume like so much chained shot that could tear sails and rigging from the mast of the most intrepid enemy. The remainder of the walls were covered with photographs and paintings, the former sere with age, the latter so dirty that even the gazes of congenial ancestors had become frowns and scowls. In the northeast corner of the room was a closet, stuffed with coats long out of style ("But still good—good material, my boy, feel that"), a century's worth of canes and umbrellas, a breeding tangle of wire coat hangers, and on a high shelf, a varied trove of half-forgotten or old-fashioned goods: a dozen fedoras and Panamas; boxes of widowed gloves; a felt-lined case holding the sidearm that Lloyd's uncle Conrad had worn as an aide to Eisenhower in Europe; a heavily tarnished loving-cup with three ears, won in a sailboat race off Marblehead in 1923; a collection of empty wooden cigar boxes; and an old spittoon full to the brim with Indianhead pennies. In the southeast corner was another projection into the room, a half-bath, which opened through a second door into the library. The closet and the bathroom cut down the area of the eastern wall so much that when Lloyd sat at his desk, he seemed to be almost enclosed by the two doorways on each side, by the books behind, and by the enormous mesa of oak before him.

He was ensconced there at seven A.M. when Mrs. Overton knocked. He called her in; she closed the thick door tightly behind her and padded over the rug, which absorbed and muffled even her heavy tread. Her face was still flushed from the heat of the kitchen, her sleeves were still rolled up over her hamlike arms to the elbow; and in her fist she gripped the spine of her household account book. None of this was unusual; but there was some purpose in her carriage that Lloyd noticed instantly and that suggested to him that she had something on her mind. But he said nothing about it, thinking he would discover what it was in due course.

He told her to sit down, as he always did. After seventeen years she still would not presume on their acquaintance to do even that without his leave. Then he opened the conference with his usual "Now, what do we have this week?"

She opened her accounts, and he opened his checkbook, and they went about the business of the house. There was the status of the household cash. There was a check to be obtained for Hal Minot for some repairs to one of the mowers. There was a report on Mrs. Overton's efforts to locate a carpenter needed to fix the kitchen stoop, one who was a particular favorite of Lloyd's ("I'm afraid he's passed on, sir; I'm not sure of it, but it seems likely. He was in his late eighties the last time he came, and that was five years ago"). There was a bill from a department store for the new towels and linens, a bill from Mitchell's for meat, a bill from the oil company. There was the tentative menu for the week to be reviewed. Lloyd disposed of all this, and rapidly; and when he had finished with the last check, he had no requests to make of her.

"That's all, then," he said, finally and formulaically.

"Yes, sir," she said, standing and retreating behind her chair. Her pausing there was a signal that tradition was about to be broken; and Lloyd was hardly more pleased to see that happen than Ryan would have been. She would be making some trouble.

"Yes?" he said, suddenly gruff. The affable patience with which he had coped with her, as he looked forward to a breakfast with his family, now vanished.

"Mr. Tate," she said, plunging directly into her speech, "you and I have known each other intimately for twenty years."

"Good God," he muttered, "I hope not intimately. Familiarly, I suppose, but not intimately."

"Familiarly, then," she said. She could not look at him; she looked over his head, at the back of one particular law book whose title—*Torts*—had always especially mystified her, and which (the spine, not the contents) she always studied, though she felt utterly hopeless of ever deciphering it. She always wondered if the book was really about some kind of German pastry.

Lloyd made an indistinct growling noise, and she proceeded. "Eighteen years," she said.

"Not quite eighteen," he corrected her. "You're pushing it."

"But almost eighteen—almost."

"Nmph," he said.

"Eighteen years—almost eighteen years—I've lived in this house; and I've never presumed to speak to you about anything but the management of the household, and Collin's upbringing, when he was a boy."

"That's right," said Lloyd. "You've never presumed, and you never shall."

This almost cowed her. She actually looked him in the face, pain in her broad features; and he thought of how faithful she had been, and how useful she had striven to make herself; and how helpless he would have been without her assistance; and perhaps he thought how good a cook she was. But he thought nothing more than this. All the same, she was encouraged by something in his expression, and continued. "This time I may, sir," she said. "I may presume on our long inti—familiarity. I've thought it over, and I have to say something."

At this point he became curious. He had not the slightest idea what she could possibly have to say to him. If she had not said it in the last seventeen and a half years, what could compel her to speak before another seventeen and a half had come and gone? He sank back in his chair, made his fingers into a tent in front of his chin, drew his thick eyebrows together, and stared at her keenly over his reading glasses. It was the pose he took when he was watching an opposing lawyer starting on a tack that might lead anywhere. She fastened her eyes on the mysterious binding again, and began the lament she had practiced in part on Ryan.

"I came here to this house, sir, when I was hardly more than a girl myself"—she missed the faint grin that flickered over his features behind his steepled fingers—"and you were a man just starting to get back on his feet after a terrible, terrible blow. I saw you, sir—I remember it—there's no point in your denying it."

He regarded her with cool equanimity.

"You were stricken with grief," she went on. "I never saw a man so unhappy. I never saw a man who had given everything, the way you did—first your love, then yourself in marriage, then your money, your peace of mind, your own sweet daughter (though you kept the son, thank God; you got the best of *that*), until you had nothing left. And I came here, and I saw right away that it was my job to take care of the little worries, the cooking, and cleaning, and caring for little Collin; while you went on to do the work you had set for yourself, to become a great figure (which you are—and really, in so little time), and to forget the terrible, terrible thing that had happened to you."

She seemed almost breathless with surprise at her own oratory. If she had managed to effect a graceful ending and stop here, vaguely expressing unhappiness and urging caution, she might have powerfully influenced Lloyd Tate. He might then recalled the frustration and anguish of the time before she had begun to work for him, and found his work of forgetting and rationalizing doubly difficult. By making herself one more victim of Sondra, she might have made him feel hurt for her; and in doing so, he might have resented again all that had been done against him. But she did not have the wit to stop there.

"But now, sir," she went on, as if dizzy with her own daring—it seemed to Lloyd that her voice went up an octave—"I find that you've forgotten the way you suffered then. I don't know how, but you've done it. But I, sir, I haven't. I remember how unhappy you were; and I'll remind you of it, if you need reminding. How can you forget it? She's come back—the woman who made you suffer so much then. She's brought her daughter back, because she knows that the dear girl will win your heart. She's camped in your house without so much as a by-your-leave. She eats your food, and uses your money, and spends her time planning exactly how she can take it all away again—all your money, like she did last time. You know yourself she hasn't got a cent. What *can* you be thinking of? Do you think she's really changed? It isn't possible, sir—it isn't possible. And as for me—how do you think I feel? Changing the sheets on *her* bed, doing *her* laundry, cooking food for *her* to eat—"

But this had really gone on long enough—much too long, in fact. Lloyd's curiosity had been sated; his sympathy had been awakened and shot dead; and now his ire was fully active, and she would feel the brunt of it. He stood up, as he would have stood to object to a line of questioning he had found impertinent and misleading. She knew at once that she had failed. When he spoke, it was the man that spoke, but with the eloquence of the lawyer, to which she could no more have responded than she could have flung formulae back in the teeth of a physicist. She could only direct her gaze meekly at the carpet and hope she would still have her job in another five minutes.

"Mrs. Overton," he said coldly, "we have known each other for nearly eighteen years, as you've pointed out. But we have never known each other in any other capacity but that of employer and very trusted employee; and we never shall. What I suffered before your coming here is my business, and your conjecture only; my feelings toward my wife are my feelings alone, and belong to no one else to know. Least of all to you, Mrs. Overton. Your analysis of Mrs. Tate's motive in coming here is totally erroneous. It's true that she wants money—money for Constance's education, which I am very pleased to be able to provide; and it's true that I have been generous, even too generous, if I may say it, with my money; but so would any man be, who wishes to demonstrate that he has succeeded in spite of adversity and been able to properly maintain the name of a fine old New England family. It may even be true that she has suffered reverses—I've heard as much myself, and she's hinted it to me—and that she is no longer in a secure financial position. Yes, she committed a terrible error once, and we all paid for it, she, and I, and especially the children, though they may never realize the full extent of their loss. But if I am convinced that she has repented, I fully intend to forgive her. With all her flaws, she is twice as much a woman as those I've met in the past seventeen years. She has intelligence, she has grace, she has good breeding—she's the mother of my children, and they become more precious to me almost with every passing hour. She, of all the women on earth, can be a companion to me and share my pride in these two splendid beings who have blessed my life. I, at least, will show that I can forgive, that I can rise above the evils she did to me. I require only contrition, contrition that is fully persuasive, and I will forgive her everything, I will take her back into this house and make her the mistress here. If at that time you no longer wish to remain in my employment, I will give you a year's pay and release to you the funds I have set aside for your retirement. I will give you the best possible references—I will actively seek a new place for you among my acquaintance. And not least of all, Collin and I will have fond and respectful memories of you till the day we die.

"But I will not let you interfere with my life. It is not some soap opera that you can tune into at will. You know nothing of it. And besides that, I am disappointed with the pettiness of your spite. It's true that I have been vocal in my condemnation of her over the years—I was in error, but my bitterness was only natural, and I plead that in my own defense. But I imagined her, in my ignorance of her actions, to be worse than she is; I imagined that she was enjoying life, while I was unhappy; and now I have reason to think that she, too, was unhappy; and that she has come to see the error of her ways. If this is so—and I will determine if it is, I promise you—then she will be staying with me; but if she is the schemer you imagine, she will find that her plans will die with the summer. I agreed that she should stay that long; let her. As for what you have suffered, don't speak to me of it. You've suffered nothing, except before I met you. I respect your previous difficulties, but I would never think of advising you concerning them. That is the very least I expect from you—respect, without meddling."

When he reached this point he stopped, suddenly realizing that he had used heavy munitions where light would have sufficed. He saw she was terrified—so terrified that she would nevermore move unless he explicitly dismissed her. "Do I make myself understood?" he added.

"Yes, sir," she said, hunching her body in what might have been some indistinct racial memory of a curtsy, or perhaps an instinctive form of groveling.

"Good," he said. "I think it will be best if we carry on as if this conference had never taken place."

She was more than grateful to hear this suggestion. She had undertaken her task with the vague idea that she would be opening Lloyd's eyes to Sondra's conduct; but it seemed that his eyes were wide open already. Furthermore, his talk of forgiveness and petty spite had struck hard upon her vestigial religiosity; she sensed, vaguely, that his conduct, even if more foolish than hers, was somehow more noble. Her entire being seemed to sink at the idea that she had earned his contempt; and she began to calculate how many excellent dinners it would take to soothe her presumption from his mind.

He cast about for a change of subject with which to close the meeting. "I understand that you wish to go to your sister's house as usual this year, from something Collin said. The last week in July. Is this true?"

"Well, I had waited to decide, sir. I didn't know if you would need me." He saw at once that she was loath to leave him alone with Sondra.

"I can do without you, if you wish to go," he said. "The children won't be here, as you know. As for myself, I can eat out, as usual. There couldn't be a better time."

"Well, perhaps I should wait and see," she said, daringly clinging to her purpose for one instant more.

"I must know now whether you intend to go or not," he said; and he looked at her in a way that made it plain that he perfectly understood what motivated her reluctance.

"I suppose I'll go," she said.

"I'll count on it. You'll take your vacation the last week of July. What day will you be going away?"

"What day would be good, sir?"

"When the children go, I suppose; that will be—" he looked at a calendar on his desk—"Friday, the twenty-fourth."

"The traveling is so hard on Fridays, sir; I'd rather go Saturday morning."

"Very well. Saturday morning, the twenty-fifth. I'll count on it. You know how much I dislike it when people change their plans."

"Yes, sir," she said.

"Very well. That should be all for today."

He sat down again. She mumbled a final "Yes, sir" and escaped.

Her mortification increased when she closed the door of the study behind her and, in looking about in a disoriented way, saw Sondra Tate standing by the front door in the sun and gazing out through the screen at the summer morning. It was bad enough that the strong sun that fell on her made her long, slender legs visible in silhouette, right to her hips, through the cloth of her light skirt; worse was her air of ingenuous distraction, as if she really were in love, and really were beginning to be happy again. Mrs. Overton found this nearly unbearable. She shambled off to the kitchen quite broken and forlorn.

❁❁❁

As the conference between Mrs. Overton and Lloyd Tate was taking place, Ryan had been on his way over to the house for breakfast. He went through the woods, where he found the season was now high summer. The air had that full, temperate quality that he associated with Elysium, with some wind off the asphodels; it had never been torched by autumn or bitten by winter. The sun, staring down upon the pungent meadows and lawns, had boiled off their dew; the breath of the earth, evanescent itself, held dispersed ton upon ton of water, which it would again at evening condense and strew with its even and delicate touch on the wiry needles of the pine, the narrow blades of the grass, the broad waiting leaves of the oak and the beech. Pollen lay on the breeze as well, infinite vibrant invisible motes of it, which softened the landscapes with a dull haze; for the wildflowers were blooming—tiny purples nestled among the disheveled grasses of the teeming meadows—black-eyed susans and cornflowers splashing the margins of the woodlawns.

In the woods, spiders wove their nets between the stalks of weeds that had not existed a few weeks before. In the shade the webs were still spangled with dew; in the sun they glistered with pollen. Sometimes Ryan tore through these weavings before he could see them—a guy wire snapped with surprising resistance across his brow, and a spider scurried across his shoulder and dropped away. Sometimes he found great beetles caught in these traps, and ugly mottled horseflies lashed tight but still buzzing with one useless wing; or the proverbially foolish moth, become a dry husk shedding the fairy dust that he and Collin had once smeared on their arms in the hope of flying. To sinister holes in the earth yellow jackets came with their booty and wended forth in bobbing flight again.

As he went down the hill through the woods he saw the wasps' enemy, the toad, squatting in the undergrowth. Here too was a turtle, bound for the pond, and a young rabbit, already alone in the world; here were whorls in the pine needles where the skunk had grubbed for food; here was a squirrel already destroying the apples of the pines; and here the crows gathered, cawing and mocking him and racing in relays of threes and sevens overhead, indignant and arrogant, daring to mob even the broad-winged owls or the patient, circling hawks, believing themselves owners of tree and wind and the earth as well, on which at times they strutted with ludicrous funereal pomp. Doves mourned as he passed, and ubiquitous anonymous insects buzzed about him.

In short, all around him the land sang and shook and quivered with life, with summer life; and he walked through it, the lover, seeing all of it for the sake of a woman, memorizing each caper of the butterfly to tell her later. It would be a dreary journey to paradise if we had no one to whom we could return and tell our story. The unexamined life, said the philosopher, is not worth living; but neither, says the lover, is the life unshared. In the great stone house in the valley the woman went her ways, the woman with whom he meant to share his life. Now perhaps she brushed her hair, or descended quietly to the hall; now she laughed, smiled, teased her brother, kissed her father on the cheek; dreamed of summer's present glory, and who knew what else, what dreams not unlike his own; perhaps even of receiving the affection of the gesture. His hunger to tell her all that he saw, all that he felt, was still a physical anguish and tightness in his chest, which her presence alone would soothe, and which only the ultimate termination of the debate of Whether or Not would end forever—on the day she checked that box marked Yes, and for the first time of the new times smiled up into his face.

As he crossed the lawn, he caught sight of Constance on the stone porch. She saw him—he hoped she had been waiting for him, as she often did. They met in the driveway. His love was shining in him; it was in the set of his shoulders, the length of his stride, the softness of his look, and in the reluctance of his eye to quit the object it had chosen. They said little beyond good morning; and immediately she turned away, with that motion women have that encourages a man to follow more than the most outspoken invitation, moving in a way that showed her consciousness of his presence and yet a certain shyness in acknowledging her own consciousness. Outside the range of her observation, he looked at her minutely, his gaze lingering on the beauties of her profile and hair, the narrow lobe of the soft small ear, studded with gold and hidden in the dark—memorizing her, as he had once memorized the imagined Helen found in the spare, mysterious Homer, lit by the dawn of the West, in the times before that world became infected by the polis. They went up the steps onto the porch; spoke a few moments in low voices, about nothing important; and went inside.

All this meeting, little and much as it was, Sondra Tate saw from her place by the door. She guessed at once that Ryan was deeply in love with her daughter. She had seen them flirting before; but she had never suspected that flirtation—which is, after all, the wavelength in which men and women naturally communicate—had passed into anything more serious.

And serious was the word, the troubling word. If Ryan had been like the others who had been drawn to Constance, she would not have been troubled. Those others had only come as bees come to flowers, because of sweetness and scent and beauty, giving every evidence that they would soon be buzzing off in another direction. They were empty themselves, and though they might entertain Constance for a time, they would ultimately prove unsatisfactory.

Ryan, however, came as one who coveted bloom, stem, leaves, and root. Young people were so especially dangerous when they took themselves seriously. She thought Constance had never been that kind herself, until she started corresponding with her brother; his poetry had discontented her, taught her to want more. And now, under the influence of this strange boy, whose lips laughed while his eyes hungered, whose eyes smiled even while the sad dreams filled his mouth, whose words stung and caressed at once, who was too plain to be handsome and too intelligent and sensitive of face to be homely, who did not win a woman with a glance, but in the dark way, through the secret byways of memory, creeping upon her mind in hours apart and in days later, as she again and again recalled the affectionate drollness of his words, the sweet center in every little bitter pill he gave her to swallow—Constance was turning, turning away—turning toward a water Sondra was sure was too deep for her to wade and too wide for her to swim. Who, man or woman, can resist the other who is perfectly, intelligently present? Ryan's very alertness was compelling. To be cared for, noticed, attended to—who would not rather have this than money, looks, power in a companion? And Ryan, though he brought no worldly presents, brought that presence that was infinitely more winning.

She felt panic and turned away from the door; walked restlessly across the clinking tiles and into the living room. She could hear low voices in the dining room, but nothing clearly.

She could not let Constance go, not yet. Constance was all the hold she had on Lloyd. She must not let Constance move out of her control into the life of another, or Sondra would find herself

suddenly of no consequence in this family. Lloyd could then simply ask her to go, and stand to lose nothing.

She was without resource, still caught in the trap other
American women had broken while she had been living in Spain:
dependent on the whim of a man, penniless, with no curriculum
vitae she could sell, and what was worse, addicted to indolence
in spite of an intellect that might have accomplished much. She
was thrown back on the weapons of the weaponless, conniving to
cling to a begrudged security. She knew things had changed; she
felt like some dinosaur persisting in a deep loch, which had finally
broken surface after millennia and found evolution had passed it
by. But she did not want to adapt; she wanted only to preserve
herself and survive.

She went hastily now into the dining room. Dissociated,
detached, as if from outside herself she watched herself greeting Ryan, heard his greeting, bandied words with him. At once
she doubted what she had seen. He was talking, and he hid well
behind his words. He laughed with Constance, but there seemed
nothing in it; now Collin came in, and Ryan deferred to his friend,
as if Collin had exclusive right to his sister's attention—he made
no claim—he seemed not even to notice when in the heat of some
joke she put her hand on his forearm.

But Sondra wondered if her uncertainty was only a way of
denying the truth. He was such a politician—what he did and said
now might mean nothing; she remembered his firm declaration
that he was the marrying kind. And how could a man not want
Constance? She had that edge of sauciness and haft of submissive-
ness that men eagerly seized to hew themselves down—the good
girl daring to be naughty, which they so often saw as the bad girl
trying to be good—she had that infinitely intoxicating air of the
woman of will restraining herself within the bounds of her subor-
dination to a man. And the way she touched them, so carelessly,
as if in the ebullition of her spirits she could not keep her hands
off them. Sondra knew how that was. There was a time she herself
had been almost as innocent.

As the morning proceeded she watched them both. Like Ryan, she was debating Whether or Not, and like him she could draw no firm conclusions. So much of Constance's attention was focused on her brother that no one could have judged her interest in Ryan. But Sondra knew how the summer seduced young people: how hot sun made the flesh dream; how long days became warm, brief nights; how the scent of earth was a spice and an intoxicant. Constance had never been in love, aside from a crush on a teacher or two, and the sort of giggling infatuation in which schoolgirls indulge to entertain themselves; she was ready for such an experience.

In the light of these suspicions Sondra wanted to rethink the matter of the trip to Maine. After breakfast she sat in the sun with Lloyd until it grew too hot. She was full of good food, sweet food and strong coffee; her body felt both tightly wound and drowsy at once; her head rang ever so slightly from the caffeine. It was hard to think; and every once in a while Lloyd spoke, and she had to pay attention.

It was essential that she have time alone with Lloyd. She could think of no other interval in the entirety of the summer when they might have this chance. In conversation since they had first spoken on the matter, he had mentioned taking time off from work. She needed that week with him; she could not know if she could make a future here unless she had that week.

But in reaching for security with Lloyd, she was likely to lose her grip on Constance. She did not fear that Ryan would take advantage of Constance somehow—or even that he would set out to seduce her. What Sondra feared was that Constance would simply fall in love with him. What Ryan would do if Constance were madly in love with him, and clung to him, and kissed him as they lay together alone on a blanket in the dunes—well, it was obvious what he would do in that case. No, there was no doubt what any man would do if Constance lost her head over him. Sondra would have felt much more safe if Ryan had declared, with the same stubborn blindness as Collin, that he had no intention of ever marrying. But to throw these two romantics together, Ryan and Constance, who were capable of conjuring up a whole life together from engagement to burial under the same headstone, all in less time than it took to catch a breath between kisses—that was adding nitro to glycerine with a hearty shake.

All Sondra could do would be to minimize the risk as best she could. As she thought over the possibilities, it heartened her that Collin would be with them at night; he seemed to effectively though unwittingly distract Constance from Ryan. She did not dare explicitly deny Constance access to Ryan at this stage, before their trip to Maine; out of perversity the girl might begin to like him better. What was worse, Lloyd would surely be offended by such a heavy-handed tactic. But she could deny Ryan access to Constance, by taking Constance away—visiting schools, shopping, anything that would prevent contact between them. And before Constance went to Maine, Sondra could give her a bracing lecture about propriety, the sin of intercourse before marriage, disease—anything and everything that might make Constance think twice. And when Constance was away, Sondra would call every day; in that way she would remind the girl that her mother was still present in her life and would be so for some time to come.

Then, after that week was over, she could come down as hard as she wanted. Either she would have reached some understanding about her future with Lloyd or she would need Constance more than ever. The critical thing was to prevent the two young people from ever forming a bond. Sondra guessed, with that sinking feeling she always had when something important was out of her control, that once Constance took a stand beside a lover, she would be difficult indeed to break.

Sunday, July 12

But I have cause to pry into this pedant:
Methinks he looks as though he were in love.

—The Taming of the Shrew

SONDRA BEGAN HER interference immediately. Lloyd had a plan to drive out to Tanglewood on Sunday afternoon for a program of Mozart and Verdi. When he discussed it with her, she urged him not to invite Ryan. "Let's just go as a family," she said. He was taken in.

She took Constance to an early Mass. As they drove back, she was scheming something to keep her daughter preoccupied for the rest of the morning; but when they pulled up in front of the stone porch, Collin and Ryan were waiting for her, dressed for the pond.

"Are you going swimming?" Constance cried as she sprang from the car.

"I had to move our plans along when this whole Tanglewood idea came up," said Collin.

She dashed up the steps, seized upon him before he could rise from his chair, kissed him on the forehead, said, "Bless you! I thought we were going to miss our sun! I'll go get changed—good morning, Ryan—" and ran indoors.

"Who was that masked woman?" asked Ryan.

"A woodland goddess, I believe," said Lloyd with a chortle, looking up from his Sunday paper.

"Nothing so pagan, Dad. She's just come from Mass. She's a saint of some kind. A suntanned saint."

"Well, I have no quarrel with that," said Lloyd.

"The pond sounds lovely," said Sondra as she came more slowly up the steps.

"It sounds wretched to me, to be perfectly frank," said Lloyd. "No proper place to sit and read the paper, sand in your pants and shoes. Thanks anyway."

"Well, the thing to do is wear a bathing suit. That's what I'm planning on."

He looked at her, somewhat surprised. "Well," he said, "maybe I'll reconsider." She went inside to change.

When she returned the young people had already gone. With a little coaxing, Lloyd consented to accompany her; while he found the beach chairs, she propitiated him by bringing some coffee in a thermal decanter.

At the pond, Constance and Collin and Ryan had not yet entered in the water; they were baking in the sun first.

"Isn't that blanket a little small for the three of you?" asked Sondra.

Constance raised her head and gave her a blinking stare. "We've never minded it," she said.

"What good does it do you to go to Mass if fifteen minutes later you're going to lie down half-naked between two men?"

"Oh, God, Mother! Don't be such a prude!" said Constance. "And besides, one of the 'men' is my own brother."

And the other isn't, thought Sondra; and she would have said it aloud, except that after delivering her riposte, Constance had rested her head comfortably on her forearms again and terminated the conversation.

Sondra could do nothing but watch. Which she did while she pretended to read the paper; but there was really very little to see. The young people were virtually immobile for some time. Lloyd was not; he grumbled as a breeze grabbed for his paper, fussed irritably as the sand found its way up his trousers, and grew hot with the coffee even though he put his chair in the shade.

At one point Ryan spoke to Constance in a voice so low that not even Collin could have heard it. She laughed softly, sleepily, happily. How could a man resist such a laugh? But Sondra saw none of the furtive glances she had expected from Ryan, or any changing of position that would have allowed him to watch Constance unseen—for instance, when Constance made an excursion from the blanket to splash her foot in the water. But that apparent lack of interest was in itself suspicious. Even Collin noticed when his sister rose and walked to the water's edge. Once she saw Ryan almost turn his head; but then he seemed to catch himself; and then, as though accidentally, his eye met Sondra's. Was he checking to see if he was being observed? She felt a shudder of apprehension at the thought that he might be even that duplicitous. Had he guessed that she had guessed? Did he detect her interest in thwarting him? If so, he would be all that much more intent on using the time in Maine to win Constance over.

As she was fretting over this possibility, something still more troublesome presented itself. Constance had been sitting upright for several minutes, reading a book of poetry in a desultory fashion, when Ryan rose and went to the water's edge. Sondra saw Constance's gaze flicker upward momentarily, as if she had only just noticed his departure; but then she stole a glance at Collin, who lay face down, oblivious to the proceedings; and then immediately she raised her eyes and watched Ryan exactly as Sondra had expected Ryan to watch her—in fact, with more absorption and less inhibition, hugging her legs and resting her chin on her knees, the book forgotten. She stared so intently at him that Sondra could not help looking too.

What she saw, now that she really looked at him, was a young man with a splendid physique. The muscles of his back seemed to have been chiseled beneath the deeply tanned, taut skin, the sinews of his thighs stood out in sharp relief, and when he turned sideways, the muscles of his stomach showed as ridges through the lean flesh. He was suddenly no dull scholar versed in weary and wearisome antiquities; he was a good-looking twenty-year-old, healthy and strong.

"I think we ought to be getting ready to go," said Sondra in a loud voice, starting abruptly out of her beach chair.

Lloyd looked at her strangely. "Well," he said, "I'll agree we ought to go back to the house and read the paper in a civilized way, but it's only ten-thirty. We don't have to leave for at least an hour and a half."

"It will take Constance and me at least that long to get ready. Come along, Constance."

The young people now looked at her as if she were out of her mind. "I have to go swimming, Mother," said Constance. "That's the whole point of sitting around in the sun."

"Well, then, go!" said Sondra irritably. All three of them exchanged a look—that look of disgust with the irrationality of adults that children perfect in their teenage years.

Lloyd had risen too and was gathering up the paper. "Let them swim in their own good time, Sondra," he said. "There's no rush."

She held her tongue, though it cost her an effort; and a worse effort, to leave Ryan and Constance together there. But Sondra was not yet willing to make a scene.

Monday, July 13, through Wednesday, July 15

How well he's read, to reason against reading!

—Love's Labour's Lost

All our will-to-live as writers comes to us, or rather stays with us, though our intercourse with Europe. Never believe people who talk to you about the West, Waldo; never forget that it is we New Yorkers and New Englanders who have the monopoly of whatever oxygen there is in the American continent.

—Van Wyck Brooks

Come Muse migrate from Greece and Ionia,
Cross out please those immensely overpaid accounts,
That matter of Troy and Achilles' wrath, and Æneas', Odysseus'
    wanderings,
Placard "Removed" and "To Let" on the rocks of your snowy
    Parnassus . . .

—Whitman

SONDRA'S FRUSTRATION ON Sunday led to a renewed resolution to keep Ryan and Constance apart. Though Ryan went so far as to call the Tates' on Monday, his boldness did him no good. "They've gone off somewhere," said Collin. "College hunting, I think. I'm busy doing rewrites. I'll have Constance give you a call when she gets back. We'll get together and do something."

"Fair enough," said Ryan nonchalantly. They both hung up simultaneously.

He spent that day studying Spanish and moping around in the woods. The wild blueberries were ripening; he sat for hours on sunny banks, lost in fantasies of the gesture, aimlessly plucking and eating the minute purple fruit. The birds fluttered among the trees around him anxiously, as if afraid this Gulliver would deprive them of all livelihood; he did not notice.

On Tuesday he received another assignment from Todd.

> In a doldrums here; can't think of anything original. I'll cop something out of my commonplace book, from Maria Edgeworth. I think we'll give you a rest from versifying and allow you to cast this one in straightforward Ciceronian prose:

> Suspense may be easily endured by persons of an indolent character, who never expect to rule their destiny by their own genius; but to those who feel themselves possessed of energy and abilities to surmount obstacles, and to brave dangers, it is torture to be compelled to remain passive, to feel that prudence, virtue, genius, avail them not, that while rapid ideas pass in their imagination, time moves with an unalterable pace, and compels them to wait, along with the herd of vulgar mortals, for the knowledge of futurity.

"You bastards," muttered Ryan as he read this over. "Eve must be crying over the phone to you. Well, I wish you'd take her off my hands. But it never works out that way."

He added the letter to his growing cache and went out into the woods.

❁ ❁ ❁

On Wednesday afternoon he was invited over. He found Collin and Constance upstairs, in the cool retreat of Collin's room, he idle at his desk, and she sitting on the edge of the bed.

"Come in," said Constance, who was the first to notice his approach.

"You're just in time," said Collin.

"Why is that?" asked Ryan.

"Collin was just giving me an overview of the great American novelists."

"'Great American novelist'—now there's a contradiction in terms."

"How would you know?" asked Collin. "You've never read any American fiction."

"That's not true. I've read Melville and Wolfe and Faulkner— or some of Faulkner anyway. And I'll admit that *they* are great. But I defy you to show me another American worth reading."

"What about Cooper?" asked Constance shyly.

"Oh, I've read Cooper. Don't all the gaffs and inconsistencies bother you? It has a certain atmospheric charm, but it's essentially absurd. Certainly not great."

"Twain?" she asked. "Even I've read *Tom Sawyer* and *Huckleberry Finn*."

"Charming in their way—but great? No. Not serious enough to be great. Episodically fine, but overall they just don't hold together."

"For someone who admits he knows nothing about the subject, you certainly do have a lot of opinions," said Collin.

"Well, don't let him stop you," said Constance. "You were telling me about the argument between Wolfe and Fitzgerald."

"Between the Putter-Inner and the Leaver-Outer, you mean?" asked Ryan.

"There's no point in continuing this discussion," said Collin.

"You said it, not me," said Ryan. "But I wouldn't want to stop you."

"Just because it's modern it's of no value?" said Constance. "Ryan, I can't believe you're so rigid in your thinking. It's just a front. You just talk that way out of some desire to defend what you love best: the things that are gone."

"You," said Collin to Ryan suddenly, with emphasis, "remind me of Gatsby."

"I'm afraid I've never read *Gatsby,* old man. You'll have to explain."

"Not the book *Gatsby,* but the character Gatsby." He went to the bookshelf and pulled out a gray paperback, which he opened decisively to the last page. "This should give you the gist of the character," he said. "And besides, you should know this passage. It's an essential part of your education. You can't be an American without knowing this passage." He read:

> And as I sat there brooding on the old, unknown world, I thought of Gatsby's wonder when he first picked out the green light at the end of Daisy's dock. He had come a long way to this blue lawn, and his dream must have seemed so close that he could hardly fail to grasp it. He did not know that it was already behind him, somewhere back in that vast obscurity beyond the city, where the dark fields of the republic rolled on under the night.
>
> Gatsby believed in the green light, the orgiastic future that year by year recedes before us. It eluded us then, but that's no matter—tomorrow we will run faster, stretch out our arms farther. . . . And one fine morning—
>
> So we beat on, boats against the current, borne back ceaselessly into the past.

"Oh," laughed Constance, "that's Ryan exactly!"

"I beg your pardon," said Ryan in a quietly humorous tone, "but I don't see the similarity." He took the book from Collin and examined the passage.

"Don't you see?" said Collin. "You're on that boat, the same way he is, 'borne back ceaselessly into the past.'"

"He stole that from Vergil, or from somebody else who stole if from Vergil. I forget who it was that Vergil stole it from." Then he recited:

> *Non aliter quam qui adverso vix flumine lembum*
> *remigiis subigit, si bracchia forte remisit,*
> *atque illum in praeceps prono rapit alveus amni.*

"Are you telling us," said Collin, "that the ancients were aware of your particular form of psychosis and you've still learned nothing from their diagnosis? Ryan, I'm shocked at you."

"Oh, shush, will you?—What's with this Fitzgerald guy, anyway? I must admit I can't exactly follow what's going on here. The future is receding from us, he says. We're running as fast as we can after it; but we're also rowing in some kind of boat being carried backwards into the past faster than we can row forwards. Which was Gatsby doing, anyway, rowing, or running? If he was running in his rowboat instead of rowing, it's no wonder he never got where he was going. He should have made up his mind whether he was on a racetrack or a river. Does the green light stand for 'Go'? In which case, you can't blame Gatsby for trying to go forward, can you? And how did his dream get behind him, anyway? And if it was behind him, and he was being 'borne back,' why didn't he just stop rowing—if he *was* rowing—and let the current take him there? And does this dock have any symbolic value—I mean, if we tie up at it, does the future stop receding? Maybe that's what Gatsby should have done. Tied up at Daisy's dock. But I'm troubled by the sexual imagery here. Rowing is a rhythmical activity, after all. And what is this about the 'orgiastic' future? 'Orgiastic' seems like a totally gratuitous adjective just thrown in for effect. Did Gatsby want to have orgies with Daisy? I suppose we should be grateful he didn't say 'orgasmic.' It would be sad to think that Gatsby's orgasm was receding endlessly before him. Although in a sense, maybe it was."

At this point he was interrupted as the laughter Constance had been suppressing burst forth in a merry peal.

"You can make hash of anything faster than anyone I ever knew," said Collin, shaking his head. "It's a special talent of yours."

"I'm sorry, Collin, but this seems like the ending of about six books all thrown together. This guy Fitzgerald is a good example of a writer we Americans tout as great because he's all we have."

"The point is," said Collin, regrouping, "that you, like Gatsby, are a believer in the past. You're trying to reclaim and recreate the past."

"But Gatsby was a believer in the future."

"No, he wasn't."

"But it says so right here. 'Gatsby believed in the green light, the orgiastic future.'"

"Yes, but he was pursuing the past."

"No, he was pursuing his future. It says so right here."

"Then why was it behind him?"

"I don't know. That's what I—"

"It was behind him because it was his past. He was trying to make his past his future."

"This seems to me to be a better description of you than me, old man. You're the one that's pursuing your plan of living in the mouths of men throughout eternity. I'm just a poor fool that knows what he likes and knows it can't last long. I'd like to enjoy it while I've got it, that's all. A little affection, a good book, a quiet place to live—what else do you need? My boat's tied up at the dock, it's not going anywhere. I'm like Marlowe's Passionate Shepherd, just asking to prolong a golden moment in life, not building for some impossible future. You're the only one I know that believes the future is the place to be; and if you don't watch out, you'll sink us all—you're rocking the boat, my friend. You're trying to row upstream, and we're trying to drift with the current. Whatever metaphor you like. You're running after this receding traffic light here, and we're happily sitting at the intersection. "

"Who's we?" asked Collin suddenly.

Ryan was silent for a moment. Then he said: "You know . . . We realists. As opposed to dreamers like you."

"You're the dreamer," sputtered Collin disgustedly.

"This argument has been reduced to an absurdity. I appeal to Constance. Which one of us is the dreamer?"

"I'm afraid I have to agree with him," Constance said apologetically to Collin. "You're much more of a dreamer than Ryan."

"We're using 'dreamer' in two different senses here," protested Collin. "I admit I'm a dreamer in one sense. That's why I enjoy writing so much. It forces me to concentrate for hours on end on one particular thing. It's like guided, concentrated, reinforced daydreaming. It's true that generally I'm a woolgatherer. When I read a nonfiction book, it seems to be eternally long, as if the writer were trying to spin out a few paragraphs into pages and pages. I can see how he could readily condense his entire point into a page or two. When I listen to a lecturer, it seems as if he's speaking incredibly slowly. My thoughts run in and out of his—I think circles around his words—I have so much spare time to think about other things while his voice is crawling up out of his brain that I wind up distracted and inattentive. I've reached the point where sometimes I think I can't think unless I'm writing. If I wasn't writing, I'd be sitting in the sun somewhere, daydreaming, daydreaming, daydreaming. But Ryan is someone who lets his dream about the past serve as his vision of the future. Isn't that dreaming too?"

"What do you daydream about?" Constance asked Collin.

"All kinds of things."

"Romantic things? I mean, I have romantic daydreams. And I have daydreams about what I'd like to do when I grow up."

"You *are* grown up, remember?"

"Well, I mean when I get through college and have a job. Usually the job part is pretty murky. But *do* you have romantic daydreams?"

Collin was curiously silent for a few moments. "Yes," he said.

"Do you have—naughty romantic daydreams?"

"Naughty?" laughed Collin. "Yes, I do have 'naughty' romantic daydreams."

"How about you?" Ryan asked Constance. "Do you have 'naughty' daydreams?"

She blushed instantly and furiously.

"No need to give a verbal response on that one, I guess," said Ryan.

"I won't let you distract me from the point I'm trying to make," insisted Collin.

"If you want to illustrate your point, you'd better find a better writer to do it from than Fitzgerald. He's too confused. He's one of those writers you can only appreciate because you know what he's trying to say even though he doesn't quite have the skill to actually say what he means."

"What are you, anyway, some kind of self-proclaimed literary vigilante?"

"I just believe that the tried and true is best, that's all. As the saying goes, 'When a new book is published, read an old one.'"

"What about Hemingway? You've got to admit that Hemingway was great. His prose is perfect—absolutely spare—simple—direct."

"He wrote beautifully about Spain," said Constance. "He loved Spain."

"I defy you to tear Hemingway's prose apart," said Collin.

"Is that a challenge?" asked Ryan.

For answer Collin went to the bookshelf again and selected a volume, which he handed defiantly to Ryan.

"For Whom the Bell Tolls," announced Ryan, with a mock meditativeness. "I doubt I'd trade the whole book for a sermon of Donne's." He opened the book at random. "'For him,'" he read,

> it was a dark passage which led to nowhere, then to nowhere, then again to nowhere, once again to nowhere, always and forever to nowhere, heavy on the elbows in the earth to nowhere, dark, never any end to nowhere, hung on all time always to unknowing nowhere, this time and again for always to nowhere, now not to be borne once again always and to nowhere now beyond all bearing up, up, up and into nowhere, suddenly, scaldingly, holdingly all nowhere gone and time absolutely still and they were both there, time having stopped and he felt the earth move out and away from under them.

He stopped and affected a quizzical look. Constance looked distressed again as she identified the context.

"This is simple prose?" he said. "Paratactic, true; but simple?"

"It's the rhythm," said Collin. "You're always prating about rhythm. Don't you see what he's doing? He's recreating the situation with the rhythm of the words."

"Does that excuse the fact that he's written half a paragraph of gibberish? He writes like someone who's trying to imagine what an animal feels like when it copulates."

"I can assure you that Hemingway knew everything he needed to know about human copulation."

"So much the worse for him, then, that he couldn't describe it better."

"Love scenes are notoriously difficult," said Collin. He sounded as though he were repeating something he had heard in a writing class. "You've got to strike exactly the balance between physical detail and artistic description." He was embarrassed; Ryan realized suddenly that implicit in his criticism of Hemingway was a statement about his own sexual experience. Constance was looking away; Collin stared at him irritably.

Ryan dropped the argument and flipped to another page, where he read at hazard: "'The young lieutenant who was dead up the slope had been the best friend of this other lieutenant who was named Paco Berrendo and who was listening to the shouting of the captain, who was obviously in a state of exaltation.'" He grimaced. "Is that or is that not a dreadful sentence?" he asked. "Four subordinate clauses in a chain."

"It's stupid to just to sit around picking holes in a piece of great writing," exclaimed Collin defensively. "That book is, on the whole, very well written. It deals with heroism—the main character is a hero, a very real hero, with fears and doubts and flaws. And the point is that in spite of his flaws, he acts bravely and intelligently in the worst of circumstances. What Hemingway is doing is defining a new type of heroism—a human kind, in which you're shown people as they really are, and yet you can still admire them."

"That's true," agreed Constance. "The main character is someone you can respect. Someone you can admire, someone you wish you knew, someone you could model yourself after."

"But he's real," added Collin. "He's not like some overblown hero in some old-fashioned romantic novel, all virtue and super-human valor. He sweats and gets a pain in the pit of his stomach when he's scared and he worries that he's going to crack. But he doesn't—by pure effort of will, he doesn't."

"I will say this, though," said Constance, apparently in an effort to be just to Ryan. "The writing really is almost too simple to carry you through a story that long. There's a lot of repetition—you know, the passages where the main character is thinking about the past or about the things he's afraid of. It gets pretty tedious at times. But the Spanish parts are wonderful—the parts where he talks about the Spanish, and why he loves them and why they drive him crazy sometimes. I could really understand that. And when he talks about the Civil War. That was so horrible, the whole thing, on both sides. He described that aspect very well."

"It sounds to me as if Hemingway's only found a different way to glorify human violence and stupidity," said Ryan. "The true heroes are the ones who are shattered and go on, not the ones who do the shattering. The meek, not the macho."

"On the contrary," rejoined Collin. "The true heroes are the ones who act in accordance with their beliefs, no matter where it leads them—not the victims, not the passive sheep who take whatever's dished out."

"The two highest laws of human life are to live and let live and to do unto others as you would have them do unto you. If Hemingway's heroes break those laws, they're not heroes at all. They're part of the problem, not part of the solution."

"All right, Mr. Critic," said Collin in final disgust, "You show me something you love and I'll pick *it* apart."

"How about Marlowe's 'Passionate Shepherd'? Are you familiar with it?"

"I was forced to read it at some point, but I'm sure I don't have a copy of it."

"That's all right. I'll recite it to you."

"That's no fair. To properly pick something apart I have to have a copy in front of me."

"You don't have to pick it apart; Raleigh already did. But you must have a copy somewhere here. You do and you just don't know it." He went to the shelves again and found an anthology; after a minute he had located the poem. He handed the text to Collin and declaimed it, beginning:

> Come live with me and be my Love,
> And we will all the pleasures prove
> That hills and valleys, dales and fields,
> Or woods or steepy mountain yields.

As he spoke he looked at Constance, who wore a hint of a smile, as if she could appreciate both his romanticism and his absurdity. As he came to a close, still without taking his eyes off her, a faint hint of crimson crept into her cheeks.

"Ryan," said Collin contemptuously, "you and I don't even speak the same language. I don't even know where to begin in disposing of this piece of trash."

"Well, begin with what Raleigh wrote in reply. It's printed next there." He then recited the nymph's reply, beginning

> If all the world and love were young,
> And truth in every shepherd's tongue,
> These pretty pleasures might me move
> To live with thee and be thy Love;

and ending

> But could youth last, and love still breed,
> Had joys no date, nor age no need,
> Then these delights my mind might move
> To live with thee and be thy Love.

He did not look at Constance as he repeated these words; he looked over Collin's head, out the window.

"Hopeless, antiquated, pretentious, contrived, sexist, meaningless trash, all of it," said Collin, in a tone that spoke his despair of even attempting critical analysis.

"So it seems to you, because you're unacquainted with the pastoral tradition. If you had studied the pastoral poets from Theocritus through Vergil, through medieval times to these great Elizabethans, pastoral poetry would resonate with an infinite number of echoes of the Golden Age. A pastoral poem is not one poem—it's a thousand; it's not from one point in time, it draws upon millennia of human poetry and ideas. And poetry and ideas are the consecrating bread and wine of human communion. I'll go further than that. They're the sustenance that humans and the divine feed to one another. Forget this truth and your soul will starve."

"You hopeless pedant!" exclaimed Collin. "Honestly Ryan, they broke the mold when they made you. And thank God they did!"

"This hardly constitutes criticism, old man."

"No, but it is a reaction."

"Try harder. Weave words. Articulate."

"Look, I'll say this much for Raleigh. He seems to have recognized that all the claptrap Marlowe trots out is just that—empty, stuffy old symbols from an outdated tradition."

"I don't find Raleigh's criticism compelling at all. For me much of the real pathos of Marlowe's poem is that we *know* that all the pleasures he offers are fleeting, that we sense that he is commenting that love, life, everything is fleeting, and that what matters is that we seize what we can while we can—that we believe in our poor petty human symbols of pleasure. Raleigh seems to be hitting us over the head with what we already know all too well. 'Hills and valleys are fine,' he seems to be saying, 'but what about medicare and social security?' Thanks, Wally, but we don't need anyone to tell us one more time that the winter of old age is coming. We need someone like Marlowe to tell us to enjoy the summer of our love and our youth while we have time. That's what we're always neglecting to do."

"I think we're neglecting it right now," said Constance. "If you two are going to start talking about how short life is again, maybe we should just go swimming."

Collin closed the anthology and threw it carelessly on the desk beside him. "I'll second that," he said. "There's no point in trying to carry on a rational discussion with this museum relic."

"You haven't seen anything yet," said Ryan. "Ask me about 'To His Coy Mistress' sometime. Now there's a great poem!"

"Did you bring your bathing suit, Ryan?" asked Collin wearily.

"Of course I did."

"Then go lecture to the pollywogs or something while I find mine."

"Aren't you being a little hard on him?" asked Constance. "After all—"

"It rolls right off my back," said Ryan. "Don't pay a moment's notice to it."

"Are you sure?"

"Absolutely. He and I have been having this kind of discussion for years."

"Out, both of you!" said Collin. "I'll need to read some decent poetry just to clear my mind of that lovey-dovey garbage."

"We'll meet you at the pond, then," said Constance.

"Yes, yes."

"You *will* come down? You won't just sit here and get distracted reading something?"

"I'll be there. Just get this archaic clown out of my sight."

Ryan followed Constance out of the room, pausing only long enough to look back at Collin with a grin of triumph; to which his friend responded with a reluctant chuckle of exasperation.

Thursday, July 16, through Friday, July 17

It is a most miserable thing to feel ashamed of home. There may be black ingratitude in the thing, and the punishment may be retributive and well deserved; but, that it is a miserable thing, I can testify.

—Dickens

I did in time collect myself, and thought
This was so and no slumber.

—*The Winter's Tale*

RYAN CALLED THE Tates on Thursday. Constance answered.

"What's up?" asked Ryan.

"Nothing," she said. "My mother was going to drag me out shopping somewhere, but I'm too sore to go."

"Sore?"

She laughed faintly and apologetically. "That time of the month," she said. "I'll be all right by tomorrow."

"It's the full moon tomorrow," he said. "That will either make things worse or better."

"They can't get any worse."

"That bad?"

"I'm lucky, really. It only bothers me for about a day. Anyway, I don't feel like doing anything but lying here in the living room feeling sorry for myself."

"Company wouldn't help?"

"I'm not fit company for a dog."

"I don't mind."

"You're awfully sweet, Ryan, but I think I'd better pass. You could do something with Collin, but he's grinding away at his typewriter. He's such a perfectionist. Every copy of every poem has to be flawless—not a typo, not a smudge."

"That's Collin, all right. Well, if you get bored and change your mind, I'll be in and out."

"Thanks. Maybe we can all do something tomorrow."

"See how you feel."

"Okay. Be talking to you."

"Bye."

He hung up the phone, wedged his shoulders against the historians, and braced his feet against the interior structure of the desk, his quadriceps holding his chair pinned at an angle to the vertical like enormous springs.

And so he stayed for most of that day and the next. He abandoned his post to dawdle over meals; he took a brief, wakeful sojourn in his bed that night; but otherwise he did little. In the other rooms his parents came and went; he was aware that they sometimes stopped and watched him for a moment, through the door he neglected to close, perhaps refused to close; but he did not care anymore what they saw. And when a boy cares no more whether he conceals his infatuation, he has reached a desperate stage.

Many dreams occupied him. He imagined her walking before him, as she often had, barefoot down the path to the pond. Pebbles stung the tender soles of her feet at every step; the smarting gave a different lilt to her lightfoot grace; he watched her body—young, lissome—the muscles of her back moving smoothly with her stride; her waist a node of indrawn delight; her buttocks, barely covered by the daring suit she wore, revealing no seam in the flesh where they joined her legs. Often in these fantasies she would look over her shoulder suddenly, with a tossing of her dark hair, and catch the gist of his gaze with her humorous eyes; and stop in the path, and wait for him, until he touched her with the gesture, and then walk on with him, holding him by the arm as she had that evening of the Fourth of July.

In another dream he went through the great house, calling her; he could hear her faint reply, but he could not locate her. At last he found her up in the attic, hiding playfully from him. As in so many of these fantasies, she wore white, and shone in the setting of dust and dry, dark wood like the last cool snow in an alpine hollow in summer. She was all unaware that she had a smudge of dust on her nose; and after he had touched her head, he smiled and wiped that smudge away. She laughed, collected some dust on the tip of one finger, and leaned breathtakingly close to draw a heart on his cheek.

But as this interval wore on, one daydream began to take precedence over the others. He saw himself sitting, as he was now, packed against the bookshelf, daydreaming; and his mother or father would come to the doorway and say, "Ryan, there's someone here to see you." He would go through the house, baffled as to who it might be, and stop at the screen door. The Mercedes would be in the broken driveway, beyond the rusting Valiant; Collin would be just stepping out, and would wave to him and laugh. But she, on the other side of the car, would be already running toward the house, with her face lifted and bright with love and anticipation—he would step out on the rickety stoop, and she would almost pause to see him better before she ran forward again, as if to reassure herself that he was there, waiting for her, and that his eyes showed the love that she herself felt. She would slow to a shy walk as she came close to him; and while his parents watched in wonder behind the screen door, and Collin looked on with satisfaction, he would touch her head; and she would accept that gesture in full acknowledgment of the pledge it signified.

"Ryan," said his mother again. Ryan shook off the dream and sat up, bewildered. "There are some people here to see you," said Maureen.

Ryan stood up in confusion and followed his mother back into the kitchen. She stopped a few paces short of the screen door, looking through it.

Constance and Collin stood in the driveway, talking to Daniel. He had the mail in one hand; he must have been returning from the mailbox when they appeared. They must have walked over; no car was in sight. Now Daniel was shaking Constance's hand; she smiled warmly at him, with that deep excitement that Ryan loved in her, that made all that she did an act of radiant delight; and she held his hand just a bit longer than he expected, in that enthusiasm that was so winning.

"Isn't she just the queen of curds and cream!" exclaimed Maureen.

Ryan threw open the door and walked down the steps; and Constance ran to him, laughing, and for a moment he hardly knew whether he was waking or dreaming. He put up his hand dazedly—and into it she thrust a bouquet of wildflowers.

He recovered himself with difficulty. "Here he is," Daniel was saying.

"Ryan!" said Collin. His tone was expansive and delighted; he was full of the pleasure of his memories of the Kinsellas and their home.

"We've come to visit you," said Constance. She laughed. "As you can see."

"Yes, so I see. I'm very glad you've come."

Maureen opened the screen door and ventured out. "You can only be Constance," she said.

"And you must be Ryan's mother," said Constance.

"Mother," said Ryan, "this is Constance Tate. Constance, my mother."

Maureen came down the steps and shook Constance's hand. She seemed small and portly and shy and in awe of the girl's beauty; and yet Constance beamed in delight, and dropped her eyes as she shook Maureen's hand, as if she felt the honor of the acquaintance more keenly than she could bear.

"I'm very pleased to meet you, Constance," said Maureen. "I'd like to be able to tell you I've heard a lot about you, but boys don't tell their mothers much. We almost have to guess more from what they don't say than from what they do. But I'm so pleased for both of you—for you and Collin—that you have this time to be together after all these years." She looked up at Collin, who now came to her and hugged her. "Look at you!" she said, with tears in her eyes. "It's so good to see you again! We never see you much anymore. Are you *still* growing, or am I getting smaller in my old age?"

"I'm not going to get too much taller than six feet," laughed Collin.

"Constance," said Maureen, "there was a time these two boys were in and out of this house every weekend. Every day during the summer. With Ryan's dog tagging along after them everywhere they went—tracking in mud and making a racket, all three of them. I used to scold! But what wouldn't I give to have them do it now! And I wouldn't scold at all. I'd just hold my tongue and be grateful. Collin was like another son. As *he* says, 'Which of them both is dearest to me I have no skill in sense to make distinction.'"

"Well, I hardly believe that!" said Collin. "But those were wonderful days. The best days of my life, till Constance came back."

"Aren't you the luckiest boy alive!" said Maureen. "Look at this beautiful creature!—And I mean creature in the best sense, dear, a lovely being created by God. And it seems you just appeared out of nowhere! It makes me think of Perdita, you know.—You know Perdita in *The Winter's Tale?*"

"No, I haven't read that one yet," said Constance.

"Well, Perdita is a child who's taken away when she's just an infant—her name means 'the Lost One,' doesn't it?" Maureen said, appealing to Ryan for confirmation, but continuing before she received it. "And she reappears in the story all grown up after sixteen years. 'Impute it not a crime,' he says, 'to me or my swift passage, that I slide o'er sixteen years, and leave the growth untried of that wide gap.'"

"Well, sixteen years is just about right," said Constance.

"And he calls her 'Perdita, now grown in grace equal with wondering.' And so you are."

Constance blushed. "You're too kind, Mrs. Kinsella," she said somewhat faintly and confusedly.

"And you remember those wonderful lines," continued Maureen, speaking not so much to Constance as to her favorite interlocutor, an imaginary being who knew Shakespeare as well as she did, "where Hermione says, 'Come, I'll question you of my lord's tricks and yours when you were boys. You were pretty lordings then?' And Polixenes says, 'We were, fair queen, two lads that thought there was no more behind but such a day tomorrow as today, and to be boy eternal.' That always reminds me of my Ryan and Collin."

Constance was staring at Maureen with brimming eyes. Ryan made a distracting noise in his throat and then asked, "You've been introduced to my father?"

She recovered and smiled at Daniel. "Yes," she said.

"Ryan's checking up on my manners," said Collin.

"I've had the pleasure of an introduction," said Daniel.

"We've come over to take your son away again," said Constance. "I hope you don't think of us as thieves, for always stealing him. I always feel guilty when I ask him over, because I know how much you want him here with you."

"We do allow him to roam occasionally," said Daniel. "But only under the strictest supervision. He's liable to start chanting principle parts or ranting about the Structuralists unless he's closely watched."

"It's a hereditary tendency," said Ryan.

"And I can see that his sense of humor is hereditary, too," Constance said.

"We're going to smuggle Constance away to the mall and buy her a pair of pants," said Collin.

"I've never owned any," Constance explained to Maureen.

"Never? All the girls seem to wear them nowadays."

"Well, my mother came from the kind of family where—well, where they didn't believe in *that kind of thing.*" She laughed and pushed up the tip of her nose with her forefinger to signify snobbery. "She'll probably kill me when I come home, but Collin insists I buy a pair before the century is out."

"It's just that my mother thinks that no woman can ever get to wear the pants in the house unless she looks good in a dress," said Collin.

"Well, I'm game," said Ryan. He looked about for Collin's car and realized it was not there. "How did you get over here?" He was thinking with a kind of horror that his parents might invite Constance inside. The event he was witnessing still seemed unreal to him. Constance existed only at the Tates—he had literally never seen her outside the valley; and yet here she was before him, almost breathlessly excited, looking about with sparkling eyes. His parents' little home seemed too dingy and cramped to contain her radiance—if she entered it she would shed light like Athena with her high-held lamp and leave the place never the same again, infusing into that narrow shed of childhood drudgery a visible essence of the valley.

"We walked over," said Collin. "Constance wanted to see the place you disappeared to every night."

"You probably thought it was a cave somewhere," said Ryan.

"I'll tell you one thing I do know," she said. "I'll never let you walk home by road at night. There aren't any sidewalks! Every time a car comes by, you have to jump in the bushes. Which seem to all be this terrible plant called poison ivy."

Collin gave Ryan a meaningful glance.

"What happened?" asked Ryan.

"We had a little incident," said Collin.

"What kind of incident?"

"Oh, you know. The old drive-up-next-to-us-at-ninety-miles-an-hour-scream-obscenities-and-throw-beer-cans kind of incident. The brush-off."

"How awful!" exclaimed Maureen.

"Did you get their license number?" asked Daniel.

"Oh, no, you never do in cases like that. You're too busy trying to get your heart back down out of your throat so you can breathe."

"Sounds like you're being introduced to all our cherished aspects of American life," said Ryan to Constance. "That used to happen to Collin and me regularly. Punks from the next town over."

"So far I've learned that there are the Tates and the Kinsellas and then there are the hoodlums," Constance said.

"That about sums up all you need to know about American society," Ryan agreed.

"That's not true," said Maureen, who was never willing to let the cyncisms of her husband and son stand unchallenged. "There are lots of good people in the world."

"Yes, but it only takes a few thugs to spoil it," said Daniel.

"You must be a little rattled after that," said Maureen. "Why don't you come in and have a little something cool to drink?"

"I'd love to," said Constance, as if she were being invited into a holy shrine.

"I'd like to look around again," said Collin. "It really has been ages and ages since I was here last."

"We missed you on Christmas," said Maureen.

"Yes," said Collin. "I always come over at the end of Christmas Day," he explained to Constance. "Something happened this year and I couldn't come over. I forget what it was."

"It's just as well you didn't," said Daniel. "Maureen and I were so proud of Ryan we probably weren't fit for company."

"As you had every right to be," said Collin. "I know my father was so proud of him he was about to swell up and burst."

"Collin wrote me about it," said Constance. "I was so excited— that was when I thought I would be going to college in England and I could meet him there."

"God," said Ryan feebly, as he thought of attending Oxford with Constance Tate.

"It was really exciting news, I must say," said Daniel, beginning to beam with the intoxication of his pride once again.

"Well, come inside," said Maureen. She turned and led the way.

"Watch those steps," said Ryan, suddenly horrified by the condition of the stoop as Constance put her diminutive white espadrille on the first tread.

"They've been like this forever," said Collin. "If they hold you, you dumb jock, they'll hold Constance." She laughed at the look on Ryan's face and went up the steps and inside. The men filed after her, Daniel laughing too and repeating the phrase "Dumb jock" under his breath. "Is that what you put on your business cards, Ryan?" he asked.

"Yes," said Collin, "it goes right under 'Shameless Pedant.'"

"Better that than 'Mad Poet,'" said Ryan.

"They haven't changed at all, Maureen," chuckled Daniel. "They're still at it."

"And we still love it," said Maureen. "You know what he says: 'He makes a July's day short as December, and with his varying childness cures in me thoughts that would thick my blood.'"

"And you haven't changed at all either, Mrs. Kinsella," said Collin. Daniel emitted a stifled laugh.

They had to do some deft and spontaneous rearrangement of their positions before they could all stand together in the tiny kitchen. Ryan was not happy that Constance should see his home, but he told himself that at least the inside was neater than the outside. She showed no distaste, in any case; in fact, she was gazing about herself in seeming enchantment. She used every possible adjective of enthusiasm, calling the kitchen cozy and charming and just what she had imagined. Ryan himself began to look about himself with new eyes. The floor, at least, was scrupulously clean, and if the counters and window sills were crowded with utensils and bric-a-brac and books, at least the arrangement of this superfluous material indicated a certain method.

"Would lemonade be good?" asked Maureen.

"It would be wonderful," said Collin.

"Constance?" Maureen inquired.

"Just a little glass," she said, showing a gap between her thumb and fingertip. "But I would love some too."

"Make a whole pitcher of it," said Daniel grandly, as if there were some other way to mix it.

"Here, I'll show you the study," said Ryan, knowing that his mother would need room to maneuver.

He found it easier to lead the way than to wave them ahead through the doorway. "Don't blink," he told Constance. "You'll miss the living room."

"Nothing has changed here at all," said Collin with pleasure. "Ah—is this a new footstool?"

"Just a new cover on the old one," said Daniel.

"What did we use to do with that, Ryan?" asked Collin.

"We used to turn it upside down and ride it down the stairs. Remember?"

"No!" exclaimed Daniel. "When did you ever do that?"

"Last year, probably," said Constance. "I can see why it needed a new cover."

Ryan went on immediately into the study. "Oh," said Constance as she entered, "this is exactly the way I pictured this place."

"She was asking me to describe it just the other day," said Collin. "There's the fireplace, see?"

"Many a warm fire we've had in that one, haven't we?" said Daniel, pausing in the doorway.

"While other kids were watching the idiot box, Con, we'd be watching the fire, and Ryan's dad or mom would read us stories from great old books." Collin smiled broadly as he remembered. "No wonder we're so strange," he added, and both he and Ryan laughed.

"It's the other kids who are strange," said Daniel loyally.

"I'm afraid not," said Collin. "The majority determines what is strange and what is not, and we're the abnormal ones. But I wouldn't have it any other way."

"You did a wonderful job raising them both," Constance told Daniel. She peered closely at the shelves, marveling at the profusion of volumes and the variety of titles. "So this really is the place," she murmured, as if she had almost doubted its existence. She turned to Ryan. "I can just imagine you here, learning your lessons."

"He was a good student," said Daniel.

"He has certainly proved that, hasn't he?" she said, with another of her winning smiles. To Ryan she said, "Show me your first Greek book."

He took a ragged textbook down as she came to his side. She stood very close to him, in the very spot where a few minutes before he had been dreaming of her almost without hope. She seemed now more real than ever. She was in the place where he lived, creating an intersection with his past; she seemed willing, even eager, to share his life; and the thought of losing her, now that her love seemed so close and so attainable, was more painful than it had ever been.

She looked over the pages in the textbook with a kind of awe while he stole glances at her. Collin paced around the room joking about something with Daniel.

"Do you think I could ever learn this?" she asked.

"In no time at all," he promised.

She shook her head. "I don't know. Maybe when I go to college, I'll take a course."

"You'll never regret it," said Ryan.

"I'll make you a deal," she said, smiling. "I'll learn Greek if you learn Spanish."

"Agreed," he said instantly, shaking her hand.

"What have I done!" she laughed.

"You've made a vow, that's what."

He realized he was still holding the bouquet of flowers in his left hand. "Here," he said, "you sit down, and I'll get a vase for these." She sat in his chair, and he went to the kitchen.

His mother was stirring the lemonade. She seemed gravely troubled, almost as if she were in physical pain.

"What's the matter?" he asked. "Are you all right?"

For his sake she tried to smile.

"Oh, yes," she reassured him. "I'm fine.—She's such a pretty girl, isn't she?"

"You're not usually given to such understatement, Mother." He looked through a cupboard hastily.

"Well," said Maureen vaguely, rattling her spoon round and round in the pitcher.

"Don't we have a vase anywhere?"

"For what? The flowers? I'm afraid not. Your father broke our only vase by accident while you were at school this year. It was a wedding present, too."

"For God's sake!" said Ryan desperately, taking an old mayonnaise jar from the cupboard and filling it with water. He thrust the flowers into it and carried it back out to the study. "Would you believe?" he said, holding up the jar so that Constance could see it. She laughed.

"That jar will probably be a precious archeological relic in another century," she said. "No one will dream of putting flowers in it then."

"Yes, the jar will certainly outlast the flowers, which are infinitely more beautiful." He put the jar on the desk before her.

"Which would you rather be, the jar or the flowers?" she asked playfully, correcting the arrangement of the flowers.

"The jar, I guess. That way I could enjoy the flowers year after year."

"Not me. I'd rather be beautiful and fade away. I have no aspiration to achieve immortality, like certain others I know." She paused, surveying the arrangement. "It's funny, you know," she said. "You really are like that. I don't mean like an old glass jar, but you've equipped yourself to enjoy so much beauty—you've learned a million languages, you've learned to look around yourself, at people and things—and you see them all so clearly. Much more clearly than I do, or—" and she looked at Collin to see if he might hear her; but he and Daniel were obliviously reminiscing— "or even Collin. I wish I could see through your eyes."

"They're yours for the asking. But don't tell me you're a flower of the field, fated to fade away while I sit in stodgy silence year after year."

"You'll outlive me, I'm sure of it. You're strong. Nothing will really shake you, not so deeply that you can't go on, somehow or other. Sometimes I think the Tates are too volatile. We love each other, but we're ready to blow up and blow away like smoke."

Instantly he had a thousand questions, a thousand reassurances. Why had she chosen a time like this to say this, when he could not speak freely? Or had she chosen this time for that very reason?

"But how could you, you in particular, blow up and blow away?" he asked. "You're a focus for everyone's love—your mother's, your father's, Collin's. You're holding your family together, in a way."

"I know. But it's my weakness that holds them together. If I were a stronger person, I would take sides. And it's so hard for me to balance all my affection. If I just gave it all to one person, it would be so much easier. But it would have to be someone outside the family."

"Here's the lemonade," said Maureen, entering with a tray. Ryan desperately wished he could have forestalled her entrance for only a few seconds.

Constance rose from the chair, and the usual civilities were observed as the glasses were handed around.

"Well," said Daniel, lifting his glass as though it were champagne, "here's to the young people. May all your dreams prosper."

"And yours, too, Mr. Kinsella," said Collin.

"I'll drink with that addendum," said Ryan. "And we'll throw Mother's dreams into the toast while we're at it."

"And I'll second you all," said Constance.

"Well, considering that our dreams are Ryan's," said Daniel, "I guess we won't argue with that."

They then sipped; only Collin seemed genuinely thirsty.

"I suppose it's silly, standing around in here when we could be sitting in the living room," said Daniel.

"We really shouldn't stay too long," said Collin. "My mother thinks we're out for a walk in the woods. We've got to sneak in this shopping trip before she wises up."

"It's so strange to hear you say, 'My mother,'" said Maureen.

"It's strange to say it," said Collin.

"But you will sit down, just for a minute?" said Maureen. "Just until you finish your lemonade?" She led the transition to the living room, where there were just places enough for everyone.

"Now, Constance," said Maureen when everyone was settled, "tell us all about your school plans."

"Well, I don't really have any yet. We're still looking at schools and trying to figure out what we need. Things have been a little bit confused."

"Any particular places you've seen that you're interested in?" asked Daniel.

"One of the schools in Amherst would be nice," she said.

"Very nice," said Maureen. "Collin could help orient you to the American scene."

"Any particular major you're thinking of?" asked Daniel.

"Well, no, not really. Probably American literature—"

"Have a career in mind? Teaching, maybe?" asked Daniel.

"Not really. I just—"

"There are lots of good private schools around," said Maureen. "It can be fun to teach in one of them, although the pay is notoriously bad, and the work's awfully hard."

"I hadn't really thought that far ahead. I—"

"I would have thought that maybe one of the professions might interest you," said Maureen. "Maybe the law. You come from a distinguished line of professional people."

"The law is drudgery, Maureen," said Daniel. "What would a bright young person want with a stuffy old subject like that?"

"I don't think I'd want to—"

"What kind of things did you study in school?" asked Daniel.

"Oh, the usual. I mean, I suppose they were the usual. Literature and chemistry and biology and physical science and math—"

"Did you take calculus?" asked Daniel.

"Yes, I—"

"Any languages?"

"I studied French, and of course Spanish—"

"Oh, of course, Spanish," said Maureen. "After all, there you were."

"I suppose you couldn't help it," said Daniel.

"With your kind of science background," said Maureen, "there's always a medical career."

"She's *not* going to medical school," said Ryan.

"Do you like music, Connie?" asked Maureen.

"That's 'Constance,' Mother," said Ryan in an ominously irritated tone.

"Oh, I love music."

"Play anything?" asked Daniel.

"A little guitar."

"A little guitar? You mean a small guitar, or—"

"No, I mean I play a little, on a guitar."

"She plays beautifully," said Collin. "You should hear her, Mrs. Kinsella. It's extraordinary."

"Oh, my dear, you should do something with that," said Maureen.

"Were there any courses you particularly liked?" asked Daniel.

"That I particularly liked? I don't know. I had fun in them all, I suppose. Chemistry got tedious sometimes. I liked the literature best. But I guess everyone does."

"Everyone in this room, anyway," said Ryan.

"How much of him did you read?" asked Maureen.

Constance looked puzzled.

"When my mother uses the masculine third person pronoun without an antecedent, you can assume she means Shakespeare," said Ryan.

"Of course," said Maureen.

"Oh! Yes—well, I read *Romeo and Juliet*, *Macbeth*, *Lear*, *Hamlet*, *Midsummer-Night's Dream*, *The Tempest*—I think that was all. Oh, *Julius Caesar*, too."

"Oh, dear, you've got quite a bit of fun ahead of you. I wish I had them all to read over for the first time. How about the sonnets?"

"A few."

"I can imagine. Eighteen, thirty, seventy-three, a hundred and sixteen. That kind of thing."

"That's about it."

"You didn't take any Latin?" asked Daniel.

"No, I'm afraid—"

"No Greek?"

"No, I—"

"Well, it's never too late to start. There's that to be said. It's never too late. I didn't start myself until I was ten or eleven. Of course, you're a little older than that, but you can catch up."

"Of course she can. She's a very bright person," said Maureen.

"I think that's about enough, Mother," said Ryan, rolling his eyes. He turned toward Constance. "My parents will let you know if you got the job tomorrow." She giggled.

"What a charming laugh you have," said Daniel, smiling at her.

"Dad, back off," said Ryan.

"What say, old man?" Collin asked Ryan. "Coming with us on a brief foray into reality?"

"Are the malls reality? I thought they were a permanent nightmare state."

"Have you ever been to one of the malls here in America, Constance?" asked Maureen. Collin laughed and Constance groaned.

"Have I ever!" she exclaimed. "Sometimes I think I live in a mall, and make brief visits at my father's house to eat and sleep. My mother's always dragging me off to shop."

"You don't like to shop?" queried Maureen. "I would think that someone like you would enjoy it."

"I don't mind a little bit once in a while. I confess I turn into an idiot when I see a new dress I really like. But my mother's a fanatic. It's her whole life."

"We don't do much shopping," said Maureen. "As a matter of fact, I've had quite a time trying to persuade Daniel he needs a new jacket. We're going to a wedding tomorrow, you know."

"Really?" exclaimed Constance, looking with great interest to Ryan for an explanation.

"One of my cousins. I forget which one."

"You do not!" protested Maureen.

"That's right. It's Pippin."

"A really sweet girl," Maureen explained to Constance.

"She's been engaged for four years," added Ryan.

"That must have been very . . . difficult."

"Perhaps you'd like to invi—" began Maureen.

"So what's this about shopping?" said Ryan, cutting her off.

"I just thought it would be good if Constance had something warm to wear in Maine," said Collin.

"Oh, yes, you're going to Nansett," said Maureen. "Won't that be nice?"

"Yes," said Collin. "We're looking to Ryan to keep Constance company while I'm at the workshop."

"Ryan did mention that you were going to be attending a conference down there," said Maureen.

"Yes—I'll be gone pretty much all day. It'd be pretty dreary for Constance to be all alone by herself."

"I didn't realize you were going to be gone that much," said Daniel. Ryan, as usual, had given his parents only the barest details.

"Yeah, the workshops last all day. From eight in the morning on."

"And for how many days will the conference run?" asked Maureen. Ryan realized her intention at once, though he guessed the Tates would not.

"Seven days. Saturday the twenty-fifth through Friday the thirty-first."

"That's a long time, isn't it?"

"Well, I should get a lot done. I'm looking forward to it."

"And what will you do all day, Connie, when Collin's at the conference?"

She blushed slightly. "Oh, I don't know," she said vaguely.

"She'll be lazing around on the beach with Ryan," said Collin. She blushed still more.

"He's going to be her chaperone," said Collin. "You see how I've got everybody's life planned around my own. All we need to do now is to get her a pair of pants to keep her warm at night.—What do you say, Ryan, are you coming to the mall with us or what?"

"Absolutely," he said, rising from his chair to put an end to the conversation.

Everyone else rose as well, and the group moved through the kitchen and out of doors. Daniel and Maureen paused on the steps.

"Wait a minute," said Ryan suddenly. "Dad, do you still have film in the camera from the Fourth?"

"Yes. I think there's one picture left."

"I want you to take a picture of the three of us."

"Oh, yes!" enthused Constance.

"Excellent," said Collin.

"The camera's on my bureau, Ryan," said Daniel. He gave Ryan room to pass into the house by descending to the buckled concrete of the front walk, and Ryan shot away inside with a bang of the screen door. As he went into his parent's room upstairs he could hear Daniel's voice faintly through the window. "He'll be down in two seconds," he was saying.

"He climbs stairs faster than anyone I've ever seen," said Maureen.

"Two, three at a time," said Daniel.

In a moment he found the camera and returned. He made sure the film was advanced and gave the camera to his father.

"Do you still have that thing?" marveled Collin. "Look at this, Constance. It's an antique."

"It's a Brownie," said Daniel. "Still takes beautiful pictures— well, snapshots, you know. None of us around here is a great photographer."

"Just get us all in the picture, Dad," said Ryan. A sudden exuberance had seized him at the idea of having a photograph of her. He would have made sure she stood in the middle, so that there would be less chance of his father cutting her out of the frame, as Daniel was apt to do; but she took her position there naturally, as she always had. And as she had before, she seized Ryan's and Collin's hands in hers. "Cheese, cheese," she cried, "Say cheese with a *Z*."

Collin laughed; Ryan said: "Cheese with a *Z*."

She laughed and turned to scold him, and Daniel snapped the shutter.

"That's it," he said.

"At least you were smiling," said Constance.

"So were you," said Ryan.

"So was Collin. You all were," said Maureen.

"Are you sure there's no more film? We could take one of you and Ryan," said Collin to the Kinsellas.

"No, that really is the last picture," said Daniel, looking at the indicator on the back of the camera.

"I'll have to bring my camera over," said Collin. "I always forget about it. Ryan, be sure to remind me to take it to Maine."

"Here, let me take the film," said Ryan to Daniel. To Collin he said, "We can drop it off on our way to the mall. I'll bring the picture over as soon as it comes back."

"Wonderful," said Constance.

"Let's go," said Collin.

"Now, look," said Maureen, "you two do come back soon. Don't be such strangers here. You're always welcome."

"It was *so* nice to meet you," said Constance.

"It was an honor to meet *you*," said Daniel. "And a pleasure to know that Collin has such a fine sister."

"That's enough," said Ryan. "We're off."

"When will you be back, Ryan?" asked Maureen anxiously.

"I'll be in touch," said Ryan. "You'll hear from me before my next birthday."

"Isn't he terrible?" Maureen said to Constance.

"Very naughty. I'll give him a lecture."

With another chorus of goodbyes the three young people escaped; Maureen and Daniel went back into the house.

Ryan had proceeded no further than the mailbox when he stopped short. "Just a second," he said. "Got to get my wallet."

He sprinted back to the house, made his way through the kitchen into the study, retrieved his wallet, and started out again.

In the kitchen he halted suddenly. His parents looked oddly bleak, as if they had been under great strain and were too exhausted to conceal it from him any longer.

"What's this?" he demanded. "What's the matter?"

They only stared at him.

"Is something wrong?" he asked.

Daniel managed to shake his head weakly.

"I hope not," said Ryan defensively.

They still could not bring themselves to respond. He went out the door, angry at first, but then dismissing the matter from his mind.

❀❀❀

After he had gone out again, Maureen and Daniel watched from the screen, still wearing the same pained look that had baffled their son.

"You've got to admit she's a beauty, Maureen," said Daniel.

"So much the worse," she said. "So much the worse for it, Danny. 'This is a creature, would she begin a sect, might quench the zeal of all professors else, and make proselytes of whom she but bid follow.' But 'the wooing doth not end like an old play: Jack hath not Jill.'"

Daniel hesitated. When Maureen got on a quoting streak, it was often difficult to carry on a conversation with her. He almost abandoned the effort. "Well," he said finally, sagging into a chair, "there's no question we were right about his trouble."

"No question," she agreed, peering through the screen door still, though the young people were now out of sight. "'His face's own margent did quote such amazes, that all eyes saw his eyes enchanted with gazes.'"

"Ah, Maureen, how can we blame him for wanting to be with them? At least the Tates know how to play. That's something we never taught him."

Maureen shook her head. "'I swear 'tis better to be lowly born, and range with humble livers in content, than to be perked up in a glistering grief, and wear a golden sorrow.' He'll come to grief with them, Danny. His pockets aren't as deep, and his thoughts aren't as shallow."

"Well, there's something in that," said Daniel. "As my Da used to say, 'Put a beggar on horseback and he'll ride to hell.'"

"'They are as sick that surfeit with too much as they that starve with nothing,'" said Maureen. Daniel found the precise application of this reference too cryptic to discern, but did not ask for an explanation.

She came to the table now and sat down, drawn and weary.

"What do we do?" she asked.

"Nothing. We do nothing. There's nothing we can do. We let things take their course."

"I think we should find some way to discourage him from going over there. It's just going to break his heart all the more. She doesn't care for him. Did you see how she turned red when we asked about Nansett? She's playing with his affections, Danny."

"No, I don't believe it's anything so deliberate. She likes him well enough. She just doesn't feel the same way about him as he does about her. He's too poor for her, that's what I think."

"To think he went through college without so much as looking at a girl, and now he's come to ruin on this one!"

"Well, he hasn't quite come to ruin yet. He'll get over it. It's just a few more weeks, Maureen. When he's off in England he'll forget all about her."

"If only we could find another girl who was . . . more in his class. I mean, we'll never find one bright enough for him. But if we could just find one who wasn't used to wealth. He'll never be wealthy, Danny."

"No, he'll never be wealthy. That's true. And no loss, I say."

"But as long as he has his heart set on someone who needs money, he'll never be happy. What if he married someone like that? He'd be miserable with her."

"He'll find his way, Maureen. He's a good boy. This summer will be trouble for him, but maybe he'll learn something from it. The next woman he chooses will be better for him."

"I hope so," she said.

"Look," he said soothingly. "Tomorrow's the wedding. That will be a good change of scene. A little fun with his own kind, away from the Tates."

"Yes," she said. "I think that *will* be good for him."

❀❀❀

To Ryan, the mall was like another planet, or like some station in space where alien beings met on their journey across galaxies.

It was all darkened glass and stuccoed concrete, inhabited by throngs of people who had more money or credit than was good for them. But Collin and Constance seemed quite at home there and knew exactly where they were going. He followed along behind, amused by the exaggerated shapes and obscene posturing of the mannequins, marveling at the rudeness of the clerks, and generally amazed and depressed by the endless profusion of merchandise. In just one showcase they passed, he saw perhaps a thousand varieties of cheap watches laid out to tempt purchasers; in another were an equal number of pieces of nondescript jewelry, with that sterile and machine-made look that seems calculated to repulse rather than provoke human desire. When they passed a bookstore, the covers of the bestsellers, with their slick, shouting hype and lurid artwork, made him avert his face in revulsion from a display of books for the first time in his life.

They checked several stores. The first few did not have the brand Collin was recommending to Constance; but in a garishly lit cavern of a place, piled on all sides with nothing but jeans, Collin found what he wanted.

He selected two pair and sent Constance to try them on. Ryan priced a replacement for his worn corduroys, but with the trip to Maine approaching, he did not dare spend the money. Then Constance reappeared, wearing her first pair of pants.

"God!" said Collin. "Those look awful!"

"I thought so too," she said unhappily. "And they feel so funny. I don't know if I really want to do this."

"Don't be silly. Which pair are they, the big ones or the small ones?"

"The bigger ones."

"Put the smaller ones on. You'll like them. Go ahead."

"I don't think I could get into the smaller size."

"Sure you can. They're supposed to be tight. You can't wear the ones you have on. They make you look fat."

She retreated to the dressing room in something like horror. In a minute she reappeared, encased from the waist down in skintight denim.

"That's the ticket," said Collin.

"They're way too tight, Collin! There's no way I can wear these. I crush my intestines if I bend over." She went over to a mirror and surveyed herself critically, turning sideways and feeling her rear end unabashedly, smoothing the cloth over her stomach and plucking at the inside of her thighs to draw the crotch downwards.

"They look great," said Collin. "They're just the way they're supposed to be."

"Maybe so, but do I have to kill myself for the sake of style? If it was possible to strangle yourself below the waist, I'd be dead by now. These things are *tight*."

"They'll loosen up a little when you walk around."

"Around the world, you mean."

"But they look awesome, Constance. You've got to get them. Mother will be so fried!"

"Don't you think I could break into this pants thing more slowly? Like get the bigger ones first until I'm used to them?"

"There's no point in getting them at all if they're too big. Believe me. You wouldn't want to wear them."

"Isn't the whole point to have something warm to wear in Maine? The big ones are warm, too, aren't they?"

"Yeah, Collin," said Ryan, "who are you trying to keep warm: Constance, or the guys who are checking her out?"

"I can't even bend over in these, Collin, I swear it."

"Sure you can. Try it."

Constance leaned over and touched her toes several times.

"I can't watch this," said Ryan.

"What's the matter—you don't like them?" asked Constance.

"Don't ask my opinion. Do whatever you want." He tried to turn away, but could not keep his eyes off her.

"But I do want your opinion, Ryan. What do you think? Do they look okay?"

"They look great," said Collin.

"No, I want Ryan's opinion."

"Don't get me involved in this."

"Just tell me," she begged him, "do you think they're sexy, or what?"

"Yes," he said with slow emphasis. "They are very, very sexy."

Constance paused, looking at him closely to see if he was serious. Then she said, "I'll take them."

❀❀❀

When they returned to the Tates, Sondra met them in the front hall.

"Where did you go?" she asked directly. She looked suspiciously at Ryan.

"To buy something for the trip," said Constance.

"What might that be?" asked Sondra.

"Something warm."

"The nights are pretty chilly there," said Collin.

"I know. I remember," Sondra told him. Then, to Constance: "What did you get?"

"I'll show you," said Constance defiantly. She turned and went upstairs. Sondra gave the young men a hostile appraisal and went back into the living room. They followed her and sat down to wait.

"I detect a certain smugness," said Sondra.

"Just a little idea I had," said Collin.

"Little ideas are dangerous."

"On the contrary. Little ideas are fun."

Sondra picked up a magazine and leafed through it. Collin raised his eyebrows at her rudeness and exchanged a glance with Ryan. In a minute Constance came downstairs and entered the room.

She had put on a leotard top instead of the blouse she had worn before; it was an eye-catching combination. Sondra stared—literally bit her lip as if to keep from saying something scathing—and darted a bristling look at Collin before she spoke.

"All right," she said to Constance. "But I trust that if you ever lose your figure, you'll have enough sense not to wear anything so . . . so disgusting."

She had capitulated, if with ill grace; if the young people had held their peace, that would have been the end of it. But Collin said, "Give her a break, Mother. It's as if you went into a time warp in 1964. This is the future. Everyone wears pants."

Sondra rose from her seat, slapping the magazine back on the coffee table. "I'll thank you not to insult your own mother," she said in a scalding tone.

"I just got them for Maine," Constance urged soothingly.

"You'd better behave yourself, young lady," said Sondra, "or you won't be going to Maine at all!"

She could not have found a more effective way of arresting their attention. For the first time in Ryan's acquaintance with Constance, she showed signs of anger. A spot of color appeared in each cheek, and her voice was choked.

"If you try to stop me from going to Maine—" she began.

"What?" said Sondra. "What will you do?"

"I'll kill myself," blurted Constance.

"Well, if you do, you can bet I won't bury you in those pants!" said Sondra.

There was a long, strained silence. Sondra remained where she was, standing by the sofa and staring at Constance; Constance tried to meet her gaze, but succeeded only intermittently. And yet this show of weakness and inability to bear her mother's anger seemed to be the most effective response to it, for it clearly moved Sondra and made her struggle against her own irrascibility. Furthermore, Ryan had the strong impression that some kind of calculation was taking place in Sondra's head, though he could not guess what the factors were.

Finally Sondra said, "Oh, do what you like." It was an amazing second capitulation, and it only made Ryan wonder all the more what had compelled it.

She left the room, even left the house entirely by the front door; her departure and her manner of going were in themselves a continued expression of anger. This time Collin held his tongue until she was fully out of hearing; then he fairly jumped out of his seat and exclaimed, "My God, what a tyrant!"

As if released by Sondra's departure, two tears began their way down Constance's cheeks; she stood slightly bent, as if she had been struck, and her lips trembled.

Collin went to Constance as if he meant to soothe her some-how, but when he reached her, he halted in sudden uncertainty—abruptly turned away, began to pace about. Ryan, who was practically sick with the longing to go to Constance and hold her, sat paralyzed with the fear that to do so would be forcing himself on her.

"I'll tell you the real reason she's so pissed off at you, Constance!" Collin said. "She can't stand the fact that you've got a better body than she does. That's her problem."

Ryan thought this crass and unhelpful, and Constance herself seemed to wince with it. "I just hope she doesn't try to stop our trip to Maine," she said.

"Don't worry. We won't let her. She promised Dad. Dad will stand up for us, don't you worry."

Her pain seemed to ease. She stood up straighter; she went to a chair and sank into it. There she turned to Ryan and gave him a chagrined and apologetic look. In response he rose and offered her a folded and rather crumpled paper tissue from his pocket. She smiled a bit as she accepted it and then used it to wipe her eyes and cheeks. "You're so gallant," she said.

"Just don't try to put that thing in your pocket when you're through with it," he said. "You might split every seam."

She giggled ruefully.

"It's about time you just told her to go to hell," said Collin. "What do you need her for, anyway? Dad loves you. You've got a roof over your head here as long as you want it. He'll pay your college bills no matter what Mother does."

"I just don't want to rock the boat," she said. "Not before the trip."

"Well, then, afterwards you can tell her where to go."

"Oh, Collin, I'll never do that."

"Why not?"

"I don't know. I just never will. I never have. I just always put up with it. I feel sorry for her. I love her. It's not her fault if she loses her temper sometimes."

"Then whose fault is it?"

"It's just the way she is."

"Doesn't that make it her fault, then?"

"It wouldn't do any good to get angry with her."

"Maybe if she had to pay the consequences of her anger for once, she'd learn it was unacceptable."

"No. It would just make everything worse for her."

"What kind of rough life has she had that you have to feel so sorry for her? She's thrown away every good thing she ever had. If she continues to act the way she did just now, she's going to blow her chance to get back together with Dad."

"Maybe she will," said Constance in a sad, strained voice.

"Well, if she does, don't let her drag you down with her. You've got a life of your own to live. You're twenty years old. It's about time you were independent. I can't believe that she still has any say at all in what you wear! What business is it of hers, anyway?"

"I'm all she has," said Constance. "She's just having a hard time letting go, that's all."

"Well, *she* won't let go until *you* do," said Collin.

Constance pressed the paper handkerchief into a shapeless mass in her hands and said nothing for a minute.

"I think I'll go change out of these pants," she said. "It's a little too hot for them today, anyway. What do you say we all go for a swim and forget about this?"

"Sounds good to me," said Ryan.

"Just don't let Mother push you around," said Collin, reluctant to leave the discussion before he was sure his point had been made.

"These things take time," said Ryan. "There's a lot happening this summer. A lot of issues may just resolve themselves, Collin. Don't worry about it."

"That may be true," said Collin. "I just hate to see anyone take advantage of my sister, that's all."

"I know," said Constance. "I appreciate your caring, Collin. Things'll work out."

She rose and went away to change. As she passed Ryan, she touched his arm gratefully.

Saturday, July 18

He belonged to the O'Brien nation—a stock to whom reverence was due. A stock not easily forgotten. The historic memory could reconstruct forgotten glories of station and battle, of terrible villainy and terrible saintliness, the pitiful, valorous, slow descent to the degradation which was not yet wholly victorious. A great stock!

—James Stephens

THE TALE OF Ryan's cousin Pippin was a sad one, worthy of the high tragedy and heroic suffering that had illumined the history of the mighty O'Briens since ancient times. At the age of eighteen she had met and fallen in love with Kevin Donegan, a man five years older, who had nothing to show for himself but an indifferent career as a car salesman, a ruined marriage, and a very stubborn wife. To this rotted piling buffeted in the vast seas of circumstance Pippin had fixed herself immutably, clinging to the man through seven years of turmoil and uncertainty. He sought an annulment; but his wife, sensing the interest of a younger woman, fought its progress every inch of the way, even after taking up open cohabitation with another partner herself; and it was finally denied. The civil authorities had not been so scrupulous. Long before he sought the annulment, Kevin managed to free himself from his marriage in the eyes of the law, on condition of his paying weekly tribute, which, though nominally in support of the children of his marriage, actually enabled his former wife to buy a sporty new two-seater, make a downpayment on a two-hundred-thousand-dollar house, and generally neglect her duties as a mother on various Caribbean cruises with her boyfriend. All this bears repeating only as part of poor Pippin's scandal and tragedy.

Having abandoned all hope of the annulment, the couple decided to marry outside the church. Uncle Frank and Aunt Mary were not sure if this was better or worse than their living together without any benefit of marriage at all; but after considerable intercession from Maureen, they came around to support it. After all, the girl would certainly never give the man up. Frank and Mary consoled themselves with the thought that Pippin could have done worse; she could, for example, have married someone like one of their own sons. Their acquaintances, casting about for palliatives, remembered that the Donegans were from Tipperary, not far from the heart and haunt of the O'Brien clan. And so with her parents' consent, and with a wink from her own priest, Pippin was finally to be wed.

The ceremony was scheduled for one o'clock in a private chapel in Chelsea, officiated over by some civil authority; the clan was then to adjourn to the backyard at Uncle Frank's for the reception. The Kinsellas had planned to leave for Chelsea at noon; and at that time, punctually, Daniel in his best professorial suit, complete with a brown bowtie with minute bears worked into the polyester, and Maureen in one of those formless formal dresses stout middle-aged women affect for weddings and funerals, and Ryan in his sole glory—the green corduroy—climbed into the rubescent Valiant.

"Now, Ryan—" Maureen began.

"No, Mother, I don't want to sit in the front. I never sit in the front."

"I know you never do, and I don't understand it."

"Please just don't say anything about my legs."

"But you have such *long* legs, I just thought—"

"I asked you not to go through this, Mother."

"Sit in the front, Maureen," said Daniel.

"I just thought—"

"He never sits in the front."

"So why doesn't he? It isn't sensible."

"I don't know, but he never does. So leave him alone."

Ryan threw his jacket to one side and stretched out on the back seat. The truth was that felt he was less visible in the back. Daniel fired up the engine and popped the car abruptly into gear.

"That muffler's getting worse," observed Ryan.

"Isn't this exciting?" said Maureen as the car rolled out of the driveway. "It's been ages since we had a wedding."

"Are you sure?" asked Ryan. "It seems like last week."

"No, the last was John and that young thing. Bless her!"

"God bless us all," said Ryan. "And God help us all."

"Amen," said Maureen.

She fell utterly and inexplicably silent for nearly a full minute. In the rearview mirror Ryan and his father exchanged a look. Then, quite suddenly, Maureen turned to Daniel and said: "Have you decided yet?"

"Oh my God!" exclaimed Ryan. "I can't believe you two are still doing this."

"It matters to me," said Maureen.

"No," said Daniel, "I haven't decided yet."

"Stop teasing her, Dad. You two are going to go to your graves without settling this."

"He's right, Danny. You should tell me how you feel."

"He might be, and he might not be," said Danny. "I don't know."

"Was there ever a son whose parents fought over such a thing?" wondered Ryan aloud. Both Daniel and Maureen laughed.

"What do you think, Ryan?" asked Maureen.

"I've told you a hundred times, Mother!"

"But I forget."

"You don't forget at all. You just want to hear me say it again."

"So humor your mother, then."

Ryan grimaced, but said: "All right. I think he was."

"There, Danny, Ryan believes it," she said triumphantly. "Why don't you?"

"Because I'm independently minded, Maureen. It's one of those wonderful things the mind likes to hold in suspension without ever deciding. Kind of like the existence of God."

"Well, thank goodness there's no doubt about that! That's a far cry from whether or not Macbeth was the Third Murderer."

"He's teasing you, Mother. Don't pay any attention to him."

"Now, look Danny," she said, "let me read you the passage again." She pulled a coverless and tattered copy of Shakespeare from the glove compartment, or rather from the recess that had been the glove compartment until the door had fallen off, some years ago. It was her car copy.

"Please!" said Ryan. "I've heard this argument a million times. Will you *please* not start it again!"

Maureen hesitated, almost unable to let go of one of her favorite bones; but then she capitulated to the tone of desperation in Ryan's voice.

"Well, then," she said, "there's another thing I've been wondering about."

"What's that?" said Ryan and Daniel simultaneously, relieved at the change of subject.

"In act one, scene two, the lines—here they are:

> The Thane of Cawdor began a dismal conflict;
> Till that Bellona's bridegroom, lapp'd in proof,
> Confronted him with self-comparisons,
> Point against point, rebellious arm 'gainst arm,
> Curbing his lavish spirit.

"Now, most of the commentators think that Bellona's bridegroom is Macbeth. But I think he only meant Mars, generally, not Macbeth. Because in scene three, Macbeth knows nothing about what has happened to Cawdor. So he couldn't have defeated him here."

"Good point, Mother. Why don't you write an article about it?"

"I think you're onto something there, Maureen."

"Well, it's just a little quibble. I'm not the first to notice it, really. Besides, if I went around correcting all the foolishness I find in the commentators, it would fill a volume in itself."

"You *ought* to write a book like that," said Ryan. "Over the years you've found all kinds of stuff of this sort that no one seems to have ever noticed."

"Well, maybe I should."

Ryan and Daniel exchanged another look. She had been saying "Maybe I should" for years. But she had no interest in engaging in that kind of debate; she was too busy communing with the mind of a man who had been dead for over three and a half centuries.

She murmured about Bellona's bridegroom for much of the ride in, almost as if it were Bellona's wedding she were going to, and not Pippin's. The day was foully hot, and the city was an undifferentiated odor of asphalt and baking concrete, exhaust and thick air. Ryan was soaked with sweat after only a few minutes; but he felt a curious freedom from care. He would not meet Constance where he was going, so his comfort, his condition, his looks—in fact, nothing at all—made any difference to him. To go to the wedding of another when you yearn for your own is either inspiring or painful; and he was more in a mood to see Pippin's wedding painfully. What would he do with the whole clan if he did marry Constance? He tried to imagine them swarming over the Tates' lawns with the same kind of morbid horror with which one fantasizes about one's own funeral. How many times would he have to listen to that endless sneering refrain about how he had married into money? He shook off the thought and imagined instead that by some accident—the misprinting of the invitations, for instance—the clan should come to the wedding a week late.

None of the O'Briens, it seemed, would miss Pippin's wedding. When the Kinsellas finally located the chapel, after fifteen minutes of circling and backtracking through Chelsea, the parking lot was full, the streets nearby were choked with familiar vehicles, and streams of cousins and aunts and uncles were converging on the place.

"Oh my Lord!" exclaimed Maureen, as they cruised past the focus of this activity, looking for a parking space, "There's Cissy! Cissy's back!"

Ryan peered as nonchalantly as possible out the window and spotted Cecelia Donahay surrounded by a knot of excited aunts. She was about his age; she had vanished from home at eighteen, when her twin brother Randy had been paralyzed in an automobile accident. Ryan had rather liked her once, because she was a rebel; but her heart was lapped in some proof no goodwill could never penetrate.

"I wonder where's she's been all this time," said Maureen.

"Well, you can ask her at the reception," said Daniel.

"You can ask everybody everything at the reception," muttered Ryan. And then he added in another mutter to himself: "I hope they have some decent beer."

When the Kinsellas entered the chapel, Ryan felt again that peculiar mixture of reactions to him and his parents that made these clan events so unsettling. Most of the O'Briens genuinely loved Maureen; some loved Daniel and Ryan for her sake; some thought Maureen a dizzy busybody, and sympathized with Daniel and Ryan for having to put up with her; and some heartily disliked all the Kinsellas. Some thought Daniel an alien, a Prot, a perpetual source of suspicion, and his son little better, a kind of half-breed. Then again, some of the O'Briens, mostly the women, thought Ryan was the kindest, sweetest boy that had ever lived, a true gentleman; others thought him disdainful, a spoiled only child, over educated, who had spent too much time at his fancy university and the house of his rich friends to be a true O'Brien or a true Catholic. Then there were those who held him in awe for his Latin (they thought little of his Greek), for his scholarship, for the intellect that he wore stamped on his forehead and in his alert eyes like the mark of Cain. Others, all men, though scarcely aware that he could even read, yet worshipped him because he was a champion soccer player who had led his college to the top of the league. That was all they had to know; and when he entered a room, they would turn and look at him the way they might have looked at a horse entering the track that was going to earn them a fistful of cash. "Staying in shape?" was all these men wanted to know. He did not mind them. At least they did not glower and mutter about him behind his back, as some of his cousins did.

"Cissy's back!" was the word everywhere. Ryan heard that poor Pippin was crying in some back room because she thought Cissy's moment of return was chosen to spite her and steal the show; but he was sure this was just a malicious rumor. Pippin would scarcely remember who Cissy was on a day such as this.

The ushers, Pippin's brothers John and Tom and Danny, were having a quick smoke somewhere and chaos seemed to be the order of the hour. The Kinsellas drifted up the aisle, looking for seats. As they passed near Aunt Luce and Uncle Ted, Cissy's parents, Ted clapped Ryan on the back—Ted was one of Ryan's fans—and gripped his arm. "Sit here, sit here!" he said to the Kinsellas, urging them into his row. He put his crutch out of the way. Ryan thought once again, as he and his parents settled in, how these gatherings were like a reunion of those wounded in the great economic war that society waged against the poor. Uncle Ted had lost a leg to a forklift, a particularly gruesome accident; Uncle Frank still wore a bandage on the back of his hand from that welding burn a couple of months ago; and then there were the faces that were missing—Randy, home in a motorized bed; one of the several Toms in the clan, in a hospital with cancer; Uncle Billy's wife, who had died insane. As difficult as the O'Briens were, when Ryan was among them he felt a glow of anger that they should be shelved, as it were, on level from which they could never rise, morally or financially; for he felt their value, and knew their failures were not entirely their own doing.

"Aunt Doreen is here," announced Maureen, who was busy waving and calling greetings and surveying the gathering.

"Is she?" said Ryan, craning to look. He saw a withered, tiny shape in the front row beside his cousin Fran. "I've got to go say hello to her," he declared. "How much time do we have?" People were still pouring into the chapel, shouting loudly over the nasal piping of the organ.

"You've got a minute," said Maureen. "Go ahead, Ryan."

He slipped past Luce and Ted and made his way to the front. He came upon her thus by surprise. He caught an unguarded view of her ancient face, which was alert and curious, though her expression was masked by the thousands of wrinkles gathered over the enduring bones of her cheeks; the dark eyes were sparkling and a smile was tugging at the corners of her chapped mouth; and then she saw him, and sat up a little straighter, and her eyes focused clearly on him, and the loving irony that is the way the Irish say *I love you* made her lips the lips of a girl.

"Sure an' it's himself," she said.

"Hello, Aunt Doreen," he said. "I didn't know you were coming."

"And why shouldn't I come? So long as they can carry my old bones in a bag, I'll come to a weddin'. Cake, Ryan, and a glass of bubbly, and a jig or two—and young faces like yours." All this delivered in a brogue that after seventy years in America was still so impenetrably thick he had to strain to understand it. She reached up, as he leaned over her, and she caught him by the collar, and tugged him down so that she could give him a kiss on the cheek and whisper to him. "You're grander than ever, Ryan," she said. "Find yourself a sweetheart yet?"

"Maybe, Aunt Doreen," he said.

"Maybe? Oh, those maybe's are heartbreakers. My da used to say, you don't get any honey out of a May bee." She still held him bent over at an awkward angle, and he laughed as she whispered to him. "Is she pretty, Ryan? Is she the most beautiful girl in all the world?"

"That she is," he said.

"Prettier than I was when I was your age?"

"Well, I doubt anybody could be that," he said, laughing; and she laughed too, and released him.

"You'll tell me more, at the party," she said.

"All right."

"And you'll dance with me, too. Remember how we used to dance?"

Long ago she had taught him to dance a jig, and for years she had refreshed his memory at these family gatherings; but she had not danced in five years or more, and she was so shrunken and so bent, so frail and so stiff, that her dancing days seemed well over. He laughed in answer to her and squeezed her hand.

As he went back up the aisle and saw the faces of his relatives turned toward him, he felt his cynicism easing in him. People he loved called to him, waved to him—girls he had once teased in frocks, now wearing eyeshadow and lipstick and pumps, nudged one another and blew him kisses; boys with whom he had committed mischief at funerals and parties and picnics slapped him on the back; his cousin John gripped his hand and stuffed a boutonniere in the lapel of his jacket; and he felt enclosed, included, for better or worse one of his people.

When he was nearly at his row again a priest stood up and held out his hand; beside him his cousin Matt and his wife Candy smiled up at Ryan, he trying to look secular, and she trying to look sacred, and neither quite succeeding.

"How are you, Ryan?" asked Father Tim.

"Not bad, old man," said Ryan with that cool irony in his tone.

"D'you hear that?" laughed Father Tim, looking at Matt. "D'you hear the tone he uses with me? He's still suspicious, after all this time."

"You gave me good reason to be," said Ryan.

"Ah, Ryan, we miss you. We miss you so much! All the boys miss you so much. Every time I see one of them, it's 'How's Mr. Kinsella?' and 'What's Mr. Kinsella doing?' They'll never forget you."

"Well, I won't soon forget them."

"Maybe you'll come back someday?"

"On the day you skate across hell," retorted Ryan. Father Tim guffawed, and Ryan went on to his seat.

"Who was that, Ryan?" asked Maureen when he sat down.

"A priest I knew at school."

"Was he in your parish?"

"No, no, Mother. This was the one who got me involved in that soccer thing."

"Oh," said Maureen uncertainly. She did not remember.

But Ryan remembered. One week in the fall of his junior year he had seen the priest hanging around at soccer practice for several days; and on Friday when Ryan came out of the athletic center into the darkness of the autumn night, the man was still there. Ryan had not known him then, but he acted as if he knew Ryan well; he approached with the self-assured manner of the received and the blessed. Ryan knew the type. He would interfere and intrude and importune and opportune in the lives of others with a humility that was only a mask for the intense consciousness of his righteousness. He was the very sort that faint Catholics like Ryan found most troublesome. "Kinsella, you are," said the priest, and Ryan now knew him doubly persistent: he could tell from the way the priest spoke those three words that he was Irish American, perhaps from New York.

"I am," he answered, stopping short and looking at the priest's outstretched hand.

"Father Tim," the man said. Ryan took his hand reluctantly, but as they shook, both his grip and the priest's were hard. "You're quite a player," said Father Tim.

"They say," said Ryan.

"It's a gift. A gift from God. Don't you think?"

"No offense, Father, but my relationship with God is a little ill-defined. I won't claim all the credit, but I'm not sure what such a gift would obligate me to, if it is a gift, and if you're implying an obligation."

"I am indeed. Every gift of God obligates us to use it in his service."

"And you don't think playing center for a team of spoiled rich brats at an ivy league university is doing the work of God?"

Father Tim threw back his head and laughed. "You can't fool me, Kinsella," he said. "I know your type. You're Catholic bred and born. I need your help, and I think you'll help me."

"Don't bet the beano pot on it, Father. I'm a busy little man." He began walking on, but the priest followed him.

"Too busy to help children?" asked Father Tim.

Ryan almost groaned with the predictability of the assault.

"Help 'em?" he said. "I eat little children for breakfast. I stir 'em right in with the cornflakes."

"Down that street not more than a mile from here," said the priest, wagging a finger to the south, "there are some kids that need you mighty bad. Wolf Bay. Ever heard of Wolf Bay?"

"Believe it or not, some of us in this ivory tower have heard of the outside world. Our geography is not limited to the quad and the green."

"Three hours on Sunday is all I'm asking."

"The Sabbath?" retorted Ryan. "You want me to work on the Sabbath?"

"Come on, Kinsella. You're no Puritan."

"Seriously, Father, I'd love to help you, but I really don't have the time. I have to study in addition to running around booting a little leather ball into people's testicles."

"These kids want someone to help them boot a ball, too. They don't have a coach. It would mean so much to them—it would mean so much to God."

"Well, get God to arrange it. Why don't you do it yourself, man? It's not that hard to pick up a book and learn enough to run a few kids ragged."

"I've got a bad heart."

Ryan looked at him sharply. The priest was fairly jogging along beside his prey with little sign of difficulty.

"No, you've got it wrong," Ryan said. "I've got the bad heart. I won't do it. Besides, I don't speak Portuguese."

"You don't have to speak Portuguese. You can stand there with a ball under your arm and they'll take one look at your legs and they'll respect you. That's the language they understand."

Ryan came to a stop. "Father," he said warningly, "I can outrun you. If I have to, I will. With all due respect—bug off."

He paused a moment, letting the message sink in; then he walked on. The priest did not follow him; but he raised his voice and continued speaking.

"Kinsella," he said, "You want to know why I know you'll do it?"

Ryan made no answer.

"Because you're a poor boy. You're poor Irish, like me. You're not like these fancy rich kids here."

Ryan stopped suddenly on the sidewalk. A gust of autumn wind pelted dried beech leaves around his shoulders. As the priest walked up to him he turned slowly around.

"Is it that obvious?" he asked.

"It is to me," said Father Tim. "I can see you in the old country a hundred and fifty years ago, grubbing in the soil for mealy potatoes, on land you don't own, speaking a tongue that isn't yours."

"And I can see you, battening off me and my kind, teaching us to turn the other cheek and bear it."

"Times have changed, Kinsella. The priesthood's changed."

"I'm not so sure about that, Father."

"Look, I won't get political with you. I just know those boys out in Wolf Bay have got the same hungry look you've got. They're hungry for everything—for love, for a meal, for God—though most of them don't even know how badly they want God. Like you."

A sudden quiver of unaccountable knowledge made Ryan look the priest in the eye by the uncertain light of the sulfur streetlamps.

"You're new to Wolf Bay, aren't you?

"Yes," said the priest innocently.

"And where were you before that?"

"Oh . . . up around Boston . . ."

"Where around Boston? It wouldn't have been Chelsea, would it?"

"It might have been."

"Or Dorchester?"

"I've been there."

"I've got forty cousins, give or take, and most of them have lived in Chelsea or Dorchester at one time or another. Which one of them put you on to me?" he asked.

The priest evaded his gaze. "Cousins?" he said vaguely.

"Pippin? Annie? Maybe you knew Matt? Did you know Matt when he was a priest?

A long, cool silence. The priest took a deep breath and confessed.

"Your Aunt Mary said you might help me."

"Christ!"

"Now, Kinsella!"

"That's what being Irish will get you! You belong to everyone. Your Aunt Mary can sell your time to priests on the street. 'Sure, go barge in on Ryan. He'll be glad to help you. His helped us when young Frank was so wild and went missing from the army. And when Tommy was arrested the first time. He won't say no. Go ask young Kinsella. His father's a Prot; but his mother's an O'Brien through and through.'"

The priest looked at Ryan a little sheepishly. "So am I, Ryan," he said.

It was the last blow. Ryan spun on his heel in disgust. "I can't escape you people!" he cried.

'It's not us you can't escape. It's Christ. Christ wants you. Christ needs you to help someone. You can say no to me, but you can't say no to the voice of Christ when he calls out to you and says, You've got to help. You've got to help or your own dear soul will starve."

"Cut the crap! Spare me the homily!"

He walked on ahead in silence, but the priest was following him again. Finally Ryan stopped, leaning against a wrought iron fence that enclosed the yard of a brick mansion. Two expensive Swedish cars were parked in the drive. The lights were on inside; he could see a blonde woman setting dinner on the table for two children and a husband; the man still wearing the tie he had worn in his brokerage, or his office in the hospital, or wherever it was he made more money than he himself could comprehend.

Ryan buried his face in his forearm. He heard the priest creeping up beside him.

"What time Sunday do you want me to be there?" he asked.

"One o'clock. Behind the church. It's on Whither Street. Just keep walking out—"

"I know where it is. I've seen it, Father."

"Why don't you come to Mass first, Ryan?

"Don't push it, Father!"

"That's all right! Don't come if you don't want to. But Ryan—" The priest seized his hand suddenly now and gripped it tightly. "Do you remember what it says, lad? 'Seek the kingdom of heaven and all things will be given to you?' Do you remember that?"

"Yes."

"Well, Wolf Bay is the door to heaven. That's where you can come look for your way in."

"Bullshit!" exclaimed Ryan.

But the priesthood went off into night victorious.

❁❁❁

It was another dark autumn day over a year later. He sat in a long, still room, facing the Rhodes committee.

It was the end of his second interview. He knew they liked him, though he did not know all the reasons why. They liked the legend of him, then at its peak—captain of the team, scholar; they liked the way he sat in his chair with a kind of serene strength and Irish nonchalance, sure of himself and yet a mystery to them, with his home schooling, his classics, his youth; they liked his articulate speech; they liked that grin that flickered over his face from time to time as if he could not quite control it. He seemed cut out of the stuff that Cecil Rhodes would have condescended to like, if he had ever liked an Irishman.

This second interview had gone on for an hour. They were satisfied; all but one older woman who had sat the time out with a troubled look on her face, rarely speaking. The chairman looked around the room. "Are we all through?" he asked.

"Service," said the woman. She was professor at Northeastern; Sterne was her name. Ryan thought she had something to do with philosophy or ethics. "Do you do any service in the community?"

The other members looked bored, or affected a look of interest because they felt this was part of their charge; but the chairman did not hesitate to indicate his contempt, fidgeting irritably and clacking a pen on the tabletop.

"The reason I ask, Mr. Kinsella," said Professor Sterne, when Ryan did not immediately answer, "is that I really don't feel I know who you are, after all this. Your credentials are amazing. They're almost unbelievable. But who are you? It seems to me that if you could explain to us some service you had performed for others, that might tell us something."

Ryan said nothing. His silence intrigued the chairman, who looked closely at him.

"Have you done any service, Mr. Kinsella?" he asked.

"Yes," said Ryan. There was an audible sigh of relief; the chairman actually made a motion as if he was ready to close the interview and go on.

"What was it?" Professor Sterne asked. "I don't see it mentioned anywhere in your letter. None of your referees have anything to say about it. It's not on your transcripts."

He had never told anyone about the boys in Wolf Bay. The place was a world away from this dark-paneled room where the trustees of the corporation held their meetings. When he opened his mouth now, it almost seemed a betrayal.

"I coach in a little soccer league in Wolf Bay," he said.

"Wolf Bay?"

"That's a Portuguese neighborhood off campus," explained one of the local members of the committee.

"You coach in this league?"

"Yes. I run it, actually. It wasn't a league when I started; it was just some kids looking for trouble, and a priest trying to keep them out of it. He asked me to help out. I've been doing it for two seasons now."

"Why didn't you mention it before?"

"No one asked."

"Why didn't you bring it up in your letter? You certainly seem to have mentioned everything else."

"It's sort of a private thing."

"But why would you conceal it? It seems to me you purposely concealed it, or at least intentionally failed to mention it."

The anger gripped him in its iron hand; he felt it squeeze the color into his face, cramp his chest. He had gone the whole interview process without feeling that anger; and here it was, when the prize was within his grasp. He felt the anger pushing him out of his own control, and he barely held to a courteous tone.

"That thing in Wolf Bay isn't just another credential," he said. "It's not a grade on a sheet; it's not a point on a scoreboard; it's not a letter someone cooks up to get you something. I did it for those kids. If I could bring those boys in here, and line them up along that wall, and you could look into their faces when I say, 'Wind sprints!' you wouldn't need to see it written on a piece of paper. I did it for them, but it meant just as much to *me* as it did to them. I just . . . I just don't talk about Wolf Bay."

Someone whispered something he could not quite catch. Sterne's eyes had locked on his, and neither he nor she would back down. "We won't trample on it, Ryan. If you trust us with it, we'll respect what you have to say."

The anger told him to say no. But he took a deep breath, and he thought of his father, especially of his father, though of his mother too. He thought how much it would mean to his father if he won this; and he worked his pride down, swallowing it slowly.

He told them about the boys. Father Tim had been right about them. The minute he walked into the yard they worshipped him. On the first day, he drilled them, showed them a few tricks, staged a scrimmage, and burned a love of him so deeply into their dry, inflammable little hearts that they would never forget him. And he went back week after week until the snow fell; and the next year too, he had gone back. Dark eyes, dark heads; dirty, scuffed, city knees; and the hunger the priest had talked about.

He talked on for ten minutes. Most of the committee seemed to think that helping poor boys in Wolf Bay was cute, but that they had already heard enough from Ryan. Sterne ignored them. Her eyes seemed to be listening to something that was speaking in him without words.

When he was through his account she smiled.

"Thank you," she said.

"Are we all set?" asked the chairman. "Let's take a five-minute break. If you would wait outside, Mr. Kinsella."

Ryan went out and found a drinking fountain down the hall. Sterne approached him; they were at a distance from the others. "You know, Ryan," she said. "I'm going to pay you a compliment I've never paid a candidate for the Rhodes before."

"Thank you, ma'am, but I think I've already heard enough compliments today to ruin me for life."

She smiled and persevered. "I think you're too good to waste two years at Oxford. You have more important things to do."

He was puzzled. "Excuse me?" he said.

"In Wolf Bay, or someplace like it."

His confusion was manifest.

"You don't understand me, do you?" she said, smiling again. "Well, don't worry. You will. By the time you get out of Oxford, I should think. Maybe even before that."

Then she went back to the committee.

❁❁❁

The group in the chapel did not definitively settle until the organist began the wedding march. Even then the music was punctuated by the soft, rebellious cries of infants and by the whispered scoldings of various parents, by the nervous giggles of teenagers, and by the throat-clearings of the officiating clerk. But when the bride appeared, reverence for this startling creature in white tamed even the most cynical husband and the most rambunctious toddler.

Pippin was tall and big-boned. Her mouth was very large, and her nose had a peculiar flatness, as if it had been pushed down and frozen in place. As a rule, she seldom looked anyone in the eye; instead she looked to one side or the other, which made her seem dishonest, though she was not, and prevented her from impressing anyone with the best features of her face, which were her large hazel eyes. For about three months when she was nineteen, she had been beautiful. Now, suddenly, she was beautiful again. She held her head up, looking straight at the groom without evasion, with a glowing smile of relief tinged by disbelief on her lips, a smile that seemed to finally give her lips a use.

As usual, there was too much of the dress; she was large anyway, and the lace and the frills increased the square footage of cloth to the point that she began to seem somehow like a ship under full sail. It was too tight in some places—her waist, for instance, and her bust, which it forced almost indecently upward—and too loose in others, such as over her hips, where its folds and gathers unhappily amplified what could well have received the opposite treatment. But it was white, and it marked Pippin as a bride, and half the crowd was like Ryan, who wondered for a moment if it wasn't too much, and then felt his eyes getting wet, because this was, after all, Pippin's wedding at last. The gown assisted in some inexplicable way in the transformation of poor Pippin into blessed Pippin; she now was to be anointed to struggle in matrimony and bear children and grow old and frowzy along with all the rest of her species.

The ceremony was too brief, as such civil services are. For her years of waiting, Pippin deserved a ceremony that should torture her entire clan for at least half an hour; but even though it lasted only a few minutes, by the end of it she was shaking like a faint windblown blossom, and Kevin had to hold her upright and apply more than one hearty kiss to bring her around.

Then there was chaos—shrieking, laughing children darting every which way, aunts and young cousins weeping, young men of the O'Brien and Donegan clans calling out ironic blessings on Kevin—who seemed proof to their sarcasms—and officious ushers and parents marshaling and giving directions and apportioning who should go in whose car to the reception. The Kinsellas made their slow way to the door in time to see the bride and groom ducking into a ten-year-old Volkswagen.

The plan had apparently been to have a receiving line at the house; but the Kinsellas found that all thought of maintaining this formality had been abandoned by the time they arrived. Frank and Mary O'Brien's dwelling was not too much larger than the Kinsellas', so a reception was impossible anywhere but in the yard behind it, a rectangle of about fifty by a hundred feet. Into this space the families of the bride and groom poured in bursts of five or six over the half hour after the wedding, gradually filling it to the point that it seemed it could hold no more—and yet still people arrived, and in truth perhaps not just O'Briens and Donegans but a crasher or two who had caught wind of free beer. The yard was surrounded on all sides by small houses with other yards, from which neighbors either inquisitive or resentful looked on from time to time, one actually signifying his protest by starting his lawnmower. Even in Charleston, relatively close to the ocean, the heat was choking; only a motley collection of borrowed patio umbrellas offered some refuge from the sun. Rented chairs were plentiful, but tables had been thought an extravagance, except for those where the bride and groom held court with their immediate families, with the bridal party, and with Aunt Doreen. For the rest a buffet would suffice. Live music, too, had not been hired; the groom had provided a collection of tapes, which played on a stereo set almost unheard in the hubbub. In the midst of this frugal celebration, the cake looked out of place: it was a five-tiered wonder, constantly drawing a cluster of small faces about it.

An American wedding, thought Ryan, as he surveyed it from a seat in the shade of a ragged ginko tree. It was part Catholic, part secular; part generic American hokum, part genuine Irish tradition. It was also in good part that bogus culture that is the expatriate's cheap approximation of Irishness, the impulse that often makes Irish American culture a parody of itself and drives otherwise tasteful people to resort each March seventeenth to fluorescent derbies, green beer, and tee shirts that read *Kiss Me, I'm Irish.*

"That all you could find?" Daniel asked Ryan, looking at the can of feeble American beer in his son's hand.

"This is all there is," said Ryan. "I wouldn't have sunk this low, but it's so unbelievably hot."

"You can say that again," said Daniel. He looked as if he could not conceive how he was going to survive the mixture of O'Briens and hot sun for the next few hours.

"I hear there's champagne," said Maureen.

"They'd better have a tank truck full of it," said Ryan. "There must be a hundred and fifty people here."

"Well," said Daniel, "it wouldn't be Irish if there weren't a big crowd."

"Yeah," said Ryan. "The only thing we're missing so far is the dog fight."

"Yes," agreed Maureen. "I'm glad they had the sense to say 'No dogs allowed.'"

No sooner had she spoken than a pack of five dogs came hurtling through the crowd, knocking over small children, spilling drinks in people's hands, and trampling and tearing the pages of the wedding book, which had been set down incautiously on a chair. Four of them—two retrievers, a spaniel, and a setter—were evidently in pursuit of the fifth, which seemed to be a chihuahua. Their barking and snarling—which their owners would have insisted was all in fun—was momentarily distracting, prompting as such a noise does a burst of adrenaline in innocent human bystanders; but then they were gone elsewhere in the press of bodies and became someone else's problem.

"Okay," said Ryan. "There's the dog fight."

"I'm glad you didn't say the only thing we were missing was a dog *bite*," said Daniel to Ryan.

"That'll come too," said Ryan.

At that moment, as a pacific contrast to this canine incursion, a little girl three years of age came dashing up to Ryan; her mother, his other aunt Mary, was not far behind. "Unkya Roo!" exclaimed the tike.

"Sure, if it isn't my little Roseleen," said Ryan. He looked up at Aunt Mary. "Get yourself something to eat," he suggested. "I'll keep an eye on her."

"Thank you, Ryan," said Aunt Mary. "I'm starving, and you're an angel!"

"Yet's go yook at da cake!" said Roseleen, grabbing Ryan by the hand.

"Yet's, by all means," agreed Ryan. He left the beer behind and made his way through the crowd, tugged by the little girl before him, until they had reached the table where the cake waited.

"Yet's have some!" chirped Roseleen.

"Not now, my little friend. You have to eat some real food first. Then, when the bride cuts it, you can have a piece."

"Bwide's Pippin!"

"Pippin is indeed the bride. And a very pretty bride she makes."

"A pwetty bwide," agreed Roseleen solemnly, looking at Pippin in her splendor, who was giggling with a gaggle of bridesmaids beneath the camera's eye. Then Roseleen turned to the cake again, in silent adoration. "Up!" she said. Ryan picked her up and held her close to the magical creation. "Yeyoh," she told him. He thought for a moment before he understood what she was saying.

"Yellow, yes. And white."

"White! Yidew gween, too."

"A little green, yes. What colors would you like to have on a cake, if it was yours?"

"Wed. And byack!"

"Black frosting on a cake? Who ever heard of black frosting?"

"Chyockyet is byack."

"Oh, not really. It's more brown than black."

This type of conversation went for quite some time. Ryan chaperoned his cousin around the reception, performing all those actions necessary to an alert adult acting *in loco parentis:* preventing her from tippling out of random plastic cups, snatching her away from the horseplay of some rowdy teenage boys, putting her left shoe back on, translating for her in interactions with other toddlers, finding her a drink of punch when she grew thirsty, putting her right shoe back on, picking her up to look over a fence at a cat in the next yard, and all the time carrying on a fragmented discussion about topics so diverse that he could only with difficulty follow as her attention moved from one theme to another. Most of caring for a toddler is simply a struggle to stay awake in a haze lit by stray lightnings of delight; and Ryan, as he followed Roseleen about, found himself returning again and again to daydreams.

In his mind's eye he saw himself arriving at the Tates' with Constance and their child. They had been married several years; Constance was more certain, more secure; she and Ryan watched a little dark-haired tike exploring along the lathed stone balustrade of the stone porch, and Ryan rushed to make sure the child—a girl, in his daydream—did not tumble down the steps. The little girl led him away from the porch, across the drive into the lawn, where she marveled at a rabbit and pointed out a hopping thrush with an extended finger; behind him, Ryan could hear the voices of Constance and her parents as a contented murmur. From time to time he looked back and saw that Constance was watching them; she might smile or lean toward him, with a subtle motion of her hand, as if to say, "I see you; I love you; all is well."

The sweetness of this dream overwhelmed him as he stood aloof with his toddling cousin in the racket of the reception. To have a child with Constance—how beautiful she would be when she was with child—and every act, every task and chore and tedious obligation of raising a child, would be filled and lightened by the joy of loving her and being loved by her.

His dream was so real to him that he wondered why they had not begun to plan for it together. Their love was so perfectly right—how could she not see it? Why was she so slow to become aware of it? Perhaps it was because she was so focused on her brother. She hardly had mental room to notice Ryan. *That will change,* thought Ryan. *If I'm patient, if I let her turn her thoughts toward me without demanding them, Collin will become only her brother, and stop being the god she's made him into.*

"Was Mama?" asked Roseleen uncertainly.

"You want your mama? She's right over there." He pointed to where his weary aunt Mary sat; he caught her eye, and she waved at Roseleen.

"Mama," said Roseleen somewhat desperately. Ryan took her through the crowd and she clambered into her mother's lap.

"Getting sleepy, honey?" asked Mary. "Did you have a good time with Uncle Roo?" Roseleen snuggled against Mary, putting a little thumb in her little frowning mouth. "Did he take you around to meet people and look at the big cake?"

"Cake," said Roseleen seriously, sitting up. "Time fo' da cake?"

Mary laughed. "Not yet, dearie."

"When?"

"In a little while."

"Ahways a yidew whiyew," complained Roseleen.

"That's life," said Ryan.

"Isn't it?" said Mary. "Always a little while longer to wait for the big cake. And when the time finally comes, you get such a little piece."

"Yidew piece?" asked Roseleen tragically.

"Oh, no, honey, not you. You'll get more than is good for you, I'm sure." She smiled up at Ryan. "Thank you, Ryan. It's nice to have a break. I remember following you around when you were just about her age."

"Then I guess I owed you one," he said. "See you later, Roseleen."

Roseleen waved the fingers of the hand that corked her mouth.

As he made his way toward his parents again he came across Roseleen's brother Stevie, a boy of about eleven. He was one of Ryan's greatest fans.

"Hey Stevie, how's the Latin coming?"

"I got a B-plus for the year," Stevie said, not without some pride.

"Not bad!" said Ryan.

"What kind of grade did you get when you started Latin?"

"I was learning at home with my dad. I didn't get grades."

"Oh, that's right."

"Going to read some Caesar next year?"

"Yeah. Everybody says its really boring, but I think all those wars and stuff, it's got to be really cool. You just have to get into it."

"That's the attitude, man. And the year after that you do a little poetry, don't you?"

"Maybe Cicero, maybe a little poetry. It depends. What's the best, Ryan? What did you like the most?"

"Vergil is the best. As long as you've got a good teacher. A bad teacher can turn even Vergil into drudgery. But a good one can show you how golden he is."

"I've got a good teacher. Mr. Perkins. He's really cool."

"You're in luck, then. And if you ever have any questions, you can ask me or my dad. My dad's a real Vergil expert, you know."

"Really? That's great!"

He shook the boy's hand and left him standing in a glow of awe.

Maureen was occupied in conversation with her sister Ginny when Ryan returned, and Daniel was away at the buffet table. After listening perforce to a dreary recounting of the troubles between Ginny and her husband Bob, Ryan decided that finding something to eat would be a good excuse to escape. All that was left was chicken wings; in point of fact, he was not sure anything else had been furnished, beyond some vegetable strips and a large bowl of dip. The beer and wine seemed to be intended to cover any omissions in the food, but he could not endure another pusillanimous Milwaukee brew. He took a little to eat on a paper plate and sat down not far from the table.

In a moment the sickly sweet scent of tobacco smoke drifted over his shoulder. Almost involuntarily he turned to see who was smoking, and found that Cissy was sitting slightly behind him, staring intently at the burning cigarette in her hand. The steamy heat had blurred her mascara, and a few faint beads of sweat stood on her upper lip. As he debated whether he should greet her or pretend not to notice, her eyes flickered upward and caught his.

"Hello, Cissy," he said.

"Ryan," she responded elliptically.

She had a hard face. She was very beautiful in some respects; but her face was too hard. She had been used for someone else's ends, whether for pleasure or pain, and she would resent it all her life; she would suspect everyone, never trust a man until the moment he was walking away from her, the moment it was too late.

"You've sure grown up," she said. She was all of a year older than he was.

"So have you," he replied.

"I heard you got some big prize or something."

"Yeah."

"You're going to England or something?"

"Yeah."

She considered this, watching the bittersweet smoke curling upward from her hand, which she held extended with that exaggerated consciousness that smokers consider to be glamorous in itself.

"Better than staying here," she muttered. She raised the cigarette and inhaled through it as if it were all that kept her alive.

"Where have you been?" asked Ryan.

"Different places. Went to New York. Got messed up."

He said nothing, not knowing what to say.

"Heroin," she explained, not caring if she shocked him or anyone around them. "Anyway," she continued after a minute, "got off that. Got pregnant. Fixed that. Went to California for a while. Some guy wanted me to work for him."

She looked at Ryan to see if he understood what she meant. He regarded her with such a neutral gaze that she must have concluded that he did not.

"He was a pimp," she explained. "I didn't do anything for him. Got a job in a MacDonald's. That's what I've been doing, mostly. I didn't get any diseases, and I'm still alive. That's pretty amazing."

"Jesus, Cissy, it sounds pretty awful."

"Better than being here," she muttered again. "You're lucky. You're getting out. Out of this whole O'Brien thing. Christ, I'm so sick of it. Look at poor Pip there. She's digging a tomb for herself, and she doesn't even know it. She'll have six brats in five years."

"Yeah, but she'll feel like her life has meaning. That's more than you or I can say."

She regarded him with slight surprise.

"You feel that way?" she asked.

"Sometimes," he said.

"Hey, what is it? Some chick?"

"Jesus, is it written on my face or something?"

"Naw. It's always some chick with guys like you."

"What do you mean?"

"You always pick the wrong ones."

He stared at her. "So who am I supposed to pick, that I'm not picking?"

"You're not supposed to pick at all. You just do your thing, and let some chick decide she's can't live without you. Then you just use her."

"Holy sh—Jesus, Cissy, what an attitude! Is that what *you* do?"

"That's what I'm gonna do," she asserted. "From now on."

She put out the cigarette in her wine and turned to him with sudden interest. He had seen that kind of look before.

"You're not a bad-looking guy, you know," she said. "You'd better sign up some chick now, while you can. In a few years they won't be interested in you anymore. Or just the losers will."

"Thanks for the advice. You're not bad-looking yourself. I wish for your sake you were happier, Cis. I really do."

"Great legs you've got. You a soccer player or something? Did somebody tell me that?"

"Yeah."

"Hey, look," she said, leaning closer. "I haven't gotten laid since I came back. I could sure use it. What do you say you and I step into the house for a few minutes?"

He stared at her in perplexity, pity, and astonishment.

"I could show you a really good time," she said. "And I'd sure like to see those legs and that butt of yours."

"Hey, no offense, but I couldn't."

"Why not? Because we're cousins or something? Hell, cousins do it all the time. They can even get married.—Not that I want to do that."

"Thanks anyway, Cis, but we're not a great match."

"That's the whole point. We've got no illusions. We'd just be doing it for fun."

"Yeah, I know, but—"

"It's that chick, isn't it?"

"Yeah."

She sat back, defeated, but not unduly perturbed. "You're making a mistake getting hung on any chick that much."

"Maybe so," he conceded.

She stood up. "Well," she said, "if you change your mind, let me know. Someone's got to do some screwing at every wedding. It's good luck. Besides, I don't think the bride's going to get much of it tonight herself. Nothing that I would call screwing, anyway." She looked at Pippin with mingled pity and contempt; and then she sauntered away.

Why do women always do this to me? he wondered. *The wrong women, anyway.*

To cleanse his thoughts of Cissy's cynicism, he went to greet the bride. He caught her at a rare moment when she was actually sitting down. She beamed at him deliriously.

"Ryan!" she said. "I'm so glad you could come."

"Wouldn't miss it for anything, Pip. Where's the groom?"

"Getting his picture taken with the ushers. They say you hardly see your husband at a wedding, and it's true. You hardly sit down, either."

"You hardly eat, either, so don't let me stop you." He gestured toward the greasy chicken wings she had before her.

"A big adventure coming up for you, huh?" she asked.

"Not as big as yours," he said. "I'll just be doing the same old same-old. Where are you guys going to live?"

"We've got a nice little apartment a few blocks from here. It's really sweet. It's sort of a mess at the moment, but we're going to fix it up."

"I'm sure you will, Pip." He was discovering, as he usually did, that much as he liked Pippin, he had little to say to her. She seemed to be having the same problem with him.

"Did you get some champagne?" she asked.

"No, I didn't see it."

"It's over by the swingset, under that umbrella. You'd better get some before it's all gone."

"Good idea. Say, Pip, best wishes to you. I may not see you for a year or two, but I'll think of you."

"You're real sweet, Ryan." She paused in the act of tearing apart a chicken wing, and her eyes grew moist.

"Yeah, well, so are you. You tell that guy to treat you right, okay?"

She giggled brightly at the mere idea that Kevin Donegan would ever cross her. Ryan went away to find the champagne.

To his amazement, he secured a glass, though the unknown person who was serving it refused to let him take extra glasses for his parents. He stepped aside, feeling overcome by thirst, and drank off the wine; it was warm, completely flat, and tasted like canned grape juice.

"Heah, Roo," said Roseleen, appearing beside him; evidently she had had a miraculous second wind. She offered him a paper plate on which various objects had been carefully arranged. He ducked down to her level and took the plate from her.

"Thanks, Roseleen. It's beautiful! Tell me what it all is."

"Dat's humboigahs," she said, indicating some pebbles.

"Humboigahs!" he repeated. "Wow, thank you. I was really starving, too. How did you know I was hungry?"

"'N dat's coweefowah," she said, pointing to a dandelion.

"What? What is it?"

"Coweefowah."

"Oh, cauliflower! Sure, it looks just like it."

"'N dat's eggs. 'N dat's s'getti. 'N dat's soap."

"Soap? Don't you mean soup?"

"No!" she said definitively. "Soap!" The item she had pointed out, a broken bit of plastic foam, did in fact look like a miniature bar of soap.

"Well, thank you very much for all this delicious food. I'll eat it right up."

She watched delightedly while he pretended to consume it with great gusto. "Yum-mee! Oh, Rose, this is great food. Did you cook this yourself?" She nodded, her eyes sparkling. "I won't eat the soap, though," he added. She burbled a sweet little laugh.

"Roo's funny!" she said.

"Here, now that I've finished, I'll put the plate down right here. Okay?"

"Okay. Wan' see my beyoon?"

"You have a balloon? Where did you get it?"

Apparently someone had supplied helium balloons to the youngest children as a kind of party favor. She led him to where her mother sat; the string of a balloon was tied around Mary's wrist.

"Want to show Uncle Roo your balloon, honey? Want it tied onto your own wrist now?"

"No, mama, yoah wrist. See, Roo? My beyoon." She stood before her mother, gazing up at the balloon with wonder.

"Here, you take it," said Mary, drawing it down by the string and taking it in her hands.

Suddenly the balloon inexplicably burst, in the way of its kind, perhaps pricked by some minute projection of a ring on Mary's hand.

For a moment the horror was frozen on Roseleen's face; then she broke into sobs of anguish, in grief past all articulation, permitting herself to be picked up, limp as a rag doll, and held in her mother's arms. "Oh, honey," mourned Mary, "I'm so sorry! I don't know why it popped!"

Ryan resolved to find another, but thought it best to slip away without making any promises. It seemed they had all been distributed; but it was not hard to locate an older child who had somehow acquired one, and to bribe him to give it up. In a few minutes he returned to where Roseleen and her mother were sitting. The storm had passed, though his little friend looked more exhausted than ever.

"Oh, look what Uncle Roo found for you!" exclaimed Mary.

Roseleen sat up with a teary grin and reached out for the string.

"Let's tie it on your wrist, Rose," said Ryan. He did so, and she sank back contentedly on her mother's breast again.

"When's da cake?" she murmured.

He winked at Mary and went away.

A group of Donegans had taken the places where he and his parents had been sitting. He saw his mother elsewhere talking with his aunt Millie; his father had been cornered by Uncle Bob, who was complaining about his wife Ginny. Ryan found another place to sit. In a few minutes Elaine, the daughter of his cousin Mary, approached him. A missing tooth suggested she might be in first or second grade, though she was technically Roseleen's niece.

"You going to England?" she asked.

"Yes."

"Robbie told me that's a sin."

Robbie was another cousin's son, about seven years old.

"A sin, is it?"

"He said Uncle Tom said so."

"Well, Uncle Tom knows all about sin, so he must be right."

"What are you going to do there? Commit sins? That's what they do in England. They don't even go to Mass."

"I'm going to study Latin and Greek."

"Latin? I know Latin."

"You do? Say something in Latin for me."

"'Oysbay are igspay.' Do you know what that means?"

"Of course I do. I know all about Latin."

"It means 'Boys are pigs.' That's what it means."

"I know that. But it's not real Latin. You can tell it's not real Latin, because it's not true. If something isn't true, you can't say it in Latin."

"Why don't you study something *useful* in England?"

"I think I've had this conversation before," said Ryan. "What would you recommend?"

"I saw a picture in a wedding magazine of a cake in England. Why don't you learn how to decorate cakes?"

"I don't really want to know that."

"You can eat cakes. You can't eat Latin."

"For me, learning things like Latin and Greek is like eating cake. But it's a cake you never finish eating. The more you eat, the more there is—and you just keep enjoying it more and more, and the cake just keeps tasting sweeter and sweeter, and you just keep getting hungrier and hungrier."

"You'll get sick of it," she predicted. "Anyway, I'd rather have *real* cake."

And she ran off to check the status of the heap of flour and icing on the buffet.

❁ ❁ ❁

Even Ryan was quite hungry for the cake by the time it was served. He was also thoroughly bored. He had talked to every relative he had wanted to talk to, and quite a few he would just as soon have never seen. So after the children had been served he joined the crowd around the side table and secured himself a piece.

He did not bother seeking a seat, but ate on his feet, holding a paper plate in the flat of one hand, and gingerly applying a plastic fork with the other. Someone bumped into him in the general confusion; he looked around. It was Cissy. She looked around simultaneously. She too was eating cake, though she had the additional difficulty of keeping a lit cigarette pinned between two fingers while she balanced her plate.

"Is this weird or what?" she said.

"I'd say it was an O'Brien wedding."

"Weird, you mean."

He said nothing for a minute. They ate in silence, Cissy emanating that defiance and scorn that was typical of her.

"Say, Cissy, I was thinking about what you said."

Her eyes glittered as she looked him over. "You change your mind?"

"No. I mean what you said about letting someone choose you and then using them."

"Oh. That."

"You're wrong, you know. You've got to do the choosing. You've got to pick the person you want and go after whoever it is, and keep after them until they know you're right."

"You've got a hell of a miserable life in front of you, Ryan, that's all I can say."

"Maybe in the short run. But not in the long run. Someday before you die you're going to wish you'd tried for what you want."

She glared at him. "You don't get it, do you? If I wanted anything, I'd be all right. My problem is I don't give a shit about anything." She ate her cake, savagely, glowering. "Not since Randy got all messed up," she added.

"Where is Randy?" asked Ryan. Sometimes his family brought him to these functions in a wheelchair, but today he was absent.

"They said it was too hot. They left him at home with a neighbor, in his air-conditioned room. The poor bastard's so bored he looks like he wants to die."

"You want to know what I think, Cissy? Or do you want me to shut up?"

"You can tell me. I can handle it."

"I think that when Randy got paralyzed, you got paralyzed too. His body got paralyzed, and your soul got paralyzed. There's nothing you can do for him, but you can do something for yourself."

"What? Pray? Go to confession?—Christ, Ryan, you wanna see a priest have a heart attack?"

"No, I don't mean any of that."

"What then?"

"You have to love someone, or something."

She finished the last of her cake without looking at him and took a long drag on her cigarette. Her hand was trembling.

"Oh, I don't know what the fuck you're talking about," she muttered.

She went away. Ryan did not see her again after that.

As he finished his cake, he looked around for a place in the shade, and caught sight of Aunt Doreen; she motioned to him, and he approached her.

"Sit down, dearie," she said, patting a seat beside her. This was where the bridal party was headquartered; as Ryan sat down he greeted several cousins. Pippin and her husband, as well as his aunt and uncle, were elsewhere. From the farthest of the several tables that had been pushed together, his cousin Tom and his cousin Ellen's husband, Christopher, stared grimly at him. These two had always nursed a hostility toward Ryan. John, an usher like Tom, was sitting with them; he had always been pleasant to Ryan, and seemed uncomfortable at being caught between the two camps.

Ryan was afraid Aunt Doreen would quiz him about his "sweetheart"; but either she had forgotten his mentioning Constance or she knew that this was not the time or place. "Now, tell me all about your trip," she said instead. She seemed to think his scholarship was a sea-going vessel of some kind, on which he would be taking a prolonged cruise. He began unraveling her misconceptions as well as he could, patiently and gently, and after about ten minutes she seemed to have a vague understanding of what was involved.

During this time, his cousin Tom had muttered something occasionally, but had not drawn anyone's attention. Now he spoke quite loudly. "Why would a man do something like that?" he asked Christopher. Ryan talked on, though distracted by what he could not help overhearing.

"Sure if I don't know," replied Christopher.

"Giving aid and comfort to the enemy, is what I say," said Tom.

"Exactly," said Christopher.

"Well, he always was half a Prot."

"A half-breed," agreed Christopher.

"Not the kind you want around when there's a war to be fought. When there's things to be done. Widows to be made, and a blow to be struck."

"Right," said Christopher.

Aunt Doreen seemed to hear none of this; and she was, in fact, a little hard of hearing.

"All the same, a traitor's a traitor."

"True," said Christopher. Ryan now perceived that the pair, and Christopher especially, were extremely drunk. The other members of the wedding party had fallen silent and looked extremely uncomfortable.

"And you know what happens to traitors. Or what should happen."

"Right."

"They get their legs blown off. Then they don't run around playing football so much, with their legs blown off."

"Nowhere near so much," said Christopher.

"Why don't you leave Ryan alone?" snapped Reena. She was the only one of Tom's siblings who would stand up to him. Aunt Doreen seemed to become aware of the trouble, and her little head swiveled on her bony neck.

"Ryan?" sneered Tom. "Who said anything about Ryan? I was talking about traitors to the cause. If you identify Ryan as a traitor to the cause, who's fault is that? Certainly not mine."

"Not his," said Christopher.

"You shut up too, Chris," said Reena. "You're drunk, both of you, and when you're drunk you're both even more obnoxious than usual."

"The fact remains," said Tom, "that our beloved cousin Ryan here is going to go over and brownnose the enemy. He's going to *Oxford*. Haven't you heard? Just as if there wasn't a war on."

"That's enough from you, Tom," said Ryan.

Everyone, including Tom, was startled to hear him speak; he usually avoided confrontations of this sort.

"No one wants Brits out more than I do," he continued. "I just don't believe in violence."

Tom snorted in derision. "I know your type," he said.

"And I know yours," responded Ryan. "You'd blow up Ireland to save it."

"If I had to, I would," said Tom.

"Make sense for once, man. Hate won't make Ireland free."

"Cowardice won't either," sneered Tom.

"I agree with you there," said Ryan significantly; his implication was clear enough that even Tom, in his befogged condition, understood it clearly.

"Are you calling *me* a coward?"

"Who said anything about you? If you identify yourself as the person in question, whose fault is that? Not mine."

"Maybe you and I ought to have a little go of it to see who's a coward and who isn't," suggested Tom, making a motion as if he would rise from the table.

"Get off it!" said Reena. "You're not going to fight anyone at Pip's wedding, you idiot!"

"Cool down, Tom," said John.

"It's time to show this little prig what a real Irishman is," said Tom.

"God!" said Reena. "I wish they'd thrown you in jail forever. If your probation officer hears you've been drinking, they'll do exactly that."

"That'll be about enough from you," said Tom, casting a very ugly stare at Reena. "By Christ, if someone does tell 'im, I'll know who it was."

"What's his phone number?" asked Reena.

"Bitch!" said Tom.

Suddenly Aunt Doreen clutched Ryan's arm. "Turn up the music," she said.

A wild jig was beginning on the tape; how she had caught it over the argument and the noise of the crowd around them, Ryan did not know. He went to the stereo, which was a few yards away, and increased the volume slightly.

"More," she said. He turned it up another notch.

"More! More, Ryan! Don't be shy with it! Turn it up!"

He looked around somewhat helplessly at the crowd and then went ahead. The jig blared crisply from the speakers; the gathering in the yard suddenly grew silent, and all eyes turned to where Ryan stood.

Aunt Doreen stood now too and tottered toward him. She took him by the hand and seized her skirt as if to hold it clear of her feet; and those little feet, laced up in a very old-fashioned kind of boot, began to tap and frisk in a most unelderly way.

"Dance wi'me, Ryan," she called to him.

And dance he must. Awkwardly at first, not quite remembering how the steps went; but in a few moments, just as well as he used to.

No one spoke, not even the tiniest baby cried, as youth and age, vigor and infirmity, danced together on the matted lawn, hemmed in by onlookers, under the burning July sun.

The music was merciful to Doreen and ended in a minute. A shout went up, and laughter, and then applause. The talk rose again; as the next song started, Ryan turned down the volume on the stereo.

Then Doreen took him by the wrist and drew him over to where Tom sat sulking.

"Listen, to me, Tom O'Brien," said Doreen. "You may have your differences with Ryan, but there's no truer Irishman. I'll have no talk of how he's a traitor. He's got his scollyship, which is more than you've got. I want you to hold your peace and shake hands with him, right now."

"I won't do it," said Tom.

"If you're so high and mighty, let's see you dance a jig like that," said Doreen. But she made no further attempt to argue with him; instead she seized him and drew him to his feet. "Hold out your hand like a proper man," she said, grasping his wrist and pulling his arm forward. "Now, Ryan, I know you'll swallow your pride and shake his hand. This is Pip's wedding. For Pip's sake they'll be no quarreling here."

Ryan took his cousin's hand and shook it, much contrary to Tom's will; but against Doreen, even Tom could do nothing. She was incontestably the most Irish of them all.

"There now," said Doreen. "Ryan, get me another piece of cake, and a glass of that bubbly."

"My pleasure," said Ryan.

He saw Doreen back to her seat and went to get the cake. As he left he heard the final exchange.

"He *can* dance," said Christopher.

"Oh, shut up," said Tom.

Sunday, July 19,
through
Tuesday, July 21

Listen America, daughter or son,
It is a painful thing to love a man or woman to excess, and yet it
    satisfies, it is great.

—Whitman

SUNDAY BEGAN THE week in which Ryan, Constance, and Collin were to go to Maine. To Ryan, Sunday was a shell of time, hot and hollow and so vast it would not even allow the echo of his own self to reverberate to his ears. He heard instead some kind of cicadalike insects, which had begun to sing in the trees, celebrating the fertile heat of the New England summer. He found their whirring and rasping, like so many things in life now, both soothing and irritating by turns.

Monday was no better. At two o'clock in the afternoon he could not endure to be without sound or sight of Constance anymore; he called the Tates. After eight or nine rings, Collin answered, annoyed.

"So what's up?" he asked, when Ryan had said hello.

"What's up with you, is the question," returned Ryan.

"I'm writing," said Collin, in a tone that Ryan knew well. "Constance has gone with my mother; they won't be back until late Wednesday. Looking at colleges somewhere. My mother was sort of vague about where."

Ryan squinted his eyes shut and held them shut.

"I'm putting the final touches on things," Collin went on, when Ryan was silent. "I've also had some ideas for a few new pieces.

So I think I'll be going flat out until the minute we leave for the shore."

"Right," Ryan managed to say. "Well, I just wanted to check and see what was going on."

"Maybe I'll ask Constance to call you Thursday to tell you what time we're leaving. It'll be some time in the morning, obviously."

"Right," said Ryan again. "Well, sorry to interrupt your work. I'll see you Friday, anyway."

"Okay. We'll let you know about the time."

"That'd be good. See you then."

Ryan put down the receiver heavily and sat stunned in his chair. This was an unexpected sentence. Release dawned at the end of it; but three or four days without her—knowing, positively, that she was away and would not return—was three or four days of loneliness, boredom, dull daydreams, and longing that was literally a lengthening of every simple act and thought until all things became intolerable.

Worse, a sentence with unwanted cellmates, as a clatter from the kitchen reminded him.

It was clear to him that his parents did not like Constance. Since the time he had realized this, he had felt by turns astonishment, indignation, and a disgust that knew no recourse. And threaded through these emotions was a vindicated cynicism and hopelessness that tugged at him like a premonition of failure. Of course they did not like her—the woman who alone could complete and give meaning to his past and future. The perverseness of life required that.

At meals on Sunday and today they had been too polite; they wore masks over their disapproval and pity; they spoke to him as if to someone who was ill or deluded. Once he had found this so unendurable he had bolted from the table and plunged outside, to walk for an hour, waiting for his anger to subside. They made no comment when he returned. No explanation, or pretense of explanation, was necessary on either side—so they seemed to feel. Ryan, for his part, felt that no explanation was possible. They might listen to him, but they would not hear his meaning; if they heard his meaning, they would not understand it; if they understood it, they would not remember it; if they remembered it, they would not act on it. And if they did not act as if they understood him, they might as well never have listened to him. He had always looked upon his role in the family as that of a kind of benign tyrant in the Greek sense, a philosopher king who knew what was best for the children who had raised him; but against their impenetrable prejudice against Constance, he could do nothing. No command or cajoling would have any effect. Only his success in winning Constance, and his abiding happiness together with her, would ever erode his parents' monolithic distrust. And if he lost her, it would be gall inmixed in the hemlock he must then drink that he would lose also the opportunity to prove them wrong.

A letter from Eve did nothing to ease his sense of being misunderstood. He received it on Monday morning, but did not open until late that afternoon. It seemed a pastiche of her old themes: longing for him, self-sacrifice, self-pity, certainty that her time had passed, inappropriate hints about Constance. She added a few items of genuine interest to him: Todd would be coming through New England, bound for Cambridge, sometime in August; he had mentioned he would try to visit Ryan. As bored with and repulsed by this letter as he was, he yet attempted a reply, filling it with stale thoughts and reassurances that meant nothing. He did not mention Constance at all, and when he read the letter over, it tasted like lie. He shredded the sheet into fragments so minute that not even his mother could have pieced them together, and threw this confetti into the wastebasket.

Tuesday brought another assignment from Todd. He opened the letter in a heartsick sulk, and read as follows:

> Next assignment. Still in a prosing mood. In the style of—shall we say, Quintilian?

> > The study of the classics—by which I mean the ancient classics, and not the so-called classics of the past few centuries—is the only proper study of humankind. If

> the highest good is in the spiritual, moral, ethical, emotional, and intellectual attainments of our kind, as I believe it is, there is quite simply no better place to study this good than in the works of the Greeks and Romans. Even in other fields, the ancient word is still the last word. Political science, for example, is only a repetition of Thucydides and Tacitus in stupid and stupefying prose. And who can match the implicit elegance and simplicity of Euclid? Or who believes Wittgenstein ultimately as *interesting* as Plato, or even as engaging as Cicero in *De Finibus?* And are not Aristotle and Longinus more than enough criticism for anyone?
>
> As for those fields slighted by the ancients, they are not worth studying. Science and economics lead us astray from moral truth by their supposed obsession with material truth. And theology has not been truly *ethical* since the death of Christ, if not since the death of Socrates.
>
> Therefore I say put aside all care for modern cultures, languages, histories. In the ancient world you have all humanity in brief and yet in depth.

Though this letter was couched in terms that implied that it was merely a facetious provocation dashed off at a whim, it reflected a belief Ryan's friend unashamedly espoused. A few months ago Ryan might have laughed at it, protesting mildly even while he harbored a secret assurance that it was in the main true. But now this attitude excluded someone he loved. Without pausing to think, he took up a pen and a piece of paper and wrote this reply:

> The objection I have to your point of view, my friend, is that it is essentially a form of intellectual fundamentalism. Fundamentalism, whether of religion, the intellect, or social thought, divorces humankind from itself and (I dare to add this, though even a month ago I knew nothing about it) from divinity. By its definition fundamentalism limits the circle of received belief. Only such-and-such a belief is correct, it says,

drawing a boundary around a subset of human knowledge and action. Only such-and-such a skin color is correct, only such-and-such a language should be spoken in our society, only such-and-such behavior and customs should be received. Your scholarly standards, your concept of the essential reading list of the educated American, your obsession with the Western world, with the Hellenistic and Roman origins of our culture, are all circles you have drawn to exclude components of our larger society. I have felt this dimly for some time and struggled (though only faintly) to grasp what it was that made our attitude as classicists so *unjust* to humanity. But I can now see that we have to move on to a tolerant classicism that sees the classics as part of a world-wide culture, not as the only pure cultural font. You are being trained—as was I—to be a classicist of the old school who would perpetuate the old system. The old system has its worthwhile features—its insistence on the value of the text over secondary scholarship, for instance; but it also, in its inherent intolerance, contains the seeds of its own destruction. In the coming world, intolerance will not thrive as it has thrived heretofore in the West. It will live only in increasingly isolated pockets. We are too big a species, too interconnected and too interdependent, to be able to afford intolerance. And the fastest way to condemn to death the Latin studies you love is to haul up the drawbridge in your ivory tower—which classicists do, you know as well as I, in their contempt for those who are not whites, who are not of Anglo background, in their abuse of women, even (in the case of certain departments) in their hatred of heterosexual men.

Fundamentalism is the great tool of exclusion. And thus it becomes the great enemy of meaning in life. We cannot limit ourselves to one human shape or color, to one human belief, to one human myth. We must embrace them all.

After all, what are we here for but the company? That is what gives life meaning—the companionship of humanity and the companionship of divinity. We experience the company of our fellows (whether living or dead) in love, in poetry, in music, in art, in any vehicle of ideas and feelings. And we find the companionship of the divine in those very same things—in love especially—love of one another, of art, of all creation. Love is, must be, the indwelling substance of all; and fundamentalism such as yours is ultimately a denial of love.

When he had written this, he reread it in some astonishment, scarcely believing that it was the product of his own brain. And yet he knew it was; and he felt certain that its insight was a gift that love had given him.

Wednesday, July 22/One

All along the watchtower
Princes kept the view.

—Dylan

COLLIN'S TYPEWRITER EMITTED only the faintest hum. When he typed, the sound of the striker hitting the daisy wheel was crisp and surprisingly loud; for days now it had continued without relenting, as he had put his poetry into final shape. Late last night he had finished rewriting and retyping; and now he sat at the typewriter again, thinking of a new poem as he looked through the window at the valley.

All the windows in the room were open. The curtains stirred from time to time when a puff of warm air pushed its way into the cool house. He did not notice this movement. A hawk ranged across the treetops outside, tilting in the morning sun so that its wings became a flash of reflected light so intense the entire bird seemed white instead of dark brown; and though his eyes tracked this motion by reflex, he did not notice it. He noticed nothing. He often thought of this room as a watchtower, but he seldom saw anything from it; instead it was a place where he watched himself, seeing memories and fantasies and passions tumbling in his own mind.

He began typing, slowly at first, but then as his theme caught him, with more speed and certainty.

Meaning meaning what?
Meaning what we search for?
Meaning the search?
Meaning the willingness to search?

Meaning the delusion
  that there is meaning?

Meaning is the pain in your bladder
  that gets you out of bed in the morning
  when you don't care about anything

Meaning is wanting
  and being unable to stop wanting
And the end of meaning is the end of wanting

For me till now meaning has been
  gripping the prize and finding
  no glory but a pitiable
  crushed creature in my hand

For me till now meaning has been
  following god's tracks
  on a beach and realizing at last
  that they are only ridges
  left by the waves

For me till now meaning has been
  looking at the most holy altar
  and seeing a mirror

For me till now meaning has been
  thinking I have done well
  by electing Darwin my god
  instead of Jesus

We make poems to make meaning
If it were not for poems there would be
  no meaning
But does it mean anything that we
  make meaning?

Meaning is everything we do
    or we wouldn't do it
Philosophy, science, art, religion
    why else would we bother with them?
They are a faint feint we make
    to persuade us to continue living

The life of someone you love is meaning
    but if you love no one
    life means nothing

Hate has no meaning
    it is
    the de-meaning of life

For me meaning is the moon
    that waxes and wanes
    and rises and sets over my life
Sometimes clouds cross it
    and it disappears instantly
And then I have no meaning
And just when all is darkest
    the cloud passes

Meaning is inconstant
And I seek it constantly

When I know for sure I can't find it
I'll leave

When he had finished, he set the poem aside without reading it, though this was contrary to his habit. He rolled a fresh sheet of paper into the typewriter and sat staring at it, fidgeting slightly with his fingers, as if struggling with himself.

After a few minutes he rose and went to the bookcase. From among a neglected group of books that included Tolkien's *Lord of the Rings* and Lattimore's Homer, he drew a slim volume he had once bought, in Ryan's company, at a fleamarket. On the cover was the seal carving of Gilgamesh with arms outstretched, holding the hock of a protesting lion in each hand. Paging through it, he found the passage he remembered:

> After three days' journey they came to the drinking hole, and there they sat down; the harlot and the trapper sat facing one another and waited for the game to come. For the first day and for the second day the two sat waiting, but on the third day the herds came; they came down to drink and Enkidu was with them. The small wild creatures of the plains were glad of the water, and Enkidu with them, who ate grass with the gazelle and was born in the hills; and she saw him, the savage man, come from far-off in the hills. The trapper spoke to her: "There he is. Now, woman, make your breasts bare, have no shame, do not delay but welcome his love. Let him see you naked, let him possess your body. When he comes near uncover yourself and lie with him; teach him, the savage man, your woman's art, for when his love is drawn to you the wild beasts that shared his life in the hills will reject him."
>
> She was not ashamed to take him, she made herself naked and welcomed his eagerness, she incited the savage to love and taught him the woman's art. For six days and seven nights they lay together, for Enkidu had forgotten his home in the hills; but when he was satisfied he went back to the wild beasts. Then, when the gazelle saw him, they bolted away; when the wild creatures saw him they fled.

He sat down at the typewriter again. He leaned on his elbows, holding his head in his hands and combing his fingers through his golden hair; and then he sat up straight again and typed these lines:

Choose, Enkidu
Choose
between the harlot and the gazelle

The harlot brought you
        within the circle of humanity
She made you one with Gilgamesh,
        your brother
But she also brought you
        the anger of the gods
She also brought you
        the dream of the house
        from which no one who enters
        ever returns
She also brought you
        to the sickbed where you lay in pain
She also brought you
        to death
And you became
        only a lament
        in the mouth of your brother

But the gazelle, Enkidu
        promised you freedom
        promised you the hills
        promised you your strength
        and protected you
        from knowledge of death
        at least until death should come

Choose, Enkidu
Choose

Unless it is already
too late

He had typed to the very bottom of the paper, and the sheet slipped from the machine as he pressed the return at the end of the last line.

He looked out over the valley. What breeze there was died away; the cicadas began to buzz; and the damp heat settled over the leafy wood. Collin did not notice any of these things, though his eyes wandered slowly over everything before him. His gaze was turned inward.

"Choose," he said softly to himself. But instantly, as he said that word, his face became contorted with pain and disgust.

Wednesday, July 22 / Two

The Ecclesiastes says, All is vanity, and I agree with the worthy
gentleman, who possibly never existed.

—Hugo

That hackneyed judge of human life,
The Preacher and the King . . .

—Burns

Imperfect mortal mind sends forth its own resemblances, of which
the wise man said, "All is vanity."

—Mary Baker Eddy

ON WEDNESDAY AFTERNOON Maureen and Daniel
went to Chelsea again to visit their nephew John's
wife. She was struggling, at the age of sixteen, with
an infant child, and taking summer school classes
to finish her high school diploma; in conversation at
the wedding, they had volunteered to sit with the child while she
took a test. It was the least they could do, said Maureen—actually, she said this several times, as if she was thinking of doing
something more. Ryan would not have been too surprised if she
had come home with the baby.

They asked him if he wished to go. He glared and scoffed; and
they left him alone in the close, hot little house, sitting at his desk,
listening to the slow ticking of the grandmother clock in the living
room. Sometimes he found himself counting the seconds, thinking
how each sound he heard brought him closer to seeing Constance
again. He wondered where she was; he wondered if she thought of
him at all; he played the game of Whether or Not, and dreamt the

dream of the Gesture; and he checked his watch; and time idled onwards.

At length he was so miserable he cast about for something, for anything, to distract him. His mother had been checking something in the King James Bible that morning; it lay on the top of the stack of books on the outside corner of his desk. He drew it to him, and opened it, looking for the Song of Solomon, but coming first upon Ecclesiastes.

He began to read; he read the book from beginning to end; and then, with the critic's instinct, he drew a piece of paper from his drawer. He needed an audience; he needed a reader; and so he wrote the following letter to Eve:

July 22

Dear Eve,

Here is the letter you wanted. Or at least, the letter you thought you wanted.

We have been playing games, you and I. You have pretended to know things about me that you did not know. I have pretended that the things you had guessed correctly were not so. Let's give up the pretense and start over.

Constance is away. I suspect her mother knows how I feel about her, and is keeping her out of the way on purpose; though why she would bother separating us now, when we are going to be alone together for a week in Maine starting the day after tomorrow, I can't imagine.

I write "the day after tomorrow" so easily—the interval sounds so trivial; but if you knew how far away that is, how every hour goes on like an Egyptian dynasty, you would understand why I am so enervated and useless.

I love this woman very much. I love you too, Eve; but since you have brought things to such a pass with us, I will tell you honestly that I love this woman more than I have ever loved anyone or anything on this earth. For her I would give up Greek and Latin forever. Sometimes I think that for her I could even give up my love of poetry. I could live somewhere quietly with her, in some little house far from the world, and never read a word again; but read love in her eyes, all worthy knowledge in her brow, all human kindness in her touch; and all my book learning would be needless then.

You think this is just the hyperbole of infatuation. But this love has shaken my self-image so that I begin to wonder who I am and what I really want.

I was dedicated to the muse of literature at a young age, her *hierodoulos*. Even while labor crushed me and drudgery ate me hollow, the joy of languages and letters supported me and delight in the written word filled me full. I gradually came to accept the role that had been set out for me—set out not so much by my parents, but by what they taught me, and by own success with it. My talent determined what I should do—be an academic, acquire degrees, publish, teach, research and write. And I can still see myself doing this. Sometimes this love seems as if it would be the perfect completion to that path I have mapped out. But there are other times when I think that maybe I will not succeed; that she will not love me; and then I feel that all my effort, all my cares to this point, have been utterly pointless.

I have just been reading Ecclesiastes. It is fashionable to belittle this text, I think. Perhaps people find frightening the notion that "all is vanity." Perhaps they do not persevere long enough to discover that this poem—for that is what it is—is essentially affirmative. Perhaps they think that the message has become trite, or that it is really nothing more than a cheap hit taken at the perplexities of human life. Here was a man who seemed to have everything, and yet could find satisfaction in none of it; what sympathy should we have with him? And yet so many of us are in that very position. I, for instance: I have had care, love, guidance, the finest training my parents and my teachers could give me. I never lacked for food, however bland it may have been; I never lacked for clothing, though my clothes are to this day a little threadbare; I never lacked for a roof over my head, though the paint is peeling off every surface in sight. I had a good and great friend to share my golden childhood—and it was golden—and a noble-hearted dog to run free beside me. I had a second home in a great house, and privileges along with that home that few can claim. I was admitted early to one of the very finest universities in this country. I attracted the notice of women—I experimented sexually, and escaped without hurt to others or myself, without disease or paternity. And I met you. We had our talks; and we had our two weeks of the flesh. I have possibilities before me— Oxford, and a further degree beyond that, and will probably emerge with all my credentials and owe no one a penny. What does anyone have, that I would trade my life for his? Nothing.

And yet when I think that I might lose this woman, I know the meaning of the Preacher's weariness with life. I know why he distrusts what he has been given. *What profit hath a man of all his labor which he taketh under the sun?* There is no "profit" in anything, no residual good that can be saved up and pointed to as the justification for the whole. As he says, *One generation passeth away, and another generation cometh.* There will be another generation after us, to whom their own instant pleasures are fully absorbing; and nothing saved from our work, or only the smallest fraction of it, will truly occupy them long. And even if it did, what good would that do us? Surely the "profit" the Preacher means is some kind of transcendent change that our labors bring to our life, that makes us content, that dispels forever the restlessness of learning and doing. And he is right—we never find that profit.

So everything we do must have *intrinsic* meaning, or be pointless. The means must be all, because the end is by definition nothing. No matter what our work, it must contain its own joy, or be a waste of our lives. The Preacher seems to have struggled for some time to come to this knowledge.

> *I have seen all works that are done under the sun; and behold, all is vanity and vexation of spirit. . . . I communed with mine own heart, saying, Lo, I am come to great estate, and have gotten more wisdom than all they that have been before me in Jerusalem: yea, my heart had great experience of*

wisdom and knowledge. . . . Then I looked on all the works that my hands had wrought, and on the labor that I had labored to do: and, behold, all was vanity and vexation of spirit, and there was no profit under the sun. . . . Wherefore I perceive that there is nothing better, than that a man should rejoice in his own works.

The reason we crave love is that love holds that intrinsic meaning that we seek. It is a means and an end in itself. More than that, it infuses meaning into our other labors.

There is one alone, and there is not a second; yea, he hath neither child nor brother: yet is there no end of all his labor; neither is his eye satisfied with riches; neither saith he, For whom do I labor, and bereave my soul of good? This is also vanity, yea, it is a sore travail.

I have dreamt many times, daydreamt, of someday living in the fine old gatehouse that was once attached to the Tate lands. I will be married to Constance then. I will be working in my study up under the eaves—it was once a dry old attic, but it has been converted into an airy space with skylights and expanses of white ceiling. It is five o'clock; I hear the rattle of a car engine in the drive. In a minute, the door clicks open and shut downstairs. There is a soft rushing sound, like the quiet tumult of the blood in my veins—Constance is dashing up the stairs. She enters the room and comes to my side. I put up my hand and touch her head, caress her, and she seizes my arm, leans close to me—

Two are better than one: because they have a good reward for their labor. For if they fall, the one will lift up his fellow: but woe to him that is alone when he falleth; for he hath not another to help him up. Again, if two lie together, then they have heat: but how can one be warm alone?

So my thoughts take me away until I am lost in them.

But then I come to. I am alone. My hands and arms are empty; my eyes are empty; my brain is empty, and my heart, too, feels empty but for the ache, which is a kind of emptiness. And I think: *What if I don't get her?*—Yes, my thinking is just as bald as that: *What if I don't get her?* For I crave possession, only that will satisfy me, to freely love and be loved.

And when I ask that question—*What if I don't get her?*—and I think about that possibility, it is as if my life has come to a dead halt: the way has ended, and I stand looking about me, and I don't know where to go. One thing I do know, and that is that I will not be able to carry on as I have been. Something must change. In any event, something must change. Either I *get* her or everything must be overturned.

No matter what happens, she has given me one thing. Lately I have had an increasing sense that I know what god is. As if for the first time I have grasped what it is that everyone else has been talking about all these millennia. The intellect is utterly useless for knowing god, I can tell you that. I tried to find god with my intellect for quite some time, and it is like groping blindly for the right way in a room with a thousand doors. Once the eyes of the heart are open, you can easily read the sign that says RIGHT HERE.

Someone has said that god is not a distinct being, but a basic principle of operation. If you live by the principle, your life works; if you don't live by the principle, you are miserable. And the only principle that works is love, certainly. I am not particularly good at living at it, though I think you would agree I am not a hopeless candidate. And no matter what happens between me and Constance, she has given me that much of love, that much of knowledge. I can go on from here, holding what I know of god to myself, so that it does not get tainted with the intellectualisms of organized belief—so I can keep it alive, breathing inside me.

Thank you, my friend, for listening to this. By the time you receive it, I will be traveling to Maine with her. And then I will take these words of the Preacher to heart:

Behold that which I have seen: it is good and comely for one to eat and to drink, and to enjoy the good of all his labor that he taketh under the sun all the days of his life, which God giveth him: for it is his portion.

Go thy way, eat thy bread with joy, and drink thy wine with a merry heart; for God now accepteth thy works. Live joyfully with the wife whom thou lovest all the days of the life of thy vanity, which he hath given thee under the sun, all the days of thy vanity: for that is thy portion in this life, and in thy labor which thou takest under the sun. Whatsoever thy hand findeth to do, do it with thy might; for there is no work, nor device, nor knowledge, nor wisdom, in the grave, whither thou goest.

Rejoice, O young man, in thy youth; and let thy heart cheer thee in the days of thy youth, and walk in the ways of thine heart, and in the sight of thine eyes: but know thou, that for all these things God will bring thee into judgment.

The Preacher certainly knew his stuff. I am sure of that because he feels compelled to put in a final word to people like me—like you and me. But I should have mentioned one other thing: in the daydream I recounted above I imagined I was studying Hebrew so I could read Ecclesiastes in the original.

You know what he said:

And further, by these, my son, be admonished: of making many books there is no end; and much study is a weariness of the flesh.

With affection,

Ryan

Thursday, July 23

Constancy is his motto.

—Cervantes

SONDRA TATE FELT a twist of apprehension in her stomach when she saw Ryan striding up the driveway on Thursday morning. He seemed too confident, too sure of the outcome of everything. Collin, who was sitting beside her on the porch, must have noticed her expression change; he turned to look in the direction she was looking; and then he considered her curiously. He rose and went to the steps.

She comforted herself with the results of her recent espionage. While traveling she had probed as discreetly as possible to discover Constance's feelings toward Ryan, and found nothing serious. And one night after Constance had fallen asleep in the motel room, she had searched her daughter's suitcase and found her diary in an inner pocket. She had not been able to read it since they had left Spain. Though it was full of Collin this and Collin that, she was relieved as she read it, sitting in the motel bathroom at two in the morning, that it showed no particular attachment to Ryan.

"What's up, old man?" asked Collin.

"Got the photo back," said Ryan. "Thought I'd just drop off a few copies for you and Constance." He ascended the steps and nodded at Sondra. "Morning," he said.

She stared at him without answering.

"The photo?" puzzled Collin. "Oh, from last week. How did it come out?"

"It's unbelievable," said Ryan. He was carrying a small package—obviously a paperback book—wrapped as a gift, along with two business envelopes. He now held out one of the envelopes to Collin, who took it from him and pulled out two prints.

For once in his life, Daniel had not been hasty with the camera. He had not held his finger over the lens, or left anyone out of the frame, or shot at their feet or at the sky over their heads, or moved out of the fixed focal length of the little Brownie. The three friends stood linked by Constance's hands, smiling all; Collin, on the left, in the best of spirits, his face lit by memory and friendship, golden and handsome; Ryan, on the right, humorous and happy; and Constance between, turning towards him and laughing.

"Great photo!" exclaimed Collin in a tone of extreme pleasure. He showed one of the copies to Sondra and continued to feast his eyes on the other.

"Hard to believe, isn't it?" said Ryan. "After all those years of looking at those photographs of her, and suddenly there we are in the picture with her."

"Exactly my feelings," said Collin.

"Well, you all seem to be having a good time," said Sondra coldly. She handed the print back to Collin.

"Is one of these copies for Constance?" asked Collin.

"No. I've got a couple more for her. I thought you each might like some for yourselves."

"Definitely. I may even ask you for an enlargement."

"No problem.—Is Constance around somewhere? I'll give her hers."

"She's upstairs. Come on up. I've got to get back to work, but you can give her the photos yourself."

As Ryan walked past Sondra they exchanged a glance—cool and mutually inscrutable.

"So how's everything shaping up?" asked Ryan as he and Collin went upstairs.

"I can't complain. It seems the closer I get to actually going to this workshop, the more ideas come to the surface. The output of new material just in the last week has been incredible. It's hard to keep everything sorted—in terms of what I'm satisfied with, and what's simply too new to judge yet. I'll have to take a certain amount of raw material with me and take a few risks with it."

"Any definite departure time?"

"All we have to do is avoid the last renters. The realtor said they were clearing out about ten in the morning. The person who cleans up was supposed to get in there right away; so if we left at ten, we should be all set."

"Sounds great. The earlier, the better."

"Well, we just want to miss rush hour. The traffic will be bad enough whenever we go, but rush hour will be a nightmare."

Collin knocked at Constance's room. The door opened instantly, as if she had been waiting behind it.

"Ryan!" she said joyfully.

"Hello there," he responded. He felt almost as though he might weep in the sheer delight of seeing her again; he was dizzy; he thought a child might have read his emotion in his face, in his studied nonchalance of tone.

"Ryan's got something for you," said Collin. "I'm going to get to work.—Want us to pick you up at your place?"

"Naw—I'll come over. All I'll have is a knapsack, anyway. That way I can help pack the car or whatever. About quarter to ten?"

"That should do it. See you then."

Collin went down the hall to his room and shut himself in.

They were alone together. Her eyes were shining with pleasure; she looked at him and then away, shy in her delight.

"I missed you, Ryan!" she said.

"I missed you, too. It seems as if you've been gone three hundred years."

"Doesn't it, though!—Come in," she said, motioning him forward. He entered; she looked briefly down the hallway and then shut the door behind him.

"How was your trip?" he asked.

"Awful! I can't tell you how awful it was. Mother acted as if everyone in the United States knew who I was and desperately wanted me registered at their college."

"Ugh! It *must* have been awful."

"I've never been so embarrassed. Imagine sitting there in some admissions office while she bragged about how we were members of the Tate and Burnham families—as if anyone knew or cared. I was positively ready to *die!*—But let's not even talk about it. Tell me what you've been doing. Here, sit down." She perched on the edge of the bed and patted the spot beside her. He leaned against the bed in the place that she had indicated.

"I didn't do much." He wondered how he could let her know that he had been utterly bored and yet not seem as if he were dependent upon her. "A little paperwork, mostly."

"Scholarship?"

"You could say.—Look, the reason I came was to give you this." He handed her the envelope.

She was puzzled, and opened it without betraying any sign that she guessed what it held. The surprise made her pleasure all that much more gratifying to him.

"Oh, Ryan! What a wonderful picture! It's *us*, it's this summer, captured to perfection!"

"Isn't it, though? I think it's wonderful. I can't take any credit for it, so I'll just agree it's one of the finest photos I've ever seen."

She could not stay seated. She paced around the room, scrutinizing both of the copies he had given her alternately, as if they were different photographs. "It came out just beautifully. Look at Collin—have you ever seen such a handsome person? It's exactly the way he looks. I've never seen a photograph that caught him so well."

"You don't look so bad there yourself."

"Oh—my hair looks a little windblown or something."

"You look beautiful that way. And you'd better get used to it, because that's the way you're going to look every day for the next week."

"I suppose you're right.—Can I keep these both? Or is one for Collin?"

"They're both yours."

"Then I know exactly what I'll do with one of them," she said. She went over to her jewelry box; but then, apparently feeling some scruple he could not divine, she paused and set them down, as if changing her immediate intention.

"I have something else for you," he said.

"For me?" she said shyly. He held out the package. "You shouldn't have," she said.

She took the gift from him and settled on the bed beside him as she unwrapped it. It was a book of translations from the Greek lyric poets.

"Ryan, thank you! This is beautiful! How nice of you to think of me this way."

"I think you'll really like them," he said. "I don't even think Collin would object too much to your reading them. They were originally in meter, but the translators abandon that for the most part."

She was paging through the book, reading here and there. "These are beautiful," she said.

"Here," he said, as he saw she had opened to Sappho. He showed her a fragment, and she read it.

The moon and the Pleiades
have set. It is the middle of the night
and the hours pass.
I lie in my bed, alone.

"I know the feeling," she said.

"It's just a fragment. The rest is lost."

"Lost?"

"No copy survived."

"How awful!"

"It *is* awful. But that's life, I guess."

She smiled at him. "I won't argue that with you now," she said.

"No, please don't. I'm enjoying the moment too much to be reminded of how brief it is."

"I'll bring this to the shore. We'll need plenty of books, you know."

"I know."

"It's going to be heaven, don't you think? Just the three of us, without Mother around. Do you realize I've never been apart from my mother for more than a night or two in my whole life?"

"That's amazing, Constance."

"And high time, too."

There was a sharp rap at the door. Constance looked at Ryan and rolled her eyes.

"Yes, Mother?" she said.

"Are you ready to go?"

"In a minute."

"I want to be home in time to pick up your father."

"Papa won't be at the station until six. We can't be going shopping for eight hours straight."

"Don't talk back to me! I'll give you two minutes."

They could hear crisp footsteps moving away up the hall.

"Shopping again?" asked Ryan. "Can't you get out of it?"

"No. We're going to drive to look at Cornell the Monday after I get back from the Maine. Mother is convinced I need some new things and she wants me to be all ready before I leave tomorrow." She paused, considering. "Something's bothering her, I swear it. I just don't know what it is. It could be that she's worried about the Maine trip. I don't want to rock the boat—you know what I mean? I just want to be goody two-shoes until I get in that car tomorrow."

"A good plan," he said. He rose reluctantly. "I'd better go."

"I'll see you out," she said, rising with him.

They went downstairs and out the front door. Once outside, however, they lingered for a minute.

"Think of me," said Constance, "while you're relaxing in your book-lined study. Think of me as a rag doll being dragged around by a sulking child."

"I'll think of you. Don't worry about that. As for you, just keep thinking about tomorrow."

"I will, believe me. The next week is going to be the most fun I've ever had in my life. Probably the most fun I'll ever have as long as I live."

"Don't be silly. It will just be the beginning of your long, happy life as an independent person."

"I wish you were right. But I have a feeling there are a few more battles to fight before I win my independence."

He took a long look at her, as if to store her up in his memory.

"What?" she said, smiling, as she sensed his emotion.

"Nothing. I'll see you tomorrow. Quarter of ten, Collin said."

"Any time will be fine. Less than twenty-four hours now! Do you believe it?—Thank you for the photographs, Ryan. And the book.—And bring some books tomorrow. Don't forget. We'll sit on the beach while Collin's at the workshop and gorge ourselves on great literature."

He suddenly did not trust himself to speak. He strode away, with a wave of his hand.

He had proceeded no more than twenty feet when she called, "Ryan!" He looked back.

He saw she was struggling with her old perplexity—she could not think what that final, nagging, unthought thought might be. She laughed at herself and shrugged as if hopeless at her own silliness.

"Call me if you think what it is," he said.

She was overcome by her embarrassment, gestured farewell, and went into the house.

He walked away up the drive. When he was out of sight of the house, around the bend, he let himself ache. "Maybe you don't know what it is that *you* want to say," he murmured. "But I know what I wish I could say. *I love you, Constance Tate.* That would do it."

❁❁❁

When Constance went back upstairs she gave her mother no notice that she was ready to leave. Instead she closed herself in her room and went straight to the jewelry box on her bureau, from which she drew a diminutive picture frame, an antique she had received as a gift on her confirmation. From her sewing box she took a pair of embroidery scissors.

The frame had an insert of faded paper. This she removed and held carefully in place over one of the photographs, cutting around its heart-shaped outline with the scissors. When she had finished, and had pressed the piece of the snapshot into the interior of the frame and closed the velvet-covered backing, she sat looking at it with pleasure for a minute.

"Are you ready to go?" demanded her mother at the door.

"I'll be right down."

She set the frame on the bureau. Making her final preparations to depart, she put away the scissors and the book of poetry, and she took the uncut copy of the photograph and propped it under the picture of Collin she had hung on the wall.

The cut photograph she at first threw in the wastebasket with the used wrapping paper; but as an afterthought, she retrieved it and shut it in her jewelry box to save until she could think what to do with it.

As she did so, the picture in the photo arrested her attention for a moment—the image of Ryan and her, with the heart-shaped blank beside them. But she took up her hairbrush and, in a moment more, forgot about it.

CONTINUED IN VOLUME 2